D0953298

IN THE RING

ABOUT THE EDITOR

MARTIN H. GREENBERG, who has been called "the king of the anthologists," now has some 150 of them to his credit. Greenberg is professor of regional analysis and political science at the University of Wisconsin-Green Bay, where he teaches a course in American foreign and defense policy.

IN THE RING

A TREASURY OF BOXING STORIES

Edited and with an Introduction by
MARTIN H. GREENBERG

Bonanza Books

New York

Publisher's Note: Selections in this work contain racial references and language which the modern reader may find offensive. These references and language are part of the time period and environment written about, and do not reflect the attitudes of the editors or publisher of this current edition.

Compilation copyright © 1986 by Martin H. Greenberg
All rights reserved.
First published in 1987 by Bonanza Books,
distributed by Crown Publishers, Inc.,
225 Park Avenue South, New York, New York 10003

Printed and Bound in the United States of America

Book design by Cynthia Dunne

Library of Congress Cataloging-in-Publication Data
In the ring.
1. Boxing stories.   2. Short stories, American.
3. Short stories, English. I. Greenberg, Martin Harry.
PS648.B67I5   1987   813'.01'08355   86-21615
ISBN 0-517-62 541-5
h g f e d c b a

ACKNOWLEDGMENTS

Hemingway—Ernest Hemingway, "Fifty Grand," from *Men Without Women,* copyright 1927 by Charles Scribner's Sons; copyright renewed 1955 by Ernest Hemingway. Reprinted with the permission of Charles Scribner's Sons.

Gallico—"The Melee of the Mages," copyright 1940 by Paul Gallico. Copyright renewed ©1968 by Paul Gallico. Reprinted by permission of Harold Ober Associates Incorporated.

Gault—"Slug the Man Down!" reprinted by permission of the author.

Reeve—"Ten Rounds for Baby," reprinted by permission of the author.

Cox—"The Big Oaf," reprinted by permission of the author.

Lardner—Ring Lardner, "Champion," from *How To Write Short Stories.* Copyright 1924 by Charles Scribner's Sons; copyright renewed 1952 by Ellis A. Lardner. Reprinted with the permission of Charles Scribner's Sons.

Woolrich—"The Blue Ribbon," copyright 1949 by Cornell Woolrich. Reprinted by permission of the agents for the author's Estate, the Scott Meredith Literary Agency, Inc., 845 Third Ave., New York, NY 10022.

Ritchie—"Ape Man," copyright 1955 by Magazine Management Co. Reprinted by permission of Larry Sternig Literary Agency.

Sternig—"Scrap Iron," copyright 1945 by Fiction House. Reprinted by permission of the author.

Nolan—"Encounter with a King," copyright ©1966 by Sirkey Publishing Co. Reprinted by permission of the author.

Brand—"Fixed," reprinted by permission of Dodd, Mead & Company, Inc. from *Wine on the Desert and Other Stories* by Max Brand. Copyright 1936 by Crowell-Collier Publishing Company. Copyright renewed ©1964 by Judith Faust, Jane F. Easton and John Frederick Faust.

Matheson—"Steel," copyright ©1956; renewed ©1984 by Richard Matheson. Reprinted by permission of Don Congdon Associates, Inc.

Oates—"Golden Gloves," copyright ©1986 by Ontario Review Inc. First published in *Raven's Wing and Other Stories.*

Gault—"Title Fight," reprinted by permission of the author.

Schulberg—"The Harder They Fall," copyright 1947; renewed ©1975 by Budd Schulberg. Reprinted by permission of Alyss Barlow Dorese.

CONTENTS

INTRODUCTION

Two men slugging it out in some form of ring is, along with wrestling, the oldest form of sport. However, it only became a sport in the true sense of the word when the Marquess of Queensberry established a set of rules in 1867. Boxing was engaged in by members of the lower classes in almost every European country, and in the United States by slaves in the antebellum South. Of course, members of all classes attended bouts as spectators, but only began to do so openly in America in the early years of the twentieth century. Since the end of World War II the game has had its ups and downs, first nearly killed by television but now benefitting greatly from exposure on network and cable TV. One of the most interesting developments of recent years is the incredible popularity of the sport in cultures as diverse as those of Latin America and the Far East, at a time when boxing is under heavy attack in the more industrialized nations as a barbaric, dangerous way to make a living.

As a primitive, violent sport, boxing has long attracted the attention of writers. Authors as different as Ernest Hemingway and Joyce Carol Oates have been fascinated by the drama inherent in prize fighting, and also by the ways this sport can be used as a metaphor about winning, losing, and American values.

Hollywood was quick to sense the drama of the fight game (and the money to be made from it), and the list of excellent boxing movies is long. A partial one would have to include the *Rocky* films starring Sylvester Stallone as Rocky Balboa; *Raging Bull*, with Robert De Niro in an unforgettable performance as Jake La Motta; the two versions of *The Champ;* Errol Flynn as "Gentleman Jim" Corbett; *Body and Soul* with the tragic John Garfield; *The Set-Up* with the vastly underrated Robert Ryan; *Champion,* with Kirk Douglas in one of his best roles; and *Somebody Up There Likes Me,* with Paul Newman as Rocky Graziano.

In the Ring: A Treasury of Boxing Stories is the largest anthology ever compiled on the sport. In its pages you will find stories of the ring by such famous literary figures as Max Brand, Jack London, the previously mentioned Ernest Hemingway, and Joyce Carol Oates. In addition, there is a good representation of writers who specialized in (among other things) sports stories—men like William Campbell Gault, the late Paul Gallico, Larry Sternig, and William R. Cox, who supplied material to both the pulp magazines and the "slicks" like *The Saturday Evening Post,* publications whose yellowing pages contain gems of boxing fiction amid much that would be better left unread. Here you will find stories by people not normally associated with sports fiction, such as the science-fiction writer Richard Matheson, master of suspense Cornell Woolrich, and the legendary Sir Arthur Conan Doyle. We are especially proud to offer you the entire text of Budd Schulberg's *The Harder They Fall*, which, along with Leonard Gardner's *Fat City* (1969) and W. C. Heinz's *The Professional* (1958), is widely considered to be one of the finest boxing novels of all time.

Two men face each other in the center of the ring. The bell rings—let the reading begin!

Green Bay, Wisconsin   Martin H. Greenberg
1987

IN THE
RING

FIFTY GRAND

Ernest Hemingway

How are you going yourself, Jack?" I asked him.

"You seen this, Walcott?" he says.

"Just in the gym."

"Well," Jack says, "I'm going to need a lot of luck with that boy."

"He can't hit you, Jack," Soldier said.

"I wish to hell he couldn't."

"He couldn't hit you with a handful of bird-shot."

"Bird-shot'd be all right," Jack says. "I wouldn't mind bird-shot any."

"He looks easy to hit," I said.

"Sure," Jack says, "he ain't going to last long. He ain't going to last like you and me, Jerry. But right now he's got everything."

"You'll left-hand him to death."

"Maybe," Jack says. "Sure. I got a chance to."

"Handle him like you handled Kid Lewis."

"Kid Lewis," Jack said. "That kike!"

The three of us, Jack Brennan, Soldier Bartlett, and I were in Hanley's. There were a couple of broads sitting at the next table to us. They had been drinking.

"What do you mean, kike?" one of the broads says. "What do you mean, kike, you big Irish bum?"

"Sure," Jack says. "That's it."

"Kikes," this broad goes on. "They're always talking about kikes, these big Irishmen. What do you mean, kikes?"

"Come on. Let's get out of here."

"Kikes," this broad goes on. "Whoever saw you ever buy a drink? Your wife sews your pockets up every morning. These Irishmen and their kikes! Ted Lewis could lick you too."

"Sure," Jack says. "And you give away a lot of things free too, don't you?"

We went out. That was Jack. He could say what he wanted to when he wanted to say it.

Jack started training out at Danny Hogan's health farm over in Jersey. It was nice out there but Jack didn't like it much. He didn't like being away from his wife and the kids, and he was sore and grouchy most of the time. He liked me and we got along fine together; and he liked Hogan, but after a while Soldier Bartlett commenced to get on his nerves. A kidder gets to be an awful thing around a camp if his stuff goes sort of sour. Soldier was always kidding Jack, just sort of kidding him all the time. It wasn't very funny and it wasn't very good, and it began to get to Jack. It was sort of stuff like this. Jack would finish up with the weights and the bag and pull on the gloves.

"You want to work?" he'd say to Soldier.

"Sure. How you want me to work?" Soldier would ask. "Want me to treat you rough like Walcott? Want me to knock you down a few times?"

"That's it," Jack would say. He didn't like it any, though.

One morning we were all out on the road. We'd been out quite a way and now we were coming back. We'd go along fast for three minutes and then walk a minute, and then go fast for three minutes again. Jack wasn't ever what you would call a sprinter. He'd move around fast enough in the ring if he had to, but he wasn't any too fast on the road. All the time we were walking Soldier was kidding him. We came up the hill to the farmhouse.

"Well," says Jack, "you better go back to town, Soldier."

"What do you mean?"

"You better go back to town and stay there."

"What's the matter?"

"I'm sick of hearing you talk."

"Yes?" says Soldier.

"Yes," says Jack.

"You'll be a damn sight sicker when Walcott gets through with you."

"Sure," says Jack, "maybe I will. But I know I'm sick of you."

So Soldier went off on the train to town that same morning. I went down with him to the train. He was good and sore.

"I was just kidding him," he said. We were waiting on the platform. "He can't pull that stuff with me, Jerry."

"He's nervous and crabby," I said. "He's a good fellow, Soldier."

"The hell he is. The hell he's ever been a good fellow."

"Well," I said, "so long, Soldier."

The train had come in. He climbed up with his bag.

"So long, Jerry," he says. "You be in town before the fight?"

"I don't think so."

"See you then."

He went in and the conductor swung up and the train went out. I rode back to the farm in the cart. Jack was on the porch writing a letter to his wife. The mail had come and I got the papers and went over on the other side of the porch and sat down to read. Hogan came out the door and walked over to me.

"Did he have a jam with Soldier?"

"Not a jam," I said. "He just told him to go back to town."

"I could see it coming," Hogan said. "He never liked Soldier much."

"No. He don't like many people."

"He's a pretty cold one," Hogan said.

"Well, he's always been fine to me."

"Me too," Hogan said. "I got no kick on him. He's a cold one, though."

Hogan went in through the screen door and I sat there on the porch and read the papers. It was just starting to get fall weather and it's nice country there in Jersey, up in the hills, and after I read the paper through I sat there and looked out at the country and the road down below against the woods with cars going along it, lifting the dust up. It was fine weather and pretty nice-looking country. Hogan came to the door and I said, "Say, Hogan, haven't you got anything to shoot out here?"

"No," Hogan said. "Only sparrows."

"Seen the paper?" I said to Hogan.

"What's in it?"

"Sande booted three of them in yesterday."

"I got that on the telephone last night."

"You follow them pretty close, Hogan?" I asked.

"Oh, I keep in touch with them," Hogan said.

"How about Jack?" I says. "Does he still play them?"

"Him?" said Hogan. "Can you see him doing it?"

Just then Jack came around the corner with the letter in his hand. He's wearing a sweater and an old pair of pants and boxing shoes.

"Got a stamp, Hogan?" he asks.

"Give me the letter," Hogan said. "I'll mail it for you."

"Say, Jack," I said, "didn't you used to play the ponies?"

"Sure."

"I knew you did. I knew I used to see you out at Sheepshead."

"What did you lay off them for?" Hogan asked.

"Lost money."

Jack sat down on the porch by me. He leaned back against a post. He shut his eyes in the sun.

"Want a chair?" Hogan asked.

"No," said Jack. "This is fine."

"It's a nice day," I said. "It's pretty nice out in the country."

"I'd a damn sight rather be in town with the wife."

"Well, you only got another week."

"Yes," Jack says. "That's so."

We sat there on the porch. Hogan was inside at the office.

"What do you think about the shape I'm in?" Jack asked me.

"Well, you can't tell," I said. "You got a week to get around into form."

"Don't stall me."

"Well," I said, "you're not right."

"I'm not sleeping," Jack said.

"You'll be all right in a couple of days."

"No," says Jack, "I got the insomnia."

"What's on your mind?"

"I miss the wife."

"Have her come out."

"No. I'm too old for that."

"We'll take a long walk before you turn in and get you good and tired."

"Tired!" Jack says. "I'm tired all the time."

He was that way all week. He wouldn't sleep at night and he'd get up in the morning feeling that way, you know, when you can't shut your hands.

"He's stale as poorhouse cake," Hogan said. "He's nothing."

"I never seen Walcott," I said.

"He'll kill him," said Hogan. "He'll tear him in two."

"Well," I said, "everybody's got to get it sometime."

"Not like this, though," Hogan said. "They'll think he never trained. It gives the farm a black eye."

"You hear what the reporters said about him?"

"Didn't I! They said he was awful. They said they oughtn't to let him fight."

"Well," I said, "they're always wrong, ain't they?"

"Yes," said Hogan. "But this time they're right."

"What the hell do they know about whether a man's right or not?"

"Well," said Hogan, "they're not such fools."

"All they did was pick Willard at Toledo. This Lardner, he's so wise now, ask him about when he picked Willard at Toledo."

"Aw, he wasn't out," Hogan said. "He only writes the big fights."

"I don't care who they are," I said. "What the hell do they know? They can write maybe, but what the hell do they know?"

"You don't think Jack's in any shape, do you?" Hogan asked.

"No. He's through. All he needs is to have Corbett pick him to win for it to be all over."

"Well, Corbett'll pick him," Hogan says.

"Sure. He'll pick him."

That night Jack didn't sleep any either. The next morning was the last day before the fight. After breakfast we were out on the porch again.

"What do you think about, Jack, when you can't sleep?" I said.

"Oh, I worry," Jack says. "I worry about property I got up in the Bronx, I worry about property I got in Florida. I worry about the kids. I worry about the wife. Sometimes I think about fights. I think about that kike Ted Lewis and I get sore. I got some stocks and I worry about them. What the hell don't I think about?"

"Well," I said, "tomorrow night it'll all be over."

"Sure," said Jack. "That always helps a lot, don't it? That just fixes everything all up, I suppose. Sure."

He was sore all day. We didn't do any work. Jack just moved around a little to loosen up. He shadowboxed a few rounds. He didn't even look good doing that. He skipped the rope a little while. He couldn't sweat.

"He'd be better not to do any work at all," Hogan said. We were standing watching him skip rope. "Don't he ever sweat at all any more?"

"He can't sweat."

"Do you suppose he's got the con? He never had any trouble making weight, did he?"

"No, he hasn't got any con. He just hasn't got anything inside any more."

"He ought to sweat," said Hogan.

Jack came over, skipping the rope. He was skipping up and down in front of us, forward and back, crossing his arms every third time.

"Well," he says. "What are you buzzards talking about?"

"I don't think you ought to work any more," Hogan says. "You'll be stale."

"Wouldn't that be awful?" Jack says and skips away down the floor, slapping the rope hard.

That afternoon John Collins showed up out at the farm. Jack was up in his room. John came out in a car from town. He had a couple of friends with him. The car stopped and they all got out.

"Where's Jack?" John asked me.

"Up in his room, lying down."

"Lying down?"

"Yes," I said.

"How is he?"

I looked at the two fellows that were with John.

"They're friends of his," John said.

"He's pretty bad," I said.

"What's the matter with him?"

"He don't sleep."

"Hell," said John. "That Irishman could never sleep."

"He isn't right," I said.

"Hell," John said. "He's never right. I've had him for ten years and he's never been right yet."

The fellows who were with him laughed.

"I want you to shake hands with Mr. Morgan and Mr. Steinfelt," John said. "This is Mr. Doyle. He's been training Jack."

"Glad to meet you," I said.

"Let's go up and see the boy," the fellow called Morgan said.

"Let's have a look at him," Steinfelt said.

We all went upstairs.

"Where's Hogan?" John asked.

"He's out in the barn with a couple of his customers," I said.

"He got many people out here now?" John asked.

"Just two."

"Pretty quiet, ain't it?" Morgan said.

"Yes," I said. "It's pretty quiet."

We were outside Jack's room. John knocked on the door. There wasn't any answer.

"Maybe he's asleep," I said.

"What the hell's he sleeping in the daytime for?"

John turned the handle and we all went in. Jack was lying asleep on the bed. He was face down and his face was in the pillow. Both his arms were around the pillow.

"Hey, Jack!" John said to him.

Jack's head moved a little on the pillow. "Jack!" John says, leaning over him. Jack just dug a little deeper in the pillow. John touched him on the shoulder. Jack sat up and looked at us. He hadn't shaved and he was wearing an old sweater.

"Christ! Why can't you let me sleep?" he says to John.

"Don't be sore," John says. "I didn't mean to wake you up."

"Oh no," Jack says. "Of course not."

"You know Morgan and Steinfelt," John said.

"Glad to see you," Jack says.

"How do you feel, Jack?" Morgan asks him.

"Fine," Jack says. "How the hell would I feel?"

"You look fine," Steinfelt says.

"Yes, don't I," says Jack. "Say," he says to John. "You're my manager. You get a big enough cut. Why the hell don't you come out here when the reporters was out! You want Jerry and me to talk to them?"

"I had Lew fighting in Philadelphia," John said.

"What the hell's that to me?" Jack says. "You're my manager. You get a big enough cut, don't you? You aren't making me any money in Philadelphia, are you? Why the hell aren't you out here when I ought to have you?"

"Hogan was here."

"Hogan," Jack says. "Hogan's as dumb as I am."

"Soldier Bahtlett was out here wukking with you for a while, wasn't he?" Steinfelt said to change the subject.

"Yes, he was out here," Jack says. "He was out here all right."

"Say, Jerry," John said to me. "Would you go and find Hogan and tell him we want to see him in about half an hour?"

"Sure," I said.

"Why the hell can't he stick around?" Jack says. "Stick around, Jerry."

Morgan and Steinfelt looked at each other.

"Quiet down, Jack," John said to him.

"I better go find Hogan," I said.

"All right, if you want to go," Jack says. "None of these guys are going to send you away, though."

"I'll go find Hogan," I said.

Hogan was out in the gym in the barn. He had a couple of his health farm patients with the gloves on. They neither one wanted to hit the other, for fear the other would come back and hit him.

"That'll do," Hogan said when he saw me come in. "You can stop the slaughter. You gentlemen take a shower and Bruce will rub you down."

They climbed out through the ropes and Hogan came over to me.

"John Collins is out with a couple of friends to see Jack," I said.

"I saw them come up in the car."

"Who are the two fellows with John?"

"They're what you call wise boys," Hogan said. "Don't you know them two?"

"No," I said.

"That's Happy Steinfelt and Lew Morgan. They got a pool-room."

"I been away a long time," I said.

"Sure," said Hogan. "That Happy Steinfelt's a big operator."

"I've heard his name," I said.

"He's a pretty smooth boy," Hogan said. "They're a couple of sharp-shooters."

"Well," I said. "They want to see us in half an hour."

"You mean they don't want to see us until a half an hour?"

"That's it."

"Come on in the office," Hogan said. "To hell with those sharp-shooters."

After about thirty minutes or so Hogan and I went upstairs. We knocked on Jack's door. They were talking inside the room.

"Wait a minute," somebody said.

"To hell with that stuff," Hogan said. "When you want to see me I'm down in the office."

We heard the door unlock. Steinfelt opened it.

"Come on in, Hogan," he says. "We're all going to have a drink."

"Well," says Hogan. "That's something."

We went in. Jack was sitting on the bed. John and Morgan were sitting on a couple of chairs. Steinfelt was standing up.

"You're a pretty mysterious lot of boys," Hogan said.

"Hello, Danny," John says.

"Hello, Danny," Morgan says and shakes hands.

Jack doesn't say anything. He just sits there on the bed. He ain't with the others. He's all by himself. He was wearing an old blue jersey and pants and had on boxing shoes. He needed a shave. Steinfelt and Morgan were dressers. John was quite a dresser too. Jack sat there looking Irish and tough.

Steinfelt brought out a bottle and Hogan brought in some glasses and everybody had a drink. Jack and I took one and the rest of them went on and had two or three each.

"Better save some for your ride back," Hogan said.

"Don't you worry. We got plenty," Morgan said.

Jack hadn't drunk anything since the one drink. He was standing up and looking at them. Morgan was sitting on the bed where Jack had sat.

"Have a drink, Jack," John said and handed him the glass and the bottle.

"No," Jack said, "I never liked to go to these wakes."

They all laughed. Jack didn't laugh.

They were all feeling pretty good when they left. Jack stood on the porch when they got into the car. They waved to him.

"So long," Jack said.

We had supper. Jack didn't say anything all during the meal except, "Will you pass me this?" or "Will you pass me that?" The two health farm patients ate at the same table with us. They were pretty nice fellows. After we finished eating we went out on the porch. It was dark early.

"Like to take a walk, Jerry?" Jack asked.

"Sure," I said.

We put on our coats and started out. It was quite a way down to the main road and then we walked along the main road about a mile and a half. Cars kept going by and we would pull out to the side until they were past. Jack didn't say anything. After we had stepped out into the bushes to let a big car go by Jack said, "To hell with this walking. Come on back to Hogan's."

We went along a side road that cut up over the hill and cut across the fields back to Hogan's. We could see the lights of the house up on the hill. We came around to the front of the house and there standing in the doorway was Hogan.

"Have a good walk?" Hogan asked.

"Oh, fine," Jack said. "Listen, Hogan. Have you got any liquor?"

"Sure," says Hogan. "What's the idea?"

"Send it up to the room," Jack says. "I'm going to sleep tonight."

"You're the doctor," Hogan says.

"Come on up to the room, Jerry," Jack says.

Upstairs Jack sat on the bed with his head in his hands.

"Ain't it a life?" Jack says.

Hogan brought in a quart of liquor and two glasses.

"Want some ginger ale?"

"What do you think I want to do, get sick?"

"I just asked you," said Hogan.

"Have a drink?" said Jack.

"No, thanks," said Hogan. He went out.

"How about you, Jerry?"

"I'll have one with you," I said.

Jack poured out a couple of drinks. "Now," he said, "I want to take it slow and easy."

"Put some water in it," I said.

"Yes," Jack said. "I guess that's better."

We had a couple of drinks without saying anything. Jack started to pour me another.

"No," I said, "that's all I want."

"All right," Jack said. He poured himself out another big shot and put water in it. He was lighting up a little.

"That was a fine bunch out here this afternoon," he said. "They don't take any chances, those two."

Then a little later, "Well," he says, "they're right. What the hell's the good in taking chances?"

"Don't you want another, Jerry?" he said. "Come on, drink along with me."

"I don't need it, Jack," I said. "I feel all right."

"Just have one more," Jack said. It was softening him up.

"All right," I said.

Jack poured one for me and another big one for himself.

"You know," he said, "I like liquor pretty well. If I hadn't been box-ing I would have drunk quite a lot."

"Sure," I said.

"You know," he said, "I missed a lot, boxing."

"You made plenty of money."

"Sure, that's what I'm after. You know I miss a lot, Jerry."

"How do you mean?"

"Well," he says, "like about the wife. And being away from home so much. It don't do my girls any good. 'Who's your old man?' some of those society kids'll say to them. 'My old man's Jack Brennan.' That don't do them any good."

"Hell," I said, "all that makes a difference is if they got dough."

"Well," says Jack, "I got the dough for them all right."

He poured out another drink. The bottle was about empty.

"Put some water in it," I said. Jack poured in some water.

"You know," he says, "you ain't got any idea how I miss the wife."

"Sure."

"You ain't got any idea. You can't have an idea what it's like."

"It ought to be better out in the country than in town."

"With me now," Jack said, "it don't make any difference where I am. You can't have an idea what it's like."

"Have another drink."

"Am I getting soused? Do I talk funny?"

"You're coming on all right."

"You can't have an idea what it's like. They ain't anybody can have an idea what it's like."

"Except the wife," I said.

"She knows," Jack said. "She knows all right. She knows. You bet she knows."

"Put some water in that," I said.

"Jerry," says Jack, "you can't have an idea what it gets to be like."

He was good and drunk. He was looking at me steady. His eyes were sort of too steady.

"You'll sleep all right," I said.

"Listen, Jerry," Jack says. "You want to make some money? Get some money down on Walcott."

"Yes?"

"Listen, Jerry," Jack put down the glass. "I'm not drunk now, see? You know what I'm betting on him? Fifty grand."

"That's a lot of dough."

"Fifty grand," Jack says, "at two to one. I'll get twenty-five thousand bucks. Get some money on him, Jerry."

"It sounds good," I said.

"How can I beat him?" Jack says. "It ain't crooked. How can I beat him? Why not make money on it?"

"Put some water in that," I said.

"I'm through after this fight," Jack says. "I'm through with it. I got to take a beating. Why shouldn't I make money on it?"

"Sure."

"I ain't slept for a week," Jack says. "All night I lay awake and worry my can off. I can't sleep, Jerry. You ain't got an idea what it's like when you can't sleep."

"Sure."

"I can't sleep. That's all. I just can't sleep. What's the use of taking care of yourself all these years when you can't sleep?"

"It's bad."

"You ain't got an idea what it's like, Jerry, when you can't sleep."

"Put some water in that," I said.

Well, about eleven o'clock Jack passes out and I put him to bed. Finally he's so he can't keep from sleeping. I helped him get his clothes off and got him into bed.

"You'll sleep all right, Jack," I said.

"Sure," Jack says, "I'll sleep now."

"Good night, Jack," I said.

"Good night, Jerry," Jack says. "You're the only friend I got."

"Oh, hell," I said.

"You're the only friend I got," Jack says, "the only friend I got."

"Go to sleep," I said.

"I'll sleep," Jack says.

Downstairs Hogan was sitting at the desk in the office reading the papers. He looked up. "Well, you get your boy friend to sleep?" he asks.

"He's off."

"It's better for him than not sleeping," Hogan said.

"Sure."

"You'd have a hell of a time explaining that to these sport writers though," Hogan said.

"Well, I'm going to bed myself," I said.

"Good night," said Hogan.

In the morning I came downstairs about eight o'clock and got some breakfast. Hogan had his two customers out in the barn doing exercises. I went out and watched them.

"One! Two! Three! Four!" Hogan was counting for them. "Hello, Jerry," he said. "Is Jack up yet?"

"No. He's still sleeping."

I went back to my room and packed up to go in to town. About nine-thirty I heard Jack getting up in the next room. When I heard him go downstairs I went down after him. Jack was sitting at the breakfast table. Hogan had come in and was standing beside the table.

"How do you feel, Jack?" I asked him.

"Not so bad."

"Sleep well?" Hogan asked.

"I slept all right," Jack said. "I got a thick tongue but I ain't got a head."

"Good," said Hogan. "That was good liquor."

"Put it on the bill," Jack says.

"What time you want to go into town?" Hogan asked.

"Before lunch," Jack says. "The eleven o'clock train."

"Sit down, Jerry," Jack said. Hogan went out.

I sat down at the table. Jack was eating a grapefruit. When he'd find a seed he'd spit it out in the spoon and dump it on the plate.

"I guess I was pretty stewed last night," he started.

"You drank some liquor."

"I guess I said a lot of fool things."

"You weren't bad."

"Where's Hogan?" he asked. He was through with the grapefruit.

"He's out in front in the office."

"What did I say about betting on the fight?" Jack asked. He was holding the spoon and sort of poking at the grapefruit with it.

The girl came in with some ham and eggs and took away the grapefruit.

"Bring me another glass of milk," Jack said to her. She went out.

"You said you had fifty grand on Walcott," I said.

"That's right," Jack said.

"That's a lot of money."

"I don't feel too good about it," Jack said.

"Something might happen."

"No," Jack said. "He wants the title bad. They'll be shooting with him all right."

"You can't ever tell."

"No. He wants the title. It's worth a lot of money to him."

"Fifty grand is a lot of money," I said.

"It's business," said Jack. "I can't win. You know I can't win anyway."

"As long as you're in there you got a chance."

"No," Jack says. "I'm all through. It's just business."

"How do you feel?"

"Pretty good," Jack said. "The sleep was what I needed."

"You might go good."

"I'll give them a good show," Jack said.

After breakfast Jack called up his wife on the long-distance. He was inside the booth telephoning.

"That's the first time he's called her up since he's out here," Hogan said.

"He writes her every day."

"Sure," Hogan says, "a letter only costs two cents."

Hogan said good-by to us and Bruce, the nigger rubber, drove us down to the train in the cart.

"Good-by, Mr. Brennan," Bruce said at the train, "I sure hope you knock his can off."

"So long," Jack said. He gave Bruce two dollars. Bruce had worked on him a lot. He looked kind of disappointed. Jack saw me looking at Bruce holding the two dollars.

"It's all in the bill," he said. "Hogan charged me for the rubbing."

On the train going into town Jack didn't talk. He sat in the corner of the seat with his ticket in his hat band and looked out of the window. Once he turned and spoke to me.

"I told the wife I'd take a room at the Shelby tonight," he said. "It's just around the corner from the Garden. I can go up to the house tomorrow morning."

"That's a good idea," I said. "Your wife ever see you fight, Jack?"

"No," Jack says. "She never seen me fight."

I thought he must be figuring on taking an awful beating if he doesn't want to go home afterward. In town we took a taxi up to the Shelby. A boy came out and took our bags and we went in to the desk.

"How much are the rooms?" Jack asked.

"We only have double rooms," the clerk says. "I can give you a nice double room for ten dollars."

"That's too steep."

"I can give you a double room for seven dollars."

"With a bath?"

"Certainly."

"You might as well bunk with me, Jerry," Jack says.

"Oh," I said, "I'll sleep down at my brother-in-law's."

"I don't mean for you to pay it," Jack says. "I just want to get my money's worth."

"Will you register, please?" the clerk says. He looked at the names. "Number 238, Mister Brennan."

We went up in the elevator. It was a nice big room with two beds and a door opening into a bathroom.

"This is pretty good," Jack says.

The boy who brought us up pulled up the curtains and brought in our bags. Jack didn't make any move, so I gave the boy a quarter. We washed up and Jack said we better go out and get something to eat.

We ate a lunch at Jimmy Hanley's place. Quite a lot of the boys were there. When we were about half through eating, John came in and sat down with us. Jack didn't talk much.

"How are you on the weight, Jack?" John asked him. Jack was putting away a pretty good lunch.

"I could make it with my clothes on," Jack said. He never had to worry about taking off weight. He was a natural welterweight and he'd never gotten fat. He'd lost weight out at Hogan's.

"Well, that's one thing you never had to worry about," John said.

"That's one thing," Jack says.

We went around to the Garden to weigh in after lunch. The match was made at a hundred forty-seven pounds at three o'clock. Jack stepped on the scales with a towel around him. The bar didn't move. Walcott had just weighed and was standing with a lot of people around him.

"Let's see what you weigh, Jack," Freedman, Walcott's manager said.

"All right, weigh *him* then," Jack jerked his head toward Walcott.

"Drop the towel," Freedman said.

"What do you make it?" Jack asked the fellows who were weighing.

"One hundred and forty-three pounds," the fat man who was weighing said.

"You're down fine, Jack," Freedman says.

"Weigh *him,*" Jack says.

Walcott came over. He was a blond with wide shoulders and arms like a heavyweight. He didn't have much legs. Jack stood about half a head taller than he did.

"Hello, Jack," he said. His face was plenty marked up.

"Hello," said Jack. "How you feel?"

"Good," Walcott says. He dropped the towel from around his waist and stood on the scales. He had the widest shoulders and back you ever saw.

"One hundred and forty-six pounds and twelve ounces."

Walcott stepped off and grinned at Jack.

"Well," John says to him, "Jack's spotting you about four pounds."

"More than that when I come in, kid," Walcott says. "I'm going to go and eat now."

We went back and Jack got dressed. "He's a pretty tough-looking boy," Jack says to me.

"He looks as though he'd been hit plenty of times."

"Oh, yes," Jack says. "He ain't hard to hit."

"Where are you going?" John asked when Jack was dressed.

"Back to the hotel," Jack says. "You looked after everything?"

"Yes," John says. "It's all looked after."

"I'm going to lie down a while," Jack says.

"I'll come around for you about a quarter to seven and we'll go and eat."

"All right."

Up at the hotel Jack took off his shoes and his coat and lay down for a while. I wrote a letter. I looked over a couple of times and Jack wasn't sleeping. He was lying perfectly still but every once in a while his eyes would open. Finally he sits up.

"Want to play some cribbage, Jerry?" he says.

"Sure," I said.

He went over to his suitcase and got out the cards and the cribbage board. We played cribbage and he won three dollars off me. John knocked at the door and came in.

"Want to play some cribbage, John?" Jack asked him.

John put his hat down on the table. It was all wet. His coat was wet too.

"Is it raining?" Jack asks.

"It's pouring," John says. "The taxi I had got tied up in the traffic and I got out and walked."

"Come on, play some cribbage," Jack says.

"You ought to go and eat."

"No," says Jack. "I don't want to eat yet."

So they played cribbage for about half an hour and Jack won a dollar and a half off him.

"Well, I suppose we got to go eat," Jack says. He went to the window and looked out.

"Is it still raining?"

"Yes."

"Let's eat in the hotel," John says.

"All right," Jack says, "I'll play you once more to see who pays for the meal."

After a little while Jack gets up and says, "You buy the meal, John," and we went downstairs and ate in the big dining room.

After we ate we went upstairs and Jack played cribbage with John again and won two dollars and a half off him. Jack was feeling pretty good. John had a bag with him with all his stuff in it. Jack took off his shirt and collar and put on a jersey and a sweater, so he wouldn't catch cold when he came out, and put his ring clothes and his bathrobe in a bag.

"You all ready?" John asks him. "I'll call up and have them get a taxi."

Pretty soon the telephone rang and they said the taxi was waiting.

We rode down in the elevator and went out through the lobby, and got in a taxi and rode around to the Garden. It was raining hard but there was a lot of people outside on the streets. The Garden was sold out. As we came in on our way to the dressing room I saw how full it was. It looked like half a mile down to the ring. It was all dark. Just the lights over the ring.

"It's a good thing, with this rain, they didn't try and pull this fight in the ball park," John said.

"They got a good crowd," Jack says.

"This is a fight that would draw a lot more than the Garden could hold."

"You can't tell about the weather," Jack says.

John came to the door of the dressing room and poked his head in. Jack was sitting there with his bathrobe on, he had his arms folded and was looking at the floor. John had a couple of handlers with him. They looked over his shoulder. Jack looked up.

"Is he in?" he asked.

"He's just gone down," John said.

We started down. Walcott was just getting into the ring. The crowd gave him a big hand. He climbed through between the ropes and put his two fists together and smiled, and shook them at the crowd, first at one side of the ring, then at the other, and then sat down. Jack got a good hand coming down through the crowd. Jack is Irish and the Irish always get a pretty good hand. An Irishman don't draw in New York like a Jew or an Italian but they always get a good hand. Jack climbed up and bent down to go through the ropes and Walcott came over from his corner and pushed the rope down for Jack to go through. The crowd thought that was wonderful. Walcott put his hand on Jack's shoulder and they stood there just for a second.

"So you're going to be one of these popular champions," Jack says to him. "Take your goddam hand off my shoulder."

"Be yourself," Walcott says.

This is all great for the crowd. How gentlemanly the boys are before the fight. How they wish each other luck.

Solly Freedman came over to our corner while Jack is bandaging his hands and John is over in Walcott's corner. Jack puts his thumb through the slit in the bandage and then wrapped his hand nice and smooth. I taped it around the wrist and twice across the knuckles.

"Hey," Freedman says. "Where do you get all that tape?"

"Feel of it," Jack says. "It's soft, ain't it? Don't be a hick."

Freedman stands there all the time while Jack bandages the other hand, and one of the boys that's going to handle him brings the gloves and I pull them on and work them around.

"Say, Freedman," Jack asks, "what nationality is this Walcott?"

"I don't know," Solly says. "He's some sort of a Dane."

"He's a Bohemian," the lad who brought the gloves said.

The referee called them out to the center of the ring and Jack walks out. Walcott comes out smiling. They met and the referee put his arm on each of their shoulders.

"Hello, popularity," Jack says to Walcott.

"Be yourself."

"What do you call yourself 'Walcott' for?" Jack says. "Didn't you know he was a nigger?"

"Listen—" says the referee, and he gives them the same old line. Once Walcott interrupts him. He grabs Jack's arm and says, "Can I hit when he's got me like this?"

"Keep your hands off me," Jack says. "There ain't no moving pictures of this."

They went back to their corners. I lifted the bathrobe off Jack and he leaned on the ropes and flexed his knees a couple of times and scuffed his shoes in the rosin. The gong rang and Jack turned quick and went out. Walcott came toward him and they touched gloves and as soon as Walcott dropped his hands Jack jumped his left into his face twice. There wasn't anybody ever boxed better than Jack. Walcott was after him, going forward all the time with his chin on his chest. He's a hooker and he carries his hands pretty low. All he knows is to get in there and sock. But every time he gets in there close, Jack has the left hand in his face. It's just as though it's automatic. Jack just raises the left hand up and it's in Walcott's face. Three or four times Jack brings the right over but Walcott gets it on the shoulder or high up on the head. He's just like all these hookers. The only thing he's afraid of is another one of the same kind. He's covered everywhere you can hurt him. He don't care about a left-hand in his face.

After about four rounds Jack has him bleeding bad and his face all cut up, but every time Walcott's got in close he's socked so hard he's got two big red patches on both sides just below Jack's ribs. Every time he gets in close, Jack ties him up, then gets one hand loose and uppercuts him, but when Walcott gets his hands loose he socks Jack in the body so they can hear it outside in the street. He's a socker.

It goes along like that for three rounds more. They don't talk any. They're working all the time. We worked over Jack plenty too, in between the rounds. He don't look good at all but he never does much work in the ring. He don't move around much and that left-hand is just automatic. It's just like it was connected with Walcott's face and Jack just had to wish it in every time. Jack is always calm in close and he doesn't waste any juice. He knows everything about working in close too and he's getting away with a lot of stuff. While they were in our corner I watched him tie Walcott up, get his right hand loose, turn it and come up with an uppercut that got Walcott's nose with the heel of the glove. Walcott was bleeding bad and leaned his nose on Jack's shoulder so as to give Jack some of it too, and Jack sort of lifted his shoulder sharp and caught him against the nose, and then brought down the right hand and did the same thing again.

Walcott was sore as hell. By the time they'd gone five rounds he hated Jack's guts. Jack wasn't sore; that is, he wasn't any sorer than he always was. He certainly did used to make the fellows he fought hate boxing. That was why he hated Kid Lewis so. He never got the Kid's goat. Kid Lewis always had about three new dirty things Jack couldn't do. Jack was as safe as a church all the time he was in there, as long as he was strong. He certainly was treating Walcott rough. The funny thing was it looked as though Jack was an open classic boxer. That was because he had all that stuff too.

After the seventh round Jack says, "My left's getting heavy."

From then he started to take a beating. It didn't show at first. But instead of him running the fight it was Walcott was running it, instead of being safe all the time now he was in trouble. He couldn't keep him out with the left hand now. It looked as though it was the same as ever, only now instead of Walcott's punches just missing him they were just hitting him. He took an awful beating in the body.

"What's the round?" Jack asked.

"The eleventh."

"I can't stay," Jack says. "My legs are going bad."

Walcott had been just hitting him for a long time. It was like a baseball catcher pulls the ball and takes some of the shock off. From now on Walcott commenced to land solid. He certainly was a socking-machine. Jack was just trying to block everything now. It didn't show what an awful beating he was taking. In between the rounds I worked on his legs. The muscles would flutter under my hands all the time I was rubbing them. He was sick as hell.

"How's it go?" he asked John, turning around, his face all swollen.

"It's his fight."

"I think I can last," Jack says. "I don't want this bohunk to stop me."

It was going just the way he thought it would. He knew he couldn't beat Walcott. He wasn't strong anymore. He was all right though. His money was all right and now he wanted to finish it off right to please himself. He didn't want to be knocked out.

The gong rang and we pushed him out. He went out slow. Walcott came right out after him. Jack put the left in his face and Walcott took it, came in under it and started working on Jack's body. Jack tried to tie him up and it was just like trying to hold on to a buzz saw. Jack broke away from it and missed with the right. Walcott clipped him with a left hook and Jack went down. He went down on his hands and knees and looked at us. The referee started counting. Jack was watching us and shaking his head. At eight John motioned to him. You couldn't hear on account of the crowd. Jack got up. The referee had been holding Walcott back with one arm while he counted.

When Jack was on his feet Walcott started toward him.

"Watch yourself, Jimmy," I heard Solly Freedman yell to him.

Walcott came up to Jack looking at him. Jack stuck the left hand at him. Walcott just shook his head. He backed Jack up against the ropes, measured him and then hooked the left very light to the side of Jack's head and socked the right into the body as hard as he could sock, just as low as he could get it. He must have hit him five inches below the belt. I thought the eyes would come out of Jack's head. They stuck way out. His mouth come open.

The referee grabbed Walcott. Jack stepped forward. If he went down there went fifty thousand bucks. He walked as though all his insides were going to fall out.

"It wasn't low," he said. "It was a accident."

The crowd were yelling so you couldn't hear anything.

"I'm all right," Jack says. They were right in front of us. The referee looks at John and then he shakes his head.

"Come on, you polak son-of-a-bitch," Jack says to Walcott.

John was hanging onto the ropes. He had the towel ready to chuck in. Jack was standing just a little way out from the ropes. He took a step forward. I saw the sweat come out on his face like somebody had squeezed it and a big drop went down his nose.

"Come on and fight," Jack says to Walcott.

The referee looked at John and waved Walcott on.

"Go in there, you slob," he says.

Walcott went in. He didn't know what to do either. He never thought Jack could have stood it. Jack put the left in his face. There was such a hell of a lot of yelling going on. They were right in front of us. Walcott hit him twice. Jack's face was the worst thing I ever-saw—the look on it! He was holding himself and all his body together and it all showed on his face. All the time he was thinking and holding his body in where it was busted.

Then he started to sock. His face looked awful all the time. He started to sock with his hands low down by his side, swinging at Walcott.

Walcott covered up and Jack was swinging wild at Walcott's head. Then he swung the left and it hit Walcott in the groin and the right hit Walcott right bang where he'd hit Jack. Way low below the belt. Walcott went down and grabbed himself there and rolled and twisted around.

The referee grabbed Jack and pushed him toward his corner. John jumps into the ring. There was all this yelling going on. The referee was talking with the judges and then the announcer got into the ring with the megaphone and says, "Walcott on a foul."

The referee is talking to John and he says, "What could I do? Jack wouldn't take the foul. Then when he's groggy he fouls him."

"He'd lost it anyway," John says.

Jack's sitting on the chair. I've got his gloves off and he's holding himself in down there with both hands. When he's got something supporting it his face doesn't look so bad.

"Go over and say you're sorry," John says into his ear. "It'll look good."

Jack stands up and the sweat comes out all over his face. I put the bathrobe around him and he holds himself in with one hand under the bathrobe and goes across the ring. They've picked Walcott up and they're working on him. There're a lot of people in Walcott's corner. Nobody speaks to Jack. He leans over Walcott.

"I'm sorry," Jack says. "I didn't mean to foul you."

Walcott doesn't say anything. He looks too damned sick.

"Well, you're the champion now," Jack says to him. "I hope you get a hell of a lot of fun out of it."

"Leave the kid alone," Solly Freedman says.

"Hello, Solly," Jack says. "I'm sorry I fouled your boy."

Freedman just looks at him.

Jack went to his corner walking that funny jerky way and we got him down through the ropes and through the reporters' tables and out down the aisle. A lot of people want to slap Jack on the back. He goes out through all that mob in his bathrobe to the dressing room. It's a popular win for Walcott. That's the way the money was bet in the Garden.

Once we got inside the dressing room Jack lay down and shut his eyes.

"We want to get to the hotel and get a doctor," John says.

"I'm all busted inside," Jack says.

"I'm sorry as hell, Jack," John says.

"It's all right," Jack says.

He lies there with his eyes shut.

"They certainly tried a nice double-cross," John said.

"Your friends Morgan and Steinfelt," Jack said. "You got nice friends."

He lies there, his eyes are open now. His face has still got that awful drawn look.

"It's funny how fast you can think when it means that much money," Jack says.

"You're some boy, Jack," John says.

"No," Jack says. "It was nothing."

THE MELEE
OF THE MAGES

Paul Gallico

S o now I'm writing a story. What can happen to me? All right, so I don't got much education from getting tossed out of grade 8A of P. S. 191 which is just a couple of blocks east of Delancey Street where I was born, for clipping the big, dumb Jake Rosenzweig, so he goes to a hospital.

Maybe if I don't take that poke at Jake ten years ago for giving me the business, when the teacher ain't looking, I go a lot further, though I guess I ain't done so bad, have I? Ask any sporting writer about Goldie. Who is writing all the press releases for Hymie Korngold's stable of Fighters that Fight, so they go in the papers sometimes with only a couple of words changed? Who takes care of the sportswriters around the training camps when we got a boy working out, and runs errands for them? Who is even allowed by Hymie Korngold sometimes I should handle a boy for him out of town when we got a fight that ain't too important? Little Irving Goldstein. But everybody calls me just Goldie.

So I guess I ain't sorry I put the slug on that big Rosenzweig, he should gradually waste away from a fatal sickness, for what the lug done to me and them other kids, the bully. A supply of small buckshot he used to keep in his teeth, and then "zip!" He'd snap one out with his teeth and sting you in the ear or the back of the neck. So one day I let him have it. There shouldn't a been no trouble only I busted his jawr and made him swallow some of the buckshot, it couldn't happen to him better. But he goes to the hospital and they give me the heav-o out of P. S. 191 and I hadda go to work.

But education ain't everything, especially when you got natural ability

22

like I have which comes by me naturally, and Joe Parkhurst who is the sports columnist for the *Morning Democrat* says it's even better if you are going to write stories you don't have too much education or the editors will not know what you are trying to say.

Joe shows me a check for one hundred bucks he got one day for writing a story for a magazine out of his head, so I says "Boy, what a racket. How long has this been going on? I'll bet I could write a story. Gimme the angle will ya, Joe?"

So Joe says—"Sure, Goldie. It's a cinch. All you do is sit down at a typewriter with a lotta paper and just tell what happens to somebody."

I says—"And they give ya dough for that?"

Joe just flashes the pay paper again. You gotta admit it's a convincer, ain't it?

So that's why I'm writing now the story of how we come to win the middleweight championship of the world with Packy McSween at the Yankee Stadium last June from Joe Falone, the champion and holder of the world crown, before eighty-nine thousand people in what the sports-writers called *The Melee of the Mages,* also the *Combat of the Conjurers* and the *War of the Wizards*.

Maybe if you was there you are saying to yourself, what is the story in that, because after the hocus-pocus between Hex-Eye Lipschitz and Professor Swammi the Wabadaba of Waaf is over, all you see was Packy slide out from our corner and park his right alongside Falone's kisser after which the call for the stiff-wagon is in order.

Chum, I'm telling you that that part of it was just wrapping up the package and delivering it C.O.D. What I got is the stuff that goes inside the bundle before we hand it to Joe Falone, the inside dope that don't get into the papers on account of what Hymie Korngold calls it secrets of the trade.

It begins maybe six months ago when Hymie Korngold gets mad with Hex-Eye Lipschitz who has been working for us regular, and tosses him out of the office over the matter of a couple of bucks. Maybe it is a foolish thing to do, but Hymie is very fond of a buck as everybody knows and if a guy is not entitled to be peculiar about something, what is it worth?

Also since we make the surprise win with Packy McSween over K. O. Hogan in the Garden in three rounds last winter with Hex-Eye putting the double whammy on Hogan, so it gradually comes a weakness over him and he doesn't duck Packy's right, Lipschitz—he should be getting in both knees eventually enough water to floating the Queen Mary—is becoming so swelled up he is not only raising his prices double but he is also demanding a piece of the fighter which is something Hymie will part with his right leg sooner than.

I guess you read about Hex-Eye Lipschitz who is a curious character around the fight racket who has the wonderful gift endowed by nature to put the hex on a fighter so he loses, just by sitting in the opposite corner and giving him the eye. He is a little Yiddle, who you would not notice in a crowd except he's got bug eyes with a very funny look in them sort of creepy-like, and when he gives them to you good, you feel like one good slap on the elbow would knock you out for a week.

Hymie picked him up in Detroit where he was making cakes and coffee putting the zing on prelim boys for two slugs apiece, brought him to New York and put him on the big time working for our stable, and I gotta hand it to him, he done pretty good, because we don't lose a fight since he joined up.

He got a regular price scale of twenty-five bucks for the left eye only where the fight ain't so important or you feel pretty sure your boy he win anyway, fifty bucks for the right eye only which is a lot more powerful and is good for a semi-windup, and one hundred smackers cash for the double whammy, which is both eyes full strength, where you are in the main event and gotta win.

So right after we stiffen Hogan, Hex-Eye is around saying that he is underpaid for his services and that he will take ten percent of Packy McSween from now on, along with double price since nobody expects Hogan will be knocked out and he alone is responsible for this glorious victory.

Naturally Hymie is sore and says Hex-Eye should gradually die first, and he is nothing but a banjo-eyed faker what he picked up when he was starving in Detroit and made him a national character in the newspapers and that the whole thing was only a lot of cykology anyway, and that he would expose him, and would he now get the Hell out of the office. So Hex-Eye Lipschitz quick gives Hymie both eyes, making Hymie duck, and then takes the air. An itching should it be by him in the nose all day long but he shouldn't be able to sneeze yet.

But I am thinking that is maybe a very wrong thing Hymie says to a guy with as powerful an eye as Lipschitz, and I am wishing maybe he had not done it, because we are going very good with the stable and especially Packy McSween. I guess maybe Hymie figures he has done wrong too, for he cools off the next day and sends around word to Hex-Eye that he was only kidding and he will pay him more money but he should forget about a piece of Packy because Packy is already cut up like a jig saw puzzle and there are not enough pieces left to go round.

We wait three days and nothing happens and I am getting very nervous when Hex-Eye sends word back what Hymie should do with his money because he has insulted him and that from now on he will have no part of him any more and besides which he has signed up with Big Augie Schonblum's stable which is the manager of Joe Falone, the middleweight titleholder of the world, and when he meets up with any of Hymie's fighters in the opposite corner, he will not only give them the double whammy with both eyes, but also the lip which he has been working on with some good klulases, which is Jewish curses, for good measure.

Well, that is bad, but not so bad, because we don't fight many of Big Augie's boys on account of him and Hymie don't get along very well together, and we figure we are at least a year away with Packy for a shot at the middleweight crown of the world.

But that just goes to show you how things happen in the fight racket and that you can't never tell. Angelo De Spoldi, who is next in line for the summer crack at Joe Louis, goes and breaks his arm falling off one of them electric horses in Steeplechase Park and Mike Jacobs is out at the big ball park match.

He gotta have something to throw in there, so Uncle Mike gets busy and promises Big Augie the Mint, ten shares of U.S. Steel and a piece of the Empire State Building if he will sign for Joe Falone to defend his middleweight title of the world in the Yankee Stadium against Packy McSween.

Big Augie signs, and we're in. We get the crack at the middleweight championship crown of the world, one of the prized bubbles of Fistiana. It is true, there is a side arrangement where Big Augie will wind up with practically all the dough with Packy in there just for the healthful exercise in the open air, but nothing worse should happen to us then we get a chance to lift that title a year sooner.

So trouble starts. Right away we find out why Big Augie is so eager to put the John Patrick Henry on the dotted line. He figures he got the difference. We are so excited about getting the match we forget all about Hex-Eye Lipschitz. He should slowly become so crippled in the spine he can't even sitting in a wheel chair yet.

The night of the afternoon we sign up the match for the photogafers, he calls Packy up on the telephone at his home and says—"Listen, Irisher, you tell that cheap goniff of a manager of yours that there ain't no use of you even going in the ring against Joe Falone, because I will be sitting in his corner and I am putting on you the left, the right, and the double whammy and you will be stiffen so quick the customers don't even get a chance to take off their coats and sit down," and he hangs up.

So Packy is around the office the next day, all broke up and doesn't want to go through with the fight because he says he knows that Lipschitz will put the zing on him and he seen how it worked on K. O. Hogan.

This Packy is not like the rest of them bums, he is a good kid, when you get to know him, but being an Irisher goy he is terrible sensitive and superstitious about the Evil Eye and hexes. He is a clean living boy that come outa the Golden Gloves with a good left and a short right that reminded you of the one Jack Delaney used to throw.

Hymie developed him good and brought him along easy, and we are no worse than even to lift the world diadem from the brow of Falone, if Packy will just forget about Hex-Eye and go in there and spear with his left until he can find a spot to drop the payoff with the right.

So Hymie has to go to work on him and says—"Aw, now Packy, that's all a lot of hooey. Anyway, Hex-Eye is a Jewisher and it's a Jewisher curse so it don't do no good against Irishers."

"Oh yeah?" says Packy. "That looked more like a Harp to me than a Star of David on Hogan's bathrobe. He was a Mick, but he dropped his hands when Hex-Eye put the $100 whammy on him and gimme a clip at his jaw."

Well, Hymie I guess had forgotten that.

Miss Mitnick who is Hymie's secretary and a cute trick that I could go for myself, with big brown eyes, lets out a sigh, and says—"Oh, Packy, I'm just knowing you can beat Mr. Falone. He got nothing that you haven't got."

By which I am having an idea that maybe Miss Mitnick is a little sweet on Packy, for which I don't blame her for like I said, he is a nice clean-looking kid with red hair. But Packy just groans and says—

"Oh yeah? He's got Hex-Eye Lipschitz."

So finally Hymie has to tell me to go out and square it with Hex-Eye.

I beat it up Broadway a couple of blocks and go over to outside the Garden where I hang around until pretty soon Hex-Eye comes along alone and I grab him and get a finger in his buttonhole.

"It's O. K., Hex-Eye," I says, "Hymie says you're to come back to work for him. And to show you there's no hard feelings he's giving you five percent of Packy McSween after we win the world's title. Now what do ya say?"

What do I get? I get a look outa them awful bugeyes so it's coming in my legs a weakness already.

"Amscray, bum," he says. "You go back and tell Hymie Goldkorn I wouldn't have no fifty percent of what's gonna be with Packy McSween after I and Joe Falone get through with him. I wouldn't take no hundred and fifty percent. He called me a banjo-eyed faker, me what is responsible for his success. You tell Hymie next time I am seeing him I am putting a klula on him, down an open manhole he should fall and break both ankles. And anyway, I am sign up with Big Augie, and am very busy. I am putting the whammy on a big dinge we are fighting in Philadelphia tonight and I must go home and practice before the mirror until it is time to take the train."

I give him a good klula when we walked away. His teeth should all gradually fall out down his throat so he should choke to death yet. But it don't look so good for our side, what I have to go back and tell Hymie, does it?

So there we are, and time goes by like it does and all of a sudden it is only three days away from when we are packing up to go to Madam Bey's camp at Summit, N.J. for six weeks of outdoor training so we can get a little steam-up for the fight in the papers which is not going so good right then because all the boys were kind of set for the Da Spoldi-Louis match, and we are very low in our minds.

Packy has not been working out good in the gym at all, and Hex-Eye has announced in the newspapers that he is going along to Gus Wilson's camp at Orangeburg, N.J. where Joe Falone, the champion of the world, will train for his title defense and Hex-Eye said that he will also go into training and work out both eyes every day so that they will be extra-special sharp and full of the old zing when it comes to slapping the whammy on Packy McSween.

Hymie is sitting at his desk, all slumped down with his hands in his pockets shaking his head and moaning—"We gotta do something, we gotta do something. That kid he lose the fight already. A flyweight near tipped him over in the gym today. We gotta do something against Hex-Eye."

All of a sudden he looks up at the ceiling like he was going to bust with a sneeze. Then he starts chewing on his lip and bangs the desk with his fist and yells—"I got it, Goldie! I got it! Gimme that phone."

He grabs the phone by the neck and gives the number in Yiddish first he is so excited, and while he is waiting for it he says to me—

"Goldie, beat it over to the Garden and round up them boxing writers. Tell 'em to be down here at five o'clock this afternoon. Tell 'em I'm gonna have a statement of the utmost importance for them. That always gets 'em. See if ya can get some of those columnists too, anybody that's around there."

So I go over to the Garden and dig 'em up like he says.

I am back in the office at five o'clock with all the sports writers and columnists I can round up which all are very curious about what kind of an important statement Hymie is giving out but I can't tell 'em nothing because I don't know nothing what is on Hymie's mind.

I gotta hand it to Hymie, it was good. He keeps us waiting in the outside room about five minutes. Then he throws open the door and says with plenty of the old schmaltz in his voice—"O.K., boys, you can come."

And when we go in, what's standing there? Such a thing shouldn't happen in a nightmare.

It's a tall guy, over six feet with a big black beard so long he shouldn't ever have to wear a necktie. He is wearing a black cloak like a rabbi only on his head he got a white turban wound around like them pictures of snake charmers. Also he got a mustache like a Turkish wrassler from Jake Pfeiffer's stable. He stands there grinning with white teeth like a horse.

"Boys," says Hymie—"I'm introducing to you Professor Swammi, the Wabadaba of Waaf, from India. That's in Asia." Then he turns to the guy and says—"Go ahead, Professor, give it to 'em just like you give it to me."

So the Professor gives a bow and touches two fingers to his noggin and then his beard and says like this in a deep voice like in *schul*—

"I am introducing myself, I am Abadullah Swammi, Great Wabadaba of Waaf, Seer and Prophet of Tetragramatan, delver into the eighth, ninth, and thirteenth mysteries of Asch Mezareph and Sepher Jetzirah, Seeker after the Golden Egg of Bramah, Interpreter of the Nuctemeron, the Zahun and the Mizkun. I read the past in the crystal ball, the present in the Sacred Mirror of Cahor, and the future in the Secret Scrolls of the Seven Butatars of Pharzuph, for one dollar. I am the Alph, the Eph, the Zizuph, and the Toglas . . ."

I hear one of the boys in the back row make the crack—

"Not to mention the Phonus and the Balonus!"

But Hymie he don't hear anything he is so excited, although I gotta say it sounded more like out of the Talmud than from Indians, but Hymie just slaps his side and says—"Ain't it a spiel, boys, ain't it? Has he got it? I'm asking you?"

Joe Parkhurst says—"He sure is a pip, Hymie. Whadaya gonna do with him?"

"What am I gonna do with him? That's what I'm telling you. He's a genuine Indian magic. He is joining up with the camp of Packy McSween challenger of the middleweight crown of the world when we are going to Madam Bey's. He is the reply of Hymie Korngold Ink. to that cheap, low-life faker Hex-Eye Lipschitz who is giving out statements already from the camp of Joe Falone, about what he should do when Packy gets in the ring. One look from them lamps of the Professor and Hex-Eye should drop dead."

"You mean he's going away to camp with you?" says Parkhurst.

"Absolutely and positively! He's in strict training like Packy. He's got to exercising his eye again because he ain't used it since the last time in the desert in India when he gives it to a wild helephant so he'd gradually falling down from convulsions."

The same guy who makes the other crack says—"Who, the helephant or the Professor?" but nobody pays him no attention, because them guys know a terrific story when they see it, and after they ask a couple more questions they all beat it away to get it into the paper and the Professor goes home to pack for Madam Bey's.

Hymie says to me—"Ain't he terrific, Goldie? But terrific? He got a studio in the Bronx. Everybody in high society on the Grand Concourse goes to him. It comes to me like a flash. My sister is telling me about him. Two weeks ago he is saying to her she is going on a trip. And now unexpectedly already she is packing to go up to Grossinger's in the Catskills on the invitation of Yella Weintraub. Like a flash it comes to me we get the Professor. So he joins the camp for five C's if we win the title, three C's if something happens."

I gotta admit the Professor has a terrific make-up, but I'm not going so good for the Professor yet, why I do not know, so I say—"Can he give the eye?"

"Can he give the eye?" Hymie yells. "You're asking me can he give the eye? How the Hell do I know can he give the eye? He looks like it, don't he? He says he can. We gotta do something, don't we? So all right, we take him to camp with us. When them photographs come out of the Professor in his turband, that Lipschitz should bust from jealousy."

Well, I'm telling you it's wonderful. Do we get publicity? Two hours each morning I gotta spend just pasting up clippings in Hymie's press book.

What looks like starting off may be a crowd of twenty-five thousand with an eighty grand gate, is selling already so many tickets, Mike Jacobs got to increase the ringside seats and print more.

We got one gang of writers in our camp covering Packy's workout and another bunch that do nothing but just cover Professor Swammi when he trains in the ring, putting the eye, after Packy is finished working out. And it's the same over in Joe Falone's camp where Hex-Eye is training first one eye, then the other and then both and issuing statements what he will do to Professor Swammi and Packy McSween.

You can't read nothing else in the newspapers except about what they call the "Combat of the Conjurors," the "Battle of the Enchanted Optics," and the "Tournament of the Thaumaturgs."

We are up and down with Packy, who works out good one day and lousy the next according to what the reports are coming out of Falone's camp, on Hex-Eye. Like the day the story comes out of Orangeburg that Hex-Eye puts the zing on a bottle of Grade A in the middle of the ring in front of everybody, giving it only the right eye alone and when they open it afterwards, it's buttermilk.

"Boy," Hymie says to me, "that's bad. I tried to keep the papers away from Packy, but he heard it over the radio and now he don't feel so good no more. We gotta have Professor Swammi pull one that'll throw a scare into them. Maybe he should work out this afternoon wilting some flowers, or something."

But I says—"Leave it to me, I got a better idea."

So I fix it up with George Lawson, a big shine sparring partner for ten bucks extra he should get bewitched, but good. So while him and Packy are working a fast round, Professor Swammi climbs up the side of the ring, mumbling something about giving George both eyes. I gotta hand it to him, the dinge earns his ten. Right in the middle he drops his hands and starts to moan—

"O Lawdy, Lawdy, de eye is on me. I feels the strength a-oozing from mah bones."

So of course Packy stiffens him with the right, and we get a lot of fine publicity in the papers and Packy starts to work good again until we get word the next day that Big Augie has got Clyde Beatty to bring a trick lion over from the circus for Hex-Eye to practice putting the whammy on, and now the circus is going to sue Big Augie because the same night the lion got sick of the stomach and died in great agony.

A couple of days later Joe Parkhurst comes out with a big column in the *Morning Democrat* which is an exclusive interview with Hex-Eye Lipschitz himself in which he says—

"Who did this so-called Professor Swammi ever Hex? What's his record? Let him go out and get a reputation before he tries to climb in the same ring with a man who has put the whammy on some of the best boys in fistendom. I say let him name one guy he has give the eye to. What goes on?"

And then comes in the interview a long list of all the boys Hex-Eye has put the peepers to so that they are either knock out or lose the dezision, ending up with K.O. Hogan.

Well, Packy is pretty sick again when he reads that one, and Hymie has to think fast so he says maybe it is a good idea if we give the Prof. an out-of-town tryout to see if we can't build him up a little before we throw him into the ring against Hex-Eye in the main event.

We have a good lightweight, Sammy Levin, going in Scranton in a special eight against Rocky Bazone a couple of nights later and Hymie, who is too busy to leave, sends me with the kid to handle him and tells me to bring the Professor along he should take a workout on Rocky who is all washed up and can't punch any more so Sammy is a sure thing to win, otherwise why should we be in there fighting him?

That ain't a trip I'm gonna forget. First they musta had a plague of gnats down there in Scranton because I never got stung so many times in my life, I am so busy all the time slapping at them. And second is, the Professor he don't go so good.

It is a sell out house because word has been printed that the Professor will be there, and so we are in our corners after the introductions, waiting for the bell with me telling Sammy how to use his left, and the Professor wearing his white turband is hanging over the ropes in the corner with me.

So the bell rings and the Professor fixes his lamps on Rocky who is coming out of his corner winding up his right, and says—"Mene! Mene Tekel Upharsin!" which Sammy thinks I am giving him some last minute instructions in Yiddish so he turns his head and asks—*"Vos haste gezugt Goldie?"*

So he is not looking at all when Rocky comes over and parks that right square on his potato, and Sammy is out like a light.

Well, I am telling you that if the knockdown timekeeper is not a personal friend of Hymie's and does not give Sammy one of those—"One—one and a half, two—two and three quarters," counts for about eighteen seconds, he will never get up except I have the presents of mind to kick over the water bucket right where Sammy is laying so it goes over his head and he makes it, otherwise the timekeeper is going to have to say, "Nineteen, twenty, you're out!" no matter how good friends he is with Hymie.

It takes Sammy four rounds to know what town he's in, but he comes around and we get the nod, but just. It's a good thing Hymie got friends among them judges too. And all the way home on the train them gnats is with us.

Well, it's all right, and Hymie give out the story how Sammy Levin is foully butted by Rocky Bazone, but that the power of the Professor's eye holds off Rocky until Sammy can come back and dezision him.

But I am beginning to be a little uneasy by this time and am wishing that Big Augie has the Professor and we have Hex-Eye Lipschitz, when it comes up the fight. I will like it better.

So it's coming on close to the big show, and nobody don't write no more whether Packy McSween is sweating good, and works four fast rounds with his spar mates, or whether Joe Falone's lightning left is as fast as it was two years ago. All that's in the papers is what Hex-Eye will do to the Prof. when he gets him in the ring and how Professor

Swammi will put the Egyptian Blast on Hex-Eye before Hex-Eye he even gets one look at Packy.

The *Morning Scimitar* comes out with the life story of Hex-Eye Lipschitz, and puts on a hundred thousand circulation, so Hymie counters right away with a series of signed articles by Professor Swammi in the *Morning Democrat* which is spooked by Joe Parkhurst. A couple of guys in Tin Pan Alley even write a song—*With the Swammi on that Swannee River Shore*. I'm telling you the build-up is terrific.

So it's coming closer all the time to the fight. Hex-Eye goes on *We, the People* on the radio in which he says with his left eye alone he will not only put the snore on the Swammi but he will cripple all his relatives too.

Hymie comes right back and gets the Professor on *Information Please*, where he turns out an awful dope what don't know any of the answers to the questions, but Hymie explains quick to the press that that is because on account of the radio he cannot use the power of his eyes which is what he is going to give to Hex-Eye and Joe Falone the night of the fight so it will be coming to them both the St. Vitus dance for a month.

It is fix up with the Commission that both Hex-Eye and the Professor are issued seconds' licenses so they can walk to the center of the ring with the two boys, because that is where the big event is going to take place where they will go to work with their whammies and try to put it on each other and the two fighters, just before they ring the bell.

Hymie and Big Augie reach an agreement in Mike Jacobs' office that neither Hex-Eye nor Professor Swammi are to show up at the weighing in, because Uncle Mike points out that when 79,000 people have bought tickets, with the unreserved sections still to go, they are entitled to a gander at the big doings, or as one sportswriter called it the Duel of the Demons.

So finally comes the day of the fight which is scheduled for ten o'clock at night in the Yankee Stadium, and you couldn't buy a ticket for it no matter who you knew. Everybody is going to be there to see what happens when the famous Hex-Eye Lipschitz meets Professor Abadullah Swammi, the Wabadaba of Waaf, face to face. The whole Bronx has a special section to cheer on the Professor while the Lower East Side and the Grand Street Boys have bought two thousand seats together to yell for Hex-Eye.

And I am feeling not so good. That afternoon, I am up in our office which is closed, to get a block of tickets Hymie left in his desk. No one is supposed to be there so when I hear a sort of funny sound from the inside office, I am surprised. I go in, and there is Miss Mitnick, and she has her head down on her arms over her typewriter and is crying. She ain't a very big dame, and she got them soft dark eyes that look even better when they're leaking.

So I says—"Well, well, sister. Something wrong? What's eating ya?"

She looks up at me so I feel I'm gonna melt and says—"O Goldie, Goldie, I'm so unhappy. I'm so afraid Packy isn't going to win and will be hurt. I saw Packy last night. He thinks he's going to lose. He doesn't believe in the Professor, and I don't either. A friend wrote to him from Scranton that the Professor was a big flop as a hexer and Levin would have been knocked out except they gave him a Chicago count. So now Packy is sure that Lipschitz will put the eye on him and he will be knocked out too. O Goldie! Can the Professor *do* anything?"

"Sister," I said—"I'll betcha the Professor couldn't put a cat to sleep if he had a can of chloroform in both hands. That Hex-Eye's got the goods, because I seen it work on Hogan. It looks bad, don't it? A congestion should slowly come to both his lungs and it shouldn't be handy an oxygen tent."

Miss Mitnick puts her head down and is sobbing harder, so I'm putting my arm around her and saying—"Don't cry so, sister. Maybe Packy's gonna win yet because he's got a good punch. You're pretty sweet on him, ain'tcha?"

She says—"Y-yes, Goldie, I am. He loves me too. He said so."

"Ya known him long?"

"Y-yes," she says. "We were sweethearts when we went to public school together on the Lower East Side, but we had a quarrel and I didn't see him again until I came to work for Hymie. It's all made up now, and now he isn't going to win and will get hurt . . ."

It comes to me like a lightning!

I'm telling you, I should live so, it comes on me just like a lightning out of the sky. I musta hit poor Miss Mitnick an awful clout on the back I got so excited because she jumped up with a scream, but I said—

"Sister, I got it. I'm tellin' ya I got it. You just leave it to Little Goldie. We're gonna see who puts what whammy on who. An' Packy's gonna be the new champion of the world. G'bye now, and don't you worry no more."

I beat it over to the Hotel Edison where we had our headquarters. But fast. They were all back from the weighing in and sitting around the room looking sick, Packy, and Hymie, and Doc who works in the corner with Hymie.

I says to Hymie—"Where's the Professor?"

Hymie answers—"He's in his room. He don't feel so good, he says. Maybe he wants to take a run-out powder."

"He's gonna feel worse before he feels better." The next minute I'm in his room. He ain't got his turband on and is sitting on the sofa looking sort of green because he is scared to death of meeting Hex-Eye Lipschitz and he got a just-opened bottle of whiskey on the table and a glass, which I knock onto the floor.

"Professor Swammi," I says—"You and me are going to have a little talk."

So we have a little talk.

So now I'm gonna tell ya about the fight because maybe you ain't a ex-bootlegger, or nightclub owner, or gangster or an actor or a politician, in which case you wasn't sitting close up enough to that ring to really see what happened.

Boy, if I'm living to be a hundred I ain't never gonna forget the noise that crowd makes when me and Packy and Hymie and Doc and the Professor come down the aisle to go to the corner. Wow!

The Professor has on a new white turband with a silver star sticking up in the front of it and a new cloak that Hymie got made up at Brooks Brothers Costumers for him with silver stars and moons on it. Did we get a hand with everybody yelling—"Attaboy, Swammi old boy! Stick it on him! We're with you!"

Then Joe Falone, the middleweight world's championship titleholder comes in with his gang with Hex-Eye Lipschitz wearing a dress suit they rented for him somewhere over on Second Avenue, with a red band across his shirt front like a diplomat, puffed up like a politician and wearing a pair of blue goggles over his eyes so as not to strain them until he is ready to let go the big whammy, and the crowd goes wild.

"Come on, Hex-Eye," they yell—"Show up that big phony! Make him like it!"

Harry Balogh was using the loudspeaker for the interductions, but you couldn't even hear them with those because of the noise the crowd is making. It seemed like the whole city is split up over who is going to win between Hex-Eye and the Professor.

So the moment comes at last when the referee calls the two boys to the center of the ring. I am crouched down at the ringside in our corner, and don't think I wasn't sweating. I am so excited I can't even think of a good klula to say at Hex-Eye.

There they are in the center of the ring, Joe Falone and Packy shaking hands and I can see Packy's knees shivering, and Big Augie and Hymie and Hex-Eye Lipschitz and Professor Abadullah Swammi, the Wabadaba of Waaf.

Everybody in the park is standing on their feet, screaming and yelling —"Give it to him, Hex-Eye! Let him have it, Swammi! Both eyes,

Hex-Eye! Put the Indian sign on him, Swammi! He'll lay down, Swammi! Show him up for a phony, Hex-Eye!"

So while the instructions are going on, the Professor is just standing there quietly grinning at Hex-Eye and showing his teeth, and they sure were nice, white strong teeth, and I can see that Hex-Eye is beginning to get a little nervous because the Professor is just standing there grinning at him like a dope without saying anything. So the referee finishes his instructions and there comes a sort of lull for a second in which I hear Hex-Eye say to the Professor—

"What are you grinning at, you big schmuck? You can starting to wipe that grin offn your big ugly face, because I'm gonna give you the eye, and I'm gonna give it to you now," and he puts his hand up to his glasses.

That crowd stops yelling just like one big hand had shut it off with a choke.

You coulda heard a dime drop as Hex-Eye slowly removes his glasses and sticks his puss right up close to the Professor's who is still grinning and says—"I am giving you the eye now! I am giving you *both* eyes!"

And the next thing you know Hex-Eye is clapping his hands to his face and letting out a yell you coulda heard in Weehawken—

"Ow! Ow, my eyes! I'm blind! Help, I'm blind! I can't see!" and starts to stagger around the ring, pawing with one hand and keeping the other over his glims.

Wow! What a yell went up from that crowd! It sounded like eight million people all screaming "Swammi! Swammi! Swammi!"

The ring is full of confusion. Packy is jigging around with a look on his face like he got a reprieve from the Governor. Big Augie doesn't know what to make of it and is trying to catch Hex-Eye to keep him from falling out of the ring. The Professor is taking bows to all four sides, putting his fingers to his bean and his whiskers and the referee is looking confused as though he does not know just what to do.

So I yell up at him—"Throw that bum out of there and start the fight," at just the right moment because it helps him make up his mind. He goes over and grabs Hex-Eye by the arm and hustles him to his corner and out through the ropes while Hymie snatches the Professor who would be in there taking bows all night otherwise and gives him the toss.

"Bong!" The timekeeper yanks the bell, and they're off.

Joe Falone comes out of his corner, and because he is a little dazed by what has happened to Hex-Eye he don't carry his left hand as high as he ought, and *blowie!* Packy is in there and drops the sweetheart right smack on Joe's chinaware, and the referee he don't even bother enough to count.

We got the new middleweight champion titleholder of the world's crown.

Joe Falone is still snoring in his corner when Hex-Eye starts yelling "It's all right now. I can see again! Where is that gonif so I will put the eye on him now. Show him to me!" So when he finds out that his boy has been chilled so he will not be up in time maybe to see next Sunday's funny papers, he is around the ringside yelling—"We was robbed! I got shot! I want another chance!"

But everybody is just giving him the horse laugh, and Hymie is in the ring, hugging and kissing Packy and the Professor, and talking into the radio, and Miss Mitnick comes up and kisses me and says—

"O Goldie, isn't it wonderful! I'm the happiest girl in the world. And you said it would be all right. But O Goldie, I'm so ashamed of the things I said about Professor Swammi. Wasn't he just too wonderful the way he stood there and put a spell on that awful Hex-Eye?"

So I don't say nothing, and soon she is in the ring with her arms around Packy and the photogafers are taking pictures and also a picture of her kissing the Professor in the middle of his whiskers.

And I am laughing, because there are 89,000 people in that park, but I am the only one that knows that Professor Abadullah Swammi ain't no professor at all, and he ain't from India either. He is Jake Rosenzweig from P.S. 191 whose jawr I busted for giving us kids the business with them little buckshot out of his teeth.

If I wasn't so dumb I should of known him right away except it is ten years since I see him and then he is hiding behind all that spinach he grows to play the part of Professor Swammi so he can tell fortunes to the suckers in the Bronx.

And if I got any brains I shoulda known it wasn't gnats that night in Scranton but that big bum still giving me the business with them buck-shot. It don't come back to me until I am talking with Miss Mitnick in the office the day of the fight and she says public school on the Lower East Side and a quarrel, and then all of a sudden, like I say, it comes on me like a lightning, where I seen Professor Swammi before, the lug.

So when I'm in his room the day of the fight I tell him what he should do with Hex-Eye when he meets him in the ring and he says he ain't gonna go in the ring because he is afraid of Hex-Eye, so I tell him if he takes a powder I will tell everyone he ain't no Professor Swammi but just plain Jake Rosenzweig, and he is more afraid of that than he is of Hex-Eye.

When Hex-Eye sticks his puss right up into his in the ring, Jake has a half a mouthful of buckshot ready for him and lets him have it right in the eyeballs. He never made two better shots, even in P.S. 191.

All right, is it a story, or is it? I'm asking you. If it don't thinking so the editors I am getting ready for them a good klula. It should come by them gradually a *geschwulst* on the larynx so they shouldn't be able to talking for eight months, except with the hands, where they should getting eventually a roomatism.

SLUG THE MAN DOWN!

William Campbell Gault

T rouble with the Skipper, he's only nine and he doesn't know about angles and percentages and playing it smart. I mean, he doesn't know about life.

Trying to be father and mother both was kind of rough. I wasn't even a good, main event father. Katie had taken care of all that, but Katie was gone now. She'd been dead for two months. She'd never told Skipper much about my trade. She'd never been proud of it. And maybe I hadn't been proud enough. Or dumb enough.

This particular May evening, I'm trying to help the Skipper with his arithmetic, and he won't put his mind to it.

"Pop," he said, "this Mickey Walker was about the best middle, wasn't he?"

"You've got this second problem all wrong," I said. "How come seven plus four always throws you for a loss?"

"Wasn't he the one they called the bulldog?" Skipper says.

"Arithmetic never bothered me," I said. "I don't know why it should give you so much trouble."

"Joe Edwards says Bob Fitzsimmons was better, but Fitzsimmons wasn't a middle, was he? He was heavyweight champ."

"He was light enough for a middleweight," I said. "He ran out of opponents and fought heavies. Now, how much is seven and four?"

"Eleven, natch. How come you don't like to talk about boxing, pop? It's your business, isn't it?"

"It's my business. It's a boring business, Skips." I shook my head. "I

38

certainly don't understand why simple problems like these should stop you."

"I can do them in my sleep," he said. "I only made the mistakes so you'd help me, so we could talk."

For a moment, it was very quiet in the apartment. For a moment, I wished more than ever that Katie was here with her answers. I said, "I talk to you, Skipper. I talk to you a lot."

"On the way out, or coming in," he said. "You never stop and talk to me."

No words for a second or two. I wanted to be careful with my next words. I wanted to take my time. Finally, I said, "That's going to change. I've been kind of busy since Katie—I've been kind of busy."

He smiled, then, "Sure, I know."

"But it's going to be different," I told him quietly. "We'll have some fun. What do you like to do, mostly, Skips?"

"I like to box," he said.

Some more time. Some more silence. "And what else?"

"That's about all. I like to play catch."

"Baseball, you mean?"

"Just catch. Just me and Joe Edwards."

"Well," I said, "there's money in baseball."

"Money?" he said. "What's money got to do with it?"

He eyed me, frowning.

"Money?" I said, "Why money is—" And then I realized it wasn't, not to him, and maybe it was too early to give him ideas like that.

"A guy has to eat," I said finally. "But you'll have a lot of jobs you'll be considering before you're ready to decide. Let's just think about what's fun."

"Boxing," he said.

He had some of Katie's stubbornness, I could see. "Boxing's fun, as long as nobody gets hurt," I admitted. "You get good enough at it, and maybe you can get a ride, at some real good school, and—"

"A ride?" he said. "What do you mean?"

"A scholarship," I explained, after a second. "You see, certain people like to encourage athletics, because it builds character and develops the right qualities." And then I stopped, because it sounded so silly.

But I couldn't think of any sensible way to explain it without telling him things that were a little advanced for his age. So I said, "Boxing, huh? Well, go get your gloves, and I'll show you a trick or two, right now."

The look he gave me, you'd think I'd given him a tip on a hot horse. I was glad that he'd asked for help with his arithmetic.

But I realized there were some angles to this mother business I'd never be able to master. I can fry a chop, and make passable coffee, but pork chops and coffee probably aren't the best diet for a growing boy.

I gave him his lesson, that night, and the next morning I went to see Father Ryan.

He'd given me my first set of boxing gloves, fifteen years ago, and I'd known him before that. He was getting gray, and his face had a few more lines. Otherwise, he was the same quiet, virile man.

He said, "I haven't seen you much since you moved out of the parish, Jack. But I've been following you in the papers. You'll be fighting for the title one of these days, won't you? The champion can't refuse you forever."

I didn't answer that. Any logical answer would be a lie. I said, "Father, I'm looking for a housekeeper. I thought maybe you'd know some-one in the parish who—"

He nodded gravely. "For the Skipper? How is he?"

"He's fine. But since Katie . . . you know how it is. And then, I have to be away so much, in my business. I'd like somebody you wouldn't be likely to get in an employment agency, Father. Someone of exceptional character."

He smiled. "You came at an opportune time, Jack. I've a girl and her brother who are looking for quarters, and the girl would be ideal. Maybe you remember her—Ellen Dean?"

"I remember a Mike Dean."

"That's the brother. Ellen's only twenty-three, Jack, and you'd have to take both of them. But she's a fine, spirited, sensible girl, and she'd make an excellent companion for your boy."

I was trying to remember Mike Dean better. I asked, "You've nobody else in mind, Father? Someone older? We've only the three bedrooms in the apartment."

"I've no one else," he said. "You and Mike could share a room, Jack."

Mike Dean. Then I remembered him more clearly. A very critical gent, a very straight and narrow, beetle-browed Irishman.

"Father," I said, "I think I remember him better, now. Kind of a hard gent to get along with, wasn't he?"

Father Ryan's eyes twinkled. "He's a highly moral man, Jack. He'd be a good example for the Skipper." He sighed. "And Ellen's a wonder-ful cook, and she's clean and neat."

I could see he wanted me to take them, so I said, "All right. Tell them to come over, after supper, and we'll talk about it."

Then I went down to see Gilly. Gilly's my manager, and I wanted to find out if there was anything promising in the wind.

He was sitting in his office, smoking one of those expensive cigars he favors when things are breaking. "Got a fight in Chicago," he told me. "Important money."

"Not Art Govern?" I said.

Gilly shook his bald head. "Nope. Art's finally decided he'll never get past you. No, this is a new one. Guy named Les Mitchell."

"Oh," I said. "Just a guy named Les Mitchell. In the top four, maybe. Rugged and young, and aiming for the title. It had better be important money."

Gilly smiled smugly. "It will be. You get the big end, of course."

I always did. The smart ones knew they had to climb through me if they wanted a title fight. The champ would see to that. The champ fought the boys who were tailored for his style. The others had to come up through me. So far, none of them had.

"The big end," I agreed. "And maybe the bad end. We waited too long, didn't we, to get that Mitchell boy?"

Gilly frowned, and studied the end of his cigar. "What makes you think so? You afraid of him, Jack?"

"No," I said. "He's no set up, but I'm not afraid. I've nothing to lose but the fight. Only, we used to get them younger and dumber, didn't we?"

Gilly's frown deepened a little, and he studied me thoughtfully. "Restless, Jack? We're doing pretty well, don't you think?"

"We always have," I answered. "You're a smart operator, Gilly. Only *you* don't have to take the punches. I'm getting marked up, here and there. The champ's profile is as clean as ever."

He nodded. "That's right. You've been his—well, stooge, in a way, I suppose. I thought that was all right with you. You figure a title fight would pay off better?"

"If I won, it would."

"You fought him, once."

"I was young. And he wasn't the champ, then. It was a bad memory, for a long time, Gilly. But it's beginning to dim."

"You want to fight him?" He was deadly serious, I could tell. Gilly's about the best finagler in the business, and it's a business that produces some pips. But he'd do what I wanted.

I didn't answer him directly. Instead, I asked, "How would I do?"

His lower jaw came out a little. "I think he'd murder you. I don't think you've changed, not about him. A fight's mental, too, remember. And he's the boy who knows it."

I thought it all over, and said, "Chicago, huh? Les Mitchell."

"If you want it. It'll pay a bundle."

"I want it," I said.

His eyes were on me curiously when I left. I was in a bad mood, and I didn't know why. Restless, Gilly had called it and he'd called it right, as usual. But why should I be?

Smart, smart, smart—it's just a word. I'd called myself that when I'd tied up with Gilly, when I'd become the first line of defense for the champ. We really coined it, Gilly and I. It had been the big grab, always. It was the smart way to play it, I'd convinced myself. Maybe I'd just been scared, though that's not anything a fighter is likely to admit. Maybe I'd remembered what a hell of a lacing the champ had given me when we were both prelim boys. It's too easy to call yourself smart.

I picked up a paper at the corner and went home.

I read the paper, and took a shower. I decided to take Skipper out for supper, out to some fancy place, and then to a show.

But I'd forgotten about the Deans.

They didn't come after supper, as I'd suggested. They came at five, while I was out in front, playing catch with my boy.

Mike I remembered all right, one of those dark Irishmen, a tall and sober gent about thirty. Ellen was something else.

Shoulder high to me, with the auburn hair and cream complexion of the breed's true beauties. Quiet, though, like her brother, and gravely modest. Though this last was just my impression at the time.

Mike said, "I guess you remember me, Jack."

I said I did, and shook his hand.

"And this is my sister, Ellen," he said, and her smile was as brief as her nod, her blue eyes never leaving my face.

I introduced the Skipper to them, and he examined them in his candid, curious way.

Mike said, "We thought, as long as Ellen would do the cooking, we'd come before supper. Then you'd have less reason to refuse us."

I said, "It's almost too late to shop, isn't it? We planned on going out to eat."

"It won't be necessary," Mike said. "I noticed a supermarket only a few blocks down. Ellen and I will run over and pick up an adequate supply for supper."

That seemed to settle that. I took out my wallet, but Mike shook his head.

"So long as this is a sort of test," he said, "it's only right we should pay for the meal."

They turned and went down the walk.

* * *

My boy looked at me, and I looked at him. Neither of us said anything for a moment, and then he said, "She's pretty, isn't she?"

I agreed to that.

"Is Mr. Dean a teacher?" he asked.

"No," I said, "I understand he's a C.P.A. That's a sort of major league bookkeeper."

"He looks like a teacher," the Skipper said. It didn't sound like a compliment.

The meal was simple enough, a stew with vegetables included. Simple and not expensive and about as good as anything I'd ever eaten. The Skipper almost ate the pattern off his plate.

"Boy," he said. "That sure beats pork chops."

I thought Ellen frowned. But she said nothing.

Mike said, "Father Ryan tells me you have three bedrooms, and that you and I are to share a room. Will you be home much, Jack?"

"When I'm in town, probably," I answered. "That's all right, isn't it?"

"Naturally," he answered. "It's your apartment. You see, I'm taking a home study course, and I must have absolute privacy. I sometimes read quite late."

Which seemed to settle everything, but after the table was cleared, Ellen spoke for about the first time. "My brother," she said evenly, "seems to think that you've decided in our favor. But you haven't said so directly, Mr. Shea."

"I'd be happy to have you," I told her. "I'm sure Mike will be glad to work out the details of it, the financial details."

Mike would.

We talked that over while Skips helped Ellen with the dishes. And I hadn't even asked him to help her.

Two days later, Gilly and I took a plane to Chicago. They'd been two placid days, and I'd spent a lot of time with the Skipper. I had also spent a lot of time listening to Mike's considered opinion on a multitude of unrelated subjects, but I'd learned how to take that. All the while he was talking, I would think of something else. After a little practice, I didn't even know he was talking.

Ellen had offered very little in the way of dialogue, but she had certainly brightened up the apartment with her dust cloth, the vacuum cleaner and her presence. Life was pleasant.

In the Coliseum, life got a little less pleasant. Mitchell hit me with a right hand, a very lucky, very heavy right hand in the second minute of the first round, and I went into a partial haze.

I fought out the round on instinct alone, and finished on my feet, in my corner.

Gilly looked worried. He said, "You all right, my boy? You feel fit to continue?"

"I'm all right," I told him. "It's the fog. Too much smoking in here."

Gus Tyden, the ref, came over to look in my eyes. The new code in Illinois was pretty strict.

"Don't worry about me, Gus," I said. "I'll give you five to three I put him away before the eighth."

He didn't look satisfied, but he walked off without comment.

Gilly had the salts under my nose now. The handler was massaging my neck. Gilly said, "This Mitchell's about the heaviest hitter in the division. Your legs all right?"

"My legs are fine," I said. "I underestimated this guy, is all."

"He's the uncrowned champ, you might say," Gilly replied. "At least, that's what they call him here in Chicago."

"I'll try and crown him," I said.

I stayed clear of him, next round. He's a broad-shouldered mixer and he likes to come in and hook. I tied him up. I told him, in one of the clinches, "You shot your wad, Les. You should have saved that right hand for later in the fight."

It seemed to burn him. He swung like a windmill the rest of the round.

I went into a strategic retreat and things were beginning to clear as the round ended.

Gilly said, "Brain versus brawn, as they say in the books. You trying to talk him out of this one?"

"He's so young and willing," I said.

"And strong." Gilly shook his head. "I don't feel good about this one, Jack. I don't feel lucky.

"It's all right. I'm coming out of it."

The third was a waltz. Les had probably had some advice from his corner, between rounds, and he was being cautious, sizing me up. The next button shot would wait for a better moment.

This waltzing I can do, in the early rounds. My legs wouldn't take it, later. Now, they were strong and nimble.

In the corner, Gilly said, "Next round he'll come in again. Be very careful, next round."

I was careful. Les came in, hooking, and I tied him up the best I could. Some of them were bound to hurt, though, and one of them was low.

I broke, and tried a short right for the jaw. It landed. It jolted him, and he took a backward step, his first of the fight. I followed, swinging with a wild overhand right, and then we were trading leather.

He had the moxie. I had the savvy. He hit me harder. I hit him oftener. Half the blows he started never landed.

We were still mixing at the bell. The crowd was screaming.

Gilly said, "You gone nuts? You can't trade with a man like that."

"I did," I said.

Gilly had some other things to say, none of which I listened to.

In the fifth Les came over to meet me, to continue the barrage. I put
the left in his flat face and went into a fox trot. He stalked me, trying to
come in under the left.

With a minute to go in the round, he made it, hooking solidly as he
stepped in. I didn't tie him up. I broke clear and chopped him as he
followed.

I never saw the right that floored me.

I heard the count, right from the start, but there was a paralysis in me,
and it was a scramble, getting to one knee. The rattle in my brain was
steady. Across the ring, Mitchell was a white cloud in dark trunks.

This time he wouldn't make any mistake. This time he'd come in and
I'd be ready for that right hand, ready for the kill.

"Seven," the ref counted.

This could be the end of Jack Shea, the champ's stooge. This could be
the turning point to the cheap fights and the small end of poor purses.
This had been due, all along.

"Eight," the ref said.

The racket shook the Coliseum, for there was a kayo in the offing,
and that's what they pay to see. Mitchell was young and ready and not
likely to make two mistakes in one fight.

"Nine," and I was up.

He came over swiftly, flatfooted, his eye gleaming. I tried to look
more shaky than I felt, which was difficult.

He came over with the right cocked, and he tried a small shift before
he threw it.

That's when I put everything I had into a button try.

It was clean. I felt the shock of it, and then I felt the pain of it as a
bone in my hand let go. I damn near fainted, walking to a neutral corner.

He was spread-eagled on the canvas, not a muscle twitching. If he got
up, it was his fight. If the bell rang it was his fight, for they'd bring him
to between rounds. The fans were hysterical.

I saw the ref's white arm go up and down, up and down, and I
thought my heart was keeping time. I saw the timekeeper, ready to ring
the bell.

Then I heard the "ten," not two seconds before the gong was due.

Gus came over to lift my right hand high. That's when I passed out.

On the plane, going home, Gilly said, "We were lucky, Jack. That boy's too young and too good."

"Maybe I'm just getting older," I said. "And maybe that was my last fight, Gilly. I don't want to wind up on Queer Street."

The rest of the trip we played gin rummy.

The Skipper took quite an interest in my bandaged hand, showing less sympathy than admiration. "You must have really walloped him, pop," he said. "You going to fight the champ, now?"

"Not for a while," I told him.

"Mike says you'll never fight him. Mike says you're too smart."

Ellen came out from the kitchen, just then, and she seemed to stop in mid-stride at the Skipper's words. Her eyes met mine, and I thought there was an apology in them.

I said, "Mike's right, Skipper. It would cost me money."

Ellen said, "I forgot to get sugar, Skipper. Would you mind running down to the store for me?"

When he'd left, she faced me squarely. "My brother is a very smart man, Mr. Shea. But he isn't nearly as smart as he thinks he is. I'm sorry about what he told Skipper."

"It's true," I said.

"Then I'm sorrier still," she said, and went back to the kitchen.

I followed her. "What did you mean?"

But she had no answers for me. She was flushed, and her eyes avoided mine. She wouldn't talk.

When the Skipper came back with the sugar, we went out for a game of catch. That's what we were doing when Mike came home.

He showed more concern than the Skipper had for my bandaged hand. "I hope it doesn't mean the end of your career," he said. "I've very little regard for your profession as a paying business, but you play it so intelligently, I'm forced to admire you."

"I've broken hands before," I said. "How did you know how I play this trade?"

"It should be obvious to anyone who makes a study of it," he said. "And who remembers what a thrashing the champion gave you at the old South Side Armory."

"That would take some memory," I said. "That was twelve years ago."

"I've trained my memory," he said. "I forget nothing I want to remember."

He had me there. I only remembered what I didn't want to remember.

When he'd left, I turned to find the Skipper looking at me strangely.

"Is that true, pop?" he said. "You afraid of the champ?"

I thought a minute before saying, "I don't know. All of us are afraid of something, I guess."

"Sure. But you'd fight him anyway, wouldn't you? I mean, if it didn't cost you money?"

Again, I had to tell him, "I don't know."

It must have been the wrong thing to say. Because he was quiet, after that, and too serious.

There wasn't much dialogue at supper, except Mike's. I don't know where I got the idea he was a quiet type. He just looked quiet. He'd been studying some insurance tables, and he was full of statistics.

Gilly phoned when we were about halfway through. He said, "Had a wire from the Coast."

"Steuber again?" I asked.

"Steuber."

I'd fought "Dutch" Steuber three times. I'd won by a kayo, on points and been held to a draw. I was getting sick of looking at him across a ring. I said, "Don't make any promises. Let's wait and see how my hand shapes up."

"Check."

When I came back to the table they were all looking at me curiously. "A guy named Steuber, from the Coast," I said. "Wants a fight again."

Mike shook his head. "He's a stubborn man, isn't he? Perhaps that draw encouraged him."

"He wants to get to the crown," I said. "He has to come through me."

Mike smiled knowingly, and Skipper said, "Why, pop? Why does he have to fight you first?"

"That's the way things are," I said. "I'm about the best, next to the champ, and sort of a . . . test."

"More wall than test, ain't it?" Mike asked. "Or you might say, you're sort of a filter."

Ellen spoke now. "If I were you, Michael Dean, I would stick to subjects I understand. Like adding machines." Her voice was sharp, and I looked at her.

He frowned. "I have nothing but admiration for the businesslike way Jack manages his affairs. I didn't mean my remark as any condemnation."

"All I know is," the Skipper said, "if I was a fighter, I'd want to be the champ."

"That," I told him, "is exactly the way I felt at nine, too."

Ellen's voice was cool. "And what changed you, Mr. Shea?"

"The champ," I said, "when we were both eighteen."

She said nothing, looking at me, her eyes clouded.

"My first kayo, and my last," I explained further. "Maybe I should go to a psychiatrist, huh?"

"You ought to fight him again," the Skipper said. "You really ought to, pop. I'll bet you learned plenty since then."

"Your father," Mike said, "has learned plenty since then. Which is more than can be said for most pugilists."

The clouds in Ellen's blue eyes were storm clouds, now. She said very clearly, "There are certain things which cannot be estimated with a slide rule. One of them is integrity."

Every black hair in Mike's brows seemed to bristle. His black eyes were indignant. "I would certainly not condone anything which is immoral, and I see nothing immoral in Jack's conduct of his profession."

"Morality," Ellen said quietly, "is not the only food the soul requires."

The Skipper looked from Mike to Ellen to me. "What's all this got to do with fighting the champ, pop?" he asked.

"I'm not sure," I said. "What say we got to a movie and figure it out?" It was Friday; there'd be no school tomorrow.

"Western? There's a western at the Grand."

"Western," I agreed. "But let's get going. We want to hit the first show."

I guess it was all right, for a western. Skipper sure enjoyed it. I couldn't keep my mind on it. I kept thinking of the dialogue at the supper table, and the unreasonable concern Ellen had shown.

When we came out, I asked, "How you getting along with our new friends? I mean Ellen and Mike?"

"Ellen's swell," he said. "She's pretty too, huh?"

I nodded. "Don't you like Mike?"

"I guess. He figures too much. Is that what people have to do in his business?"

"That's what they get paid for."

"I sure wouldn't want to be like him," Skipper said.

We were home by ten thirty, and I went right to bed. But I couldn't sleep. I tossed and fretted, and listened to Mike snore. *Morality isn't the only food the soul requires.* I thought back to my amateur days, and to the prelim years. All through that time I'd had the one goal. Every fighter really has only the one goal, but too many get sidetracked.

In the morning, I phoned Gilly. I said, "Tell Steuber's manager it's no dice. I'm retiring, Gilly."

A silence on the wire. Finally, "Come on down and see me before you decide. Don't make any decision yet."

I drove Skipper to school and went down from there. Gilly was standing near his front window, and he turned as I came in.

"How about one more?" he asked me. "One big one?"

I shook my head. "The ring's treated me all right. One more might be the one too many." I paused. "You were thinking of a title fight?"

He smiled. "That's right."

"Look at it this way," I said. "We started about even, Al and I. But in the last five years, I've absorbed some awful heavy pummelings, battles he should have fought. I'm not kicking, understand. It was my own decision. But it's left him in one hell of a lot better shape than me."

"That's the only thing you're thinking of?"

"Maybe not. Maybe I'm thinking that most of the smart boys consider me the uncrowned champ. Most of them think I could take Al. If I retire, now they can keep the illusion—and I can."

"That's what I meant," Gilly said. "How about the public?"

"What about the public?"

Gilly actually looked embarrassed, a facial expression I'd never seen on him before. "It might sound silly, coming from me, but don't you figure the public's got a right to know?"

"That's too complicated for me," I said. "Get the x-rays on my hand, yet?"

He nodded. "Middle knuckles spread a little is all. In two weeks you'll be good as new. In three you could fight for real money, in the Garden."

I stared at him. "You've been talking to Al's manager. You promised him?"

"I've been talking to him. I didn't make any promises." Gilly's smile was ironic. "I guess Al's been hearing what the smart ones think, too. He wants to flex his muscles."

"Let him fight Mitchell," I said.

Gilly shrugged. "Okay, Jack. Eight years I've been without a title-holder. But no hard feelings."

He'd handled me those eight years. I said, "You don't need the sob stuff with me, Gilly. Those aren't tears in your eyes. They're dollar signs."

He sighed. "I admit it. It would be a nice gate, terrific gate. Well, see you around, Jack."

I left him, and went home. Ellen was vacuuming, and I watched her do that for a while, and after she'd stopped, I turned on the radio. But it was all soap opera, jive and commercials.

I tried to read, but I couldn't concentrate. I went out to the kitchen to watch Ellen peel potatoes.

I said, "Had a chance for a title fight this morning. I turned it down."

No comment.

"It's the only smart thing to do," I went on. "Al Krug's the champ, and he's a terrific punisher when he's right. I don't want to end my career on Queer Street."

No words.

"I've made more than I'd have made driving a truck," I further explained. "I've still got most of my brains, and my looks were never anything I'd mind losing. I've done pretty well."

Silence.

"Lots of guys who fought for the title are selling pencils today," I said. "And even if I won, which is doubtful, it wouldn't be fair to quit. I'd have to defend the title. I'm tired of fighting."

Nothing from her.

I said, "Haven't you any comment to make? Have I offended you?"

She shook her head. "You don't owe me any explanations, Mr. Shea. All your explanations would be entirely for yourself."

"You could call me Jack," I said.

"Jack's a fighter's name," she said, "and you're through fighting."

I shook my head. I said, "You're more critical than Mike, really. And I always thought Mike was the critical one."

She flushed. She started to speak, but changed her mind. I went back to the living room.

Skipper came home for lunch. It was a quiet meal, mostly, with the only dialogue his questions and my answers. This Ellen had a great capacity for the pregnant silence, as they say.

I took him back to school, after lunch, and went downtown. I stopped in at the Ringside Rendezvous for a short beer, and Tony Zoeller was in there. Tony's one of the few sports scribes who makes sense with a typewriter.

He said, "I've been hearing rumors."

"That's your business," I told him. "About me?"

He nodded. "I hear you and Al Krug are finally going to get together."

"We've been together," I said.

"I know. South Side Armory, 1936. That's a long time ago, Jack."

"Not too long to remember," I said.

"Lot of things have happened since then," he said. "One of them was your learning your trade. Don't think Gilly's as cold-blooded as he looks. He's the best in the business, for my money."

I finished my beer. I said, "Everybody wants me to fight the champ. But *I'd* have to do the fighting. None of the ones who want the fight have ever taken a punch. None but Al, that is."

"You've taken a lot more punches than Al," he offered, "but it's your business, not mine. Forget I mentioned it. Have a drink on me, kid."

I had another short beer, and drove over to the park.

The sun was warm, and there was a slight breeze. The grass was green and I was healthy. Money in the bank, a son to be proud of, ready to retire at thirty. What more could a man ask?

This Al Krug was fairly fast, plenty smart and he could hit with either hand. What would I want in a ring with him? Nothing—nothing but the crown, of course.

Too many people were overstocked on advice. Only Mike had sense enough to realize how smart I'd been.

I drove home. I turned on the radio and listened to Mary Marlowe's Misery, The Tragedy of Helen Hume and The Widow Murphy's Struggle.

Ellen was dusting. She was a very pretty girl, and certainly a clean one.

"All right," I said. "You win."

She just stared at me.

I went to the phone and called Gilly. I said, "You can tell the champ I'll take it. And the sooner the better."

When I turned from the phone, Ellen was smiling. "Jack," she said. "Oh Jack, I'm so proud of you."

So was the Skipper when he heard about it. You'd think he'd regained his faith in Santa Claus.

But at supper, Mike delivered his considered opinion. "You're making the biggest mistake of your life," he told me solemnly. "You will regret this, I'm sure."

I felt better, after that. I knew I'd done the right thing.

We went up to Elkhart Lake for this one. We had a little over three weeks, and the first week or two would be general conditioning. I wasn't going to risk the hand until then.

I'd fought often enough so that I hadn't needed any training to get into condition. The ring had been my conditioner. But this one was for the title, and we had to give it the proper build-up.

Besides, at Elkhart we could charge admission to watch me train, and Gilly is a boy who likes to wring the last nickel out of a bout.

I was all right, physically. Mentally, I was where I'd been for twelve years, and there wasn't much I would be able to do about that. Any pug can have a jinx, and it's got nothing to do with ability. Some guys are just designed by nature to beat other boys, and training won't change that.

When my hand began to shape up, Gilly imported a couple sparmates, a fast welter and a middle who fought about like Al, only at a different level.

The hand took it. Heavy gloves, of course, and just trying a right for size, occasionally, but no pain, and the doc said it looked all right to him.

I kept pretty busy. I missed the Skipper, and Ellen. I didn't miss Mike much, for some reason.

On a Thursday, we went back to town. I dropped Gilly at his office and went to the apartment.

Ellen wasn't dusting, or vacuuming, or listening to the radio. She was on the davenport, reading the paper, reading the sports page.

I said, "Hello."

"They're all crazy," she said. "Welcome home, Jack."

"Who's crazy?" I asked.

"These sportswriters. They say the champion will knock you out before the seventh—all but Mr. Zoeller."

"Tony Zoeller's the one to read, then," I said. "Tony always thought a lot of me."

Her blue eyes were just brimming with concern. "You mean, he's a friend of yours?"

"More or less."

"Then you . . . these other men are right?"

"We'll know Saturday night. You going to be there?"

"No. I couldn't. No, I won't be there. It's all my fault, isn't it. I talk too much. I don't usually, but I did this time. You can't call it off, now, can you?"

"It's a little late for that," I said. "How are Helen Hume and Mary Marlowe and the Widow Murphy?"

"How can you joke at a time like this?" she said, and then she went into the kitchen, sniffling.

I followed her out. I said, "Look, I haven't been beat in seven years. In that time, I've handed out some pastings. Now it's my turn to catch some. It's simple justice. I owe it to the public to fight this boy. I owe it to myself."

"You've certainly changed your tune," she said.

"You didn't though," I said. "You're still on the opposite side of the fence."

The Skipper came home soon after that. He sure looked proud. He had a black eye.

"Joe Edwards," he explained. "He said you and the champ had made a deal, pop. He said the fight wasn't on the level."

"Fighting won't prove anything," I said. "Fighting for money's bad enough. But fighting for nothing is wasted time."

"Sure, pop," he said. "You're going to wallop him, aren't you?"

"The reporters won't let me," I said, "but I'm going to try."

Ellen had nothing to say.

Friday I loafed, and Saturday I went down for the weighing in. After that, I took Skipper to the zoo. I should have taken a nap, but I knew I wouldn't sleep anyway, and I wanted to keep my mind occupied.

In the cab, going down Saturday night, Gilly looked very optimistic. But with a good gate, he can look that way no matter what our chances were. And the place was a sellout.

He smiled at me as we got into the thick traffic. "We've been pointing for this a long time, Jack," he said.

"Not me," I answered. "And not you. If the gate was the same you wouldn't care who I was fighting."

It didn't dim his smile. "You misjudged me," he said gently. "Money isn't the only thing I live for, Jack. It's just the only important thing."

There were a lot of scribes in the dressing room, and they were full of quips. Gilly mixed words with them while I stretched out on the table. They were all friendly enough, but cynics by nature.

The fight was being televised, and I was surprised Gilly hadn't cut us in on a slice of that money. My mind went back to the last time I'd fought Al, and then came forward through the years. All the towns we'd hit, Gilly and I. Seattle and Portland, Frisco and L.A., Dallas and Denver and Chicago. Some tank towns, too. Cheap fights against home-town favorites. There was only one way you could win those—with a kayo.

Tony Zoeller had said Gilly wasn't as cold-blooded as I thought. I'd never thought of him that way. A very canny man around a dollar, a man of unlimited angles, but I'd known him too long and too close to think of him as cold-blooded.

Well, this was something I'd been avoiding for twelve years, and I felt all right there on the table. I wasn't dumb enough to lack fright, but I was a full man for the first time, a whole man. I could thank Ellen for that. I could thank Mike, in reverse.

The prelims were dotted with kayos, and we were going up the aisle a lot earlier than we'd expected. Gilly walked next to me. He grinned up at me as the applause moved through the house.

I looked at him, and winked, and maybe we were both thinking the same thing. Maybe we were both remembering the trail.

Al came in after we were seated, and he walked to my corner with the big hello.

I smiled at him, and said, "Haven't seen you since this morning, Al."

"We haven't met in a ring for longer than that," he said. "Nineteen thirty-six, wasn't it, Jack?"

Cute, he was. "I've forgotten," I said. "But I hope I've improved."

He smiled, and went to his corner.

Gilly was smiling, too. Gilly said, "He talks a good fight. Jack, he's strictly cheese. If he had another name and another face, he wouldn't last two rounds with you." He went over to inspect the wrappings.

I watched them across the ring. Gilly didn't miss a thread. Then they came over to inspect mine, Gilly and Al's noodle.

Al's noodle asked sympathetically, "How's the hand, boy?"

"Good as new," I told him. "I'm mostly left hand, anyway."

The gloves, the introductions, the instructions, the house lights dimming. I went to my corner to flex a little on the ropes.

Twelve years. Well, we'd both improved, but he'd gone on to the title.

The bell, and I turned, and here Al came, but moving slowly, waiting for me to come to him. A counterpuncher, Al.

My stomach was tight as a drum, but that would go away, I hoped. One good punch in the nose, and my imagination wouldn't be so active, nor my memory. In this business, it's best not to think too much.

"Wallop him, pop," the Skipper had said. I moved in to wallop him. He put the left in my face, circling to the right, waiting, waiting, waiting.

He could afford to wait. He was wearing the crown, figuratively speaking, and the burden was with the challenger. The challenger had to carry the fight, come in and get that crown.

I came in under his left hand, hooking as I came. I landed twice, solidly, before he tied me up.

Clean break, and then he came in, and caught me with a right hand, high, on the ear.

I stumbled sideways, and he followed, throwing leather. One of them rattled my brain, and then I tied him up.

As we broke, I stepped to the right, and as I stepped, I hooked. You won't see that much, these days, a hook off a step to the right. I'd learned it in St. Paul.

It caught Al napping. It landed over the heart and shook him plenty, I could tell. He clinched.

I said, "Tricky, huh? You should get out of town once in a while, Al."

He looked puzzled when the ref broke us. I landed a short right, but his own right was faster. It caught me on the mouth and it jarred. I'd been careless; I'd forgotten this was the *champ*.

We were both playing it cagey at the bell.

Gilly was smiling as he helped the handler. I said, "What kind of a canary did you eat? I don't see anything funny."

"That hook off the step to the right," he said. "You looked good on that one."

"How did I look when he hit me on the mouth?" I asked.

"You've been hit on the mouth before."

Sure, but it wasn't anything you could build up a tolerance for. I told Gilly that, and he shrugged. "He's cheese," he said, "all cheese, Jack."

I had no answer to that.

The second round Al went into a shell. It was his title, and if I wanted it, I could come in, dig it out of him. For a minute I moved around him, not throwing a punch. The fans began to chant, and Al straightened a little.

I brushed his nose with a long left. He was short with a countering right. I feinted, shifted, and threw a whistler.

It landed too high for a knockdown but he went sailing into the ropes, and I crowded him, slamming at the midriff with both hands. I could feel him wilt, and I stepped clear to throw a right.

He moved in with me, and his head crashed my nose.

Stars fell in the Garden as I covered.

I could sense that he was sizing me up. I circled to the right, away from his right, and then I felt his foot, close, and I stepped on it. I brought a right up.

It was a good right, and his head snapped back. His mouthpiece went flying.

The fans were screaming as Al retreated.

He stayed on his bike the rest of the round.

Between rounds, the ref came over. He said, "I didn't miss that footwork, Jack. Remember, this is a title fight."

"You could mention that to Al," I said. "I hope you saw the headwork of his, too."

"I saw it, and I told him about it. And if I want any comments I'll ask for them."

He went away, jotting on his card.

"Nice clean business," Gilly said. "I guess you can pick up tricks right here in town, too, can't you?"

"Al has," I said.

Gilly mopped my face with a cold, wet towel. "Still got the sign on you, has he?"

"A little," I agreed.

"You shouldn't be fighting him if you feel like that," Gilly said.

"It was the Skipper's idea," I told him.

The third was dead—jab, counter, feint and footwork, like college kids. Toward the end of the round, Al landed a couple of short rights but

I was going away on both of them. They were enough to make it his round, though.

The fourth was a little rougher. Al was stepping up the pace. He was sensitive about pleasing the crowd. I'd learned, long ago, the folly of trying to please fight fans.

In the fifth, I began to see the light. In the fifth, I began to realize the truth of what Tony Zoeller had been trying to tell me. Gilly was the best in the business. Gilly wouldn't bring me to a title fight until I was ready.

That's when the jinx left me, in the fifth.

The sixth, I went out to get him. I caught him coming out of his corner, and put two solid lefts over his heart. He tried to clinch, and I stepped clear. He brought his hands up, and I put all my moxie into a right for the solar plexus.

He was hurt. His legs wobbled, and he half fell. I made the mistake of coming in, and I was tied up.

It didn't matter. It was, I knew, only a question of time, now. I wrestled it out with him, while the fans shook the roof. The ref was digging us apart, and then we were clear.

Al stood there in a temporary daze, and I made my second mistake of the round. I put my heart into a right-hand button shot, a wild try.

Just as Al's head came down.

I landed on his skull, above the ear. I didn't need a degree from Johns Hopkins to know the hand had gone again. Pain shot up my arm like an electric current and sparked in my brain.

Nausea rose in me, and Al's outline grew hazy. He came in to clinch in that moment.

We wrestled out the round, neither of us landing a solid punch.

Gilly's eyes bored into mine. "That hand go?"

I shook my head. "I'll get him." Things were getting clearer.

Gilly had the salts under my nose, and ice at the back of my neck. He said, "Not that it matters. You could beat him with one hand. You know, now, why we hit the road, Jack, why we fought off his contenders?"

"I know," I said. "I was learning my trade."

"That's right. Go out and finish him, now." It would have to be the next round. He looked at my right hand, and away.

On his stool, Al was getting a lot of advice. He was looking across at me while his manager was bending his ear and I knew they were talking about the right hand.

The seventh brought the proof of that. Al didn't circle away from my right hand, this round. He circled to the left.

I swung a right, a terrific right that missed his jaw by inches, and he began to look puzzled again. He couldn't be sure I'd intended to miss.

For a moment, he stopped circling and I smashed that left into his solar plexus.

Again, I saw his legs wobble. He half turned, and the path was clear.

There was a hundred and sixty pounds riding on that hook, and a title. It would have to be enough.

Al went back and down, as thunder shook the house.

Then the ring was full of fans and a mike was being shoved into my face, and Gilly was hugging me.

I hoped the Skipper was listening, and Ellen. I said into the mike, "I'll be home in fifteen minutes."

And I was.

TEN ROUNDS
FOR BABY

Joel Reeve

oe Dailey made a gesture which included everyone in the smoky room and said, "Why, certainly, chum! I will tip Harry Catt on his wig."

Joe walked among the sportswriters, a medium-sized man with sloping shoulders and long arms, and a shuffle to his gait. They were polite to Joe. Everybody liked Joe.

Snicker said in his crisp voice, "We decided Joe could take a slugger like Catt and we went after him. Joe should have had a shot at the title long ago."

Sam Drake, of the Star, said dryly, "You were a genius to wangle it, Snicker. What did you use, a club?"

"We have been trying to get Harry Catt for two years," Snicker said smoothly. "Joe is a boxer. Catt will never touch him. Why, we took this bout for no dough just to crack at Harry Catt."

Drake said, "Now, Snicker!"

"Well—not enough dough," said Snicker. "Joe will positively wear the champ down and knock him out."

Joe grinned. They straggled out of the hotel suite. Snicker closed the door behind the last of them and leaned against the door frame. He was a youngish, slightly bald man with a hard mouth and quick, clever eyes. He said, "So they don't go for it. But people will come to see Harry Catt. They always do. And it'll be four to one. It's a killer, chum!"

Joe rubbed a thick thumb over his slightly flattened nose. He said, "I don't know. Maybe you shouldn't bet your last two grand on it. Catt is a hitter. He's five years younger than me."

Snicker said, "It's a cinch. You'll get him early. It's the best one to four I ever saw in my life!"

Joe said abruptly, "How much dough you got, Snicker?"

"Oh, maybe a C note," said Snicker, reaching for his pocket. "You want it?"

Joe shook his head. "Always a quick man with a dollar! I mean, how much you got all together? Including everything."

Snicker frowned. "A couple of thousand, more or less."

Joe nodded. "You and your betting. Me, I got that apartment in Jersey City. I got a farm in Florida. Gladioluses, I raise. Two grand profit out of flowers!"

Snicker looked impatient. "Sure. I know. Look, Joe, will you—"

"Flowers!" Joe repeated. It was wonderful. "I got twenty thousand in bonds. And me a dumb gee that got fired out of high school. You got an education, Snicker! You went one year to college! That gambling will get you a seat in the park, chum! I'm telling you again—"

"Look, Joe," said Snicker painfully. "Hedda's downstairs. Take care of her for me, will you? I got to see a man."

"About the gee-gee in the fourth race," said Joe without rancor. "Okay, chum. Let it go. Let it go."

The girl sitting in the corner booth of the coffee shop smiled up at Joe Dailey. She had reddish-gold hair and she wore clothes which had been designed by a genius and purveyed by a first-class shop. She was a top-flight model and she looked it. She was lean and light-legged, with unexpected curves and level gray eyes.

Hedda Horan said, "You signed to fight Harry Catt, and Snicker has rushed off to get his bets arranged."

Joe said, "Uh—yeah. We'll go to a show, huh?"

He sat down and ordered ice cream, then remembered the training and took a lemonade. He was already in the groove, getting ready for the bout a month away. He was thinking of it and loving it, as he had always loved training. It was his life, his job, and he was proud of it.

He said, "Snicker put it over, all right. He is the talk of Broadway right now. Nobody but Snicker could have made that bout for me."

She said, "He is the wonder boy of the universe. Could we see the Orson Welles picture? I like to see Orson Welles and think of my prodigious Snicker!"

Joe said, "What has Orson Welles got that Snicker hasn't got—except some hair, maybe?"

Hedda put her elbows on the table and stared into Joe's face. She had full red lips and her teeth were whiter than any ivory ever grown on an elephant. "You really put out for Snicker, don't you, Joe? You know he's an erratic gambler, a chance-taker, a wastrel, but you stick by him every inch."

"You're engaged to him! You been engaged to him for five years!" said Joe. "I guess you stick by him too. I guess Snicker must be all right, or we wouldn't be sticking to him, would we?"

"We could be wrong," she murmured, not taking her eyes from Joe's plain features.

Joe said, "You're always gagging! Come on, baby. We'll take a gander at this Orson Welles. I understand it is at popular prices now. I have been wanting to see how this young punk makes himself into an old gee!"

"Five years," Hedda said, walking out with him. Joe took her arm crossing the street, fearful of the midtown traffic. "Snicker must have charm, all right. We can't be that wrong."

"Snicker is the greatest manager in the world," said Joe. "I have fought three hundred fights without getting a shot at the title. So what? So Snicker fixes it—like that! He waltzes around and gets wired in with the right people, and bang! We are signed."

"And Harry Catt will give you a beating," said Hedda. "And Snicker will lose the down payment on the bungalow."

Joe said, "Now wait, baby."

"Although of course Harry will not hurt you much," Hedda said, half to herself. "You are too smart to be hurt. I will say that for you."

Joe said, "Aw, Hedda."

"Five years," she muttered. He stole a glance at her delicious profile. She was frowning and her lips pouted a little.

Joe Dailey jerked his eyes straight ahead. She was engaged to Snicker. He had to keep his mind on that, all the time. It was very tough, sometimes, but Joe always made it, after a struggle.

One thing about Joe Dailey, he liked the grind in camp that most athletes hated. He liked the daily boxing, sharpening his tools like any other artisan. He was a canny workman with the mitts, a master mechanic of the ring.

He even liked the morning run, because he could think most clearly just running along with Ted Dover, the trainer. Ted never said anything much. He was a small, tough man with plenty of horse sense and he was Joe's man. He was a grand cut repairer in that corner too.

Joe thought again about Hedda Horan. This bout would make Snicker. If Joe could turn on the heat as they had planned, if he could get to Harry Catt quick enough—

Even if he didn't, thought Joe. Just for making the bout, Snicker was a made manager. They were all yessing him along the Rialto now. He could have his pick of good fighters to handle. He could be in the big money and marry Hedda and everything would be all right.

Maybe Joe could beat Harry Catt to it. If he was five years younger, and his speed was in there, he thought he might do it. Harry was a killer, but he was slow in the head. Barney Ross, now—that was different. Barney was a hitter *and* smart.

When Barney had given it to him, Joe had been young and dumb. Now that he was smart, he was about washed up.

That was it, Joe thought with utter good humor. About the time a man got smart, he was all through and could not use his hard-earned knowledge.

Joe chuckled. That was very deep thinking. This morning his head was working very clearly. He turned his attention back to Hedda and Snicker.

It had been right after the McLarnin fight that Hedda and Snicker got engaged. That Baby-Face! What a hitter! Harry Catt never could hit with the Irish Kid! At that, Joe had him on one knee in the fifth. Ah, well!

Ted Dover said, "You're traveling pretty fast, Joe. Don't want to leave your fight on the road, pal."

Joe slowed down. The Jersey hills were green and lovely. It would be clear in the ball park. It was always good weather when Joe fought. He was lucky that way.

He might have had another shot at Ross, later, when he was readier. But he and Snicker had decided that Joe should stay off of Queer Street. They had agreed that there was dough enough in the second rank and why get Joe's ears pinned all the way back?

It had paid off too. If Snicker hadn't been so fast with his dollar—

But Snicker was a gambler. Snicker could not play with the smart boys because of this black spot, this gambling itch. It put him on a limb, and then the smart boys chopped it off. Snicker had been known on Jacobs Beach as a second-rater—until he copped the championship bout.

Hedda had been patient. Joe shook his head at the trustful, loving patience of Hedda Horan. She was always smiling, always wisecracking. She had plenty chances, with heavy-dough boys from the Fifties falling over themselves to drag her around. But Hedda never went for it. She looked flashy and she talked smart, but Hedda was a wife in her heart. She was a tall Irish girl who wanted a home. Joe knew.

He ran too fast, remembered, slowed down. His pulse always beat too fast when he thought of Hedda like that. She was in his blood. She was a part of him.

Well, Snicker was a pal. Snicker deserved Hedda. All through the years, splitting everything down the middle, there had never been a contract between Joe and Snicker. It had been wonderful, and Joe had loved every minute of it.

He stopped and shadowboxed in the bright morning air. Ted Dover said approvingly, "You're in the pink. You don't need no trainer. You know more about conditioning than I do."

Joe snorted through his nose and said, "I'm all right. I'm fine."

They turned back toward the camp. Joe knew in his heart that he was not kidding. He was as good as he could get. He was as good as his twenty-nine-year-old legs. He grinned to himself.

The wangling of the match with Harry Catt would do it. The newspaper boys were still dazed. They could not figure how Snicker promoted it—getting this outdoor bout for washed-up old Joe Dailey to have his shot at the championship. It put Snicker right up there. Ten striving young fighters had already applied to Snicker to handle them, Joe knew. Snicker was built right up. He could marry Hedda tomorrow, even if Joe quit and went down to Florida to raise gladioli.

It *was* gladioli, a fat lady at a flower show had insisted. Gladioluses —gladioli—there was dough in those long-stemmed fantastic blooms. His manager on the Florida farm said that there was a fortune in them if Joe would come down and work it himself.

It would be lonely down there, away from Hedda and Snicker. It would be queer, not seeing Jack and Braddock and Mickey and Benny —but they'd all come down and visit Joe on his farm. They were a restless crew, anyway.

Joe and Ted rounded the turn and there was the camp. Snicker was out looking for them, his face tinted by the sun, his eyes crinkling with approval as the sweat ran on Joe's face. Snicker said, "Okay, chum?"

"Okay, chum!" said Joe, and another day was off to a fine start.

Joe touched his oily face with the tips of his fingers. The bandages were very white on his hands. Outside, the noise of the crowd echoed hollowly in the ball park.

Snicker said nervously, "Catt trained for it. He's a little scared of you."

Joe grinned. There was a tap on the door and Snicker called, "No visitors, please!"

Hedda Horan said, "You wouldn't kid a man, would you?"

She came in, smiling like an angel. She wore a summery dress, a light, clinging silky dress, and she was as beautiful as a sunrise in the hills. Joe stared at her.

She said, "Well, well, well! A couple of strangers! How have you been this past month, Snicker?"

Snicker said, "Now, baby! You know where I've been. I called you."

"You certainly did!" said Hedda. "Last week sometime, wasn't it? There I was, sitting in my lovely little apartment and the phone rang and it was you! You wanted me to make sure our money was all cleaned out of the bank, so that you could get it down with the bookies."

Snicker said, "You want to upset Joe before he goes on, Hedda? Now listen—"

"Two thousand, four hundred dollars. The down payment on our bungalow in Jersey," she said lightly. "If Joe wins, it will be eight thousand. No—nine thousand, six hundred. Pay for the whole house."

Snicker said, "Now, baby."

"You're sending Joe in there with that on his shoulders. He knows all about it. He's got to make a try to win. You know what that means, Snicker?"

"Now wait, Hedda," said Joe. "I'll beat this Harry Catt's brains out!"

The girl said, "You can't beat one side of Harry Catt, and you know it. But you could get out with a whole skin if you fought a defensive fight."

Joe said, "Now wait, Hedda. This is my racket."

"I don't know anything about it?" There was a sharp note in the rising inflection. Hedda's eyes were very bright. "I don't know what you're planning to do? I'll tell you, Joe Dailey."

Snicker said, "Please, baby. You're upsetting him!"

"I'll upset both of you!" she cried. "Joe is going out there to try for a kayo. He's perfectly aware that his legs won't last the distance unless he paces himself in a losing defensive fight. So he's going to try to knock out Harry Catt. He'll get killed!"

"She got to Ted Dover!" groaned Snicker. "That Dover is a pushover for a skirt!"

"I suspected it," Hedda said flatly. "Ted merely confirmed my suspicions. You're a couple of smart dealers."

Snicker said, "Please, baby."

Hedda was very calm. She said, "Snicker, I'm telling you straight. If Joe fights that kind of a fight—I'll never marry you!"

Joe cried, "Now wait, Hedda!"

"You know what Catt can do to a man who comes to him," said Hedda in the same hard voice. "He crucifies him. Not for twenty times nine thousand, six hundred dollars will I see Joe injured for life—to build us a home! I've taken a lot from you in five years, Snicker. But I'm warning you now."

"It's Joe's only chance to win!" protested Snicker. His face was very white. "It's not the money—"

"You heard me, Snicker," said the girl. She turned on Joe. "You fight him the right way. You protect yourself. You've been in there too many times, Joe Dailey! Harry Catt could kill you if he got to you!"

Snicker said, "Hedda, this is not right. You can't—"

In the hall someone called, "You're on, Dailey!"

"You heard me, Snicker! I won't marry you! I won't!"

She faced them for one moment, her eyes shining, her chin high. Then she was gone and the door slammed with a slap like a gunshot.

After a moment, Snicker said, "Well, we're on."

Joe's brow was furrowed. He said, "Yeah. We're on."

Snicker said, "Uh—I guess—uh. What do you think, Joe?"

Snicker's assurance was gone. Snicker was a kid, like ten years ago, when they had started. He was asking Joe, just like in the beginning, when Snicker had not been smartened up, when he used to depend a lot on Joe's decisions.

Joe said, "Chum, I'll do the fighting. You watch the corner, chum."

Snicker looked relieved. He said humbly, "Okay, Joe. It's all right, then?"

"Sure!" said Joe. "Leave it to me." He felt strong. He felt terrific. He almost felt good enough to lick Harry Catt. He was able, then, to fix it. He was able to make it just the way he wanted.

All the way down to the ring, mitting the crowd, dancing and bowing with that shy grin which got them, which made him so popular with the mob, even though he was no killer, he was thinking about it, enjoying it. The whole thing was dropped in his lap. He spotted Hedda in her third-row seat and beamed upon her.

Hedda was very pale. Joe called, "Don't fret, baby. It's all under control," but he knew she couldn't hear him, because just then Harry Catt came in and the wolf pack howled.

The bloodthirsty faithful loved Harry Catt. Harry looked like a fighter. He had a round head and no neck at all, and thick, muscular arms and no legs or hips. He was a murderer. He was not bright, sometimes, although he knew his way around. But he was a killer, and the mob was with him or against him, but anyway, they wanted him. He was a popular champion.

Joe sat on his stool. Ted Dover and Jerry Winn and Snicker were in his corner. Joe was all right. He was fine. He took off his robe, let Snicker put it around his shoulders and forced his hands into the new gloves. He laughed at Sam Drake and chatted with the other newspaper boys. He felt wonderful.

Dempsey came over and said, "Luck, pal."

Conn leaned close and said, "Come on, Irish! Murder the bum!"

They were all pretty white, at that. They had always been all right with Joe. Maybe there were angles and some pretty tough apples in the game, but Joe got along with them. He was sorry to be saying good-by.

He went out and mitted Harry Catt. The champ was all business, staring at the floor, taciturn, like a stone man, no blood in him. Harry was a battler, all right.

The referee, Tom Hanley, smiled and said, "I know you'll fight clean. You two are clean boys. Make it interesting for the people, now. Shake hands . . . come out fighting."

Joe winked at Hanley and went back. Snicker took the robe and crawled through the ropes.

Snicker said hoarsely, "Two grand and a half, pretty near. It's a lot of tomatoes, chum."

Joe nodded. Snicker said, "You can cop him. He's wide for the shift. Make it look good! But try it, Joe! It's a nice bet to win, Joe! You can tag him, boy!"

Joe stood looking straight into Snicker's urgent eyes. There was a spot of color on each of Snicker's cheeks. The gambling fever. At that moment, Joe knew, Snicker was thinking of nothing but the bet. Not even the championship. Not even Hedda Horan!

And Hedda wouldn't marry Snicker if Joe fought it out. Hedda would be free. She—why, she had threatened Snicker because she had been afraid Joe would get hurt!

The arc lights above were not so bright as the light which shone upon Joe Dailey's soul in that one blinding flash. Hedda did not want him crippled! She had thought that much of him! It was enough for a simple man.

He went wheeling out at the bell. Harry Catt stalked him, like an animal with deadly paws, the left high, the right cocked and ready to sink off Harry's chest to Joe's lean body. It would be the body, of course, to slow Joe for the finish. Joe knew exactly what it would be.

Hedda was worried about him! It was a strange, new thought.

Harry Catt threw the left and was short. Joe hit him twice with a light jab, touched him to throw Harry off balance, moved away. It was duck soup. Harry followed, implacable. Joe laughed and speared three lefts to the head without return. Joe's legs felt wonderful.

Hedda had meant it. She was dead serious. Joe knew Hedda. He had stooged for Snicker for five years. Hedda was open and aboveboard. What she said, she meant. Snicker underrated her.

Joe was on the ropes and Harry was punching, methodical, like a machine, his face expressionless. For a moment Joe stood there, weaving with his consummate skill, slipping punches, touching Harry just right, making him miss. Then Joe moved left, came back right and swung about. Harry got mixed up, turning.

Joe dropped the left in there fast. Harry staggered. Joe hit him with a right cross. Harry's feet got twisted. Joe hit him three more times, very quick, like an adder striking, so that no one there knew which hand went first. Harry went through the ropes and Hanley walked between them, counting. The bell rang.

Joe nodded thanks for the ovation. Maniacs were standing on chairs, shrieking at the near-disaster of the champion. Snicker was pale as a ghost, his hands shaking. Snicker said hoarsely, "The whole thing. We had the whole thing. We would of collected every way if the bell—"

Joe said, "I never saw you so excited, chum. It was a break, chum. Forget it!"

"You got to do it!" said Snicker, desperation in his eyes. "You got to catch him coming out and belt him over."

Joe tried to look down at Hedda, but he could not see her. He leaned forward at the whistle, waiting for the bell.

Harry Catt looked all right. There was no knocking Harry out so easily. The champ came right out to ring center, his small eyes angry. Joe went to him and knew that all hell was to pay now.

Catt was a fury of brown gloves belting at Joe's body. It was impossible to evade them all. They came like a rataplan of bullets against him, and all the cleverness in the world could not smother those punches.

Joe was gasping at the halfway mark. He leaped backward, described a circle. He got his left hand high, buried his chin. He walked around, spinning Harry before him on the cleverest pair of hands in the business.

Catt slowed down. He went back on the prowl. The round dragged by with Harry stalking his prey, Joe dancing like a ballet master.

Snicker said, "So what, Joe?" Snicker had regained control of himself. Under the sunburn his face was white and sullen. Snicker said, "You throwing my bet, Joe?"

Joe said, "Yep. You heard Hedda."

Snicker said, "That's out, Joe. You could nail him. You showed you could nail him."

Joe said, "I'm boxing him, chum."

Snicker said, "Okay. Throw me then."

Joe said, "What about Hedda?"

Snicker said, "Ah-h-h! You could tip him over!"

Joe said, "You never were smart about boxing, chum."

The bell sounded.

Harry Catt was very strong—the strongest man he had ever fought, Joe knew. The rounds went on. The body punches were quick and shrewd. Joe took his lumps, moving away all the time. It was in the tenth, with five more to go, that he first noticed his legs.

Continued socks to the midriff will do it every time. The bounce was gone. In the tenth Joe tried to leap back, away from a two-handed attack. He did not quite make it.

The left swept him sideways. The right nailed him and sent him toppling. He hit the deck very hard, sprawled out, and again the crowd went mad.

He could hear them while he waited, listening to the count. He looked over at Snicker but it was no dice. Snicker's face was cold with anger. Snicker didn't care now. Snicker thought Joe had thrown him.

Joe heard the "Eight—nine—" He got up. Harry Catt came deliberately, implacably. Joe retreated. The ropes were at his back. His belly felt as though three mules had kicked him, one after the other. His nose was bleeding pretty bad. He flicked blood from his face with the thumb of his right glove.

Harry's eyes were eager. Joe was cornered at last. He hunched his shoulders, ready to cover, turtlewise, on the hemp, his knees bent a little.

The crowd moaned, "There he go-o-o-o-o-oes!"

Harry was very deliberate. The left swept at the reddened middle. Joe seemed to double over.

Then Harry's right went in. Only Joe was not there. Joe was half behind Harry Catt. Joe was hooking as he had not hooked before. His glove went behind Harry's ear.

Harry started to fall forward. Joe came in and threw the right from the floor. He hit Harry upon the chin.

Harry floundered, his eyes like a china doll's, rolling in his head. Joe tapped him on the button.

Harry Catt fell on his face.

Hanley said, "Go to your corner, Joe! You're the new champion!"

Snicker was limp. Snicker had his mouth open but he was unable to speak. Snicker finally said, "Nine thousand, six hundred bucks! What a bet! What a beating for the bookies! What a fall for the smart dough!"

Joe said, "Yeah, chum. You sure got them, Snicker."

He posed for pictures and spoke into the microphone. He ranged himself among the belligerent tall cops and tramped down to the dressing room. He sat on a table and let Ted Dover cut off his bandages.

He was dressed at last. The screaming mob was gone. Ted Dover was packing his things. Joe said, "I'll send you a check, Ted. It'll be a big one."

Ted hesitated. He said, "Look—that dame."

"Huh?"

"Snicker's gone to rub it into the bookies. That dame is outside."

"Send her in! Send her in, stupid!" yelled Joe.

Hedda came in. She walked straight up to him and kissed Joe right on the sore nose. Then she kissed him on the mouth, hard.

Joe said, "Now wait!"

Hedda said, "You did it for Snicker. You fought my way, to make it right. You could have had him in the first round."

Joe said, "Now wait, baby."

"I've seen you fight a hundred times! You had him. You could have nailed him in the first, but you were afraid I'd think Snicker decided that way."

"No, baby. You're wrong."

"And Snicker did decide that way! You think I couldn't tell—even if Ted Dover didn't tell me."

"That Dover is a big mouth," said Joe undecidedly.

Hedda kissed him again. She was good at that infighting. Joe couldn't get her loose without hurting her.

The door opened and Snicker came in, his hands full of green bills. He said, "I ruined them! Are they crying the blues! We were losing the fight and they had it spent, and then—socko! We killed them!"

He stopped and stared. He said, "Hey!"

"Stand-in makes good," said Hedda.

Joe couldn't pry her loose. Snicker's mouth hung wide open. Hedda said, "You pushed him on me for five years. All right, so I love him. What are you going to do about it?"

Snicker sat down on a chair. He slowly stuffed the money in his coat pocket, all wadded up. He said, "Nothing. I'm not going to do anything."

Hedda said, "You don't even care. You know you don't. I interfere with your gambling. I nag you."

Snicker said, "No. I mean—well. . . . It's all right."

Joe said, "Now wait."

"I've been waiting five years," said Hedda. "Are you going to marry me, or aren't you?"

Snicker looked at Joe. Joe spread his hands, one each side of Hedda's trim waist. Snicker said, "I guess she's right, chum."

Hedda said, "You're damn right I'm right!"

Joe put his hands together, on the small of her back. It was amazing how wonderful she felt. Snicker took out his money and counted it slowly.

Joe kissed Hedda. He even forgot his mouth was cut inside. He wondered if he could have really copped Harry Catt in the first. He doubted it very much.

THE
BIG OAF

William R. Cox

Things were a little blurred, but Owny Ridge thought he had a grand command of the situation. He reached for his drink, one broken-knuckled hand on the bar to steady himself. He heard his own voice saying, very clearly, slowly, "I can lick any jerk in the place." He had said this before, he now remembered. Either in this barroom or some other. There were a couple of guys he thought might take him up; he had seen them earlier, either in here or in one of the other places. They were pretty tough-looking characters, which made him feel very brave and eager. He balanced himself as best he could. His eyes did not focus very well. There could have been three of the tough characters . . .

The barkeep growled, "G'wan. T'row the bum out."

They began scuffling, moving toward him. Owny Ridge got his hands up, left hand high. He had only to side-step, shift and throw the right. His right was the best in the business, he told himself fiercely. He would show them if he was through, if one beating by a bigger, younger man could finish Owny Ridge.

"You know who I am?" he thundered at them. "You know Owny Ridge? I'm twenty-eight years old, that's all. I'll show you!"

He was not washed up. He felt fine with the whisky in him. His eyes were slightly shadowed, he thought, and he moved to get the light from them. But he could not move far enough and when the first of the attackers closed in he was suddenly unable to see him at all. A fist caught his jaw and he fell back and bumped into someone. His timing was gone and panic gripped him as the two—or was it three—charged him.

Then he was against the bar and a large something was before him. A calm voice was saying, "All right, fellas. Leave him alone."

The three—or was it only two—charged on. The large form moved with economy. A long arm snatched one from amongst them and made mopping motions. Feet came from the floor and described a circle just within Owny's vision, so that he ducked and almost fell.

Then the voice, a dimly-remembered voice, was saying, "That'll do, now. We don't want anybody hurt in here, y'know. That'll do."

There were two—or maybe three—men wallowing in the sawdust on the floor of the Third Avenue saloon. Owny Ridge stammered, "Lemme at 'em. I'll show 'em . . . I'm only twenty-eight years old—"

The calm, deep voice said, "Sure, Owny. Just come with me. You're great, Owny, great!"

That's all he could remember.

Owny groaned and woke almost completely, turning in the bed. He had not the slightest idea where he was. He stared at the neat room, the figure on the floor, wrapped only in a blanket, the giant form gently slumbering.

He staggered up and went through into the bathroom. He ran the cold water in the shower and forced himself under it. He stayed there holding himself erect, suffering the cold, cursing himself, gritting his teeth, hating himself. Now he could face it, now in the throes of the hangover; now he knew he was indeed finished, through. Dimly, he remembered the brawl, his loud voice denying the truth. This was the way he was true to Marge Merton; this was his comeback trail.

He backed out of the shower. A hand held a towel. He stared up into the round, bland features of his benefactor.

"You're Jack Crown. You're that sparring-partner guy!"

"Yep," said the giant cheerfully. "Saw you were havin' a little trouble. Nothing to it, Owny. Forget it."

Owny said, "Okay . . . okay . . . thanks." He scowled. He hated to give thanks. He hated being in the wrong. He squared his shoulders and rubbed hard at himself. He slapped at the layer of lard around his waist. He hustled inside and stared at his soiled clothing, folded neatly over a chair.

There was a kitchenette, he saw, a couple of large windows which allowed the sun to shine on a bright rug, an easy chair, a radio, a shelf of magazines and pocket-sized books. The oversize fold-up bed, in which he had slept while his host used the floor, took up the remaining room space.

He wrapped the towel about his middle and the huge man came from the bathroom wrapped in a robe with faded letters across the back. Jack Crown was grinning and it occurred to Owny Ridge that this character was always happily smiling at the world.

Crown said, "I'll take your stuff to the cleaner. He's a pal of mine. Have 'em back right away."

Ridge said, "I'll need linen." He reached into his trousers pocket and hauled forth the wallet with his name written in gold, the present from Marge Merton which he could not touch without wincing. There were two limp bills. He stared at them. They were tens, but they were the last of it, the last of all that money.

He handed a bill to Crown, who was getting into slacks and a jersey. He grunted, "Arrow shirt and shorts'll do."

Crown said, "I know what to get, Owny. Just stick around and we'll eat. There's a bottle of booze in the kitchen." He nodded brightly and went out.

Owny Ridge sat still for a moment, looking at the wallet and the one bill. He was a square-faced man with scowling dark brows. He tapped blunt fingers against the leather, the gilt letters. Then he put the money into the wallet and tossed it onto a small table. He meticulously made up the bed and restored it to the wall. He knotted the towel about his waist and padded into the kitchen. He found the bottle and took a small drink.

In half an hour Crown was back. The giant moved quietly in the kitchenette while Owny dressed. The odor of bacon and eggs made merry in the sunny room. Two steaming platters appeared and the contents were demolished without conversation. Owny's head began to feel as though it were shrinking back to normal size.

He said, "What you been doing, Jack?"

"Same thing," said Crown. "Workin' here and there."

"Win and lose," nodded Owny. "But you get work. I remember. You could be a good fighter, too, if you'd get mad and turn loose."

"I do all right," said Crown mildly.

"No ambition," said Owny, scowling. Then he said suddenly, "Didn't you work for Merton?"

"Yeah. Yeah. Worked for Pat before the Wolcott fight."

Owny was silent for a moment. Then he said harshly, "See anything of his sister, Marge?"

"Saw her last month," nodded Crown.

"She's . . . she's all right?"

"Marge? She's fine," said Crown cheerfully. "Pretty as a picture. Knows as much about boxing as her brother. And Pat knows plenty." He chuckled. "Remember one day he slipped on somethin' and I lucked one on his jaw and he went down on his fanny. She jumped into the ring and bawled him out plenty. He took it awhile, then we started again. Boy, he near killed me!"

Owny said, "He's a killer, all right." His face darkened.

"Oh, I forgot." Crown was all sympathy. "You never fought since, huh, Owny? What you doin' now?"

"He didn't finish me!" Owny's hand beat at the table. "He beat me, sure. He was better, that night. And I broke my hand." He thrust the right hand under Crown's nose. "You see it? He didn't finish me, I tell you!"

Crown said quietly, "Okay, Owny."

"I'm . . . I'm looking around. A fighter. A heavy—" He thought of the lone ten-dollar bill, the meager change Crown had brought him. He said lamely, "No. I'll never fight again. I'm twenty-eight. It's been a year. But I'd like to manage a good boy . . . build him up . . . send him against Pat Merton, knowing what I know now."

Jack Crown said, "Don't know of any good heavies, pal."

Owny Ridge jerked around, stared.

"Except you! You're a good heavy. Only you won't fight. You box, you fiddle, you won't hit. Do you know how to hit, Jack?"

The big man said deprecatingly, "Might hurt somebody, pal. Nobody hurts me much. I wouldn't wanta kill a man. I'm so big!"

He was big, but not freakish. He was strong as an ox. He had speed and grace for a man weighing about two-thirty. Owny Ridge said, "Look, Jack. How about it? You did me a favor last night. I appreciate it. How about letting me train you? I'll bet I can make you the champion. I know I can!"

"Cut it out. I'm just a sparring partner."

But Owny was on his feet, saying excitedly: "Listen, Jack. I am going to get someone to beat Pat Merton. You understand? I'm going to do it. All right, I've been on the booze. I've been fighting myself. But one thing I do know: I'm going to get even with Merton if it's the last act I perform on earth. And it's not because he beat me. Don't get me wrong. He's the champ; he's a good fighter. But I know how to beat him. And, brother, you're good enough to do it. Tell me, how much dough you got?"

Jack Crown said, "A couple thousand in the bank, mebbe."

"It's enough," snapped Ridge. "We'll start today. Right downtown at the Boys' Club gym. Away from the wisenheimers. Then we'll go to Jersey, a place I know. Merton's in California, living there. He won't know too much about it. We'll fight Rizzoli, Martin, Blake, those bums. Then we'll get Merton into the ring—"

"And he'll kill me," grinned Jack. "I know—I was with him, remember?"

"Not when I get through with you, he won't." Owny Ridge's face was alive, alight with his enthusiasm. "I know how to do it. You'll beat him, win his title. We'll be rich, pal, rich!"

Jack Crown said plaintively, "I don't think I wanta be rich, Owny. Honest, I'm doin' all right." But he was persuaded easily enough, swept along by Ridge's driving enthusiasm.

Over in Jersey, months later, it was a fine autumn day. The ring was back of a barn, a real barn complete with farmhouse nearby and the sound of pigs and chickens. Owny Ridge drove a hard right to the belly. Jack Crown took it sturdily and slammed a left to the head. Owny went back on the ropes, his eyes glazed. Instinctively he came off swinging short, vicious hooks, crowding the giant, lacing the big gloves home against head-guard and jaw.

Jack grunted, reached his long arms into a pincers and held Owny in his embrace. He panted, "Hey, you tryin' to kill me?"

Owny shook his head. He cried, "There! You see? You almost kayo'd me! You're getting it, you big clown! You'll fight Blake next week and you'll knock him out. Then we got Merton, I tell you. We got him!"

Jack plucked at his gloves. "Uh-huh. I see. The right cross, huh? You sure taught it to me." His grin spread wide over his face.

Owny snapped, "Don't be so damned happy. Today you got it; tomorrow you don't throw it. I don't get you, Jack. You'll never be a killer. What did you do against Rizzoli?"

"Aw, he was out on his feet," said Jack. "I couldn't smear the poor guy. Might hurt him."

Owny snarled, "It's a hurting business. Anguish and flying leather—that's fighting. Remember that, dammit, remember it!"

They showered, put on blue jeans and sweaters and moccasins and ran to the house, Owny a step ahead all the way. They were bronzed, tanned, and lean. Jack had lost the plumpness of his profile; Owny had lost the lard around his middle.

Mrs. Opperman, stout, beaming, said, "My, oh, my! Comp'ny! Never saw a purtier gal, either. Look!"

Owny drew up short. Under the tan his face went pale, then dull carmine. He said, "Hello, Marge."

Jack went past him, hands outstretched. "Margie! Li'l' Margie Merton! How'd you find us, Margie? What's cookin', baby? Where's Pat? Everything okay, Margie?"

She was five feet tall. She wore flat-heeled saddle shoes and no stockings on her tanned, lovely legs. She stood like a boy, feet apart, hands in the pockets of her jacket. She had a slightly tilted nose and a round, firm jaw and the coloring of an earthly angel. Her shoulders were rounded, but sturdy and straight across, as indicative of character as the clarity of her brown eyes.

She said, "Hello, kids. Playing house down here?"

Owny said, "Just fooling around, Marge. How are you?"

"I do all right. Without you."

"That was the idea," he said shortly.

Jack looked from one to the other, perplexed. "Hey! You two got a beef on each other? You can't do that to me! Why, you're my pals. Both of you!"

Owny said in an ugly voice, "I'm not your pal. I'm your partner and your trainer. Get in there out of the wind and eat."

Jack's eyes widened in wonder. "Why, there ain't any wind! And it ain't time to eat."

Marge said, "Go inside, darling. I'll talk to you later."

"Uh—sure, Margie. Anything you say, baby." He beamed upon her. He reached out a huge hand and touched her as though she were something to love and cherish and adore. His smile, Owny saw with a start, was an expression of real beauty.

Marge said, "Walk with me."

They walked toward the barn. She looked at the ring he had set up years ago for his own use. She said, "It stood up well."

"Better than me," he said challengingly.

"Anything stands up better than you!" Her gaze went over him. "I see you did get off the booze."

"I was never a lush."

"Always deny, always accuse others," she said. "Nothing was ever your fault. Alibi Owen Ridge, the unfortunate."

"What's the use?" His voice was hoarse. "Why do you come back and nag at me? You gave me back the ring. I got beat by your precious brother. Leave me alone, can't you?"

She said, "I know what you're doing, Owny. You're building up Jack to beat Pat. You can't do it. Jack will get killed. You know Pat. He might have pity on Jack—but not if you are in his corner. And Pat is the best fighter in the world. You ought to know that."

He leaned against the ring post. He said, "You're always right, aren't you, Marge?"

"Maybe," she said tersely. Her face reddened. "I'm right about Pat. He's the best and poor Jack can never beat him. Never!"

"You and your brother. Champions of the world!" His tone was harsh, unforgiving. "Now you're spying for him, chasing down here, warning us. Jack's knocked out a few stumblebums, so you get ideas. You're only thinking of Jack, the big oaf."

She said, "I was right once, anyway, Owny. I was right when I gave you back that ring."

"Okay, I'll buy that." When she wheeled and started walking swiftly to the house he wanted to call after her, to stop her, to say he had not meant to be ugly to her. He wanted it, he wanted it more than anything in the world. He had to wheel away from there and walk into the wood-lot and toward the field where Opperman would be finishing with the tractor. He had to steel his nerves and clench his teeth and fight himself to stay away for an hour.

When he came back her convertible was gone. Jack was rocking on the porch, waiting for him. The big man got up and said anxiously, "You all right, pal? I worried."

Owny sat down heavily on the top step. "Did she talk to you about Pat? Did she try to scare you?"

Jack said confusedly, "She was nice to me. She's always nice to me. I'm crazy about her."

"Sure. Crazy about her." Owny was muttering. He raised his voice. "You'll fight Pat. You'll beat him. When I'm through with you there won't be anything you won't know about him. You're young enough, more than big enough. You're too strong for him, do you hear?"

"Yes, Owny," said the giant.

There was no conviction in him, Owny knew. But he was winning fights by knockouts. He was becoming mechanically smart. Daily lessons consisting of sharp punches in the jaw, repetitious admonishments, and hard bone work were bringing him along.

Pat Merton was big, strong, and smart. He was tough. He hated Owny Ridge. He hated Owny because of Marge, because he had not wanted her to marry. He hated Owny because Owny had been his closest rival and many had thought Owny his superior as a boxer. He had stunned and beaten Owny with hatred blazing in his eyes.

Well, Owny Ridge's hatred was hot, too. He clenched the hand he had broken on Pat Merton's head. What would have happened if he had not broken that hand?

Searching within himself, he at least admitted he did not know. Always before he had thought the broken hand defeated him.

Yet he had never fought after Merton had contemptuously denied him a return bout. Something had broken within him. Marge's visit, her cutting words, had finally made him admit it. He did admit it, to himself, sitting there, nursing his old wounds, his hatred . . .

The day of the Blake fight they weighed in at the Commission office. It was a double-wind-up card with Corson going against Rizzoli underneath the Blake-Crown go. Rizzoli was there, tough and vindictive against Crown, who laughed and clapped his shoulder and kidded with Blake and made everybody happy. The big guy got under your skin, Owny Ridge mused. He even had Owny grinning.

The promoter came in late, wailing. "Corson's out. Broke his hand in an auto accident. Who am I gonna get? I got to get somebody. Damn all double bills!"

"Fight him yourself," suggested Jack. Then he turned and stared at Owny. His big arm reached out, his hand closed on Owny's elbow, squeezing gently. He said, "How much is in it?"

Owny said, "No, you don't. You big clown!"

The promoter said, "Hey! The doc's right here. If Owny can pass the physical. Four grand in it, Owny."

Rizzoli's eyes glowered. "Yeah, Owny. Four grand, Owny. And wouldn't I just love it!"

There was a pause. Owny Ridge gulped. The past fifteen months sped by, the long months since he had been in there for pay. Then the hot days over in Jersey, the many rounds against Jack Crown came to mind. Then Marge and her searing words.

He choked, "Okay, okay."

The doctor went over him. Last of all he examined the right hand. He pursed his lips, hesitated, then nodded. Rizzoli, in the corner getting dressed, was chortling, "The bum's yella. Merton busted him up. I'll finish him for good!"

That could happen, too. No one knew it better than Owny Ridge.

That night, in the dressing-room, he said to Jack, "You stay warm. It'll be a moment or two before I can chuck on some clothes and get down to your corner. Box Blake—play with him—until I get there. I want you to use that right hand the way it should be used."

Jack finished adjusting the bandage on Owny's right hand. He chuckled: "Always could bandage a hand better'n you, anyhow. You couldn't hurt it if you tried. Poor Rizzoli. He couldn't hit you with a shovel. This is fun, huh, Owny? Fun!"

Owny said, "Don't get in a draft. The boys'll handle my corner. You stay here and keep warm, you hear me?"

"Rizzoli'll wish Corson never seen an automobile," Jack crowed. "Boy, oh, boy! This is sure fun!"

They had two brothers named Moe and Joe in their corner. Owny never bothered trying to tell them apart for both were expert corner men. Owny ranged himself between them and shuffled out. As he hit the ramp leading down to the familiar Garden ring he began to dance a little, a thing of old habit, a jig, waving his arms a bit, moving on the balls of his feet, dancing all the way down to battle. The crowd saw him and in the gallery an old fan whooped, "Owny boy! That's my Owny!"

They cheered him! Owny was stunned. He had forgotten the cheers, remembering only the dismal aftermath of utter defeat at the hands of Pat Merton. The blood ran quicker through his veins. He leaped upon the apron and mitted the section where the cheering had begun.

He sat upon the stool, went to ring center and was instructed by a referee he knew of old, came back and shucked the robe and hauled at the ropes. The small gloves felt tight on his hands; he had been using pillows with Jack so long that these seemed inadequate. He stared up at the spot where the man had called to him and the voice came through, "Moider the bum, Owny boy!"

He had never waved at the crowd in his life. But he felt his mouth stretching in a grin marred by the red-rubber mouthpiece as he flung up an arm. The bell rang.

Rizzoli had made up his mind in the Commission office. He'd decided Owny Ridge was a broken man, ruined by the fists of the champion. Rizzoli came out roaring, both hands going, determined to blast Ridge in a matter of seconds. He came with head down, strong as a lion and thirsty for blood.

Owny Ridge moved with the instinct and skill of his years. Side-stepping, he hooked a right to the body. He threw a left to the jaw as Rizzoli floundered. He chopped another right to the base of the jaw. He slung two lefts to the head and Rizzoli straightened.

Without thinking, Owny Ridge struck from the chest, lining his right fist down the middle alley. It thudded convincingly against a hard jaw. Rizzoli fell forward, his nose plowing the resin.

The referee leaped forward, crouching. Owny Ridge retreated to a neutral corner, his eyes upon the fallen fighter. Leaning on the ropes he stared, not removing the mouthpiece, disbelieving the sudden drama in which he had taken part.

"Ten . . . and out!"

Owny Ridge turned. At ringside, leaping and cavorting, was Jack Crown, wrapped in the robe Owny had first seen in the apartment where he had awakened with a hangover. The long arms waved, the broad face beamed, the white teeth flashed.

Owny climbed through the ropes held wide by Moe and Joe.

He said rapidly to Jack, "Box him, now, box him!" The big man only laughed and clowned amid the tumult. The man in the gallery was screaming for "Owny boy," and Owny waved at him. Then he ran up the ramp alone, leaving Jack with Moe and Joe.

In the dressing room he fumbled for his old trousers and heavy sweater. He was scarcely sweating, but the Garden was draughty. He tore off gloves and bandages. He sat an instant, staring at his right hand. It was sound as a nut.

Then he ran out of the dressing room and back down the aisle. As he mounted the steps he could see Jack sitting on the stool, the first round over, clowning with the reporters in the working-press rows.

Moe—or Joe—said, "Jack win it easy. He jest poke ol' Blake."

Across the ring Blake, a young, earnest pugilist, already sported a pink eye socket. Owny rubbed the back of Jack's neck with oil and said, "You got him figured, Jack? You boxing him?"

"Sure, pal, sure! Never didn't you powder old Rizzoli! Broth-er! Right on the kisser! Ol' Rizzoli never knew what—"

"Keep your left in this guy's puss," said Owny sternly. "I'll tell you when to sink him. I want him sunk, see?"

"Y' oughta do it yourself then," guffawed Jack. The whistle sounded and Owny climbed down. Jack was still grinning when he went to meet his opponent.

Blake was a worker, a good prospect. He kept walking around Jack, very swiftly, trying to find an opening. Jack stuck out his long left and almost languidly bathed Blake's eye with blows. After the third round Blake was plunging recklessly, trying to get close.

Owny said, "Now you take him. Straight in with it."

Jack said, "Aw, I might hurt the kid. I'm winnin', Owny."

"Knock him out," ordered Owny. "Get him out of there this round."

Jack sighed. He got up at the bell and trotted to ring center. He leveled a left at Blake, shifted and threw the right fist. It was a replica of Owny's own blow, the cross off the chest. It landed high on Blake's head.

The young man shuddered, but recovered. He came in, punching, and Jack got a bit tangled up. He didn't knock Blake out that round—or in any of the next seven rounds.

"You've got to do it!" Owny was desperate. It was the tenth and last round coming up. "You've missed his chin a hundred times. You've got him beaten, but not by too much. Knock him out!"

"But he keeps movin'," said Jack good-naturedly. There was not a mark on the big fellow. "I keep shootin' at him and he keeps movin'. Pretty tough feller, ain't he?"

"Merton did it," said Owny grimly. "Merton kayo'd him."

Jack went out for the last round. Blake, strong as a horse, one eye almost closed, rushed the bigger man. Jack held him off, then tried the right cross again. Blake's head spun with the force of the blow, but he kept his feet. Jack measured him in leisurely fashion; Blake recovered and clinched.

The round and the fight ended that way, with Blake reeling, gamely trying to fight back.

All Owny could get out of Jack was, "Aw . . . I won, didn't I? But the way you took that Rizzoli! Bam! What fun, pal!"

Owny did not reiterate that Jack was not his pal. He found himself listening as Jack told it over and over, at Lindy's, at Reuben's, wherever they went and had an audience. "Bam! Poor ol' Rizzoli!" And then Jack's infectious laugh . . .

It became a sort of dream world, something like the dread year after his defeat by Pat Merton. He kept shaking himself, trying to get out of it. But the snowball grew, coasting down the hill as the sportswriters rolled out reams of copy.

Jack said gleefully, "You gotta fight Blake. See? You gotta!"

Owny said: "I won't do it. I built you into a spot and you dogged it against Blake. You could have got him out of there."

"Phooie," laughed Jack. "*You* got to fight Blake. For the honor of the camp. You and me—that's the camp."

Owny fought Blake. He got him in close and drove him to the canvas with chopping-block punches. Blake went out in the second round.

The snowball grew to tremendous proportions. "Cinderella of the Year, Male Species" and then a picture of poor Blake on the floor. Stories about Owny's broken hand, now mended, his neat campaign of building up Jack Crown, who simply did not have the punch and could not hope to defeat Pat Merton.

Marge came to town with her aroused brother. There were press conferences. The champion would be delighted to meet either Crown or Ridge but he preferred Ridge. He would like to fight Ridge for breakfast every day. There were pictures of Marge, pert and confident, hands in pockets, nose tilted at the camera.

She met Owny in Tim Costello's bar on Third Avenue. She called him and he had to go. They sat in one of the back booths and she looked across the table at him and said, "You're going to fight Pat."

"No," he said flatly.

"You're going to do it."

He looked at her. The loneliness of the many months choked him. He said thickly, "I don't hate him any more. I don't know what's happened to me. I don't even want to hit Pat."

She said, "Then you should fight him. Win, lose or draw, you have got to prove you weren't wrecked by him."

He said, "Wait, now. There's something wrong with this. You didn't talk like this before."

She said, "You weren't like this before. Look at you! Your eye is clear, you actually smile sometimes. You're lean and fit and clean-looking."

She leaned toward him. "We were engaged once. I believed in you. Then you went away. You became someone I didn't know, a man with hatred against my brother, hatred against me. But once I loved you, Owen Ridge. Now I know you have to box Pat."

He said, "That's . . . that's all, Marge?" His jaw was hardening again, but his eyes were clear.

She said, "That's all. Now buy me a steak sandwich and a drink."

He said quietly, "All right, Marge, all right."

The next day he signed to meet Pat Merton for the heavyweight title.

They trained in Jersey, at Opperman's farm. Jack Crown ran the camp. It was a happy camp. Everyone who visited it had a good time. Owny worked himself slowly into shape, getting his timing down. He did a lot of thinking during the long session.

He boxed daily with Jack. He bulled the big man a lot. He had arranged a rematch between Blake and Crown for the windup bout on the championship bill. He thought a lot about that, particularly one afternoon when Jack almost tore off his head with a right cross. He did not say anything, which was a real switch in character, but he thought a lot.

He came down to the bout in perfect shape. He went into the ring with health glowing from him. He nodded to Pat Merton without emotion.

Pat Merton was a picture fighter. He was blond, handsome, craggy-faced. He was built like a wedge and he moved like a panther. All the tricks of boxing were his, and all the strength a man needed. He sneered at Owny Ridge and said, "Come to get it again, huh, Owny?"

"Maybe." Owny grinned.

Owny could see where Marge sat, behind Pat's corner, with just the top of her brown hair showing. Jack Crown said: "Pal, this it it. Pal, this is what we wanted, all along. Face it, Owny, face it!"

Owny stared at his friend. Jack was not laughing. Jack's face was pallid, his lips were trembling. His big hands were tender as a woman's as he stroked Owny's muscles. Owny laughed and said, "Take it easy, kid."

"Geez, I'm scared, pal. I wanted this, but I'm scared."

Owny said, "You're not as dumb as you look, are you, kid?"

A slow flush mounted through the pallor. Jack said, "Get to him, pal. Get to him and make him like it."

Moe and Joe had the corner stuff down. Owny went to ring center and the referee talked to them. The television cameras were eyeing him. He saw them, saw the sports reporters who had been so kind to him, saw

Marge plainly, saw her heart-shaped face turned up to him, her expression withdrawn and taut, her eyes shadowy.

Merton said curtly, "Comin' at you, you yellow bum!"

He laughed. He went to his corner dancing and gripped the ropes. Jack's face was white. Owny smiled down at him, gesturing. From somewhere in the ball park came the stentorian cry, "Owny boy! Moider 'im, Owny boy!" He waved in the direction of the call. The bell sounded.

Pat Merton was an assassin. He could creep close with his deceptive shuffle and lash out like a striking knife-blade, cutting, slashing. His speed was amazing. He always came forward, always attacked with relentless dauntlessness. Owny made a circle, dancing, hands wide, inviting the champion in.

Turning, going forward, Merton came. His left licked out. Owny's head went back, blood ran from a cut over his eye. He bowed acknowledgment, laughing. He feinted with his right, threw his own left as Merton, eyes gleaming at the sight of gore, came inside.

The hook landed on the side of Merton's head. The champion staggered. Owny hit him with a right hook under the heart. Merton sagged against the ropes. Owny stepped back delicately, poised. He struck with left and right. Merton folded, covering up as thousands stood on their chairs and screamed to the heavens.

Rattled, the referee stepped between them, eyeing Merton. That second was enough.

The champion came off the ropes with both hands unleashed. Punch after punch drove against Owny's body, his head. He tincanned, fighting back with short wallops to the head. They went all over the ring, head and head, swapping blows which would have felled lesser men. Neither heard the bell.

The referee followed Owny to his corner. Breathing hard, he said, "I'm sorry, Ridge. I messed you up."

Owny spat blood. He said, "That's all right, Harry."

The referee hesitated, then went away, fumbling for his scorecard. Jack Crown was almost weeping. "He loused it up. You had him. You had him cooled. Damn him!"

"Where's that old grin? Where's my boy Jack?" asked Owny. "Where's Pat Merton's sparmate and great admirer?"

Jack said, "Owny, it was all for you. I mean, it wasn't at first, and then we got to be pals and—"

"Sure. Pals," nodded Owny. "Now stop weepin' and watch the fight. This is liable to be good, as far as it goes."

It was funny, the way he felt. He saw Pat Merton knocking his gloves together, aching to get at him, but it meant nothing except that here was a bout he had to make. He had to make it for many reasons, but not for the one which a year ago would have been paramount. He was not fighting because he hated Pat Merton.

He went out and boxed. Merton was fast as ever, but Merton had a cut, too, alongside his lip. Owny laid a left to the eye and Pat began to puff a little as the right hand clipped him amidships. The champion fell in close and worked over Owny's body, the body which would have collapsed a year ago under one of those solid blows. Even then Owny was doing a lot of thinking.

He drove the champion away from him with a left uppercut. A right caught him alongside the face and he almost went down, but his legs spread, his toes dug in. He met the rush of the champ with a straight left to the head. He heard Jack Crown shouting, heard the crowd, heard away off the shrill-voiced fan crying, "Owny boy! Moider him, Owny."

He drilled the right where it had to go. He did not even look at his mark. He knew Merton would be there. He had taught it to Jack so often, with painstaking care, and he knew Merton would be in the middle of the shift coming forward. Through the pain of the side of his face, through the ache in his body, through the thoughts and resolved doubts and the shame of other days, he sent the right cross crashing.

It struck Merton square in the face. It stopped his rush. His hands dropped at his sides and his nostrils gushed blood. He hung there wide open, glassy-eyed for a full moment. He was marked for the kill.

Nimbly, like a dancer, Owny Ridge stepped back. He saw Merton return to consciousness. He saw the champion start forward. Then Owny leaped in and smashed lefts and rights full on the jaw of the charging champion.

Pat Merton slid to the canvas slowly, all his instincts against his going, all his fighting heart urging him to remain erect. He slid sideways, one leg out, tried to get up. He fell flat on his back.

In the neutral corner Owny Ridge spat the mouthpiece into his glove, hurled it at his corner. The referee was counting. Owny did not look anywhere but at the fallen Merton.

The referee said, "Ten . . . and *out!*"

Owny was at the champion's side. He lifted the blond head. He shook it gently as Merton's eyes opened. He saw the hatred returning to the cold blue eyes. He said softly, "I'm not yellow, Pat. Not any more. And Marge is through with me for good. Get wise to yourself, Pat. Get wise, and be happy."

He turned the champion of yesterday over to his handlers. Jack Crown hoisted Owny aloft, dancing about, holding him in a bear grasp. Then

Jack put him down and took off his pants and shirt, to appear in the trunks he was to wear against Blake. Moe and Joe hesitated.

Owny said sternly, "Stay with Jack, fellows." He looked for Marge. She was gone. He went through the dugout and up the tunnel and into the dressing room. Reporters swarmed in and he talked quietly to them as he hurried into his ancient pants and sweater, eager to return to Jack.

The door opened and Jack Crown came in. He was laughing. "I got lucky and caught him in the first minute! This is our night, fellas, me and my pal Owny."

When everyone else was gone and they had showered, Owny said, "Let's go home, pal. I want to have a talk with you."

Jack said uncertainly, "What about Lindy's? I'll have to call. They expect us."

"Call them," said Owny.

They went to the little apartment in a cab. They looked at each other, standing in the neat room where Owny had awakened from his living nightmare. Then Jack went into the kitchen and returned with a bottle of liquor. He said, "Same ol' bottle."

They sat down. Owny said, "Jack, you should have been in there tonight. You'd better tell me the truth about it. I've guessed a lot, but you better tell me."

Jack said, "Aw, let's take a drink first."

Owny said, "You're in love with Marge Merton. By God, if I can't do anything else I can help you there, somehow or other."

Jack smiled suddenly, beautifully. "You're a real pal, Owny. Y'know what? I didn't like you at first."

"You did it for some reason," said Owny. "You must have been looking for me on Third Avenue."

Jack said, "Take a drink, pal. Relax."

Owny said, "I've got to know. I've got to know why you rebuilt me from a drunken, no-good bum into the heavy champion without letting me know you were doing it."

Jack said, "Aw—" He seemed to be listening for something. He arose, towering, filling the small room. His face was bright with pride and something else, some emotion Owny could not quite understand. Then, moving with that speed which always amazed the beholder, he was gone out the door of the apartment.

Owny came to his feet, startled. There was someone in the kitchenette. He heard the tap of light heels.

He said, "Marge. Marge!"

She was openly weeping. She came straight into his arms, thrusting her small, full body against him, offering her face to his kisses, but she was weeping.

When he could speak again, he said, "You did it. You sent him. And he came and he stuck because he loves you."

She nodded. "He . . . he's the most wonderful big guy in the world."

Owny said, "You came up there and gave me the works in Jersey to set me up for Jack's failure against Blake. You planted it that Jack would be hurt if he fought Pat, that I should fight my own battles. You planted that in my mind."

She said, "Oh, Owny, have I done wrong?"

He said, "You loved me enough to send Jack, enough to help me beat your brother."

"I had to find out," she begged. "I had to find out if you were the man I loved or that other man who somehow slipped."

"You loved me all the time—"

"We don't love a person for virtues alone," she said, her head muffled on his chest. "We don't stop loving them because they do something wrong, or weak, or even bad."

Owny Ridge stared at the wall. He said slowly, "No, that's right. I love you, Marge. You love me. But if there was justice, Marge, you'd love Jack Crown."

A PIECE
OF STEAK

Jack London

With the last morsel of bread Tom King wiped his plate clean of the last particle of flour gravy and chewed the resulting mouthful in a slow and meditative way. When he arose from the table, he was oppressed by the feeling that he was distinctly hungry. Yet he alone had eaten. The two children in the other room had been sent early to bed in order that in sleep they might forget they had gone supperless. His wife had touched nothing, and had sat silently and watched him with solicitous eyes. She was a thin, worn woman of the working class, though signs of an earlier prettiness were not wanting in her face. The flour for the gravy she had borrowed from the neighbor across the hall. The last two ha'pennies had gone to buy the bread.

He sat down by the window on a rickety chair that protested under his weight, and quite mechanically he put his pipe in his mouth and dipped into the side pocket of his coat. The absence of any tobacco made him aware of his action, and, with a scowl for his forgetfulness, he put the pipe away. His movements were slow, almost hulking, as though he were burdened by the heavy weight of his muscles. He was a solid-bodied, stolid-looking man, and his appearance did not suffer from being overprepossessing. His rough clothes were old and slouchy. The uppers of his shoes were too weak to carry the heavy resoling that was itself of no recent date. And his cotton shirt, a cheap, two-shilling affair, showed a frayed collar and ineradicable paint stains.

But it was Tom King's face that advertised him unmistakably for what he was. It was the face of a typical prize fighter; of one who had put in long years of service in the squared ring and, by that means, developed and emphasized all the marks of the fighting beast. It was distinctly a lowering countenance, and, that no feature of it might escape notice, it was clean-shaven. The lips were shapeless, and constituted a mouth harsh to excess, that was like a gash in his face. The jaw was aggressive, brutal, heavy. The eyes, slow of movement and heavy-lidded, were almost expressionless under the shaggy, indrawn brows. Sheer animal that he was, the eyes were the most animal-like feature about him. They were sleepy, lionlike—the eyes of a fighting animal. The forehead slanted quickly back to the hair, which, clipped close, showed every bump of a villainous-looking head. A nose, twice broken and moulded variously by countless blows, and a cauliflower ear, permanently swollen and distorted to twice its size, completed his adornment, while the beard, fresh-shaven as it was, sprouted in the skin and gave the face a blue-black stain.

All together, it was the face of a man to be afraid of in a dark alley or lonely place. And yet Tom King was not a criminal, nor had he ever done anything criminal. Outside of brawls, common to his walk of life, he had harmed no one. Nor had he ever been known to pick a quarrel. He was a professional, and all the fighting brutishness of him was reserved for his professional appearances. Outside the ring he was slow-going, easy-natured, and, in his younger days, when money was flush, too open-handed for his own good. He bore no grudges and had few enemies. Fighting was a business with him. In the ring he struck to hurt, struck to maim, struck to destroy; but there was no animus in it. It was a plain business proposition. Audiences assembled and paid for the spectacle of men knocking each other out. The winner took the big end of the purse. When Tom King faced the Woolloomoolloo Gouger, twenty years before, he knew that the Gouger's jaw was only four months healed after having been broken in a Newcastle bout. And he had played for that jaw and broken it again in the ninth round, not because he bore the Gouger any ill will, but because that was the surest way to put the Gouger out and win the big end of the purse. Nor had the Gouger borne him any ill will for it. It was the game, and both knew the game and played it.

Tom King had never been a talker, and he sat by the window, morosely silent, staring at his hands. The veins stood out on the backs of the hands, large and swollen; and the knuckles, smashed and battered and malformed, testified to the use to which they had been put. He had never heard that a man's life was the life of his arteries, but well he knew the meaning of those big, upstanding veins. His heart had pumped too much blood through them at top pressure. They no longer did the work. He had stretched the elasticity out of them, and with their distention had passed his endurance. He tired easily now. No longer could he do a fast twenty rounds, hammer and tongs, fight, fight, fight, from gong to gong, with fierce rally on top of fierce rally, beaten to the ropes and in turn beating his opponent to the ropes, and rallying fiercest and fastest of all in that last, twentieth round, with the house on its feet and yelling, himself rushing, striking, ducking, raining showers of blows upon showers of blows and receiving showers of blows in return, and all the time the heart faithfully pumping the surging blood through the adequate veins. The veins, swollen at the time, had always shrunk down again, though not quite—each time, imperceptibly at first, remaining just a trifle larger than before. He stared at them and at his battered knuckles, and, for the moment, caught a vision of the youthful excellence of those hands before the first knuckle had been smashed on the head of Benny Jones, otherwise known as the Welsh Terror.

The impression of his hunger came back on him.

"Blimey, but couldn't I go a piece of steak!" he muttered aloud, clenching his huge fists and spitting out a smothered oath.

"I tried both Burke's an' Sawley's," his wife said half apologetically.

"An' they wouldn't?" he demanded.

"Not a ha'penny. Burke said . . ." She faltered.

"G'wan! Wot'd he say?"

"As how 'e was thinkin' Sandel ud do ye to night, an' as how yer score was comfortable big as it was."

Tom King grunted, but did not reply. He was busy thinking of the bull terrier he had kept in his younger days to which he had fed steaks without end. Burke would have given him credit for a thousand steaks—then. But times had changed. Tom King was getting old; and old men, fighting before second-rate clubs, couldn't expect to run bills of any size with the tradesmen.

He had got up in the morning with a longing for a piece of steak, and the longing had not abated. He had not had a fair training for this fight. It was a drought year in Australia, times were hard, and even the most irregular work was difficult to find. He had had no sparring partner, and his food had not been of the best nor always sufficient. He had done a few days' navvy work when he could get it, and he had run about the Domain in the early mornings to get his legs in shape. But it was hard, training without a partner and with a wife and two kiddies that must be fed. Credit with the tradesmen had undergone very slight expansion when he was matched with Sandel. The secretary of the Gayety Club had advanced him three pounds—the loser's end of the purse—and beyond that had refused to go. Now and again he had managed to borrow a few shillings from old pals, who would have lent more only that it was a drought year and they were hard put themselves. No—and there was no use in disguising the fact—his training had not been satisfactory. He should have had better food and no worries. Besides, when a man is forty, it is harder to get into condition than when he is twenty.

"What time is it, Lizzie?" he asked.

His wife went across the hall to inquire, and came back.

"Quarter before eight."

"They'll be startin' the first bout in a few minutes," he said. "Only a tryout. Then there's a four-round spar 'tween Dealer Wells an' Gridley, an' a ten-round go 'tween Starlight an' some sailor bloke. I don't come on for over an hour."

At the end of another silent ten minutes, he rose to his feet.

"Truth is, Lizzie, I ain't had proper trainin'."

He reached for his hat and started for the door. He did not offer to kiss her—he never did on going out—but on this night she dared to kiss him, throwing her arms around him and compelling him to bend down to her face. She looked quite small against the massive bulk of the man.

"Good luck, Tom," she said. "You gotter do 'im."

"Ay, I gotter do 'im," he repeated. "That's all there is to it. I jus' gotter do 'im."

He laughed with an attempt at heartiness, while she pressed more closely against him. Across her shoulders he looked around the bare room. It was all he had in the world, with the rent overdue, and her and the kiddies. And he was leaving it to go out into the night to get meat for his mate and cubs—not like a modern working man going to his machine grind, but in the old, primitive, royal, animal way, by fighting for it.

"I gotter do 'im," he repeated, this time a hint of desperation in his voice. "If it's a win, it's thirty quid—an' I can pay all that's owin', with a lump o' money left over. If it's a lose, I get naught—not even a penny for me to ride home on the tram. The secretary's give all that's comin' from a loser's end. Good-by, old woman. I'll come straight home if it's a win."

"An' I'll be waitin' up," she called to him along the hall.

It was full two miles to the Gayety, and as he walked along he remembered how in his palmy days—he had once been the heavyweight champion of New South Wales—he would have ridden in a cab to the fight, and how, mostly likely, some heavy backer would have paid for the cab and ridden with him. There were Tommy Burns and that Yankee nigger, Jack Johnson—they rode about in motor cars. And he walked! And, as any man knew, a hard two miles was not the best preliminary to a fight. He was an old un, and the world did not wag well with old uns.

He was good for nothing now except navvy work, and his broken nose and swollen ear were against him even in that. He found himself wishing that he had learned a trade. It would have been better in the long run. But no one had told him, and he knew, deep down in his heart, that he would not have listened if they had. It had been so easy. Big money— sharp, glorious fights—periods of rest and loafing in between—a following of eager flatterers, the slaps on the back, the shakes of the hand, the toffs glad to buy him a drink for the privilege of five minutes' talk—and the glory of it, the yelling houses, the whirlwind finish, the referee's "King wins!" and his name in the sporting columns next day.

Those had been times! But he realized now, in his slow, ruminating way, that it was the old uns he had been putting away. He was Youth, rising; and they were Age, sinking. No wonder it had been easy—they with their swollen veins and battered knuckles and weary in the bones of them from the long battles they had already fought. He remembered the time he put out old Stowsher Bill, at Rush-Cutters Bay, in the eighteenth round, and how old Bill had cried afterward in the dressing room like a baby. Perhaps old Bill's rent had been overdue. Perhaps he'd had at home a missus an' a couple of kiddies. And perhaps Bill, that very day of the fight, had had a hungering for a piece of steak. Bill had fought game and taken incredible punishment. He could see now, after he had gone through the mill himself, that Stowsher Bill had fought for a bigger stake, that night twenty years ago, than had young Tom King, who had fought for glory and easy money. No wonder Stowsher Bill had cried afterward in the dressing room.

Well, a man had only so many fights in him, to begin with. It was the iron law of the game. One man might have a hundred hard fights in him, another man only twenty; each, according to the make of him and the quality of his fibre, had a definite number, and, when he had fought them, he was done. Yes, he had had more fights in him than most of them, and he had had far more than his share of the hard, gruelling fights—the kind that worked the heart and lungs to bursting, that took the elastic out of the arteries and made hard knots of muscle out of Youth's sleek suppleness, that wore out nerve and stamina and made brain and bones weary from excess of effort and endurance overwrought. Yes, he had done better than all of them. There was none of his old fighting partners left. He was the last of the old guard. He had seen them all finished, and he had had a hand in finishing some of them.

They had tried him out against the old uns, and one after another he had put them away—laughing when, like old Stowsher Bill, they cried in the dressing-room. And now he was an old un, and they tried out the youngsters on him. There was that bloke, Sandel. He had come over from New Zealand with a record behind him. But nobody in Australia knew anything about him, so they put him up against old Tom King. If Sandel made a showing, he would be given better men to fight, with bigger purses to win; so it was to be depended upon that he would put up a fierce battle. He had everything to win by it—money and glory and career; and Tom King was the grizzled old chopping block that guarded the highway to fame and fortune. And he had nothing to win except thirty quid, to pay to the landlord and the tradesmen. And, as Tom King thus ruminated, there came to his stolid vision the form of Youth, glorious Youth, rising exultant and invincible, supple of muscle and silken of skin, with heart and lungs that had never been tired and torn and that laughed at limitation of effort. Yes, Youth was the Nemesis. It destroyed the old uns and recked not that, in so doing, it destroyed itself. It enlarged its arteries and smashed its knuckles, and was in turn destroyed by Youth. For Youth was ever youthful. It was only Age that grew old.

At Castlereagh Street he turned to the left, and three blocks along came to the Gayety. A crowd of young larrikins hanging outside the door made respectful way for him, and he heard one say to another: "That's 'im! That's Tom King!"

Inside, on the way to his dressing-room, he encountered the secretary, a keen-eyed, shrewdfaced young man, who shook his hand.

"How are you feelin', Tom?" he asked.

"Fit as a fiddle," King answered, though he knew that he lied, and that if he had a quid, he would give it right there for a good piece of steak.

When he emerged from the dressing room, his seconds behind him, and came down the aisle to the squared ring in the center of the hall, a burst of greeting and applause went up from the waiting crowd. He acknowledged salutations right and left, though few of the faces did he know. Most of them were the faces of kiddies unborn when he was winning his first laurels in the squared ring. He leaped lightly to the raised platform and ducked through the ropes to his corner, where he sat down on a folding stool. Jack Ball, the referee, came over and shook his hand. Ball was a broken-down pugilist who for over ten years had not entered the ring as a principal. King was glad that he had him for referee. They were both old uns. If he should rough it with Sandel a bit beyond the rules, he knew Ball could be depended upon to pass it by.

Aspiring young heavyweights, one after another, were climbing into the ring and being presented to the audience by the referee. Also, he issued their challenges for them.

"Young Pronto," Bill announced, "from North Sydney, challenges the winner for fifty pounds side bet."

The audience applauded, and applauded again as Sandel himself sprang through the ropes and sat down in his corner. Tom King looked across the ring at him curiously, for in a few minutes they would be locked together in merciless combat, each trying with all the force of him to knock the other into unconsciousness. But little could he see, for Sandel, like himself, had trousers and sweater on over his ring costume. His face was strongly handsome, crowned with a curly mop of yellow hair, while his thick, muscular neck hinted at bodily magnificence.

Young Pronto went to one corner and then the other, shaking hands with the principals and dropping down out of the ring. The challenges went on. Ever Youth climbed through the ropes—Youth unknown, but insatiable—crying out to mankind that with strength and skill it would match issues with the winner. A few years before, in his own heyday of invincibleness, Tom King would have been amused and bored by these preliminaries. But now he sat fascinated, unable to shake the vision of Youth from his eyes. Always were these youngsters rising up in the boxing game, springing through the ropes and shouting their defiance; and always were the old uns going down before them. They climbed to success over the bodies of the old uns. And ever they came, more and more youngsters—Youth unquenchable and irresistible—and ever they put the old uns away, themselves becoming old uns and travelling the same downward path, while behind them, ever pressing on them, was Youth eternal—the new babies, grown lusty and dragging their elders down, with behind them more babies to the end of time—Youth that must have its will and that will never die.

King glanced over to the press box and nodded to Morgan, of the *Sportsman,* and Corbett, of the *Referee.* Then he held out his hands, while Sid Sullivan and Charley Bates, his seconds, slipped on his gloves and laced them tight, closely watched by one of Sandel's seconds, who first examined critically the tapes on King's knuckles. A second of his own was in Sandel's corner, performing a like office. Sandel's trousers were pulled off, and, as he stood up, his sweater was skinned off over his head. And Tom King, looking, saw Youth incarnate, deep-chested, heavy-thewed, with muscles that slipped and slid like live things under the white satin skin. The whole body was acrawl with life, and Tom King knew that it was a life that had never oozed its freshness out through the aching pores during the long fights wherein Youth paid its toll and departed not quite so young as when it entered.

The two men advanced to meet each other, and, as the gong sounded and the seconds clattered out of the ring with the folding stools, they shook hands and instantly took their fighting attitudes. And instantly, like a mechanism of steel and springs balanced on a hair trigger, Sandel was in and out and in again, landing a left to the eyes, a right to the ribs, ducking a counter, dancing lightly away and dancing menacingly back again. He was swift and clever. It was a dazzling exhibition. The house yelled its approbation. But King was not dazzled. He had fought too many fights and too many youngsters. He knew the blows for what they were—too quick and too deft to be dangerous. Evidently Sandel was going to rush things from the start. It was to be expected. It was the way of Youth, expending its splendor and excellence in wild insurgence and furious onslaught, overwhelming opposition with its own unlimited glory of strength and desire.

Sandel was in and out, here, there, and everywhere, light-footed and eager-hearted, a living wonder of white flesh and stinging muscle that wove itself into a dazzling fabric of attack, slipping and leaping like a flying shuttle from action to action through a thousand actions, all of them centered upon the destruction of Tom King, who stood between him and fortune. And Tom King patiently endured. He knew his business, and he knew Youth now that Youth was no longer his. There was nothing to do till the other lost some of his steam, was his thought, and he grinned to himself as he deliberately ducked so as to receive a heavy blow on the top of his head. It was a wicked thing to do, yet eminently fair according to the rules of the boxing game. A man was supposed to take care of his own knuckles, and, if he insisted on hitting an opponent on the top of the head, he did so at his own peril. King could have ducked lower and let the blow whiz harmlessly past, but he remembered his own early fights and how he smashed his first knuckle on the head of the Welsh Terror. He was but playing the game. That duck had accounted for one of Sandel's knuckles. Not that Sandel would mind it now. He would go on, superbly regardless, hitting as hard as ever throughout the fight. But later on, when the long ring battles had begun to tell, he would regret that knuckle and look back and remember how he smashed it on Tom King's head.

The first round was all Sandel's, and he had the house yelling with the rapidity of his whirlwind rushes. He overwhelmed King with avalanches of punches, and King did nothing. He never struck once, contenting himself with covering up, blocking and ducking and clinching to avoid punishment. He occasionally feinted, shook his head when the weight of a punch landed, and moved stolidly about, never leaping or springing or wasting an ounce of strength. Sandel must foam the froth of Youth away before discreet Age could dare to retaliate. All King's movements were slow and methodical, and his heavy-lidded, slow-moving eyes gave him the appearance of being half asleep or dazed. Yet they were eyes that saw everything, that had been trained to see everything through all his twenty years and odd in the ring. They were eyes that did not blink or waver before an impending blow, but that coolly saw and measured distance.

Seated in his corner for the minute's rest at the end of the round, he lay back with outstretched legs, his arms resting on the right angle of the ropes, his chest and abdomen heaving frankly and deeply as he gulped down the air driven by the towels of his seconds. He listened with closed eyes to the voices of the house, "Why don't yeh fight, Tom?" many were crying. "Yeh ain't afraid of 'im, are yeh?"

"Musclebound," he heard a man on a front seat comment. "He can't move quicker. Two to one on Sandel, in quids."

The gong struck and the two men advanced from their corners. Sandel came forward fully three-quarters of the distance, eager to begin again; but King was content to advance the shorter distance. It was in line with his policy of economy. He had not been well trained, and he had not had enough to eat, and every step counted. Besides, he had already walked two miles to the ringside. It was a repetition of the first round, with Sandel attacking like a whirlwind and with the audience indignantly demanding why King did not fight. Beyond feinting and several slowly delivered and ineffectual blows he did nothing save block and stall and clinch. Sandel wanted to make the pace fast, while King, out of his wisdom, refused to accommodate him. He grinned with a certain wistful pathos in his ring-battered countenance, and went on cherishing his strength with the jealousy of which only Age is capable. Sandel was Youth, and he threw his strength away with the munificent abandon of Youth. To King belonged the ring generalship, the wisdom bred of long, aching fights. He watched with cool eyes and head, moving slowly and waiting for Sandel's froth to foam away. To the majority of the onlookers it seemed as though King was hopelessly outclassed, and they voiced their opinion in offers of three to one on Sandel. But there were wise ones, a few, who knew King of old time, and who covered what they considered easy money.

The third round began as usual, one-sided, with Sandel doing all the leading and delivering all the punishment. A half-minute had passed when Sandel, overconfident, left an opening. King's eyes and right arm flashed in the same instant. It was his first real blow—a hook, with the twisted arch of the arm to make it rigid, and with all the weight of the half-pivoted body behind it. It was like a sleepy-seeming lion suddenly thrusting out a lightning paw. Sandel, caught on the side of the jaw, was felled like a bullock. The audience gasped and murmured awe-stricken applause. The man was not musclebound, after all, and he could drive a blow like a triphammer.

Sandel was shaken. He rolled over and attempted to rise, but the sharp yells from his seconds to take the count restrained him. He knelt on one knee, ready to rise, and waited, while the referee stood over him, counting the seconds loudly in his ear. At the ninth he rose in fighting attitude, and Tom King, facing him, knew regret that the blow had not been an inch nearer the point of the jaw. That would have been a knockout, and he could have carried the thirty quid home to the missus and the kiddies.

The round continued to the end of its three minutes. Sandel for the first time respectful of his opponent and King slow of movement and sleepy-eyed as ever. As the round neared its close, King, warned of the fact by sight of the seconds crouching outside ready for the spring in through the ropes, worked the fight around to his own corner. And when the gong struck, he sat down immediately on the waiting stool, while Sandel had to walk all the way across the diagonal of the square to his own corner. It was a little thing, but it was the sum of little things that counted. Sandel was compelled to walk that many more steps, to give up that much energy, and to lose a part of the precious minute of rest. At the beginning of every round King loafed slowly out from his corner, forcing his opponent to advance the greater distance. The end of every round found the fight maneuvered by King into his own corner so that he could immediately sit down.

Two more rounds when by, in which King was parsimonious of effort and Sandel prodigal. The latter's attempt to force a fast pace made King uncomfortable, for a fair percentage of the multitudinous blows showered upon him went home. Yet King persisted in his dogged slowness, despite the crying of the young hotheads for him to go in and fight. Again, in the sixth round, Sandel was careless, again Tom King's fearful right flashed out to the jaw, and again Sandel took the nine seconds count.

By the seventh round Sandel's pink of condition was gone, and he settled down to what he knew was to be the hardest fight in his experience. Tom King was an old un, but a better old un than he had ever encountered—an old un who never lost his head, who was remarkably able at defense, whose blows had the impact of a knotted club, and who had a knockout in either hand. Nevertheless, Tom King dared not hit often. He never forgot his battered knuckles, and knew that every hit must count if the knuckles were to last out the fight. As he sat in his corner, glancing across at his opponent, the thought came to him that the sum of his wisdom and Sandel's youth would constitute a world's champion heavyweight. But that was the trouble. Sandel would never become a world champion. He lacked the wisdom, and the only way for him to get it was to buy it with Youth; and when wisdom was his, Youth would have been spent in buying it.

King took every advantage he knew. He never missed an opportunity to clinch, and in effecting most of the clinches his shoulder drove stiffly into the other's ribs. In the philosophy of the ring a shoulder was as good as a punch so far as damage was concerned. And a great deal better so far as concerned expenditure of effort. Also, in the clinches King rested his weight on his opponent, and was loath to let go. This compelled the interference of the referee, who tore them apart, always assisted by Sandel, who had not yet learned to rest. He could not refrain from using those glorious flying arms and writhing muscles of his, and when the other rushed into a clinch, striking shoulder against ribs, and with head resting under Sandel's left arm, Sandel almost invariably swung his right behind his own back and into the projecting face. It was a clever stroke, much admired by the audience, but it was not dangerous, and was, therefore, just that much wasted strength. But Sandel was tireless and unaware of limitations, and King grinned and doggedly endured.

Sandel developed a fierce right to the body, which made it appear that King was taking an enormous amount of punishment, and it was only the old ringsters who appreciated the deft touch of King's left glove to the other's biceps just before the impact of the blow. It was true, the blow landed each time; but each time it was robbed of its power by that touch on the biceps. In the ninth round, three times inside a minute, King's right hooked its twisted arch to the jaw; and three times Sandel's body, heavy as it was, was levelled to the mat. Each time he took the nine seconds allowed him and rose to his feet, shaken and jarred, but still strong. He had lost much of his speed, and he wasted less effort. He was fighting grimly; but he continued to draw upon his chief asset, which was Youth. King's chief asset was experience. As his vitality had dimmed and his vigor abated, he had replaced them with cunning, with wisdom born of the long fights and with a careful shepherding of strength. Not alone had he learned never to make a superfluous movement, but he had learned how to seduce an opponent into throwing his strength away. Again and again, by feint of foot and hand and body he continued to inveigle Sandel into leaping back, ducking, or countering. King rested, but he never permitted Sandel to rest. It was the strategy of Age.

Early in the tenth round King began stopping the other's rushes with straight lefts to the face, and Sandel, grown wary, responded by drawing the left, then by ducking it and delivering his right in a swinging hook to the side of the head. It was too high up to be vitally effective; but when first it landed, King knew the old, familiar descent of the black veil of unconsciousness across his mind. For the instant, or for the slightest fraction of an instant, rather, he ceased. In the one moment he saw his opponent ducking out of his field of vision and the background of white, watching faces; in the next moment he again saw his opponent and the background of faces. It was as if he had slept for a time and just opened his eyes again, and yet the interval of unconsciousness was so microscopically short that there had been no time for him to fall. The audience saw him totter and his knees give, and then saw him recover and tuck his chin deeper into the shelter of his left shoulder.

Several times Sandel repeated the blow, keeping King partially dazed, and then the latter worked out his defense, which was also a counter. Feinting with his left he took a halfstep backward, at the same time upper-cutting with the whole strength of his right. So accurately was it timed that it landed squarely on Sandel's face in the full, downward sweep of the duck, and Sandel lifted in the air and curled backward, striking the mat on his head and shoulders. Twice King achieved this, then turned loose and hammered his opponent to the ropes. He gave Sandel no chance to rest or to set himself, but smashed blow in upon blow till the house rose to its feet and the air was filled with an unbroken roar of applause. But Sandel's strength and endurance were superb, and he continued to stay on his feet. A knockout seemed certain, and a captain of police, appalled at the dreadful punishment, arose by the ringside to stop the fight. The gong struck for the end of the round and Sandel staggered to his corner, protesting to the captain that he was sound and strong. To prove it, he threw two back handsprings, and the police captain gave in.

Tom King, leaning back in his corner and breathing hard, was disappointed. If the fight had been stopped, the referee, perforce, would have rendered him the decision and the purse would have been his. Unlike Sandel, he was not fighting for glory or career, but for thirty quid. And now Sandel would recuperate in the minute of rest.

Youth will be served—this saying flashed into King's mind, and he remembered the first time he had heard it, the night when he had put away Stowsher Bill. The toff who had bought him a drink after the fight and patted him on the shoulder had used those words. Youth will be served! The toff was right. And on that night in the long ago he had been Youth. Tonight Youth sat in the opposite corner. As for himself, he had been fighting for half an hour now, and he was an old man. Had he fought like Sandel, he would not have lasted fifteen minutes. But the point was that he did not recuperate. Those upstanding arteries and that sorely tried heart would not enable him to gather strength in the intervals between the rounds. And he had not had sufficient strength in him to begin with. His legs were heavy under him and beginning to cramp. He should not have walked those two miles to the fight. And there was the steak which he had got up longing for that morning. A great and terrible hatred rose up in him for the butchers who had refused him credit. It was hard for an old man to go into a fight without enough to eat. And a piece of steak was such a little thing, a few pennies at best; yet it meant thirty quid to him.

With the gong that opened the eleventh round, Sandel rushed, making a show of freshness which he did not really possess. King knew it for what it was—a bluff as old as the game itself. He clinched to save himself, then, going free, allowed Sandel to get set. This was what King desired. He feinted with his left, drew the answering duck and swinging upward hook, then made the half-step backward, delivered the upper cut full to the face and crumpled Sandel over to the mat. After that he never let him rest, receiving punishment himself, but inflicting far more, smashing Sandel to the ropes, hooking and driving all manner of blows into him, tearing away from his clinches or punching him out of attempted clinches, and even when Sandel would have fallen, catching him with one uplifting hand and with the other immediately smashing him into the ropes where he could not fall.

The house by this time had gone mad, and it was his house, nearly every voice yelling: "Go it, Tom!" "Get 'im! Get 'im!" "You've got 'im, Tom! You've got 'im!" It was to be a whirlwind finish, and that was what a ringside audience paid to see.

And Tom King, who for half an hour had conserved his strength, now expended it prodigally in the one great effort he knew he had in him. It was his one chance—now or not at all. His strength was waning fast, and his hope was that before the last of it ebbed out of him he would have beaten his opponent down for the count. And as he continued to strike and force, coolly estimating the weight of his blows and the quality of the damage wrought, he realized how hard a man Sandel was to knock out. Stamina and endurance were his to an extreme degree, and they were the virgin stamina and endurance of Youth. Sandel was certainly a coming man. He had it in him. Only out of such rugged fiber were successful fighters fashioned.

Sandel was reeling and staggering, but Tom King's legs were cramping and his knuckles going back on him. Yet he steeled himself to strike the fierce blows, every one of which brought anguish to his tortured hands. Though now he was receiving practically no punishment, he was weakening as rapidly as the other. His blows went home, but there was no longer the weight behind them, and each blow was the result of a severe effort of will. His legs were like lead, and they dragged visibly under him; while Sandel's backers, cheered by this symptom, began calling encouragement to their man.

King was spurred to a burst of effort. He delivered two blows in succession—a left, a trifle too high, to the solar plexus, and a right cross to the jaw. They were not heavy blows, yet so weak and dazed was Sandel that he went down and lay quivering. The referee stood over him, shouting the count of the fatal seconds in his ear. If before the tenth second was called, he did not rise, the fight was lost. The house stood in hushed silence. King rested on trembling legs. A mortal dizziness was upon him, and before his eyes the sea of faces sagged and swayed, while to his ears, as from a remote distance, came the count of the referee. Yet he looked upon the fight as his. It was impossible that a man so punished could rise.

Only Youth could rise, and Sandel rose. At the fourth second he rolled over on his face and groped blindly for the ropes. By the seventh second he had dragged himself to his knee, where he rested, his head rolling groggily on his shoulders. As the referee cried "Nine!" Sandel stood upright, in proper stalling position, his left arm wrapped about his face, his right wrapped about his stomach. Thus were his vital points guarded, while he lurched forward toward King in the hope of effecting a clinch and gaining more time.

At the instant Sandel arose, King was at him, but the two blows he delivered were muffled on the stalled arms. The next moment Sandel was in the clinch and holding on desperately while the referee strove to drag the two men apart. King helped to force himself free. He knew the rapidity with which Youth recovered, and he knew that Sandel was his if he could prevent that recovery. One stiff punch would do it. Sandel was his, indubitably his. He had outgeneralled him, outfought him, out-pointed him. Sandel reeled out of the clinch, balanced on the hairline between defeat or survival. One good blow would topple him over and down and out. And Tom King, in a flash of bitterness, remembered the piece of steak and wished that he had it then behind that necessary punch he must deliver. He nerved himself for the blow, but it was not heavy enough nor swift enough. Sandel swayed, but did not fall, staggering back to the ropes and holding on. King staggered after him, and, with a pang like that of dissolution, delivered another blow. But his body had deserted him. All that was left of him was a fighting intelligence that was dimmed and clouded from exhaustion. The blow that was aimed for the jaw struck no higher than the shoulder. He had willed the blow higher, but the tired muscles had not been able to obey. And, from the impact of the blow, Tom King himself reeled back and nearly fell. Once again he strove. This time his punch missed altogether, and, from absolute weakness, he fell against Sandel and clinched, holding on to him to save himself from sinking to the floor.

King did not attempt to free himself. He had shot his bolt. He was gone. And Youth had been served. Even in the clinch he could feel Sandel growing stronger against him. When the referee thrust them apart, there, before his eyes, he saw Youth recuperate. From instant to instant Sandel grew stronger. His punches, weak and futile at first, became stiff and accurate. Tom King's bleared eyes saw the gloved fist driving at his jaw, and he willed to guard it by interposing his arm. He saw the danger, willed the act; but the arm was too heavy. It seemed burdened with a hundredweight of lead. It would not lift itself, and he strove to lift it with his soul. Then the gloved fist landed home. He experienced a sharp snap that was like an electric spark, and, simultaneously, the veil of blackness enveloped him.

When he opened his eyes again he was in his corner, and he heard the yelling of the audience like the roar of the surf at Bondi Beach. A wet sponge was being pressed against the base of his brain, and Sid Sullivan was blowing cold water in a refreshing spray over his face and chest. His gloves had already been removed, and Sandel, bending over him, was shaking his hand. He bore no ill will toward the man who had put him out, and he returned the grip with a heartiness that made his battered knuckles protest. Then Sandel stepped to the center of the ring and the audience hushed its pandemonium to hear him accept young Pronto's challenge and offer to increase the side bet to one hundred pounds. King looked on apathetically while his seconds mopped the streaming water from him, dried his face, and prepared him to leave the ring. He felt hungry. It was not the ordinary, gnawing kind, but a great faintness, a palpitation at the pit of his stomach that communicated itself to all his body. He remembered back into the fight to the moment when he had Sandel swaying and tottering on the hairline balance of defeat. Ah, that piece of steak would have done it! He had lacked just that for the decisive blow, and he had lost. It was all because of the piece of steak.

His seconds were half-supporting him as they helped him through the ropes. He tore free from them, ducked through the ropes unaided, and leaped heavily to the floor, following on their heels as they forced a passage for him down the crowded center aisle. Leaving the dressing room for the street, in the entrance to the hall, some young fellow spoke to him.

"W'y didn't yuh go in an' get 'im when youh 'ad 'im?" the young fellow asked.

"Aw, go to hell!" said Tom King, and passed down the steps to the sidewalk.

The doors of the public house at the corner were swinging wide, and he saw the lights and the smiling barmaids, heard the many voices discussing the fight and the prosperous chink of money on the bar. Somebody called to him to have a drink. He hesitated perceptibly, then refused and went on his way.

He had not a copper in his pocket, and the two-mile walk home seemed very long. He was certainly getting old. Crossing the Domain, he sat down suddenly on a bench, unnerved by the thought of the missus sitting up for him, waiting to learn the outcome of the fight. That was harder than any knockout, and it seemed almost impossible to face.

He felt weak and sore, and the pain of his smashed knuckles warned him that, even if he could find a job at navvy work, it would be a week before he could grip a pick handle or a shovel. The hunger palpitation at the pit of the stomach was sickening. His wretchedness overwhelmed him, and into his eyes came an unwonted moisture. He covered his face with his hands, and, as he cried, he remembered Stowsher Bill and how he had served him that night in the long ago. Poor old Stowsher Bill! He could understand now why Bill had cried in the dressing room.

CHAMPION

Ring Lardner

Midge Kelly scored his first knockout when he was seventeen. The knockee was his brother Connie, three years his junior and a cripple. The purse was a half dollar given to the younger Kelly by a lady whose electric had just missed bumping his soul from his frail little body.

Connie did not know Midge was in the house, else he never would have risked laying the prize on the arm of the least comfortable chair in the room, the better to observe its shining beauty. As Midge entered from the kitchen, the crippled boy covered the coin with his hand, but the movement lacked the speed requisite to escape his brother's quick eye.

"Whatcha got there?" demanded Midge.

"Nothin'," said Connie.

"You're a one-legged liar!" said Midge.

He strode over to his brother's chair and grasped the hand that concealed the coin.

"Let loose!" he ordered.

Connie began to cry.

"Let loose and shut up your noise," said the elder, and jerked his brother's hand from the chair arm.

The coin fell onto the bare floor. Midge pounced on it. His weak mouth widened in a triumphant smile.

"Nothin', huh?" he said. "All right, if it's nothin' you don't want it."

"Give that back," sobbed the younger.

"I'll give you a red nose, you little sneak! Where'd you steal it?"

"I didn't steal it. It's mine. A lady give it to me after she pretty near hit me with a car."

"It's a crime she missed you," said Midge.

Midge started for the front door. The cripple picked up his crutch, rose from his chair with difficulty, and, still sobbing, came toward Midge. The latter heard him and stopped.

"You better stay where you're at," he said.

"I want my money," cried the boy.

"I know what you want," said Midge.

Doubling up the fist that held the half dollar, he landed with all his strength on his brother's mouth. Connie fell to the floor with a thud, the crutch tumbling on top of him. Midge stood beside the prostrate form.

"Is that enough?" he said. "Or do you want this, too?"

And he kicked him in the crippled leg.

"I guess that'll hold you," he said.

There was no response from the boy on the floor. Midge looked at him a moment, then at the coin in his hand, and then went out into the street, whistling.

An hour later, when Mrs. Kelly came home from her day's work at Faulkner's Steam Laundry, she found Connie on the floor, moaning. Dropping on her knees beside him, she called him by name a score of times. Then she got up and, pale as a ghost, dashed from the house. Dr. Ryan left the Kelly abode about dusk and walked toward Halsted Street. Mrs. Dorgan spied him as he passed her gate.

"Who's sick, Doctor?" she called.

"Poor little Connie," he replied. "He had a bad fall."

"How did it happen?"

"I can't say for sure, Margaret, but I'd almost bet he was knocked down."

"Knocked down!" exclaimed Mrs. Dorgan. "Why, who—?"

"Have you seen the other one lately?"

"Michael? No, not since mornin'. You can't be thinkin'—"

"I wouldn't put it past him, Margaret," said the doctor gravely. "The lad's mouth is swollen and cut, and his poor, skinny little leg is bruised. He surely didn't do it to himself and I think Helen suspects the other one."

"Lord save us!" said Mrs. Dorgan. "I'll run over and see if I can help."

"That's a good woman," said Doctor Ryan, and went on down the street.

Near midnight, when Midge came home, his mother was sitting at Connie's bedside. She did not look up.

"Well," said Midge, "what's the matter?"

She remained silent. Midge repeated his question.

"Michael, you know what's the matter," she said at length.

"I don't know nothin'," said Midge.

"Don't lie to me, Michael. What did you do to your brother?"

"Nothin'."

"You hit him."

"Well, then, I hit him. What of it? It ain't the first time."

Her lips pressed tightly together, her face like chalk, Ellen Kelly rose from her chair and made straight for him. Midge backed against the door.

"Lay off'n me, Ma. I don't want to fight no woman."

Still she came on, breathing heavily.

"Stop where you're at, Ma," he warned.

There was a brief struggle and Midge's mother lay on the floor before him.

"You ain't hurt, Ma. You're lucky I didn't land good. And I told you to lay off'n me."

"God forgive you, Michael!"

Midge found Hap Collins in the showdown game at the Royal.

"Come on out a minute," he said.

Hap followed him out on the walk.

"I'm leavin' town for a w'ile," said Midge.

"What for?"

"Well, we had a little run-in up to the house. The kid stole a half buck off'n me, and when I went after it he cracked me with his crutch. So I nailed him. And the old lady came at me with a chair and I took it off'n her and she fell down."

"How is Connie hurt?"

"Not bad."

"What are you runnin' away for?"

"Who the hell said I was runnin' away? I'm sick and tired o' gettin' picked on; that's all. So I'm leavin' for a w'ile and I want a piece o'money."

"I ain't only got six bits," said Happy.

"You're in bad shape, ain't you? Well, come through with it."

Happy came through.

"You oughtn't to hit the kid," he said.

"I ain't astin' you who can I hit," snarled Midge. "You try to put somethin' over on me and you'll get the same dose. I'm goin' now."

"Go as far as you like," said Happy, but not until he was sure that Kelly was out of hearing.

*   *   *

Early the following morning, Midge boarded a train for Milwaukee. He had no ticket, but no one knew the difference. The conductor remained in the caboose.

On a night six months later, Midge hurried out of the "stage door" of the Star Boxing Club and made for Duane's saloon, two blocks away. In his pocket were twelve dollars, his reward for having battered up one Demon Dempsey through the six rounds of the first preliminary.

It was Midge's first professional engagement on the manly art. Also it was the first time in weeks that he had earned twelve dollars.

On the way to Duane's he had to pass Niemann's. He pulled his cap over his eyes and increased his pace until he had gone by. Inside Niemann's stood a trusting bartender, who for ten days had staked Midge to drinks and allowed him to ravage the lunch on a promise to come in and settle the moment he was paid for the "prelim."

Midge strode into Duane's and aroused the napping bartender by slapping a silver dollar on the festive board.

"Gimme a shot," said Midge.

The shooting continued until the wind-up at the Star was over and part of the fight crowd joined Midge in front of Duane's bar. A youth in the early twenties, standing next to young Kelly, finally summoned sufficient courage to address him.

"Wasn't you in the first bout?" he ventured.

"Yeah," Midge replied.

"My name's Hersch," said the other.

Midge received the startling information in silence.

"I don't want to butt in," continued Mr. Hersch, "but I'd like to buy you a drink."

"All right," said Midge, "but don't overstrain yourself."

Mr. Hersch laughed uproariously and beckoned to the bartender.

"You certainly gave that wop a trimmin' tonight," said the buyer of the drink, when they had been served. "I thought you'd kill him."

"I would if I hadn't let up," Midge replied. "I'll kill 'em all."

"You got the wallop all right," the other said admiringly.

"Have I got the wallop?" said Midge. "Say, I can kick like a mule. Did you notice them muscles in my shoulders?"

"Notice 'em? I couldn't help from noticin' 'em," said Hersch. "I says to the fella settin' alongside o' me, I says: 'Look at them shoulders! No wonder he can hit,' I says to him."

"Just let me land and it's good-by, baby," said Midge. "I'll kill 'em all."

The oral manslaughter continued until Duane's closed for the night. At parting, Midge and his new friend shook hands and arranged for a meeting the following evening.

For nearly a week the two were together almost constantly. It was Hersch's pleasant role to listen to Midge's modest revelations concerning himself, and to buy every time Midge's glass was empty. But there came an evening when Hersch regretfully announced that he must go home to supper.

"I got a date for eight bells," he confided. "I could stick till then, only I must clean up and put on the Sunday clo'es, 'cause she's the prettiest little thing in Milwaukee."

"Can't you fix it for two?" asked Midge.

"I don't know who to get," Hersch replied. "Wait, though. I got a sister and if she ain't busy, it'll be okay. She's no bum for looks herself."

So it came about that Midge and Emma Hersch and Emma's brother and the prettiest little thing in Milwaukee foregathered at Wall's and danced half the night away. And Midge and Emma danced every dance together, for though every little onestep seemed to induce a new thirst of its own, Lou Hersch stayed too sober to dance with his own sister.

The next day, penniless at last in spite of his phenomenal ability to make someone else settle, Midge Kelly sought out Doc Hammond, matchmaker for the Star, and asked to be booked for the next show.

"I could put you on with Tracy for the next bout," said Doc.

"What's they in it?" asked Midge.

"Twenty if you cop," Doc told him.

"Have a heart," protested Midge. "Didn't I look good the other night?"

"You looked all right. But you aren't Freddie Welsh yet by a consid'able margin."

"I ain't scared of Freddie Welsh or none of 'em," said Midge.

"Well, we don't pay our boxers by the size of their chests," Doc said. "I'm offerin' you this Tracy bout. Take it or leave it."

"All right; I'm on," said Midge, and he passed a pleasant afternoon at Duane's on the strength of this booking.

Young Tracy's manager came to Midge the night before the show.

"How do you feel about this go?" he asked.

"Me?" said Midge. "I feel all right. What do you mean, how do I feel?"

"I mean," said Tracy's manager, "that we're mighty anxious to win, 'cause the boy's got a chanct in Philly if he cops this one."

"What's your proposition?" asked Midge.

"Fifty bucks," said Tracy's manager.

"What do you think I am, a crook? Me lay down for fifty bucks. Not me!"

"Seventy-five, then," said Tracy's manager.

The market closed on eighty and the details were agreed on in short order. And the next night Midge was stopped in the second round by a terrific slap on the forearm.

This time Midge passed up both Niemann's and Duane's, having a sizable account at each place, and sought his refreshment at Stein's farther down the street.

When the profits of his deal with Tracy were gone, he learned, by firsthand information from Doc Hammond and the matchmakers at the other "clubs," that he was no longer desired for even the cheapest of preliminaries. There was no danger of his starving or dying of thirst while Emma and Lou Hersch lived. But he made up his mind, four months after his defeat by young Tracy, that Milwaukee was not the ideal place for him to live.

"I can lick the best of 'em," he reasoned, "but there ain't no more chanct for me here. I can maybe go east and get on somewheres. And besides—"

But just after Midge had purchased a ticket to Chicago with the money he had "borrowed" from Emma Hersch "to buy shoes," a heavy hand was laid on his shoulders and he turned to face two strangers.

"Where are you goin', Kelly?" inquired the owner of the heavy hand.

"Nowheres," said Midge. "What the hell do you care?"

The other stranger spoke: "Kelly, I'm employed by Emma Hersch's mother to see that you do right by her. And we want you to stay here till you've done it."

"You won't get nothin' but the worst of it, monkeying with me," said Midge.

Nevertheless, he did not depart for Chicago that night. Two days later, Emma Hersch became Mrs. Kelly, and the gift of the groom, when once they were alone, was a crushing blow on the bride's pale cheek.

Next morning, Midge left Milwaukee as he had entered it—by fast freight.

"They's no use kiddin' ourself any more," said Tommy Haley. "He might get down to thirty-seven in a pinch, but if he done below that a mouse could stop him. He's a welter; that's what he is and he knows it as well as I do. He's growed like a weed in the last six mont's. I told him, I says, 'If you don't quit growin' they won't be nobody for you to box, only Willard and them.' He says, 'Well, I wouldn't run away from Willard if I weighed twenty pounds more.'"

"He must hate himself," said Tommy's brother.

"I never seen a good one that didn't," said Tommy. "And Midge is a good one; don't make no mistake about that. I wisht we could of got Welsh before the kid growed so big. But it's too late now. I won't make no holler, though, if we can match him up with the Dutchman."

"Who do you mean?"

"Young Goetz, the welter champ. We mightn't not get so much dough for the bout itself, but it'd roll in afterward. What a drawin' card we'd be, 'cause the people pays their money to see the fella with the wallop, and that's Midge. And we'd keep the title just as long as Midge could make the weight."

"Can't you land no match with Goetz?"

"Sure, 'cause he needs the money. But I've went careful with the kid so far and look at the results I got! So what's the use of takin' a chanct? The kids' comin' every minute and Goetz is goin' back faster'n big Johnson did. I think we could lick him now; I'd bet my life on it. But six mont's from now they won't be no risk. He'll of licked hisself before that time. Then all as we'll have to do is sign up with him and wait for the referee to stop it. But Midge is so crazy to get at him now that I can't hardly hold him back."

The brothers Haley were lunching in a Boston hotel. Dan had come down from Holyoke to visit with Tommy and to watch the latter's protégé go twelve rounds, or less, with Bud Cross. The bout promised little in the way of a contest, for Midge had twice stopped the Baltimore youth and Bud's reputation for gameness was all that had earned him the date. The fans were willing to pay the price to see Midge's haymaking left, but they wanted to see it used on an opponent who would not jump out of the ring the first time he felt its crushing force. But Cross was such an opponent, and his willingness to stop boxing gloves with his eyes, ears, nose and throat had long enabled him to escape the horrors of honest labor. A game boy was Bud, and he showed it in his battered, swollen, discolored face.

"I should think," said Dan Haley, "that the kid'd do whatever you tell him after all you done for him."

"Well," said Tommy, "he's took my dope pretty straight so far, but he's so sure of hisself that he can't see no reason for waitin'. He'll do what I say, though; he'd be a sucker not to."

"You got a contrac' with him?"

"No, I don't need no contrac'. He knows it was me that drug him out o' the gutter and he ain't goin' to turn me down now, when he's got the dough and bound to get more. Where'd he of been at if I hadn't listened to him when he first come to me? That's pretty near two years ago now, but it seems like last week. I was settin' in the s'loon acrost from the Pleasant Club in Philly, waitin' for McCann to count the dough and come over, when this little bum blowed in and tried to stand the house off for a drink. They told him nothin' doin' and to beat it out o' there, and then he seen me and come over to where I was settin' and ast me wasn't I a boxin' man and I told him who I was. Then he ast me for money to buy a shot and I told him to set down and I'd buy it for him.

"Then we got talkin' things over and he told me his name and told me about fightin' a couple o' prelims out to Milwaukee. So I says, 'Well, boy, I don't know how good or how rotten you are, but you won't never get nowheres trainin' on that stuff.' So he says he'd cut it out if he could get on in a bout and I says I would give him a chanct if he played square with me and didn't touch no more to drink. So we shook hands and I took him up to the hotel with me and give him a bath and the next day I bought him some clo'es. And I staked him to eats and sleeps for over six weeks. He had a hard time breakin' away from the polish, but finally I thought he was fit and I give him his chanct. He went on with Smiley Sayer and stopped him so quick that Smiley thought sure he was poisoned.

"Well, you know what he's did since. The only beatin' in his record was by Tracy in Milwaukee before I got hold of him and he's licked Tracy three times in the last year.

"I've gave him all the best of it in a money way and he's got seven thousand bucks in cold storage. How's that for a kid that was in the gutter two years ago? And he'd have still more yet if he wasn't so nuts over clo'es and got to stop at the good hotels and so forth."

"Where's his home at?"

"Well, he ain't really got no home. He came from Chicago and his mother canned him out o' the house for bein' no good. She gave him a raw deal, I guess, and he says he won't have nothin' to do with her unlest she comes to him first. She's got a pile o' money, he says, so he ain't worryin' about her."

The gentleman under discussion entered the café and swaggered to Tommy's table, while the whole room turned to look.

Midge was the picture of health despite a slightly colored eye and an ear that seemed to have no opening. But perhaps it was not his healthiness that drew all eyes. His diamond horseshoe tiepin, his purple cross-striped shirt, his orange shoes and his light blue suit fairly screamed for attention.

"Where you been?" he asked Tommy. "I been lookin' all over for you."

"Set down," said his manager.

"No time," said Midge. "I'm goin' down to the w'arf and see 'em unload the fish."

"Shake hands with my brother Dan," said Tommy.

Midge shook with the Holyoke Haley.

"If you're Tommy's brother, you're okay with me," said Midge, and the brothers beamed with pleasure.

Dan moistened his lips and murmured an embarrassed reply, but it was lost on the young gladiator.

"Leave me take twenty," Midge was saying. "I prob'ly won't need it, but I don't like to be caught short."

Tommy parted with a twenty dollar bill and recorded the transaction in a small black book the insurance company had given him for Christmas.

"But," he said, "it won't cost you no twenty to look at them fish. Want me to go along?"

"No," said Midge hastily. "You and your brother here prob'ly got a lot to say to each other."

"Well," said Tommy, "don't take no bad money and don't get lost. And you better be back at four o'clock and lay down a w'ile."

"I don't need no rest to beat this guy," said Midge. "He'll do enough layin' down for the both of us."

And laughing even more than the jest called for, he strode out through the fire of admiring and startled glances.

The corner of Boylston and Tremont was the nearest Midge got to the wharf, but the lady awaiting him was doubtless a more dazzling sight than the catch of the luckiest Massachusetts fisherman. She could talk, too—probably better than the fish.

"O you Kid!" she said, flashing a few silver teeth among the gold. "O you fighting man!"

Midge smiled up at her.

"We'll go somewheres and get a drink," he said. "One won't hurt."

In New Orleans, five months after he had rearranged the map of Bud Cross for the third time, Midge finished training for his championship bout with the Dutchman.

Back in his hotel after the final workout, Midge stopped to chat with some of the boys from up north, who had made the long trip to see a champion dethroned, for the result of this bout was so nearly a foregone conclusion that even the experts had guessed it.

Tommy Haley secured the key and the mail and ascended to the Kelly suite. He was bathing when Midge came in, half an hour later.

"Any mail?" asked Midge.

"There on the bed," replied Tommy from the tub.

Midge picked up the stack of letters and postcards and glanced them over. From the pile he sorted out three letters and laid them on the table. The rest he tossed into the wastebasket. Then he picked up the three and sat for a few moments holding them, while his eyes gazed off into space. At length he looked again at the three unopened letters in his hand; then he put one in his pocket and tossed the other two at the basket. They missed their target and fell on the floor.

"Hell!" said Midge, and stooping over picked them up.
He opened one postmarked Milwaukee and read:

Dear Husband:
    I have wrote to you so many times and got no anser and I don't
know if you ever got them, so I am writeing again in the hopes you
will get this letter and anser. I don't like to bother you with my
trubles and I would not only for the baby and I am not asking you
should write to me but only send a little money and I am not asking
for myself but the baby has not been well a day sence last Aug.
And the dr. told me she cant live much longer unless I give her
better food and thats impossible the way things are. Lou has not
been working for a year and what I make don't hardley pay for the
rent. I am not asking for you to give me any money, but only you
should send what I loaned when convenient and I think it amts. to
about $36.00. Please try and send that amt. and it will help me, but
if you cant sent the whole amt. try and send me something.
                                            Your wife,   Emma.

    Midge tore the letter into a hundred pieces and scattered them over the
floor.
    "Money, money, money!" he said. "They must think I'm made o'
money. I s'pose the old woman's after it too."
    He opened his mother's letter:

    dear Michael Connie wonted me to rite and say you must beet
the dutchman and he is sur you will and wonted me to say we wont
you to rite and tell us about it, but I gess you havent no time to rite
or we herd from you long before this but I wish you would rite jest
a line or 2 boy because it would be better for Connie then a barl of
medisin. It would help me to keep things going if you send me
money now and then when you can spair it but if you cant send no
money try and fine time to rite a letter onley a few lines and it will
please Connie. jest think boy he hasent got out of bed in over 3 yrs.
Connie says good luck.
                                    Your Mother,   Ellen F. Kelly.

    "I thought so," said Midge. "They're all alike."
    The third letter was from New York. It read:

Hon:—This is the last letter you will get from me before your
champ, but I will send you a telegram Saturday, but I can't say as
much in a telegram as in a letter and I am writeing this to let you
know I am thinking of you and praying for good luck.

Lick him good hon and don't wait no longer than you have to
and don't forget to wire me as soon as its over. Give him that little
old left of yours on the nose hon and don't be afraid of spoiling his
good looks because he couldn't be no homlier than he is. But don't
let him spoil my baby's pretty face. You won't will you hon.

Well hon I would give anything to be there and see it, but I guess
you love Haley better than me or you wouldn't let him keep me
away. But when your champ hon we can do as we please and tell
Haley to go to the devil.

Well hon I will send you a telegram Saturday and I almost forgot
to tell you I will need some more money, a couple hundred say and
you will have to wire it to me as soon as you get this. You will
won't you hon.

I will send you a telegram Saturday and remember hon I am
pulling for you.

Well good-by sweetheart and good luck.

Grace.

"They're all alike," said Midge. "Money, money, money."

Tommy Haley, shining from his ablutions, came in from the adjoining
room.

"Thought you'd be layin' down," he said.

"I'm goin' to," said Midge, unbuttoning his orange shoes.

"I'll call you at six and you can eat up here without no bugs to pester
you. I got to go down and give them birds their tickets."

"Did you hear from Goldberg?" asked Midge.

"Didn't I tell you? Sure; fifteen weeks at five hundred, if we win.
And we can get a guarantee o' twelve thousand, with privileges either in
New York or Milwaukee."

"Who with?"

"Anybody that will stand up in front of you. You don't care who it is,
do you?"

"Not me. I'll make 'em all look like a monkey."

"Well you better lay down aw'ile."

"Oh, say, wire two hundred to Grace for me, will you? Right away;
the New York address."

"Two hundred! You just sent her three hundred last Sunday."

"Well, what the hell do you care?"

"All right, all right. Don't get sore about it. Anything else?"

"That's all," said Midge, and dropped onto the bed.

"And I want the deed done before I come back," said Grace as she rose from the table. "You won't fall down on me, will you, hon?"

"Leave it to me," said Midge. "And don't spend no more than you have to."

Grace smiled a farewell and left the café. Midge continued to sip his coffee and read his paper.

They were in Chicago and they were in the middle of Midge's first week in vaudeville. He had come straight north to reap the rewards of his glorious victory over the broken-down Dutchman. A fortnight had been spent in learning his act, which consisted of a gymnastic exhibition and a ten minute monologue on the various excellences of Midge Kelly. And now he was twice daily turning 'em away from the Madison Theater.

His breakfast over and his paper read, Midge sauntered into the lobby and asked for his key. He then beckoned to a bellboy, who had been hoping for that very honor.

"Find Haley, Tommy Haley," said Midge. "Tell him to come up to my room."

"Yes, sir, Mr. Kelly," said the boy, and proceeded to break all his former records for diligence.

Midge was looking out of his seventh-story window when Tommy answered the summons.

"What'll it be?" inquired his manager.

There was a pause before Midge replied.

"Haley," he said, "twenty-five percent's a whole lot o' money."

"I guess I got it comin', ain't I?" said Tommy.

"I don't see how you figger it. I don't see where you're worth it to me."

"Well," said Tommy, "I didn't expect nothing' like this. I thought you was satisfied with the bargain. I don't want to beat nobody out o' nothin', but I don't see where you could have got anybody else that would of did all I done for you."

"Sure, that's all right," said the champion. "You done a lot for me in Philly. And you got good money for it, didn't you?"

"I ain't makin' no holler. Still and all, the big money's still ahead of us yet. And if it hadn't of been for me, you wouldn't of never got within grabbin' distance."

"Oh, I guess I could of went along all right," said Midge. "Who was it that hung that left on the Dutchman's jaw, me or you?"

"Yes, but you wouldn't been in the ring with the Dutchman if it wasn't for how I handled you.''

"Well, this won't get us nowheres. The idear is that you ain't worth no twenty-five percent now and it don't make no diff'rence what come off a year or two ago."

"Don't it?" said Tommy. "I'd say it made a whole lot of difference."

"Well, I say it don't and I guess that settles it."

"Look here, Midge," Tommy said, "I thought I was fair with you, but if you don't think so, I'm willin' to hear what you think is fair. I don't want nobody callin' me a Sherlock. Let's go down to business and sign up a contrac'. Wha's your figger?"

"I ain't namin' no figger," Midge replied. "I'm sayin' that twenty-five's too much. Now what are you willin' to take?"

"How about twenty?"

"Twenty's too much," said Kelly.

"What ain't too much?" asked Tommy.

"Well, Haley, I might as well give it to you straight. They ain't nothin' that ain't too much."

"You mean you don't want me at no figger?"

"That's the idear."

There was a minute's silence. Then Tommy Haley walked toward the door.

"Midge," he said, in a choking voice, "you're makin' a big mistake, boy. You can't throw down your best friends and get away with it. That damn woman will ruin you."

Midge sprang from his seat.

"You shut your mouth!" he stormed. "Get out o' here before they have to carry you out. You been spongin' off o' me long enough. Say one more word about the girl or about anything else and you'll get what the Dutchman got. Now get out!"

And Tommy Haley, having a very vivid memory of the Dutchman's face as he fell, got out.

Grace came in later, dropped her numerous bundles on the lounge and perched herself on the arm of Midge's chair.

"Well?" she said.

"Well," said Midge, "I got rid of him."

"Good boy!" said Grace. "And now I think you might give me that twenty-five percent."

"Besides the seventy-five you're already gettin'?" said Midge.

"Don't be no grouch, hon. You don't look pretty when you're grouchy."

"It ain't my business to look pretty," Midge replied.

"Wait till you see how I look with the stuff I bought this mornin'!"
Midge glanced at the bundles on the lounge.
"There's Haley's twenty-five percent," he said, "and then some."

The champion did not remain long without a manager. Haley's successor was none other than Jerome Harris, who saw in Midge a better
meal ticket than his popular-priced musical show had been.

The contract, giving Mr. Harris twenty-five percent of Midge's earn-
ings, was signed in Detroit the week after Tommy Haley had heard his
dismissal read. It had taken Midge just six days to learn that a popular
actor cannot get on without the ministrations of a man who thinks, talks
and means business. At first Grace objected to the new member of the
firm, but when Mr. Harris had demanded and secured from the vaudeville people a one-hundred dollar increase in Midge's weekly stipend,
she was convinced that the champion had acted for the best.

"You and my missus will have some great old times," Harris told
Grace. "I'd of wired her to join us here, only I seen the Kid's bookin'
takes us to Milwaukee next week, and that's where she is."

But when they were introduced in the Milwaukee hotel, Grace admitted to herself that her feeling for Mrs. Harris could hardly be called love
at first sight. Midge, on the contrary, gave his new manager's wife the
many times over and seemed loath to end the feast of his eyes.

"Some doll," he said to Grace when they were alone.

"Doll is right," the lady replied, "and sawdust where her brains ought
to be."

"I'm li'ble to steal that baby," said Midge, and he smiled as he noted
the effect of his words on his audience's face.

On Tuesday of the Milwaukee week the champion successfully defended his title in a bout that the newspapers never reported. Midge was
alone in his room that morning when a visitor entered without knocking.
The visitor was Lou Hersch.

Midge turned white at sight of him.

"What do you want?" he demanded.

"I guess you know," said Lou Hersch. "Your wife's starvin' to death
and your baby's starvin' to death and I'm starvin' to death. And you're
dirty with money."

"Listen," said Midge, "if it wasn't for you, I would never saw your
sister. And, if you ain't man enough to hold a job, what's that to me?
The best thing you can do is keep away from me."

"You give me a piece o' money and I'll go."

Midge's reply to the ultimatum was a straight right to his brother-in-
law's narrow chest.

"Take that home to your sister."

And after Lou Hersch had picked himself up and slunk away, Midge thought: "It's lucky I didn't give him my left or I'd of croaked him. And if I'd hit him in the stomach, I'd of broke his spine."

There was a party after each evening performance during the Milwaukee engagement. The wine flowed freely and Midge had more of it than Tommy Haley ever would have permitted him. Mr. Harris offered no objection, which was possibly just as well for his own physical comfort.

In the dancing between drinks, Midge had his new manager's wife for a partner as often as Grace. The latter's face, as she floundered round in the arms of the portly Harris, belied her frequent protestations that she was having the time of her life.

Several times that week Midge thought Grace was on the point of starting the quarrel he hoped to have. But it was not until Friday night that she accommodated. He and Mrs. Harris had disappeared after the matinee and when Grace saw him again at the close of the night show, she came to the point at once.

"What are you tryin' to pull off?" she demanded.

"It's none o' your business, is it?" said Midge.

"You bet it's my business; mine and Harris's. You cut it short or you'll find out."

"Listen," said Midge, "have you got a mortgage on me or somethin'? You talk like we was married."

"We're goin' to be, too. And tomorrow's as good a time as any."

"Just about," Midge said. "You got as much chanct o' marryin' me tomorrow as the next day or next year and that ain't no chanct at all."

"We'll find out," said Grace.

"You're the one that's got somethin' to find out."

"What do you mean?"

"I mean I'm married already."

"You lie!"

"You think so, do you? Well, s'pose you go to this here address and get acquainted with my missus."

Midge scrawled a number on a piece of paper and handed it to her. She stared at it unseeingly.

"Well," said Midge, "I ain't kiddin' you. You go there and ask for Mrs. Michael Kelly, and if you don't find her, I'll marry you tomorrow before breakfast."

Still Grace stared at the scrap of paper. To Midge it seemed an age before she spoke again.

"You lied to me all this w'ile."

"You never ast me was I married. What's more, what the hell diff'rence did it make to you? You got a split, didn't you? Better'n fifty-fifty."

He started away.

"Where you goin'?"

"I'm goin' to meet Harris and his wife."

"I'm goin' with you. You're not goin' to shake me now."

"Yes, I am too," said Midge quietly. "When I leave town tomorrow night, you're going to stay here. And if I see where you're goin' to make a fuss, I'll put you in a hospital where they'll keep you quiet. You can get your stuff tomorrow mornin' and I'll slip you a hundred bucks. And then I don't want to see no more o' you. And don't try and tag along now or I'll have to add another kayo to the old record."

When Grace returned to the hotel that night, she discovered that Midge and the Harrises had moved to another. And when Midge left town the following night, he was again without a manager, and Mr. Harris was without a wife.

Three days prior to Midge Kelly's ten-round bout with Young Milton in New York City, the sporting editor of the *News* assigned Joe Morgan to write two or three thousand words about the champion to run with a picture layout for Sunday.

Joe Morgan dropped in at Midge's training quarters Friday afternoon. Midge, he learned, was doing road work, but Midge's manager, Wallie Adams, stood ready and willing to supply reams of dope about the greatest fighter of the age.

"Let's hear what you've got," said Joe, "and then I'll try to fix up something."

So Wallie stepped on the accelerator of his imagination and shot away.

"Just a kid; that's all he is; a regular boy. Get what I mean? Don't know the meanin' o' bad habits. Never tasted liquor in his life and would prob'bly get sick if he smelled it. Clean livin' put him up where he's at. Get what I mean? And modest and unassumin' as a school girl. He's so quiet you wouldn't never know he was round. And he'd go to jail before he'd talk about himself.

"No job at all to get him in shape, 'cause he's always that way. The only trouble we have with him is gettin' him to light into these poor bums they match him up with he's scared he'll hurt somebody. Get what I mean? He's tickled to death over this match with Milton, 'cause everybody says Milton can stand the gaff. Midge'll maybe be able to cut loose a little this time. But the last two bouts he had, the guys hadn't no business in the ring with him, and he was holdin' back all the w'ile for the fear he'd kill somebody. Get what I mean?"

"Is he married?" inquired Joe.

"Say, you'd think he was married to hear him rave about them kiddies he's got. His fam'ly's up in Canada to their summer home and Midge is wild to get up there with 'em. He thinks more o' that wife and them kiddies than all the money in the world. Get what I mean?"

"How many children has he?"

"I don't know, four or five, I guess. All boys and every one of 'em a dead ringer for their dad."

"Is his father living?"

"No, the old man died when he was a kid. But he's got a grand old mother and a kid brother out in Chi. They're the first ones he thinks about after a match, them and his wife and kiddies. And he don't forget to send the old woman a thousand bucks after every bout. He's gon' to buy her a new home as soon as they pay him off for this match."

"How about his brother? Is he going to tackle the game?"

"Sure, and Midge says he'll be a champion before he's twenty years old. They're a fightin' fam'ly and all of 'em honest and straight as a die. Get what I mean? A fella that I can't tell you his name come to Midge in Milwaukee onct and wanted him to throw a fight and Midge give him such a trimmin' in the street that he couldn't go on that night. That's the kind he is. Get what I mean?"

Joe Morgan hung around the camp until Midge and his trainers returned.

"One o' the boys from the *News*," said Wallie by way of introduction. "I been givin' him your fam'ly hist'ry."

"Did he give you good dope?" he inquired.

"He's some historian," said Joe.

"Don't call me no names," said Wallie smiling. "Call us up if they's anything more you want. And keep your eyes on us Monday night. Get what I mean?"

The story in Sunday's *News* was read by thousands of lovers of the manly art. It was well written and full of human interest. Its slight inaccuracies went unchallenged, though three readers, besides Wallie Adams and Midge Kelly, saw and recognized them. The three were Grace, Tommy Haley, and Jerome Harris and the comments they made were not for publication.

Neither the Mrs. Kelly in Chicago nor the Mrs. Kelly in Milwaukee knew that there was such a paper as the New York *News*. And even if they had known of it and that it contained two columns of reading matter about Midge, neither mother nor wife could have bought it. For the *News* on Sunday is a nickel a copy.

Joe Morgan could have written more accurately, no doubt, if, instead of Wallie Adams, he had interviewed Ellen Kelly and Connie Kelly and Emma Kelly and Lou Hersch and Grace and Jerome Harris and Tommy Haley and Hap Collins and two or three Milwaukee bartenders.

But a story built on their evidence would never have passed the sporting editor.

"Suppose you can prove it," that gentleman would have said. "It wouldn't get us anything but abuse to print it. The people don't want to see him knocked. He's champion."

THE
BLUE RIBBON

Cornell Woolrich

I 'll never forget the day I first met him. He made quite an impression on me. Especially on my right eye, which he changed to a dun-colored sworl. Also on my upper left pivot, which he detached. It was a first tooth, it would have come out eventually anyhow, but he undeniably hastened the process.

He was maybe seven, I was maybe eight.

I'd strayed incautiously out of my own neighborhood. They still had the El up in those days, and I'd ventured across to the lee side of it, riverward.

He was lounging up against the wall, alongside one of the tenement doorways. He had his arms pinioned behind his back, in an attitude suggestive of keeping them leashed, holding them in reserve for eventual use. I should have been forewarned by that, but I wasn't.

I eyed him with the detached objectivity of one boy for another, a strange boy, as I came along, no more. Everything about him—the slanted peaked cap, the maroon jersey, the knee britches, the black stockings—was strictly *de rigueur,* befitting his age and surroundings. Everything but one thing. And that was so glaring, so incredible, so horrific a stigma, I had to look twice, to make sure I had actually seen it there the first time. That was where I made my mistake.

It was a bow of ribbon; a pert, four-leafed bow of blue ribbon, such as the little girls contemporaneous to us wore on their pigtails. *And it was on his head.* On, or in, or clinging to, his hair. Since he had no pigtail, someone (inconceivable that it could have been he himself) had taken a

119

strand of his carrot-colored hair, just over the ear, brought it downward, and affixed this unspeakable token to it. At that, his cap could have been made to conceal it; it could have been thrust upward out of sight, or the cap brought down over it. Instead, the cap had been deliberately and acutely slanted far over the other way, so that the whole side of his skull was left unprotected. And there it was, in full view, in broad daylight, on 22nd Street east of Second Avenue.

The rest was automatic. A stomach-deep guffaw churned up from me.

His head had been lowered slightly, his eyes had been watchfully on me, following me across his radius of vision. Now he nodded to himself, as if to say, "That'll do nicely. That's just what I've been waiting for."

His arms came out from behind his back. He stepped forward away from the wall.

To me he was monosyllabic. "Okay" was all he said.

He made various fistic preparations. Shucked back his cuffs so that they wouldn't hamper him; took off his cap and stowed it up under his jersey for temporary safekeeping, directly over his stomach. He also tested out the knuckles of one hand by *grinding* them, so to speak, against the palm of the other.

There was no anger or any other emotion apparent, he was quite professional about it.

I didn't like any of this. There was too much formality, and I was used to only impromptu little scuffles that were over with almost before you even knew you were engaged in them. I saw that I'd let myself in for something. I had an inkling of my own limitations. Also the average amount of prudence. Or caution, if you want to call it that.

"All right, I apollugize," I said grudgingly, but fairly hurriedly.

I was laboring under a misapprehension. I had thought there was a point of honor involved: I had ridiculed him by chortling as I was going by. It seemed that wasn't it at all.

"What're you trying to do, spoil everything?" he said accusingly. "I don't want no apollugies. I want some *training*. What do you think I've been standing here like this for, for over an hour? Come on, put 'em up."

"But I—I take it back," I faltered.

"What're you trying to do, do me out of a workout? Come on, put 'em up. How're we going to start, until you put 'em up?"

I had to put them up then, what could I do?

I could have saved myself the trouble. They went right down again. So did all the rest of my person with them, to a sprawling position on the sidewalk. That was when my eye got it.

A certain amount of heated emotion entered into it on my part now. None whatever on his, "Wide open," I heard him mutter judiciously.

I got up again, and I put 'em up again.

I, and they, both went down again. That was when my tooth got it.

He was beginning to veer over into advice, although I was in too rabid a state at the moment to take much note of it. "No guard at all," he said critically. "Y' just put 'em up, and then you don't do anything with them." He spat off to one side, although I imagine this was a restorative reflex and not a commentary on my prowess. "And y'get sore when you fight," he added. "Never get sore when you fight; dintcha ever learn that?"

I was up again; then I was down again just as promptly. This time there was no particular damage, except to my equilibrium.

"I pulled that one," he told me. He stood a moment, then he swung his hand at me disgustedly. "Aw, what's the use?" he said. "That ain't no practice. I could get that from a punching bag."

He let me cool off a minute in a recumbent position. Then abruptly he held out his hand, helped me to swing myself to my feet.

"Where you from?" he said.

"The other side of the El."

"Oh, no wonder!" he exclaimed, as though that explained everything. "They don't know how to fight. Why'n't you say so before? I wouldn't have matched up with you."

I felt like pointing out I'd done about as much as I could to avoid having it happen myself, but I refrained.

"Know who my father was?" he said pridefully. "Chuck O'Reilly."

"Who was that?" I asked incautiously.

His voice rose almost to the third-floor windows over us. "Chuck O'Reilly?" he shrieked. "He was only the world's champiun! Don't you know anything?"

I felt rather humble now intellectually, just as humble as I'd felt physically before.

"He's dead now," he said more quietly. "That's what I'm training for. He made my mother swear before he died that she'd train me to be champiun some day, like he was."

I was looking at his eye. "Did I do that to you?" I asked incredulously. I couldn't remember having been anywhere near there, or any of the rest of him.

"Naw," he said reluctantly, "I got that yesterday. I forgot, and dropped my guard." That seemed to remind him of something. He seized me by the arm suddenly, pulled me in toward the doorway. "Come on up a minute, I want to find out."

He didn't say what he wanted to find out. I was vaguely uneasy; I tried to hang back. I didn't like the gloomy interior of the hallway, or the even gloomier stairs he started to tow me up, flight after flight. After all I was legitimate spoils of war, in a manner of speaking, and I didn't know what might be awaiting me. "Come on," he urged, "nobody's gonna hurt you."

He partly urged and partly dragged me up four long flights, and then threw open a flat-door without the formality of knocking. It appeared we had had an audience the whole time, without my being aware of it. She was sitting by a window, overlooking the street. She was on some kind of a rocker; she must have been, because I could see her sway a little every now and then; but outside of that you couldn't tell. You couldn't see hide nor hair of it, not even the runners. She was wide of girth, she must have weighed about one-eighty. With the smooth, pink cheeks of a young girl. His mother.

"Y'don't cahll that a bout, now do ye?" she blurted out before we were fairly in the doorway. "It was over before it begun. 'Twas what your father used to cahll a set up."

"It was all I could get. I stood there an hour. Nobody around here will laugh at me any more. The kids stand right in front of me and pretend they don't see it," he exculpated himself.

"Then why don't you go over on the next block?"

"They're foreigners over there, they jump you three at a time. An' that's Officer McGinty's beat, he's getting to be a sorehead lately, he says he'll run me in the next time I—" He took a deep, crucial breath. "Can I take it off now, Mom? Can I?"

"Well now, I don't know. Look at that eye. Y'left yourself wide open yesterday, and your footwork was a crying shame, it was. And now today, you take on this—this—" Words seemed to fail her. "Come here, creature," she said to me with kindly contempt.

She reached out and felt my spindly arms. She shook her head with professional gravity. "He hasn't the makings, he'll never be any good for it, I can tell ye that now. He's stunted. He's a dwharf. Don't they feed you anything at ahll at your house, poor limb? It's here with us you'd better be staying for a few meals."

"He's from the other side of the El," he explained, the way you would explain some helpless maimed thing you have brought home with you out of sheer humanitarianism.

She threw up her hands in pious horror. "The poor soul," was all she said.

I felt like a useless encumbrance on the face of the earth.

And yet I had taken to her instantly, even though I was getting the short end of her criticism. She was the kind of mother my age dreamed about—and never got. She was interested in the right sort of things to be interested in. Not whether one of your knee pants was dragging down your leg or how your marks were in history. The things *she* taught you stayed with you all through life. You stopped wearing knee pants after a while. And history went right on making itself up without any help from you. When I grew older I learned to call what she was taking, the *long view.* She was a maker of men.

"Can I take it off, Mom?" he kept pestering her. "Can I now? I don't like it. I don't even like *him* to see it on me."

"I know ye don't," she said judiciously. "And that's why I put it on ye." She considered. "Very well, that'll do for this time," she assented finally. "Fetch me my box, ye know where it is."

He brought out a trinket box of sorts. Of polished rosewood, with brass hinges. The sort of box that women use to hold their treasured keepsakes and mementos.

"Bend your head down," she ordered.

Her fingers worked deftly, separating the hideous appendage from his virile thatch, while I stared in frozen fascination.

Then she wound it about her finger, in a tight-packed coil. It was the sort of ribbon they weren't making even then. A rich, full-bodied silk; it must have come over from the old country with her, maybe on one of her dresses. It had a thin line of satin traced along each edge, the way a mirror is beveled. And an invisible pattern of flowers sprinkled all over it. When you held it flat, you couldn't see them; when you held it up, they came out.

She prodded it down into the box, wedged it in, into a special little cranny, a crevice, just big enough to hold it. She closed the lid.

"And the next time ye break any of me rules, forget the things I've told ye, like ye did yesterday," she warned him, "out it comes again. Mark me word now!"

And then, as he turned his back in unutterable relief, she caught my eye, and solemnly dropped one eyelid at me. I glowed all over. She was soaring moment by moment in my young esteem. I was already well into the opening stages of heroine-worship. It was more than that; if there's such a thing as acquiring a second mother, contemporary with the first, I was in process of doing just that. She was a mother the old Spartans would have understood. A mother who reared warriors.

"I'm going to be champiun of the world some day," he told me matter-of-factly, as we went flying down the tenement stairs together, his penance at an end.

I was carrying his coat. I knew then that was what I wanted to do,

more than anything else. Carry his coat, figuratively speaking. I knew
then that I had my life's work cut out ahead of me.

"And I'm going to be your manager," I said.

He came up the hard way. Fighting for a turkey or a smoked ham,
fighting almost for the love of it alone; fighting at church benefits and
social club smokers, fighting in basements and on amusement piers and
at the back of recreation halls, once even on the roof of a disused car-
barn. And no matter where it was, I was always there. Every step of the
way. Little Barney Carpenter, undersized as ever and still wearing those
same horn-rimmed glasses, who had to wear a topcoat right up to the
end of May and couldn't have paced him even once around the Reser-
voir in the Park without being carried off on a stretcher. I was his manager, as I'd always said I'd be. I had to be a civil engineer on the side,
my family'd had something to say about that. But that was on the side,
that was a pale substitute for living. *This* was my real life, the truncated
hours of the day and night I snitched to spend with him. This was the
main event, and nothing could make it otherwise.

He was a grand specimen by now. He could have held up the El on
one shoulder while they shifted supports under it. When you saw him in
a pair of trunks, you only realized then what the Creator's blueprints
must have originally called for. And when you watched him inside the
ropes, you knew what they meant by the expression "poetry of motion."
The carrot thatch of his kid days had darkened to bronze, and there was
a sort of honest, open look about his face that's all any man requires in
the way of good looks.

He was a comer. But then everyone is, I guess, until—well, until he's
a goner.

It was a foregone conclusion that someone would see him sooner or
later. Someone did, at one of those peanut-bouts one night. The door
blew open in the dressing room right afterward and a big black cigar
walked in, followed by a man.

"Shackley's the name," he said, and shoved out his hand to O'Reilly,
who couldn't take it because he was unlacing his gym shoes. So he
changed it to a clout on the back instead.

"I'm your new manager," he announced. "I seen you out there just
now. Now don't argue, I gotta make a train back to the Hudson Termi-
nal. I'm a busy man. Ben Hogan on the entertainment committee tipped
me off I should come out here, and anything that'll get me all the way to
Hackensack— This is your trainer. Here's a notary public. Where's that
contract, Freeman; you got that contract, Freeman? Here, get your un-
nawear off this bench, this'll do. Just sign here."

"Well, gimme time to get my pants on at least, will you?" O'Reilly glowered.

Meanwhile the dynamic one had become aware of me, as if by post-script. "Who's this guy?" he asked.

"He's my manager," O'Reilly said. "Past, present and future." He gave him a level look. "And he suits me just fine."

The cigar notched upward an inch in his mouth. He looked me up and down as though he didn't think much of the dates I was able to get for him. "How much you want for his contract?" he blurted out.

"Even if there was one between us," I let him know, "I wouldn't peddle it like a side of bacon over a counter."

The cigar hitched up another notch. "Oh, one of them idlelists! Fine," he went on briskly, "then I'm not taking anything away from you. If you think that much of him, then you ought to be glad to see him get what he's worth. Whaddye want to waste him on things like this for? He's material, I tell you, *material*." He turned to O'Reilly. "Whaddye say, fighter?"

O'Reilly finished tucking his shirt in, went over to get his coat. "Like I told you, I'm doing all right. Carp suits me, and I'm the guy that's to be suited." He put on his hat. "Coming, Carp?"

I incautiously handed him the ten dollars he'd just earned, at this point, so he could take it home to her.

Shackley calmly intercepted it, looked it over on both sides as if he'd never seen one that small before. "Hunh!" he said expressively. Then before either one of us could stop him he'd put a match to it and used it to relight his extinguished cigar. After which he dropped it on the floor and stepped all over the blazing remnants.

"Hey, what the!" O'Reilly gasped. I had to hold him back for a minute or he would have swung at the guy.

Meanwhile Shackley calmly proceeded to peel off a pair of fifties and held them out toward him in exchange. "Here," he said loftily. "Quit thinking in five and tens. Guys that fight under me don't have to bother with small change like that." And at the door, for *coup de grâce*, he turned and suggested casually: "How would you like a crack at Donner —oh, say within the next two, three years?"

"D-D-Donner, the world's heavy?" O'Reilly sputtered. He sat down on the bench, pointed to his shirt front. "M-me?"

He was smart, this Shackley. He was a shrewd psychologist, although he probably wouldn't have known how to pronounce the word. His parting shot was directed at me, not O'Reilly.

"Don't hold him back," he pleaded ruefully as he pulled the door closed after him. "If you love him, don't hold him back."

So I didn't hold him back. We went down to Shackley's office the next day, the two of us, and I went halves with Shackley on him. I was to be the silent voice, Shackley was to be in active control, attend to the business angles. I think this was the first time that was ever done, although since then there have been many such arrangements.

I didn't think Shackley'd accept on those terms, but to my surprise he did. He sure must have seen something in that Hackensack ring the night before. I guess he decided he'd rather have a half-share in O'Reilly than none at all. It was all drawn up in black and white and the three of us signed. "And now," he said to O'Reilly, lighting up another of those big black cigars, "get ready to get famous."

I was there the night he won the title from Donner. Three years from that night in Hackensack, maybe four. Not three years. A lifetime. The short, swift lifetime of a prizefighter, from the bottom to the top. In no other profession is there such an absolute, measurable, mathematically exact top. In no other profession are you so alone on it; nobody else can be up there with you, it's one at a time. In no other profession is your stay up there so short, so strictly limited. You stand up on the pinnacle, in rays of glory, you look around, then down you come, clawing and crumbling.

But sometimes I think it's the closest you can get to the stars. Higher than all the arts and sciences, all the gentler things. Man alone, in the glow of his youth, with the body that God gave him.

Was I there? Every blow that landed on him, landed on me too. Every fall he took, I went down with him. Every drop of blood he lost, was drawn from me as well. Every drop of sweat he sweated, I paid out with him. Every time he hurt, and every time his heart broke, I hurt for him and my heart broke right in time with his.

What love for a woman can match up with that: what you feel when your man's in the ring?

Until the bell was way up in the early teens. Until their savings were gone, and they were dead broke. Both down to one last good punch apiece.

He looked down at me blurredly one time, dangling there half-over the ropes. I didn't know whether he could see me or not, or even knew who I was any more.

I stood up on my seat and put my hands gently on the sides of his face. "Have you got one punch left?" I whispered.

"The tailings," he heaved.

"Save it until after his. Make him come across first. Be the last one out with it."

The referee came over, and he swung around, with that grace they still have even when they're dying on their feet.

I saw Donner's come and go, and I knew it was his last, the way his whole guts nearly came up with it to send it off, the way his belly swelled, and then dropped flat again, empty.

It turned my boy completely around, he breasted the ropes, as though the whole ring were a boat heaving under him and throwing him against the gunwale.

Then I stood up and I screamed, until my lungs smouldered and sent out wisps of smoke: "Now yours! *Now!* Use it! Oh, for the love of God, use it *now!*"

He had to scrape it up from his toes, practically. But he collected it, and he packaged it, and he delivered it. And that did it, that told the story. The last punch. The one that always counts. The last punch after the other guy's last punch.

I couldn't see very well, the next few seconds right after that. I guess my glasses were too steamy or something. Funny, but when I took them off, my eyes still were steamy anyway.

But I heard the thud when Donner went down. And I saw the blur of something going up: two arms together, O'Reilly's and the referee's. And I heard the words that went with it. "The winner!" And he was the heavyweight champion of the world. Like his father had been before him. Like his mother had sworn she'd live to see him be some day too.

And after that, I guess, there was no place else for him to go but down.

Then the girl comes into it. There's always a girl comes into it sooner or later, in every man's life, and you can tell by the time she picks for coming into it, whether she's going to be good for him or bad. If she comes into it while he's still at the bottom, before he starts up, then it's only he himself she wants, and she'll probably be good for him, all right. If she comes into it after he's already at the top, watch out for her.

There'd been a girl in his life before this, but he'd kept her off-center, around the edges. Maggy Connors. Plain like her name. He'd brought her home to her door now and then, and that was two doors down from his own. It never seemed to get anywhere much, though. Maybe it was her fault, maybe it was his. Then after he'd copped the title, she couldn't get through the crowd to where he was. She wasn't much of a one for using her elbows to push her way forward, I guess.

This one I mean was different. Lolly Dean. She hailed from Park Avenue. I'm giving you her generic address now, not the actual house number. Her voice had been injected with novocain, but she had cayenne in her eyes. I think they called her a deb. I used to call her something else, but it was an equally short word.

She probably didn't mean him any harm, that was the worst of it. If she'd been after his money, it would have been a lot easier for somebody to save him. She had more money than he did, from first to last. I don't know what she was after, myself. Maybe she didn't either. The world's heavyweight championship, you might say. I guess she enjoyed wearing it slung over her arm, like whatever the fashionable fur was that year.

I was with him the night he first met her. She was death, on high heels. I knew that the minute I saw her start across the room toward him as we came in, holding a Martini in her hand, saying in that muscle-bound accent she had: "I want to meet a world's champion. Just let me stand here close to a world's heavyweight champion and *breathe* in the same air he does."

She was the kind of a high-class dame that's bad for a fighter. In fact, she was the kind of a high-class dame that's bad for anyone except a high-class man just like her. And the reason she's not bad for a high-class man just like her, is that he's just as bad for her as she is for him. They neutralize one another.

Oh, it took a while. It was slow but it was sure. She hit him like a slow-burning fever, and you know what a fever does to you. But what she did to him, there was no quinine for.

I don't know what there was between them; it wasn't any of my business. I'm inclined to think, nothing. It might have been better if there had been; in that case the man usually gets the upper hand.

The first thing you know he'd moved into a bachelor penthouse and had some slant-eyed little runt for a valet. He had paintings on the walls, the kind you couldn't tell if they were hanging upside-down or right-side-up, because they didn't make any sense either way. Not even side-wise; I even tried them that way. He even had books around the place.

The first I heard about it was when I dropped in at the old flat one day, expecting to meet him there. "His lordship don't live here any more," she said, rocking away on the rocker that couldn't be seen. You had to look real close at her to detect the genuine hurt. She upped a palm and swung it around her in innocent perplexity. "What's wrong with this place, Carp? Can you tell me what's wrong with it? Sure 'tis pleasanter than ever now, the way the neighbors look up to me since he's holder of the title. It's like a queen I'm treated on all sides. I can't for the life of me see what's wrong with it. Can you?"

"Nothing, Mom," I said. "Not a thing." To me it was a shrine, almost.

We both looked down at the floor and felt kind of lonely.

I was the one kept on climbing the four flights of stairs from then on.

He didn't have the time; he just sent her checks instead. But can you cook Irish stew for a check? Can it grin and call you "Mom"?

I didn't see so much of him any more. Oh, he wanted me to, it wasn't that. It used to do something to me to go over there and have to give my name to a laundryman at the door before I could get in. And then when you did get in, you had to wade through broken-down pugs knee-deep before you could get over to him. When you did get over to him, he was always putting on a stiff shirt to go out somewhere with her.

I visited him once at his training quarters. That was when he was priming for the Jack Day bout. Once was enough. His headquarters was down at one of the Jersey beaches, and it was one long Mardi gras. She was down there, with her whole crowd. There was one large and two small yachts anchored off the place the whole time he was there; I counted them, not to mention several motor cruisers. And just to make the record complete, I can vouch for the fact that there was actually a woman fashion expert in attendance, to write back on what Lolly and the rest of her set were wearing for sportswear. The only thing they left out was to sprinkle rose leaves along the ground when he did his roadwork. And that popping sound you heard after dark regularly, that wasn't a punching bag, that was champagne corks. Just before he left, his trainer busted a toe kicking at a telegraph pole. "I was just pretending," he explained to me, "that it was O'Reilly's can." I knew how he felt. I got on the train and went home.

You know the history of his world championship; short, but not very sweet. Donner, then Jack Day, then out.

She didn't have to live to see him lose the championship—I've always been glad of that.

It wasn't anything in particular. It was just her time. She was dying without any fuss or fancy airs, just as she'd always lived. A little tired, and a whole lot disappointed, that was all.

I was with her at the end. I was, but he wasn't. I kept praying he'd come; not even for her sake, as much as for his own. But he didn't. He wasn't where he could be reached in time. Or else they delayed giving him my messages, I don't know. He was on some party somewhere with Lolly and her bunch, amusing them, playing the trained seal, clapping his flippers and catching the fish she threw him.

So I sat there with her alone, beside her bed in the dim tenement room. Well, that was all right, I was her son too. She'd strain her ears and try to lift her head, each time there was a step outside on the stairs, thinking this time maybe it was he. Then when it wasn't, when it went on past, she'd sort of fall back again, to wait some more, the little time she had left.

We spoke of him. It had always been him with us, with her and me

both, and it still was him, right up to the very end. I saw that she wanted
to say something, and I held her head a little higher, and put my face
down close to listen.

"Tell him to keep punching, Carp. To always keep punching, never
quit."

Her voice got lower.

"Tell him to mind that left of his, it always was a little ragged—"

I could hardly hear her any more, I had to put my ear down close.

"Tell him—Carp, tell him for me—when they've got him backed to
the ropes, or he's down for the count of nine, to look around—he'll see
me there somewhere around—I'll be there, I'll be there."

Her eyes closed and I laid her head gently back to rest. I couldn't see
the door very clearly any more, but I managed to find where it was and
tiptoe outside. I waited on the other side of it for him to come.

He came late, and straight from the party. His dancing shoes twinkled
hurrying up those tenement stairs, but they couldn't save him, he was
late. He still had the remnants of a flower left in his buttonhole, and
there was a piece of paper streamer still snagged across his shoulder.
Straight from the party, and late.

He tried to say something when he saw me standing there, but it
wouldn't come. Then as he made to go ahead on in, I reached out
suddenly and barred him for a minute with the back of my arm. I jerked
the withered flower out of his coat and the streamer off his shoulder; I
pulled the dress-handkerchief out of his breast pocket and kicked it away
on the floor. "She wants her son," I said under my breath, "not a society
clown."

He came out again after a while and closed the door behind him. I
could tell by the lingering way his hand left the knob she was gone. He
couldn't look at me. He came up and tried to stand alongside me, and I
started to move away.

"You broke her heart," I said bitterly. "You threw the fight. The long
fight. Go on back to your fine friends now. They can have you. There's
your handkerchief, there's your flower."

His hand started out to stop me, but I wasn't there any more. "Carp,
not you and me—"

I went on down the stairs.

The Dean girl's familiar black limousine was outside the door, with
her sitting in it waiting for him, powdering her nose, when I came out of
the door.

She looked at me and I looked at her. I raised my hands over my head
and I gave her the double handshake coming to the winner. I guess she
didn't know what I meant.

It went awfully fast after that. He hit the skids. The skids are high compared to what he hit. He hit the bottom. He went down until he got to where he couldn't go any lower than where he was.

First the title. He lost that, flat and final; Jack Day took it away from him. His chin dug into the resin like a tomahawk. They'd turned him into a cream puff that any man's fist could go through. I wasn't there, but they told me of an incident that happened there, that night. She was sitting there right under him, ringside, and a drop of blood from his split lip got on her new white dress (she was the kind went to the fights in ball-gowns), when he slopped over the ropes nearly into her lap one time. Anyway, she flinched, and edged away, and spent the next couple of minutes rubbing and scratching at it. It was more important to her than what was happening to him up above her in the ring. Finally she and her whole crowd of jackanapes got up and walked out on him during the ninth. They dropped him like a hot potato, then and there. "Come on, my dears," she was heard to say during a lull in the booing, "This is really too slow for words, let's go somewhere else." That was the way I heard it.

He was no longer amusing. It had been too, too quaint when the world's champion drank his coffee with the spoon left in the cup, but it was just plain bad manners when the world's ex-champion did it, I suppose.

Anyway, I give her credit she's done a thorough job. In about six months after that, he was through. Just another has-been. Which is awfully fast time, even in the fight game. Nothing left. His bones picked clean.

Then finally, I heard, even Shackley dropped him. I didn't blame Shackley. He was a businessman. He didn't love him like I had: O'Reilly wasn't any good to him any more.

One night two or three years later I was standing waiting for a trolley on Sixth Avenue, one of those old green-line cars, when one of these walking sandwich-boards came drifting along behind me. You know the kind of thing. It had a patch of sample material pasted to it, and said something about having your old suits rewoven as good as new.

I would never even have raised my eyes any higher than the message on it, except for the peculiar way it suddenly changed pace. It had been moving along slowly, the way they're supposed to, to give the passers-by ample time to read it. Then all at once, for no reason, it picked up speed, started to move away from me down the street almost at a run. As though the bearer couldn't get away from that immediate vicinity fast enough. In fact he all but collided head-on with several people in the attempt. My eyes went up above the top of the board, naturally, and I *thought* there was something familiar about the back of that neck.

I made a beeline after him, and caught up with him just after he got

around the corner. He couldn't make very good time with that thing
dangling on him, front and back. I stepped around in front of him and
blocked his way, so he couldn't pass me by. I looked him up and down.

"So it ended up the way it always does."

He looked down at the ground. "Rub it in," he answered. "I've got it
coming to me. I didn't even get one last break. Out of seven million
people, I had to run into someone I used to know!"

"No," I said. "Not 'used to.' I'm your manager, remember? Your first
one, before you got fancy in the pants. What's this, some new way of
training? What're you doing with this chest-protector on?" I hauled the
sandwich-board off him so violently it nearly scalped him. Then I gave
it a ride with my foot that sent it out across the curb.

I took him back to my place with me. I did what I could for the
outside of him. I lent him my razor, and I lent him my towel, and I lent
him my shirt. I couldn't do anything for the inside of him, only feed it; I
did that too. Then he sat there, looking enough like O'Reilly had, to fool
you into thinking it was he again.

"It's no use," he kept telling me over and over. "What do you think
you can do for me?"

"Nothing," I agreed. "The point is, what do you think you can do for
yourself?"

It was going to take time to answer that. A long, long time, I could
see. Weeks and months.

I don't think I was ever happier than the night he gave me the answer.
He gave it as though I'd just finished asking it, instead of months before.

"Carp," he said, "I'd like to fight again. Do you think I could, do you
think I've got anything left?"

"When did you lose your right arm?" I asked. "I didn't notice. And
whatever became of the left?"

He looked down and nodded humbly.

I pulled wires like a spider spinning a web. I ran around all over town.

"It's no use," he said. "You never come back. It's a game with a
one-way door."

"Braddock did," I said, "and you've got him licked by ten years. But
then he was no quitter."

He just looked down again, like he was always doing. That's where
they look, when they're down themselves. It makes where they are already look higher to them by comparison, I guess.

I got McKane, his old trainer, back for him. He nearly fell over the
first time McKane walked in with me. "Where'd you dig him up?" he
asked me on the side.

"Bumped into him in Stillman's, where else?" I said casually. I'd had to put an ad in the personal columns, run it for ten days straight, to locate him.

"What's the score?" I asked McKane a couple weeks later.

"Look, Mr. Carpenter," he said, "he'll be all right on the outside when I get through, but he's no good inside. He's out of something I can't put into him. I can condition his mind but I can't put that spark back into him. It ain't his mitts, it's his mind. He thinks he's licked, so he is."

"He'll be all right if I can get him a fight," I said. "That's the main hurdle. Once he's over that, it'll be clear sailing."

I looked up Shackley and I brought him around to take a look at him, without telling him who it was, ahead of time. He made the look a short one. "Nothing doing," he said, "I ain't interested in rummage sales," and turned around and walked out of the gym.

I brought him around again two weeks later. I had to hold the door of the taxi closed with both hands all the way over to keep him in it. "All right, I'll look, but I won't buy," he said. He stayed longer this time. "A very good job," he admitted. "But the Salvation Army does it every day, and I don't have to go and watch."

The third time was the hardest of all to get him there. He was wise now. I had to lace his coffee with slivovitz first, when he wasn't looking, after spending the whole previous night in a Turkish bath with him. He liked to have someone to talk to, he said, when he was on the steam table.

We had a sparring partner for O'Reilly now. I turned it into a fix, the partner took a back dive.

Shackley turned around and walked out again. "All right, I like him," he said. "But my money's hard to convince, it's smarter than I am. You keep him."

I followed him back to his office, and I wouldn't get out. "He bought you that diamond you've got on your little finger," I told him, leaning across the desk at him.

"Not this exact one," he admitted phlegmatically. "But I do have a smaller one back at the house, my weekday ring, that came out of his winnings."

"Just one fight, that's all I'm asking." I think I wrung my hands at him, or shook him by the shoulders, I don't remember any more. "With anyone at all, a football-tackle dummy, I don't care. Just one fight. That's all he needs. That's all I'm begging you for."

"What've you got, religion?" he said drily.

I turned around and slouched over to the door, beat. Then I stopped and looked around at him. He was holding the phone to his ear. "I may as well do this as contribute to the Red Cross," he said matter-of-factly.

The guy's name he got for him was Behrens. I didn't know anything about him. I didn't want to. All I cared about was that he had two arms and was willing to step into the ring with O'Reilly.

Shackley looked me up for a heart-to-heart talk the night before the fight, after I'd put O'Reilly to bed. I could see he was plenty worried.

"I been watching him all week," he said. "There's something wrong with him. Listen, there's two kinds of a sure thing, and it looks to me like I let myself in on the wrong one—a sure loss. His spine has a wave in it. Is it that society dame that—?"

"Naw, she went down the drain long ago. It's just that he don't believe in himself any more. His self-confidence is sapped."

"And I'm a bigger sap than that, even," he grunted.

"You can't bring it back. I can't bring it back. It's got to come back by itself. I only know of one person who could bring it back, if she was still alive."

He asked me who I meant. I told him about her, then. How she used to train him when he was a kid, with that scrap of blue ribbon. How it worked. What results it got.

He just took it in, didn't say much. He was thinking about it for a while after, though, I could see. He looked at me kind of intently, one time. All of a sudden he bounced his hands against his knees, stood up to go.

The last thing he said when he left the room was, "I've got a certain amount of money tied up in this, after all. I'd like to protect it the best I can, that's all."

O'Reilly tipped at one hundred ninety and Behrens was way up in the two-twenties, but we weren't worried about that; it was just that McKane had shaved him down pretty close to the bone, that was all.

Behrens's manager gave our man a contemptuous pitch of the head at the weighing-in. "What sort of chance d'you think *he* stands?" he asked us insultingly. "What does he think *he* can do?"

"He's not talking," I answered for him. "He ends at the shoulders."

"He sure will tonight," he promised. "He's going to get his block knocked off."

O'Reilly just looked down at the floor. He believed that himself, and I could see it. That was the whole trouble.

He climbed in in a welter of groaning and booing that night. It wasn't so much that they were against him; they were showing they didn't think he had a chance, didn't think he was good enough, that was all. It got him, too, I could see that; started the dirty work of sapping the little confidence he'd had to begin with. He just sat down in his corner without taking a bow, and looked down between his legs at the canvas. Always looking down, always down.

· The gong boomed and the agony dance began. Behrens came out like a young hurricane tearing a path across the ring. They met, and he kept plastering short ones all over O'Reilly, like a potter modeling wet clay. O'Reilly just staggered through the hailstorm like a guy caught far from shelter without his umbrella; he stayed up, but that was about all.

"Look at him," Shackley commented bitterly, "blinding himself with his own bent arm like it was raining in his face. Cringing. Watch; see that? He's scared of the blows before they even land on him!"

It looked truer than I would have cared to admit.

The bell, and then the bell again.

He went in again, plodding like a guy on his way to dig a ditch. And burdened down by dragging his own shovel and wheelbarrow along behind him.

Behrens's arms blurred at times, like a pinwheel, they circled so fast.

"I thought you trained all that yellow out of him," Shackley turned and scowled at the trainer.

"That ain't yellow," McKane snapped. "It's orange!"

"You two talk a good fight, with your cans to the chair," I said sourly. "At least he's up there on his own two feet, no matter how lame a showing he's making."

"Oh, is he up there?" Shackley sneered sarcastically. "I'm glad you told me. You see, you're the one wearing glasses, I'm not. I wasn't sure until now. Behrens is hitting at something up there, that's all I know, and it *looks* like a live figure. But it doesn't do anything."

"Why don't you change seats?" I growled. "You seem to be in back of the wrong corner."

"My money sure is," he let me know.

The bell, and then the bell, and then the bell again.

"Throw him a hot-water bottle," Shackley said savagely. "He must be cold, the way he's afraid to take his arms away from his sides!" He was on his feet beside me, on tenterhooks, one hand in his pocket jingling some loose change. Showing where his thoughts were, now as always, I said to myself bitterly.

"I don't have to *throw* my money away like this!" he seethed. "I can bet it on horses if I want to lose it that bad!"

When O'Reilly staggered back to his stool next time, I reached up through the ropes and squeezed him encouragingly on his moist calf. "You're doing all right," I said above the catcalls and the insults. "Good boy. You're still up. Don't let them get you down." And I meant the spectators, as much as his opponent.

He turned around and looked at me blearily, and tried to smile a little. But he was ashamed even of me, I could see.

He got up and lumbered in again at the next bell, slower than slow, no flash at all, no fire, no fight. Just old habit (maybe) keeping one hundred and ninety pounds vertical, instead of the other way. All he did was spar, and spar, and spar, and backtrack all the while.

"We ain't booked here through tomorrow night, you know," Shackley shrilled. "We gotta clear out sometime between now and morning."

"It's no use," McKane said disgustedly. "He needs a miracle."

"He needs a Pulmotor," I heard Shackley ejaculate. The next time I looked around he wasn't there alongside me any more, he was ploughing his way up the aisle, on his way out. As if he couldn't stand watching even another minute of it.

The noise the crowd was making was like surf spattering against the shore; but a surf of muddy water, not of clean. It would rise and dip, dip and rise. Sometimes the things they said would come through, sharp and clear for a minute, by themselves; individual remarks. The jeers, the insults, the cruel things that laugh at a man's pain and misfortune. The things the crowd says are always the things the crowd says; they never change. Two thousand years ago the circus crowd must have howled out the same things to some dying gladiator. In a different language, but with the same stony hearts.

"Reach out, kid. He ain't poison ivy, don't be afraid to touch him."

"Why don't somebody introduce the two of them? What kind of manners yis got?"

"I want a rebate! There's only one guy in the ring, I paid to see two!"

"Hey, how much longer does this keep up? We got homes and families to get back to."

Behrens hit him like nobody's ever hit anybody before. He hit him all around the ring, in a kind of a May dance; as if there were a pole in the middle of it, and they were both attached to it by equidistant streamers. From a neutral corner, past his own, past the second neutral corner, past O'Reilly's corner, back to the first neutral corner again. All one-way blows, one-way; just give, give, and no take. It wasn't a prize fight any more, it was like something out of the penal code.

And still he stayed up.

Then after a while one of those strange unaccountable hushes fell over the crowd. It got to them, the way he was hanging on up there. They quit the razzing and the hooting and the catcalling. They became compassionately silent, as in the presence of death. And to go down in the ring for the final count, well that is a form of death after all. The fight became a pantomime, almost completely without background sounds for a few minutes. Just the crunch of each blow. Each blow from Behrens, those were the only blows there were.

I could understand what had come over the crowd. I felt it myself a thousandfold more, for there was a personal love between him and me. That silence, that sudden respect, was a form of masculine mass-pity. I remember I'd lowered my head and I'd been holding my hands heeled to my eyes for a minute, for the lights over the canvas hurt them, and the blows hurt them, and the figures blurred a little with too much juice.

There was a *plop* like a big fat watermelon hitting a tin roof. And then I heard a great, deep, shuddering breath go up. As though the whole vast crowd had just one windpipe. What a strange sound it made, I remember. There was something of compunction in it, but even more of relief. It hadn't been clean any more. It hadn't been sport. It hadn't been good any more to watch. There's a cruel streak in everyone. But there's no one that's *all* cruelty and nothing else.

And I think they'd changed over without knowing it, changed sides. The guy they'd wanted to win, wasn't the guy they wanted to win now. And the guy they wanted to win now, was the guy who couldn't.

I knew he was down. And I was glad; yes, I was glad. I looked, and he was down, and it was finished. No one could take a beating like that and ever get up again. He was lying there flat as a paper cutout, and with his arms straight out from the shoulders in a ruler-even line.

The referee started to slice time thin over him. His arm chopped past the back of his neck like a guillotine blade. "One!" he intoned, in the embalmed hush that had fallen.

He wasn't out even yet. He may have been dazed, but his eyes were wide open, I could see them from where I sat, under the querulous, corrugated ridges of his forehead. Staring, staring out along the resin; from way down low, as low as they could get. Just skimming the surface of it.

"Two!" shattered over his head.

A change came over him. I didn't know what it was at first. It was so subtle, so gradual; it had nothing to do with moving his body. It was more like an awareness of something, a gathering to a head of attentiveness, all over him at once. Before there had been vacancy, now there was intentness; no line of his figure expressed it, yet every line expressed it.

His eyes seemed to be looking out across the edge of the ring floor he lay upon, out somewhere beyond, into the shadowy perspective. Then his head came up, slowly. Then his chest started to curve upward away from the resin, like something peeling off it. Then his shoulders backed, until he had propped himself up on one arm. He stayed like that for a short while.

His eyes were so fixed, they had so unmistakably the focus of steady though distant scrutiny, that half-unconsciously I turned my own head to follow their direction. It was just a reflex.

She was standing there down at the lower reaches of the aisle, not more than ten yards from the ring. Mom O'Reilly. In full glare of the ring. Just the way she used to look. That same coat-sweater that had always gapped open across her middle. That pair of funny little barrettes she wore, one on each side of her topknot, and never on quite straight. Round of figure, red of face, resolution and imprecation written all over her. Holding aloft in one fist, for him to see, a twining scrap of blue ribbon. Shaking the other at him while she did so, as if to say "This is what you're going to get."

It did something funny to me for a minute; it was like breathing in menthol and getting my pipes chilled all the way down. But only for a minute. I was scared for only a minute. There wasn't anything to scare you about her.

I don't know what she was, but she wasn't any ghost. There wasn't anything transparent or ethereal about her. And I had my glasses on. She blocked out everything and everyone she stood before, solid. I could see the shine on her high-blooded face, against the light. I could even see the black shadow she cast on the inclination of the aisle behind her. I even saw one of the ushers come down after her and tap her to get back, clear out of the aisle, and saw the impatient backhanded swat she gave him, like someone brushing off a mosquito. Then he even tried to take her by the arm, and she wrenched it away from him, and dug at him punitively with the point of her elbow.

I turned back to the ring.

He'd gotten up to his knees now. He was reared there on them, in an attitude curiously suggestive of penitence. There was some sort of sincere humility expressed by the posture, ungainly and trained-bear-like as it was. There was no fear on his face, no blatant stupefaction; only a sort of inscrutable contrition, very calm and sturdy. The sort of face one makes when one promises: "I'll do better."

Then he got all the way up. He went back to ring-center to fight some more. No, not some more, for he hadn't fought at all until now. To begin to fight, unafraid, sure of himself. It's funny what just a little thought inside your head can do; how much more it can do than all the might of your arms. "I'm good. I can win this. I'm good enough to win this."

That thought won it for him. The referee hoisted his arm up in the air. He snatched it right down again, and came over to the side I was sitting on. He leaned over and looked straight down into my face. His eyes were wide and scared, but not scared in a bad way. Scared in the wondering way of a child that doesn't understand something. That knows it must be all right, but can't quite grasp it, and wants some wiser head to reassure him.

I knew what he was trying to say to me, even though he couldn't say it. I nodded to show him I knew. "Don't be scared, kid," I told him. "It's all right, don't be scared." Then we both looked around for her, sort of slow and gingerly, turning our heads little by little, instead of all at once.

She wasn't there any more. Everyone had got to their feet, all at one time, all over the arena, and the aisles were clogged with slowly moving backs. She'd been swallowed up. You couldn't see where she'd been, you couldn't see where she'd gone. She'd been drowned in the rising tide of departure, gone under.

It was just as well, I told myself bitterly. I had my doubts she could have borne a very much closer inspection. I was remembering how I'd told Shackley the story, only the night before, of that early training method of hers, when he was just a kid; complete down to the last detail, ribbon and all. I was remembering that hard, speculative look he'd given me at the time. I was remembering how he'd got up from his seat and stalked out, a round or two or three ago, and never come back.

I swore a little under my breath. He'd always been full of tricks, full of bright ideas, ever since I'd known him.

O'Reilly jumped down beside me on the arena floor, without waiting for his bathrobe even, and we forced our way back through the bedlam together. I went into the dressing room at his heels. I chased them all out, every last one of them down to McKane; squeezed the door closed on them, so there was just the two of us together, alone in there.

He still had his gloves on. He held both his mitts up against my shoulder, made a cushion of them, and put his head down on them, and cried into them. Cried like anything; I never saw a guy cry like that before.

"Did you see her?" he said after a while.

I didn't answer. I didn't answer, in a way that meant yes; I wanted it to.

"It wasn't really her, Carp, was it?" he kept saying over and over. "It wasn't really her?"

"No," I said, "it wasn't really her." I could feel an undercurrent of bitterness surging through me. "Don't think about it any more," I said.

He said, "But you saw her too, Carp."

What could I say? "I loved her too, you see," I explained. "I loved her as much as you. I was her second son, remember? The one she always said she would have had if the old champ hadn't died."

That satisfied him.

"Do you think anyone else?"

"Don't talk about it any more, don't you see what it does to it? It takes something away from it. You saw her, I saw her, that's enough. We're the only ones she—wanted to have see her."

But I was remembering an usher who'd tapped her on the shoulder, to move back out of the way. And a man in an aisle seat who'd glanced momentarily aside at her, with indifferent curiosity, because the tail of his eye had caught her gesturing in some way; then looked back to the ring again.

And I was sore. I would have rather had him lose, than win by such a shabby trick.

"I'm going to be all right now," he said. "I'll take on two or three more, just so I'll have a little money put aside. And then I'll quit the fights. I'll quit on my feet, though, and not on my back. That's what she wanted, I guess. That's what she wanted to do."

He was going to be all right. Not up at the top any more, not down at the bottom either. Then leave it before it left him. Get into some longer-lived business, that would last him through the thirties and forties. We do what we can, the best of us, the worst of us, all of us.

I left him in the dressing room. I said, "I've got to see somebody about something." The Connors girl was waiting around outside, when I jostled my way through. I saw her there, standing off by herself, away from the rest of them; like somebody who has a special arrangement, who knows she isn't wasting her time. I went over to her. "He'll be right out," I said. "Been waiting long?"

"Yes, I guess I have," she said thoughtfully. "A long, long time." Then she smiled. "But that's all right, I don't mind."

I knew what she meant.

He'd be all right now, that was all I cared about. She was for him; made to order for him. She'd see him through the rest of the way.

I went out into the arena again. I talked to the ushers until I'd found the one I wanted, the one who'd been posted on Aisle A. I said: "Did you see a little short, stout lady standing down there, about the third row, shaking her fists, toward the end?"

"Yes," he said. "Yes, I did. I hadda go down to her and tell her to move."

"What'd—what'd it feel like, when you tapped her on the shoulder? You did feel—something, didn't you?"

He looked at me like he thought I was crazy. "Sure I felt something. It felt good and firm and solid, that's what. But I felt it even worse a minute later; she took and poked her elbow into my ribs." And he rubbed himself there, where it must have been still a little sore.

I left him and went down that aisle to the ring again, and stood around. The ring looked so empty, so still and lonely now. Then on the way back, trudging up it, I found it. I stopped and picked it up.

It had been trampled half to death, nearly. I had to blow on it, and stroke it against my sleeve, to clear it off and get it back in shape. It was blue and it was silk, that was about all I could be sure of in the smoky, blurred light of the arena. I smiled grimly to myself as I looked at it. First I was going to throw it right away again, but instead I kept it. Put it in my billfold and put it away. Then I went on to do what I'd told him I was going to do: see Somebody about Something.

It didn't take long. Shackley was standing waiting for me in the open doorway of his office, all the way at the back, where they were sitting ready to count out the receipts.

"Come on in," he invited. "There's something coming to you. We did all right tonight."

"There's something coming to you too," was all I said.

The last time I'd struck a blow was that day outside the tenement, when I first met O'Reilly. I struck one now again, just one, and I put everything into it that I'd been saving up all those years. Even at that, it mayn't have been much of a wallop, but it was enough to take care of him. He was shrimpy, and soft all over. He went down, loud-checked coat and all, and he put the hand wearing his Sunday diamond—or maybe it was his Saturday-night one—to his jaw and held it there; and it made the place the sock had landed sparkle pretty.

I never saw a guy like him. Money could do anything for him, even take the sting out of a knockdown. He didn't even get sore about being floored like that, just acted stupefied for a minute or two. "What was that for, anyway?" he called out after me, as I turned and stalked away. "We won, didn't we?"

I didn't bother telling him. It wouldn't have done any good. If he didn't know already he'd never learn it now. It wasn't that we'd won that made the difference, it was how we'd won.

It was like making fun of a guy's mother. The one thing that no man should ever do to any other man, not the lowest, not the worst. That's the closest we ever come to God, any one of us. Worse. It was like making fun of a guy's mother after she was dead. Worse still, it was like making fun of a guy's mother, after she was dead, in front of twenty thousand people, all at one time.

Hiring some fat old lady for ten or twenty dollars, rigging her up to look like Mom O'Reilly, putting a piece of blue ribbon in her hand, and sending her waddling down the aisle at the psychological moment, to give him the shot in the arm that he'd needed.

That was the only explanation then, and it still is now.

I took it out and looked at it again the next morning, in the daylight. It was the sort of ribbon they don't make any more; a rich, full-bodied silk. With a thin line of satin traced along each edge, the way a mirror is beveled. And an invisible pattern of flowers sprinkled all over it. When you held it flat, you couldn't see them; when you held it up, they came out. I wondered how he'd been able to match it so exactly. He'd never seen that first one, from long ago.

I went around to my safety-deposit box, in the bank vault, to compare the two. That was where I'd put the little trinket box she'd kept it in, that she'd turned over to me when she died.

They were very strict there. They are in all those places. You had to sign a little admission card first, and they checked your signature with the one on file. Then you had to turn over your duplicate key, and it had to match up with its mate, the original that they kept in their possession. They even had your physical description, and checked you against that. No one but the rightful owner can ever gain access to one of those boxes. Finally, they even kept a record of each visit you made. It showed the last time I'd been in there, as I knew already, was over a year before.

I took the trinket box out and opened it. It hadn't been disturbed, it was just the way she'd left it when she'd turned it over to me. All her little treasures, all the odds and ends, all the keepsakes and mementos, were still in it, in their rightful places. All but one thing. All but the ribbon I'd come to look at.

There was still a little cranny, a niche, where it had been tucked, all rolled up tight; but it was empty, there was nothing in it now.

The only ribbon was the one I was holding in my hand, that I'd brought in with me, from the arena floor, last night.

APE
MAN

Jack Ritchie

I was on the davenport with my eyes closed and the comic books scattered around, some of them on the floor and some on my chest. I breathed deeply and wondered idly whether I should try snoring. They might get a kick out of that.

"I guess the heavy reading wore out Brute's brain," Harry said.

Harry Whitman earned his living writing a daily sports column for the *Courier*. I heard the cards being riffled and I slitted my eyes open just enough to see.

Max Kaminski, my manager, was looking at his drink with a sour expression on his face and Ed Weaver of the *Journal* had his jaws working on a wad of gum.

"I got it now," Harry said, snapping his fingers. "Prognathous. Yep, that's what it is."

Ed Weaver raised a bored eyebrow. "Explain it to me."

"Prognathous," Harry said. "His jaw sticks out. Like an ape's."

A heavy jaw, yes, I thought tiredly. Possibly mesognathous, but definitely not prognathous.

"One of these days he'll understand you when you make those cracks," Ed said. "You're liable to lose your pearly whites."

Harry had a high laugh and I wondered how fast it would stop if I suddenly got up and grabbed him by the collar.

"The whiskey is gone now boys," Max said. "When are you leaving?"

"Once more around," Ed said. He looked at me. "You got to admit he's not pretty. You getting used to him, Max?"

Harry's chair creaked as he crossed his legs and lounged back. "Should we wake the beast and get his statement on the fight tonight?"

"Make up your own," Max said. "You know how to do it."

"If this kid Barlow uses his head and keeps in close, he might get the decision," Ed said.

"There won't be any decision," Max said. "Brute will get to him in less than six."

I stretched, yawned, and sat up. I watched Harry deal off and then he and Ed got to their feet.

"What round is it gonna be, Brute?" Harry asked.

"When Max tells me," I said.

After they left, Max got out his box of bicarbonate. "Sometimes I think you're making a mistake," he said. "Look at the publicity Tunney got for knowing how to read and write."

"He looked the part," I said. "And I don't. What I have between my ears is my own business and I want to keep it that way."

Max is a short man carrying around weight that would look better on someone six inches taller. "When they look at your eyes they ought to know," he said. "The sparkle of a good brain is there." He braced himself as he looked at the glass in his hand. "Don't they ever get you sore?"

I slipped into my coat. "I'm going out for some fresh air and more comic books," I said.

Max finished his glass. "Do you ever really read those things?"

"Sure," I said. "I'm crazy about Superman."

Downstairs I hesitated a moment before going out into the streets. I didn't like going out there to be stared at, but I couldn't stay in the hotel room all day either. After a few hours, the place always seemed like a cage to me.

I walked slowly, trying to concentrate on the fresh air and sunlight, but the familiar moisture formed on my palms as I saw the disbelief in the faces of the people I passed, or the shocks, or the suppressed smirks.

I went about six blocks when I saw the library. I halted at the bottom of the stairs, toying with the idea of going in. Back home the librarians were used to me, though they still kept their distance, but this was a strange city.

I was about to move on when two high school girls came out. Their eyes widened as they saw me and I could almost hear sighs of relief once they were safely past me.

They glanced back over their shoulders to make sure they had been right and I felt the anger getting me again. I wanted to run. To run someplace where I could be alone and where there were no eyes to look at me.

But you can't, I thought, shaking myself out of it. At least not yet. I stared at the library and made up my mind to go in.

I wandered along the stacks, sampling a volume here and there. Gradually the quiet worked on me and I could feel the tenseness seeping out. I turned down one aisle and was half way down when I realized that it was a little too shadowy to see the titles. I turned back and started for the light switch.

The slim silhouette of a girl appeared before me and her hand went to the light switch.

We were only a foot or two apart when she snapped on the light. She gasped when she saw me and the books in her arm slipped. I caught them before they dropped to the floor.

The tenseness again frayed on my nerves. "I know it's startling to see me," I said. "But don't scream here. We must have silence at all times." I put the books back in her arms and went back down to the middle of the aisle.

I was conscious of her still standing there. Look all you want, I said to myself, but I'm not going to be chased away by what you think.

In a few seconds I heard her footsteps as she came nearer. She stopped in the section next to me and added one of her books to the shelves.

Brave girl to come so near to me, I thought bitterly. I glanced covertly at her and our eyes met. I noticed that hers were violet and that she had soft, brown hair.

She didn't look away. "I'm sorry about seeming so shocked," she said.

"It's all right."

"It's just that out of the dark . . ."

"Your apology is accepted," I said. I pulled a book from the row and paged through it. I could feel her eyes still examining me.

"Dogs sometimes bark at me," I said. "But generally children love me for my basic kindness and gentle qualities." I snapped the book shut and put it back. I started leaving, but she put her hand on my arm.

"I'll go," she said. "I didn't mean to disturb you."

I looked at her more carefully. There was a peculiar seriousness to her expression and there was no fear.

"I was only browsing," I said. "I couldn't take out any of them anyway. I don't have a library card."

"I'm one of the librarians here," she said. "If you will come to the desk I'll see that you're issued one."

I studied her face for a hint of mockery and then I said, "All right. Let's get me a card." I followed her to the desk. She pulled a blank library card out of a drawer and rolled it into a typewriter.

"Your name, please?" she asked.

"Westwood." I said. "Robert Westwood."

Her head tilted up slightly in disbelief and I knew that she must have seen photographs of me and knew who I was supposed to be.

The tightness returned to the back of my neck and I knew I had to get out of there. "Never mind the card," I said. I walked to the door and turned to look at her.

"Yes," I said. "Robert Westwood is my real name. But if it will give you a laugh, make out the card to Brute Brown and send it to the Queen Hotel."

I left the library and started toward the hotel. Why did I have to let it get me, I thought. By now I should be used to being Brute Brown. I slowed down. Snap out of it. A few thousand more and then you can get your island without people or mirrors.

I rested in the hotel room the rest of the day and around 7:30 Max and I went down to the arena. We got our call at 9 P.M. and walked down the aisle to the ring. The fans stood up and craned their necks to get a good look at me as I passed and in the safety of their numbers I heard a few giggles.

When the announcer was through with the introductions and the statistics, Barlow and I met in the center of the ring for instructions and I looked him over again. He was about my age and I wondered what it must feel like to be a clean-cut kid with blue eyes.

Barlow had a string of 21 wins; he was one of the best fighters around. But looking at him now I felt the sickness in my stomach when I saw that he was scared. He avoided my eyes and one foot moved nervously back and forth on the canvas.

That's how I get almost all of them, I thought wearily. They come in here scared silly. They've heard about me and they've seen pictures of me and they've met me at the weigh-in and for the photographers. But now that we're in the ring everything is different. Nothing their managers told them makes them ready to fight.

You're as strong as he is, kid, and a lot faster, they told him. All this ape stuff is just publicity. They had a doc fix up his face to make him look that way, kid. He was never pretty to begin with, but he's human, kid. Human.

I listened dully to the referee and then went back to my corner for the bell. When it rang I had to go three-quarters of the way across the ring to get to Barlow.

Barlow was known for smiling slightly when he fought, but the smile wasn't there now. His face was unnaturally white and his movements stiff and awkward. I could see that he was wondering how it was going to feel to be knocked out for the first time. He was wondering how bad a beating he was going to have to take before that happened.

I could do it right now, I thought. I could crowd him into that corner and it would all be over in a few seconds.

Barlow grabbed and held as I came in and as I leaned on him and waited for the referee to part us, I suddenly wondered why I had to win. Suppose I lost this one and then a few more. I looked out at the crowd. They'd still come, all those people. And that was really why they were here in the first place. They wanted to see me beaten to the floor.

Barlow fell into another clinch and after we were parted I threw out a few light lefts, just stiff enough to sting him. It was a dull first round and at the bell they booed both of us.

We came out for the second and I noticed that Barlow's movements were more fluid. He was still cautious and he covered up and clinched whenever he thought I might do some damage, but he was gaining some confidence.

I kept my left in his face when I could, but I wasn't doing him any harm. Defensively I reacted automatically to the few punches he threw, almost lulled by the steady crowd noises. It was only an occasional loud ringside voice that woke me from my daze.

With ten seconds left in the round, Barlow's long left snaked out and caught me on the side of the head. It brought the crowd to its feet but I held until the bell sounded.

In my corner, Max handed me the bottle. "If you really want to go to sleep so much, I can get you a pillow."

Barlow came out for the third with a faint smile on his face. He was still alive and functioning after two rounds and it pleasantly surprised him. He was beginning to get the idea that his managers were right.

Experimentally I sent in a harder punch and watched the confidence fade from his eyes. But I didn't press it and as the round wore on, the smile on his face gradually returned.

He began scoring with those long lefts. I didn't mind them much. They stung for a second or two, and then I waited for the next one.

I learned now with drowsy curiosity just when to expect them. First there was the squeak of Barlow's shoe on the rosin, and then the left. Always the squeak and then the left.

At first I mechanically clinched after every one of them, and listened to the delighted noises of the people.

But then I stopped falling into the clinch and I stopped listening for the squeak on the canvas. I just listened to the people. The human beings who paid money for their seats and the more money they paid the closer they could get.

In my corner at the end of the round I stared numbly at my shoes. "Brute," Max said. "What's wrong?"

"Nothing. Everything is fine with Brute. The Brute is feeling fine."

I waited until the gong before I got off my stool. Barlow met me in the center of the ring. The smile was permanent now. He wasn't afraid and he knew he was going to win. He was going to beat me to a pulp and he wasn't going to mind at all.

The lefts were there again, but now he was using his right too. A left, and when I dropped my hands, the right. But they weren't hurting me any more and I wanted them to be harder.

And suddenly the roar of the crowd woke me and I found myself sitting on the canvas. I was faintly surprised as I sat there watching the ringsiders with their distorted faces and their bright, satisfied eyes.

I closed my eyes and waited for the count. I could get up, but I wasn't going to. I was tired. So much more tired than I had ever been in my life.

But the referee wasn't counting and I opened my eyes to see why. Barlow was still standing over me, with the referee tugging at his arm.

Barlow's lips were moving as he looked down at me. They seemed to be twisting out the words. "Get up, Ape Man. So I can knock you right down again. Ape Man."

The referee got Barlow to a neutral corner and he began counting over me. I looked back at the ringsiders and they seemed to be saying it too. "Get up, Ape Man. Get up, Ape Man.

"Get up, Ape man. We don't want it this easy. Get up, Ape Man, so that you can be cut to ribbons. Once more. At least once more."

The redness of hate came to my eyes and the Ape Man got up. He stood there and waited for Barlow. He waited for Barlow and all the people in the world. He waited until they were all close enough and then he struck.

The surprise in Barlow's eyes was glazed in the thin slice of a second and he collapsed to the canvas.

The crowd's roar died and there was the murmur of shock and disappointment. The Ape Man turned and looked directly into the television cameras. How many people are looking at you right now, Brute, he asked himself. How many millions of people who are disappointed.

Max and I got back to the hotel at 11 P.M. and a blonde in chinchilla waited outside the doors of our room. She came up to me and ran her hands along my shoulders and down my arms. Her eyes glowed with eager intensity. "Magnificent," she said. "Magnificent Brute."

I said nothing as I watched the quick way she breathed.

"Brute," she said. "Come downstairs with me. Just one drink, Brute. Please, Brute."

"Maybe," I said. "Maybe later."

"You will?" she said, her tongue darting nervously over sharp white teeth. "You will, Brute?"

"I'll see," I said.

I followed Max into the room and he locked the door. I went to the davenport and sat down.

"Are you?" Max asked. "You saw her eyes, didn't you?"

I looked at him. "Max," I said. "How many women chase after me? Any kind of women?"

Max went to the suitcases and brought out a bottle. He poured himself a drink.

"Would it help if I drink, Max?" I asked. "Will it make me happy?"

"I don't know," Max said. He stared at his drink and then swallowed it.

I went over to the bed and lay down. "I'm going to try to sleep now, Max," I said. "It's either sleep or I go downstairs."

I closed my eyes and began hoping for sleep. For a long, long sleep that would never end.

And it was a long sleep, but not long enough. I woke up at 11 the next morning. I went to the bathroom and washed and shaved and then I came back and looked out of the window.

It was a clear bright day with tufts of clouds moving slowly in the blue sky. It was the kind of a morning when you should want to live. It was a day of sunlight when you take your girl to a picnic.

I opened the window and felt the air moving past my face. It was fresh and clean with the smell of life.

And then I looked down.

I looked down nine stories and there they were. People moving about on foot and in their cars and their buses. The good, kind people who could walk the streets without frightening anyone.

I heard the door open behind me. Max said quietly, "Brute."

Just a little push with my toes, I thought. That's all it takes and then no more Brute.

Max spoke again. "Bob," he said.

I stared down for half a minute more and then I shut the window. "Thanks," I said.

Max stood in the middle of the room, his brown eyes watching me.

"Max," I said. "I'm through. I'm quitting."

"I could see it," Max said.

"I'm sorry, Max. I hate to run out on you after you brought me this far, but I can't take any more. You'll be out money, Max."

Max kept his eyes on the cigar he was unwrapping. "The hell with the money. A man's heart is more important."

"I'll write you post cards when the mail boat comes to my island," I said. "If you want them."

"I want them," Max said. He took an envelope out of his pocket. "This was left at the desk this morning, Bob."

It was a plain envelope with no address on it. I fingered the paper and inside I felt an oblong piece of cardboard. I felt suddenly afraid and my fingers began to tremble. I tore the envelope open and let the cardboard slide out.

I held it for a moment and then I turned it over. It was a library card made out in the name of Robert Westwood.

I looked at the printing of my name until it became blurred to me. After a while I noticed that Max was still watching me.

"Haven't you got something else to look at, Max?" I said.

Max looked worried. "You still haven't got any bad ideas, have you?"

"No, Max," I said.

She was at the desk when I walked into the library and she smiled as I came toward her.

"Thanks for delivering the card," I said. From where I stood I could smell the perfume she was wearing.

"Did you see the fight last night?" I asked.

"No," she said.

"Did you want to?"

"No."

"It was my last one," I said. "Now I'm going to buy an island and live there."

She considered me for a moment. "Do you have to?" she asked.

The bitterness hovered over me again. "Look at me once more," I said.

Her eyes went over my battered face. "Do you really have to?"

"Yes," I said. "I really have to." I looked carefully at her upturned face. "I'll take out some books now," I said. "And I'll come back."

"Yes," she said, her eyes still on my face.

I had trouble saying it. "Do you know what I mean? I'll be back."

"Yes," she said. "I know."

She smiled again and I looked into her violet eyes. They were eyes that saw something no other woman had ever seen in me. She was looking at a man.

SCRAP IRON

Larry Sternig

HEAVYWEIGHT CHAMPIONSHIP OF THE SYSTEM

TONIGHT AT EIGHT
INVINCIBLE vs THE CRUSHER
1000 POUND CLASS

TUNE YOUR VISI TO KWP NETWORK

Every shuttle platform on Mars, and every crossroad, carried a duplicate of that sign today. Everybody would read it, although most all the fans knew about it already. And at eight tonight practically every visiset in the system would tune in on the battle of the century.

Walt Correvon sighed. All those people were going to be disappointed, and most of them would blame him. Kra Kigor's Crusher had been champion long enough, most people felt. Most planets, except the people of Mars, of course, wanted to see the challenger from Earth win, partly because they disliked The Crusher and partly because—well, they wanted to give big Invincible a chance to clear himself of those old charges of having thrown a fight.

That old suspicion, an unjustified one, had almost died out now. But after tonight—

Walt remembered that it had been nearly an hour since he'd had the

bad news. Maybe by now Pete would know more. Anyway, there wasn't
a shuttlecar in sight.

He stepped quickly into a communicabooth and set the dials.

"Yeah?" said a voice. A voice that sounded weary and desperate.

"Pete, this is Correvon. Can you patch up Vince?"

"I got all his guts out, Mr. Correvon. I'm doing the best I can, but it
looks bad. And all the cogs in that left tibia are—"

"You told me that, Pete. But listen, can we fight or do we have to
forfeit?"

"I've got ten men working on him. We sent his right arm to Tyron
where they do that tyronium welding. We're sticking in a full new set of
tubes, even though it don't leave us any spares."

"Skip the details, Pete. Is or isn't Vince going to be ready to fight? Do
we or don't we lose that half-million guarantee and sacrifice that
hundred thousand we posted for a forfeit?"

"You'll be able to try with him, Mr. Correvon. But, frankly, the best
we can make him will be a pushover."

"I'm on my way there," said Walt. "Keep at it. I've *got* to get in an
hour or two at the controls. No telling how they'll respond after the
rebuild."

There was a worried frown on his forehead as he stepped from the
booth and got on the first westbound shuttlecar. He caught a glimpse of
himself in the door mirror and immediately straightened out his face as
best he could. If a newscast reporter caught him looking like that—

At the transfer platform, he had another short wait, and again he
stepped into a communicabooth.

"Murray apartments," said a voice.

"Is Dot there? Walt Correvon speaking."

"Just a moment, Mr. Correvon."

And then, *her* voice: "Walt, what are you doing up? I thought you'd
sleep all day to get ready for the fight."

"Don't worry about me," Walt said quickly. "Listen, honey—have
you got the receiver set for privacy? I mean, could anyone else in the
building be listening in on another outlet?"

Click of a switch. "It's private now, Walt. Why, is anything wrong?"

He lowered his voice. "Honey, they got at Vince last night."

"*Invincible?* Walt, how . . . what did they—?"

"Acid. Pete says it seems to have been dilute corrositrate. Mixed with
oil and put in at his oil-holes. It's a mess. The stuff wasn't strong
enough to eat *through* anything, just enough to weaken the whole works.
And we can't prove a thing; they got away with it clean and didn't leave
a trace. If we complain, you know what'll happen. It will look like our
alibi for throwing the fight. That old scandal—"

"But Walt, would Kra Kigor actually—?"

"He would, and did. He's backed The Crusher with his whole fortune, almost. But we haven't a shred of proof; it wouldn't even be our word against his. It'd be our guess against his word. All we can do is try to have Vince ready, go through with it and do our best."

"Oh, Walt, does *Dad know?* This must be awful for him; he's got every credit he has tied up in Vince. You know he invested everything in those super-selenium response centers you figured out."

"He knows, but he won't get there for a while yet. Soon as I know more I'll call you and—"

"No, Walt. I'm going there, too. I'll see you. 'Bye."

Walt left the booth and caught the first southbound car. Ten minutes later he entered the training quarters.

Pete Werrah, the head mechanic, surrounded by a dozen helpers, scarcely looked up. Walt was tall enough to peer over their shoulders at the thing on the worktable.

Contender for the heavyweight crown; intricately interlocking dural-loy plates, many of them now removed, covered a mass of machinery. Activating mechanisms that implemented the radio controls, more deli-cate than the works of the finest watch; muscle cable gear chains, com-pact but tremendously powerful. As powerful and efficient as ten years' work and a half million credits investment could make them. And the radio controls themselves, responsive to the shadowy ghost of an ampere and tuned to a waveband as fine as frog hair.

"How's it coming, Pete?"

The mechanic looked up and ran a grimy hand across an already streaked forehead. "We can't work miracles, Mr. Correvon. We got ten hours now till the fight, and it's taken ten weeks to get him as smooth as he was before this happened."

"But isn't there a chance that—?"

"No. He'll be working tonight, after a fashion. He'll be able to walk out there and take a few wallops before he goes down. That'll save Mr. Murray losing the forfeit. But dance him away from The Crusher. All defense, and you might last him a few minutes, maybe, long enough to make it look good."

Walt groaned. "If it's that bad, maybe we better tell—"

"Sure, and you know what everybody'll say. Alibi. Crying in ad-vance. Maybe trying to shift the betting odds. And the ones that have already bet on him will . . ." He shrugged and went back to work on Vince.

Walt walked moodily across the big room to the portable control board and sat down in front of it. Tonight—in front of a visicast audience of millions—he'd sit down at the control board and the big Martian, owner-operator of the mighty Crusher, would sit down at one similar to it. And what was supposed to be the most important sporting event of all time would turn out to be a fiasco. It would have been a great battle if—

The juice wasn't on, but Walt let his fingers drift among the controls, slid his feet into the slipper-levers that controlled the robot's footwork— or part of it—and tried to visualize Vince out there responding—

But it was like trying to play a tune on a piano without any strings. Without Vince responding to those delicate controls, the practice was worthless; didn't mean a thing.

There was a click of heels across the floor and he turned, knowing from the sound that it was Dot Murray. He stood up and turned just in time to take her in his arms.

"Walt, Dad's here. I came up in the lift with him. He's talking to the members of the commission, trying to see if he can get a postponement without forfeiting. If only—"

"With the weight Kigor swings with that board—" Walt said, shaking his head. "Nope, honey, we'll have to try. Let's see if the news is out yet."

He crossed to the newscaster and flicked the switch. "Commentator Broo's on the air. He generally gets things before they even happen. He—"

"Shhh."

". . . and that," said the newscaster, "pretty well takes care of the space situation. Now for something really important, friends, THE BIG FIGHT. A nasty little rumor has just come in that Murray, owner of Invincible, is asking a postponement. He claims that *someone* (Why not come right out and accuse Kigor by name, Murray?) has sabotaged Big Vince. Or maybe bribed him? Can it be that Correvon, Vince's speed-artist operator, is going to take another—Pardon, delete that word 'another' for lack of proof in the first instance—dive? Not that I think so myself, but, after all, there is a lot at stake and some of the big bettors think—"

Walt reached out and flicked the dial to another station.

His face was white with anger. "See, honey? Damn them, we'll fight The Crusher if I have to put on a suit of antique armor and go out there myself and—"

"Walt, just how much *does* depend on this fight?"

"The championship of the System, Dot. Not to mention a little matter like my savings. I—"

Pete Werrah's voice, yelling across the room, cut in on them. "Hey, guys! Bring that left leg over here!"

*   *   *

The light above the arena was almost blindingly brilliant. Seated at the control board and looking out over the top of it into the ten-yard circular ring, Walt Correvon fiddled with the controls and watched Big Vince shuffle and shadow-box in the marked-off neutral area to the left of the ring. On the right, The Crusher, champion of the Solar System, was going through similar gyrations under the control of Kra Kigor, seated opposite Correvon on the far side of the ring.

Weighing in was over. The Crusher had scaled two pounds under the half-ton maximum allowed in the heavyweight class. Vince was five pounds under. Three pounds of metal difference on a thousand pounds —but that three pounds had been eaten off by acid, Walt knew, at points where the damage done gave him an almost hopeless disadvantage.

Pete and his crew had performed near-miracles in getting Vince ready at all. There hadn't been time for the usual ultra-delicate adjustments. Vince was slow to respond. The automatics were okay, though. Walt set the backward shuffle switch and watched Vince's footwork.

Left feint. Right cross, third of a second too slow.

"Testing," said the microphone. The lights grew even brighter as the four giant visireceptor cameras swung into action.

"Focus okay," said another microphone.

"Seven fifty-seven," said the shrill voice of the invisible audiclock. After eight, it would sing out simply "One" for one minute of elapsed time of the fight, "Two" for two, and monotonously on until the sixty-minute limit.

"Into the ring," came the order. Walt's fingers danced over the keyboard and Vince climbed the ropes, stood at immobile attention just inside them.

"Seven fifty-eight," shrilled the audiclock.

The Crusher was in the ring, too, now, his six-inch-thick arms swinging aggressively. Twelve yards away, Kigor was grinning at him across the top of the control board. A sardonic, amused grin that made Walt almost wish that he and Kigor were going out there into the ring, instead of the fighting robots.

Men *had* done that once, he recalled. At least Earthmen did. Way back in ancient, barbarous times. Men had fought with their bare hands in square rings—or had it been bare hands? No, he remembered now; they'd used a kind of leather glove called a cestus. Gladiators, they'd called them. There had been a great gladiator named Dempsey, who was ten feet tall, and there'd been the champion gladiator Joseph Louis, who had also been a famous aviator. He'd left the ring at the height of his career to fly a plane called the Brown Bomber in the Earth war of liberation.

Or was all that merely legend, like the old belief in werewolves and gangsters? Why should human beings have fought one another for the amusement of crowds, when robots could fight so much more efficiently? With such satisfying clangor and reverberation of blows? Why, one tap from a bantamweight robot would knock—

"Seven fifty-nine."

"On the ether," barked the referee, who operated in a glass cubicle overhead. "In this corner—" Walt didn't listen to the introduction of the robots and their operators. He was getting his hands into exact juxtaposition over the keyboard, flexing and limbering his fingers.

The referee finished. "Two-way," ordered the direction microphone, and suddenly there was the roar of the crowd. All over Mars, indeed all over the system, millions of people grouped in front of visisets were yelling and cheering. Those yells and cheers came back to the station pickups and were blended into a rising, falling "roar of the crowd" background without which no major sportcast would be complete. Individual voices were only rarely distinguishable, but without that crowd-roar the event itself would have lost color.

"Eight o'clock," shrieked the audivoice of the automatic timer. "Go!"

Walt let Vince fall backward and bounce off the springy steel ring cables, then charge forward. There wouldn't be any chance, this time, to feel out his opponent with a few minutes of cautious boxing. His one slim chance was a quick assault.

Vince rushed, his ponderous footsteps shaking the ring, left arm extended, right cocked. The Crusher braced to meet the attack. Vince's right—too slow. The Crusher ducked under it and countered with a blow to the chest that sounded like gyrocars crashing head-on. Vince fell back from the impact, and there was a dent in his chest-plates.

He bobbed, and came up with an uppercut—or what would have been one if his responses hadn't been slowed by the weakening of the acid and the hasty rebuild. The blow whistled upward past The Crusher's chin, and a counter-blow that would have ended the contest flashed right at Vince's face. Walt's index finger, moving with the speed of lightning, tapped a key and Vince's head jerked to the right. Fast enough to avoid the full force of the blow. It rasped along his metal cheek and took off his left ear.

Then he was safely back out of range, and circling. That wild rush had failed. There wasn't a dent or a scratch on The Crusher to show for it.

"One," shrilled the audiclock. Invincible had survived one minute—out of sixty.

Walt watched The Crusher warily. What was Kigor up to? He could force the fight easily now by wading in. But Kigor had some other plan of battle. The Crusher merely turned, as though on a pivot, while Vince circled. The Crusher's left wasn't extended; both fists were cocked at his sides and he looked wide open. He was inviting Vince to lead, standing pat.

Walt shot a glance at the other operator. Kigor was intent on the robots, waiting—for something. What was his plan of action?

The roar of the crowd grew; getting impatient. They demanded noise and action. They were paying millions, via the visiset tax, to see this fight, and they wanted their credits' worth of metallic clangor.

Well—he couldn't circle forever. Walt's fingers moved swiftly and smoothly. His battler moved ahead, bobbed and weaved once, then swung his left at The Crusher's head.

And then Walt knew what Kigor had been waiting for: instead of ducking, The Crusher's bludgeon of a fist lashed out almost simultaneously with Vince's. The fists met in midair between the robots with the combined force of the blows.

There was a crack and rend of metal. Vince's arm, the muscle-cables hopelessly broken, dropped to his side. And then The Crusher was suddenly swarming forward, raining blow after reverberating blow on his crippled opponent.

Walt's fingers danced like mad, making Vince ride with those devastating sledge-hammer wallops. Shuffling him back in a circular path of retreat that would keep him from being trapped and smashed against the ropes.

Somehow, despite the terrific concentration it took to do that, Walt caught a glimpse of Kigor's face. The Martian was grinning.

There was a cold ball of something that seemed too physical for anger, somewhere inside Walt Correvon. If he'd needed any proof of Kigor's connection with the sabotage of Vince, that grin furnished it; that grin and the tactics he'd just used with The Crusher.

He'd known that acid had weakened those muscle cables; he'd known the inevitable damage to Vince from deliberately meeting a blow with another, fist to fist, force to force.

Walt kept Vince in the automatic back-shuffle so he could concentrate every bit of attention on finding an opening for a telling blow with Vince's one good arm. His only chance now was to land with that right on a vital spot.

It swung like a mace, that right hand of Vince's. Once in a while it got through. The Crusher wasn't unmarked any more. But Vince was taking four blows for every one he gave. His other ear was gone. What had been his face now looked like scrap iron.

The Crusher came through with a terrific left hook that would have torn Vince's head off, if Walt hadn't seen it coming and set the balance compensator to ride with the blow. Not that he set it consciously: there isn't time to do much consciously when one directs a fighting robot. It's a matter of split-second automatic responses. The blow flung Vince backward, but he kept his balance.

It seemed to stagger The Crusher, too. He took a full back step, and, under Walt's frantic fingers, Vince waded in, swinging. And then Walt knew that The Crusher's backing had been deliberate; that he'd walked into it again. The Crusher's fist met Vince's squarely. And again there was the crack of metal and Vince's right arm came only part way up in response to Walt's quick jab of the biceps-button.

The crowd was roaring for the knockout.

The Crusher stormed in, now completely confident and completely belligerent, facing an opponent whose arms no longer worked. Blows came so fast that Vince could dodge only a few of them.

For a black instant, Walt almost jabbed at the off key. Why wait until Vince was battered down? He was helpless out there; why not let him fall and get it over with? True, Big Vince was practically scrap iron already, but—

He caught another glimpse of Kigor, grinning triumphantly. And there was that cold something inside Walt again. If it was anger, it was a kind he'd never known before. Something more. He seemed to see that saturnine grinning face through a reddish haze, and there was a roaring in his ears that drowned out the clangor of steel and the scream of the crowd. He was in the grip of an emotion he hadn't known existed. It wasn't just in his mind. It was in all of him. In his fists; it clenched them for him. He wanted to—

He did.

Through that red haze he jumped to his feet and vaulted over the cables, across the ring toward Kra Kigor. He was going to knock the—

Suddenly something monstrous loomed in his path. Kigor had seen him coming. Like the well-oiled piece of machinery that he was, The Crusher wheeled from battering his helpless opponent, and blocked the way across the ring to Kigor. Big Vince, on his automatics, still shuffled meaninglessly backward away from nothing.

The Crusher raised his huge fist. It swung toward him; but Walt Correvon's nerves were timed to the same split-second impulse as those of the robot's operator. And he was trained to do things first and think them out afterward. He couldn't have told you how it was possible for a fragile hundred-eighty-pound man to knock down a thousand-pound metal robot, but his body did it for him.

He slid to one side of that deadly blow and brought up his own right to The Crusher's steel jaw. At the last instant he opened his fist to make it a flat-handed blow. It stung, but to have struck with clenched fingers would have broken every bone in his hand.

And The Crusher was falling—forward. Automatically, seeing a blow about to land on his robot's face, Kigor set the balance compensator—the same setting he would have used to compensate for a sledge-hammer steel-fisted blow from another robot. And Walt's blow—comparatively the mere brush of a feather—put The Crusher off balance. He slid aside as the huge steel robot toppled, and went on through to the other side, reaching for Kigor.

He yanked the operator out of his seat before he could get The Crusher back on his feet again. There was sudden panic in Kigor's face and he wasn't grinning any more. He gave a yell for help, looking upward toward the referee's cubicle, and then tore loose from Correvon's grip and ran. There was only one direction open—into the arena. He dove between two of the cables.

Walt could have caught and pulled him back—but there'd be more room inside the ring for what he wanted to do. Instead he vaulted over the cables again, and landed beside Kigor. As the latter straightened up, Walt landed a stinging flat-handed blow to his face. Kra Kigor's cheek turned white, then red.

"If you want to talk to the referee," Walt raged, "tell him what you did to Vince."

"You're crazy. I—"

Walt hit him again, and suddenly and surprisingly the Martian galvanized into action. It was obvious now that he wasn't a coward; his first reaction had merely been surprise. After all, fighting was against the law. Nobody actually hit anyone else in modern times.

And as Kigor's fist suddenly exploded in his face, Walt realized, through a haze of pain, that getting Kigor to fight was only half of it. He had to lick him, and the Martian was bigger and perhaps stronger. The blow rocked Walt back on his heels, and he retreated to get his balance; then bored back in, fists pumping.

He tried to imagine that he was Big Vince; to dodge and punch as he would have directed the robot to do. But this was different, very different. Outside a ring, one could see clearly. But here, fists got in your eyes.

He fell back, circling, planning a new offensive. He remembered to keep his left extended, to feint with it and try to punch his opponent off balance while he brought up the right with enough force to act as the heavy artillery.

The dull thud of punches sounded strange. They didn't clang as they should. There was a confused roaring in his ears, though. And when Kigor's fist slammed his jaw, suddenly there were bright little spots of light in front of his eyes that looked like stars.

But he shook his head, and it cleared. He put his head down and bored in, both fists lashing out like rocket blasts against Kigor's ribs. He'd have to hurry. In a minute the police would come in here and break it up and arrest him. He lunged forward, boring his head in under the Martian's chin, and pumped those short, vicious blows into the abdomen as hard and as fast as he could. Kigor was grunting, gasping.

Then suddenly Kigor's thick arms wrapped around his shoulders in a clinch and he was being pulled off balance and thrown. They crashed to the floor together. Correvon gave a convulsive wriggle that put him behind Kigor and locked his legs around his middle. When Kigor tried to reach back, Walt caught his arm and bent it until Kigor howled suddenly.

"Talk, and I'll let you go," he panted.

The thud of ponderous footsteps, and suddenly the words that Kigor was howling made sense. "Vince! Let go, you fool, or he'll fall on top of us and kill us!"

Walt looked up. Invincible, still shuffling automatically backward around the ring, was five feet away and backing directly toward them. Five more backward steps and he'd trip over them and fall. Almost a thousand pounds of compact metal would crash down on their interlocked bodies.

"Let go! You'll get us both killed. Vince'll drop on us! He weighs a thousand—"

"Not quite," Walt panted. "A little less after that acid. Talk, and talk fast. Or we stay here."

"You—" Kigor struggled violently, but he was caught fast. The big robot was only two paces away now. "You—"

"Okay," said Walt. "Then he falls on us."

Cold sweat streamed down Kigor's large forehead. The ponderous thud of another footstep. "Yes!" he screamed frantically. "I put acid in him last night. I hired—"

They almost didn't make it. There wasn't time to get up before Vince's feet would trip over them.

Walt rolled, pulling the Martian with him.

It was morning. Not early morning, for a lot had happened the night before. Not the least part, by any means, being his marriage to Dot Murray. You could hardly call it an elopement, since Mr. Murray had given his blessings and gone with them to the registrar.

Walt sat up in bed and stretched. His movements awakened his wife and she opened her eyes sleepily and yawned.

"Morning, Mrs. Correvon," he sang out, smiling down at her. "And how's my—"

"Walt, turn on the newscaster. I want to hear—"

"—that we won the fight? You know that, honey." But he flicked the switch.

"Big news of the morning," said the commentator, "is the sudden demand for revival of an ancient sport. I believe it used to be known on Earth as the art of fisticuffs. You've already heard, of course, that The Crusher was disqualified last night after his operator's confession of sabotage—in fact, most of you heard that confession yourselves, and the excitement that followed. Invincible is now heavyweight champion.

"But the real news is that Sportscasts, Inc., has been swamped with requests for restoration of the ancient sport. The visiset spectators have found a new thrill; they went mad last night at the spectacle of a real flesh-and-blood battle. The Commission has appointed a research committee to rediscover the rules that used to govern pre-robot fistic contests. They have named Walt Correvon as the first modern champion of the system and are seeking an opponent to challenge—"

"Walt! You wouldn't—"

"Shhh!"

"It is rumored that he will be offered a half-million guarantee, and a percentage of the visiset tax for the battle. Many believe the new sport will completely overshadow robot boxing in popularity. And now for my predictions on the inter-solar races—"

Walt's fingers snapped the switch. They were trembling just a little. "Dot!" he said, putting his arms around her. "We're rich! *Now* are you glad you married me?"

"But Walt—you might get hurt—"

"Phooey. Listen, honey, that audience last night found out it's fun to watch a fight, but I learned—Dot, I learned, that it's *fun to fight*. Sometimes, anyway. Maybe those ancients weren't so dumb after all."

ENCOUNTER WITH
A KING

William F. Nolan

A side from the raw circus flash of the "Dancer WEBB vs. King SOLAMAN" fight poster newly tacked to the pitted screen door, the Hot Shot Eatery was like a thousand other timeworn roadside cafes in Kansas. Beneath a twist of dirt-streaked neon a rusting red metal DRINK COCA COLA sign clung stubbornly to the flaking wind-eroded clapboard front, and an opaque sheen of grease clouded the two plate glass windows.

Inside, at the end of the long wooden lunch counter, Anthony T. Webb sat on a peeling oilcloth covered stool, talking to the waitress. He had been called "Dancer" since his sophomore year in high school because whenever he fought—and fighting was his business—he moved fast, on the balls of his feet, dancing in on his target, striking, and dancing away. Fast. Fast and light.

"I recognized you right off from the poster," the waitress said, dabbing idly at the counter top with a frayed cloth. "Read all about you in today's paper..." (Cute girl, Dancer noted, real cute, with a neat little figure under her plain white uniform. Blue eyes, brown soft hair. Nice.) "The sports page told all about how you're supposed to beat this Solaman guy tonight. Tells all about you."

As Dancer listened, he thought: poor kid's probably lonely as hell out here in a Kansas tank town like Railton, with nothing to do but serve coffee and burgers to local characters. Dancer knew he looked real good to her with his sharp Chicago suit and his handsome unmarked face framed by blond curly hair. I must look like something right out of the movies to this kid, he thought. So okay. So let's see if we can wrap this one up, this little no-ring-on-her-finger lonesome-type doll.

"Ever watch the fights?" asked Dancer, lazily raising his head like a cat to smile at her.

She said she didn't. "I'm a baseball nut. I dunno anything about boxing."

"Not much to know," said Dancer. "Like, take tonight. I put on a pair of gloves, and I hit a guy. He ends up on his back and I get paid for putting him there."

The girl's eyes widened. "Then—this is one of those "fixed" fights?"

Dancer chuckled. "No, it's on the square. But putting away an old plowhorse like Solaman is no problem."

"Why do you fight a man if you *know* you can beat him?"

"Because that's how it's done. When you win you move up. And right now I'm moving up."

Sometimes a question like this bothered him. Sometimes, in the early morning hours when sleep was away on the other side of the horizon, Dancer wondered about his real direction in life; his future didn't seem as clear as it should be. Fighting was a dirty game, and the dirt didn't always wash away. But he should be used to it by now. You live with dirt to get where you have to go.

The girl said: "More coffee?"

Dancer leaned forward toward her over the counter. "Look," he said, "I got an extra ticket for tonight." He handed her a small white envelope. "Be my guest, eh?"

The girl hesitated a moment, looking at the envelope. Then she smiled back at him. "Thanks," she said.

Dancer knew he excited her, but she wasn't completely sold yet. After she saw him in action tonight, with his lithe, hard-muscled boxer's body moving smooth as oil up there under the ring lights, when she saw him put away old Solaman sweet as a baby in a crib and heard the crowd cheer his name, *then* she'd be sold. And after the fight he'd have time enough for her before the train to K.C. Just enough time for this lonely little doll.

Dancer checked his watch. Spec and Patchey would be here soon, and he'd agreed to meet them in front of the cafe. "After the fight we'll go somewhere and relax a little," he told the girl while she rang up the sale. "Okay?"

"Sure—okay," she said. "See you."

Dancer walked to the door, knowing she was watching every step he took. Smiling, he opened the screen and stepped into the blaze of Kansas sunlight.

Outside the Hot Shot, Dancer studied the poster announcing his bout with Solaman: Anthony Theodore "Dancer" Webb, 22, unmarried, weight 156. Style: fast and weaving. Record to date: 15 bouts, 13 wins. Potential: the middleweight crown.

Actually, thought Dancer, the record should stand at 14 wins out of 15. The first loss, back in the beginning, was ordinary enough, and could happen to any young fighter on the way up: he'd lacked the savvy and was overmatched. So—a K.O., lights out. But the other one should never have happened, and an odd feeling of guilt lay behind it. A bean-legged kid named Zuckerman had nailed him three months ago in Cincy because . . . damn it, because the kid looked like his brother Tom, who'd been killed overseas, and hitting the kid was like hitting his own flesh. That weakness in himself, that sudden inability to punch, had cost him the fight. But that was a freak thing, meeting a guy who looked like Tommy, and it would never happen again. So why couldn't he forget it? Why the hell keep thinking about it?

The sound of tires on gravel startled Dancer. A battered red and yellow taxi rolled to a stop near the cafe. A voice from the car window said: "Been waiting long, kid?"

Webb turned toward his manager, Spec Leonard, who was now holding the rear door open. Dancer could see Patchey Johnson inside, smiling at him. "We couldn't find a cab in this hick burg," said Patchey.

"No problem," Dancer told them. "Let's go."

And he did not look back at the poster as he climbed into the taxi.

"We got things all set for tonight," Leonard said when Dancer had settled into the seat. "You work out with Patchey in the downtown gym for awhile to loosen up, then you catch a couple hours sleep before the match."

Spec Leonard, with his close-cropped bullet head was one of those ageless people in the sport who could be forty or fifty—or maybe thirty-five when the sun was down. He never told you and you never asked. Spec had handled some of the best. Red Garvey had been one of his boys, and Omaha Charlie Ross and Dutch Nielson and Kid Latimar. He'd taken them on when they were awkward punks with six arms and made them great. Patchey Johnson had introduced Dancer to Leonard. "Here's the next champ," he'd said. "You manage him, I train him, and the kid'll go all the way."

Fat and rosy-cheeked, Johnson was a calculating man under his loud façade of humor and fast talk. Single-minded and unrelenting in his profession, he trained fighters to do one thing only: to win—and that meant no cigarettes or liquor or late hours in town with their women; that meant roadwork and the rope and the bags; that meant a steady unbroken string of days at camp with no easing off, no break in the toughening rhythm. You worked like hell for Patchey Johnson because you knew he would settle for nothing less.

"Don't be so sure of this guy," Spec Leonard told them, pulling the red tab and twisting the cellophane from a pack of Luckies. "He may be over the hill but he's got plenty of savvy and he can still put out the lights with that big left of his if he gets the chance."

"Yeah, and like when has that been lately?" asked Patchey.

"Like two months ago in Ohio when he flattened Sid Blanchard."

Patchey snorted. "Blanchard's a second-rater. He's lucky he can stand up without a crutch. Dancer can take this Solaman tonight with one glove. Right, kid?"

Dancer nodded—but he was remembering when, not so long ago, the man he would fight this evening, this man called "King" Solaman, had been at the top. A king indeed, with the middleweight crown to prove it. A compact dark mass of fighting flesh that took all the punishment there was to be taken and then found an opening and moved in with that single killing powerhouse left. But the not-so-long-ago had been six years, and now Solaman was almost thirty-nine, tired and old and with too much punishment from too many blows behind him.

"You take Solaman, then we go for Geha in K.C.," said Patchey. "Then we're movin', we're really *movin'*. Detroit, L.A. Maybe the Garden by the end of the year. Who knows, eh? Maybe the Garden."

"You talk like he was already champ," said Spec, stubbing out his cigarette on the window of the cab. "Boy's gotta walk before he can run."

"He don't need to run," grinned Patchey. "He *dances* to the top, this kid!"

"Right now just let him worry about the King a little," finished Spec.

Patchey raised his head, giving them both his broad smile. "That's just how much he'll worry," he said, "a little."

As Dancer moved toward the heavy swinging bag in the corner of Lacey's Health Club he thought about how much he hated this flat, dry country, with its killing heat and lousy hotels. He was born in Chicago and to Chicago. The cutting wind on Michigan Avenue was a sweet wine to Dancer Webb—and the Loop, brash and loud and fast-moving, was his special playground. Chicago had guts and flare and a will of its own. It was like a woman, sometimes you had to *take* what you wanted, not ask for it, because she was giving nothing away. But Kansas was a pushover. Just like that little waitress back in the cafe. Soft and ready. Pushover. And tonight he'd push over another easy mark to get a little closer to where he had to go. The really rough stuff was ahead—in Kansas City and Detroit and the Garden. Not here. Not tonight.

Patchey had told him how to go after Solaman on the train coming out here. "You pound his belly and ribs," Patchey had said, grinning his fat grin and shaking that hound head of his. "You just go for the bread-basket, kid, cuz that's where he lives—he don't like it much down there. You work on him good down where it hurts, then you move upstairs and finish the job."

Now, slamming the heavy bag, Dancer pictured his antagonist, weakening under each hammer-blow, staggering under the barrage, with the crowd shouting for the knockdown, shouting his name...*Dancer! Dancer! Dancer!*

In his dressing room below stairs Dancer could hear the crowd, an immense rush of voices, rising and falling in pitch like waves on a shore. On this muggy Saturday night in Railton every seat was taken for the 10-round main, following the prelims. Right now, up there in the ring, two local boys were mixing it up. Two boys who had never been anywhere and would never get there.

With three hours of sleep behind him, shoes and silk trunks on, with the tape and the gloves ready, Dancer felt the old familiar surge of animal power singing in his blood. He knew he'd win tonight. Like Patchey said, this one was a lock.

Yet, like a faint pulsebeat below his skin, something was bothering him about Solaman. He couldn't pin down the feeling; maybe later. Maybe.

A fuzz-faced cub reporter from the local paper was shooting questions at Dancer as Patchey carefully wound tape around the fighter's outstretched hand.

"How about a final statement?" the boy asked, "ya know, something that'll look good in print."

"Sure," grinned Patchey. "Just say that tonight Dancer Webb is gonna send King Solaman back to the mines."

The reporter jotted down the words, then confided, "Solaman's through after this one. The King is abdicating."

Dancer raised his eyes to the young reporter. "Where'd you hear that?"

"From his old lady—Mrs. Alonzo Solaman herself. I talked to her before I came down and she says this is the last one for him. She seemed damn glad he was quitting."

So this is the end of the line, thought Dancer. Up from the Harlem slums to the top—and now the finish, here in a lousy Kansas tank town with the hicks screaming for blood. Well, you play the game and you've got to quit sometime.

Spec opened the door and motioned the reporter out.

"We're up," he said, handing Dancer his silk robe, bright red to match his trunks. "So let's go."

This was the moment the crowd had been waiting for: when the raking twin spots swept across a sea of expectant faces and steadied on the tall swing doors at either end of the arena.

The doors opened, and the two combatants stepped into the glare, into the crowd's roar and the massed heat of shouting, shifting close-packed bodies.

They moved down the aisles to the ring, Dancer, Spec, and Patchey to the right, Solaman and his boys to the left—each fighter towel-hooded like a monk, each moving leisurely toward the roped canvas carved by the white flare of lights. They wore bright silk, with a single word stitched on the back of each robe: red silk, DANCER in gold; black silk, KING in silver.

As he neared his corner Dancer saw the girl from the cafe, sitting where he knew she would be sitting, looking fresh and summery in a light print dress accenting her full figure. He winked at her as he passed and she gave him back a warm smile in return. Tonight, thought Dancer as he ducked through the ropes, I've got an *extra* reason for looking good. To the victor...

After Solaman had shrugged aside his robe Dancer looked closely at his enemy. (That was the way Spec told him to think of a man in the ring: an enemy to be conquered before he conquered you.)

Solaman had his back to Dancer, executing a little shuffling step, muscles moving under his skin like sleek fish in bronze waters. Now he turned, and Dancer thought: he's still got it, whatever it takes to make a champion. He may be old and soft, but he's still got that look—like he doesn't belong to the human race, like he's something special.

I wonder how many of them out there tonight can still recognize it. A few of them maybe, but not many. They're here to see youth defeat age, to see white against black, to see some royal blood spilled.

To the far left, near Solaman's corner, *his* part of the crowd had gathered. Dark men and women, not more than a dozen in all, his friends and his wife, there to see him fight for the last time, there to hope for some sudden miracle against this fast, deadly destroyer from Chicago.

The announcer was in the center of the ring, a red-necked fat man in a bow tie sweating through a starched white shirt. He was telling the crowd what they already knew about both fighters: the towns they came from, their weight, the color of their trunks, their full names, the maximum number of rounds in the bout—all the required information delivered like a political speech in measured dramatic tones, as standardized as a newsboy's chant.

Dancer took his bow to wild applause, but Solaman's expression did not alter as he accepted the subdued spatter of handclaps from his side of the arena.

The two men met silently in the center of the white square, heads lowered in an attitude of prayer as they listened to the fat man's droning voice, telling them to abide by the rules. "... and now shake hands, gentlemen, and come out fighting."

As Dancer touched gloves, he looked deep into Solaman's impassive eyes, seeing no emotion there that he could catalogue. Louis, the Brown Bomber, had looked like this; even when he was losing you could never see it in his eyes.

The sudden pre-fight hush before the bell, a heart beat of hot silence in the packed arena. Then the warning buzzer.

"Stay away from that left of his," Spec Leonard said, speaking with his close-shaven bullet head close to Dancer's ear. "He can still punch if you give him an opening. So wind him, keep him running. And go for the body."

At the bell, Dancer came out of his corner like a Jack-in-the-box propelled by a spring. He'd show them some style, some class; he'd let them see his famous legwork while he ran circles around this slow-moving dusky man who faced him now under the lights.

Solaman did not crouch to protect his body; he fought erect, as he had in the old days when body blows were only so many insect stings, when his massive frame could still take the punishment and come back for more. But now, when he should be covering up, he wasn't. Stubborn pride kept him tall, and Dancer knew he could finish the job in two rounds if he really tried.

The face of King Solaman was shiny with healed scar tissue. The nose and ears had lost sharp definition; under the force of a hundred ring encounters they had slowly retreated into the clay-colored face—just as the eyes had retreated under battered ledges of bone. They were incredibly dark eyes, cave-black, flecked with silver when the lights caught them, and they were fixed to the weaving, dipping, rolling figure of Dancer Webb.

Webb allowed a hard right to slide off his shoulder, slashing in with a left to the body, a right and another left, hard, to the body, then danced away from the return punches with that easy half-smile on his handsome unmarked face.

Someone in the crowd yelled: "Kill the bastard, Webb, *kill* him!"

Dancing, weaving, hooking, chopping, back-pedaling in and out, around and around, with Solaman shuffling heavily after him, taking the punches where they hurt with no traces of pain evident in that great impassive face.

Solaman had been good all right, Dancer told himself, as he felt the power of the King's left against his own rib cage; he's only half a man now, but when he fought the invincible Belanski to a standstill in the Garden and sent him down in that final, tension-filled ninth round—when he'd put away the big boys one by one: Tiger Altman, the Baltimore Ace, Aiken and Ted Roeburt, all of them—that's when he should have retired; not now, not tonight with the hicks waiting for his blood, waiting to see him crushed to the canvas. No, thought Dancer, you should have quit when they were still cheering you! I just hope to God I have enough sense to do that, he thought, dancing in again and going for the body, striking and dancing away. Yeah, I hope I still got that much sense left in my head when I get to the other side of the hill.

Then the bell rang and the first round was over. Already, Dancer knew, the King was tiring. By the end of the second he'd be ripe.

"You were *terrific,* kid," Patchey told him, working on his neck and back while Spec Leonard tipped up the bottle and Dancer swallowed, grateful for the cool liquid against his dry throat.

"I felt a couple," said Dancer. "He's still got a left."

"Sure," grinned Patchey, "if there's anything in front of him to hit. Maybe a wooden Indian he could put away!"

"How you feel?" asked Spec.

"Great. Think I should try to take him out in the second?"

Leonard shook his head. "Let it go three," he said. "They came for a show, so let's give 'em one. Stay on your bicycle. Dance him around in there. Then you can axe him at the end of the third."

"And remember the belly," Patchey reminded him, pulling away the stool at the buzzer. "Give it to him solid down there."

At the bell, Dancer moved out lightly on the balls of his feet. He knew the girl from the cafe was watching him, probably a little breathless with excitement, watching him move, sharp and quick, godlike under the lights. I've never looked better, he told himself.

Solaman followed Dancer in a shuffling series of flat-soled steps, waiting for a chance to use his legendary left, the powerhouse left that had put down so many of the greats. But Dancer wouldn't slow for it; he came weaving in like a shadow, connected with a flurry of punches, then darted back out of range. His slashing gloves had opened up an old scar above Solaman's right eye, and the King's lips were puffed and swollen over the mouthpiece. Dancer was beginning to work on the face as well as the body.

The crowd loved it, shouting for the kill, anxious to see Alonzo Solaman go down. Even the quiet group to the left of the arena, the King's
friends—even *they* wanted it to be over. Every blow reached them;
watching the two men—bright with perspiration up there in the blue-
white smoke haze—they sat almost unmoving, silent, waiting.

The dry-leaf scuff of shoes on canvas, the heavy wet smacking sound
of leather on flesh, the unceasing voices yelling for blood, now high,
now low, and the minutes ticking past on the official time clock: this was
the fall of the king.

I'm still fresh and he's already badly winded, thought Dancer, rolling
smoothly away from a left hook that grazed his cheek. He's wishing to
God the bell would ring and he could sit down and rest, get his breath
back, but the bell won't ring for another long minute and I won't give
him time to get his breath.

In, out, slashing, thumping, cutting at the head and belly and ribs . . .

Dancer moved in again, thistle-light and fast on his toes, giving the
crowd something to remember when they talked about the quick young
kid from Chicago. He loosed a stunning combination of blows and Solaman reeled back, arms out, falling into a clinch against the ropes. The
sharp odor of perspiration reached Dancer; he felt a trickle of warm
blood from his shoulder from Solaman's swollen lips, and as he attempted to shove back the heavy-breathing coppery body the referee
parted them—just as the bell ended round two.

"He's gonna go down like Oregon timber!" enthused Patchey, swab-
bing Dancer's face and chest. "You practically got him sleepwalking out
there."

"He's old and he's tired and his wind is gone," said Dancer. "I'm not
proving anything to anybody. What the hell am I proving?"

"Next one, you take him," said Spec Leonard, his eyes narrow and
hard on Dancer's. "You go in and stretch him this time. Hear me?"

"I hear you," said Dancer.

But when the third round began, and Dancer saw the stolid, advancing
figure of Alonzo Solaman moving toward him, erect and unafraid over
the stretched white canvas, he began to ask himself questions; he began
to examine an area within himself which he'd tried to ignore, tried to
believe wasn't there at all. Did he have any *right* to do what he was
doing? When I send him down tonight I'm sending down his pride,
everything he lived for, everything people remember him for. When he
goes down tonight that's how they'll think of him, flat on the deck,
glaze-eyed and helpless as a baby—a bloody, beaten hulk to gloat over.

"Eat him up and spit him out, Dancer!" a woman shrilled from below.
"Murder him!"

That's just what I'd be doing, Webb told himself, as he back-pedaled away from a chopping right; that's just what I'd be doing: murdering a king. Is this bout worth a man like Solaman? Is one lousy win in one lousy tank town in Kansas worth destroying a man like this?

He could hear Patchey yelling at him.

"The belly, Kid—go for the belly!"

But he didn't. Dancer flicked out a harmless right and ducked inside the return left, moving out of range.

One solid punch from the King would end it, he said to himself. Just let Solaman get that powerhouse left across solid and that would do it. No one could doubt the result, they'd all seen it happen a hundred times: that sudden opening and then the smashing, crushing left, straight in to the jaw, putting out the lights. That was all Solaman had now, that waiting terrible left, but he was no longer able to catch his man and use it. Not unless that man made a mistake.

It wouldn't be easy. He'd lose the girl out there in the darkness; a girl like that doesn't touch a loser. But it would be a chance to do a *right* thing instead of a wrong one, a chance to give instead of take. All his life he'd taken, like his father had taken when he walked out on the family so many years ago. Dancer had always taken everything he could get from life, from the girls he'd loved, but never *loved,* from his mother, from his friends . . . Now he could do one decent thing: he could give King Solaman this fight, a great victory to be remembered instead of an ignoble defeat. Oh, they'd talk about this one; they'd talk about the night the King came back from the grave to stop Dancer Webb cold in the third. They'd all talk plenty about this one.

His fighter's instinct told him no, that he was a fool, a crazy damn fool to be thinking this way. He'd been taught to avoid blows, not walk into them. This meant going directly against his grain, against everything he'd been trained for up to this moment. Could he really force himself to do it? He was afraid of that left, of the power of that terrible left, but there was no other way to do what he felt he had to do. It would have to be a case of conscious action over unconscious instinct . . .

The round was half over. Spec and Patchey were nodding their heads with each blow Dancer drove home, mentally counting the seconds before Solaman would fall. Then, abruptly, a shocked cry stabbed up from the arena. Patchey put one hand to his mouth. "My God!" he said.

For suddenly King Solaman had struck. He'd found an opening; miraculously it was there—and the mighty left had crashed into Webb's jaw like a boulder into sand. Dancer's head snapped back, his eyes rolled up white, and he fell—straight forward on his face to the hard gray canvas.

Alonzo Solaman, breathing hard, his face glittering with diamond specks, stepped back as the countdown began. Somewhere in the darkness to the left a woman's voice said: "Bless you, King!"

And when the rest of the crowd saw that it was over, that a great fighter had rallied to win over the fast brash boy from Chicago, they began to cheer for this exhausted giant. He was a champion again—and they were cheering for a champion.

Patchey didn't wait for the official verdict. He ducked under the ropes and ran toward his boy. But Spec Leonard did not move. He watched Dancer Webb stagger to his feet under Patchey's supporting hands, and still he did not move.

In the dressing room, under the raw overhead glare, Dancer was lying on his back on the long rubdown table and Patchey was cutting away the tape on his hands and talking soft and easy to him, as a mother talks to her child.

"He just got lucky is all," intoned the little man. "He just threw a lucky punch, Hell, you *had* him, kid. They all saw that. You had him all the way and then he just got lucky. That's all, he just got real, real lucky."

Spec had been silent since they'd left the ring. Now he stood over the table, watching the trainer work.

"I—I'm sorry, Spec," said Dancer, squinting up, attempting to clear his head of the pain that remained behind his eyes. His face was still handsome, but it was no longer unmarked.

"Don't give me that crap," snapped Leonard. "I saw what I saw."

Dancer sighed. "Okay, so I threw it—but what the hell, it's only one lousy fight. I just couldn't go out and slaughter that tired old bastard tonight. I just couldn't."

"That's right," said Leonard slowly, "you couldn't. And that's something for you to live with." He leaned closer to Webb. "Do you believe that Solaman would ever do what you did tonight if *you* were at the bottom of the hill? Lemme tell you he wouldn't, not in a million years. Because he's hard, because he's got the stuff it takes to be a champ, with no room left for anything else. You weakened. I saw it in your eyes after the second round. Hell, I saw it on your face in Cincy when you let that Zuckerman punk dump you. Kid, you got a flaw in you. I guess I needed to be sure about it. Well—so now I'm sure."

Leonard turned, opened the door and hesitated for a moment. "You and me, Dancer, we've just said good-bye."

Then he was gone, the door bumping shut behind him.

As Patchey's confused voice rang in his ears Dancer closed his eyes against the light—knowing that he could never close his eyes against what he had done, knowing there wouldn't be any K.C. or Detroit or L.A. for him now, that he would never stand there in the Garden as a champion with the crowd shouting his name.

A crack had opened, a fault in his career that had been there all along, and it could never be closed.

"Listen, kid, don't you worry," Patchey was telling him. "Spec'll be back. Hell, he never walked out on a fighter yet. You watch, he'll be back."

"Sure," said Dancer softly, his eyes still closed, feeling the pain again, "he'll be back."

FIXED

Max Brand

As he got out of his limousine, Big Bill pulled a mahogany-colored leather cigar case from the inside pocket of his dinner jacket and lighted an excellent perfecto, for when he went to a fight at Madison Square Garden he always kept some of the fragrance of good living between him and the crowd. On the sidewalk, in the crowd, he waited a moment, straightening his dinner jacket around the carefully fitted whiteness of his front while he saw and was seen.

He spoke to a police officer. "Hello, McNally. What you got for tonight?"

"I like Slam Finnegan, sir," said the officer. "Whatta you think yourself?"

Big Bill looked at him and smiled. Then he winked. In this manner he conveyed to McNally, delicately, his acceptance of the officer as one of the inside circle who "know," but he dropped not a morsel of information in the way of the hungry policeman.

Big Bill looked upon himself as a sort of expensive bomb which, if his news were exploded, would reduce the entire Garden to a rioting shambles. The greatness of his knowledge increased his dignity from the bulges of his neck to the gleam of his shoes and bestowed upon him an inner strength somewhat akin to the virtue of the good and the great; for among all the thousands there was not one who knew that he had wagered fifty thousand dollars on "Little David" LaRue, that black magician with the gloves; only two others in the entire world knew that ten thousand more of his dollars had been spent to make his profit certain.

The truth was that he had bought young Slam Finnegan; in about the eighth or the ninth round the Irishman would "take a dive."

Rosenbloom appeared, suspended sidewise in the crowd like a fish in water as he undulated rapidly toward Big Bill. He held up his hat as a signal flag above his bald head, which shone no more brightly than his smile, for Sammy Rosenbloom was never too proud to show his joy when he saw his chief. In spite of his hairless head, which gave his opinion unusual weight with many people, Sammy was only thirty, but already he knew his way around New York so well that Big Bill often forgot to be amused and was amazed outright by the precocity of the boy. He pushed his way through to Bill

"Where you get 'em, Sammy?"

"Third row," said Sammy, swiveling his head about, "where the blood won't splash on your shirt front, Bill."

After seven years of almost Biblical service, Big Bill had permitted this faithful man Friday to use the shortened name which was familiar on the lips of the wise. As for the row in which he sat, Big Bill only wished it to be close enough for his features to be seen when a flashlight was taken in his direction. God had given him such a nose and chin and he had improved on nature by adding such a pair of jowls that in a group photograph he looked like two-in-one.

They passed the ticket kiosk, entered one of the roped alleys leading toward the entrance door. Sammy began to walk sidewise with his usual skill, giving all his attention to the chief.

"How are things?" asked Bill.

"Two and a half to one," said Sammy.

"They think Slam is going to take him, eh?" asked Big Bill. "What *you* think, Sammy?"

"I think Slam has got the old sleep-syringe in both hands," answered Sammy, "but I don't think he knows as much as the chief."

He winked and laughed.

"What *d'you* know?" asked Bill.

"Not enough to answer questions," said Sammy. "There's the big guy! There's Harrigan!"

He got his hat off and began to wave it above his spotlight of a head. If attention were attracted his way, his master could benefit by it if he chose. In the meantime a group of men advanced three aisles away toward the entrance, a policeman going ahead to smooth the way of the great Jimmy Harrigan, the chief of chiefs, the boss of bosses. He was a little man with a face putty-white and the eyes thumbed into it with soot. Smiling was not enough. He never stopped laughing.

This group passed into the building ahead of Big Bill in spite of Sammy's fishlike efforts to advance. Bill panted out a cloud of smoke.

His fat lips, which glistened almost like a chorus girl's, were saying: "See us? Did he see us? Did he walk us down or didn't he see us?"

The sweat of Big Bill ran cold upon his flesh. The answer of Sammy Rosenbloom was sweeter than milk and honey: "Didn't you see? That was Ike Fishbein alongside of him.'

"What does that mean?"

"Fishbein is gunna find out in a day or two. They're gunna open him up and clean him. That's why Harrigan can't see anything now. He's too busy getting the can opener ready to use on that boneless sardine!"

Big Bill filled his lungs and sighed forth the smoke and the relief.

"You sure the chief didn't see me? You sure he didn't pass me up?" he queried again.

"Sure he didn't see you. I watched every eye in that mob. They were all full of Fishbein."

"Ike has always been right up there," said Big Bill.

"We don't know him any more," answered Sammy. "Account of that funny job he done in Jersey. He thought account of it was Jersey he could eat all that honey; and now they're gunna clean him."

They entered a Garden which already seemed full although the several thousand who were jamming toward the gates still had to be poured into the interstices. Big Bill drew toward the ringside as into a family circle. Everyone was there. Levi Isaacs turned with a wave and a laugh. Pudge Murphy loosed a shout of recognition. Old Harry Blatts had a seat just down the row.

"Everyone knows you, Chief," said Sammy. "And the ones that don't know are asking. You *look* like something.'"

The lights went out through the arena, leaving only the many cones of brilliance above the ring. Beneath that luminous fountain the faces of the crowd weltered away into the outer dimness while Bill still recognized important names here and there. He knew them all; they all knew him; everything was all right. He felt at last a human sympathy, a warm pity for the Police Commissioner off at the left. What was it that the poor devil made in a year? And yet how useful the fellow could be! In the mystery of the metropolis nothing impressed Bill more than the men of small salary in key positions. Their industry was incomprehensible, like that of the bees and the ants.

A hand was laid from behind on the shoulder of Bill. The voice of Snipe Dickinson said at his ear, "Which one of these you like, Bill?"

"Why should I like one of 'em?" asked Bill.

"I've got a spare hundred at seven to five on McGuire," said Snipe.

Big Bill, with the easy indulgence of the great for the small, gave some of his attention to the pair of featherweights who were struggling in the ring.

"They all got the forward stance, these days," said Big Bill to Sammy. "Which is McGuire?"

"The one in the red trunks," said Sammy. "He's a baby, ain't he? Look at that left! Look at that baby go! Oh, socko! He's got Choochoo Lavine as red as Santa Claus."

The face of Lavine dripped blood but his eye was clear; he was waiting through the storm.

"Lavine's holding something out," said Big Bill. He added over his shoulder, "Snipe, make it two hundred at ten to five."

"Why should I?" asked the Snipe.

"And why should I give you something for nothing?" asked Bill.

"All right, you robber," said Snipe Dickinson. "It's two hundred against one hundred, and you've got Lavine, you sucker. . . . Hai, McGuire! The old one-two, kid!"

The round ended. McGuire danced back to his corner. Lavine remained for a moment in the center of the ring, looking thoughtfully after his opponent. The crowd laughed.

"Get an adding machine, Lavine!" yelled a wit.

"Lavine is gunna take him," said Bill to Sammy.

The girl in front of him turned. She had black hair and blue eyes and a neat, saucy face. Bill winked and beckoned but she became aware of him only to drift her eyes critically up and down his swollen body before she turned away again.

"Listen, Sammy," said Bill. "Let that kid know who I am, after this bout."

"Is this gunna be a pickup?" asked Sammy.

"We'll see, Sammy."

The next round was already under way. McGuire kept shooting his one-two. But Lavine kept on waiting. The round almost had ended before he slipped a straight right and came in with a body blow. McGuire clinched and held on.

"He's gunna kill McGuire," said Bill.

One round later the thoughtful Lavine feinted for the body, the hands of McGuire dropped to the hurt section, and through an opening a yard wide Lavine drove the finishing punch to the chin.

"I'll take it in tens and fives," said Big Bill to the Snipe. "I need some small change."

He went over to see Gipsy Connor.

"Whatta *you* want?" asked the Gip.

"Money, Gip," said Bill. "I want your money. How are you laying the main go now?"

"A dollar on the nigger gets two from me," said Connor.

"It's three to one all over the house," said Big Bill.

"To hell with the house," said Connor.

"The nigger hasn't got a chance," said Big Bill. "Five to one would be more like it."

"If he hasn't got a chance, why would *you* wanta lay money on him?" asked Connor.

"Sympathy with a downtrodden race," answered Big Bill. "Make it two and a half and I'll talk to you."

"I don't like your lingo," said Connor. "I never did."

"Two and a half, Gip?"

"How far?"

"Five, let's say."

"Grand?"

"Why should we be pikers?"

"It's ten to five," said Gip.

"You'd rob your grandmother of her glass eye," remarked Big Bill. "But I'd rather have ten of yours than a hundred of somebody regular."

He went back to his seat where Sammy greeted him with a wink and a nod. Big Bill laughed. He leaned forward and said over the girl's shoulder: "Why should I remember you so well?"

She moved to face him. At the base of her young throat a gardenia was pinned. It had three big, green, lustrous leaves.

"Why should I remember you so well?" repeated Bill.

"How could you ever forget?" asked the girl.

He laughed again. He felt warm, at ease.

"You really own that nice horse, Dinner Gong?" she asked.

"Why not?" asked Bill.

"I don't see any resemblance," said the girl.

He had to laugh again.

"That's not bad," he said. "That's pretty good. Was Dinner Gong ever right for you?"

"He made my day at Aqueduct," she answered.

"That was when he gave ten pounds to Topsy Turvy," remarked Big Bill. "Was he carrying much for you?"

"He carried a pair of shoes and turned 'em into a fur coat," said the girl.

"Remembering you so well, why shouldn't I remember your name?" he asked.

"Some people call me Jap. Are you one of them?" she said.

"Japs cheat but they don't have blue eyes," replied Big Bill.

The gong rang. She turned from him slowly, leaving her smile behind her, as it were.

"Okay," asked Sammy.

"Sure. What you think?" replied Bill.

"I dunno how you do it," said Sammy. "Whatta you say to them?"

"It ain't what you say. It's the way you say it," said Big Bill. "Having good intentions is what counts."

"How good are your intentions?" asked Sammy.

"Why d'you keep on talking when you got nothing to say?" said Bill.

A pair of lightweights struggled through eight dull rounds. Battling Miller had youth; old Jim Cross had a head on his shoulders and a long left that won for him and Big Bill; Snipe Dickinson counted another two hundred into the hand of the lucky man.

"It's gunna be your night, Chief," said Sammy.

Welterweights were next. Big Bill bet a thousand on the red head of Dick Roach, and young Dick plastered Lester Grogan in the fifth round during a mix-up in his own corner.

"I'm going to take a walk but I'll be back," said Big Bill to Jap.

"Don't lose yourself, Big Boy," she said.

He found Gip Connor again.

"Rub the trouble out of your eyes, Gip," said Big Bill.

Connor looked at him without answering.

"Another five grand the same way," said Big Bill.

"That's it, is it?" asked Connor.

"That's what?"

"I might have known," mused Connor.

Big Bill bit into a fresh cigar.

"What you say, Gip?" he asked.

"I say you're a dirty dog," answered Connor.

"What!" cried Big Bill.

A horribly familiar sickness of heart overwhelmed him; his knees loosened; he remembered out of the great distance a March day, a windy corner, and a young lad screeching insults at him while a crowd of their schoolmates waited for the fight to start. The fight had not started and therefore, from time to time, the giddy nausea returned upon Bill.

"Get out of my sight, you yella rat!" said Connor.

Big Bill got out of his sight. He still was trembling when he returned to his seat. By that time the principals for the main bout were in their corners, Pop Finnegan pushing the gloves home over the hands of his son. Pop had a featureless blear of a face with a mouth that slopped to one side or the other when he talked, but he had been tense and bright-eyed enough when Big Bill talked money to him and put the five thousand advance into his hands.

Now the red old bathrobe was worked off over the gloved hands; now young Slam Finnegan was on his feet with the robe loose on his shoulders as he tested the spring of the top rope and shuffled his feet in the resin. He picked out people he knew at the ringside with a wave and a smile.

This calmness before a fight in which Slam was to "take a dive" gradually restored a regular rhythm to the heartbeat of Big Bill. He could breathe again. In place of the cigar he had thrown away he lighted a new one and could enjoy the taste of the smoke. After all, the time had passed when he needed to fear physical violence. There are other forms of courage, of moral courage. He skipped from the word "moral" and found refuge in the phrase "strength of spirit." Take a fellow like himself who was always one of the boys and who never let down anyone who was in the know. . . . Besides, he would be a fool to take to heart anything that Gipsy Connor did or said. By this force of inward persuasion, like a sensible man, Big Bill put fear behind him and concentrated upon the present moment, the pleasant expectancy of the future.

"What are you doing about this?" asked Snipe Dickinson.

"Ah, nothing much," answered Big Bill.

"The nigger's been coming on," said Snipe. "You heard what he did to Jeff Millard out on the Coast. Two rounds! . . . These people are all nuts, around here, betting two to one on Slam. Maybe he'll win, but he hasn't got a walkaway. This nigger is another Joe Louis, and he's better every time he starts. If he don't take on too much weight, he'll be the middleweight champ, one of these days!"

Everyone was standing now, near the ringside, getting the cramps out of legs before the final bout. Slam Finnegan waved suddenly straight toward Big Bill, who closed his eyes and almost groaned aloud. It was the last thing that Slam should have done—to recognize his money-man on this night of all nights. But the Irish are dumb, decided Big Bill. That's why they're useful, they're so dumb.

When he opened his eyes again, Jap was waving and shouting at Finnegan.

"You like Slam?" asked Big Bill.

"Oh, he's a honey, isn't he?" she demanded, turning her bright face on him.

Big Bill considered her with a smile, He leaned over and took the gardenia on her breast between thumb and forefinger.

"I better take this before you get it all messed up, waving your arms around," he said.

She looked down at his hand, then up at his face. Something that might have been almost disgust vanished with her smile.

"All right, Big Boy, you take it," she said.

He pushed it into his buttonhole. People were calling: "Down! Down in front!"

"I'll be thinking of you, Jap," said Big Bill. "I'll be breathing you, beautiful."

She gave him her smile over her shoulder as she sat down, and while

Big Bill settled into place Sammy was saying: "The way you do it, Chief! . . . That nigger looks good, don't he?"

"Did you watch the gal's face just now?" asked Big Bill.

"Sure I watched it."

"You didn't get a flash, did you?"

"You got the flash, Chief."

"I mean, she had a kind of a look for a second. Maybe she's stringing me."

"Stringing *you?* That'd be a scream, wouldn't it?"

"Well, women are all kind of nuts," said Bill.

"The nigger looks like something, don't he?" asked Sammy.

The two had met in the center of the ring to shake hands, receive the final instructions. Now they came out fighting, as different in style as in build and color. Slam Finnegan, hardly more than a lightweight about the hips and spindling legs, had his weight layered around the shoulders and drawn down over his capable arms. He stepped in a light, mincing dance. The Negro was carefully muscled in every part; he wore a gravely studious air as he glided in and out with his stance rather low as against the tip-toe alertness of the white boy.

They came to the danger line, shifted away from it, met again with a sudden darting of gloves. Finnegan shook his head, stepped back; the Negro wove in after him; the whole Garden yelled with delight, seeing that this was to be a fight and not a sparring match.

Sammy said: "What I tell you? Notice the way that coon let 'em slide off the back of his head? See that left he stuck into Finnegan's belly? That didn't do Slam any good!"

Slam Finnegan, backing away, pecked at a distance. The punches missed the bobbing head of "Little David" LaRue.

"He can hit when he's on his heels, is what Finnegan can do, can't he?" pleaded Sammy.

"You'll see," grunted Big Bill.

He turned his head and surveyed the crowd, particularly the working faces along the nearby benches. Their eyes were wide, glaring; some of the men worked their shoulders to help home punches; some made little automatic gestures as though they were blocking hard blows. No one in the great house sat immobile, at ease, except Big Bill, a deity raised above the pitiful human concerns of the millions. For he alone had knowledge of what the end must be.

He watched young Finnegan take the initiative suddenly, hammering home short blows to the body as he backed the Negro into a corner. The crowd yelled, the dry tinder of its enthusiasm for a favorite flaming up suddenly. For from exactly such an attack Finnegan knew how to shift a blow to the head and end a battle.

The round ended. Finnegan sat with his head down a little, his father handling him, sneering out words from the drooping corner of his mouth. Across the ring Little David had begun to laugh. Still laughing, he patted his body, looking up at his trainer. It was plain that the punches of Finnegan had not injured him.

"The nigger's tough," said Sammy Rosenbloom. "He sure can take it. Out on the Coast . . ."

"Ah, shut up for a minute," said Big Bill. He leaned forward. "What you think, honey?" he asked.

"I don't know. . . . Slam isn't right," said the girl. She turned her troubled face. "There's not so much of the old 'I be damned' about him. He studies around too much. What's he think he's doing? Reading a book?"

"No, counting money," chuckled Big Bill, settling back into his place.

That was, in fact, his explanation. For of course as Finnegan pulled his punches he was thinking of the ten thousand dollars. Not so much that, either, as the avoidance of certain dangers at the hands of the law. It was a practice of Mr. Bill's to investigate the past lives of prominent people in all lines of work, from time to time. It was true that the detective agencies often sent in big bills, but it was equally true that he managed to reap large profits now and then. Besides, the knowledge gave him that divine power over other men which he relished more than all else in the world.

In this instance what he had learned was so unimportant and so outlawed by time that it would have amounted to nothing, except that he had been able to reinforce his knowledge with a powerful bluff. That bluff had turned Pop Finnegan white with fear. He was crumbling under the attack when Big Bill turned to the sweet music of a cash offer. He felt, after the interview ended, that he might have bought out the Finnegans for five or six thousand. In that respect he had been careless, for, having victory in sight, he had named the figure upon which he already had planned.

It was the second or the third round. He cared not which. Finnegan, dancing through his usual maze, was caught by the gliding Negro with two blows that sent a smacking impact through the loudspeaker.

Finnegan covered, stabbed feebly at the black whirlwind, retreated, felt the ropes against his back, and hit through an opening with all his might. The punch caught LaRue high on the chest. Even when he was stung, Slam dared not strike at a vital spot for fear of abrogating his agreement with a knockout punch!

Big Bill laughed a little. It always amused him, in fact, when he considered how money controls men in love and hate, in war and peace. He, for ten small thousands, was able to insure the winning of fifty. Of course it was not a matter of the ten thousand but the leverage he had

given to that sum, so that it outweighed the fifty, in the minds of the
Finnegans. It outweighed the chance at the championship for rising
young Slam Finnegan; it outweighed his pride in three score honest
battles. Ten thousand dollars was a quicksand that imprisoned his feet
and left him helpless before the Negro.

The joy of command brimmed the very soul of Big Bill. His sense of
power was no less great because it was secret.

Snipe Dickinson yelled out, somewhere along in the seventh round:
"Yella! Yella! Finnegan's yella. . . . See that dirty Irish Mick, Bill? He's
yella as a dog! He won't fight!"

But Sammy Rosenbloom said a moment later: "He ain't yella. He's
doing about his best, but the nigger's too good for him. The nigger's
lefting him to death. . . ."

It was true. Whatever Finnegan might have done with an honest start,
he seemed hopelessly out of it now. The left hand of Little David was
hitched to his head with a strong elastic and could not miss the mark. It
kept the hair of Finnegan leaping up. Now the Negro began to throw the
right. The blows glanced. They cut a gash over Finnegan's left eye; they
swelled the entire left side of his face; now and then they plumped home
deep in the body, shots to the wind that would have brought down a
giant, eventually.

Well, the next round was the eighth and then, according to agreement,
Finnegan could make his dive and be out of his misery. Only an Irishman, thought Big Bill, would have endured so patiently and made the
fight seem so real. In his heart he registered a vow never to forget the
Irish—never to forget to use them and to pay them liberally. He felt
about the entire Irish nation as a great general feels about the stout
fellows who go over the top for him.

The round ended with Little David dancing to his corner, sitting
laughing on his stool, while Slam Finnegan stumbled back to his place
on loose knees and with hanging head.

"Little David, play on your harp!" shouted the ringside jester.

A few people laughed. Most of them turned sour faces, for Finnegan
was a great favorite.

Sammy said: "When there ain't no jump to the spark, any more, what
can they do? Look at Dempsey in Philadelphia. In there with Firpo he
was a tiger; down there in Philadelphia he was a tame pup and got
clawed to pieces. The best of 'em . . . they just bog down all at once. But
to see Slam go this way, eh?"

Jap had leaped to her feet with her hands cupped at her mouth. Her
thin young voice cut through the muddy roar of the crowd.

"Hey, Slam! Hey, Slam, Slam, Slam!"

Slam Finnegan was lying back against the ropes, his body newly drenched and polished with water, his back bent in under his own weight, his flaccid belly lifting, falling with his breathing, while a handler snapped a bath towel to give him a cooling breeze and his father worked on his wounds to stop the bleeding. But it seemed that the voice of the girl reached clearly to the punch-drunk brain of Slam, for now he lifted himself, waving his father aside, and stared down through the dazzle of the lights straight toward her.

Big Bill, at that moment, had risen to say at the girl's ear: "Take it easy, Jap. He'll be out of pain pretty soon."

She only screeched: "Slam, wake up! Wake up, Slam!"

Slam seemed to be waking up. He shaded his dazzled eyes with a glove and stared again. Then the fifteen-second gong was rung and the seconds left the ring. Slam Finnegan rose, but still with turned head he studied the distant figures as though he had forgotten all about the Negro who was slithering across the ring to meet him.

"Stop it!" yelled someone close to the ear of Big Bill. "Hey, stop it! He's out on his feet!"

"Stop it!" roared Big Bill, and yet he felt like laughing except that the face of Finnegan was puckering strangely almost as though he were about to weep, or shout in a frenzy. He turned at the last instant to meet Little David.

The Negro popped in his left three times. He was hitting perfectly, well accustomed to an unresisting target.

Then something happened. The trained eye of Big Bill could not have missed it and did, in fact, see that Finnegan countered just inside a driving punch; but his mind refused to believe that he was watching Little David walk backward on his heels toward the center of the ring while an Irishman with a bleeding, convulsed face rushed after him.

Those punches were very wild. LaRue, though badly dazed, instinctively wrapped himself in a perfect defense. Finnegan stood up on his toes and with a right fist that was a leaden club beat on the side of LaRue's head.

LaRue gave ground. He began to run. Finnegan swung himself off his feet and landed on the canvas full length. When he rose, LaRue was able to fight again, though still in full retreat.

The air of the Garden was no longer a smoking mist but a continual explosion with an endless siren screaming through the mist. Big Bill felt that he was going mad. The Finnegans had sold him out, and yet that could not be the case, for when he climbed onto his seat as every man in the house had done before him, he was able to see the face of Pop Finnegan as he crouched, making himself small, an animal fear in his eyes.

Big Bill looked up, as though for superior guidance, and beyond the glaring cone of the ring lights he saw the dim upper galleries with the pallor of crowded faces through the shadow like stones under water. It seemed to Bill that this world had no mountains except heaps of human flesh and that no winds moved upon its face except the insane screaming of human voices. A mind had been in control only a moment before and that was the mind of Bill, but now the contact was lost, all was rushing to witness ruin.

The gong sounded the end of the round like a small voice in the distance.

No one sat down. Snipe Dickinson screamed: "You see it, Bill? The kid was holding it all the time. Like a Bonthron sprint finish. He let the nigger wear himself out, and then he started. . . ."

That was what the sportswriters were getting into words as fast as their fingers could work; that was what the announcer was broadcasting; but it held no meaning for Big Bill. Pathetically, with the eyes of a child, he looked up to the misty rafters, he looked back into the ring. Three men with fear-tightened faces were working over Little David, who lay back on the ropes while Finnegan sat alert on the edge of his stool. Pop, on one knee, poured advice at him with a savage leering mouth, and shook a fist under his chin, but Slam pushed the old man off to the end of his long left arm and rose with the gong.

Then Big Bill partly understood. Old Pop was all right. It was Slam who had gone mad. That, thought Bill, was the trouble with the Irish. You never could tell. A lot of sparkle like champagne, and then a hell of a headache.

But fifty thousand dollars . . . a year's profits . . . a year of wasted life.

"There oughta be a law. . ." shouted Big Bill, and found that his voice was the babbling of a voiceless child beside a roaring sea.

For Little David could still fight and did fight. He met the Irishman almost in the middle of the ring, stopped him with a stone wall of straight lefts and then crossed his right to the head, to the cheek, to the jaw.

Finnegan fell on his back so hard that his head bounced from the canvas.

Bill said through the tornado of screeching, to the profound stillness of his heart: "What a beauty . . . on the button! He can't get up. Oh, God, don't let him get up!"

The referee, down almost on one knee, used his left hand as one half of a megaphone to make the shouted numbers reach the ear of Finnegan. His whole body swayed gracefully in rhythm with his long arm which beat out the count.

"Three . . . four . . . five . . ."

Finnegan stirred.

"He can't get up!" said Bill to his heart.

He reached out his hands. The spiritual weight of them would press Slam back to the canvas.

Finnegan turned over on his face.

Something burned the mouth of Bill. It was his cigar. He spat it out. It hit the back of Jap's fur coat and dropped to the floor.

"Eight . . . nine . . ."

Finnegan thrust himself up on his arms and swayed to his feet. He was half turned from the Negro and LaRue, seeing that wide target, forgot all the years of gymnasium instruction and risked a wide swing. It landed with a jarring thud—on the lifted shoulder of Finnegan!

And then came the clinch.

"Shake him off!" screamed Bill. "Push him away . . . and kill him! Kill him!"

LaRue pushed Slam Finnegan away and smashed with both hands, his face grown apelike with the grin of effort. The blows skidded off the ducking head of Slam. He fell into another clinch. The referee worked hard to pry them apart; they separated; and as LaRue smashed with his right again, Finnegan's leaden fist banged home inside the punch. A perfect counter. With dull eyes Bill watched Little David's knees sag.

It was his time to run, now, but apparently he could not believe that a man who one moment before had been helpless was now formidable. So he went in with flailing gloves to the attack.

"Keep away from him!" screamed the sore throat of Bill. "He's ready again . . . keep away . . . you nigger fool, don't you know he's *Irish?*"

Someone was beating his shoulder. His hat was joggling over awry on his head. But the trained eye saw everything. It watched the two stabbing lefts with which Finnegan staggered Little David back to the right distance. It saw the right poised with a tremor of dreadful power.

Big Bill wanted to close his eyes but he was crucified and had to see fate fulfilled. The blow landed. It seemed to take Little David by the chin and pull out his face to twice its normal length. The Negro fell straight forward and knocked himself out a second time against the floor.

Sammy said: "Wasn't it great! Ever see anything like it? . . . Hey, Chief!"

Big Bill did not answer. He only smiled as in death he would smile.

Jap was jerking the lapel of his dinner coat.

"Give me back the flower," she was crying. "Slam pinned it on me his own self. I forgot! He'll wanta see it on me!"

He let her take the gardenia but still he held her by the arm with his shaking hand.

"Slam Finnegan . . . *he* pinned that stinking flower on you? Slam did that?"

"Sure he did! What's eating you, Papa?"

But Big Bill could not answer, for again he was seeing the picture of young Finnegan in the corner at the end of the seventh round peering under his shaded eyes at the girl. How clearly Slam must have seen the familiar face of Big Bill, large as two in the crowded picture, and beneath it, almost brushing the fat of the throat, the little white gardenia with its three big shining leaves, for luck.

"Let's go home, Sammy," he said. "Why do we care a damn about the windup fight?"

The noise of the storm had not abated a great deal when Sammy Rosenbloom went with him up the aisle.

"Are you gunna leave the gal, Chief?" asked Sammy. "Are you gunna chuck her?"

"Doncha see she was only stringin' me from the start?" demanded Big Bill, in a feeble rage.

"Stringing . . . you?" gasped Sammy.

"Yeah, me, me, me!" groaned Bill. "She's Slam Finnegan's girl. She was only building things with a big shot so's to help Slam."

"You mean that Slam . . . you mean a classy kid like her . . ." protested Sammy.

"Ah, shut up!" commanded Big Bill, and to himself he muttered: "Am I getting old, or something?"

They got out into the lobby. Other men came with them, slowly, weak in the knees. Some of them carried their coats and the faces of all were streaming with perspiration. Torn programs littered the floor and the sidewalk. Rain was falling, silver bright, a veil that only half covered the face of this wretched world. He was as sad as Monday morning, as lonely as a telephone ringing in an empty room. His chauffeur, signaling from the distance, was a ghost half lost in the gloomy chaos of time and space.

"The trouble with you, Sammy, is you don't understand," said Big Bill, sadly.

"Understand what, Chief?" asked Sammy.

"Gardenias, you fool!" shouted Big Bill.

STEEL

Richard Matheson

The two men came out of the station rolling a covered object. They rolled it along the platform until they reached the middle of the train, then grunted as they lifted it up the steps, the sweat running down their bodies. One of its wheels fell off and bounced down the metal steps and a man coming up behind them picked it up and handed it to the man who was wearing a rumpled brown suit.

"Thanks," said the man in the brown suit and he put the wheel in his side coat pocket.

Inside the car, the men pushed the covered object down the aisle. With one of its wheels off, it was lopsided and the man in the brown suit—his name was Kelly—had to keep his shoulder braced against it to keep it from toppling over. He breathed heavily and licked away tiny balls of sweat that kept forming over his upper lip.

When they reached the middle of the car, the man in the wrinkled blue suit pushed forward one of the seat backs so there were four seats, two facing two. Then the two men pushed the covered object between the seats and Kelly reached through a slit in the covering and felt around until he found the right button.

The covered object sat down heavily on a seat by the window.

"Oh, God, listen to'm squeak," said Kelly.

The other man, Pole, shrugged and sat down with a sigh.

"What d'ya expect?" he asked.

Kelly was pulling off his suit coat. He dropped it down on the opposite seat and sat down beside the covered object.

188

"Well, we'll get 'im some o' that stuff soon's we're paid off," he said worriedly.

"If we can find some," said Pole, who was almost as thin as one. He sat slumped back against the hot seat watching Kelly mop at his sweaty cheeks.

"Why shouldn't we?" asked Kelly, pushing the damp handkerchief down under his shirt collar.

"Because they don't make it no more," Pole said with the false patience of a man who has had to say the same thing too many times.

"Well, that's crazy," said Kelly. He pulled off his hat and patted at the bald spot in the center of his rust-colored hair. "There's still plenty B-twos in the business."

"Not many," said Pole, bracing one foot upon the covered object.

"*Don't,*" said Kelly.

Pole let his foot drop heavily and a curse fell slowly from his lips. Kelly ran the handkerchief around the lining of his hat. He started to put the hat on again, then changed his mind and dropped it on top of his coat.

"God, but it's hot," he said.

"It'll get hotter," said Pole.

Across the aisle a man put his suitcase up on the rack, took off his suit coat, and sat down, puffing. Kelly looked at him, then turned back.

"Ya think it'll be hotter in Maynard, huh?" he asked.

Pole nodded. Kelly swallowed dryly.

"Wish we could have another o' them beers," he said.

Pole stared out the window at the heat waves rising from the concrete platform.

"I had three beers," said Kelly, "and I'm just as thirsty as I was when I started."

"Yeah," said Pole.

"Might as well've not had a beer since Philly," said Kelly.

Pole said, "Yeah."

Kelly sat there staring at Pole a moment. Pole had dark hair and white skin and his hands were the hands of a man who should be bigger than Pole was. But the hands were as clever as they were big. Pole's one o' the best, Kelly thought, one o' the best.

"Ya think he'll be all right?" he asked.

Pole grunted and smiled for an instant without being amused.

"If he don't get hit," he said.

"No, no, I mean it," said Kelly.

Pole's dark, lifeless eyes left the station and shifted over to Kelly.

"So do I," he said.

"Come *on,*" Kelly said.

"Steel," said Pole, "ya know just as well as me. He's shot t'hell."

"That ain't true," said Kelly, shifting uncomfortably. "All he needs is a little work. A little overhaul 'n' he'll be as good as new."

"Yeah, a little three-four-grand overhaul," Pole said, "with parts they don't make no more." He looked out the window again.

"Oh . . . it ain't as bad as that," said Kelly. "Hell, the way you talk you'd think he was ready for scrap."

"Ain't he?" Pole asked.

"No," said Kelly angrily, "he *ain't*."

Pole shrugged and his long white fingers rose and fell in his lap.

"Just 'cause he's a little old," said Kelly.

"Old." Pole grunted. *"Ancient."*

"Oh . . ." Kelly took a deep breath of the hot air in the car and blew it out through his broad nose. He looked at the covered object like a father who was angry with his son's faults but angrier with those who mentioned the faults of his son.

"Plenty o' fight left in him," he said.

Pole watched the people walking on the platform. He watched a porter pushing a wagon full of suitcases.

"Well . . . is he okay?" Kelly asked finally as if he hated to ask.

Pole looked over at him.

"I dunno know, Steel," he said. "He needs work. Ya know that. The trigger spring in his left arm's been rewired so many damn times it's almost shot. He's got no protection on that side. The left side of his face's all beat in, the eye lens is cracked. The leg cables is worn, they're pulled slack, the tension's gone to hell. Even his gyro's off."

Pole looked out at the platform again with a disgusted hiss.

"Not to mention the oil paste he ain't got in 'im," he said.

"We'll get 'im some," Kelly said.

"Yeah, *after* the fight, *after* the fight!" Pole snapped. "What about *before* the fight? He'll be creakin' around that ring like a goddam . . . *steam shovel*. It'll be a miracle if he does two rounds. They'll prob'ly ride us outta town on a rail."

Kelly swallowed. "I don't think it's that bad," he said.

"The *hell* it ain't," said Pole. "It's worse. Wait'll that crowd gets a load of 'Battling Maxo' from Philadelphia. They'll blow a nut. We'll be lucky if we get our five hundred bucks."

"Well, the contract's signed," said Kelly firmly. "They can't back out now. I got a copy right in the old pocket." He leaned over and patted at his coat.

"That contract's for Battling Maxo," said Pole. "Not for this steam shovel here."

"Maxo's gonna do all right," said Kelly as if he was trying hard to believe it. "He's not as bad off as you say."

"Against a B-*seven?*" Pole asked.

"It's just a *starter* B-*seven,*" said Kelly. "It ain't got the kinks out yet."

Pole turned away.

"Battling Maxo," he said. "One-round Maxo. The battling steam shovel."

"Aw, shut the hell up!" Kelly snapped suddenly, getting redder.

"You're always knockin' 'im down. Well, he's been doin' OK for twelve years now and he'll keep on doin' OK. So he needs some oil paste. And he needs a little work. So *what?* With five hundred bucks we can get him all the paste he needs. And a new trigger spring for his arm and—and new leg cables! And everything. Chris*sake.*"

He fell back against the seat, chest shuddering with breath, and rubbed at his cheeks with his wet handkerchief. He looked aside at Maxo. Abruptly, he reached over a hand and patted Maxo's covered knee clumsily and the steel clanked hollowly under his touch.

"You're doin' all right," said Kelly to his fighter.

The train was moving across a sunbaked prairie. All the windows were open but the wind that blew in was like blasts from an oven.

Kelly sat reading his paper, his shirt sticking wetly to his broad chest. Pole had taken his coat off too and was staring morosely out the window at the grass-tufted prairie that went as far as he could see. Maxo sat under his covering, his heavy steel frame rocking a little with the motion of the train.

Kelly put down his paper.

"Not even a word," he said.

"What d'ya expect?" Pole asked. "They don't cover Maynard."

"Maxo ain't just some clunk from Maynard," said Kelly. "He was big time. Ya'd think they'd"—he shrugged—"remember him."

"Why? For a coupla prelims in the Garden three years ago?" Pole asked.

"It wasn't no three years, buddy," said Kelly definitely.

"It was in 1977," said Pole, "and now it's 1980. That's three years where I come from."

"It was late '77," said Kelly. "Right before Christmas. Don't ya remember? Just before . . . Marge and me . . ."

Kelly didn't finish. He stared down at the paper as if Marge's picture were on it—the way she looked the day she left him.

"What's the difference?" Pole asked. "They don't remember *them,* for Chrissake. With a coupla thousand o' the damn things floatin' around? How could they remember 'em? About the only ones who get space are the champeens and the new models."

Pole looked at Maxo. "I hear Mawling's puttin' out a B-nine this year," he said.

Kelly refocused his eyes. "Yeah?" he said uninterestedly.

"Hyper-triggers in both arms—*and* legs. All steeled aluminum. Triple gyro. Triple-twisted wiring. God, they'll be beautiful."

Kelly put down the paper.

"Think they'd remember him," he muttered. "It wasn't so long ago." His face relaxed in a smile of recollection.

"Boy, will I ever forget that night," he said. "No one gives us a tumble. It was all Dimsy the Rock, Dimsy the Rock. *Three* t'one for Dimsy the Rock. Dimsy the Rock—fourth-rankin' light heavy. On his way t'the top."

He chuckled deep in his chest. "And did we ever put him away," he said. *Oooh."* He grunted with savage pleasure. "I can see that left cross now. *Bang!* Right in the chops. And old Dimsy the Rock hittin' the canvas like a—like a *rock,* yeah, *just* like a rock!"

He laughed happily. "Boy, what a night, what a night," he said. "Will I ever forget that night?"

Pole looked at Kelly with a somber face. Then he turned away and stared at the dusty sunbaked plain again.

"I wonder," he muttered.

Kelly saw the man across the aisle looking again at the covered Maxo. He caught the man's eye and smiled, then gestured with his head toward Maxo.

"That's my fighter," he said loudly.

The man smiled politely, cupping a hand behind one ear.

"My fighter," said Kelly. "Battling Maxo. Ever hear of 'im?"

The man stared at Kelly a moment before shaking his head.

Kelly smiled. "Yeah, he was almost light-heavyweight champ once," he told the man. The man nodded politely.

On an impulse, Kelly got up and stepped across the aisle. He reversed the seat back in front of the man and sat down facing him.

"Pretty damn hot," he said.

The man smiled. "Yes. Yes it is," he said.

"No new trains out here yet, huh?"

"No," said the man. "Not yet."

"Got all the new ones back in Philly," said Kelly. "That's where"—he gestured with his head—"my friend 'n' I come from. And Maxo."

Kelly stuck out his hand.

"The name's Kelly," he said. "Tim Kelly."

The man looked surprised. His grip was loose.

When he drew back his hand he rubbed it unobtrusively on his pants leg.

"I used t'be called 'Steel' Kelly," said Kelly. "Used t'be in the business m'self. Before the war, o' course. I was a light heavy."

"Oh?"

"Yeah. That's right. Called me 'Steel' 'cause I never got knocked down once. Not *once*. I was even number nine in the ranks once. Yeah."

"I see." The man waited patiently.

"My—fighter," said Kelly, gesturing toward Maxo with his head again. "He's a light heavy too. We're fightin' in Maynard t'night. You goin' that far?"

"Uh, no," said the man. "No, I'm—getting off at Hayes."

"Oh." Kelly nodded. "Too bad. Gonna be a good scrap." He let out a heavy breath. "Yeah, he was fourth in the ranks once. He'll be *back* too. He—uh—knocked down Dimsy the Rock in late '77. Maybe ya read about that."

"I don't believe...."

"Oh. Uh-huh." Kelly nodded. "Well...it was in all the East Coast papers. You know. New York, Boston, Philly. Yeah it got a hell of a spread. Biggest upset o' the year."

He scratched at his bald spot.

"He's a B-two, y'know, but—that means he's the second model Mawling put out," he explained, seeing the look on the man's face. "That was back in—let's see—'67, I think it was. Yeah, '67."

He made a smacking sound with his lips. "Yeah, that was a good model," he said. "The best. Maxo's still goin' strong." He shrugged depreciatingly. "I don't go for these new ones," he said. "You know. The ones made o' steeled aluminum with all the doodads."

The man stared at Kelly blankly.

"Too...flashy—flimsy. Nothin'..." Kelly bunched his big fist in front of his chest and made a face. "Nothin' *solid*," he said. "No. Mawling don't make 'em like Maxo no more."

"I see," said the man.

Kelly smiled.

"Yeah," he said. "Used t'be in the game m'self. When there was enough men, o' course. Before the bans." He shook his head, then smiled quickly. "Well," he said, "we'll take this B-seven. Don't even know what his name is," he said, laughing.

His face sobered for an instant and he swallowed.

"We'll take 'im," he said.

Later on, when the man had gotten off the train, Kelly went back to his seat. He put his feet up on the opposite seat and, laying back his head, he covered his face with the newspaper.

"Get a little shut-eye," he said.

Pole grunted.

Kelly sat slouched back, staring at the newspaper next to his eyes. He felt Maxo against his side a little. He listened to the squeaking of Maxo's joints. "Be all right," he muttered to himself.

"What?" Pole asked.

Kelly swallowed. "I didn't say anything," he said.

When they got off the train at six o'clock that evening they pushed Maxo around the station and onto the sidewalk. Across the street from them a man sitting in his taxi called them.

"We got no taxi money," said Pole.

"We can't just push 'im through the streets," Kelly said. "Besides, we don't even know where Kruger Stadium is."

"What are we supposed to eat with then?"

"We'll be loaded after the fight," said Kelly. "I'll buy you a steak three inches thick."

Sighing, Pole helped Kelly push the heavy Maxo across the street that was still so hot they could feel it through their shoes. Kelly started sweating right away and licking at his upper lip.

"God, how d'they live out here?" he asked.

When they were putting Maxo inside the cab the base wheel came out again and Pole, with a snarl, kicked it away.

"What're ya *doin'*?" Kelly asked.

"Oh . . . sh—" Pole got into the taxi and slumped back against the warm leather of the seat while Kelly hurried over the soft tar pavement and picked up the wheel.

"Chris*sake*," Kelly muttered as he got in the cab. "What's the—?"

"Where to, chief?" the driver asked.

"Kruger Stadium," Kelly said.

"You're there." The cab driver pushed in the rotor button and the car glided away from the curb.

"What the hell's wrong with you?" Kelly asked Pole in a low voice. "We wait more'n half a damn year t'get us a bout and you been nothin' but bellyaches from the start."

"Some bout," said Pole. "Maynard, Kansas—the prizefightin' center o' the nation."

"It's a start, ain't it?" Kelly said. "It'll keep us in coffee 'n' cakes a while, won't it? It'll put Maxo back in shape. And if we take it, it could lead to—"

Pole glanced over disgustedly.

"I don't *get* you," Kelly said quietly. "He's our fighter. What're ya writin' 'im off for? Don't ya want 'im t'win?"

"I'm a class-A mechanic, Steel," Pole said in his falsely patient voice. "I'm not a daydreamin' kid. We got a piece 'o dead iron here, not

a B-seven. It's simple mechanics, Steel, that's all. Maxo'll be lucky if
he comes out o' that ring with his head still on."

Kelly turned away angrily.

"It's a *starter* B-seven," he muttered. "Full o' kinks. *Full* of 'em."

"Sure, sure," said Pole.

They sat silently a while looking out the window, Maxo between
them, the broad steel shoulders bumping against theirs. Kelly stared at
the building, his hands clenching and unclenching in his lap as if he was
getting ready to go fifteen rounds.

"Have you seen this Maynard Flash?" Pole asked the driver.

"The Flash? You bet. Man, there's a fighter on his way. Won seven
straight. He'll be up there soon, ya can bet ya life. Matter o' fact he's
fightin' t'night too. With some B-two heap from back East, I hear."

The driver snickered. "Flash'll slaughter 'im," he said.

Kelly stared at the back of the driver's head, the skin tight across his
cheekbones.

"Yeah?" he said flatly.

"Man, he'll—"

The driver broke off suddenly and looked back. "Hey, you ain't—" he
started, then turned front again. "Hey, I didn't know, mister," he said. "I
was only ribbin'."

"Skip it," Pole said. "You're right."

Kelly's head snapped around and he glared at the sallow-faced Pole.

"Shut up," he said in a low voice.

He fell back against the seat and stared out the window, his face hard.

"I'm gonna get 'im some oil paste," he said after they'd ridden a block.

"Swell," said Pole. "We'll eat the tools."

"Go to hell," said Kelly.

The cab pulled up in front of the brick-fronted stadium and they lifted
Maxo out onto the sidewalk. While Pole tilted him, Kelly squatted down
and slid the base wheel back into its slot. Then Kelly paid the driver the
exact fare and they started pushing Maxo toward the alley.

"Look," said Kelly, nodding toward the poster board in front of the
stadium. The third fight listed was

MAYNARD FLASH

(B-7, L.H.)

VS.

BATTLING MAXO

(B-2, L.H.)

"Big deal," said Pole.

Kelly's smile disappeared. He started to say something, then pressed his lips together. He shook his head irritably and big drops of his sweat fell to the sidewalk.

Maxo creaked as they pushed him down the alley and carried him up the steps to the door. The base wheel fell out again and bounced down the cement steps. Neither one of them said anything.

It was hotter inside. The air didn't move.

"Get the wheel," Kelly said and started down the narrow hallway, leaving Pole with Maxo. Pole leaned Maxo against the wall and turned for the door.

Kelly came to a half-glassed office door and knocked.

"Yeah," said a voice inside. Kelly went in, taking off his hat.

The fat bald man looked up from his desk. His skull glistened with sweat.

"I'm Battling Maxo's owner," said Kelly, smiling. He extended his big hand but the man ignored it.

"Was wonderin' if you'd make it," said the man whose name was Mr. Waddow. "Your fighter in decent shape?"

"The best," said Kelly cheerfully. "The best. My mechanic—he's class-A—just took 'im apart and put 'im together again before we left Philly."

The man looked unconvinced.

"He's in good shape," said Kelly.

"You're lucky t'get a bout with a B-two," said Mr. Waddow. "We ain't used nothin' less than B-fours for more than two years now. The fighter we was after got stuck in a car wreck though and got ruined."

Kelly nodded. "Well, ya got nothin' t'worry about," he said. "My fighter's in top shape. He's the one knocked down Dimsy the Rock in Madison Square year or so ago."

"I want a good fight," said the fat man.

"You'll get a good fight," Kelly said, feeling a tight pain in his stomach muscles. "Maxo's in good shape. You'll see. He's in top shape."

"I just want a good fight."

Kelly stared at the fat man a moment. Then he said, "You got a ready room we can use? The mechanic 'n' me'd like t'get something t'eat."

"Third door down the hall on the right side," said Mr. Waddow. "Your bout's at eight thirty."

Kelly nodded. "OK."

"Be there," said Mr. Waddow, turning back to his work.

"Uh . . . what about—?" Kelly started.

"You get ya money after ya deliver a fight," Mr. Waddow cut him off.

Kelly's smile faltered.

"OK," he said. "See ya then."

When Mr. Waddow didn't answer, he turned for the door.

"Don't slam the door," Mr. Waddow said. Kelly didn't.

"Come on," he said to Pole when he was in the hall again. They pushed Maxo down to the ready room and put him inside it.

"What about checkin' im over?" Kelly said.

"What about my *gut?*" snapped Pole. "I ain't eaten in six hours."

Kelly blew out a heavy breath. "All right, let's go then," he said.

They put Maxo in a corner of the room.

"We should be able t'lock him in," Kelly said.

"Why? Ya think somebody's gonna *steal* 'im?"

"He's valuable," said Kelly.

"Sure, he's a priceless antique," said Pole.

Kelly closed the door three times before the latch caught. He turned away from it, shaking his head worriedly. As they started down the hall he looked at his wrist and saw for the fiftieth time the white band where his pawned watch had been.

"What time is it?" he asked.

"Six twenty-five," said Pole.

"We'll have t'make it fast," Kelly said. "I want ya t'check 'im over good before the fight."

"What for?" asked Pole.

"Did ya *hear* me?" Kelly said angrily.

"Sure, sure," Pole said.

"He's gonna take that son-of-a-bitch B-seven," Kelly said, barely opening his lips.

"Sure he is," said Pole. "With his teeth."

"Some town," Kelly said disgustedly as they came back in the side door of the stadium.

"I told ya they wouldn't have any oil paste here," Pole said. "Why should they? B-twos are dead. Maxo's probably the only one in a thousand miles."

Kelly walked quickly down the hall, opened the door of the ready room and went in. He crossed over to Maxo and pulled off the covering.

"Get to it," he said. "There ain't much time."

Blowing out a slow, tired breath, Pole took off his wrinkled blue coat and tossed it over the bench standing against the wall. He dragged a small table over to where Maxo was, then rolled up his sleeves. Kelly took off his hat and coat and watched while Pole worked loose the nut that held the tool cavity door shut. He stood with his big hands on his hips while Pole drew out the tools one by one and laid them down on the table.

"Rust," Pole muttered. He rubbed a finger around the inside of the cavity and held it up, copper-colored rust flaking off the tip.

"Come on," Kelly said irritably. He sat down on the bench and watched as Pole pried off the sectional plates on Maxo's chest. His eyes ran up over Maxo's leonine head. *If I didn't see them coils*, he thought once more, *I'd swear he was real*. Only the mechanics in a B-fighter could tell it wasn't real men in there. Sometimes people were actually fooled and sent in letters complaining that real men were being used. Even from ringside the flesh tones looked human. Mawling had a special patent on that.

Kelly's face relaxed as he smiled fondly at Maxo.

"Good boy," he murmured. Pole didn't hear. Kelly watched the sure-handed mechanic probe with his electric pick, examining connections and potency centers.

"Is he all right?" he asked, without thinking.

"Sure, he's great," Pole said. He plucked out a tiny steel-caged tube. "If this doesn't blow out," he said.

"Why should it?"

"It's sub-par," Pole said jadedly. "I told ya that after the last fight *eight months* ago."

Kelly swallowed. "We'll get 'im a new one after this bout," he said.

"Seventy-five bucks," muttered Pole as if he were watching the money fly away on green wings.

"It'll hold," Kelly said, more to himself than Pole.

Pole shrugged. He put back the tube and pressed in the row of buttons on the main autonomic board. Maxo stirred.

"Take it easy on the left arm," said Kelly. "Save it."

"If it don't work here, it won't work out there," said Pole.

He jabbed at a button and Maxo's left arm began moving with little, circling motions. Pole pushed over the safety-block switch that would keep Maxo from counterpunching and stepped back. He threw a right at Maxo's chin and the robot's arm jumped up with a hitching motion to cover his face. Maxo's left eye flickered like a ruby catching the sun.

"If that eye cell goes . . ." Pole said.

"It *won't*," said Kelly tensely. He watched Pole throw another punch at the left side of Maxo's head. He saw the tiny ripple of the flexo-covered cheek, then the arm jerked up again. It squeaked.

"That's enough," he said. "It works. Try the rest of 'im."

"He's gonna get more than two punches throwed at his head," Pole said.

"His arm's all right," Kelly said. "Try something else, I said."

Pole reached inside Maxo and activated the leg-cable centers. Maxo began shifting around. He lifted his left leg and shook off the base wheel automatically. Then he was standing lightly on black-shoed feet, feeling at the floor like a cured cripple testing for stance.

Pole reached forward and jabbed in the FULL button, then jumped back as Maxo's eye beams centered on him and the robot moved forward, broad shoulders rocking slowly, arms up defensively.

"Damn," Pole muttered, "they'll hear 'im squeakin' in the back row."

Kelly grimaced, teeth set. He watched Pole throw another right and Maxo's arm lurch up raggedly. His throat moved with a convulsive swallow and he seemed to have trouble breathing the close air in the little room.

Pole shifted around the floor quickly, side to side. Maxo followed lumberingly, changing directions with visibly jerking motions.

"Oh, he's *beautiful*," Pole said, stopping. "Just beautiful." Maxo came up, arms still raised, and Pole jabbed in under them, pushing the OFF button. Maxo stopped.

"Look, we'll have t'put 'im on *de*fense, Steel," Pole said. "That's all there is to it. He'll get chopped t'pieces if we have 'im movin' in."

Kelly cleared his throat. "No," he said.

"Oh for—will ya use ya *head?*" snapped Pole. "He's a B-two, f'Chrissake. He's gonna get slaughtered anyway. Let's save the pieces."

"They want 'im on the *off*ense," said Kelly. "It's in the contract."

Pole turned away with a hiss.

"What's the use?" he muttered.

"Test 'im some more."

"What for? He's as good as he'll ever be."

"Will ya do what I say!" Kelly shouted, all the tension exploding out of him.

Pole turned back and jabbed in a button. Maxo's left arm shot out. There was a snapping noise inside it and it fell against Maxo's side with a dead clank.

Kelly started up, his face stricken. "My God! What did ya *do?*" he cried. He ran over to where Pole was pushing the button again. Maxo's arm didn't move.

"I *told* ya not t'fool with that arm!" Kelly yelled. "What the hell's the *matter* with ya!" His voice cracked in the middle of the sentence.

Pole didn't answer. He picked up his pry and began working off the left shoulder plate.

"So help me God, if you broke that arm..." Kelly warned in a low, snaking voice.

"If *I* broke it!" Pole snapped. "Listen, you dumb mick! This heap has been runnin' on borrowed time for three years now! Don't talk t'me about breakages!"

Kelly clenched his teeth, his eyes small and deadly.

"Open it up," he said.

"Son-of-a—" Pole muttered as he got the plate off. "You find another goddam mechanic that coulda kep' this steam shovel together any better these last years. You just *find* one."

Kelly didn't answer. He stood rigidly, watching while Pole put down the curved plate and looked inside.

When Pole touched it, the trigger spring broke in half and part of it jumped across the room.

Pole started to say something, then stopped. He looked at the ashen-faced Kelly without moving.

Kelly's eyes moved to Pole.

"Fix it," he said hoarsely.

Pole swallowed. "Steel, I—"

"*Fix* it!"

"I can't! That spring's been fixin t'break for—"

"You broke it! Now *fix* it!" Kelly clamped rigid fingers on Pole's arm. Pole jerked back.

"Let go of me!" he said.

"What's the matter with you!" Kelly cried. "Are you crazy? He's got t'be fixed. He's *got* t'be!"

"Steel, he needs a new spring."

"Well, *get* it!"

"They don't *have* 'em here, Steel," Pole said. "I *told* ya. And if they *did* have 'em, we ain't got the sixteen fifty t'get one."

"Oh . . . Oh, God," said Kelly. His hand fell away and he stumbled to the other side of the room. He sank down on the bench and stared without blinking at the tall, motionless Maxo.

He sat there a long time, just staring, while Pole stood watching him, the pry still in his hand. He saw Kelly's broad chest rise and fall with spasmodic movements. Kelly's face was a blank.

"If he don't watch 'em," muttered Kelly finally.

"What?"

Kelly looked up, his mouth set in a straight, hard line. "If he don't watch, it'll work," he said.

"What're ya talkin' about?"

Kelly stood up and started unbuttoning his shirt.

"What're ya—"

Pole stopped dead, his mouth falling open. "Are you *crazy?*" he asked.

Kelly kept unbuttoning his shirt. He pulled it off and tossed it on the bench.

"Steel, you're out o' your mind!" Pole said. "You can't do that!"

Kelly didn't say anything.

"But you'll—Steel, you're *crazy!*"

"We deliver a fight or we don't get paid," Kelly said.

"But—you'll get *killed!*"

Kelly pulled off his undershirt. His chest was beefy, there was red hair swirling around it. "Have to shave this off," he said.

"Steel, *come on*," Pole said. "You—"

His eyes widened as Kelly sat down on the bench and started unlacing his shoes.

"They'll never let ya," Pole said. "You can't make 'em think you're a—" He stopped and took a jerky step forward. "Steel, fuh Chrissake!"

Kelly looked up at Pole with dead eyes.

"You'll help me," he said.

"But they—"

"Nobody knows what Maxo looks like," Kelly said. "And only Waddow saw me. If he don't watch the bouts we'll be all right."

"But—"

"They won't know," Kelly said. "The B's bleed and bruise too."

"Steel, come on," Pole said shakily. He took a deep breath and calmed himself. He sat down hurriedly beside the broad-shouldered Irishman.

"Look," he said. "I got a sister back East—in Maryland. If I wire 'er, she'll send us the dough t'get back."

Kelly got up and unbuckled his belt.

"Steel, I know a guy in Philly with a B-five wants t'sell cheap," Pole said desperately. "We could scurry up the cash and—Steel, fuh Chrissake, you'll get *killed!* It's a B-seven! Don't ya understand? A B-*seven!* You'll be mangled!"

Kelly was working the dark trunks over Maxo's hips.

"I won't let ya do it, Steel," Pole said. "I'll go to—"

He broke off with a sucked-in gasp as Kelly whirled and moved over quickly to haul him to his feet. Kelly's grip was like the jaws of a trap and there was nothing left of him in his eyes.

"You'll help me," Kelly said in a low, trembling voice. "You'll help me or I'll beat ya brains out on the wall."

"You'll get killed," Pole murmured.

"Then I will," said Kelly.

Mr. Waddow came out of his office as Pole was walking the covered Kelly toward the ring.

"Come on, come on," Mr. Waddow said. "They're waitin' on ya."

Pole nodded jerkily and guided Kelly down the hall.

"Where's the owner?" Mr. Waddow called after them.

Pole swallowed quickly. "In the audience," he said.

Mr. Waddow grunted and, as they walked on, Pole heard the door to the office close. Breath emptied from him.

"I should've told 'im," he muttered.

"I'd o' killed ya," Kelly said, his voice muffled under the covering.

Crowd sounds leaked back into the hall now as they turned a corner. Under the canvas covering, Kelly felt a drop of sweat trickle down his temple.

"Listen," he said, "you'll have t'towel me off between rounds."

"Between what rounds?" Pole asked tensely. "You won't even last one."

"Shut up."

"You think you're just up against some tough fighter?" Pole asked. "You're up against a machine! Don't ya—"

"I said shut up."

"Oh . . . you dumb—" Pole swallowed. "If I towel ya off, they'll know," he said.

"They ain't seen a B-two in years," Kelly broke in. "If anyone asks, tell 'em it's an oil leak."

"Sure," said Pole disgustedly. He bit his lips. "Steel, ya'll never get away with it."

The last part of his sentence was drowned out as, suddenly, they were among the crowd, walking down the sloping aisle toward the ring. Kelly held his knees locked and walked a little stiffly. He drew in a long, deep breath and let it out slowly.

The heat burdened in around him like a hanging weight. It was like walking along the sloping floor of an ocean of heat and sound. He heard voices drifting past him as he moved.

"Ya'll take 'im home in a box!"

"Well, if it ain't *Rattlin'* Maxo!"

And the inevitable, *"Scrap iron!"*

Kelly swallowed dryly, feeling a tight, drawing sensation in his loins. Thirsty, he thought. The momentary vision of the bar across from the Kansas City train station crossed his mind. The dim-lit booth, the cool fan breeze on the back of his neck, the icy, sweat-beaded bottle chilling his palm. He swallowed again. He hadn't allowed himself one drink in the last hour. The less he drank the less he'd sweat, he knew.

"Watch it."

He felt Pole's hand slide in through the opening in the back of the covering, felt the mechanic's hand grab his arm and check him.

"Ring steps," Pole said out of a corner of his mouth.

Kelly edged his right foot forward until the shoe tip touched the riser of the bottom step. Then he lifted his foot to the step and started up.

At the top, Pole's fingers tightened around his arm again.

"Ropes," Pole said, guardedly.

It was hard getting through the ropes with the covering on. Kelly almost fell and hoots and catcalls came at him like spears out of the din. Kelly felt the canvas give slightly under his feet and then Pole pushed the stool against the back of his legs and he sat down a little too jerkily.

"Hey, get that derrick out o' here!" shouted a man in the second row. Laughter and hoots.

Then Pole drew off the covering and put it down on the ring apron.

Kelly sat there staring at the Maynard Flash.

The B-seven was motionless, its gloved hands hanging across its legs. There was imitation blonde hair, crew cut, growing out of its skull pores. Its face was that of an impassive Adonis. The simulation of muscle curve on its body and limbs was almost perfect. For a moment Kelly almost thought that years had been peeled away and he was in the business again, facing a young contender. He swallowed carefully. Pole crouched beside him, pretending to fiddle with an arm plate.

"Steel, *don't*," he muttered again.

Kelly didn't answer. He kept staring at the Maynard Flash, thinking of the array of instant-reaction centers inside that smooth arch of chest. The drawing sensation reached his stomach. It was like a cold hand pulling in at strands of muscle and ligament.

A red-faced man in a white suit climbed into the ring and reached up for the microphone which was swinging down to him.

"Ladies and gentlemen," he announced, "the opening bout of the evening. A ten-round light-heavyweight bout. From Philadelphia, the B-two, *Battling Maxo.*"

The crowd booed and hissed. They threw up paper airplanes and shouted, *"Scrap iron!"*

"His opponent, our own B-seven, the *Maynard Flash!*"

Cheers and wild clapping. The Flash's mechanic touched a button under the left armpit and the B-seven jumped up and held his arms over his head in the victory gesture. The crowd laughed happily.

"God," Pole muttered, "I never saw that. Must be a new gimmick."

Kelly blinked to relieve his eyes.

"Three more bouts to follow," said the red-faced man and then the microphone drew up and he left the ring. There was no referee. B-fighters never clinched—their machinery rejected it—and there was no knockdown count. A fellow B-fighter stayed down. The new B-nine, it was claimed by the Mawling publicity staff, would be able to get up, which would make for livelier and longer bouts.

Pole pretended to check over Kelly.

"Steel, it's your last chance," he begged.

"Get out," said Kelly without moving his lips.

Pole looked at Kelly's immobile eyes a moment, then sucked in a ragged breath and straightened up.

"Stay *away* from him," he warned as he started through the ropes.

Across the ring, the Flash was standing in its corner, hitting its gloves together as if it were a real young fighter anxious to get the fight started. Kelly stood up and Pole drew the stool away. Kelly stood watching the B-seven, seeing how its eye centers were zeroing in on him. There was a cold sinking in his stomach.

The bell rang.

The B-seven moved out smoothly from its corner with a mechanical glide, its arms raised in the traditional way, gloved hands wavering in tiny circles in front of it. It moved quickly toward Kelly, who edged out of his corner automatically, his mind feeling, abruptly, frozen. He felt his own hands rise as if someone else had lifted them and his legs were like dead wood under him. He kept his gaze on the bright, unmoving eyes of the Maynard Flash.

They came together. The B-seven's left flicked out and Kelly blocked it, feeling the rock-hard fist of the Flash even through his glove. The fist moved out again. Kelly drew back his head and felt a warm breeze across his mouth. His own left shot out and banged against the Flash's nose. It was like hitting a doorknob. Pain flared in Kelly's arm and his jaw muscles went hard as he struggled to keep his face blank.

The B-seven feinted with a left and Kelly knocked it aside. He couldn't stop the right that blurred in after it and grazed his left temple. He jerked his head away and the B-seven threw a left that hit him over the ear. Kelly lurched back, throwing out a left that the B-seven brushed aside. Kelly caught his footing and hit the Flash's jaw solidly with a right uppercut. He felt a jolt of pain run up his arm. The Flash's head didn't budge. He shot out a left that hit Kelly on the right shoulder.

Kelly backpedaled instinctively. Then he heard someone yell, "Get 'im a bicycle!" and he remembered what Mr. Waddow had said. He moved in again.

A left caught him under the heart and he felt the impact shudder through his frame. Pain stabbed at his heart. He threw a spasmodic left which banged against the B-seven's nose again. There was only pain. Kelly stepped back and staggered as a hard right caught him high on the chest. He started to move back. The B-seven hit him on the chest again. Kelly lost his balance and stepped back quickly to catch equilibrium. The crowd booed. The B-seven moved in without making a single mechanical sound.

Kelly regained his balance and stopped. He threw a hard right that missed. The momentum of his blow threw him off center and the Flash's left drove hard against his upper right arm. The arm went numb. Even as Kelly was sucking in a teeth-clenched gasp the B-seven shot in a hard right under his guard that slammed into Kelly's spongy stomach. Kelly felt the breath go out of him. His right slapped ineffectively across the Flash's right cheek. The Flash's eyes glinted.

As the B-seven moved in again, Kelly sidestepped and, for a moment, the radial eye centers lost him. Kelly moved out of range dizzily, pulling air in through his nostrils.

"Get that heap out o' there!" a man yelled.

Breath shook in Kelly's throat. He swallowed quickly and started forward just as the Flash picked him up again. He stepped in close, hoping to outtime electrical impulse, and threw a hard right at the Flash's body.

The B-seven's left shot up and Kelly's blow was deflected by the iron wrist. Kelly's left was thrown off too and then the Flash's left shot in and drove the breath out of Kelly again. Kelly's left barely hit the Flash's rock-hard chest. He staggered back, the B-seven following. He kept jabbing but the B-seven kept deflecting the blows and counter-jabbing with almost the same piston-like motion. Kelly's head kept snapping back. He fell back more and saw the right coming straight at him. He couldn't stop it.

The blow drove in like a steel battering ram. Spears of pain shot behind Kelly's eyes and through his head. A black cloud seemed to flood across the ring. His muffled cry was drowned out by the screaming crowd as he toppled back, his nose and mouth trickling bright blood that looked as good as the dye they used in the B-fighters.

The rope checked his fall, pressing in rough and hard against his back. He swayed there, right arm hanging limp, left arm raised defensively. He blinked his eyes instinctively, trying to focus them. I'm a robot, he thought, a robot.

The Flash stepped in and drove a violent right into Kelly's chest, a left to his stomach. Kelly doubled over, gagging. A right slammed off his skull like a hammer blow, driving him back against the ropes again. The crowd screamed.

Kelly saw the blurred outline of the Maynard Flash. He felt another blow smash into his chest like a club. With a sob he threw a wild left that the B-seven brushed off. Another sharp blow landed on Kelly's shoulder. He lifted his right and managed to deflect the worst of a left thrown at his jaw. Another right concaved his stomach. He doubled over. A hammering right drove him back on the ropes. He felt hot, salty blood in his mouth and the roar of the crowd seemed to swallow him.

Stay up!—he screamed at himself. Stay up, goddam you! The ring wavered before him like dark water.

With a desperate surge of energy, he threw a right as hard as he could at the tall, beautiful figure in front of him. Something cracked in his wrist and hand and a wave of searing pain shot up his arm. His throat-locked cry went unheard. His arm fell, his left went down, and the crowd shrieked and howled for the Flash to finish it.

There were only inches between them now. The B-seven rained in blows that didn't miss. Kelly lurched and staggered under the impact of them. His head snapped from side to side. Blood ran across his face in scarlet ribbons. His arm hung like a dead branch at his side. He kept getting slammed back against the ropes, bouncing forward and getting slammed back again. He couldn't see anymore. He could only hear the screaming of the crowd and the endless swishing and thudding of the B-seven's gloves. Stay up, he thought. I have to stay up. He drew in his head and hunched his shoulders to protect himself.

He was like that seven seconds before the bell when a clubbing right on the side of his head sent him crashing to the canvas.

He lay there gasping for breath. Suddenly, he started to get up, then, equally as suddenly, realized that he couldn't. He fell forward again and lay on his stomach on the warm canvas, his head throbbing with pain. He could hear the booing and hissing of the dissatisfied crowd.

When Pole finally managed to get him up and slip the cover over his head the crowd was jeering so loudly that Kelly couldn't hear Pole's voice. He felt the mechanic's big hand inside the covering, guiding him, but he fell down climbing through the ropes and almost fell again on the steps. His legs were like rubber tubes. Stay up. His brain still murmured the words.

In the ready room he collapsed. Pole tried to get him up on the bench but he couldn't. Finally, he bunched up his blue coat under Kelly's head and, kneeling, he started patting with his handkerchief at the trickles of blood.

"You dumb bastard," he kept muttering in a thin, shaking voice. "You dumb bastard."

Kelly lifted his left hand and brushed away Pole's hand.

"Go—get the—money," he gasped hoarsely.

"What?"

"The money!" gasped Kelly through his teeth.

"But—"

"*Now!*" Kelly's voice was barely intelligible.

Pole straightened up and stood looking down at Kelly a moment. Then he turned and went out.

Kelly lay there drawing in breath and exhaling it with wheezing sounds. He couldn't move his right hand and he knew it was broken. He felt the blood trickling from his nose and mouth. His body throbbed with pain.

After a few moments he struggled up on his left elbow and turned his head, pain crackling along his neck muscles. When he saw that Maxo was all right he put his head down again. A smile twisted up one corner of his lips.

When Pole came back, Kelly lifted his head painfully. Pole came over and knelt down. He started patting at the blood again.

"Ya get it?" Kelly asked in a crusty whisper.

Pole drew out a slow breath.

"Well?"

Pole swallowed. "Half of it," he said.

Kelly stared up at him blankly, his mouth fallen open. His eyes didn't believe it.

"He said he wouldn't pay five C's for a one rounder."

"What d'ya mean?" Kelly's voice cracked. He tried to get up and put down his right hand. With a strangled cry he fell back, his face white. His head thrashed on the coat pillow, his eyes shut tightly.

"He can't—he can't do that," he gasped.

Pole licked his dry lips.

"Steel, there—ain't a thing we can do. He's got a bunch o' toughs in the office with 'im. I can't. . . ." He lowered his head. "And if—you was t'go there he'd know what ya done. And—he might even take back the two and a half."

Kelly lay on his back staring up at the naked bulb without blinking. His chest labored and shuddered with breath.

"No," he murmured. "No."

He lay there for a long time without talking. Pole got some water and cleaned off his face and gave him a drink. He opened up his small suitcase and patched up Kelly's face. He put Kelly's right arm in a sling.

Fifteen minutes later Kelly spoke.

"We'll go back by bus," he said.

"What?" Pole asked.

"We'll go by bus," Kelly said slowly. "That'll only cost fifty-six bucks." He swallowed and shifted on his back. "That'll leave us almost two C's. We can get 'im a—a new trigger spring and a—eye lens and—" He blinked his eyes and held them shut a moment as the room started fading again.

"And oil paste," he said then. "Loads of it. He'll be—good as new again."

Kelly looked up at Pole. "Then we'll be all set up," he said. "Maxo'll be in good shape again. And we can get us some decent bouts," He swallowed and breathed laboriously. "That's all he needs is a little work. New spring, a new eye lens. That'll shape 'im up. We'll show those bastards what a B-two can do. Old Maxo'll show 'em. *Right?*"

Pole looked down at the big Irishman and sighed.

"Sure, Steel," he said.

GOLDEN GLOVES

Joyce Carol Oates

He was a premature baby, seven months old, born with deformed feet: the tiny arches twisted, the toes turned inward like fleshy claws. He didn't learn to walk until the age of three; then he tottered and lurched from side to side, his small face contorted with an adult rage, a rim of white showing above the irises of his eyes. His parents watched him in pity and despair—his father with a kind of embarrassment as well. Even at that age he hated to be helped to walk. Sometimes he hated to be touched.

Until the age of eight, when both his feet were finally operated on, he was always stumbling, falling, hurting himself, but he was accustomed to pain, he rarely cried. He wasn't like other children! At school, on the playground, out on the street, the cruelest children mocked him, called him names—Cripple, Freak—sometimes they even tripped him—but as he got older and stronger they learned to keep their distance. If he could grab them he'd hurt them with his hard pummeling fists, he'd make them cry. And even with his handicap he was quick: quick and clever and sinewy as a snake.

After the operation on his feet his father began to take him to boxing matches downtown in the old sports arena. He will remember all his life the excitement of his first Golden Gloves tournament, some of the boxers as young as fifteen, ribs showing, backs raw with acne, hard tight muscles, tiny glinting gold crosses on chains around their necks. He remembers the brick-red leather gloves that looked as if they must be soft to the touch, the bodies hotly gleaming with sweat, white boys, black boys, their amazing agility, the quickness of their feet and hands, high-laced shoes and ribbed socks halfway to their knees. They wore trunks like swimming trunks, they wore robes like bathrobes, and all with such nonchalance, in public. He remembers the dazzling lights focused upon the elevated ring, the shouts of the crowd that came in waves, the warm rippling applause when one boy of a pair was declared the winner of his match, his arm held aloft by the referee. What must it be, to be that boy!—to stand in his place!

He was seated in a child's wheelchair in the aisle, close beside his father's seat. Both legs encased in plaster from hip to toe: and him trapped inside. He was a quiet child, a friendly child, uncomplaining and perhaps even shy, showing none of the emotion that welled up in him—hurt, anger, shame—when people stared. They were curious, mainly—didn't mean to be insulting. Just ignore them, honey, his mother always said. But when he was alone with his father and people looked at him a little too long his father bristled with irritation. If anyone dared ask what had happened to him his father would say, Who wants to know? in a certain voice. And the subject was quickly dropped.

To him his father said, Let the sons of bitches mind their own business and we'll mind ours. Right?

The operation had lasted nine hours but he remembered little of it afterward except the needle going into his arm, into a vein, the careening lights, then walking alone and frightened in a room so cold his teeth began to chatter. Such cold, and such silence: he thought he must have died. Then the pain began and he knew he was alive, he cried in short breathless incredulous sobs until the first shock was past. A nurse stood over him telling him he'd be all right. He'd been a brave, brave little boy, she said.

The promise all along had been: he'd be able to walk now like any other boy. As soon as the casts were removed.

And: he'd be able to run. (Until now he'd crawled on his hands and knees faster than he'd been able to walk, like something scuttling along a beach.)

In his wheelchair at the Golden Gloves tournament he told himself he would be a boxer: he told himself at the conclusion of the first three-round match when a panting grinning boy was declared the winner of his match, on points, his arm held high, the gleaming brick-red glove raised for all to see. And the applause!—immediate, familial, rising and swelling like a heartbeat gone wild. The boy's father was in the ring with him, other boys who might have been his brothers or cousins—they were hugging one another in their happiness at the victory. Then the ring was emptied except for the referee, and the next young boxers and their seconds appeared.

He knew: he would be up there in the ring one day in the lights, rows of people watching. He would be there in the lighted ring, not in a wheelchair. Not in the audience at all.

After the casts were removed he had to learn to walk again.

They stood him carefully against a wall like a small child and encouraged him, Don't be afraid, take a step, take another step, come to them as best he could. They told him it wouldn't hurt and though it did hurt he didn't care, he plunged out lurching, swaying, falling panicked into his mother's arms. Yes, said his mother. Like that. Come *on,* said his father. Try again.

It was a year before he could walk inside the house without limping or turning his left foot helplessly inward. It was another year before he could run in the yard or in the school playground. By then his father had bought him a pair of child's boxing gloves, soft simulated dark brown leather. The gloves were the size of melons and so beautiful his eyes filled with tears when he first saw them. He would remember their sharp pungent smell through his life.

His father laced on the gloves, crouched to spar with him, taught him a few basic principles—how to hold his guard, how to stand at an angle with his chin tucked against his shoulder (Joe Louis style), how to jab, how to keep moving—later arranged for him to take boxing lessons at the YMCA. His father had wanted to be a boxer himself when he was a boy, he'd fought in a few three-round matches at a local club but had won only the first match; his reflexes, he said, were just slightly off: when his opponent's jab got to him he forgot everything he knew and wanted to slug it out. He'd known enough to quit before he got hurt. Either you have the talent or you don't, his father said. It can't be faked.

He began to train at the Y, he worked out every day after school and on Saturday mornings; by the age of sixteen he'd brought his weight up to 130 pounds standing five foot six, he could run ten, twelve, as many as fifteen miles without tiring. He was quick, light, shrewd, he was good at boxing and he knew he was good, everyone acknowledged it, everyone watched him with interest. When he wasn't at the gym—when he had to be in school, or in church, or at home, even in bed—he was thinking about the gym, the ring, himself in his boxing trunks and leather gloves, Vaseline smeared on his face and his headgear on his head, he was in his crouch but getting ready to move, his knees bent, his hands closed into fists. He was ready! He couldn't be taken unawares! He couldn't be stopped! He became obsessed with some of the boys and young men he knew at the gym, their weights, their heights, the reach of their arms, could they knock him out if he fought them, could he knock them out? What did they think about *him?* There were weeks when he was infatuated with one or another boy who might be a year or two older than he, a better boxer, until it was revealed that he wasn't a better boxer after all: he had his weaknesses, his bad habits, his limitations. He concentrated a good deal on the feel of his own body, building up his muscles, strengthening his stomach, his neck, learning not to wince at pain—not to show pain at all. He loved the sinewy springiness of his legs and feet, the tension in his shoulders; he loved the way his body came to life, moving, it seemed, of its own will, knowing by instinct how to strike his opponent how to get through his opponent's guard how to hurt him and hurt him again and make it last. His clenched fists inside the shining gloves. His teeth in the mouthpiece. Eyes narrowed and shifting behind the hot lids as if they weren't his own eyes merely but those belonging to someone he didn't yet know, an adult man, a man for whom all things were possible.

Sometimes on Saturday afternoons the boys were shown film clips and documentaries of the great fighters. Jack Dempsey—Gene Tunney—Benny Leonard—Joe Louis—Billy Conn—Archie Moore—Sandy Saddler—Carmen Basilio—Sugar Ray Robinson—Jersey Joe Walcott—Rocky Marciano. He watched entranced, staring at the flickering images on the screen; some of the films were aged and poorly preserved, the blinds at the windows fitted loosely so that the room wasn't completely darkened, and the boxers took on an odd ghostly insubstantial look as they crouched and darted and lunged at one another. Feinting, clinching, backing off, then the flurry of gloves so swift the eye couldn't follow, one man suddenly down and the other in a neutral corner, the announcer's voice rising in excitement as if it were all happening now right now and not decades ago. More astonishing than the powerful blows dealt were the blows taken, the punishment absorbed as if really finally one could not be hurt by an opponent, only stopped by one's own failure of nerve or judgment. If you're hurt you deserve to be hurt! If you're hurt badly you deserve to be hurt badly! Turning to the referee to protest a low blow, his guard momentarily lowered—there was Jack Sharkey knocked out by Jack Dempsey with a fast left hook. Like that! And the fight was over. And there was aging Archie Moore knocked down repeatedly, savagely, by young Yvon Durrelle, staggering on his feet part-conscious but indomitable—how had he come back to win? how had he done it?—boasting he wasn't tired afterward, he could fight the fight all over again. Young Joe Louis baffled and outboxed by stylish Billy Conn for twelve rounds, then suddenly as Conn swarmed all over him trying to knock him out Louis came alive, turned into a machine for hitting, combinations so rapid the eye couldn't follow, left hooks, right crosses, uppercuts, a dozen punches within seconds and Conn was finished—that was the great Joe Louis in his prime. And here, Jersey Joe Walcott outboxing Rocky Marciano until suddenly Marciano connected with his right, that terrible incalculably powerful right, Let's see the knockout in slow motion, the announcer said, and you could see this time how it happened, Walcott hit so hard his face so stunned so distorted it was no longer a human face, no longer recognizable. And Rocky Marciano and Ezzard Charles fighting for Marciano's heavyweight title in 1954—after fifteen rounds both men covered in blood from cuts and gashes in their faces but embracing each other like brothers, smiling, laughing it seemed, in mutual respect and admiration and it didn't—almost—seem to matter that one man had to lose and the other had to win: they'd fought one of the great fights of the century and everyone knew it.

And *he* knew he was of their company. If only he might be allowed to show it.

He was sixteen years old, he was seventeen years old, boxing in local matches, working his way steadily up into state competitions, finally into the Golden Gloves Tri-State tournament. He had a good trainer, his father had seen to that. He had trophies, plaques, photographs taken at ringside, part of the living room was given over to his boxing as to a shrine. What do your friends think about your boxing? his relatives asked. Isn't it a dangerous sport? But he hadn't any friends that mattered and if his classmates had any opinion about him he couldn't have guessed what it might be, or cared. And, no, it wasn't a dangerous sport. It was only dangerous if you made mistakes.

It was said frequently at the gym that he was "coming along." The sportswriter for the local newspaper did a brief piece on him and a few other "promising" amateurs. He was quick and clever and intuitive, he knew to let a blow slide by his shoulder then to get his own in then to retreat, never to panic, never to shut his eyes, never to breathe through his mouth, it was all a matter of breath you might say, a matter of the most exquisite timing, momentum, a dancer's intelligence in his legs, the instinct to hit, to hit hard, and to hit again. He was a young Sandy Saddler they said—but he didn't fight dirty! No, he was a young Sugar Ray. Styled a bit on that brilliant new heavyweight Cassius Clay, who'd surprised the boxing world by knocking out Sonny Liston. He hadn't a really hard punch but he was working on it, working constantly, in any case he was winning all his matches or fighting to a draw, there's nothing wrong in fighting to a draw his father told him, though he could see

his father was disappointed sometimes, there were fights he should have
won but just didn't—couldn't. The best times were when he won a
match by a knockout, his opponent suddenly falling, and down, not
knocked out really, just sitting there on the canvas dazed and frightened,
blinking, looking as if he were about to cry but no one ever cried, that
never happened.

You have real talent, he was told. Told repeatedly.

You have a future!

The promise was—he seemed to know—that he couldn't lose. He'd
understood that years before, watching one or another of the films,
young Dempsey fierce as a tiger against the giant Jess Willard, twenty-
year-old Joe Louis in action, Sugar Ray Robinson who'd once killed an
opponent in the ring with the force of his blows: he was of their company and he knew it and he knew he couldn't lose, he couldn't even be
seriously hurt, that seemed to be part of the promise. But sometimes he
woke in the night in his bed not knowing at first where he was, was he
in the gym, in the ring, staring panicked across the wide lighted canvas
to his opponent shadowy in the opposite corner, he lay shivering, his
heart racing, the bedclothes damp with sweat. He liked to sweat most of
the time, he liked the rank smell of his own body, but this was not one of
those times. His fists when he woke would be clenched so hard his
fingernails would be cutting into his palms, his toes curled in tight and
cramped as if still deformed, secretly deformed. Cripple! Freak! The
blow you can't see coming is the blow that knocks you out—the blow
out of nowhere. How can you protect yourself against a blow out of
nowhere? How can you stop it from happening again? He'd been surprised like that only a few times, sparring, not in real fights. But the
surprise had stayed with him.

Yet there was a promise. Going back to when he was very small,
before the operation.

And his father adored him, his father was so happy for him, placing
bets on him, not telling him until afterward—after he'd won. Just small
bets. Just for fun. His father said, I don't want you to feel any pressure,
it's just for fun.

Then of course he was stopped and his "career" ended abruptly and
unromantically. As he should have foreseen. Just a few weeks before his
eighteenth birthday.

It happened midway in the first round of a Golden Gloves semifinal
lightweight match in Buffalo, New York, when a stocky black boy from
Trenton, New Jersey, came bounding at him like a killer, pushing and
crowding and bulling him back into the ropes, forcing him backward as

he'd never been forced; the boy brushed aside his jabs and ignored his feints, popped him with a hard left then landed a blow to his exposed mouth that drove his upper front teeth back through his slack lower lip but somehow at the same time smashed the teeth upward into his palate. He'd lost his mouthpiece in the confusion, he'd never seen the punch coming, he was told afterward it had been a hard straight right like no amateur punch anyone could recall.

He fell dazed into the ropes, he fell to the canvas, he hid his bleeding face with his gloves, gravity pulled him down and his instinct was to submit to curl up into a tight ball and lie very still maybe he wouldn't be hit again maybe it was all over.

And so it happened.

That was his career as an amateur boxer. Twenty or so serious matches: that was it.

Never again, he told himself. That *was* it.

(The black boy from New Jersey—Roland Bush Jr.—was eighteen years old at the time of the fight but had the face of a mature man, heavy-lidded eyes, broad flat nose, scars in his forehead and fanning his eyes. An inch shorter than his white opponent but his shoulder and leg muscles rippled with high-strung nervous strength, he'd thickened his neck muscles to withstand all blows, he was ready, he was hot, he couldn't be stopped. His skin was very dark and the whites of his eyes were an eerie bluish-white, luminous, threaded almost invisibly with blood. He weighed no more than his opponent but he had a skull and a body build to absorb punishment, he was solid, hard, relentless, taking no joy in his performance just doing it, doing it superbly, getting it done, he went on to win the Golden Gloves title in his division with another spectacular knockout and a few months later turned professional and was advanced swiftly through the lightweight ranks then into the junior welterweights where he was ranked number fourteen by *Ring* magazine at the time of his death—he died aged twenty of a cerebral hemorrhage following a ten-round fight in Houston, Texas, which he'd lost in the ninth round by a technical knockout.)

The fight was stopped, the career of "promise" was stopped, now he is thirty-four years old and it seems to him his life is passing swiftly. But at a distance. It doesn't seem in fact to belong to him, it might be anybody's life.

In his professional career, in his social life, he is successful, no doubt enviable, but he finds himself dreaming frequently these days of the boy with the crippled feet. Suppose he'd never had the operation: what then! He sees the creature on its hands and knees crawling crablike along the ground, there is a jeering circle of boys, now the terrible blinding lights of the operating room snuff him out and he's gone. And now seated in his aluminum wheelchair staring down helplessly at the white plaster casts: his punishment. Hips to toes, toes to hips. His punishment.

The adults of the world conspire in lies leaning over him smiling into his face. He will be able to walk he will be able to run he won't feel any pain he won't be hurt again doesn't he want to believe?—and of course he does.

He does. His wife's name is Annemarie, a name melodic and lovely he sometimes shapes with his lips, in silence: an incantation.

He had fallen in love with Annemarie seeing her for the first time amid a large noisy gathering of relatives and friends. When they were introduced and he was told her name he thought extravagantly, Anne-marie, yes—she's the one!

From the first she inspired him to such extravagant fancies, such violations of his own self. Which is why he loves her desperately.

Annemarie is twenty-nine years old but has the lithe small-boned features of a girl. Her hair is light brown, wavy, silvery in sunshine, her eyes wide-set and intelligent, watchful. Most of the time she appears to be wonderfully assured, her center of gravity well inside her, yet in the early weeks of the pregnancy she cried often and asked him half angrily, Do you love me? And he told her, Yes, of course. Of course I love you. But shortly afterward she asked him again, as if she hadn't believed him, Do you love me—*really?* More than before, or less? and he laughed as if she were joking, as if it were one of her jokes, closing his arms around her to comfort her. This was Annemarie's second pregnancy after all: the first had ended in a miscarriage.

Don't be absurd, Annemarie, he tells her.

Most of the time, of course, she is good-natured, sunny, uncomplaining; she loves being pregnant and she is eager to have the baby. She chooses her maternity outfits with care and humor: flowing waistless dresses in colorful fabrics, blouses with foppish ties, shawls, Indian beads, cloth flowers in her hair. Some of the outfits are from secondhand shops in the city, costumes from the forties and fifties, long skirts, culottes, silk pants suits, a straw boater with clusters of artificial berries on the rim: to divert the eye from her prominent belly, she says. But the childlike pleasure Annemarie takes in dressing is genuine and her hus-

band is charmed by it, he adores her for all that is herself, yes, he'd fight
to the death to protect her he'd die in her place if required.

Odd how, from the start, she has had the power to inspire him to such
melodramatic extravagant claims.

The miscarriage took place in the fifth month of the first pregnancy.
One night Annemarie woke with mock-labor pains and began to bleed,
she bled until nothing remained in her womb of what was to have been
their son. And they were helpless, helpless to stop it.

They'd known for weeks that the fetus was impaired, the pregnancy
might not go to term; still, the premature labor and the premature death
were blows from which each was slow to recover. Annemarie wept in
his arms and, he thought, in his place: her angry childish mourning
helped purge his soul. And Annemarie was the first to recover from the
loss for after all—as her doctor insisted—it wasn't anything personal,
it's just physical. The second pregnancy has nothing at all to do with the
first.

So we'll try again, Annemarie said reasonably.

And he hesitated saying, Not now. Saying, Isn't it too soon? You
aren't recovered.

And she said, Of course I'm recovered.

And he said, But I think we should wait.

And she said, chiding, *Now*. When if not *now?*

(Twenty-nine years old isn't young, in fact it is "elderly" in medical
terms for a woman pregnant with her first child. And they want more
than one child, after all. They want a family.)

So they made love. And they made love. And he gave himself up to
her in love, in love, in a drowning despairing hope, it's just physical
after all it doesn't mean anything. Such failures of the physical life don't
mean anything. You take the blow then get on with living isn't that the
history of the world? Of course it is.

He's an adult man now, not a boy any longer. He knows.

He cradles his wife's belly in his hands. Stroking her gently. Kissing
her. Fiercely attentive to the baby's secret life, that mysterious interior
throb, that ghostly just-perceptible kick. Through the doctor's stetho-
scope each listened to the baby's heartbeat, a rapid feverish-sounding
beat, *I am, I am, I am*. This pregnancy, unlike the first, has been diag-
nosed as "normal." This fetus unlike the first has been promised as
"normal."

Approximately fifteen days yet to go: the baby has begun its descent
head first into the pelvic cavity and Annemarie has begun, oddly, to feel
more comfortable than she has felt in months. She assures him she is

excited—not frightened—and he remembers the excitement of boxing, the excitement of climbing through the ropes knowing he couldn't turn back. Elation or panic? euphoria or terror?—that heartbeat beating everywhere in his body.

For months they have attended natural childbirth classes together and he oversees, genially but scrupulously, her exercises at home: he will be in the delivery room with her, he'll be there all the while.

This time, like last time, the fetus is male, and again they have drawn up a list of names. But the names are entirely different from the first list, Patrick, William, Alan, Seth, Sean, Raymond; sometimes Annemarie favors one and sometimes another but she doesn't want to choose a name until the baby is born. Safely born.

Why hasn't he ever told Annemarie about his amateur boxing, his "career" in the Golden Gloves?—he has told her virtually everything else about his life. But it is a matter of deep shame to him, recalling not only the evening of his public defeat but his hope, his near-lunatic hope that he would be a hero, a star! a great champion! He has told her he'd been a premature baby, born with a "slight deformity" of one foot which was corrected by surgery immediately after his birth: this is as near to the truth as he can manage.

Which foot was it? Annemarie asks sympathetically.

He tells her he doesn't remember which foot, it isn't important.

But one night he asks her to caress his feet. They are in bed, he is feeling melancholy, worried, not wholly himself. He has begun to profoundly dislike his work in proportion to his success in it and this is a secret he can't share with Annemarie; there are other secrets too he can't share, won't share, he fears her ready sympathy, the generosity of her spirit. At such times he feels himself vulnerable to memory, in danger of reliving that last fight, experiencing moments he hadn't in a sense experienced at the time—it had all happened too swiftly. Roland Bush Jr. pressing through his defense, jabbing him with precise machinelike blows, that gleaming black face those narrowed eyes seeking him out. White boy! White boy who are *you!* Bush was the true fighter stalking his prey. Bush was the one.

He hadn't been a fighter at all, merely a victim.

He asks Annemarie to caress his feet. Would she hold them? Warm them? Would she . . . ? It would mean so much, he can't explain.

Perhaps he is jealous of their son so cozy and tight upside down beneath his wife's heart but this is a thought he doesn't quite think.

Of course Annemarie is delighted to massage his feet, it's the sort of impulsive whimsical thing she loves to do, no need for logic, no need for explanations, she has wanted all along to nourish the playful side of his personality. So she takes his feet between her small dry warm hands and gently massages them. She brings to the intimate task a frowning concentration that flatters him, fills him with love. What is she thinking? he wonders. Then suddenly he is apprehensive: What does she know of me? What can she guess? Annemarie says, smiling, Your feet are so terribly cold! But I'll make them warm.

The incident is brief, silly, loving, quickly forgotten. One of those moments between a husband and a wife not meant to be analyzed, or even remembered. It never occurs a second time, never again does Annemarie offer to caress his feet and out of pride and shame he certainly isn't going to ask.

The days pass, the baby is due in less than a week, he keeps thinking, dreaming, of that blow to his mouth: the terrible power of the punch out of nowhere. His skull shook with a fierce reverberation that ran through his entire body and he'd known then that no one had ever hit him before.

It was his own death that had crashed into him—yet no more than he deserved. He was hit as one is hit only once in a lifetime. He was hit and time stopped. He was hit in the second minute of the first round of a long-forgotten amateur boxing match in Buffalo, New York; he was hit and he died and they carried him along a corridor of blinding lights, strapped to a stretcher, drooling blood and saliva, eyes turned up in his head. Something opened, lifted, a space of some kind clearing for him to enter, his own death but he hadn't had the courage to step forward.

Someone whose face he couldn't see was sinking a needle deep into his forearm, into the fleshy part of his forearm, afterward they spoke calmly and reassuringly saying it isn't really serious, a mild concussion not a serious fracture, his nose wasn't broken, only his mouth and teeth injured, that could be fixed. He flinched remembering the blow flying at him out of nowhere. He flinched, remembering. It happens once in a lifetime after that you're dead white boy but you pick yourself up and keep going.

There followed then the long period—months, years—when his father shrank from looking him fully in the face. Sometimes, however, his father examined his mouth, wasn't entirely pleased with the plastic surgeon's work. It had cost so damned much after all. But the false teeth were lifelike, wonderfully convincing, some consolation at least. Expensive too but everyone in the family was impressed with the white perfect teeth affixed to their lightweight aluminum plate.

All that the old tales of pregnancy promise of a female beauty luminous and dewy, lit from within, was true: here is Annemarie with eyes moist and bright as he'd rarely seen them, a skin with a faint rosy bloom, feverish to the touch. Here is the joy of the body as he had known it long ago and had forgotten.

There were days, weeks, when she felt slightly unwell yet the bloom of pregnancy had held and deepened month following month. A woman fully absorbed in herself, suffused with light, heat, radiance, entranced by the plunge into darkness she is to take. Pain—the promised pain of childbirth—frightens yet fascinates her: she means to be equal to it. She doesn't shrink from hearing the most alarming stories, labors of many hours without anesthetic, cesarean deliveries where natural childbirth had been expected, sudden losses of blood. She means to triumph.

Within the family they joke—it's the father-to-be, not Annemarie, who is having difficulty sleeping these past few weeks. But that too is natural, isn't it?

One night very late in her term Annemarie stares down at herself as if she'd never seen herself before—the enormous swollen belly, the blue-veined stretched skin with its uncanny luminous pallor—and because she has been feeling melancholy for days, because she is fatigued, suddenly doubting, not altogether herself, she exclaims with a harsh little laugh, God look at me, at this, how can you love anything like—*this!*

His nerves are torn like silk. He knows she isn't serious, he knows it is the lateness of the hour and the strain of waiting, it can't be Annemarie herself speaking. Quickly he says, Don't be absurd.

But that night as he falls slowly asleep he hears himself explaining to Annemarie in a calm measured voice that she will be risking something few men can risk, she should know herself exalted, privileged, in a way invulnerable to hurt even if she is very badly hurt, she'll be risking something he himself cannot risk again in his life. And maybe he never risked it at all.

You'll be going to a place I can't reach, he says.

He would touch her, in wonder, in dread, he would caress her, but his body is heavy with sleep, growing distant from her. He says softly, I'm not sure I'll be here when you come back.

But by now Annemarie's breathing is so deep and rhythmic she must be asleep. In any case she gives no sign of having heard.

THE BULLY OF
THE CAVENDISH

W. W. Jacobs

Talking of prize fighters sir," said the night watchman, who had nearly danced himself over to the edge of the wharf in illustrating one of Mr. Corbett's most trusted blows, and was now sitting down taking in sufficient air for three, "they ain't wot they used to be when I was a boy. They advertise in the papers for months and months about their fights, and when it does come off, they do it with gloves, and they're all right agin a day or two arter.

"I saw a picter the other day o' one punching a bag wot couldn't punch back, for practice. Why, I remember as a young man Sinker Pitt, as used to 'ave the King's Arms 'ere in 'is old age; when 'e wanted practice 'is plan was to dress up in a soft 'at and black coat like a chapel minister or something, and go in a pub and contradict people; sailor-men for choice. He'd ha' no more thought o' hitting a pore 'armless bag than I should ha' thought of hitting 'im.

"The strangest prize fighter I ever come acrost was one wot shipped with me on the *Cavendish*. He was the most eggstrordinry fighter I've ever seen or 'eard of, and 'e got to be such a nuisance afore 'e'd done with us that we could 'ardly call our souls our own. He shipped as an ordinary seaman—an unfair thing to do, as 'e was anything but ordinary, and 'ad no right to be there at all.

"We'd got one terror on board afore he come, and that was Bill Bone, one o' the biggest and strongest men I've ever seen down a ship's fo'c's'le, and that's saying a good deal. Built more like a bull than a man, 'e was, and when he was in his tantrums the best thing to do was to get out of 'is way or else get into your bunk and keep quiet. Oppersi-

221

tion used to send 'im crazy a'most, an' if 'e said a red shirt was a blue
one, you 'ad to keep quiet. It didn't do to agree with 'im and call it blue
even, cos if you did he'd call you a liar and punch you for telling lies.

"He was the only drawback to that ship. We 'ad a nice old man, good
mates, and good grub. You may know it was A-one when I tell you that
most of us 'ad been in 'er for several v'y'ges.

"But Bill was a drawback, and no mistake. In the main he was a
'earty, good-tempered sort o' shipmate as you'd wish to see, only, as I
said afore, oppersition was a thing he could not and would not stand. It
used to fly to his 'ead direckly.

"The v'y'ge I'm speaking of—we used to trade between Australia
and London—Bill came aboard about an hour afore the ship sailed. The
rest of us was already aboard and down below, some of us stowing our
things away and the rest sitting down and telling each other lies about
wot we'd been doing. Bill came lurching down the ladder, and Tom
Baker put 'is 'and to 'im to steady 'im as he got to the bottom.

"'Who are you putting your 'ands on?' ses Bill, glaring at 'im.

"'Only 'olding you up, Bill,' ses Tom, smiling.

"'Oh,' ses Bill.

"He put 'is back up agin a bunk and pulled hisself together.

"''Olding of me—up—was you?' he ses; 'whaffor, if I might be so
bold as to arsk?'

"'I thought your foot 'ad slipped, Bill, old man,' ses Tom; 'but I'm
sorry if it 'adn't.'

"Bill looks at 'im agin, 'ard.

"'Sorry if my foot didn't slip?' he ses.

"'You know wot I mean, Bill,' ses Tom, smiling a uneasy smile.

"'Don't laugh at me,' roars Bill.

"'I wasn't laughing, Bill, old pal,' ses Tom.

"''E's called me a liar,' ses Bill, looking round at us; 'called me a
liar. 'Old my coat, Charlie, and I'll split 'im in halves.'

"Charlie took the coat like a lamb, though he was Tom's pal, and Tom
looked round to see whether he couldn't nip up the ladder and get away,
but Bill was just in front of it. Then Tom found out that one of 'is
bootlaces was undone and he knelt down to do it up, and this young
ordinary seaman, Joe Simms by name, put his 'ead out of his bunk and
he ses, quiet-like—

"'You ain't afraid of that thing, mate, are you?'

"'*Wot?*' screams Bill, starting.

"'Don't make such a noise when I'm speaking,' ses Joe; 'where's
your manners, you great 'ulking rascal?'

"I thought Bill would ha' dropped with surprise at being spoke to like
that. His face was purple all over and 'e stood staring at Joe as though 'e

didn't know wot to make of 'im. And we stared too, Joe being a smallish sort o' chap and not looking at all strong.

"'Go easy, mate,' whispers Tom; 'you don't know who you're talking to.'

"'Bosh,' ses Joe, 'he's no good. He's too fat and too silly to do any 'arm. He shan't 'urt you while I'm 'ere.'

"He just rolled out of 'is bunk and, standing in front of Bill, put 'is fists up at 'im and stared 'im straight in the eye.

"'You touch that man,' he ses, quietly, pointing to Tom, 'and I'll give you such a dressing down as you've never 'ad afore. Mark my words, now.'

"'I wasn't going to 'it him,' ses Bill, in a strange, mild voice.

"'You'd better not,' ses the young 'un, shaking his fist at 'im; 'you'd better not, my lad. If there's any fighting to be done in this fo'c's'le I'll do it. Mind that.'

"It's no good me saying we was staggered; becos staggered ain't no word for it. To see Bill put 'is hands in 'is pockets and try and whistle, and then sit down on a locker and scratch 'is 'ead, was the most amazing thing I've ever seen. Presently 'e begins to sing under his breath.

"'Stop that 'umming,' ses Joe; 'when I want you to 'um I'll tell you.'

"Bill left off 'umming, and then he gives a little cough behind the back of 'is 'and, and, arter fidgeting about a bit with 'is feet, went up on deck again.

"'Strewth,' ses Tom, looking round at us, ''ave we shipped a bloomin' prize fighter?'

"'Wot did you call me?' ses Joe, looking at 'im.

"'Nothing, mate,' ses Tom, drawing back.

"'You keep a quiet tongue in your 'ead,' ses Joe, 'and speak when you're spoken to, my lad.'

"He was an ordinary seaman, mind, talking to A.B.'s like that. Men who'd been up aloft and doing their little bit when 'e was going about catching cold in 'is little petticuts. Still, if Bill could stand it, we supposed as we'd better.

"Bill stayed up on deck till we was under way, and 'is spirit seemed to be broke. He went about 'is work like a man wot was walking in 'is sleep, and when breakfast come 'e 'ardly tasted it.

"Joe made a splendid breakfast, and when he'd finished 'e went to Bill's bunk and chucked the things out all over the place and said 'e was going to 'ave it instead of his own. And Bill sat there and took it all quiet, and by and by he took 'is things up and put them in Joe's bunk without a word.

"It was the most peaceful fust day we 'ad ever 'ad down that fo'c's'le, Bill usually being in 'is tantrums the fust day or two at sea, and wanting to know why 'e'd been born. If you talked you was noisy and worriting, and if you didn't talk you was sulky; but this time 'e sat quite still and didn't interfere a bit. It was such a pleasant change that we all felt a bit grateful, and at teatime Tom Baker patted Joe on the back and said he was one o' the right old sort.

" 'You've been in a scrap or two in your time, I know,' he ses, admiring like. 'I knew you was a bit of a one with your fists direckly I see you.'

" 'Oh, 'ow's that?' asks Joe.

" 'I could see by your nose,' ses Tom.

"You never know how to take people like that. The words 'ad 'ardly left Tom's lips afore the other ups with a basin of 'ot tea and heaves it all over 'im.

" 'Take that, you insulting rascal,' he ses, as Tom jumped up spluttering and wiping 'is face with his coat. 'How dare you insult me?'

" 'Get up,' ses Tom, dancing with rage. 'Get up; prize fighter or no prize fighter, I'll mark you.'

" 'Sit down,' ses Bill, turning round.

" 'I'm going to 'ave a go at 'im, Bill,' ses Tom; 'if you're afraid of 'im, I ain't.'

" 'Sit down,' ses Bill, starting up. ' 'Ow dare you insult me like that?'

" 'Like wot?' ses Tom, staring.

" 'If I can't lick 'im you can't,' ses Bill; 'that's 'ow it is, mate.'

" 'But I can try,' ses Tom.

" 'All right,' ses Bill. 'Me fust, then if you lick me, you can 'ave a go at 'im. If you can't lick me, 'ow can you lick 'im?'

" 'Sit down both of you,' ses young Joe, drinking Bill's tea to make up for 'is own. 'And mind you, I'm cock o' this fo'c's'le, and don't you forget it. Sit down, both of you, afore I start on you.'

"They both sat down, but Tom wasn't quick enough to please Bill, and he got a wipe o' the side o' the 'ead that made it ring for an hour afterwards.

"That was the beginning of it, and instead of 'aving one master we found we'd got two, owing to the eggstrordinry way Bill had o' looking at things. He gave Joe best without even 'aving a try at him, and if anybody else wanted to 'ave a try, it was a insult to Bill. We couldn't make 'ead or tail of it, and all we could get out of Bill was that 'e had one time 'ad a turn-up with Joe Simms ashore, which he'd remember all 'is life. It must ha' been something of a turn, too, the way Bill used to try and curry favour with 'im.

"In about three days our life wasn't worth living, and the fo'c's'le was more like a Sunday school class than anything else. In the fust place Joe put down swearing. He wouldn't 'ave no bad langwidge, he said, and he didn't neither. If a man used a bad word Joe would pull 'im up the fust time, and the second he'd order Bill to 'it 'im, being afraid of 'urting 'im too much 'imself. 'Arf the men 'ad to leave off talking altogether when Joe was by, but the way they used to swear when he wasn't was something shocking. Harry Moore got clergyman's sore throat one arternoon through it.

"Then Joe objected to us playing cards for money, and we 'ad to arrange on the quiet that brace buttons was ha'-pennies and coat buttons pennies, and that lasted until one evening Tom Baker got up and danced and nearly went off 'is 'ead with joy through havin' won a few dozen. That was enough for Joe, and Bill by his orders took the cards and pitched 'em over the side.

"Sweet-'earting and that sort o' thing Joe couldn't abear, and Ned Davis put his foot into it finely one afternoon though not knowing. He was lying in 'is bunk smoking and thinking, and by and by he looked across at Bill, who was 'arf asleep, and 'e ses:

"'I wonder whether you'll see that little gal at Melbourne agin this trip, Bill.'

"Bill's eyes opened wide and he shook 'is fist at Ned, as Ned thought, playful-like.

"'All right, I'm a-looking at you, Bill,' 'e ses. 'I can see you.'

"'What gal is that, Ned?' ses Joe, who was in the next bunk to him, and I saw Bill's eyes screw up tight, and e' suddenly fell fast asleep.

"'I don't know 'er name,' ses Ned, 'but she was very much struck on Bill; they used to go to the theayter together.'

"'Pretty gal?' ses Joe, leading 'im on.

"'*Rather*,' ses Ned. 'Trust Bill for that, 'e always gets the prettiest gal in the place—I've known as many as six and seven to—'

"'WOT!' screams Bill, waking up out of 'is sleep, and jumping out of 'is bunk.

"'Keep still, Bill, and don't interfere when I'm talking,' ses Joe, very sharp.

"''E's insulted me,' ses Bill, 'talking about gals when everybody knows I 'ate 'em worse than pison.'

"'Hold your tongue,' ses Joe. 'Now, Ned what's this about this little gal? What's 'er name?'

"'It was only a little joke o' mine,' ses Ned, who saw 'e'd put 'is foot in it. 'Bill 'ates 'em worse than—worse than—pison.'

"'You're telling me a lie,' ses Joe, sternly. 'Who was it?'

"'It was only my fun, Joe,' ses Ned.

"'Oh, very well then, I'm going to 'ave a bit of fun now,' ses Joe. 'Bill!'

"'Yes,' ses Bill.

" 'I won't 'it Ned myself for fear I shall do 'im a lasting injury,' ses Joe, 'so you just start on 'im and keep on till 'e tells all about your goings on with that gal.'

" 'Hit *'im* to make 'im tell about *me?'* ses Bill, staring 'is 'ardest.

" 'You 'eard wot I said,' ses Joe, 'don't repeat my words. You a married man, too; I've got sisters of my own, and I'm going to put this sort o' thing down. If you don't down 'im, I will.'

"Ned wasn't much of a fighter, and I 'alf expected to see 'im do a bolt up on deck and complain to the skipper. He did look like it for a moment, then he stood up, looking a bit white as Bill walked over to 'im, and the next moment 'is fist flew out, and afore we could turn round I'm blest if Bill wasn't on the floor. 'E got up as if 'e was dazed like, struck out wild at Ned and missed 'im, and the next moment was knocked down agin. We could 'ardly believe our eyes, and as for Ned, 'e looked as though 'e'd been doing miracles by mistake.

"When Bill got up the second time 'e was that shaky 'e could 'ardly stand, and Ned 'ad it all 'is own way, until at last 'e got Billy's 'ead under 'is arm and punched at it till they was both tired.

" 'All right,' ses Bill, 'I've 'ad enough. I've met my master.'

" *'Wot?'* ses Joe, staring.

" 'I've met my master,' ses Bill, going and sitting down. 'Ned 'as knocked me about crool.'

"Joe looked at 'im, speechless, and then without saying another word, or 'aving a go at Ned himself, as we expected, 'e went up on deck, and Ned crossed over and sat down by Bill.

" 'I 'ope I didn't hurt you, mate,' he ses, kindly.

" 'Hurt me?' roars Bill. 'You! You 'urt me? You, you little bag o' bones. Wait till I get you ashore by yourself for five minutes, Ned Davis, and then you'll know what 'urting means.'

" 'I don't understand you, Bill,' ses Ned; 'you're a mystery, that's what you are; but I tell you plain when you go ashore you don't have me for a companion.'

"It was a mystery to all of us, and it got worse and worse as time went on. Bill didn't dare to call 'is soul 'is own, although Joe only hit 'im once the whole time, and then not very hard, and he excused 'is cowardice by telling us of a man Joe 'ad killed in a fight down in one o' them West End clubs.

"Wot with Joe's Sunday-school ways and Bill backing 'em up, we was all pretty glad by the time we got to Melbourne. It was like getting out o' pris'n to get away from Joe for a little while. All but Bill, that is, and Joe took 'im to hear a dissolving views on John Bunyan. Bill said 'e'd be delighted to go, but the language he used about 'im on the quiet when he came back showed what 'e thought of it. I don't know who John

Bunyan is, or wot he's done, but the things Bill said about 'im I wouldn't soil my tongue by repeating.

"Arter we'd been there two or three days we began to feel a'most sorry for Bill. Night arter night, when we was ashore, Joe would take 'im off and look arter 'im, and at last, partly for 'is sake, but more to see the fun, Tom Baker managed to think o' something to put things straight.

"'You stay aboard to-night, Bill,' he ses one morning, 'and you'll see something that'll startle you.'

"'Worse than you?' ses Bill, whose temper was getting worse and worse.

"'There'll be an end o' that bullying Joe,' ses Tom, taking 'im by the arm. 'We've arranged to give 'im a lesson as'll lay 'im up for a time.'

"'Oh,' ses Bill, looking 'ard at a boat wot was passing.

"'We've got Dodgy Pete coming to see us tonight,' ses Tom, in a whisper; 'there'll only be the second officer aboard, and he'll likely be asleep. Dodgy's one o' the best lightweights in Australia, and if 'e don't fix up Mister Joe, it'll be a pity.'

"'You're a fair treat, Tom,' ses Bill, turning round, 'that's what you are. A fair treat.'

"'I thought you'd be pleased, Bill,' ses Tom.

"'Pleased ain't no name for it, Tom,' answers Bill. 'You've took a load off my mind.'

"The fo'c's'le was pretty full that evening, everybody giving each other a little grin on the quiet, and looking over to where Joe was sitting in 'is bunk putting a button or two on his coat. At about ha' past six Dodgy comes aboard, and the fun begins to commence.

"He was a nasty, low-looking little chap, was Dodgy, very fly-looking and very conceited. I didn't like the look of 'im at all, and unbearable as Joe was, it didn't seem to be quite the sort o' thing to get a chap aboard to 'ammer a shipmate you couldn't 'ammer yourself.

"'Nasty stuffy place you've got down 'ere,' ses Dodgy, who was smoking a big cigar; 'I can't think 'ow you can stick it.'

"'It ain't bad for a fo'c's'le,' ses Charlie.

"'An' what's that in that bunk over there?' ses Dodgy, pointing with 'is cigar at Joe.

"'Hush, be careful,' ses Tom, with a wink; 'that's a prize fighter.'

"'Oh,' ses Dodgy, grinning, 'I thought it was a monkey.'

"You might 'ave heard a pin drop, and there was a pleasant feeling went all over us at the thought of the little fight we was going to see all to ourselves, as Joe lays down the jacket he was stitching at and just puts 'is little 'ead over the side 'o the bunk.

"'Bill,' he ses, yawning.

"'Well,' ses Bill, all on the grin like the rest of us.

"'Who is that 'andsome, gentlemanly-looking young feller over there smoking a half-crown cigar?' ses Joe.

"'That's a young gent wot's come down to 'ave a look round,' ses Tom, as Dodgy takes 'is cigar out of 'is mouth and looks round, puzzled.

"'Wot a terror 'e must be to the gals, with them lovely little peepers of 'is,' ses Joe, shaking 'is 'ead. *Bill!'*

"'Well,' ses Bill, agin, as Dodgy got up.

"'Take that lovely little gentleman and kick 'im up the fo'c's'le ladder,' ses Joe, taking up 'is jacket again; 'and don't make too much noise over it, cos I've got a bit of a 'eadache, else I'd do it myself."

"There was a bit of a laugh went all round then, and Tom Baker was near killing himself, and then I'm blessed if Bill didn't get up and begin taking off 'is coat.

"'Wot's the game?' ses Dodgy, staring.

"'I'm obeying orders,' ses Bill. 'Last time I was in London, Joe 'ere half killed me one time, and 'e made me promise to do as 'e told me for six months. I'm very sorry, mate, but I've got to kick you up that ladder.'

"'You kick me up?' ses Dodgy, with a nasty little laugh.

"'I can try, mate, can't I?' ses Bill, folding 'is things up very neat and putting 'em on a locker.

"''Old my cigar,' ses Dodgy, taking it out of 'is mouth and sticking it in Charlie's. 'I don't need to take my coat off to 'im.'

"'E altered his mind, though, when he saw Bill's chest and arms, and not only took off his coat, but his waistcoat, too. Then, with a nasty look at Bill, 'e put up 'is fists and just pranced up to 'im.

"The fust blow Bill missed, and the next moment 'e got a tap on the jaw that nearly broke it, and that was followed up by one in the eye that sent 'im staggering up agin the side, and when 'e was there Dodgy's fists were rattling all round 'im.

"I believe it was that that brought Bill round, and the next moment Dodgy was on 'is back with a blow that nearly knocked his 'ead off. Charlie grabbed at Tom's watch and began to count, and after a little bit called out 'Time.' It was a silly thing to do, as it would 'ave stopped the fight then and there if it 'adn't been for Tom's presence of mind, saying it was two minutes slow. That gave Dodgy a chance, and he got up again and walked round Bill very careful, swearing 'ard at the small size of the fo'c's'le.

"He got in three or four at Bill afore you could wink a'most, and when Bill 'it back 'e wasn't there. That seemed to annoy Bill more than anything, and he suddenly flung out 'is arms, and grabbing 'old of 'im

flung 'im right across the fo'c's'le to where, fortunately for 'im—
Dodgy, I mean—Tom Baker was sitting.

"Charlie called 'Time' again, and we let 'em 'ave five minutes while
we 'elped Tom to bed, and then wot 'e called the 'disgusting exhibishun'
was resoomed. Bill 'ad dipped 'is face in a bucket and 'ad rubbed 'is
great arms all over and was as fresh as a daisy. Dodgy looked a bit
tottery, but 'e was game all through and very careful, and, try as Bill
might, he didn't seem to be able to get 'old of 'im agin.

"In five minutes more, though, it was all over, Dodgy not being able
to see plain—except to get out 'o Bill's way—and hitting wild. He
seemed to think the whole fo'c's'le was full o' Bills sitting on a locker
and waiting to be punched, and the end of it was a knockout blow from
the real Bill which left 'im on the floor without a soul offering to pick
'im up.

"Bill 'elped 'im up at last and shook hands with 'im, and they rinsed
their faces in the same bucket, and began to praise each other up. They
sat there purring like a couple o' cats, until at last we 'eard a smothered
voice coming from Joe Simms's bunk.

"'Is it all over?' he asks.

"'Yes,' ses somebody.

"'How is Bill?' ses Joe's voice again.

"'Look for yourself,' ses Tom.

"Joe sat up in 'is bunk then and looked out, and he no sooner saw
Bill's face than he gave a loud cry and fell back agin, and, as true as I'm
sitting here, fainted clean away. We was struck all of a 'eap, and then
Bill picked up the bucket and threw some water over 'im, and by and by
he comes round again and in a dazed sort o' way puts his arm round
Bill's neck and begins to cry.

"'*Mighty Moses!*' ses Dodgy Pete, jumping up, 'it's a woman!'

"'It's my *wife!*' ses Bill.

"We understood it all then, leastways the married ones among us did.
She'd shipped aboard partly to be with Bill and partly to keep an eye on
'im, and Tom Baker's mistake about a prize fighter had just suited 'er
book better than anything. How Bill was to get 'er home 'e couldn't
think, but it 'appened the second officer had been peeping down the
fo'c's'le, waiting for ever so long for a suitable opportunity to stop the
fight, and the old man was so tickled about the way we'd all been done
'e gave 'er a passage back as stewardess to look arter the ship's cat."

THE CROXLEY
MASTER

Arthur Conan Doyle

PART ONE

Mr. Robert Montgomery was seated at his desk, his head upon his hands, in a state of the blackest despondency. Before him was the open ledger with the long columns of Dr. Oldacre's pre- scriptions. At his elbow lay the wooden tray with the labels in various partitions, the cork box, the lumps of twisted sealing-wax, while in front a rank of empty bottles waited to be filled. But his spirits were too low for work. He sat in silence, with his fine shoulders bowed and his head upon his hands.

Outside, through the grimy surgery window over a foreground of blackened brick and slate, a line of enormous chimneys like Cyclopean pillars upheld the lowering, dun-coloured cloud bank. For six days in the week they spouted smoke, but today the furnace fires were banked, for it was Sunday. Sordid and polluting gloom hung over a district blighted and blasted by the greed of man. There was nothing in the surroundings to cheer a despondent soul, but it was more than his dismal environment which weighed upon the medical assistant.

His trouble was deeper and more personal. The winter session was approaching. He should be back again at the University completing the last year which would give him his medical degree; but, alas! he had not the money with which to pay his class fees, nor could he imagine how he could procure it. Sixty pounds were wanted to make his career, and it might have been as many thousands for any chance there seemed to be of his obtaining it.

He was roused from his black meditation by the entrance of Dr. Oldacre himself, a large, clean-shaven, respectable man, with a prim manner and an austere face. He had prospered exceedingly by the support of the local Church interest, and the rule of his life was never by word or action to run a risk of offending the sentiment which had made him. His standard of respectability and of dignity was exceedingly high, and he expected the same from his assistants. His appearance and words were always vaguely benevolent. A sudden impulse came over the despondent student. He would test the reality of this philanthropy.

"I beg your pardon, Dr. Oldacre," said he, rising from his chair. "I have a great favour to ask of you."

The doctor's appearance was not encouraging. His mouth suddenly tightened, and his eyes fell.

"Yes, Mr. Montgomery?"

"You are aware, sir, that I need only one more session to complete my course."

"So you have told me."

"It is very important to me, sir."

"Naturally."

"The fees, Dr. Oldacre, would amount to about sixty pounds."

"I am afraid that my duties call me elsewhere, Mr. Montgomery."

"One moment, sir! I had hoped, sir, that perhaps, if I signed a paper promising you interest upon your money, you would advance this sum to me. I will pay you back, sir, I really will. Or, if you like, I will work it off after I am qualified."

The doctor's lips had thinned into a narrow line. His eyes were raised again, and sparkled indignantly.

"Your request is unreasonable, Mr. Montgomery. I am surprised that you should have made it. Consider, sir, how many thousands of medical students there are in this country. No doubt there are many of them who have a difficulty in finding their fees. Am I to provide for them all? Or why should I make an exception in your favour? I am grieved and disappointed, Mr. Montgomery, that you should have put me into the painful position of having to refuse you." He turned upon his heel, and walked with offended dignity out of the surgery.

The student smiled bitterly, and turned to his work of making up the morning prescriptions. It was poor and unworthy work—work which any weakling might have done as well, and this was a man of exceptional nerve and sinew. But, such as it was, it brought him his board and £1 a week, enough to help him during the summer months and let him save a few pounds towards his winter keep. But those class fees! Where were they to come from? He could not save them out of his scanty wage. Dr. Oldacre would not advance them. He saw no way of earning them. His brains were fairly good, but brains of that quality were a drug in the market. He only excelled in his strength; and where was he to find a customer for that? But the ways of Fate are strange, and his customer was at hand.

"Look y'ere!" said a voice at the door.

Montgomery looked up, for the voice was a loud and rasping one. A young man stood at the entrance—a stocky, bull-necked young miner, in tweed Sunday clothes and an aggressive necktie. He was a sinister-looking figure, with dark, insolent eyes, and the jaw and throat of a bulldog.

"Look y'ere!" said he again. "Why hast thou not sent t' medicine oop as thy master ordered?"

Montgomery had become accustomed to the brutal frankness of the Northern worker. At first it had enraged him, but after a time he had grown callous to it, and accepted it as it was meant. But this was something different. It was insolence—brutal, overbearing insolence, with physical menace behind it.

"What name?" he asked coldly.

"Barton. Happen I may give thee cause to mind that name, yoong man. Mak' oop t' wife's medicine this very moment, look ye, or it will be the worse for thee."

Montgomery smiled. A pleasant sense of relief thrilled softly through him. What blessed safety valve was this through which his jangled nerves might find some outlet. The provocation was so gross, the insult so unprovoked, that he could have none of those qualms which take the edge off a man's mettle. He finished sealing the bottle upon which he was occupied, and he addressed it and placed it carefully in the rack.

"Look here!" said he, turning round to the miner, "your medicine will be made up in its turn and sent down to you. I don't allow folk in the surgery. Wait outside in the waiting room, if you wish to wait at all."

"Yoong man," said the miner, "thou's got to mak' t' wife's medicine here, and now, and quick, while I wait and watch thee, or else happen thou might need some medicine thysel' before all is over."

"I shouldn't advise you to fasten a quarrel upon me." Montgomery was speaking in the hard, staccato voice of a man who is holding himself in with difficulty. "You'll save trouble if you'll go quietly. If you don't you'll be hurt. Ah, you would? Take it, then!"

The blows were almost simultaneous—a savage swing which whistled past Montgomery's ear and a straight drive which took the workman on the chin. Luck was with the assistant. That single whizzing uppercut, and the way in which it was delivered, warned him that he had a formidable man to deal with. But if he had underrated his antagonist, his antagonist had also underrated him, and had laid himself open to a fatal blow.

The miner's head had come with a crash against the corner of the surgery shelves, and he had dropped heavily on to the ground. There he lay with his bandy legs drawn up and his hands thrown abroad, the blood trickling over the surgery tiles.

"Had enough?" asked the assistant, breathing fiercely through his nose.

But no answer came. The man was insensible. And then the danger of his position came upon Montgomery, and he turned as white as his antagonist. A Sunday, the immaculate Dr. Oldacre with his pious connection, a savage brawl with a patient; he would irretrievably lose his situation if the facts came out. It was not much of a situation, but he could not get another without a reference, and Oldacre might refuse him one. Without money for his classes, and without a situation—what was to become of him? It was absolute ruin.

But perhaps he could escape exposure after all. He seized his insensible adversary, dragged him out into the centre of the room, loosened his collar, and squeezed the surgery sponge over his face. He sat up at last with a gasp and a scowl.

"Domn thee, thou's spoilt my necktie," said he, mopping up the water from his breast.

"I'm sorry I hit you so hard," said Montgomery, apologetically.

"Thou hit me hard! I could stan' such fly-flappin' all day. 'Twas this here press that cracked my pate for me, and thou art a looky man to be able to boast as thou hast outed me. And now I'd be obliged to thee if thou wilt give me t' wife's medicine."

Montgomery gladly made it up and handed it to the miner.

"You are weak still," said he. "Won't you stay awhile and rest?"

"T' wife wants her medicine," said the man, and lurched out at the door.

The assistant, looking after him, saw him rolling with an uncertain step down the street, until a friend met him, and they walked on arm-in-arm. The man seemed in his rough Northern fashion to bear no grudge, and so Montgomery's fears left him. There was no reason why the doctor should know anything about it. He wiped the blood from the floor, put the surgery in order, and went on with his interrupted task, hoping that he had come scathless out of a very dangerous business.

Yet all day he was aware of a sense of vague uneasiness, which sharpened into dismay when, late in the afternoon, he was informed that three gentlemen had called and were waiting for him in the surgery. A coroner's inquest, a descent of detectives, an invasion of angry relatives— all sorts of possibilities rose to scare him. With tense nerves and a rigid face he went to meet his visitors.

They were a very singular trio. Each was known to him by sight; but what on earth the three could be doing together, and, above all, what they could expect from *him,* was a most inexplicable problem.

The first was Sorley Wilson, the son of the owner of the Nonpareil Coalpit. He was a young blood of twenty, heir to a fortune, a keen sportsman, and down for the Easter Vacation from Magdalene College. He sat now upon the edge of the surgery table, looking in thoughtful silence at Montgomery, and twisting the ends of his small, black, waxed moustache.

The second was Purvis, the publican, owner of the chief beershop, and well known as the local bookmaker. He was a coarse, clean-shaven man, whose fiery face made a singular contrast with his ivory-white bald head. He had shrewd, light-blue eyes with foxy lashes, and he also leaned forward in silence from his chair, a fat, red hand upon either knee, and stared critically at the young assistant.

So did the third visitor, Fawcett, the horsebreaker, who leaned back, his long, thin legs, with their boxcloth riding gaiters, thrust out in front of him, tapping his protruding teeth with his riding whip, with anxious thought in every line of his rugged, bony face. Publican, exquisite, and horsebreaker were all three equally silent, equally earnest, and equally critical. Montgomery, seated in the midst of them, looked from one to the other.

"Well, gentlemen?" he observed, but no answer came.

The position was embarrassing.

"No," said the horsebreaker, at last. "No. It's off. It's nowt."

"Stand oop, lad; let's see thee standin'." It was the publican who spoke.

Montgomery obeyed. He would learn all about it, no doubt, if he were patient. He stood up and turned slowly round, as if in front of his tailor.

"It's off! It's off!" cried the horsebreaker. "Why, mon, the Master would break him over his knee."

"Oh, that be hanged for a yarn!" said the young Cantabrigian. "You can drop out if you like, Fawcett, but I'll see this thing through, if I have to do it alone. I don't hedge a penny. I like the cut of him a great deal better than I liked Ted Barton."

"Look at Barton's shoulders, Mr. Wilson."

"Lumpiness isn't always strength. Give me nerve and fire and breed. That's what wins."

"Ay, sir, you have it theer—you have it theer!" said the fat, red-faced publican, in a thick, suety voice. "It's the same wi' poops. Get 'em clean-bred an' fine, an' they'll yark the thick 'uns—yark 'em out o' their skins."

"He's ten good pund on the light side," growled the horsebreaker.

"He's a welterweight, anyhow."

"A hundred and thirty."

"A hundred and fifty, if he's an ounce."

"Well, the Master doesn't scale much more than that."

"A hundred and seventy-five."

"That was when he was hog-fat and living high. Work the grease out of him, and I lay there's no great difference between them. Have you been weighed lately, Mr. Montgomery?"

It was the first direct question which had been asked him. He had stood in the midst of them, like a horse at a fair, and he was just beginning to wonder whether he was more angry or amused.

"I am just eleven stone," said he.

"I said that he was a welterweight."

"But suppose you was trained?" said the publican. "Wot then?"

"I am always in training."

"In a manner of speakin', no doubt, he *is* always in trainin'," remarked the horsebreaker. "But trainin' for everyday work ain't the same as trainin' with a trainer; and I dare bet, with all respec' to your opinion, Mr. Wilson, that there's half a stone of tallow on him at this minute."

The young Cantab put his fingers on the assistant's upper arm. Then with his other hand on his wrist he bent the forearm sharply, and felt the biceps, as round and hard as a cricket ball, spring up under his fingers.

"Feel that!" said he.

The publican and horsebreaker felt it with an air of reverence.

"Good lad! He'll do yet!" cried Purvis.

"Gentlemen," said Montgomery, "I think that you will acknowledge that I have been very patient with you. I have listened to all that you have to say about my personal appearance, and now I must really beg that you will have the goodness to tell me what is the matter."

They all sat down in their serious, businesslike way.

"That's easy done, Mr. Montgomery," said the fat-voiced publican. "But before sayin' anything we had to wait and see whether, in a way of speakin', there was any need for us to say anything at all. Mr. Wilson thinks there is. Mr. Fawcett, who has the same right to his opinion, bein' also a backer and one o' the committee, thinks the other way."

"I thought him too light built, and I think so now," said the horse-breaker, still tapping his prominent teeth with the metal head of his riding whip. "But happen he may pull through; and he's a fine-made, buirdly young chap, so if you mean to back him, Mr. Wilson——"

"Which I do."

"And you, Purvis?"

"I ain't one to go back, Fawcett."

"Well, I'll stan' to my share of the purse."

"And well I knew you would," said Purvis, "for it would be somethin' new to find Isaac Fawcett as a spoilsport. Well, then, we make up the hundred for the stake among us, and the fight stands—always supposin' the young man is willin'."

"Excuse all this rot, Mr. Montgomery," said the University man, in a genial voice. "We've begun at the wrong end, I know, but we'll soon straighten it out, and I hope that you will see your way to falling in with our views. In the first place, you remember the man whom you knocked out this morning? He is Barton—the famous Ted Barton."

"I'm sure, sir, you may well be proud to have outed him in one round," said the publican. "Why, it took Morris, the ten-stone-six champion, a deal more trouble than that before he put Barton to sleep. You've done a fine performance, sir, and happen you'll do a finer, if you give yourself the chance."

"I never heard of Ted Barton, beyond seeing the name on a medicine label," said the assistant.

"Well, you may take it from me that he's a slaughterer," said the horsebreaker. "You've taught him a lesson that he needed, for it was always a word and a blow with him, and the word alone was worth five shillin' in a public court. He won't be so ready now to shake his neif in the face of every one he meets. However, that's neither here nor there."

Montgomery looked at them in bewilderment.

"For goodness' sake, gentlemen, tell me what it is you want me to do!" he cried.

"We want you to fight Silas Craggs, better known as the Master of Croxley."

"But why?"

"Because Ted Barton was to have fought him next Saturday. He was the champion of the Wilson coal pits, and the other was the Master of the iron-folk down at the Croxley smelters. We'd matched our man for a purse of a hundred against the Master. But you've queered our man, and he can't face such a battle with a two-inch cut at the back of his head. There's only one thing to be done, sir, and that is for you to take his place. If you can lick Ted Barton you may lick the Master of Croxley;

but if you don't we're done, for there's no one else who is in the same street with him in this district. It's twenty rounds, two-ounce gloves, Queensberry rules, and a decision on points if you fight to the finish."

For a moment the absurdity of the thing drove every other thought out of Montgomery's head. But then there came a sudden revulsion. A hundred pounds!—all he wanted to complete his education was lying there ready to his hand if only that hand were strong enough to pick it up. He had thought bitterly that morning that there was no market for his strength, but here was one where his muscle might earn more in an hour than his brains in a year. But a chill of doubt came over him.

"How can I fight for the coal pits?" said he. "I am not connected with them."

"Eh, lad, but thou art!" cried old Purvis. "We've got it down in writin', and it's clear enough. 'Any one connected with the coal pits.' Doctor Oldacre is the coal pit club doctor; thou art his assistant. What more can they want?"

"Yes, that's right enough," said the Cantab. "It would be a very sporting thing of you, Mr. Montgomery, if you would come to our help when we are in such a hole. Of course, you might not like to take the hundred pounds; but I have no doubt that, in the case of your winning, we could arrange that it should take the form of a watch or piece of plate, or any other shape which might suggest itself to you. You see, you are responsible for our having lost our champion, so we really feel that we have a claim upon you."

"Give me a moment, gentlemen. It is very unexpected. I am afraid the doctor would never consent to my going—in fact, I am sure that he would not."

"But he need never know—not before the fight, at any rate. We are not bound to give the name of our man. So long as he is within the weight limits on the day of the fight, that is all that concerns anyone."

The adventure and the profit would either of them have attracted Montgomery. The two combined were irresistible.

"Gentlemen," said he, "I'll do it!"

The three sprang from their seats. The publican had seized his right hand, the horse dealer his left, and the Cantab slapped him on the back.

"Good lad! good lad!" croaked the publican. "Eh, mon, but if thou yark him, thou'll rise in one day from being just a common doctor to the best-known mon 'twixt here and Bradford. Thou art a witherin' tyke, thou art, and no mistake; and if thou beat the Master of Croxley, thou'll find all the beer thou want for the rest of thy life waiting for thee at the Four Sacks."

"It is the most sporting thing I ever heard of in my life," said young

Wilson. "By George, sir, if you pull it off, you've got the constituency in your pocket, if you care to stand. You know the outhouse in my garden?"

"Next the road?"

"Exactly. I turned it into a gymnasium for Ted Barton. You'll find all you want there: clubs, punching balls, bars, dumbbells, everything. Then you'll want a sparring partner. Ogilvy has been acting for Barton, but we don't think that he is class enough. Barton bears you no grudge. He's a good-hearted fellow, though cross-grained with strangers. He looked upon you as a stranger this morning, but he says he knows you now. He is quite ready to spar with you for practice, and he will come at any hour you will name."

"Thank you; I will let you know the hour," said Montgomery; and so the committee departed jubilant upon their way.

The medical assistant sat for a little time in the surgery turning it over in his mind. He had been trained originally at the University by the man who had been middleweight champion in his day. It was true that his teacher was long past his prime, slow upon his feet and stiff in his joints, but even so he was still a tough antagonist; but Montgomery had found at last that he could more than hold his own with him. He had won the University medal, and his teacher, who had trained so many students, was emphatic in his opinion that he had never had one who was in the same class with him. He had been exhorted to go in for the Amateur Championships, but he had no particular ambition in that direction. Once he had put on the gloves with Hammer Tunstall in a booth at a fair, and had fought three rattling rounds, in which he had the worst of it, but had made the prize fighter stretch himself to the uttermost. There was his whole record, and was it enough to encourage him to stand up to the Master of Croxley? He had never heard of the Master before, but then he had lost touch of the ring during the last few years of hard work. After all, what did it matter? If he won, there was the money, which meant so much to him. If he lost, it would only mean a thrashing. He could take punishment without flinching, of that he was certain. If there were only one chance in a hundred of pulling it off, then it was worth his while to attempt it.

Dr. Oldacre, new come from church, with an ostentatious prayer book in his kid-gloved hand, broke in upon his meditation.

"You don't go to service, I observe, Mr. Montgomery," said he, coldly.

"No, sir; I have had some business to detain me."

"It is very near to my heart that my household should set a good example. There are so few educated people in this district that a great responsibility devolves upon us. If we do not live up to the highest, how can we expect these poor workers to do so? It is a dreadful thing to reflect that the parish takes a great deal more interest in an approaching glove fight than in their religious duties."

"A glove fight, sir?" said Montgomery, guiltily.

"I believe that to be the correct term. One of my patients tells me that it is the talk of the district. A local ruffian, a patient of ours, by the way, is matched against a pugilist over at Croxley. I cannot understand why the law does not step in and stop so degrading an exhibition. It is really a prize fight."

"A glove fight, you said."

"I am informed that a two-ounce glove is an evasion by which they dodge the law, and make it difficult for the police to interfere. They contend for a sum of money. It seems dreadful and almost incredible— does it not?—to think that such scenes can be enacted within a few miles of our peaceful home. But you will realise, Mr. Montgomery, that while there are such influences for us to counteract, it is very necessary that we shoud live up to our highest."

The doctor's sermon would have had more effect if the assistant had not once or twice had occasion to test his highest and come upon it at unexpectedly humble elevations. It is always so particularly easy to "compound for sins we're most inclined to by damning those we have no mind to." In any case, Montgomery felt that of all the men concerned in such a fight—promoters, backers, spectators—it is the actual fighter who holds the strongest and most honourable position. His conscience gave him no concern upon the subject. Endurance and courage are virtues, not vices, and brutality is, at least, better than effeminacy.

There was a little tobacco shop at the corner of the street, where Montgomery got his bird's-eye and also his local information, for the shopman was a garrulous soul, who knew everything about the affairs of the district. The assistant strolled down there after tea and asked, in a casual way, whether the tobacconist had ever heard of the Master of Croxley.

"Heard of him! Heard of him!" the little man could hardly articulate in his astonishment. "Why, sir, he's the first mon o' the district, an' his name's as well known in the West Riding as the winner o' t' Derby. But Lor', sir"—here he stopped and rummaged among a heap of papers. "They are makin' a fuss about him on account o' his fight wi' Ted Barton, and so the *Croxley Herald* has his life an' record, an' here it is, an' thou canst read it for thysel'."

The sheet of the paper which he held up was a lake of print around an islet of illustration. The latter was a coarse woodcut of a pugilist's head and neck set in a cross-barred jersey. It was a sinister but powerful face, the face of a debauched hero, clean-shaven, strongly eyebrowed, keen-eyed, with a huge, aggressive jaw, and an animal dewlap beneath it. The long, obstinate cheeks ran flush up to the narrow, sinister eyes. The mighty neck came down square from the ears and curved outwards into shoulders, which had lost nothing at the hands of the local artist. Above was written "Silas Craggs," and beneath, "The Master of Croxley."

"Thou'll find all about him there, sir," said the tobacconist. "He's a witherin' tyke, he is, and w're proud to have him in the county. If he hadn't broke his leg he'd have been champion of England."

"Broke his leg, has he?"

"Yes, and it set badly. They ca' him owd K behind his bock, for thot is how his two legs look. But his arms—well, if they was both stropped to a bench, as the sayin' is, I wonder where the champion of England would be then."

"I'll take this with me," said Montgomery; and putting the paper into his pocket he returned home.

It was not a cheering record which he read there. The whole history of the Croxley Master was given in full, his many victories, his few defeats.

"Born in 1857," said the provincial biographer, "Silas Craggs, better known in sporting circles as The Master of Croxley, is now in his fortieth year."

"Hang it, I'm only twenty-three," said Montgomery to himself, and read on more cheerfully.

"Having in his youth shown a surprising aptitude for the game, he fought his way up among his comrades, until he became the recognised champion of the district and won the proud title which he still holds. Ambitious of a more than local fame, he secured a patron, and fought his first fight against Jack Barton, of Birmingham, in May, 1880, at the old Loiterers' Club. Craggs, who fought at ten-stone-two at the time, had the better of fifteen rattling rounds, and gained an award on points against the Midlander. Having disposed of James Dunn, of Rotherhithe, Cameron, of Glasgow, and a youth named Fernie, he was thought so highly of by the fancy that he was matched against Ernest Willox, at that time middleweight champion of the North of England, and defeated him in a hard-fought battle, knocking him out in the tenth round after a punishing contest. At this period it looked as if the very highest honours of the ring were within the reach of the young Yorkshireman, but he was laid upon the shelf by a most unfortunate accident. The kick of a horse broke his thigh, and for a year he was compelled to rest himself. When he returned to his work the fracture had set badly, and his activity was much impaired. It was owing to this that he was defeated in seven rounds by Willox, the man whom he had previously beaten, and afterwards by James Shaw, of London, though the latter acknowledged that he had found the toughest customer of his career. Undismayed by his reverses, the Master adapted the style of his fighting to his physical disabilities and resumed his career of victory—defeating Norton (the black), Bobby Wilson, and Levi Cohen, the latter a heavyweight. Conceding two stone, he fought a draw with the famous Billy McQuire, and afterwards, for a purse of fifty pounds, he defeated Sam Hare at the Pelican Club, London. In 1891 a decision was given against him upon a foul when fighting a winning fight against Jim Taylor, the Australian middleweight, and so mortified was he by the decision that he withdrew from the ring. Since then he has hardly fought at all save to accommodate any local aspirant who may wish to learn the difference between a barroom scramble and a scientific contest. The latest of these ambitious souls comes form the Wilson coal pits, which have undertaken to put up a stake of £100 and back their local champion. There are various rumours afloat as to who their representative is to be, the name of Ted Barton being freely mentioned; but the betting, which is seven to one on the Master against any untried man, is a fair reflection of the feeling of the community."

Montgomery read it over twice, and it left him with a very serious face. No light matter this which he had undertaken; no battle with a rough-and-tumble fighter who presumed upon a local reputation. The man's record showed that he was first-class—or nearly so. There were a few points in his favour, and he must make the most of them. There was age—twenty-three against forty. There was an old ring proverb that "Youth will be served," but the annals of the ring offer a great number of exceptions. A hard veteran, full of cool valour and ring-craft, could give ten or fifteen years and a beating to most striplings. He could not rely too much upon his advantage in age. But then there was the lameness; that must surely count for a great deal. And, lastly, there was the chance that the Master might underrate his opponent, that he might be remiss in his training, and refuse to abandon his usual way of life, if he thought that he had an easy task before him. In a man of his age and habits this seemed very possible. Montgomery prayed that it might be so. Meanwhile, if his opponent were the best man who ever jumped the ropes into a ring, his own duty was clear. He must prepare himself carefully, throw away no chance, and do the very best that he could. But he knew enough to appreciate the difference which exists in boxing, as in every sport, between the amateur and the professional. The coolness, the power of hitting, above all the capability of taking punishment, count for so much. Those specially developed, gutta-percha-like abdominal muscles of the hardened pugilist will take without flinching a blow which would leave another man writhing on the ground. Such things are not to be acquired in a week, but all that could be done in a week should be done.

The medical assistant had a good basis to start from. He was 5 feet 11 inches—tall enough for anything on two legs, as the old ring men used to say—lithe and spare, with the activity of a panther, and a strength which had hardly yet ever found its limitations. His muscular development was finely hard, but his power came rather from that higher nerve energy which counts for nothing upon a measuring tape. He had the well-curved nose and the widely-opened eye which never yet were seen upon the face of a craven, and behind everything he had the driving force which came from the knowledge that his whole career was at stake upon the contest. The three backers rubbed their hands when they saw him at work punching the ball in the gymnasium next morning; and Fawcett, the horsebreaker, who had written to Leeds to hedge his bets, sent a wire to cancel the letter, and to lay another fifty at the market price of seven to one.

Montgomery's chief difficulty was to find time for his training without any interference from the doctor. His work took him a large part of the day, but as the visiting was done on foot, and considerable distances had to be traversed, it was a training in itself. For the rest, he punched the swinging ball and worked with the dumbbells for an hour every morning and evening, and boxed twice a day with Ted Barton in the gymnasium, gaining as much profit as could be got from a rushing, two-handed slogger. Barton was full of admiration for his cleverness and quickness, but doubtful about his strength. Hard hitting was the feature of his own style, and he exacted it from others.

"Lord, sir, that's a turble poor poonch for an eleven-stone man!" he would cry. "Thou wilt have to hit harder than that afore t' Master will know that thou art theer. Ah, thot's better, mon, thot's fine!" he would add, as his opponent lifted him across the room on the end of a right counter. "Thot's how I likes to feel 'em. Happen thou'lt pull through yet." He chuckled with joy when Montgomery knocked him into a corner. "Eh, mon, thou art comin' along grand. Thou hast fair yarked me off my legs. Do it again, lad, do it again!"

The only part of Montgomery's training which came within the doctor's observation was his diet, and that puzzled him considerably.

"You will excuse my remarking, Mr. Montgomery, that you are becoming rather particular in your tastes. Such fads are not to be encouraged in one's youth. Why do you eat toast with every meal?"

"I find that it suits me better than bread, sir."

"It entails unnecessary work upon the cook. I observe, also, that you have turned against potatoes."

"Yes, sir, I think that I am better without them."

"And you no longer drink your beer?"

"No, sir."

"These causeless whims and fancies are very much to be deprecated, Mr. Montgomery. Consider how many there are to whom these very potatoes and this very beer would be most acceptable."

"No doubt, sir. But at present I prefer to do without them."

They were sitting alone at lunch, and the assistant thought that it would be a good opportunity of asking leave for the day of the fight.

"I should be glad if you could let me have leave for Saturday, Doctor Oldacre."

"It is very inconvenient upon so busy a day."

"I should do a double day's work on Friday so as to leave everything in order. I should hope to be back in the evening."

"I am afraid I cannot spare you, Mr. Montgomery."

This was a facer. If he could not get leave he would go without it.

"You will remember, Doctor Oldacre, that when I came to you it was understood that I should have a clear day every month. I have never claimed one. But now there are reasons why I wish to have a holiday upon Saturday."

Doctor Oldacre gave in with a very bad grace.

"Of course, if you insist upon your formal rights, there is no more to be said, Mr. Montgomery, though I feel that it shows a certain indifference to my comfort and the welfare of the practice. Do you still insist?"

"Yes, sir."

"Very good. Have your way."

The doctor was boiling over with anger, but Montgomery was a valuable assistant—steady, capable, and hard-working—and he could not afford to lose him. Even if he had been prompted to advance those class fees, for which his assistant had appealed, it would have been against his interests to do so, for he did not wish him to qualify, and he desired him to remain in his subordinate position, in which he worked so hard for so small a wage. There was something in the cool insistence of the young man, a quiet resolution in his voice as he claimed his Saturday, which aroused his curiosity.

"I have no desire to interfere unduly with your affairs, Mr. Montgomery, but were you thinking of having a day in Leeds upon Saturday?"

"No, sir."

"In the country?"

"Yes, sir."

"You are very wise. You will find a quiet day among the wild flowers a very valuable restorative. Had you thought of any particular direction?"

"I am going over Croxley way."

"Well, there is no prettier country when once you are past the iron works. What could be more delightful than to lie upon the Fells, basking in the sunshine, with perhaps some instructive and elevating book as your companion? I should recommend a visit to the ruins of St. Bridget's Church, a very interesting relic of the early Norman era. By the way, there is one objection which I see to your going to Croxley on Saturday. It is upon that date, as I am informed, that that ruffianly glove fight takes place. You may find yourself molested by the blackguards whom it will attract."

"I will take my chance of that, sir," said the assistant.

On the Friday night, which was the last before the fight, Montgomery's three backers assembled in the gymnasium and inspected their man as he went through some light exercises to keep his muscles supple. He was certainly in splendid condition, his skin shining with health, and his eyes with energy and confidence. The three walked round him and exulted.

"He's simply ripping!" said the undergraduate. "By gad, you've come out of it splendidly. You're as hard as a pebble, and fit to fight for your life."

"Happen he's a trifle on the fine side," said the publican. "Runs a bit light at the loins, to my way of thinkin'."

"What weight today?"

"Ten stone eleven," the assistant answered.

"That's only three pund off in a week's trainin'," said the horse-breaker. "He said right when he said that he was in condition. Well, it's fine stuff all there is of it, but I'm none so sure as there is enough." He kept poking his finger into Montgomery, as if he were one of his horses. "I hear that the Master will scale a hundred and sixty odd at the ringside."

"But there's some of that which he'd like well to pull off and leave behind wi' his shirt," said Purvis. "I hear they've had a rare job to get him to drop his beer, and if it had not been for that great red-headed wench of his they'd never ha' done it. She fair scratted the face off a potman that had brought him a gallon from t' Chequers. They say the hussy is his sparrin' partner, as well as his sweetheart, and that his poor wife is just breakin' her heart over it. Hullo, young 'un, what do you want?"

The door of the gymnasium had opened, and a lad about sixteen, grimy and black with soot and iron, stepped into the yellow glare of the oil lamp. Ted Barton seized him by the collar.

"See here, thou yoong whelp, this is private, and we want noan o' thy spyin'!"

"But I maun speak to Mr. Wilson."

The young Cantab stepped forward.

"Well, my lad, what is it?"

"It's aboot t' fight, Mr. Wilson, sir. I wanted to tell your mon somethin' aboot t' Maister."

"We've no time to listen to gossip, my boy. We know all about the Master."

"But thou doant, sir. Nobody knows but me and mother, and we thought as we'd like thy mon to know, sir, for we want him to fair bray him."

"Oh, you want the Master fair brayed, do you? So do we. Well, what have you to say?"

"Is this your mon, sir?"

"Well, suppose it is?"

"Then it's him I want to tell aboot it. T' Maister is blind o' the left eye."

"Nonsense!"

"It's true, sir. Not stone blind, but rarely fogged. He keeps it secret, but mother knows, and so do I. If thou slip him on the left side he can't cop thee. Thou'll find it right as I tell thee. And mark him when he sinks his right. 'Tis his best blow, his right uppercut. T' Maister's finisher, they ca' it at t' works. It's a turble blow, when it do come home."

"Thank you, my boy. This is information worth having about his sight," said Wilson. "How came you to know so much? Who are you?"

"I'm his son, sir."

Wilson whistled.

"And who sent you to us?"

"My mother. I maun get back to her again."

"Take this half-crown."

"No, sir, I don't seek money in comin' here. I do it——"

"For love?" suggested the publican.

"For hate!" said the boy, and darted off into the darkness.

"Seems to me t' red-headed wench may do him more harm than good, after all," remarked the publican. "And now, Mr. Montgomery, sir, you've done enough for this evenin', and a nine-hours' sleep is the best trainin' before a battle. Happen this time tomorrow night you'll be safe back again with your £100 in your pocket."

PART TWO

Work was struck at one o'clock at the coal pits and the iron works, and the fight was arranged for three. From the Croxley Furnaces, from Wilson's Coal Pits, from the Heartsease Mine, from the Dodd Mills, from the Leverworth Smelters the workmen came trooping, each with his fox terrier or his lurcher at his heels. Warped with labour and twisted by toil, bent double by week-long work in the cramped coal galleries, or half-blinded with years spent in front of white-hot fluid metal, these men still gilded their harsh and hopeless lives by their devotion to sport. It was their one relief, the only thing which could distract their minds from sordid surroundings, and give them an interest beyond the blackened circle which inclosed them. Literature, art, science, all these things were beyond their horizon; but the race, the football match, the cricket, the fight, these were things which they could understand, which they could speculate upon in advance and comment upon afterwards. Sometimes brutal, sometimes grotesque, the love of sport is still one of the great agencies which make for the happiness of our people. It lies very deeply in the springs of our nature, and when it has been evacuated out, a higher, more refined nature may be left, but it will not be of that robust British type which has left its mark so deeply on the world. Every one of these ruddled workers, slouching with his dog at his heels to see something of the fight, was a true unit of his race.

It was a squally May day, with bright sunbursts and driving showers. Montgomery worked all morning in the surgery getting his medicine made up.

"The weather seems so very unsettled, Mr. Montgomery," remarked the doctor, "that I am inclined to think that you had better postpone your little country excursion until a later date."

"I am afraid that I must go today, sir."

"I have just had an intimation that Mrs. Potter, at the other side of Angleton, wishes to see me. It is probable that I shall be there all day. It will be extremely inconvenient to leave the house empty so long."

"I am very sorry, sir, but I must go," said the assistant, doggedly.

The doctor saw that it would be useless to argue, and departed in the worst of bad tempers upon his mission. Montgomery felt easier now that he was gone. He went up to his room, and packed his running shoes, his fighting-drawers, and his cricket-sash into a handbag. When he came down Mr. Wilson was waiting for him in the surgery.

"I hear the doctor has gone."

"Yes; he is likely to be away all day."

"I don't see that it matters much. It's bound to come to his ears by tonight."

"Yes; it's serious with me, Mr. Wilson. If I win, it's all right. I don't mind telling you that the hundred pounds will make all the difference to me. But if I lose, I shall lose my situation, for, as you say, I can't keep it secret."

"Never mind. We'll see you through among us. I only wonder the doctor has not heard, for it's all over the country that you are to fight the Croxley Champion. We've had Armitage up about it already. He's the Master's backer, you know. He wasn't sure that you were eligible. The Master said he wanted you whether you were eligible or not. Armitage has money on, and would have made trouble if he could. But I showed him that you came within the conditions of the challenge, and he agreed that it was all right. They think they have a soft thing on."

"Well, I can only do my best," said Montgomery.

They lunched together; a silent and rather nervous repast, for Montgomery's mind was full of what was before him, and Wilson had himself more money at stake than he cared to lose.

Wilson's carriage and pair were at the door, the horses with blue-and-white rosettes at their ears, which were the colours of the Wilson Coal Pits, well known on many a football field. At the avenue gate a crowd of some hundred pitmen and their wives gave a cheer as the carriage passed. To the assistant it all seemed dreamlike and extraordinary—the strangest experience of his life, but with a thrill of human action and interest in it which made it passionately absorbing. He lay back in the open carriage and saw the fluttering handkerchiefs from the doors and windows of the miners' cottages. Wilson had pinned a blue-and-white rosette upon his coat, and every one knew him as their champion. "Good luck, sir! Good luck to thee!" They shouted from the roadside. He felt that it was like some unromantic knight riding down to sordid lists, but there was something of chivalry in it all the same. He fought for others as well as for himself. He might fail from want of skill or strength, but deep in his sombre soul he vowed that it should never be for want of heart.

Mr. Fawcett was just mounting into his high-wheeled, spidery dog-cart, with his little bit of blood between the shafts. He waved his whip and fell in behind the carriage. They overtook Purvis, the tomato-faced publican, upon the road, with his wife in her Sunday bonnet. They also dropped into the procession, and then, as they traversed the seven miles of the high road to Croxley, their two-horsed, rosetted carriage became gradually the nucleus of a comet with a loosely radiating tail. From every side road came the miners' carts, the humble, ramshackle traps, black and bulging, with their loads of noisy, foul-tongued, open-hearted partisans. They trailed for a long quarter of a mile behind them—cracking, whipping, shouting, galloping, swearing. Horsemen and runners were mixed with the vehicles. And then suddenly a squad of the Sheffield Yeomanry, who were having their annual training in those parts, clattered and jingled out of a field, and rode as an escort to the carriage. Through the dust clouds round him Montgomery saw the gleaming brass helmets, the bright coats, and the tossing heads of the chargers, the delighted brown faces of the troopers. It was more dreamlike than ever.

And then, as they approached the monstrous uncouth line of bottle-shaped buildings which marked the smelting works of Croxley, their long, writhing snake of dust was headed off by another but longer one which wound across their path. The main road into which their own opened was filled by the rushing current of traps. The Wilson contingent halted until the others should get past. The iron men cheered and groaned, according to their humour, as they whirled past their antagonist. Rough chaff flew back and forwards like iron nuts and splinters of coal. "Brought him up, then!" "Got t' hearse for to fetch him back?" "Where's t' owd K-legs?" "Mon, mon, have thy photograph took—'twill mind thee of what thou used to look!" "He fight?—he's nowt but a half-baked doctor!" "Happen he'll doctor thy Croxley Champion afore he's through wi't."

So they flashed at each other as the one side waited and the other passed. Then there came a rolling murmur swelling into a shout, and a great break with four horses came clattering along, all streaming with salmon-pink ribbons. The driver wore a white hat with pink rosette, and beside him, on the high seat, were a man and a woman—she with her arm around his waist. Montgomery had one glimpse of them as they flashed past: he with a furry cap drawn low over his brow, a great frieze coat, and a pink comforter round his throat; she brazen, red-headed, bright-coloured, laughing excitedly. The Master, for it was he, turned as he passed, gazed hard at Montgomery, and gave him a menacing, gap-toothed grin. It was a hard, wicked face, blue-jowled and craggy, with long, obstinate cheeks and inexorable eyes. The break behind was full of patrons of the sport—flushed iron foremen, heads of departments, managers. One was drinking from a metal flask, and raised it to Montgomery as he passed; and then the crowd thinned, and the Wilson cortege with their dragoons swept in at the rear of the others.

The road led away from Croxley, between curving green hills, gashed and polluted by the searchers for coal and iron. The whole country had been gutted, and vast piles of refuse and mountains of slag suggested the mighty chambers which the labour of man had burrowed beneath. On the left the road curved up to where a huge building, roofless and dismantled, stood crumbling and forlorn, with the light shining through the windowless squares.

"That's the old Arrowsmith's factory. That's where the fight is to be," said Wilson. "How are you feeling now?"

"Thank you. I was never better in my life," Montgomery answered.

"By Gad, I like your nerve!" said Wilson, who was himself flushed and uneasy. "You'll give us a fight for our money, come what may. That place on the right is the office, and that has been set aside as the dressing and weighing room."

The carriage drove up to it amidst the shouts of the folk upon the hillside. Lines of empty carriages and traps curved down upon the winding road, and a black crowd surged round the door of the ruined factory. The seats, as a huge placard announced, were five shillings, three shillings, and a shilling, with half price for dogs. The takings, deducting expenses, were to go to the winner, and it was already evident that a larger stake than a hundred pounds was in question. A babel of voices rose from the door. The workers wished to bring their dogs in free. The men scuffled. The dogs barked. The crowd was a whirling, eddying pool surging with a roar up to the narrow cleft which was its only outlet.

The break, with its salmon-coloured streamers and four reeking horses, stood empty before the door of the office; Wilson, Purvis, Fawcett, and Montgomery passed in.

There was a large, bare room inside with square, clean patches upon the grimy walls, where pictures and almanacs had once hung. Worn linoleum covered the floor, but there was no furniture save some benches and a deal table with a ewer and a basin upon it. Two of the corners were curtained off. In the middle of the room was a weighing-chair. A hugely fat man, with a salmon tie and a blue waistcoat with birds'-eye spots, came bustling up to them. It was Armitage, the butcher and grazier, well known for miles round as a warm man, and the most liberal patron of sport in the Riding.

"Well, well," he grunted, in a thick, fussy, wheezy voice, "you have come, then. Got your man? Got your man?"

"Here he is, fit and well. Mr. Montgomery, let me present you to Mr. Armitage."

"Glad to meet you, sir. Happy to make your acquaintance. I make bold to say, sir, that we of Croxley admire your courage, Mr. Montgomery, and that our only hope is a fair fight and no favour and the best man win. That's our sentiment at Croxley."

"And it is my sentiment also," said the assistant.

"Well, you can't say fairer than that, Mr. Montgomery. You've taken a large contrac' in hand, but a large contrac' may be carried through, sir, as any one that knows my dealings could testify. The Master is ready to weigh in!"

"So am I."

"You must weigh in the buff."

Montgomery looked askance at the tall, red-headed woman who was standing gazing out of the window.

"That's all right," said Wilson. "Get behind the curtain and put on your fighting kit."

He did so, and came out the picture of an athlete, in white, loose drawers, canvas shoes, and the sash of a well-known cricket club round his waist. He was trained to a hair, his skin gleaming like silk, and every muscle rippling down his broad shoulders and along his beautiful arms as he moved them. They bunched into ivory knobs, or slid into long, sinuous curves, as he raised or lowered his hands.

"What thinkest thou o' that?" asked Ted Barton, his second, of the woman in the window.

She glanced contemptuously at the young athlete.

"It's but a poor kindness thou dost him to put a thread-paper yoong gentlemen like yon against a mon as is a mon. Why, my Jock would throttle him wi' one hond lashed behind him."

"Happen he may—happen not," said Barton. "I have but twa pund in the world, but it's on him, every penny, and no hedgin'. But here's t' Maister, and rarely fine he do look."

The prize fighter had come out from his curtain, a squat, formidable figure, monstrous in chest and arms, limping slightly on his distorted leg. His skin had none of the freshness and clearness of Montgomery's, but was dusky and mottled, with one huge mole amid the mat of tangled black hair which thatched his mighty breast. His weight bore no relation to his strength, for those huge shoulders and great arms, with brown, sledge-hammer fists, would have fitted the heaviest man that ever threw his cap into a ring. But his loins and legs were slight in proportion. Montgomery, on the other hand, was as symmetrical as a Greek statue. It would be an encounter between a man who was specially fitted for one sport, and one who was equally capable of any. The two looked curiously at each other: a bulldog, and a high-bred, clean-limbed terrier, each full of spirit.

"How do you do?"

"How do?" The Master grinned again, and his three jagged front teeth gleamed for an instant. The rest had been beaten out of him in twenty years of battle. He spat upon the floor. "We have a rare fine day for't."

"Capital," said Montgomery.

"That's the good feelin' I like," wheezed the fat butcher. "Good lads, both of them!—prime lads!—hard meat an' good bone. There's no ill-feelin'."

"If he downs me, Gawd bless him!" said the Master.

"An' if we down him, Gawd help him!" interrupted the woman.

"Haud thy tongue, wench!" said the Master, impatiently. "Who art thou to put in thy word? Happen I might draw my hand across thy face."

The woman did not take the threat amiss.

"Wilt have enough for thy hand to do, Jock," said she. "Get quit o' this gradely man afore thou turn on me."

The lovers' quarrel was interrupted by the entrance of a newcomer, a gentleman with a fur-collared overcoat and a very shiny top hat—a top hat of a degree of glossiness which is seldom seen five miles from Hyde Park. This hat he wore at the extreme back of his head, so that the lower surface of the brim made a kind of frame for his high, bald forehead, his keen eyes, his rugged and yet kindly face. He bustled in with the quiet air of possession with which the ringmaster enters the circus.

"It's Mr. Stapleton, the referee from London," said Wilson.

"How do you do, Mr. Stapleton? I was introduced to you at the big fight at the Corinthian Club, in Piccadilly."

"Ah, I dare say," said the other, shaking hands. "Fact is, I'm introduced to so many that I can't undertake to carry their names. Wilson, is it? Well, Mr. Wilson, glad to see you. Couldn't get a fly at the station, and that's why I'm late."

"I'm sure, sir," said Armitage, "we should be proud that any one so well known in the boxing world should come down to our little exhibition."

"Not at all. Not at all. Anything in the interest of boxin'. All ready? Men weighed?"

"Weighing now, sir."

"Ah, just as well I should see it done. Seen you before Craggs. Saw you fight your second battle against Wilcox. You had beaten him once, but he came back on you. What does the indicator say?—one hundred and sixty-three pounds—two off for the kit—one hundred and sixty-one. Now, my lad, you jump. My goodness, what colours are you wearing?"

"The Anonymi Cricket Club."

"What right have you to wear them? I belong to the club myself."

"So do I."

"You an amateur?"

"Yes, sir."

"And you are fighting for a money prize?"

"Yes."

"I suppose you know what you are doing. You realise that you're a professional pug from this onwards, and that if ever you fight again—"

"I'll never fight again."

"Happen you won't," said the woman, and the Master turned a terrible eye upon her.

"Well, I suppose you know your own business best. Up you jump. One hundred and fifty-one, minus two, one hundred and forty-nine—twelve pounds difference, but youth and condition on the other scale. Well, the sooner we get to work the better, for I wish to catch the seven o'clock express at Hellifield. Twenty three-minute rounds, with one minute intervals, and Queensberry rules. Those are the conditions, are they not?"

"Yes, sir."

"Very good, then, we may go across."

The two combatants had overcoats thrown over their shoulders, and the whole party, backers, fighters, seconds, and the referee, filed out of the room. A police inspector was waiting for them in the road. He had a notebook in his hand—that terrible weapon which awes even the London cabman.

"I must take your names, gentlemen, in case it should be necessary to proceed for breach of peace."

"You don't mean to stop the fight?" cried Armitage, in a passion of indignation. "I'm Mr. Armitage, of Croxley, and this is Mr. Wilson, and we'll be responsible that all is fair and as it should be."

"I'll take the names in case it should be necessary to proceed," said the inspector, impassively.

"But you know me well."

"If you was a dook or even a judge it would be all the same," said the inspector. "It's the law, and there's an end. I'll not take upon myself to stop the fight, seeing that gloves are to be used, but I'll take the names of all concerned. Silas Craggs, Robert Montgomery, Edward Barton, James Stapleton of London. Who seconds Silas Craggs?"

"I do," said the woman. "Yes, you can stare, but it's my job, and no one else's. Anastasia's the name—four a's."

"Craggs?"

"Johnson. Anastasia Johnson. If you jug him, you can jug me."

"Who talked of juggin', ye fool?" growled the Master. "Coom on, Mr. Armitage, for I'm fair sick o' this loiterin'."

The inspector fell in with the procession, and proceeded, as they walked up the hill, to bargain in his official capacity for a front seat, where he could safeguard the interests of the law, and in his private capacity to lay out thirty shillings at seven to one with Mr. Armitage. Through the door they passed, down a narrow lane walled with a dense bank of humanity, up a wooden ladder to a platform, over a rope which was slung waist-high from four corner stakes, and then Montgomery realised that he was in that ring in which his immediate destiny was to be worked out. On the stake at one corner there hung a blue-and-white streamer. Barton led him across, the overcoat dangling loosely from his shoulders, and he sat down on a wooden stool. Barton and another man, both wearing white sweaters, stood beside him. The so-called ring was a square, twenty feet each way. At the opposite angle was the sinister figure of the Master, with his red-headed woman and a rough-faced friend to look after him. At each corner were metal basins, pitchers of water, and sponges.

During the hubbub and uproar of the entrance Montgomery was too bewildered to take things in. But now there was a few minutes' delay, for the referee had lingered behind, and so he looked quietly about him. It was a sight to haunt him for a lifetime. Wooden seats had been built in, sloping upwards to the tops of the walls. Above, instead of a ceiling, a great flight of crows passed slowly across a square of grey cloud. Right up to the topmost benches the folk were banked—broadcloth in front, corduroys and fustian behind; faces turned everywhere upon him. The grey reek of the pipes filled the building, and the air was pungent with the acrid smell of cheap, strong tobacco. Everywhere among the human faces were to be seen the heads of the dogs. They growled and yapped from the black benches. In that dense mass of humanity one could hardly pick out individuals, but Montgomery's eyes caught the brazen gleam of the helmets held upon the knees of the ten yeomen of his escort. At the very edge of the platform sat the reporters, five of them: three locals, and two all the way from London. But where was the all-important referee? There was no sign of him, unless he were in the centre of that angry swirl of men near the door.

Mr. Stapleton had stopped to examine the gloves which were to be used, and entered the building after the combatants. He had started to come down that narrow lane with the human walls which led to the ring. But already it had gone abroad that the Wilson champion was a gentleman, and that another gentleman had been appointed as referee. A wave of suspicion passed through the Croxley folk. They would have one of their own people for a referee. They would not have a stranger. His path was stopped as he made for the ring. Excited men flung themselves in front of him; they waved their fists in his face and cursed him. A woman howled vile names in his ear. Somebody struck at him with an umbrella. "Go thou back to Lunnon. We want noan o' thee. Go thou back!" they yelled.

Stapleton with his shiny hat cocked backwards, and his large, bulging forehead swelling from under it, looked round him from beneath his bushy brows. He was in the centre of a savage and dangerous mob.

Then he drew his watch from his pocket and held it dial upwards in his palm.

"In three minutes," said he, "I will declare the fight off."

They raged round him. His cool face and that aggressive top hat irritated them. Grimy hands were raised. But it was difficult, somehow, to strike a man who was so absolutely indifferent.

"In two minutes I declare the fight off."

They exploded into blasphemy. The breath of angry men smoked into his placid face. A gnarled, grimy fist vibrated at the end of his nose. "We tell thee we want noan o' thee. Get thou back where thou com'st from."

"In one minute I declare the fight off."

Then the calm persistence of the man conquered the swaying, mutable, passionate crowd.

"Let him through, mon. Happen there'll be no fight after a'."

"Let him through."

"Bill, thou loomp, let him pass. Dost want the fight declared off?"

"Make room for the referee!—room for the Lunnon referee!"

And half pushed, half carried, he was swept up to the ring. There were two chairs by the side of it, one for him and one for the timekeeper. He sat down, his hands on his knees, his hat at a more wonderful angle than ever, impassive but solemn, with the aspect of one who appreciates his responsibilities.

Mr. Armitage, the portly butcher, made his way into the ring and held up two fat hands, sparkling with rings, as a signal for silence.

"Gentlemen!" he yelled. And then in a crescendo shriek, "Gentlemen!"

"And ladies!" cried somebody, for indeed there was a fair sprinkling of women among the crowd. "Speak up, owd man!" shouted another. "What price pork chops?" cried somebody at the back. Everybody laughed, and the dogs began to bark. Armitage waved his hands amidst the uproar as if he were conducting an orchestra. At last the babel thinned into silence.

"Gentlemen," he yelled, "the match is between Silas Craggs, whom we call the Master of Croxley, and Robert Montgomery, of the Wilson Coal Pits. The match was to be under eleven eight. When they were weighed just now Craggs weighed eleven seven, and Montgomery ten nine. The conditions of the contest are: the best of twenty three-minute rounds with two-ounce gloves. Should the fight run to its full length it will, of course, be decided upon points. Mr. Stapleton, the well-known London referee, has kindly consented to see fair play. I wish to say that Mr. Wilson and I, the chief backers of the two men, have every confidence in Mr. Stapleton, and that we beg that you accept his rulings without dispute."

He then turned from one combatant to the other, with a wave of his hand.

PART THREE

"Montgomery—Craggs!" said he.

A great hush fell over the huge assembly. Even the dogs stopped yapping; one might have thought that the monstrous room was empty. The two men had stood up, the small white gloves over their hands. They advanced from their corners and shook hands: Montgomery gravely, Craggs with a smile. Then they fell into position. The crowd gave a long sigh—the intake of a thousand excited breaths. The referee tilted his chair on to its back legs, and looked moodily critical from the one to the other.

It was strength against activity—that was evident from the first. The Master stood stolidly upon his K-leg. It gave him a tremendous pedestal; one could hardly imagine his being knocked down. And he could pivot round upon it with extraordinary quickness; but his advance or retreat was ungainly. His frame, however, was so much larger and broader than that of the student, and his brown, massive face looked so resolute and menacing, that the hearts of the Wilson party sank within them. There was one heart, however, which had not done so. It was that of Robert Montgomery.

Any nervousness which he may have had completely passed away now that he had his work before him. Here was something definite— this hard-faced, deformed Hercules to beat, with a career as the price of beating him. He glowed with the joy of action; it thrilled through his nerves. He faced his man with little in-and-out steps, breaking to the left, breaking to the right, feeling his way, while Craggs, with a dull, malignant eye, pivoted slowly upon his weak leg, his left arm half extended, his right sunk low across the mark. Montgomery led with his left, and then led again, getting lightly home each time. He tried again, but the Master had his counter ready, and Montgomery reeled back from a harder blow than he had given. Anastasia, the woman, gave a shrill cry of encouragement, and her man let fly his right. Montgomery ducked under it, and in an instant the two were in each other's arms.

"Break away! Break away!" said the referee.

The Master struck upwards on the break, and shook Montgomery with the blow. Then it was "time." It had been a spirited opening round. The people buzzed into comment and applause. Montgomery was quite fresh, but the hairy chest of the Master was rising and falling. The man passed a sponge over his head, while Anastasia flapped the towel before him. "Good lass! Good lass!" cried the crowd, and cheered her.

The men were up again, the Master grimly watchful, Montgomery as alert as a kitten. The Master tried a sudden rush, squattering along with his awkward gait, but coming faster than one would think. The student slipped aside and avoided him. The Master stopped, grinned, and shook his head. Then he motioned with his hand as an invitation to Montgomery to come to him. The student did so and led with his left, but got a swinging right counter in the ribs in exchange. The heavy blow staggered him, and the Master came scrambling in to complete his advantage; but Montgomery, with his greater activity, kept out of danger until the call of "time." A tame round, and the advantage with the Master.

"T' Maister's too strong for him," said a smelter to his neighbour.

"Ay; but t'other's a likely lad. Happen we'll see some sport yet. He can joomp rarely."

"But t' Maister can stop and hit rarely. Happen he'll mak' him joomp when he gets his neif upon him."

They were up again, the water glistening upon their faces. Montgomery led instantly and got his right home with a sounding smack upon the Master's forehead. There was a shout from the colliers, and "Silence! Order!" from the referee. Montgomery avoided the counter and scored with his left. Fresh applause, and the referee upon his feet in indignation. "No comments, gentlemen, if *you* please, during the rounds."

"Just bide a bit!" growled the Master.

"Don't talk—fight!" said the referee, angrily.

Montgomery rubbed in the point by a flush hit upon the mouth, and the Master shambled back to his corner like an angry bear, having had all the worst of the round.

"Where's that seven to one?" shouted Purvis, the publican. "I'll take six to one!"

There were no answers.

"Five to one!" There were givers at that. Purvis booked them in a tattered notebook.

Montgomery began to feel happy. He lay back with his legs outstretched, his back against the corner post, and one gloved hand upon each rope. What a delicious minute it was between each round. If he could only keep out of harm's way, he must surely wear this man out before the end of twenty rounds. He was so slow that all his strength went for nothing. "You're fightin' a winnin' fight—a winnin' fight," Ted Barton whispered in his ear. "Go canny; tak' no chances; you have him proper."

But the Master was crafty. He had fought so many battles with his maimed limb that he knew how to make the best of it. Warily and slowly he manœuvred round Montgomery, stepping forward and yet again forward until he had imperceptibly backed him into his corner. The student suddenly saw a flash of triumph upon the grim face, and a gleam in the dull, malignant eyes. The Master was upon him. He sprang aside and was on the ropes. The Master smashed in one of his terrible uppercuts, and Montgomery half broke it with his guard. The student sprang the other way and was against the other converging rope. He was trapped in the angle. The Master sent in another, with a hoggish grunt which spoke of the energy behind it. Montgomery ducked, but got a jab from the left upon the mark. He closed with his man. "Break away! Break away!" cried the referee. Montgomery disengaged and got a swinging blow on the ear as he did so. It had been a damaging round for him, and the Croxley people were shouting their delight.

"Gentlemen, I will *not* have this noise!" Stapleton roared. "I have been accustomed to preside at a well-conducted club, and not at a beargarden." This little man, with the tilted hat and the bulging forehead, dominated the whole assembly. He was like a headmaster among his boys. He glared round him, and nobody cared to meet his eye.

Anastasia had kissed the Master when he resumed his seat. "Good lass! Do't again!" cried the laughing crowd, and the angry Master shook his glove at her, as she flapped her towel in front of him. Montgomery was weary and a little sore, but not depressed. He had learned something. He would not again be tempted into danger.

For three rounds the honours were fairly equal. The student's hitting was the quicker, the Master's the harder. Profiting by his lesson, Montgomery kept himself in the open, and refused to be herded into a corner. Sometimes the Master succeeded in rushing him to the side ropes, but the younger man slipped away, or closed, and then disengaged. The monotonous "Break away! Break away!" of the referee broke in upon the quick, low patter of rubber-soled shoes, the dull thud of the blows, and the sharp, hissing breath of two tired men.

The ninth round found both of them in fairly good condition. Montgomery's head was still singing from the blow that he had in the corner, and one of his thumbs pained him acutely and seemed to be dislocated. The Master showed no sign of a touch, but his breathing was the more laboured, and a long line of ticks upon the referee's paper showed that the student had a good show of points. But one of his ironman's blows was worth three of his, and he knew that without the gloves he could not have stood for three rounds against him. All the amateur work that he had done was the merest tapping and flapping when compared to those frightful blows, from arms toughened by the shovel and the crowbar.

It was the tenth round, and the fight was half over. The betting now was only three to one, for the Wilson champion had held his own much better than had been expected. But those who knew the ring-craft as well as the staying power of the old prize fighter knew that the odds were still a long way in his favour.

"Have a care of him!" whispered Barton, as he sent his man up to the scratch. "Have a care! He'll play thee a trick, if he can."

But Montgomery saw, or imagined he saw, that his antagonist was tiring. He looked jaded and listless, and his hands drooped a little from their position. His own youth and condition were beginning to tell. He sprang in and brought off a fine left-handed lead. The Master's return lacked his usual fire. Again Montgomery led, and again he got home. Then he tried his right upon the mark, and the Master guarded it downwards.

"Too low! Too low! A foul! A foul!" yelled a thousand voices.

The referee rolled his sardonic eyes slowly round. "Seems to me this buildin' is chock-full of referees," said he.

The people laughed and applauded, but their favour was as immaterial to him as their anger.

"No applause, please! This is not a theatre!" he yelled.

Montgomery was very pleased with himself. His adversary was evidently in a bad way. He was piling on his points and establishing a lead. He might as well make hay while the sun shone. The Master was looking all abroad. Montgomery popped one upon his blue jowl and got away without a return. And then the Master suddenly dropped both his hands and began rubbing his thigh. Ah! that was it, was it! He had muscular cramp.

"Go in! Go in!" cried Teddy Barton.

Montgomery sprang wildly forward, and the next instant was lying half senseless, with his neck nearly broken, in the middle of the ring.

The whole round had been a long conspiracy to tempt him within reach of one of those terrible righthand uppercuts for which the Master was famous. For this the listless, weary bearing, for this the cramp in the thigh. When Montgomery had sprang in so hotly he had exposed himself to such a blow as neither flesh nor blood could stand. Whizzing up from below with a rigid arm, which put the Master's eleven stone into its force, it struck him under the jaw: he whirled half round, and fell a helpless and half-paralysed mass. A vague groan and murmur, inarticulate, too excited for words, rose from the great audience. With open mouths and staring eyes they gazed at the twitching and quivering figure.

"Stand back! Stand right back!" shrieked the referee, for the Master was standing over his man ready to give him the *coup-de-grace* as he rose.

"Stand back, Craggs, this instant!" Stapleton repeated.

The Master sank his hands sulkily and walked backwards to the rope with his ferocious eyes fixed upon his fallen antagonist. The timekeeper called the seconds. If ten of them passed before Montgomery rose to his feet, the fight was ended. Ted Barton wrung his hands and danced about in an agony in his corner.

As if in a dream—a terrible nightmare—the student could hear the voice of the timekeeper—three—four—five—he got upon his hand—six—seven—he was on his knee, sick, swimming, faint, but resolute to rise. Eight—he was up, and the Master was on him like a tiger, lashing savagely at him with both hands. Folk held their breath as they watched those terrible blows, and anticipated the pitiful end—so much more pitiful where a game but helpless man refuses to accept defeat.

Strangely automatic is the human brain. Without volition, without effort, there shot into the memory of this bewildered, staggering, half-stupefied man the one thing which could have saved him—that blind eye of which the Master's son had spoken. It was the same as the other to look at, but Montgomery remembered that he had said that it was the left. He reeled to the left side, half felled by a drive which lit upon his shoulder. The Master pivoted round upon his leg and was at him in an instant.

"Yark him, lad! yark him!" screamed the woman.

"Hold your tongue!" said the referee.

Montgomery slipped to the left again and yet again; but the Master was too quick and clever for him. He struck round and got him full on the face as he tried once more to break away. Montgomery's knees weakened under him, and he fell with a groan on the floor. This time he knew that he was done. With bitter agony he realised, as he groped blindly with his hands, that he could not possibly raise himself. Far away and muffled he heard, amid the murmurs of the multitude, the fateful voice of the timekeeper counting of the seconds.

"One—two—three—four—five—six——"

"Time!" said the referee.

Then the pent-up passion of the great assembly broke loose. Croxley gave a deep groan of disappointment. The Wilsons were on their feet, yelling with delight. There was still a chance for them. In four more seconds their man would have been solemnly counted out. But now he had a minute in which to recover. The referee looked round with relaxed features and laughing eyes. He loved this rough game, this school for humble heroes, and it was pleasant to him to intervene as a *deus ex machina* at so dramatic a moment. His chair and his hat were both tilted at an extreme angle; he and the timekeeper smiled at each other. Ted Barton and the other second had rushed out and thrust an arm each under

Montgomery's knee, the other behind his loins, and so carried him back to his stool. His head lolled upon his shoulder, but a douche of cold water sent a shiver through him, and he started and looked round him.

"He's a' right!" cried the people round. "He's a rare brave lad. Good lad! Good lad!" Barton poured some brandy into his mouth. The mists cleared a little, and he realised where he was and what he had to do. But he was still very weak, and he hardly dared to hope that he could survive another round.

"Seconds out of the ring!" cried the referee. "Time!"

The Croxley Master sprang eagerly off his stool.

"Keep clear of him! Go easy for a bit," said Barton; and Montgomery walked out to meet his man once more.

He had had two lessons—the one when the Master got him into his corner, the other when he had been lured into mixing it up with so powerful an antagonist. Now he would be wary. Another blow would finish him; he could afford to run no risks. The Master was determined to follow up his advantage, and rushed at him, slogging furiously right and left. But Montgomery was too young and active to be caught. He was strong upon his legs once more, and his wits had all come back to him. It was a gallant sight—the line-of-battleship trying to pour its overwhelming broadside into the frigate, and the frigate manœuvring always so as to avoid it. The Master tried all his ring-craft. He coaxed the student up by pretended inactivity; he rushed at him with furious rushes towards the ropes. For three rounds he exhausted every wile in trying to get at him. Montgomery during all this time was conscious that his strength was minute by minute coming back to him. The spinal jar from an uppercut is overwhelming, but evanescent. He was losing all sense of it beyond a great stiffness of the neck. For the first round after his downfall he had been content to be entirely on the defensive, only too happy if he could stall off the furious attacks of the Master. In the second he occasionally ventured upon a light counter. In the third he was smacking back merrily where he saw an opening. His people yelled their approval of him at the end of every round. Even the ironworkers cheered him with that fine unselfishness which true sport engenders. To most of them, unspiritual and unimaginative, the sight of this clean-limbed young Apollo, rising above disaster and holding on while consciousness was in him to his appointed task, was the greatest thing their experience had ever known.

But the Master's naturally morose temper became more and more murderous at this postponement of his hopes. Three rounds ago the battle had been in his hands; now it was all to do over again. Round by round his man was recovering his strength. By the fifteenth he was strong again in wind and limb. But the vigilant Anastasia saw something which encouraged her.

"That bash in t' ribs is telling on him, Jock," she whispered. "Why else should he be gulping t' brandy? Go in, lad, and thou hast him yet."

Montgomery had suddenly taken the flask from Barton's hand, and had a deep pull at the contents. Then, with his face a little flushed, and with a curious look of purpose, which made the referee stare hard at him, in his eyes, he rose for the sixteenth round.

"Game as a pairtridge!" cried the publican, as he looked at the hard-set face.

"Mix it oop, lad; mix it oop!" cried the iron-men to their Master.

And then a hum of exultation ran through their ranks as they realised that their tougher, harder, stronger man held the vantage, after all.

Neither of the men showed much sign of punishment. Small gloves crush and numb, but they do not cut. One of the Master's eyes was even more flush with his cheek than Nature had made it. Montgomery had two or three livid marks upon his body, and his face was haggard, save for that pink spot which the brandy had brought into either cheek. He rocked a little as he stood opposite his man, and his hands drooped as if he felt the gloves to be an unutterable weight. It was evident that he was spent and desperately weary. If he received one other blow it must surely be fatal to him. If he brought one home, what power could there be behind it, and what chance was there of its harming the colossus in front of him? It was the crisis of the fight. This round must decide it. "Mix it oop, lad; mix it oop!" the iron-men whooped. Even the savage eyes of the referee were unable to restrain the excited crowd.

Now, at last, the chance had come for Montgomery. He had learned a lesson from his more experienced rival. Why should he not play his own game upon him? He was spent, but not nearly so spent as he pretended. That brandy was to call up his reserves, to let him have strength to take full advantage of the opening when it came. It was thrilling and tingling through his veins, at the very moment when he was lurching and rocking like a beaten man. He acted his part admirably. The Master felt that there was an easy task before him, and rushed in with ungainly activity to finish it once for all. He slap-banged away left and right, boring Montgomery up against the ropes, swinging in his ferocious blows with those animal grunts which told of the vicious energy behind them.

But Montgomery was too cool to fall a victim to any of those murderous uppercuts. He kept out of harm's way with a rigid guard, an active foot, and a head which was swift to duck. And yet he contrived to present the same appearance of a man who is hopelessly done. The Master, weary from his own shower of blows, and fearing nothing from so weak a man, dropped his hand for an instant, and at that instant Montgomery's right came home.

It was a magnificent blow, straight, clean, crisp, with the force of the loins and the back behind it. And it landed where he had meant it to—upon the exact point of that blue-grained chin. Flesh and blood could not stand such a blow in such a place. Neither valour nor hardihood can save the man to whom it comes. The Master fell backwards, flat, prostrate, striking the ground with so simultaneous a clap that it was like a shutter falling from a wall. A yell which no referee could control broke from the crowded benches as the giant went down. He lay upon his back, his knees a little drawn up, his huge chest panting. He twitched and shook, but could not move. His feet pawed convulsively once or twice. It was no use. He was done. "Eight—nine—ten!" said the timekeeper, and the roar of a thousand voices, with a deafening clap like the broadside of a ship, told that the Master of Croxley was the Master no more.

Montgomery stood half dazed, looking down at the huge, prostrate figure. He could hardly realise that it was indeed all over. He saw the referee motion towards him with his hand. He heard his name bellowed in triumph from every side. And then he was aware of some one rushing towards him; he caught a glimpse of a flushed face and an aureole of flying red hair, a gloveless fist struck him between the eyes, and he was on his back in the ring beside his antagonist, while a dozen of his supporters were endeavouring to secure the frantic Anastasia. He heard the angry shouting of the referee, the screaming of the furious woman, and the cries of the mob. Then something seemed to break like an over-stretched banjo-string, and he sank into the deep, deep, mist-girt abyss of unconsciousness.

The dressing was like a thing in a dream, and so was a vision of the Master with the grin of a bulldog upon his face, and his three teeth amiably protruded. He shook Montgomery heartily by the hand.

"I would have been rare pleased to shake thee by the throttle, lad, a short while syne," said he. "But I bear no ill-feelin' again' thee. It was a rare poonch that brought me down—I have not had a better since my second fight wi' Billy Edwards in '89. Happen thou might think o' goin' further wi' this business. If thou dost, and want a trainer, there's not much inside t' ropes as I don't know. Or happen thou might like to try it wi' me old style and bare knuckles. Thou hast but to write to t' iron-works to find me."

But Montgomery disclaimed any such ambition. A canvas bag with his share—one hundred and ninety sovereigns—was handed to him, of which he gave ten to the Master, who also received some share of the gate money. Then, with young Wilson escorting him on one side, Purvis on the other, and Fawcett carrying his bag behind, he went in triumph to his carriage, and drove amid a long roar, which lined the highway like a hedge for the seven miles, back to his starting point.

"It's the greatest thing I ever saw in my life. By George, it's ripping!" cried Wilson, who had been left in a kind of ecstasy by the events of the day. "There's a chap over Barnsley way who fancies himself a bit. Let us spring you on him, and let him see what he can make of you. We'll put up a purse—won't we, Purvis? You shall never want a backer."

"At his weight," said the publican, "I'm behind him, I am, for twenty rounds, and no age, country, or colour barred."

"So am I!" cried Fawcett; "middleweight champion of the world, that's what he is—here, in the same carriage with us."

But Montgomery was not to be beguiled.

"No; I have my own work to do now."

"And what may that be?"

"I'll use this money to get my medical degree."

"Well, we've plenty of doctors, but you're the only man in the Riding that could smack the Croxley Master off his legs. However, I suppose you know your own business best. When you're a doctor, you'd best come down into these parts, and you'll always find a job waiting for you at the Wilson Coal Pits."

Montgomery had returned by devious ways to the surgery. The horses were smoking at the door and the doctor was just back from his long journey. Several patients had called in his absence, and he was in the worst of tempers.

"I suppose I should be glad that you have come back at all, Mr. Montgomery!" he snarled. "When next you elect to take a holiday, I trust it will not be at so busy a time."

"I am sorry, sir, that you should have been inconvenienced."

"Yes, sir, I have been exceedingly inconvenienced." Here, for the first time, he looked hard at the assistant. "Good heavens, Mr. Montgomery, what have you been doing with your left eye?"

It was where Anastasia had lodged her protest.

Montgomery laughed. "It is nothing, sir," said he.

"And you have a livid mark under your jaw. It is, indeed, terrible that my representative should be going about in so disreputable a condition. How did you receive these injuries?"

"Well, sir, as you know, there was a little glove fight today over at Croxley."

"And you got mixed up with that brutal crowd?"

"I *was* rather mixed up with them."

"And who assaulted you?"

"One of the fighters."

"Which of them?"

"The Master of Croxley."

"Good heavens! Perhaps you interfered with him?"

"Well, to tell the truth, I did a little."

"Mr. Montgomery, in such a practice as mine, intimately associated as it is with the highest and most progressive elements of our small community, it is impossible——"

But just then the tentative bray of a cornet player searching for his keynote jarred upon their ears, and an instant later the Wilson Colliery brass band was in full cry with "See the Conquering Hero Comes," outside the surgery window. There was a banner waving, and a shouting crowd of miners.

"What is it? What does it mean?" cried the angry doctor.

"It means, sir, that I have, in the only way which was open to me, earned the money which is necessary for my education. It is my duty, Doctor Oldacre, to warn you that I am about to return to the University and that you should lose no time in appointing my successor."

THE
MEXICAN

Jack London

Nobody knew his history—they of the Junta least of all. He was their "little mystery," their "big patriot," and in his way he worked as hard for the coming Mexican Revolution as did they. They were tardy in recognizing this, for not one of the Junta liked him. The day he first drifted into their crowded, busy rooms they all suspected him of being a spy—one of the bought tools of the Diaz secret service. Too many of the comrades were in civil and military prisons scattered over the United States, and others of them, in irons, were even then being taken across the border to be lined up against adobe walls and shot.

At the first sight the boy did not impress them favorably. Boy he was, not more than eighteen and not overlarge for his years. He announced that he was Felipe Rivera, and that it was his wish to work for the revolution. That was all—not a wasted word, no further explanation. He stood waiting. There was no smile on his lips, no geniality in his eyes. Big, dashing Paulino Vera felt an inward shudder. Here was something forbidding, terrible, inscrutable. There was something venomous and snakelike in the boy's black eyes. They burned like cold fire, as with a vast, concentrated bitterness. He flashed them from the faces of the conspirators to the typewriter which little Mrs. Sethby was industriously operating. His eyes rested on hers but an instant—she had chanced to look up—and she, too, sensed the nameless something that made her pause. She was compelled to read back in order to regain the swing of the letter she was writing.

Paulino Vera looked questioningly at Arrellano and Ramos, and questioningly they looked back and to each other. The indecision of doubt brooded in their eyes. This slender boy was the Unknown, vested with all the menace of the Unknown. He was unrecognizable, something quite beyond the ken of honest, ordinary revolutionists whose fiercest hatred for Diaz and his tyranny after all was only that of honest and ordinary patriots. Here was something else, they knew not what. But Vera, always the most impulsive, the quickest to act, stepped into the breach.

"Very well," he said coldly. "You say you want to work for the revolution. Take off your coat. Hang it over there. I will show you—come —where are the buckets and cloths. The floor is dirty. You will begin by scrubbing it, and by scrubbing the floors of the other rooms. The spittoons need to be cleaned. Then there are the windows."

"Is it for the revolution?" the boy asked.

"It is for the revolution," Vera answered.

Rivera looked cold suspicion at all of them, then proceeded to take off his coat.

"It is well," he said.

And nothing more. Day after day he came to his work—sweeping, scrubbing, cleaning. He emptied the ashes from the stoves, brought up the coal and kindling, and lighted the fires before the most energetic one of them was at his desk.

"Can I sleep here?" he asked once.

Aha! So that was it—the hand of Diaz showing through! To sleep in the rooms of the Junta meant access to their secrets, to the lists of names, to the addresses of comrades down on Mexican soil. The request was denied, and Rivera never spoke of it again. He slept they knew not where, and ate they knew not where nor how. Once Arrellano offered him a couple of dollars. Rivera declined the money with a shake of the head. When Vera joined in and tried to press it upon him, he said:

"I am working for the revolution."

It takes money to raise a modern revolution, and always the Junta was pressed. The members starved and toiled, and the longest day was none too long, and yet there were times when it appeared as if the revolution stood or fell on no more than the matter of a few dollars. Once, the first time, when the rent of the house was two months behind and the landlord was threatening dispossession, it was Felipe Rivera, the scrub boy in the poor, cheap clothes, worn and threadbare, who laid sixty dollars in gold on May Sethby's desk. There were other times. Three hundred letters, clicked out on the busy typewriters (appeals for assistance, for sanctions from the organized labor groups, requests for square news deals to the editors of newspapers, protests against the highhanded treatment of revolutionists by the United States courts), lay unmailed, awaiting postage. Vera's watch had disappeared—the old-fashioned gold repeater that had been his father's. Likewise had gone the plain gold band from May Sethby's third finger. Things were desperate. Ramos and Arrellano pulled their long mustaches in despair. The letters must go off, and the post office allowed no credit to purchasers of stamps. Then it was that Rivera put on his hat and went out. When he came back he laid a thousand two-cent stamps on May Sethby's desk.

"I wonder if it is the cursed gold of Diaz?" said Vera to the comrades.

They elevated their brows and could not decide. And Felipe Rivera, the scrubber for the revolution, continued, as occasion arose, to lay down gold and silver for the Junta's use.

And still they could not bring themselves to like him. They did not know him. His ways were not theirs. He gave no confidences. He repelled all probing. Youth that he was, they could never nerve themselves to dare to question him.

"A great and lonely spirit, perhaps, I do not know, I do not know," Arrellano said helplessly.

"He is not human," said Ramos.

"His soul has been seared," said May Sethby. "Light and laughter have been burned out of him. He is like one dead, and yet he is fearfully alive."

"He has been through hell," said Vera. "No man could look like that who has not been through hell—and he is only a boy."

Yet they could not like him. He never talked, never inquired, never suggested. He would stand listening, expressionless, a thing dead, save for his eyes, coldly burning, while their talk of the revolution ran high and warm. From face to face and speaker to speaker his eyes would turn, boring like gimlets of incandescent ice, disconcerting and perturbing.

"He is no spy," Vera confided to May Sethby. "He is a patriot—mark me, the greatest patriot of us all. I know it, I feel it, here in my heart and head I feel it. But him I know not at all."

"He has a bad temper," said May Sethby.

"I know," said Vera with a shudder. "He has looked at me with those eyes of his. They do not love; they threaten; they are savage as a wild tiger's. I know, if I should prove unfaithful to the cause, that he would kill me. He has no heart. He is pitiless as steel, keen and cold as frost. He is like moonshine in a winter night when a man freezes to death on some lonely mountaintop. I am not afraid of Diaz and all his killers; but this boy, of him am I afraid. I tell you true. I am afraid. He is the breath of death."

Yet Vera it was who persuaded the others to give the first trust to

Rivera. The line of communications between Los Angeles and Lower California had broken down. Three of the comrades had dug their own graves and been shot into them. Two more were United States prisoners in Los Angeles. Juan Alvarado, the federal commander, was a monster. All their plans did he checkmate. They could no longer gain access to the active revolutionists, and the incipient ones, in Lower California.

Young Rivera was given his instructions and dispatched south. When he returned, the line of communications was reestablished, and Juan Alvarado was dead. He had been found in bed, a knife hilt-deep in his breast. This had exceeded Rivera's instructions, but they of the Junta knew the times of his movements. They did not ask him. He said nothing. But they looked at one another and conjectured.

"I have told you," said Vera. "Diaz has more to fear from this youth than from any man. He is implacable. He is the hand of God."

The bad temper, mentioned by May Sethby, and sensed by them all, was evidenced by physical proofs. Now he appeared with a cut lip, a blackened cheek, or a swollen ear. It was patent that he brawled, somewhere in that outside world where he ate and slept, gained money, and moved in ways unknown to them. As the time passed he had come to set type for the little revolutionary sheet they published weekly. There were occasions when he was unable to set type, when his knuckles were bruised and battered, when his thumbs were injured and helpless, when one arm or the other hung wearily at his side while his face was drawn with unspoken pain.

"A wastrel," said Arrellano.

"A frequenter of low places," said Ramos.

"But where does he get the money?" Vera demanded. "Only today, just now, have I learned that he paid the bill for white paper—one hundred and forty dollars."

"There are his absences," said May Sethby. "He never explains them."

"We should set a spy upon him," Ramos propounded.

"I should not care to be that spy," said Vera. "I fear you would never see me again, save to bury me. He has a terrible passion. Not even God would he permit to stand between him and the way of his passion."

"I feel like a child before him," Ramos confessed.

"To me he is power—he is the primitive, the wild wolf, the striking rattlesnake, the stinging centipede," said Arrellano.

"He is the revolution incarnate," said Vera. "He is the flame and the spirit of it, the insatiable cry for vengeance that makes no cry but that slays noiselessly. He is a destroying angel moving through the still watches of the night."

"I could weep over him," said May Sethby. "He knows nobody. He hates all people. Us he tolerates, for we are the way of his desire. He is alone . . . lonely." Her voice broke in a half sob and there was dimness in her eyes.

Rivera's ways and times were truly mysterious. There were periods when they did not see him for a week at a time. Once he was away a month. These occasions were always capped by his return, when, without advertisement or speech, he laid gold coins on May Sethby's desk. Again, for days and weeks, he spent all his time with the Junta. And yet again, for irregular periods, he would disappear through the heart of each day, from early morning until late afternoon. At such times he came early and remained late. Arrellano had found him at midnight, setting type with fresh-swollen knuckles, or mayhap it was his lip, new-split, that still bled.

The time of the crisis approached. Whether or not the revolution would be depended upon the Junta, and the Junta was hard-pressed. The need for money was greater than ever before, while money was harder to get. Patriots had given their last cent and now could give no more. Section-gang laborers—fugitive peons from Mexico—were contributing half their scanty wages. But more than that was needed. The heartbreaking, conspiring, undermining toil of years approached fruition. The time was ripe. The revolution hung in the balance. One shove more, one last heroic effort, and it would tremble across the scales to victory. They knew their Mexico. Once started, the revolution would take care of itself. The whole Diaz machine would go down like a house of cards. The border was ready to rise. One Yankee, with a hundred I.W.W. men, waited the word to cross over the border and begin the conquest of Lower California. But he needed guns. And clear across to the Atlantic, the Junta in touch with them all and all of them needing guns, mere adventurers, soldiers of fortune, bandits, disgruntled American union men, socialists, anarchists, roughnecks, Mexican exiles, peons escaped from bondage, whipped miners from the bullpens of Coeur D'Alene and Colorado who desired only the more vindictively to fight—all the flotsam and jetsam of wild spirits from the madly complicated modern world. And it was guns and ammunition, ammunition and guns—the unceasing and eternal cry.

Fling this heterogeneous, bankrupt, vindictive mass across the border, and the revolution was on. The custom house, the northern ports of entry, would be captured. Diaz could not resist. He dared not throw the weight of his armies against them, for he must hold the south. And through the south the flame would spread despite. The people would rise. The defenses of city after city would crumple up. State after state would totter down. And at last, from every side, the victorious armies of the revolution would close in on the city of Mexico itself, Diaz's last stronghold.

But the money. They had the men, impatient and urgent, who would use the guns. They knew the traders who would sell and deliver the guns. But to culture the revolution thus far had exhausted the Junta. The last dollar had been spent, the last resource and the last starving patriot milked dry, and the great adventure still trembled in the scales. Guns and ammunition! The ragged battalions must be armed. But how? Ramos lamented his confiscated estates. Arrellano wailed the spendthriftness of his youth. May Sethby wondered if it would have been different had they of the Junta been more economical in the past.

"To think that the freedom of Mexico should stand or fall on a few paltry thousands of dollars," said Paulino Vera.

Despair was in all their faces. José Amarillo, their last hope, a recent convert who had promised money, had been apprehended at his hacienda in Chihuahua and shot against his own stable wall. The news had just come through.

Rivera, on his knees, scrubbing, looked up, with suspended brush, his bare arms flecked with soapy, dirty water.

"Will five thousand do?" he asked.

They looked their amazement. Vera nodded and swallowed. He could not speak, but he was on the instant invested with a vast faith.

"Order the guns," Rivera said, and thereupon was guilty of the longest flow of words they had ever heard him utter. "The time is short. In three weeks I shall bring you the five thousand. It is well. The weather will be warmer for those who fight. Also, it is the best I can do."

Vera fought his faith. It was incredible. Too many fond hopes had been shattered since he had begun to play the revolution game. He believed this threadbare scrubber of the revolution, and yet he dared not believe.

"You are crazy," he said.

"In three weeks," said Rivera. "Order the guns."

He got up, rolled down his sleeves, and put on his coat.

"Order the guns," he said. "I am going now."

After hurrying and scurrying, much telephoning and bad language, a night session was held in Kelly's office. Kelly was rushed with business; also, he was unlucky. He had brought Danny Ward out from New York, arranged the fight for him with Billy Carthey, the date was three weeks away, and for two days now, carefully concealed from the sporting writers, Carthey had been lying up, badly injured. There was no one to take his place. Kelly had been burning the wires east to every eligible lightweight, but they were tied up with dates and contracts. And now hope had revived, though faintly.

"You've got a hell of a nerve," Kelly addressed Rivera, after one look, as soon as they got together.

Hate that was malignant was in Rivera's eyes, but his face remained impassive.

"I can lick Ward," was all he said.

"How do you know? Ever see him fight?"

Rivera shook his head.

"He can beat you up with one hand and both eyes closed."

Rivera shrugged his shoulders.

"Haven't you got anything to say?" the fight promoter snarled.

"I can lick him."

"Who'd you ever fight, anyway?" Michael Kelly demanded. Michael was the promoter's brother, and ran the Yellowstone Poolrooms, where he made goodly sums on the fight game.

Rivera favored him with a bitter, unanswering stare.

The promoter's secretary, a distinctively sporty young man, sneered audibly.

"Well, you know Roberts." Kelly broke the hostile silence. "He ought to be here. I've sent for him. Sit down and wait, though from the looks of you, you haven't got a chance. I can't throw the public down with a bum fight. Ringside seats are selling at fifteen dollars, you know that."

When Roberts arrived it was patent that he was mildly drunk. He was a tall, lean, slack-jointed individual, and his walk, like his talk, was a smooth and languid drawl.

Kelly went straight to the point.

"Look here, Roberts, you've been braggin' you discovered this little Mexican. You know Carthey's broke his arm. Well, this little yellow streak has the gall to blow in today and say he'll take Carthey's place. What about it?"

"It's all right, Kelly," came the slow response. "He can put up a fight."

"I suppose you'll be sayin' next that he can lick Ward," Kelly snapped.

Roberts considered judicially.

"No, I won't say that. Ward's a topnotcher and a ring general. But he can't hash-house Rivera in short order. I know Rivera. Nobody can get his goat. He ain't got a goat that I could ever discover. And he's a two-handed fighter. He can throw in the sleep-makers from any position."

"Never mind that. What kind of a show can he put up? You've been conditioning and training fighters all your life. I take off my hat to your judgment. Can he give the public a run for its money?"

"He sure can, and he'll worry Ward a mighty heap on top of it. You don't know that boy. I do. I discovered him. He ain't got a goat. He's a devil. He's a wizzy-wooz if anybody should ask you. He'll make Ward sit up with a show of local talent that'll make the rest of you sit up. I won't say he'll lick Ward, but he'll put up such a show that you'll all know he's a comer."

"All right." Kelly turned to his secretary. "Ring up Ward. I warned him to show up if I thought it worth while. He's right across at the Yellowstone, throwin' chests and doing the popular." Kelly turned back to the conditioner. "Have a drink?"

Roberts sipped his highball and unburdened himself.

"Never told you how I discovered the little cuss. It was a couple of years ago he showed up out at the quarters. I was getting Prayne ready for his fight with Delaney. Prayne's wicked. He ain't got a trickle of mercy in his make-up. He'd chopped up his pardners something cruel, and I couldn't find a willing boy that'd work with him. I'd noticed this little starved Mexican kid hanging around, and I was desperate. So I grabbed him, slammed on the gloves, and put him in. He was tougher'n rawhide, but weak. And he didn't know the first letter in the alphabet of boxing. Prayne chopped him to ribbons. But he hung on for two sickening rounds, when he fainted. Starvation, that was all. Battered? You couldn't have recognized him. I gave him half a dollar and a square meal. you oughta seen him wolf it down. He hadn't had a bite for a couple of days. That's the end of him, thinks I. But next day he showed up, stiff an' sore, ready for another half and a square meal. And he done better as time went by. Just a born fighter, and tough beyond belief. He hasn't a heart. He's a piece of ice. And he never talked eleven words in a string since I know him. He saws wood and does his work."

"I've seen 'm," the secretary said. "He's worked a lot for you."

"All the big little fellows has tried out on him," Roberts answered. "And he's learned from 'em. I've seen some of them he could lick. But his heart wasn't in it. I reckoned he never liked the game. He seemed to act that way."

"He's been fighting some before the little clubs the last few months," Kelly said.

"Sure. but I don't know what struck 'em. All of a sudden his heart got into it. He just went out like a streak and cleaned up all the little local fellows. Seemed to want the money, and he's won a bit, though his clothes don't look it. He's peculiar. Nobody knows his business. Nobody knows how he spends his time. Even when he's on the job, he plumb up and disappears most of each day soon as his work is done.

Sometimes he just blows away for weeks at a time. But he don't take advice. There's a fortune in it for the fellow that gets the job of managin' him, only he won't consider it. And you watch him hold out for the cash money when you get down to terms."

It was at this stage that Danny Ward arrived. Quite a party it was. His manager and trainer were with him, and he breezed in like a gusty draft of geniality, good nature, and all-conqueringness. Greetings flew about, a joke here, a retort there, a smile or a laugh for everybody. Yet it was his way, and only partly sincere. He was a good actor, and he had found geniality a most valuable asset in the game of getting on in the world. But down underneath he was the deliberate, coldblooded fighter and businessman. The rest was a mask. Those who knew him or trafficked with him said that when it came to brass tacks he was Danny on the Spot. He was invariably present at all business discussions, and it was urged by some that his manager was a blind whose only function was to serve as Danny's mouthpiece.

Rivera's way was different. Indian blood, as well as Spanish, was in his veins, and he sat back in a corner, silent, immobile, only his black eyes passing from face to face and noting everything.

"So that's the guy," Danny said, running an appraising eye over his proposed antagonist. "How de do, old chap."

Rivera's eyes burned venomously, but he made no sign of acknowledgment. He disliked all gringos, but this gringo he hated with an immediacy that was unusual even in him.

"Gawd!" Danny protested facetiously to the promoter. "You ain't expectin' me to fight a deef mute." When the laughter subsided he made another hit. "Los Angeles must be on the dink when this is the best you can scare up. What kindergarten did you get 'm from?"

"He's a good little boy, Danny, take it from me," Roberts defended. "Not as easy as he looks."

"And half the house is sold already," Kelly pleaded. "You'll have to take 'm on, Danny. It's the best we can do."

Danny ran another careless and unflattering glance over Rivera and sighed.

"I gotta be easy with 'm, I guess. If only he don't blow up."

Roberts snorted.

"You gotta be careful," Danny's manager warned. "No taking chances with a dub that's likely to sneak a lucky one across."

"Oh, I'll be careful all right, all right," Danny smiled. "I'll get 'm at the start an' nurse 'm along for the dear public's sake. What d'ye say to fifteen rounds, Kelly—an' then the hay for him?"

"That'll do," was the answer. "As long as you make it realistic."

"Then let's get down to biz." Danny paused and calculated. "Of course, sixty-five per cent of gate receipts, same as with Carthey. But the split'll be different. Eighty will just about suit me." And to his manager, "That right?"

The manager nodded.

"Here, you, did you get that?" Kelly asked Rivera.

Rivera shook his head.

"Well, it's this way," Kelly exposited. "The purse'll be sixty-five per cent of the gate receipts. You're a dub, and an unknown. You and Danny split, twenty per cent goin' to you, an' eighty to Danny. That's fair, isn't it, Roberts?"

"Very fair, Rivera," Roberts agreed. "You see, you ain't got a reputation yet."

"What will sixty-five per cent of the gate receipts be?" Rivera demanded.

"Oh, maybe five thousand, maybe as high as eight thousand," Danny broke in to explain. "Something like that. Your share'll come to something like a thousand or sixteen hundred. Pretty good for takin' a licking from a guy with my reputation. What d'ye say?"

Then Rivera took their breaths away.

"Winner takes all," he said with finality.

A dead silence prevailed.

"It's like candy from a baby," Danny's manager proclaimed.

Danny shook his head.

"I've been in the game too long," he explained. "I'm not casting reflections on the referee or the present company. I'm not sayin' nothing about bookmakers an' frame-ups that sometimes happen. But what I do say is that it's poor business for a fighter like me. I play safe. There's no tellin'. Mebbe I break my arm, eh? Or some guy slips me a bunch of dope." He shook his head solemnly. "Win or lose, eighty is my split. What d'ye say, Mexican?"

Rivera shook his head.

Danny exploded. He was getting down to brass tacks now.

"Why, you dirty little greaser! I've a mind to knock your block off right now."

Roberts drawled his body to interposition between hostilities.

"Winner takes all," Rivera repeated sullenly.

"Why do you stand out that way?" Danny asked.

"I can lick you," was the straight answer.

Danny half started to take off his coat. But, as his manager knew, it was a grandstand play. The coat did not come off, and Danny allowed himself to be placated by the group. Everybody sympathized with him. Rivera stood alone.

"Look here, you little fool," Kelly took up the argument. "You're nobody. We know what you've been doing the last few months—putting away little local fighters. But Danny is class. His next fight after this will be for the championship. And you're unknown. Nobody ever heard of you out of Los Angeles."

"They will," Rivera answered with a shrug, "after this fight."

"You think for a second you can lick me?" Danny blurted in.

Rivera nodded.

"Oh, come; listen to reason," Kelly pleaded. "Think of the advertising."

"I want the money," was Rivera's answer.

"You couldn't win from me in a thousand years," Danny assured him.

"Then what are you holding out for?" Rivera countered. "If the money's that easy, why don't you go after it?"

"I will, so help me!" Danny cried with abrupt conviction. "I'll beat you to death in the ring, my boy—you monkeyin' with me this way. Make out the articles, Kelly. Winner take all. Play it up in the sportin' columns. Tell 'em it's a grudge fight. I'll show this fresh kid a few."

Kelly's secretary had begun to write, when Danny interrupted.

"Hold on!" He turned to Rivera. "Weights?"

"Ringside," came the answer.

"Not on your life, fresh kid. If winner takes all, we weigh in at 10 A.M."

"And winner takes all?" Rivera queried.

Danny nodded. That settled it. He would enter the ring in his full ripeness of strength.

"Weigh in at ten," Rivera said.

The secretary's pen went on scratching.

"It means five pounds," Roberts complained to Rivera. "You've given too much away. You've thrown the fight right there. Danny'll be as strong as a bull. You're a fool. He'll lick you sure. You ain't got the chance of a dewdrop in hell."

Rivera's answer was a calculated look of hatred. Even this gringo he despised, and him had he found the whitest gringo of them all.

Barely noticed was Rivera as he entered the ring. Only a very slight and very scattering ripple of halfhearted handclapping greeted him. The house did not believe in him. He was the lamb led to slaughter at the hands of the great Danny. Besides, the house was disappointed. It had expected a rushing battle between Danny Ward and Billy Carthey, and here it must put up with this poor little tyro. Still further, it had manifested its disapproval of the change by betting two, and even three, to one on Danny. And where a betting audience's money is, there is its heart.

The Mexican boy sat down in his corner and waited. The slow minutes lagged by. Danny was making him wait. It was an old trick, but ever it worked on the young, new fighters. They grew frightened, sitting thus and facing their own apprehensions and a callous, tobacco-smoking audience. But for once the trick failed. Roberts was right. Rivera had no goat. He, who was more delicately coordinated, more finely nerved and strung than any of them, had no nerves of this sort. The atmosphere of foredoomed defeat in his own corner had no effect on him. His handlers were gringos and strangers. Also they were scrubs—the dirty driftage of the fight game, without honor, without efficiency. And they were chilled, as well, with certitude that theirs was the losing corner.

"Now you gotta be careful," Spider Hagerty warned him. Spider was his chief second. "Make it last as long as you can—them's my instructions from Kelly. If you don't, the papers'll call it another bum fight and give the game a bigger black eye in Los Angeles."

All of which was not encouraging. But Rivera took no notice. He despised prize fighting. It was the hated game of the hated gringo. He had taken up with it, as a chopping block for others in the training quarters, solely because he was starving. The fact that he was marvelously made for it had meant nothing. He hated it. Not until he had come in to the Junta had he fought for money, and he found the money easy. Not first among the sons of men had he been to find himself successful at a despised vocation.

He did not analyze. He merely knew that he must win this fight. There could be no other outcome. For behind him, nerving him to this belief, were profounder forces than any the crowded house dreamed. Danny Ward fought for money and for the easy ways of life that money would bring. But the things Rivera fought for burned in his brain—blazing and terrible visions, that, with eyes wide open, sitting lonely in the corner of the ring and waiting for his tricky antagonist, he saw as clearly as he had lived them.

He saw the white-walled, water-power factories of Rio Blanco. He saw the six thousand workers, starved and wan, and the little children, seven and eight years of age, who toiled long shifts for ten cents a day. He saw the perambulating corpses, the ghastly death's heads of men who labored in the dye rooms. He remembered that he had heard his father call the dye rooms the "suicide holes," where a year was death. He saw the little patio, and his mother cooking and moiling at crude housekeeping and finding time to caress and love him. And his father he saw, large, big-mustached, and deep-chested, kindly above all men, who loved all men and whose heart was so large that there was love to overflowing still left for the mother and the little *muchacho* playing in the corner of the patio. In those days his name had not been Felipe Rivera. It had been Fernandez, his father's and mother's name. Him had they called Juan. Later he had changed it himself, for he had found the name of Fernandez hated by prefects of police, *jefes políticos,* and *rurales.*

Big, hearty Joaquin Fernandez! A large place he occupied in Rivera's visions. He had not understood at the time, but, looking back, he could understand. He could see him setting type in the little printery, or scribbling endless hasty, nervous lines on the much-cluttered desk. And he could see the strange evenings, when workmen, coming secretly in the dark like men who did ill deeds, met with his father and talked long hours where he, the muchacho, lay not always asleep in the corner.

As from a remote distance he could hear Spider Hagerty saying to him: "No layin' down at the start. Them's instructions. Take a beatin' an' earn your dough."

Ten minutes had passed, and he still sat in his corner. There were no signs of Danny, who was evidently playing the trick to the limit.

But more visions burned before the eye of Rivera's memory. The strike, or, rather, the lockout, because the workers of Rio Blanco had helped their striking brothers of Puebla. The hunger, the expeditions in the hills for berries, the roots and herbs that all ate and that twisted and pained the stomachs of all of them. And then the nightmare; the waste of ground before the company's store; the thousands of starving workers; General Rosalio Martinez and the soldiers of Porfirio Diaz; and the death-splitting rifles that seemed never to cease spitting, while the workers' wrongs were washed and washed again in their own blood. And that night! He saw the flatcars, piled high with the bodies of the slain, consigned to Vera Cruz, food for the sharks of the bay. Again he crawled over the grisly heaps, seeking and finding, stripped and mangled, his father and his mother. His mother he especially remembered— only her face projecting, her body burdened by the weight of dozens of bodies. Again the rifles of the soldiers of Porfirio Diaz cracked, and again he dropped to the ground and slunk away like some hunted coyote of the hills.

To his ears came a great roar, as of the sea, and he saw Danny Ward, leading his retinue of trainers and seconds, coming down the center aisle. The house was in wild uproar for the popular hero who was bound to win. Everybody proclaimed him. Everybody was for him. Even Rivera's own seconds warmed to something akin to cheerfulness when Danny ducked jauntily through the ropes and entered the ring. His face continually spread to an unending succession of smiles, and when Danny smiled he smiled in every feature, even to the laughter wrinkles of the corners of the eyes and into the depths of the eyes themselves. Never was there so genial a fighter. His face was a running advertisement of good feeling, of good-fellowship. He knew everybody. He joked, and laughed, and greeted his friends through the ropes. Those farther away, unable to suppress their admiration, cried loudly: "Oh, you Danny!" It was a joyous ovation of affection that lasted a full five minutes.

Rivera was disregarded. For all that the audience noticed, he did not exist. Spider Hagerty's bloated face bent down close to his.

"No gettin' scared," the Spider warned. "An' remember instructions. You gotta last. No layin' down. If you lay down, we got instructions to beat you up in the dressing rooms. Savvy? You just gotta fight."

The house began to applaud. Danny was crossing the ring to him. Danny bent over, caught Rivera's right hand in both his own and shook it with impulsive heartiness. Danny's smile-wreathed face was close to his. The audience yelled its appreciation of Danny's display of sporting spirit. He was greeting his opponent with the fondness of a brother. Danny's lips moved, and the audience, interpreting the unheard words to be those of a kindly-natured sport, yelled again. Only Rivera heard the low words.

"You little Mexican rat," hissed from between Danny's gaily smiling lips, "I'll fetch the yellow outa you."

Rivera made no move. He did not rise. He merely hated with his eyes.

"Get up, you dog!" some man yelled through the ropes from behind.

The crowd began to hiss and boo him for his unsportsmanlike conduct, but he sat unmoved. Another great outburst of applause was Danny's as he walked back across the ring.

When Danny stripped, there were ohs! and ahs! of delight. His body was perfect, alive with easy suppleness and health and strength. The skin was white as a woman's, and as smooth. All grace, and resilience, and power resided therein. He had proved it in scores of battles. His photographs were in all the physical-culture magazines.

A groan went up as Spider Hagerty peeled Rivera's sweater over his head. His body seemed leaner because of the swarthiness of the skin. He had muscles, but they made no display like his opponent's. What the audience neglected to see was the deep chest. Nor could it guess the toughness of the fiber of the flesh, the instantaneousness of the cell explosions of the muscles, the fineness of the nerves that wired every part of him into a splendid fighting mechanism. All the audience saw was a brown-skinned boy of eighteen with what seemed the body of a boy. With Danny it was different. Danny was a man of twenty-four, and his body was a man's body. The contrast was still more striking as they stood together in the center of the ring receiving the referee's last instructions.

Rivera noticed Roberts sitting directly behind the newspapermen. He was drunker than usual, and his speech was correspondingly slower.

"Take it easy, Rivera," Roberts drawled. "He can't kill you, remember that. He'll rush you at the go-off, but don't get rattled. You just cover up, and stall, and clinch. He can't hurt you much. Just make believe to yourself that he's choppin' out on you at the trainin' quarters."

Rivera made no sign that he had heard.

"Sullen little devil," Roberts muttered to the man next to him. "He always was that way."

But Rivera forgot to look his usual hatred. A vision of countless rifles blinded his eyes. Every face in the audience, far as he could see, to the high dollar seats, was transformed into a rifle. And he saw the long Mexican border arid and sun-washed and aching, and along it he saw the ragged bands that delayed only for the guns.

Back in his corner he waited, standing up. His seconds had crawled out through the ropes, taking the canvas stool with them. Diagonally across the squared ring, Danny faced him. The gong struck, and the battle was on. The audience howled its delight. Never had it seen a battle open more convincingly. The papers were right. It was a grudge fight. Three quarters of the distance Danny covered in the rush to get together, his intention to eat up the Mexican lad plainly advertised. He assailed with not one blow, nor two, nor a dozen. He was a gyroscope of blows, a whirlwind of destruction. Rivera was nowhere. He was overwhelmed, buried beneath avalanches of punches delivered from every angle and position by a past master in the art. He was overborne, swept back against the ropes, separated by the referee, and swept back against the ropes again.

It was not a fight. It was a slaughter, a massacre. Any audience, save a prize-fighting one, would have exhausted its emotions in that first minute. Danny was certainly showing what he could do—a splendid exhibition. Such was the certainty of the audience, as well as its excitement and favoritism, that it failed to take notice that the Mexican still stayed on his feet. It forgot Rivera. It rarely saw him, so closely was he enveloped in Danny's man-eating attack. A minute of this went by, and two minutes. Then, in a separation, it caught a clear glimpse of the Mexican. His lip was cut, his nose was bleeding. As he turned and staggered into a clinch the welts of oozing blood, from his contacts with the ropes, showed in red bars across his back. But what the audience did not notice was that his chest was not heaving and that his eyes were coldly burning as ever. Too many aspiring champions, in the cruel welter of the training camps, had practiced this man-eating attack on him. He had learned to live through for a compensation of from half a dollar a go up to fifteen dollars a week—a hard school, and he was schooled hard.

Then happened the amazing thing. The whirling, blurring mix-up ceased suddenly. Rivera stood alone. Danny, the redoubtable Danny, lay on his back. His body quivered as consciousness strove to return to it. He had not staggered and sunk down, nor had he gone over in a long slumping fall. The right hook of Rivera had dropped him in midair with the abruptness of death. The referee shoved Rivera back with one hand and stood over the fallen gladiator counting the seconds. It is the custom of prize-fighting audiences to cheer a clean knockdown blow. But this audience did not cheer. The thing had been too unexpected. It watched the toll of the seconds in tense silence, and through this silence the voice of Roberts rose exultantly:

"I told you he was a two-handed fighter!"

By the fifth second Danny was rolling over on his face, and when seven was counted he rested on one knee, ready to rise after the count of nine and before the count of ten. If his knee still touched the floor at "ten" he was considered "down" and also "out." The instant his knee left the floor he was considered "up," and in that instant it was Rivera's right to try and put him down again. Rivera took no chances. The moment that knee left the floor he would strike again. He circled around, but the referee circled in between, and Rivera knew that the seconds he counted were very slow. All gringos were against him, even the referee.

At "nine" the referee gave Rivera a sharp thrust back. It was unfair, but it enabled Danny to rise, the smile back on his lips. Doubled partly over, with arms wrapped about face and abdomen, he cleverly stumbled into a clinch. By all the rules of the game the referee should have broken it, but he did not, and Danny clung on like a surf-battered barnacle and moment by moment recuperated. The last minute of the round was going fast. If he could live to the end he would have a full minute in his corner to revive. And live to the end he did, smiling through all desperateness and extremity.

"The smile that won't come off!" somebody yelled, and the audience laughed loudly in its relief.

"The kick that greaser's got is something God-awful," Danny gasped in his corner to his adviser while his handlers worked frantically over him.

The second and third rounds were tame. Danny, a tricky and consummate ring general, stalled and blocked and held on, devoting himself to recovering from that dazing first-round blow. In the fourth round he was himself again. Jarred and shaken, nevertheless his good condition had enabled him to regain his vigor. But he tried no man-eating tactics. The Mexican had proved a tartar. Instead he brought to bear his best fighting powers. In tricks and skill and experience he was the master, and though he could land nothing vital, he proceeded scientifically to chop and wear down his opponent. He landed three blows to Rivera's one, but they were punishing blows only, and not deadly. It was the sum of many of them that constituted deadliness. He was respectful of this two-handed dub with the amazing short-arm kicks in both his fists.

In defense Rivera developed a disconcerting straight left. Again and again, attack after attack he straight-lefted away from him with accumulated damage to Danny's mouth and nose. But Danny was protean. That was why he was the coming champion. He could change from style to style of fighting at will. He now devoted himself to infighting. In this he was particularly wicked, and it enabled him to avoid the other's straight left. Here he set the house wild repeatedly, capping it with a marvelous lock-break and lift of an inside uppercut that raised the Mexican in the air and dropped him to the mat. Rivera rested on one knee, making the most of the count, and in the soul of him he knew the referee was counting short seconds on him.

Again, in the seventh, Danny achieved the diabolic inside uppercut. He succeeded only in staggering Rivera, but in the ensuing moment of defenseless helplessness he smashed him through the ropes with another blow. Rivera's body bounced on the heads of the newspapermen below, and they boosted him back to the edge of the platform outside the ropes. Here he rested on one knee, while the referee raced off the seconds. Inside the ropes, through which he must duck to enter the ring, Danny waited for him. Nor did the referee intervene or thrust Danny back.

The house was beside itself with delight.

"Kill 'm, Danny, kill 'm!" was the cry.

Scores of voices took it up until it was like a war chant of wolves.

Danny did his best, but Rivera, at the count of eight, instead of nine, came unexpectedly through the ropes and safely into a clinch. Now the referee worked, tearing him away so that he could be hit, giving Danny every advantage that an unfair referee can give.

But Rivera lived, and the haze cleared from his brain. It was all of a piece. They were the hated gringos and they were all unfair. And in the worst of it visions continued to flash and sparkle in his brain—long lines of railroad track that simmered across the desert; *rurales* and American constables; prisons and calabooses; tramps at water tanks—all the squalid and painful panorama of his odyssey after Rio Blanco and the strike. And, resplendent and glorious, he saw the great red revolution sweeping across his land. The guns were there before him. Every hated face was a gun. It was for the guns he fought. He was the guns. He was the revolution. He fought for all Mexico.

The audience began to grow incensed with Rivera. Why didn't he take the licking that was appointed him? Of course he was going to be licked, but why should he be so obstinate about it? Very few were interested in him, and they were the certain, definite percentage of a gambling crowd that plays long shots. Believing Danny to be the winner, nevertheless they had put their money on the Mexican at four to ten and one to three. More than a trifle was up on the point of how many rounds Rivera could last. Wild money had appeared at the ringside proclaiming that he could not last seven rounds, or even six. The winners of this, now that their cash risk was happily settled, had joined in cheering on the favorite.

Rivera refused to be licked. Through the eighth round his opponent strove vainly to repeat the uppercut. In the ninth Rivera stunned the house again. In the midst of a clinch he broke the lock with a quick, lithe movement, and in the narrow space between their bodies his right lifted from the waist. Danny went to the floor and took the safety of the count. The crowd was appalled. He was being bested at his own game. His famous right uppercut had been worked back on him. Rivera made no attempt to catch him as he arose at "nine." The referee was openly blocking that play, though he stood clear when the situation was reversed and it was Rivera who required to rise.

Twice in the tenth Rivera put through the right uppercut, lifted from waist to opponent's chin. Danny grew desperate. The smile never left his face, but he went back to his man-eating rushes. Whirlwind as he would, he could not damage Rivera, while Rivera, through the blur and whirl, dropped him to the mat three times in succession. Danny did not recuperate so quickly now, and by the eleventh round he was in a serious way. But from then till the fourteenth he put up the gamest exhibition of his career. He stalled and blocked, fought parsimoniously, and strove to gather strength. Also he fought as foully as a successful fighter knows how. Every trick and device he employed, butting in the clinches with the seeming of accident, pinioning Rivera's glove between arm and body, heeling his glove on Rivera's mouth to clog his breathing. Often, in the clinches, through his cut and smiling lips he snarled insults unspeakable and vile in Rivera's ear. Everybody, from the referee to the house, was with Danny and was helping Danny. And they knew what he had in mind. Bested by this surprise box of an unknown, he was pinning all on a single punch. He offered himself for punishment, fished, and feinted, and drew, for that one opening that would enable him to whip a blow through with all his strength and turn the tide. As another and greater fighter had done before him, he might do—a right and left, to solar plexus and across the jaw. He could do it, for he was noted for the strength of punch that remained in his arms as long as he could keep his feet.

Rivera's seconds were not half caring for him in the intervals between rounds. Their towels made a showing but drove little air into his panting lungs. Spider Hagerty talked advice to him, but Rivera knew it was wrong advice. Everybody was against him. He was surrounded by treachery. In the fourteenth round he put Danny down again, and himself stood resting, hands dropped at side, while the referee counted. In the other corner Rivera had been noting suspicious whisperings. He saw Michael Kelly make his way to Roberts and bend and whisper. Rivera's ears were a cat's, desert-trained, and he caught snatches of what was said. He wanted to hear more, and when his opponent arose he maneuvered the fight into a clinch over against the ropes.

"Got to," he could hear Michael, while Roberts nodded. "Danny's got to win—I stand to lose a mint. I've got a ton of money covered—my own. If he lasts the fifteenth I'm bust. The boy'll mind you. Put something across."

And thereafter Rivera saw no more visions. They were trying to job him. Once again he dropped Danny and stood resting, his hands at his side. Roberts stood up.

"That settled him," he said. "Go to your corner."

He spoke with authority, as he had often spoken to Rivera at the training quarters. But Rivera looked hatred at him and waited for Danny to rise. Back in his corner in the minute interval, Kelly, the promoter, came and talked to Rivera.

"Throw it, damn you," he rasped in a harsh low voice. "You gotta lay down, Rivera. Stick with me and I'll make your future. I'll let you lick Danny next time. But here's where you lay down."

Rivera showed with his eyes that he heard, but he made neither sign of assent nor dissent.

"Why don't you speak?" Kelly demanded angrily.

"You lose anyway," Spider Hagerty supplemented. "The referee'll take it away from you. Listen to Kelly and lay down."

"Lay down, kid," Kelly pleaded, "and I'll help you to the championship."

Rivera did not answer.

"I will, so help me, kid."

At the strike of the gong Rivera sensed something impending. The house did not. Whatever it was, it was there inside the ring with him and very close. Danny's earlier surety seemed returned to him. The confidence of his advance frightened Rivera. Some trick was about to be worked. Danny rushed, but Rivera refused the encounter. He sidestepped away into safety. What the other wanted was a clinch. It was in some way necessary to the trick. Rivera backed and circled away, yet he knew, sooner or later, the clinch and the trick would come. Desperately he resolved to draw it. He made as if to effect the clinch with Danny's next rush. Instead, at the last instant, just as their bodies should have come together, Rivera darted nimbly back. And in the same instant Danny's corner raised a cry of foul. Rivera had fooled them. The referee paused irresolutely. The decision that trembled on his lips was never uttered, for a shrill, boy's voice from the gallery piped, "Raw work!"

Danny cursed Rivera openly, and forced him, while Rivera danced away. Also Rivera made up his mind to strike no more blows at the body. In this he threw away half his chance of winning, but he knew if he was to win at all it was with the out-fighting that remained to him. Given the least opportunity, they would lie a foul on him. Danny threw all caution to the winds. For two rounds he tore after and into the boy who dared not meet him at close quarters. Rivera was struck again and again, he took blows by the dozens to avoid the perilous clinch. During this supreme final rally of Danny's the audience rose to its feet and went mad. It did not understand. All it could see what that its favorite was winning after all.

"Why don't you fight?" it demanded wrathfully of Rivera. "You're yellow! You're yellow!" "Open up, you cur! Open up!" "Kill 'm, Danny! Kill 'm!" "You sure got 'm! Kill 'm!"

In all the house, bar none, Rivera was the only cold man. By temperament and blood he was the hottest-passioned there; but he had gone through such vastly greater heats that this collective passion of ten thousand throats, rising surge on surge, was to his brain no more than the velvet cool of a summer twilight.

Into the seventeenth round Danny carried his rally. Rivera, under a heavy blow, drooped and sagged. His hands dropped helplessly as he reeled backward. Danny thought it was his chance. The boy was at his mercy. Thus Rivera, feigning, caught him off his guard, lashing out a clean drive to the mouth. Danny went down. When he arose Rivera felled him with a down-chop of the right on neck and jaw. Three times he repeated this. It was impossible for any referee to call these blows foul.

"Oh, Bill! Bill!" Kelly pleaded to the referee.

"I can't," that official lamented back. "He won't give me a chance."

Danny, battered and heroic, still kept coming up. Kelly and others near to the ring began to cry out to the police to stop it, though Danny's corner refused to throw in the towel. Rivera saw the fat police captain starting awkwardly to climb through the ropes, and was not sure what it meant. There were so many ways of cheating in this game of the gringos. Danny, on his feet, tottered groggily and helplessly before him. The referee and the captain were both reaching for Rivera when he struck the last blow. There was no need to stop the fight, for Danny did not rise.

"Count!" Rivera cried hoarsely to the referee.

And when the count was finished Danny's seconds gathered him up and carried him to his corner.

"Who wins?" Rivera demanded.

Reluctantly the referee caught his gloved hand and held it aloft.

There were no congratulations for Rivera. He walked to his corner unattended, where his seconds had not yet placed his stool. He leaned backward on the ropes and looked his hatred at them, swept it on and about him till the whole ten thousand gringos were included. His knees trembled under him, and he was sobbing from exhaustion. Before his eyes the hated faces swayed back and forth in the giddiness of nausea. Then he remembered they were the guns. The guns were his. The revolution could go on.

TITLE
FIGHT

William Campbell Gault

T he sounds from above were dim in the dressing room. Over his head, between him and the thousands of fans, were the tons of concrete, robot-made concrete. Man conceived but robot made.

He looked down at his hands, his strong, short-fingered hands. Complete with fingerprints—but of protonol. Who'd know it, to look at them? In man's image, he was made. In God's image, man was made, if one believed in that, anymore. In man's image, he was made, but not with man's status.

His name was Alix 1340, which meant only that he was the thirteen hundred and fortieth of the Alix type. The short, broad Nordic type. In about twenty minutes, he was due in the ring. He was fighting for the middleweight championship of the world.

Joe Nettleton had dreamed that one up. It had been born in the verbiage of his daily syndicated sports column, nurtured by the fans' clamor, and fanned into reality—by what? Animosity? These robots were coming up in the world, getting too big for their britches. Nick Nolan would show this Alix his place.

Nick was the champ, a man, made in His image. He butted and thumbed and gouged and heeled. His favorite target was the groin. But *he* was a man. Oh, yes, he was a man. A champion among men.

Manny came in. His real title was Manuel 4307, but robots like to forget the numbers. He was Manny, Alix's manager and number-one second. A deft and sharp and able robot, Manny.

He said, "I thought it would be better if we were alone. No fans, especially. And I've had a bellyful of sportswriters."

"Even Joe Nettleton?" Alix asked. "Joe's on our side, isn't he?"

"It's hard to say. Do you ever wonder about him, Alix?"

Alix didn't answer, right away. He knew there were robots who "passed," went over the status line and lived as humans. He didn't know how many there were, and he often wondered about them. In every robot brain, there was a remote-controlled circuit breaker. They could be stopped with the throwing of a switch at the personnel center. There was a well-guarded office and a man on duty at that center twenty-four hours of every day.

Now Alix said, "I never thought much about Joe, either way."

"What have you been thinking?" Manny asked.

"I've been thinking," Alix said slowly, "that we fight man's wars and pulverate his garbage and dehydrate his sewerage, but we're not citizens. Why, Manny?"

"We're not human. We're not—orthodox." Manny was watching him closely as he spoke.

"Not human? They feed us Bach and Brahms and Beethoven and Shakespeare and Voltaire in our incubation period, don't they? And all the others I've forced myself to forget. Does this—this *soul* come from somewhere outside the system?"

"I guess it does. They don't feed us much religion, but I guess it comes from God."

"And what's He like?"

"It would depend upon who you ask, I guess," Manny said. "Sort of a superman. From Him they get their charity and tolerance and justice and all the rest of their noble attributes." Manny's laugh was bitter. "How they love themselves."

"They're so sure about everything else," Alix said, "but not very sure of their God. Is that it?"

"That's about it. I heard one man say He watched when a sparrow falls. I guess we're less than the sparrows, Alix."

There was a silence, and then Manny put a hand on Alix's shoulder. "We've got about fifteen minutes, and I've got a million things to say. Maybe I should have said them earlier."

Alix turned at the gravity of Manny's voice. His lumagel eyes went over Manny's dark face, absorbing his rigid intensity. Whatever it was that was coming, it was more important than the fight.

Manny said quietly, "Win this one, and blood will run in the streets, Alix."

"Human blood?"

"White man's blood. We've got the Negro, and the Jap, and the China-men and all the rest of them who got their rights so recently. And what kind of rights have they got? Civil, not in the people's hearts. You think those races don't know it? We were talking of their God, Alix. Well, the robots have one, too. His name is Alix 1340."

"Manny, you've gone crazy."

"Have I? Joe Nettleton's one of us, Alix. This was his scheme, and the four men who run the switch at the personnel center; they're ours, too. Top robots. Their IQ's all crowding two hundred. We've got the brains, Alix, and the manpower. We've got the combined venom of a billion nonwhites. And now we've got you."

"A pug. What kind of god would I make? You're off the beam, Manny."

"Am I? Did I ever give you anything but the straight dope? They adore you, Alix. You've been a model to them. You could be their king, if you say the word."

"You've been setting this up, you and Joe Nettleton? This fight to-night's the crisis? You've been building toward tonight?"

"But it takes a front man, a symbol. You're the only one who can be that. You're the only one they'd all back."

Alix looked again at his hands, the hands that had taken him to the first mixed fight in history, to a title fight. "Man Versus The Machine," most of the sports scribes had labeled it, though not Joe Nettleton. Machine? A machine that had assimilated Voltaire? A machine that had listened to Brahms?

What differentiates man from his machines? Supremacy? Supremacy would be established tonight. No, it wasn't physical supremacy. And there were robots far beyond man's mental powers.

The spark, then, the spark from their God? How did they know they had it? In all the wrangling mysticism that had gone through so many misdirected interpretations, where could they find God?

"Thinking it over?" Manny asked. "Why so quiet, Alix?"

Alix's grin was saturnine. "Believe it or not, I was thinking of God."

"*Their* God?"

Alix frowned. "I suppose. Theirs and the sparrows'."

There were three spaced knocks at the door. Manny said, "Joe Nettleton. He wants to talk to you. We've got about eight minutes, Alix." He went to the door.

Joe Nettleton was tall, and pale, and brown-eyed. The eyes should be lumagel, and Alix studied them, but could note no difference from those of a man.

Joe said to Manny, "He knows?"

Manny nodded.

Joe turned back. "Well—Alix—?"

"I don't know. It's—it's—monstrous, it's—" He shrugged his shoulders and pounded one hand into the palm of the other.

"You're *it*, Alix. King, god, what you will. For six years, I've built you up—in *their* papers, in *their* minds. Clean, quiet, hardworking Alix. And humble. Oh, the humility I gave you has made me cry, at times."

Manny said in mild protest, "You didn't have to build that angle much. Alix is humble. Alix is—he's—he's—" And the articulate Manny had no words.

Joe Nettleton's pale face was cynical. He said, "The way you feel is the way they all feel—the black ones out there and the brown ones and the yellow ones."

"They've got their rights," Alix said.

"Have they? Take a look at the first twenty rows, ringside. You'll see what rights they have, word rights, paper rights. But not in the hearts of men. Oh, the grapes of wrath are out there, Alix, beyond the twentieth row. Haven't you any sense of history, of destiny?"

Alix didn't answer.

Manny said, "He's been thinking of God, he tells me."

Joe Nettleton's face was blank. "God? Their God?" He looked at Alix wonderingly. "This Superman they scare us with? You don't eat that malarkey, do you, Alix?"

Alix shrugged, saying nothing.

"They don't believe it themselves," Joe protested. "It's one of those symbols they set up, to make them superior. They ever tell you what He looks like? Oh, they give Him a prophet sure, and the prophet gives them words to live by. Don't kill, don't steal, don't lie, don't lust, don't envy: words, Alix, words, words, words. Judge them by their actions."

Alix looked up. "I'm not—cut out to be a leader."

"Yes, you are. And I cut you out, in their minds, with words. The brown ones read me and the black ones and the yellow ones, and I built you up, in their minds—*and tonight they'll wait for a signal from you.*"

"A signal from me? Are you—what—?"

"A signal from you. To those in the crowd, to those watching on the video screens, the ones who are briefed and *know* about rioting, about how to steer a revolution. Think of the irony of it—man's prejudice building the army of resentment and man's genius building the machines that army can use to destroy man—white man. White man—first."

"First—?" Manny said. "You've dreams beyond tonight, Joe?"

Joe smiled disarmingly. "I use too many words. That one got away. We can't think beyond tonight, now." He turned to Alix. "It's not an involved signal, Alix. It's just one word. The word is 'kill.' From *you* it's more than a word, it's an order."

There was a knock at the door, and the sono-bray above the door said, "Time to go up. Time for the big one."

All three were silent, and then Joe put a hand on Alix's shoulder. "You can't give the signal from your back, Alix. You'd better be standing up, when this one is over with."

Alix looked at Joe, trying to read behind those brown eyes. Alix said, "I'll be standing up. There's never been a second I doubted that."

They went out, and there was a clamor, a ring of scribes in the corridor beyond the showers. One of them voiced it for all of them, "What the hell is this, Manny? Joe a cousin, or something? How about a statement?"

Manny looked at them bleakly. "We hope to win, but we're up against a superior being. It's in God's lap."

Cynical men, but they resented the blasphemy—coming from a robot.

Joe said, "And Alix is his prophet. Who's betting what?"

No answer. They stared at Joe, and some wrote down a few words. One of them looked at Alix.

"How about you, Alix? How do you feel?"

Alix the humble, the new-day Uncle Tom, the subservient. Alix lifted his chin and didn't smile. "Confident. I'll win."

"How?" another asked.

"Hitting him harder, and oftener. What's he got but a hook and an iron jaw?"

"Guts," one of them said. "You've got to hand him that, Alix."

"I concede nothing," Alix answered. "We'll see, tonight."

There were no further questions. They went down the long aisle that led to the bright ring, Manny and Alix and the other handler, who'd been waiting in the prelim boys' shower room.

Eighty thousand people in the Bowl, a clear, warm night, and millions watching on the video screens around the globe. Video hadn't hurt this one—this was history, a robot crossing the status line. They wanted to be a part of this.

The referee was black, Willie Newton. It would look less like favoritism if the referee were black, reasoned the white men in their lefthanded way.

Bugs around the arcs, and big ebony Willie in his striped shirt waiting in the ring, smiling, just *happening* to be in Alix's corner as he climbed through.

Willie bent, pretending to help part the ropes. Willie whispered, "You'll get all the breaks you need, Alix."

Alix came through and stood erect. "I don't want a single break, Willie, just a fair shake. *You* can understand it has to be like that."

"I can, Alix. I'm sorry. About the name—just Alix? Or I could blur the rest."

"Alix one-three-four-oh, not blurred. It's my name."

He turned from Willie then, acknowledging the thunder behind him, both hands high in salute. He could see the rows stretching out from ringside—the first twenty all white. Most of the thunder came from high in the stands.

And now the champ came down his aisle, his faded purple dressing robe across his bulky shoulders, his handlers a respectful few paces behind him.

Nick Nolan, the middleweight champion of the world. His ears were lumpy, his brows ridged with scar tissue. His round head centered on those bulky shoulders, apparently with no neck to connect them. A fringe of red hair and a brutal, thick-featured face.

Made in His image?

Some words ran through Alix's mind: "Is this the thing Lord God made and gave—To have dominion over sea and land . . . ?"

This was a hell of a time to be recalling Markham.

Nick came over to his corner, the false geniality on his face as phony as the gesture of a champ coming to the challenger's corner. Nick said, "Best—between us, huh?"

"The better," Alix corrected him. "Keep them above the belt, Nick."

Nick grinned. "Don't I always? I came up the hard way, Alix."

Alix said nothing, staring . . . *when this dumb Terror shall rise to judge the world* . . .

A man with a hook and an urge to combat. The hard way? Maybe. He'd taken enough punches to give him a lifetime lease on Queer Street. But he'd handed out more than he'd received. A spoiler and a mixer. A weight-draper and infighter and an easy bleeder.

Blood will run in the streets, Alix. . . .

In the ring, Nick's blood would flow, and further stain the spotted canvas. In the streets, the blood of Nick's brothers would flow, in the streets around the world.

Title fight? Oh, yes.

The Irishman first, he'd come up through the ring to his grudging equality, and the Jew, then, and the Filipino and the Negro and the Cuban and all the others who wouldn't stay down. Who had their fists and their guts. Mickey Walker, Benny Leonard, Joe Louis—immortals all. Great men, great champs, great memories.

And he? Alix 1340? Different, a machine, no spark. He'd almost forgotten about no spark.

Nick's manager came over to inspect the bandages on Alix's hands, and then went back to his corner with Manny to inspect those on the battered hands of the champ.

Alix's hands were clean-lined, no breaks, no lumps. Alix was a scientific hitter, and his protocol was better than the natural product.

He watches the sparrows, Manny had said. *A signal,* Joe had said. I wish somebody would give me a signal, Alix thought. It's too big for me.

The introductions, the numbers not blurred. The instructions, and Willie saying, "Clean tonight, Nick. I know you well, Nick. But this one is touchy, remember."

"Ah, save it," Nick told him. Champ, big man, Nick Nolan.

The buzzer and Manny's brief pat on the shoulder. Rising, and flexing on the ropes, looking down into that sea of faces, white faces. The ones who held dominion over sea and land.

Bugs in the arcs, a hush on the crowd, and the bell.

Alix turned and here came Nick, shuffling across, wasting no time, bringing the fight to the upstart.

Nick had a right hand, too, but it was clumsy. The hook was better trained. Alix circled to his left, away from Nick's left, and put his jab easily to Nick's nose.

There are sportswriters, Alix knew, who talked of a *right* hook, but a man would need to be a contortionist to throw it. Unless he was *completely* unorthodox. Or a southpaw.

Nick was neither. Nick had a right hand like a mallet, but it came from below or above, and was telegraphed by the pulling up of his right foot. Nick saved that for the time his opponent couldn't see or react.

Nick came in with the hook, trying to slide under Alix's extended left hand, trying to time the pattern of his feet to Alix's circling, looking for the hole.

Alix peppered him with the left, and then saw the low left hand of Nick. Alix stopped circling—and tossed a singing right.

It traveled over Nick's left and found the button. Nick took two stumbling backward steps, and went down.

Resin dust swirled and the scream of the stands was like a single anguished cry.

Alix went to a neutral corner, shrugging his shoulder muscles loose, trying to still the sudden pounding of his heart. Nick had been knocked down before, often.

He took a full count, under the rules, but was on one knee at three. The big black semaphore of Willie's right hand and then those hands wiping the gloves and Willie stepping clear.

Nick stormed in. He got through Alix's left, this time, and sent a looping right hand high. It missed, but it was meant to miss. Nick's elbow smashed Alix's mouth.

Rage, a red rage, and they stood in the corner, trading leather.

The hook came in low, and pain knifed into Alix's groin. In his aching blindness he could feel Nick's feet groping for his, trying to find his instep.

Champion, model.

Alix grabbed, and hung on. This one he had to win. This one could be lost, right now.

Nick said, "Break it up, phony man. I can't hit you when you're hanging on."

The big slap of Willie's hand. Willie, playing it straight. Alix broke at the touch.

Alix broke—and Nick threw the right hand, on the break.

Foul? Of course, but Alix went down, his senses numb, his mind turning black. He lay on his face, not moving, the blackness moving through his body.

What's this God like? It would depend upon who you ask. They ever tell you what He looks like? The blackness turned red, the red of blood, running in the streets. And there was suddenly a cross, and a dim figure, and he heard Willie's sonorous, "Five, six—"

He turned over at seven, was on one knee at eight, and up at nine. And Nick came bulling in, both hands ready.

The bell.

He got to his corner without Manny's help. The magic of Manny's hands dug at his neck, bringing clarity. The ice, the other handler probing at his flaccid legs.

"I saw a cross, Manny."

"Nobody's crossing us, Alix. Don't think, Alix. Here." He gave him the water bottle.

Alix rinsed his mouth, and spit it out. "He's rough, Manny. He knows all the tricks."

"Don't you?"

"I don't want to. I saw a cross when I was unconscious, Manny. A cross like you see on a church."

"Don't tell me about it. Get him, boy. Don't try to mix with him, but get him, with that left, with your speed, with your brain. Get him."

"I'll try. But he's not typical, Manny. They're not all like Nick."

"The hell they aren't. He's one of the better ones. Get him."

The buzzer, the bell, and Nick.

Nick with the iron jaw, Nick with the hook and the bulging shoulders, Nick the champion.

Alix put the left into Nick's face, but it wasn't a jab. It was a straight left, with shoulder in it. It twisted Nick's nose, and brought blood.

Nick was nettled, and he charged. He charged into a straight, sweet right hand that was delivered from a flat-footed stance. Nick wavered, and tried to grab.

Alix felt his strength pour back and the pattern of his feet was sure and planned. A left, a feint, a jolting right, moving around this hulk, this blundering knot of flesh and muscle, beating a tattoo on him, spreading the blood. *Get him.*

It looked like a slaughterhouse. Blood all over Nick's face, and blood matting the curled, sweaty hair on his chest. Starting to look dazed, starting to wonder, the champ. The untypical man? He must be, he had to be, to have dominion over sea and land.

"Why didn't he go down? Couldn't he see the pattern of it, the pattern Alix was tracing for him with his blood-soaked gloves? Why didn't he go down? Why didn't he quit?

He hadn't quit by the end of the fifth round. Out there, those eighty thousand were silent. This was no fight, this was now murder. Why didn't he quit?

Alix asked Manny, on the stool, before the sixth. "Why doesn't he quit? He can't win. Manny, I hate to hit him."

"Don't be a sucker. Don't be a damned fool." Manny's voice was hoarse. "As long as there's a spark of life in those bastards, they won't quit. He's dangerous yet, Alix."

A spark, a spark—Life? Cognizance? No, life, a spark of life.

In the sixth, Nick almost went to his knees, in the middle of the ring. But he got control, and stumbled toward Alix.

Alix came in fast and carelessly—and the earth erupted.

He's dangerous, yet, Alix. There was no blackness this time, just the blood red. There was no cross. But a voice? "In the sky, in the sky—" Silence.

Get up, Alix. For the black and brown and red and yellow who are watching you, around the world, get up. You're their hope, you're their WORD. Up, to one knee, and up just under the wire.

Nick didn't charge, this time. Wary and careful, he was, after the pasting he'd been taking. Let Alix make the mistakes, like the one he just had. Nick only needed one more.

Manny said, "Can you hit him, now? Still mourning for him, are you?"

Alix said, "I'm a machine, Manny. He can't hurt me. I can hurt him, but he can't hurt me."

"That's my boy," Manny said. "I'm glad you know what side of the fence you're on, finally."

"I know my place," Alix said. "I know my job."

"That you do. Get him."

He got him. They don't quit, these men. Not while they're conscious. Not while they're alive. Alix hit him everywhere there was room to hit, with both hands, knocking him down four times in the seventh round.

Each time, Nick got up. And in the eighth, he came out to meet Alix, walking into his doom, not flinching, not hiding, putting his crown on the line.

Supremacy? Nick had it, bastard though he was. But for how long? How long could he stay that dumb and still live?

Nick came out, his low hands a farce of a defense.

How long could he hold the animosity down with his arrogance and his brutality and his shoddiness? How much time did he have? Alix knew.

Nick came out for the eighth, and Alix hit him with a solid right hand. He didn't set it up, or feint Nick into the spot, or hesitate. There wasn't any need to.

He put all his weight and most of his bitterness into the button shot that made him middleweight champion of the world.

Silence, a shocked silence at the history before them, and then, from the far seats, from the cheap seats, acclamation. The video cameras covered the ring, the crowd; the lights went on all over the huge bowl.

Manny hugged him, Joe Nettleton hugged him, and others.

In the far seats, no one moved. In the near seats, no one moved. Joe said, "The word, Alix."

They were bringing the banked microphones over, the microphones that would carry the word all over the world. The cameras trained on him. The word.

He looked at Joe, and Manny. He brought the mikes to mouth level, and moved back a bit. He said, "I won, tonight. I've no message for you. But someone has. It's in the sky."

Craning necks, a murmur, the cameras leaving Alix as the operators swung the huge machines toward the red letters in the sky.

Beside him, Manny gasped. Joe Nettleton stared, unbelieving, his mouth slack.

Red letters? Something like red, but luminous and miles high, and definite. The cameras were trained directly on it, now:

FIND YOUR GOD

Manny said, "Alix . . . how . . . are you, did you? Alix, what in hell are you?"

"There's more to it they don't know," Alix said. "It's 'Find your God or your machines will kill you.' I don't think there's any need to tell them the rest if they obey the first."

Manny said hoarsely, "But this message came through you? You're a—"

"A prophet? Me, a machine, Alix 1340?"

Joe said, "You're not sending out the other word?"

"Not yet. It's not time."

"How do *you* know?" Manny cut in. "How do you know if it's time or not? And if their God wanted to send a message, why should he use a machine? Why should he use you?"

"Because," Alix said, "no man would listen. And if they don't listen, now, Manny, our time *will* come...."

THE
PEACEMAKER

W. W. Jacobs

The harbour was crowded with fishing boats, and fresh arrivals were coming in every few minutes. Until the entrance was reached they came scudding along with every appearance of haste, but then their mainsails came tumbling down to the deck, and the boats with sufficient way left on them moved easily over the still water, and felt their way to a berth. Small boats conveyed the fish to the quay, where embryo fishermen were appraising the catch with a wisdom beyond their years.

There was a glut of whiting. So many whiting, and going so cheaply that it was enough to make them bite their tails from sheer vexation. Small flat fish which slid away from their pile were carefully looked after and coaxed back with the toe of a sea-boot, but whiting slid away unnoticed until they vanished from mortal ken in the pockets of predatory urchins.

In the small market, a short, red-faced man with a scrubby beard walked in a disparaging fashion from heap to heap, using a favourite briar in lieu of a hammer to knock down such fish as found bidders. The latter were few and wary, and turning a deaf ear to eloquence expressed opinions distasteful to an auctioneer's ear in crude English.

The sense of the meeting being against him, the auctioneer truckled to it, and coming to another heap consisting of a selection of the most undesirable fish that swim Britannia's realm, gazed at it indignantly. There was a titter behind him, and he voiced his wrath impetuously.

"That's Joe Gubbs's catch," he bawled. "S'elp me, I'd know that man's luck anywhere."

He turned the fish over scornfully with his foot, and, with a severe glance at the hapless Gubbs, moved away to something more saleable.

"Where d'ye get 'em from, Gubbs?" inquired an aggravating voice. "We never get such things in our nets. I've never seen some o' them things afore."

"There's a lot you ain't seen, Bob Tarbut," said Gubbs, turning upon him, "and what you do see don't do you much good."

"I'd be ashamed to bring home such a queer-looking lot," jeered the other.

"They mayn't be up to much, but there's none on 'em would care to change faces with you, I expect," related Gubbs.

"You leave my face alone," said Tarbut, whose physiognomy was much used in the village for purposes of comparison.

"A skate's handsome to you," said Gubbs, following up his advantage.

He jumped back suddenly as the fist of the sensitive Tarbut shot suddenly out, and treading on a small fish, whirled round wildly with his hands in the air in the effort to retain his balance, and sat down heavily. The bystanders instantly separated into two groups, and two or three anxious sympathisers helped the fallen man to his feet, and indicated those parts of Tarbut's frame which in their opinion were least adapted to offer resistance to his fist.

"Stand up," said Gubbs, sternly, as he shook himself free from these friends.

"I am a-standin' up!" said Tarbut, breathing hard.

The two combatants approached each other stealthily, and manœuvering round the heaps of fish, struck safely at each other over these convenient barriers.

"Get 'em in the road," cried an excited voice, "they can't 'urt each other here."

A dozen kindly hands helped them there, and finding too much strategy for sport in a large ring, at the bidding of the resourceful individual who had last spoken, gradually made it smaller and smaller. Two or three small blows warmed the combatants, and they set to work in earnest. Then Gubbs, under a heavy blow from Tarbut, went to the ground and stayed there.

It was three minutes before he came thoroughly round, and then he sat up in a dazed fashion and looked round for his opponent.

"Did I kill 'im?" he inquired, in a whisper.

"No, not quite," said one of his friends, gently.

Gubbs rubbed his eyes. "What are they patting him on the back for?"

he inquired, eyeing the group who were making a fuss over Tarbut.

"'Cos he's won," said his friend.

Gubbs staggered to his feet.

"It's no good," said the landlord of the Three Fishers, who had run over to the scene of the fray; "you wasn't properly trained, you know. Now, look 'ere. If you put yourself in my hands, in three weeks you can beat him holler."

"You do as Mr. Larkins ses, Joe," said his friend, impressively.

"I lived among prize fighters afore I come down 'ere," said Mr. Larkins, expanding his small frame. "In three weeks' time, Gubbs, you'll be able to knock him silly."

"Well, what about Tarbut? He ought to be trained too," said one of the men. "Fair play's fair play any day."

"I'll train 'im," said an old ex-coastguardsman.

"I don't want no training," said Tarbut, surlily. "I've beat 'im, beat 'im easy."

"Well, beat 'im again, Tarbut," said one of his friends. "I'll put my five bob on you. Who'll take me?"

For the next five minutes, heedless of the assertions of both men that they wouldn't fight any more, bets were freely taken, Tarbut, in view of his recent success, being a hot favourite.

A jarring element was introduced into the proceedings by a small, elderly man wearing a piece of blue ribbon, who, pushing his way in eagerly, inquired what it was all about. Nobody troubling to give him a correct answer, he tried to solve it for himself, and was then caught, just in the nick of time, trying to make the enemies shake hands.

"You go off to your Mother's Meeting, Peter Morgan," said an incensed voice.

"It's a fight," said the little man, raising his voice. "Oh, my friends—"

"It's nothing o' the kind," said Larkins, hotly. "I'm training 'em for a race, that's all. They're just going to see who's the best runner."

Morgan, disregarding the publican, looked to others for information.

"It's quite right," said a bystander. "You can believe me, can't you?"

"When's it going to be?" asked Morgan.

"I don't know," said the other, turning away.

"You ought to be ashamed of yourselves," said Morgan, warmly. "It's bad enough to make a couple of men fight what don't want to without telling a lot of lies about it."

"It's none o' your business," said Larkins, surlily. "Ask no questions and you'll hear no lies. You'll get some idea into that 'ead of yours and then go and split, and have it stopped."

"I never told of anything in my life," said Morgan, sharply. "My mates here know that. That ain't my way. My way's persuasion and example, not forcing people to do what I want."

"There's a purse o' fifteen and six made up for the winner," said Larkins, turning away and whispering the news to Gubbs. "The spot for the picnic'll be made known later on. Them what's in the know is respectfully asked to keep their mouths shut to save trouble all round."

He went back to his bar, and the other men, after standing about a bit, strolled off one by one to their teas. Mr. Morgan was one of the last to leave, and went as far as Tarbut's door with him to tell him an anecdote of a man who was struck behind the ear in a fight and killed on the spot.

A comfortable meal and a good night's rest restored Mr. Gubbs to his wonted serenity of mind, and he awoke at six o'clock feeling determined to shake hands with Tarbut and let the matter drop. A persistent hammering at the door, which gradually got louder and louder, interfering with his meditations, he roused Mrs. Gubbs, who was sleeping peacefully, and with some asperity bade her get up and stop it.

"It's Mr. Larkins, Joe," said the lady, hastily withdrawing her head from the window.

Mr. Gubbs sat up in bed, and then with a mighty yawn rose, and, pushing open the casement again, gazed indignantly at the small publican, who was standing below keeping up an incessant rapping on the door with a small cane.

"Morning, Mr. Larkins, sir," said Gubbs, sniffing at the cool morning air.

"Halloa!" said Larkins, looking up. "This won't do, you know. You're wasting time. You ought to be up and out by now."

"I've changed my mind," said Gubbs, leaning out and speaking in a low voice to defeat the intentions of Mrs. Gubbs, who was listening. "I dreamt I killed Tarbut, an' it's give me such a fright that I've resolved not to fight."

"That's all right," said Larkins, briskly; "dreams always go by contraries."

"Well there ain't much comfort in that," said Gubbs, who was anxious to get back to his warm bed, sharply.

"You dress and come down," said the imperious Larkins. "You ought to be ashamed of yourself after all the trouble I'm taking on your behalf."

Mr. Gubbs rubbed his eyes and pondered. "What's the towel for?" he demanded, suspiciously.

"Rub you down with after you've bathed," said the other.

"Bathed?" said Mr. Gubbs, with emphasis. "Bathed? What for?"

"Training," replied Larkins. "Hurry up."

"I don't believe old Bullock's going to make Tarbut bathe," said Gubbs, shivering; "it's weakening."

"You do as you're told," said the autocratic Larkins. "Bullock don't know nothing about it."

Mr. Gubbs sighed and withdrew his head, and explaining to his astonished wife that he was going for a little stroll, gloomily dressed himself and joined his trainer below.

"Shoulders back," said the small publican. "Head up."

He led the way down to the beach, and, ignoring the looks of aversion which Mr. Gubbs bestowed upon the silver sea, stood by while he disrobed and picked his way painfully over the shingle to the edge of the water. It was a bright morning, but somewhat chill, and Mr. Gubbs's breathless gaspings furnished an excellent clue to the temperature of the water.

"How do you feel?" inquired Mr. Larkins, anxiously, as he rubbed him down.

"I feel ill," said the other, shivering.

"You'll feel better when you've had your run," said Larkins, cheerily.

"'Ad my w—w—*wot?*" inquired Mr. Gubbs, staring at him offensively, and rubbing himself furiously with the towel.

"Your run," repeated Larkins, sternly. "You don't want your coat. I'll hold that. And mind, I don't want you to go running like a steam engine, or a runaway horse."

"I wasn't goin' to," said Gubbs.

"Just trot easy," continued the other, "for about half a mile. Go as far as that gate over there, then rest two minutes and trot back again."

His manner was so dictatorial that Mr. Gubbs, remembering in time his score at the Three Fishers, swallowed something he was going to say—and it was nearly strong enough to choke him—and set off at a strange, weird gait towards the indicated goal. He reached it at last, and after a long two minutes started back again in response to the semaphore-like appeals of the enthusiastic Larkins.

"I've got my work cut out for me, I can see," said the latter, as his victim, puffing and blowing, sat down on the ground. "But I'll soon get you in trim, and mind you keep quiet about it. I don't want Bullock to know."

"Why not?" demanded Mr. Gubbs.

"Because he'd train Tarbut the same way," said Larkins, with a cunning grin.

"Well, why shouldn't Tarbut 'ave a doing same as me?" said Mr. Gubbs, vindictively. "Why should 'e be a-laying in comfort in 'is bed while I'm catching cold bathing and killing myself running?"

"Don't you be a fool," said Larkins, affectionately patting him on the shoulder. "Come into my place when you have time, and I'll put the gloves on with you a bit; and be careful what you eat, mind, else you'll undo all the good I've done you."

If it is possible for a man to expectorate sarcastically, Mr. Gubbs achieved that feat.

"Only two cups of tea with your breakfast," continued Larkins, solemnly, "and no greens for dinner, and I'll send you in one pint of old ale every day free gratis."

The tensity of Mr. Gubbs's features relaxed, and he smiled faintly as he rose and accompanied his friend back. Larkins saw him to his door, and after explaining fluently to Mrs. Gubbs that her husband was training for a race, gave her explicit instructions as to his diet, and departed.

It was a source of much joy to Mr. Larkins, though he was unable to persuade Gubbs to share in his feelings, that Tarbut's trainer was satisfied with a less vigorous system for his man. He let Tarbut off with a cold sponging on rising, and as Tarbut had his own ideas as to what constituted a cold sponging, both parties were well pleased with each other.

The businesslike nature of these proceedings was keenly appreciated by the inhabitants of the fishing quarter. Fights had happened before and doubtless would again, but they were mere rough-and-tumble affairs, and over before any proper excitement could be worked up. The purse had steadily mounted up to thirty-five shillings, and the betting varied from day to day.

Each man had his knot of supporters, and enthusiasm had reached such a pitch that Gubbs, who was naturally of a retiring disposition, had to take his matutinal tub before quite a circle of admirers. Opposition on the part of the ladies was balked by continuing to allude to the affair as a race, though Mrs. Gubbs, who got up one morning to see her man run, went home in a state of mind bordering upon stupefaction.

An uneasy feeling was caused by the anxiety of the excellent Mr. Morgan to discover the time and place of meeting. No information was afforded him, and as he had indignantly denied any intention of giving the alarm, the gentlemen interested were much exercised as to the reasons for his curiosity.

The battle was fixed for a Saturday evening, the two trainers, after much wordy warfare, having selected a site which Mr. Larkins insisted had been made purposely by Nature with a view to affairs of the kind. Lofty cliffs hid it from view, and the ground itself consisted of turf so soft and spongy that Larkins predicted that Tarbut would bounce up from

it like an india–rubber ball. The principals expressed themselves as satisfied, though their niggardliness in the matter of thanks for the trouble
which had been taken over the arrangements formed food for conversation for the trainers all the way home.

The boats got in early on Friday afternoon with their fish. The catch
was small and soon disposed of, and then the attentive trainers, rescuing
their men from admirers, who were feeling their arms and putting leading questions as to their wind and state of mind, sent them indoors with
concise instructions as to how they were to spend the last evening. Larkins officiously sent his man off for a short, sharp walk after his tea, and
later on, going to the quay, found that Bullock had given his man the
same instructions.

"Don't you go worrying of 'em, mind," said Larkins sternly to the
group, "an' let 'em have an easy time of it tomorrow in the boats. Both
of 'em," he added, generously.

"Spoke like a Briton, Mr. Larkins," said an old fisherman.

"What I want is fair play and no favour," said Mr. Larkins; "it's to be
a genuine sporting affair. No bad blood or anything of that kind. After
the little affair, all what go to see it are welcome to one drink at my
expense."

"It's time my man was back," said Bullock, looking up the road
which led over the cliffs. "I told him to go just as far as the ground and
back."

"Old Peter Morgan's gone down to the place too, I think," piped a
small lad in huge boots. "I saw 'im following of Tarbut."

The landlord of the Three Fishers started uneasily. "It's on my mind,"
he said, in a melancholy voice, "that that blessed old teetotaller'll have
the thing stopped. He'll tell the police or something."

"No he won't," said the old fisherman who had spoken before. "Me
an' Peter was boys together, an' he's never done anything o' that sort in
his life. Before old Peter got religious there was nothing he liked better
than to see a fight, or to take part in one either, an' it's my opinion he'd
like to see this one, only he don't like to say so."

"Well, he won't," said Larkins, grimly; "it may be as you say, but
we're not going to take any risks."

Conversation became general, and in view of the nearness of the
event, animated, but still the two gladiators failed to put in an appearance.

"He's overdoing it, that's what he is," said Mr. Larkins, referring to
the ardent Gubbs. "You can 'ave a man too willing. He'll go and knock
hisself up."

The small boy came up, his boots clattering over the stones, and, shading his eyes with his hands, looked up the road. The other men, following his gaze, saw three men advancing lovingly arm-in-arm towards them.

"It—it can't be old Morgan with 'em?" said Mr. Larkins.

"It is, though," said the old fisherman, peering through screwed-up eyes. "They've made it up through old Peter, that's wot they've done. He's been talking at 'em and getting at 'em, and now there won't be no fight."

His disappointed auditors groaned in chorus. "Won't there," said Larkins, savagely. "Ho—won't there—You don't think me and my friend Bullock here are going to slave three weeks for nothing, do you?"

"There won't be no fight," repeated the old man. "Look how loving they are! All three of 'em as close together as sweethearts."

The advancing trio certainly bore out the old man's words to the letter. Mr. Peter Morgan was in the centre, and appeared to be half-embracing his companions.

"Why, they can hardly walk," said Bullock; "they've been too far."

"Yes, that's what it is," said Larkins, in a hollow voice.

"Seems to me," said the boy, slowly, "that they've 'ad a bit of a scrap already."

The crowd, with bated breath, stepped out to meet them, Larkins and Bullock leading. It was evident that the two heroes were clinging to Mr. Morgan more for support than from any motives of affection, and it was no less evident that the lad's remark as to a bit of a scrap was capable of wide interpretation. In a few minutes both parties were face to face, and the two trainers gazing at their charges speechless with indignation.

"Which is Gubbs?" demanded Larkins at last, in an unnatural voice.

The figure on Morgan's right arm managed to open an eye and to twist its swollen lips into something intended for a smile.

"What 'ave you been doing," vociferated the incensed landlord.

"Fightin'," said Gubbs, speaking with some difficulty; "it's all over now. It was a draw, and we're going to halve the money between us."

"Oh, are you," said Larkins, bitterly. "Well, you won't have a damned ha'penny of it. What do you mean by it? Eh?"

"I'll tell you all about it," said Morgan, who was looking radiantly happy. "I saw Tarbut going up the road and I followed him and talked to him, and by and by up comes Gubbs, and I talked to him. Then I found out what, of course, I knew before, that all you men were trying to induce these poor souls to knock each other about for money."

Mr. Larkins, choking helplessly, looked sternly at Mr. Morgan, and pointed an incriminating finger at Tarbut's visage.

"I urged 'em not to make such a brutal show of themselves for money," continued Mr. Morgan, "but they said as 'ow they would.

Gubbs said it would be the easiest thirty-five shillings he'd ever earned, and Tarbut said it was him as was going to earn it. After a little talk o' this kind, Gubbs here 'it Tarbut smack in the eye."

Tarbut gave a faint groan in confirmation.

"Then they both started to peel," continued Mr. Morgan.

"Why didn't you stop 'em?" inquired the ex-coastguard; "it was your duty as a Christian to stop 'em."

"I thought it was better for 'em to fight like that than to make a brutal exhibition of themselves," said Mr. Morgan, with dignity. "It was a revolting spectacle, shocking, and I'm glad and thankful there was nobody there but me to see 'em make such brute beasts of themselves."

A threatening murmur broke from the crowd.

"There in that sweet secluded spot," said Mr. Morgan, shaking his head, "these two men, stripped to the waist, knocked one another about for fifteen rounds. First blood fell to Tarbut, he got in with his left on Gubbs's nose, then Gubbs up with a fearful blow and knocked him flat. It was as clean a blow as ever I see. I took Tarbut on my knee—poor fellow, he was doing wrong, but still he was suffering, and Peter Morgan's always got a knee for the sufferer. Second round he was more cautious, and watching 'is opportunity, he clenched and fell with Gubbs underneath. It was a disgusting spectacle."

Mr. Larkins bent savagely over to Mr. Bullock and whispered in his ear.

"When time was called—" said Mr. Morgan.

"Who called it?" inquired a voice, with the air of one making a point.

"I did," said Mr. Morgan; "there was nobody else—both of 'em walked round each other a bit, sparring and looking for opportunities. I think the third round was the longest of all. Both of 'em kept getting in a lot of little knocks and then dodging away again. Then Tarbut caught Gubbs one in the bread-ba—in the wind—and then followed up on his jaw and knocked him down again. It was a disgusting spectacle."

"Must ha' been," said a dejected voice.

"After that there was twelve more rounds," continued the narrator; "sometimes Tarbut had the best of it, and sometimes Gubbs. Both men was very determined and fought very fair. It was good, solid hard hitting, and they were marked all over before they'd finished. Once Gubbs gave Tarbut a blow over the heart, and I thought he wouldn't get up to time."

"I wouldn't if you hadn't blowed water into my face out of that puddle," said Tarbut.

"It was a most disgusting spectacle," said Mr. Peter Morgan, hurriedly.

"Seems to me—" began Larkins, ferociously.

"Two fine strong men, stripped to the waist, hard as nails, knocking each other about for money," said Mr. Morgan. "They're never going to fight any more. I made 'em promise they wouldn't. They're good friends now; ain't you, lads?"

With an utter disregard of the feelings of the bystanders the two men shook hands.

"And though I regard fighting with horror," concluded Mr. Morgan, beaming on them, "I think that, as it was a bargain, you should divide the purse between 'em."

"They won't get a farthing of it," said Mr. Larkins, exposively, "unless you like to give it to 'em out of your own pocket."

"Me!" said Mr. Morgan, opening his eyes. "Why?"

"Ask yourself," said Mr. Larkins, pointedly. "I should say if any man ever 'ad thirty-five shillings worth of sport all to hisself, you have; and, what's more, you know it, Mr. Peter Morgan."

The peacemaker sighed, and, turning, led his charges gently away. The crowd watched them as far as the Three Fishers, and observing that they detached themselves by force from their guide and friend, crossed the road and followed them in.

THE LORD OF
FALCONBRIDGE

Arthur Conan Doyle

Tom Cribb, Champion of England, having finished his active career by his two famous battles with the terrible Molineux, had settled down into the public house which was known as the Union Arms, at the corner of Panton Street in the Haymarket. Behind the bar of this hostelry there was a green baize door which opened into a large, red-papered parlour, adorned by many sporting prints and by the numerous cups and belts which were the treasured trophies of the famous prize fighter's victorious career. In this snuggery it was the custom of the Corinthians of the day to assemble in order to discuss, over Tom Cribb's excellent wines, the matches of the past, to await the news of the present, and to arrange new ones for the future. Hither also came his brother pugilists, especially such as were in poverty or distress, for the Champion's generosity was proverbial, and no man of his own trade was ever turned from his door if cheering words or a full meal could mend his condition.

On the morning in question—August 25, 1818—there were but two men in this famous snuggery. One was Cribb himself—all run to flesh since the time seven years before, when, training for his last fight, he had done his forty miles a day with Captain Barclay over the Highland roads. Broad and deep, as well as tall, he was a little short of twenty stone in weight, but his heavy strong face and lion eyes showed that the spirit of the prize fighter was not yet altogether overgrown by the fat of the publican. Though it was not eleven o'clock, a great tankard of bitter ale stood upon the table before him, and he was busy cutting up a plug of black tobacco and rubbing the slices into powder between his horny fingers. For all his record of desperate battles, he looked what he was: a good-hearted, respectable householder, law-abiding and kindly, a happy and prosperous man.

His companion, however, was by no means in the same easy circumstances, and his countenance wore a very different expression. He was a tall and well-formed man, some fifteen years younger than the Champion, and recalling in the masterful pose of his face and in the fine spread of his shoulders something of the manly beauty which had distinguished Cribb at his prime. No one looking at his countenance could fail to see that he was a fighting man by profession, and any judge of the fancy, considering his six feet in height, his thirteen stone of solid muscle, and his beautifully graceful build, would admit that he had started his career with advantages which, if they were only backed by the driving-power of a stout heart, must carry him far. Tom Winter, or Spring— as he chose to call himself—had indeed come up from his Herefordshire home with a fine country record of local successes, which had been enhanced by two victories gained over formidable London heavyweights. Three weeks before, however, he had been defeated by the famous Painter, and the setback weighed heavily upon the young man's spirits.

"Cheer up, lad," said the Champion, glancing across from under his tufted eyebrows at the disconsolate face of his companion. "Indeed, Tom, you take it over-hard."

The young man groaned, but made no reply.

"Others have been beat before you and lived to be Champions of England. Here I sit with that very title. Was I not beat down Broadwater way by George Nicholls in 1805? What then? I fought on, and here I am. When the big Black came from America it was not George Nicholls they sent for. I say to you fight on, and by George, I'll see you in my own shoes yet!"

Tom Spring shook his head. "Never, if I have to fight you to get there, Daddy."

"I can't keep it for ever, Tom. It's beyond all reason. I'm going to lay it down before all London at the Fives Courts next year, and it's to you that I want to hand it. I couldn't train down to it now, lad. My day's done."

"Well, Dad, I'll never bid for it till you choose to stand aside. After that, it is as it may be."

"Well, have a rest, Tom; wait for your chance, and, meantime, there's always a bed and crust for you here."

Spring struck his clenched fist on his knee. "I know, Daddy! Ever since I came up from Fownthorpe, you've been as good as a father to me."

"I've an eye for a winner."

"A pretty winner! Beat in forty rounds by Ned Painter."

"You had beat him first."

"And by the Lord, I will again!"

"So you will, lad. George Nicholls would never give me another shy. Knew too much, he did. Bought a butcher's shop in Bristol with the money, and there he is to this day."

"Yes, I'll come back on Painter, but I haven't a shilling left. My backers have lost faith in me. If it wasn't for you, Daddy, I'd be in the kennel."

"Have you nothing left, Tom?"

"Not the price of a meal. I left every penny I had, and my good name as well, in the ring at Kingston. I'm hard put to it to live unless I can get another fight, and who's going to back me now?"

"Tut, man! the knowing ones will back you. You're the top of the list, for all Ned Painter. But there are other ways a man may earn a bit. There was a lady in here this morning—nothing flash, boy, a real tip-top out-and-outer with a coronet on her coach—asking after you."

"Asking after me! A lady!" The young pugilist stood up with surprise and a certain horror rising in his eyes. "You don't mean, Daddy—"

"I mean nothing but what is honest, my lad. You can lay to that!"

"You said I could earn a bit!"

"So, perhaps you can. Enough, anyhow, to tide you over your bad time. There's something in the wind there. It's to do with fightin'. She asked questions about your height, weight, and my opinion of your prospect. You can lay that my answers did you no harm."

"She ain't making a match, surely?"

"Well, she seemed to know a tidy bit about it. She asked about George Cooper, and Richmond the Black, and Tom Oliver, always comin' back to you, and wantin' to know if you were not the pick of the bunch. *And* trustworthy. That was the other point. Could she trust you? Lord, Tom, if you was a fightin' archangel you could hardly live up to the character that I've given you."

A drawer looked in from the bar. "If you please, Mr. Cribb, the lady's carriage is back again."

The Champion laid down his long clay pipe. "This way, lad," said he, plucking his young friend by the sleeve towards the side window. "Look there, now! Saw you ever a more slap-up carriage? See, too, the pair of bays—two hundred guineas apiece. Coachman, too, and footman—you'd find 'em hard to beat. There she is now, stepping out of it. Wait here, lad, till I do the honours of my house."

Tom Cribb slipped off, and young Spring remained by the window, tapping the glass nervously with his fingers, for he was a simple-minded country lad with no knowledge of women, and many fears of the traps which await the unwary in a great city. Many stories were afloat of pugilists who had been taken up and cast aside again by wealthy ladies, even as the gladiators were in decadent Rome. It was with some suspicion therefore, and considerable inward trepidation, that he faced round as a tall veiled figure swept into the room. He was much consoled, however, to observe the bulky form of Tom Cribb immediately behind her as a proof that the interview was not to be a private one. When the door was closed, the lady very deliberately removed her gloves. Then with fingers which glittered with diamonds she slowly rolled up and adjusted her heavy veil. Finally, she turned her face upon Spring.

"Is this the man?" said she.

They stood looking at each other with mutual interest, which warmed in both their faces into mutual admiration. What she saw was as fine a figure of a young man as England could show, none the less attractive for the restrained shyness of his manner and the blush which flushed his cheeks. What he saw was a woman of thirty, tall, dark, queen-like, and imperious, with a lovely face, every line and feature of which told of pride and breed, a woman born to Courts, with the instinct of command strong within her, and yet with all the softer woman's graces to temper and conceal the firmness of her soul. Tom Spring felt as he looked at her that he had never seen nor ever dreamed of any one so beautiful, and yet he could not shake off the instinct which warned him to be upon his guard. Yes, it was beautiful, this face—beautiful beyond belief. But was it good, was it kind, was it true? There was some strange subconscious repulsion which mingled with his admiration for her loveliness. As to the lady's thoughts, she had already put away all idea of the young pugilist as a man, and regarded him now with critical eyes as a machine designed for a definite purpose.

"I am glad to meet you, Mr.—Mr. Spring," said she, looking him over with as much deliberation as a dealer who is purchasing a horse. "He is hardly as tall as I was given to understand, Mr. Cribb. You said six feet, I believe?"

"So he is, ma'am, but he carries it so easy. It's only the beanstalk that looks tall. See here, I'm six foot myself, and our heads are level, except I've lost my fluff."

"What is the chest measurement?"

"Forty-three inches, ma'am."

"You certainly seem to be a very strong young man. And a game one, too, I hope?"

Young Spring shrugged his shoulders.

"It's not for me to say, ma'am."

"I can speak for that, ma'am," said Cribb. "You read the *Sporting Chronicle* for three weeks ago, ma'am. You'll see how he stood up to Ned Painter until his senses were beat out of him. I waited on him, ma'am, and I know. I could show you my waistcoat now—that would let you guess what punishment he can take."

The lady waved aside the illustration.

"But he was beat," said she, coldly. "The man who beat him must be the better man."

"Saving your presence, ma'am, I think not, and outside Gentleman Jackson my judgment would stand against any in the ring. My lad here has beat Painter once, and will again, if your ladyship could see your way to find the battle-money."

The lady started and looked angrily at the Champion.

"Why do you call me that?"

"I beg pardon. It was just my way of speaking."

"I order you not to do it again."

"Very good, ma'am."

"I am here incognita. I bind you both upon your honours to make no inquiry as to who I am. If I do not get your firm promise, the matter ends here."

"Very good, ma'am. I'll promise for my own part, and so, I am sure, will Spring. But if I may be so bold, I can't help my drawers and potmen talking with your servants."

"The coachman and footman know just as much about me as you do. But my time is limited, so I must get to business. I think, Mr. Spring, that you are in want of something to do at present?"

"This is so, ma'am."

"I understand from Mr. Cribb that you are prepared to fight any one at any weight?"

"Any thing on two legs," cried the Champion.

"Who did you wish me to fight?" asked the young pugilist.

"That cannot concern you. If you are really ready to fight any one, then the particular name can be of no importance. I have my reasons for withholding it."

"Very good, ma'am."

"You have been only a few weeks out of training. How long would it take you to get back to your best?"

"Three weeks or a month."

"Well, then, I will pay your training expenses and two pounds a week over. Here are five pounds as a guarantee. You will fight when I consider that you are ready, and that the circumstances are favourable. If you win your fight, you shall have fifty pounds. Are you satisfied with the terms?"

"Very handsome, ma'am, I'm sure."

"And remember, Mr. Spring, I choose you, not because you are the best man—for there are two opinions about that—but because I am given to understand that you are a decent man whom I can trust. The terms of this match are to be secret."

"I understand that. I'll say nothing."

"It is a private match. Nothing more. You will begin your training tomorrow."

"Very good, ma'am."

"I will ask Mr. Cribb to train you."

"I'll do that, ma'am, with pleasure. But by your leave, does he have anything if he loses?"

A spasm of emotion passed over the woman's face and her hands clenched white with passion.

"If he loses, not a penny, not a penny!" she cried. "He must not, shall not lose!"

"Well, ma'am," said Spring, "I've never heard of any such match. But it's true that I am down at heel, and beggars can't be choosers. I'll do just what you say. I'll train till you give the word, and then I'll fight where you tell me. I hope you'll make it a large ring."

"Yes," said she; "it will be a large ring."

"And how far from London?"

"Within a hundred miles. Have you anything else to say? My time is up."

"I'd like to ask, ma'am," said the Champion, earnestly, "whether I can act as the lad's second when the time comes. I've waited on him the last two fights. Can I give him a knee?"

"No," said the woman, sharply. Without another word she turned and was gone, shutting the door behind her. A few moments later the trim carriage flashed past the window, turned down the crowded Haymarket, and was engulfed in the traffic.

The two men looked at each other in silence.

"Well, blow my dicky, if this don't beat cock-fightin'!" cried Tom Cribb at last. "Anyhow, there's the fiver, lad. But it's a rum go, and no mistake about it."

After due consultation, it was agreed that Tom Spring should go into training at the Castle Inn on Hampstead Heath, so that Cribb could drive over and watch him. Thither Spring went on the day after the interview with his patroness, and he set to work at once with drugs, dumbbells, and breathers on the common to get himself into condition. It was hard, however, to take the matter seriously, and his good-natured trainer found the same difficulty.

"It's the baccy I miss, Daddy," said the young pugilist, as they sat together on the afternoon of the third day. "Surely there can't be any harm in my havin' a pipe?"

"Well, well, lad, it's against my conscience, but here's my box and there's a yard o' clay," said the Champion. "My word, I don't know what Captain Barclay of Ury would have said if he had seen a man smoke when he was in trainin'! He was the man to work you! He had me down from sixteen to thirteen the second time I fought the Black."

Spring had lit his pipe and was leaning back amid a haze of blue smoke.

"It was easy for you, Daddy, to keep strict trainin' when you knew what was before you. You had your date and your place and your man. You knew that in a month you would jump the ropes with ten thousand folk around you, and carrying maybe a hundred thousand in bets. You knew also the man you had to meet, and you wouldn't give him the better of you. But it's all different with me. For all I know this is just a woman's whim, and will end in nothing. If I was sure it was serious, I'd break this pipe before I would smoke it."

Tom Cribb scratched his head in puzzlement.

"I can make nothing of it, lad, 'cept that her money is good. Come to think of it, how many men on the list could stand up to you for half an hour? It can't be Stringer, 'cause you've beat him. Then there's Cooper; but he's up Newcastle way. It can't be him. There's Richmond; but you wouldn't need to take your coat off to beat him. There's the Gasman; but he's not twelve stone. And there's Bill Neat of Bristol. That's it, lad. The lady has taken into her head to put you up against either the Gasman or Bill Neat."

"But why not say so? I'd train hard for the Gasman and harder for Bill Neat, but I'm blowed if I can train with any heart when I'm fightin' nobody in particular and everybody in general, same as now."

There was a sudden interruption to the speculations of the two prize fighters. The door opened and the lady entered. As her eyes fell upon the two men her dark, handsome face flushed with anger, and she gazed at them silently with an expression of contempt which brought them both to their feet with hangdog faces. There they stood, their long, reeking pipes in their hands, shuffling and downcast, like two great rough mastiffs before an angry mistress.

"So!" said she, stamping her foot furiously. "And this is training!"

"I'm sure we're very sorry, ma'am," said the abashed Champion. "I didn't think—I never for one moment supposed—"

"That I would come myself to see if you were taking my money on false pretences? No, I dare say not. You fool!" she blazed, turning suddenly upon Tom Spring. "You'll be beat. That will be the end of it."

The young man looked up with an angry face.

"I'll trouble you not to call me names, ma'am. I've my self-respect, the same as you. I'll allow that I shouldn't have smoked when I was in trainin'. But I was saying to Tom Cribb here, just before you came in, that if you would give over treatin' us as if we were children, and if you would tell us just who is it you want me to fight, and when, and where, it would be a deal easier for me to take myself in hand."

"It's true, ma'am," said the Champion. "I know it must be either the Gasman or Bill Neat. There's no one else. So give me the office, and I'll promise to have him as fit as a trout on the day."

The lady laughed contemptuously.

"Do you think," said she, "that no one can fight save those who make a living by it?"

"By George, it's an amateur!" cried Cribb, in amazement. "But you don't surely ask Tom Spring to train for three weeks to meet a Corinthian?"

"I will say nothing more of who it is. It is no business of yours," the lady answered fiercely. "All I *do* say is, that if you do not train I will cast you aside and take some one who will. Do not think you can fool me because I am a woman. I have learned the points of the game as well as any man."

"I saw that the very first word you spoke," said Cribb.

"Then don't forget it. I will not warn you again. If I have occasion to find fault I shall choose another man."

"And you won't tell me who I am to fight?"

"Not a word. But you can take it from me that at your very best it will take you, or any man in England, all your time to master him. Now get back this instant to your work, and never let me find you shirking it again." With imperious eyes she looked the two strong men down, and then, turning on her heel, she swept out of the room.

The Champion whistled as the door closed behind her, and mopped his brow with his red bandanna handkerchief as he looked across at his abashed companion. "My word, lad," said he, "it's earnest from this day on."

"Yes," said Tom Spring, solemnly, "it's earnest from this day on."

In the course of the next fortnight the lady made several surprise visits to see that her champion was being properly prepared for the contest which lay before him. At the most unexpected moments she would burst into the training quarters, but never again had she to complain of any slackness upon his part or that of his trainer. With long bouts of the gloves, with thirty-mile walks, with mile runs at the back of a mail-cart with a bit of blood between the shafts, with interminable series of jumps with a skipping-rope, he was sweated down until his trainer was able to proudly proclaim that "the last ounce of tallow is off him, and he is ready to fight for his life." Only once was the lady accompanied by any one upon these visits of inspection. Upon this occasion a tall young man was her companion. He was graceful in figure, aristocratic in his bearing, and would have been strikingly handsome had it not been for some accident which had shattered his nose and broken all the symmetry of his features. He stood in silence with moody eyes and folded arms, looking at the splendid torso of the prize fighter as, stripped to the waist, he worked with his dumbbells.

"Don't you think he will do?" said the lady.

The young swell shrugged his shoulders. "I don't like it, *cara mia*. I can't pretend that I like it."

"You must like it, George. I have set my very heart on it."

"It is not English, you know. Lucrezia Borgia and medieval Italy. Woman's love and woman's hatred are always the same, but this particular manifestation of it seems to me out of place in nineteenth-century London."

"Is not a lesson needed?"

"Yes, yes; but one would think there were other ways."

"You tried another way. What did you get out of that?"

The young man smiled rather grimly, as he turned up his cuff and looked at a puckered hole in his wrist.

"Not much, certainly," said he.

"You've tried and failed."

"Yes, I must admit it."

"What else is there? The law?"

"Good gracious, no!"

"Then it is my turn, George, and I won't be balked."

"I don't think any one is capable of balking you, *cara mia*. Certainly I, for one, should never dream of trying. But I don't feel as if I could cooperate."

"I never asked you to."

"No, you certainly never did. You are perfectly capable of doing it alone. I think, with your leave, if you have quite done with your prize fighter, we will drive back to London. I would not for the world miss Goldoni in the Opera."

So they drifted away; he, frivolous and dilettante, she with her face as set as Fate, leaving the fighting men to their business.

And now the day came when Cribb was able to announce to his employer that his man was as fit as science could make him.

"I can do no more, ma'am. He's fit to fight for a kingdom. Another week would see him stale."

The lady looked Spring over with the eye of a connoisseur.

"I think he does you credit," she said at last. "Today is Tuesday. He will fight the day after tomorrow."

"Very good, ma'am. Where shall he go?"

"I will tell you exactly, and you will please take careful note of all that I say. You, Mr. Cribb, will take your man down to the Golden Cross Inn at Charing Cross by nine o'clock on Wednesday morning. He will take the Brighton coach as far as Tunbridge Wells, where he will alight at the Royal Oak Arms. There he will take such refreshment as you advise before a fight. He will wait at the Royal Oak Arms until he receives a message by word, or by letter, brought him by a groom in a mulberry livery. This message will give him his final instructions."

"And I am not to come?"

"No," said the lady.

"But surely, ma'am," he pleaded, "I may come as far as Tunbridge Wells? It's hard on a man to train a cove for a fight and then to leave him."

"It can't be helped. You are too well known. Your arrival would spread all over the town, and my plans might suffer. It is quite out of the question that you should come."

"Well, I'll do what you tell me, but it's main hard."

"I suppose," said Spring, "you would have me bring my fightin' shorts and my spiked shoes?"

"No; you will kindly bring nothing whatever which may point to your trade. I would have you wear just those clothes in which I saw you first, such clothes as any mechanic or artisan might be expected to wear."

Tom Cribb's blank face had assumed an expression of absolute despair.

"No second, no clothes, no shoes—it don't seem regular. I give you my word, ma'am, I feel ashamed to be mixed up in such a fight. I don't know as you can call the thing a fight where there is no second. It's just a scramble—nothing more. I've gone too far to wash my hands of it now, but I wish I had never touched it."

In spite of all professional misgivings on the part of the Champion and his pupil, the imperious will of the woman prevailed, and everything was carried out exactly as she had directed. At nine o'clock Tom Spring found himself upon the box-seat of the Brighton coach, and waved his hand in good-bye to burly Tom Cribb, who stood, the admired of a ring of waiters and ostlers, upon the doorstep of the Golden Cross. It was in the pleasant season when summer is mellowing into autumn, and the first golden patches are seen amid the beeches and the ferns. The young

country-bred lad breathed more freely when he had left the weary streets
of Southwark and Lewisham behind him, and he watched with delight
the glorious prospect as the coach, whirled along by six dapple greys,
passed by the classic grounds of Knowle, or after crossing Riverside Hill
skirted the vast expanse of the Weald of Kent. Past Tonbridge School
went the coach, and on through Southborough, until it wound down a
steep, curving road with strange outcrops of sandstone beside it, and
halted before a great hostelry, bearing the name which had been given
him in his directions. He descended, entered the coffee room, and ordered the under-done steak which his trainer had recommended. Hardly
had he finished it when a servant with a mulberry coat and a peculiarly
expressionless face entered the apartment.

"Beg your pardon, sir, are you Mr. Spring—Mr. Thomas Spring, of
London?"

"That is my name, young man."

"Then the instructions which I had to give you are that you wait for
one hour after your meal. After that time you will find me in a phaeton
at the door, and I will drive you in the right direction."

The young pugilist had never been daunted by any experience which
had befallen him in the ring. The rough encouragement of his backers,
the surge and shouting of the multitude, and the sight of his opponent
had always cheered his stout heart and excited him to prove himself
worthy of being the centre of such a scene. But this loneliness and
uncertainty were deadly. He flung himself down on the horsehair couch
and tried to doze, but his mind was too restless and excited. Finally he
rose, and paced up and down the empty room. Suddenly he was aware
of a great rubicund face which surveyed him from round the angle of the
door. Its owner, seeing that he was observed, pushed forward into the
room.

"I beg pardon, sir," said he, "but surely I have the honour of talking to
Mr. Thomas Spring?"

"At your service," said the young man.

"Bless me. I am vastly honoured to have you under my roof! Cordery
is my name, sir, landlord of this old-fashioned inn. I thought that my
eyes could not deceive me. I am a patron of the ring, sir, in my own
humble way, and was present at Mousley in September last, when you
beat Jack Stringer of Rawcliffe. A very fine fight, sir, and very handsomely fought, if I may make bold to say so. I have a right to an
opinion, sir, for there's never been a fight for many a year in Kent or
Sussex that you wouldn't find Joe Cordery at the ringside. Ask Mr.
Greyson at the Chop-house in Holborn, and he'll tell you about old Joe
Cordery. By the way, Mr. Spring, I suppose it is not business that has
brought you down into these parts? Any one can see with half an eye

that you are trained to a hair. I'd take it very kindly if you would give me the office."

It crossed Spring's mind that if he were frank with the landlord it was more than likely that he would receive more information than he could give. He was a man of his word, however, and he remembered his promise to his employer.

"Just a quiet day in the country, Mr. Cordery. That's all."

"Dear me! I had hoped there was a mill in the wind. I've a nose for these things, Mr. Spring, and I thought I had a whiff of it. But, of course, you should know best. Perhaps you will drive round with me this afternoon and view the hop-gardens—just the right time of year, sir."

Tom Spring was not very skilled in deception, and his stammering excuses may not have been very convincing to the landlord, or finally persuaded him that his original supposition was wrong. In the midst of the conversation, however, the waiter entered with the news that a phaeton was waiting at the door. The innkeeper's eyes shone with suspicion and eagerness.

"I thought you said you knew no one in these parts, Mr. Spring?"

"Just one kind friend, Mr. Cordery, and he has sent his gig for me. It's likely that I will take the night coach to town. But I'll look in after an hour or two and have a dish of tea with you."

Outside the mulberry servant was sitting behind a fine black horse in a phaeton, which had two seats in front and two behind. Tom Spring was about to climb up beside him, when the servant whispered that his directions were that he should sit behind. Then the phaeton whirled away, while the excited landlord, more convinced than ever that there was something in the wind, rushed into his stable yard with shrieks to his ostlers, and in a very few minutes was in hot pursuit, waiting at every crossroad until he could hear tidings of a black horse and a mulberry livery.

The phaeton meanwhile drove in the direction of Crowborough. Some miles out it turned from the high road into a narrow lane spanned by a tawny arch of beech trees. Through this golden tunnel a lady was walking, tall and graceful, her back to the phaeton. As it came abreast of her she stood aside and looked up, while the coachman pulled up the horse.

"I trust that you are at your best," said she, looking very earnestly at the prize fighter. "How do you feel?"

"Pretty tidy, ma'am, I thank you."

"I will get up beside you, Johnson. We have some way to go. You will drive through the Lower Warren, and then take the lane which skirts the Gravel Hanger. I will tell you where to stop. Go slowly, for we are not due for twenty minutes."

Feeling as if the whole business was some extraordinary dream, the young pugilist passed through a network of secluded lanes, until the phaeton drew up at a wicket gate which led into a plantation of firs, choked with a thick undergrowth. Here the lady descended and beckoned Spring to alight.

"Wait down the lane," said she to the coachman. "We shall be some little time. Now Mr. Spring, will you kindly follow me? I have written a letter which makes an appointment."

She passed swiftly through the plantation by a tortuous path, then over a stile, and past another wood, loud with the deep chuckling of pheasants. At the farther side was a fine rolling park, studded with oak trees, and stretching away to a splendid Elizabethan mansion, with balustraded terraces athwart its front. Across the park, and making for the wood, a solitary figure was walking.

The lady gripped the prize fighter by the wrist. "That is your man," said she.

They were standing under the shadow of the trees, so that he was very visible to them, while they were out of his sight. Tom Spring looked hard at the man, who was still some hundreds of yards away. He was a tall, powerful fellow, clad in a blue coat with gilt buttons, which gleamed in the sun. He had white corded breeches and riding boots. He walked with a vigorous step, and with every few strides he struck his leg with a dog whip which hung from his wrist. There was a great suggestion of purpose and of energy in the man's appearance and bearing.

"Why, he's a gentleman!" said Spring. "Look 'ere, ma'am, this is all a bit out of my line. I've nothing against the man, and he can mean me no harm. What am I to do with him?"

"Fight him! Smash him! That is what you are here for."

Tom Spring turned on his heel with disgust. "I'm here to fight, ma'am, but not to smash a man who has no thought of fighting. It's off."

"You don't like the look of him," hissed the woman. "You have met your master."

"That is as may be. It is no job for me."

The woman's face was white with vexation and anger.

"You fool!" she cried. "Is all to go wrong at the last minute? There are fifty pounds—here they are in this paper—would you refuse them?"

"It's a cowardly business. I won't do it."

"Cowardly? You are giving the man two stone, and he can beat any amateur in England."

The young pugilist felt relieved. After all, if he could fairly earn fifty pounds, a good deal depended upon his winning it. If he could only be sure that this was a worthy and willing antagonist!

"How do you know he is so good?" he asked.

"I ought to know. I am his wife."

As she spoke she turned, and was gone like a flash among the bushes. The man was quite close now, and Tom Spring's scruples weakened as he looked at him. He was a powerful, broad-chested fellow, about thirty, with a heavy, brutal face, great thatched eyebrows, and a hard-set mouth. He could not be less than fifteen stone in weight, and he carried himself like a trained athlete. As he swung along he suddenly caught a glimpse of Spring among the trees, and he at once quickened his pace and sprang over the stile which separated them.

"Halloa!" said he, halting a few yards from him, and staring him up and down. "Who the devil are you, and where the devil did you come from, and what the devil are you doing on my property?"

His manner was even more offensive than his words. It brought a flush of anger to Spring's cheeks.

"See here, mister," said he, "civil words is cheap. You've no call to speak to me like that."

"You infernal rascal!" cried the other. "I'll show you the way out of that plantation with the toe of my boot. Do you dare to stand there on my land and talk back at me?" He advanced with a menacing face and his dog whip half raised. "Well, are you going?" he cried, as he swung it into the air.

Tom Spring jumped back to avoid the threatened blow.

"Go slow, mister," said he. "It's only fair that you should know where you are. I'm Spring, the prize fighter. Maybe you have heard my name."

"I thought you were a rascal of that breed," said the man. "I've had the handling of one or two of you gentry before, and I never found one that could stand up to me for five minutes. Maybe you would like to try?"

"If you hit me with that dog whip, mister—"

"There, then!" He gave the young man a vicious cut across the shoulder. "Will that help you to fight?"

"I came here to fight," said Tom Spring, licking his dry lips. "You can drop that whip, mister, for I *will* fight. I'm a trained man and ready. But you would have it. Don't blame me."

The man was stripping the blue coat from his broad shoulders. There was a sprigged satin vest beneath it, and they were hung together on an alder branch.

"Trained, are you?" he muttered. "By the Lord, I'll train you before I am through!"

Any fears that Tom Spring may have had lest he should be taking some unfair advantage were set at rest by the man's assured manner and by the splendid physique, which became more apparent as he discarded a black satin tie, with a great ruby glowing in its centre, and threw aside the white collar which cramped his thick muscular neck. He then, very deliberately, undid a pair of gold sleeve links, and, rolling up his shirt sleeves, disclosed two hairy and muscular arms, which would have served as a model for a sculptor.

"Come nearer the stile," said he, when he had finished. "There is more room."

The prize fighter had kept pace with the preparations of his formidable antagonist. His own hat, coat, and vest hung suspended upon a bush. He advanced now into the open space which the other had indicated.

"Ruffianing or fighting?" asked the amateur, coolly.

"Fighting."

"Very good," said the other. "Put up your hands, Spring. Try it out."

They were standing facing one another in a grassy ring intersected by the path at the outlet of the wood. The insolent and overbearing look had passed away from the amateur's face, but a grim half-smile was on his lips and his eyes shone fiercely from under his tufted brows. From the way in which he stood it was very clear that he was a past master at the game. Tom Spring, as he paced lightly to right and left, looking for an opening, became suddenly aware that neither with Stringer nor with the redoubtable Painter himself had he ever faced a more businesslike opponent. The amateur's left was well forward, his guard low, his body leaning back from the haunches, and his head well out of danger. Spring tried a light lead at the mark, and another at the face, but in an instant his adversary was on to him with a shower of sledge-hammer blows which it took him all his time to avoid. He sprang back, but there was no getting away from that whirlwind of muscle and bone. A heavy blow beat down his guard, a second landed on his shoulder, and over went the prize fighter with the other on the top of him. Both sprang to their feet, glared at each other, and fell into position once more.

There could be no doubt that the amateur was not only heavier, but also the harder and stronger man. Twice again he rushed Spring down, once by the weight of his blows, and once by closing and hurling him on to his back. Such falls might have shaken the fight out of a less game man, but to Tom Spring they were but incidents in his daily trade. Though bruised and winded he was always up again in an instant. Blood was trickling from his mouth, but his steadfast blue eyes told of the unshaken spirit within.

He was accustomed now to his opponent's rushing tactics, and he was ready for them. The fourth round was the same as to attack, but it was very different in defence. Up to now the young man had given way and been fought down. This time he stood his ground. As his opponent rushed in he met him with a tremendous straight hit from his left hand, delivered with the full force of his body, and doubled in effect by the momentum of the charge. So stunning was the concussion that the pugilist himself recoiled from it across the grassy ring. The amateur staggered back and leaned his shoulder on a tree trunk, his hand up to his face.

"You'd best drop it," said Spring. "You'll get pepper if you don't."

The other gave an inarticulate curse, and spat out a mouthful of blood. "Come on!" said he.

Even now the pugilist found that he had no light task before him. Warned by his misadventure, the heavier man no longer tried to win the battle at a rush, nor to beat down an accomplished boxer as he would a country hawbuck at a village fair. He fought with his head and his feet as well as with his hands. Spring had to admit in his heart that, trained to the ring, this man must have been a match for the best. His guard was strong, his counter was like lightning, he took punishment like a man of iron, and when he could safely close he always brought his lighter antagonist to the ground with a shattering fall. But the one stunning blow which he had courted before he was taught respect for his adversary weighed heavily on him all the time. His senses had lost something of their quickness and his blows of their sting. He was fighting, too, against a man who, of all the boxers who have made their names great, was the safest, the coolest, the least likely to give anything away, or lose an advantage gained. Slowly, gradually, round by round, he was worn down by his cool, quick-stepping, sharp-hitting antagonist. At last he stood exhausted, breathing hoarsely, his face, what could be seen of it, purple with his exertions. He had reached the limit of human endurance. His opponent stood waiting for him, bruised and beaten, but as cool, as ready, as dangerous as ever.

"You'd best drop it, I tell you," said he. "You're done."

But the other's manhood would not have it so. With a snarl of fury he cast his science to the winds, and rushed madly to slogging with both hands. For a moment Spring was overborne. Then he side-stepped swiftly; there was the crash of his blow, and the amateur tossed up his arms and fell all asprawl, his great limbs outstretched, his disfigured face to the sky.

"For a moment Tom Spring stood looking down at his unconscious opponent. The next he felt a soft warm hand upon his bare arm. The woman was at his elbow.

"Now is your time!" she cried, her dark eyes aflame. "Go in! Smash him!"

Spring shook her off with a cry of disgust, but she was back in an instant.

"I'll make it seventy-five pounds—"

"The fight's over, ma'am. I can't touch him."

"A hundred pounds—a clear hundred! I have it here in my bodice. Would you refuse a hundred?"

He turned on his heel. She darted past him, and tried to kick at the face of the prostrate man. Spring dragged her roughly away, before she could do him a mischief.

"Stand clear!" he cried, giving her a shake. "You should take shame to hit a fallen man."

With a groan the injured man turned on his side. Then he slowly sat up and passed his wet hand over his face. Finally, he staggered to his feet.

"Well," he said, shrugging his broad shoulders, "it was a fair fight. I've no complaint to make. I was Jackson's favourite pupil, but I give you best." Suddenly his eyes lit upon the furious face of the woman, "Halloa, Betty!" he cried. "So I have you to thank. I might have guessed it when I had your letter."

"Yes, my lord," said she, with a mock curtsey. "You have me to thank. Your little wife managed it all. I lay behind those bushes, and I saw you beaten like a hound. You haven't had all that I had planned for you, but I think it will be some little time before any woman loves you for the sake of your appearance. Do you remember the words, my lord? Do you remember the words?"

He stood stunned for a moment. Then he snatched his whip from the ground, and looked at her from under his heavy brows.

"I believe you're the devil!" he cried.

"I wonder what the governess will think?" said she.

He flared into furious rage and rushed at her with his whip. Tom Spring threw himself before him with his arms out.

"It won't do, sir; I can't stand by."

The man glared at his wife over the prize fighter's shoulder.

"So it's for dear George's sake!" he said, with a bitter laugh. "But poor, broken-nosed George seems to have gone to the wall. Taken up with a prize fighter, eh? Found a fancy man for yourself!"

"You liar!" she gasped.

"Ha, my lady, that stings your pride, does it? Well, you shall stand together in the dock for trespass and assault. What a picture—great Lord, what a picture!"

"You wouldn't, John!"

"Wouldn't I, by—! You stay there three minutes and see if I wouldn't." He seized his clothes from the bush, and staggered off as swiftly as he could across the field, blowing a whistle as he ran.

"Quick! quick," cried the woman. "There's not an instant to lose." Her face was livid, and she was shivering and panting with apprehension. "He'll raise the country. It would be awful—awful!"

She ran swiftly down the tortuous path, Spring following after her and dressing as he went. In a field to the right a gamekeeper, his gun in his hand, was hurrying towards the whistling. Two labourers, loading hay, had stopped their work and were looking about them, their pitchforks in their hands. But the path was empty, and the phaeton awaited them, the horse cropping the grass by the lane-side, the driver half asleep on his perch. The woman sprang swiftly in and motioned Spring to stand by the wheel.

"There is your fifty pounds," she said, handing him a paper. "You were a fool not to turn it into a hundred when you had the chance. I've done with you now."

"But where am I to go?" asked the prize fighter, gazing around him at the winding lanes.

"To the devil!" said she. "Drive on, Johnson!"

The phaeton whirled down the road and vanished round a curve. Tom Spring was alone.

Everywhere over the countryside he heard shoutings and whistlings. It was clear that so long as she escaped the indignity of sharing his fate his employer was perfectly indifferent as to whether he got into trouble or not. Tom Spring began to feel indifferent himself. He was weary to death, his head was aching from the blows and falls which he had received, and his feelings were raw from the treatment which he had undergone. He walked slowly some few yards down the lane, but had no idea which way to turn to reach Tunbridge Wells. In the distance he heard the baying of dogs, and he guessed that they were being set upon his track. In that case he could not hope to escape them, and might just as well await them where he was. He picked out a heavy stake from the hedge, and he sat down moodily waiting, in a very dangerous temper, for what might befall him.

But it was a friend and not a foe who came first into sight. Round the corner of the lane flew a small dogcart, with a fast-trotting chestnut cob between the shafts. In it was seated the rubicund landlord of the Royal Oak, his whip going, his face continually flying round to glance behind him.

"Jump in, Mr. Spring, jump in!" he cried, as he reined up. "They're all coming, dogs and men! Come on! Now, hud up, Ginger!" Not another word did he say until two miles of lanes had been left behind them at racing speed and they were back in safety upon the Brighton road. Then he let the reins hang loose on the pony's back, and he slapped Tom Spring with his fat hand upon the shoulder.

"Splendid!" he cried, his great red face shining with ecstasy. "Oh, Lord! but it was beautiful!"

"What!" cried Spring. "You saw the fight?"

"Every round of it! By George! to think that I should have lived to have had such a fight all to myself! Oh, but it was grand," he cried, in a frenzy of delight, "to see his lordship go down like a pithed ox and her ladyship clapping her hands behind the bush! I guessed there was something in the wind, and I followed you all the way. When you stopped, I tethered little Ginger in a grove, and I crept after you through the wood. It's as well I did, for the whole parish was up!"

But Tom Spring was sitting, gazing at him in blank amazement.

"His lordship!" he gasped.

"No less, my boy. Lord Falconbridge, Chairman of the Bench, Deputy Lieutenant of the County, Peer of the Realm—that's your man."

"Good Lord!"

"And you didn't know? It's as well, for maybe you wouldn't have whacked it in as hard if you had; and, mind you, if you hadn't, he'd have beat you. There's not a man in this county could stand up to him. He takes the poachers and gipsies two and three at a time. He's the terror of the place. But you did him—did him fair. Oh man, it was fine!"

Tom Spring was too much dazed by what he heard to do more than sit and wonder. It was not until he had got back to the comforts of the inn, and after a bath had partaken of a solid meal, that he sent for Mr. Cordery the landlord. To him he confided the whole train of events which had led up to his remarkable experience, and he begged him to throw such light as he could upon it. Cordery listened with keen interest and many chuckles to the story. Finally he left the room and returned with a frayed newspaper in his hand, which he smoothed out upon his knee.

"It's the *Pantiles Gazette,* Mr. Spring, as gossiping a rag as ever was printed. I expect there will be a fine column in it if ever it gets its prying nose into this day's doings. However, we are mum and her ladyship is mum, and, my word! his lordship is mum, though he did, in his passion, raise the hue and cry on you. Here it is, Mr. Spring, and I'll read it to you while you smoke your pipe. It's dated July of last year, and it goes like this:

"'FRACAS IN HIGH LIFE. It is an open secret that the differences which have for some years been known to exist between Lord F——and his beautiful wife have come to a head during the last few days. His lordship's devotion to sport, and also, as it is whispered, some attentions which he has shown to a humbler member of his household, have, it is said, long alienated Lady F——'s affection. Of late she has sought consolation and friendship with a gentleman whom we will designate as Sir George W——n. Sir George, who is a famous lady-killer, and as well-proportioned a man as any in England, took kindly to the task of consoling the disconsolate fair. The upshot, however, was vastly unfortunate, both for the lady's feelings and for the gentleman's beauty. The two friends were surprised in a rendezvous near the house by Lord F—— himself at the head of a party of his servants. Lord F——then and there, in spite of the shrieks of the lady, availed himself of his strength and skill to administer such punishment to the unfortunate Lothario as would, in his own parting words, prevent any woman from loving him again for the sake of his appearance. Lady F——has left his lordship and betaken herself to London, where, no doubt, she is now engaged in nursing the damaged Apollo. It is confidently expected that a duel will result from the affair, but no particulars have reached us up to the hour of going to press.'"

The landlord laid down the paper. "You've been moving in high life, Mr. Thomas Spring," said he.

The pugilist passed his hand over his battered face. "Well, Mr. Cordery," said he, "low life is good enough for me."

THE
HARDER
THEY FALL

A Novel by
BUDD SCHULBERG

*"I sorrow'd at his captive state,
  but minded
Not to be absent at that
  spectacle."*
JOHN MILTON: Samson Agonistes

1

When I came into the story I was having a quiet conversation over a bottle of Old Taylor with my friend Charles the bartender at Mickey Walker's, the place Mickey hasn't got any more at 50th and Eighth Avenue, right across the street from the Garden. I like Charles because he always serves up a respectable two-ounce whisky and because of the talks we have about old-time fighters. Charles must know as much about the old days as Granny Rice. He must be sixty or seventy years of age, with baby-pink skin and hardly a wrinkle in his face. The only giveaway to his age is his spare white hair that he insists, for some reason, on dyeing a corny yellow. He's seen a lot of the fighters who are just names to me—legendary names like Ketchell and Gans and Mexican Joe Rivers. One of the last things he did before he left London (a faint cockney echo lingers in his speech) was to see the famous Peter Jackson-Frank Slavin fight at the National Sporting Club. This afternoon, as on so many other afternoons, we were back in the crucial twentieth round, and Charles, with his hands raised in the classical nineteenth-century boxing stance, was impersonating the dark-skinned, quiet-spoken, wonderfully poised Jackson.

"Fix the picture in your mind, sir," Charles was always saying. "Here's Jackson, a fine figure of a man, the first of the heavies to get up on his toes, faster than Louis and every bit the puncher. And here in front of him is solid Frank, a great rock of a man who's taken everything the black man had to offer and had him on the verge of a kayo in the early rounds. They're locked for a moment in a furious clinch. Jackson,

329

who's made a remarkable recovery, a miraculous recovery, sir, breaks away and nails old Frank with a right that travels just this far—" Charles demonstrated, reaching over the bar and rapping me sharply on the side of the jaw—"just that far."

At this point in the battle Charles switched sides. He had been in vaudeville once, and during the early days of the Depression he had picked up a couple of bucks playing butlers on Broadway. He should be paying regular dues to Actors Equity because he's acting all the time. Now he was the staggering, glassy-eyed Slavin, reeling back from Jackson's short punishing blow. "Fix the picture in your mind, sir," he repeated. His chin was resting on his chest and his body had gone limp. "His hands are at his side, he can't raise his head or lift his feet, but he won't go down. Peter Jackson hits him again, and Frank is helpless to defend himself, but he won't go down. He just stands there with his arms at his side, waiting to be hit again. He's made quite a boast of it before the fight, you see, sir, that there's no nigger in the world good enough to make Frank Slavin quit to him. I never use the word 'nigger' myself, you understand, sir, I'm just trying to give you the picture as it was. In my business, you see, sir, I judge a man by the color of his deeds, not the color of his skin. This Peter Jackson, for instance. A finer sportsman never climbed through the ropes than this dark gentleman from Australia."

Now Charles was Jackson again, magnificently proud and erect as the crowd waited for him to finish off his battered opponent. "But at this moment, a memorable thing happened, sir. Instead of rushing in and clubbing the helpless Slavin to the canvas, Jackson stood back, risking the chance that Slavin with his bull-strength might recover, and turned to the referee. You could hear his calm, deep voice all the way back to where I was sitting, sir. Sounded more like a preacher than a fighter, he did. 'Must I finish him off, Mr. Angle?' he said. 'Box on,' said Mr. Angle. Black Peter turned back to his man again. In spite of all those taunts about the color of his skin, you could see he had no stomach for the job. He tapped Frank on the chin once, twice, three times—little stiff punches that would put him away without breaking his jaw—and finally on the fourth, down went old Frank, cold as the proverbial mackerel, for all his boasts. And all the gentlemen who had come to the Sporting Club to see the white man get the better of the black couldn't help rising to their feet and giving Jackson one of the longest rounds of applause that had ever been heard in the Sporting Club."

"Give me another shot," I said. "Charles, you're wonderful. Did you really see the Jackson-Slavin fight?"

"Would I lie to you, Mr. Lewis?"

"Yes," I said. "You told me you were one of Joe Choynski's handlers the time he fought Corbett on that barge off San Francisco. Well, over on Third Avenue I found an old picture of Choynski and Corbett with their handlers just before the fight. You don't seem to be in it."

Charles uncorked the Old Taylor again and poured me another one. "You see, a man of my word," he said. "Every time you catch me in an inaccuracy, Mr. Lewis, I buy you a drink."

"An inaccuracy is an accidental mistake," I said. "What I caught you in, Charles, was a good old-fashioned lie."

"Please, Mr. Lewis," said Charles, deeply offended. "Don't use that word. I may on occasion, for dramatic emphasis, fib. But I never lie. A lie is a thief, sir, and will steal from anybody. A fib just borrows a little from people who can afford it and forgets to pay them back."

"But you actually saw this Jackson-Slavin fight?"

"Say 'bout,' sir, the Jackson-Slavin bout. You'd never hear a gentleman calling a boxing contest a fight."

"Here on Eighth Avenue," I said, "a gentleman is a fellow who calls a woman a broad instead of something else."

"It is unfortunately true," Charles agreed. "The gentlemen in the pugilism business are conspicuous by their abstinence."

"That includes me in," I said. "What do I owe you for this week, Charles?"

"I'll tell you before you leave," Charles said. He never liked to talk about money. He would always scribble the amount on the back of a tab and then slip it under my glass like a secret message.

A sharply dressed, nervous-looking little man stuck his head in the door. "Hey, Charley—you seen the Mumbler?"

"Not today, Mr. Miniff."

"Jeez, I gotta find him," the little man said.

"If he shows up I'll tell him you're looking for him," Charles told him.

"T'anks," said Miniff. "You're m' boy." He disappeared.

Charles shook his head. "It's a sad day, Mr. Lewis, a sad day."

I looked at the big oval clock over the door. A little after three. Time for Charles' over-the-bar address on the decline and fall of the manly art. "The people who come into this place," Charles began. "Grifters, chiselers, two-bit gamblers, big-time operators with small-time minds, managers who'd rather see their boys get killed than make an honest living and boxers who've taken so many dives they've got hinges on their knees. In the old days, sir, it was a rough game but it had some . . . some character to it, some dignity. Take Choynski and Corbett fighting on that barge. Skin gloves on Choynski, two-ouncers on Corbett, to a finish. No fancy percentages, no non-title business, just winner take all, may the best man win. A man squared off for his own pride in those days. He was an athlete. If he made a little money at it, fine and dandy. But what have we got today? Champions with mobsters for managers who stall for years fighting over-weight bouts because they know the first time they climb into the ring with a good man it's good-bye, championship."

Charles turned around to see if the boss was watching and had one himself. The only time I ever saw him take one was when we were alone and he got going on this decline-and-fall thing.

He washed his glass and wiped it clean, to destroy the evidence, and looked at me steadily. "Mr. Lewis, what is it that turned a fine sport into a dirty business?"

"Money," I said.

"It's money," he went on, as if he hadn't heard me. "Money. Too much money for the promoters, too much money for the managers, too much money for the fighters."

"Too much money for everybody except the press agents," I said. I was feeling sorrier for myself at the moment than I was for the game. That's what the bottle always did to me.

"I tell you, Mr. Lewis, it's money," Charles was saying. "An athletic sport in an atmosphere of money is like a girl from a good family in a house of ill fame."

I pulled out the gold-banded fountain pen Beth had given me for my birthday, and made a couple of notes on what Charles was saying. He was made to order for that play I was going to write, the play on the fight game I had been talking about so long, the one Beth seemed to be so sure I was never going to finish. "Don't spill it all out in talk," she was always saying. Damn Beth and her bright sayings. If I had had any sense I would have found myself a nice dumb broad. But if I could only set the play down the way I felt it sometimes, in all its sweaty violence —not a nine-dollar bill like *Golden Boy*—no violinists with brittle hands, no undigested poetry subtle as a train wreck, but the kids from the street as they really were, mean and money-hungry, and the greed of the mobsters who had the game rigged; that was the guts of it and I was the boy to write it.

One solid job could justify all the lousy years I had frittered away as a press agent for champions, deserved and otherwise, contenders and bums, plenty of the latter. You see, that play would tell Beth, I haven't really fallen so low as you thought. All the time it seemed as if I were prostituting myself by making with the adjectives for Honest Jimmy Quinn and Nick (The Eye) Latka, the well-known fistic entrepreneurs, I was actually soaking up material for my masterpiece. Just as O'Neill spent all those years as a common sailor and Jack London was on the bum.

Like O'Neill and London. It always made me feel better to make those notes. My pockets were full of notes. There were notes in every drawer of my desk at the hotel. The notes were kind of an escape valve for all the time I wasted getting loaded, cutting up touches with Charles, sitting around with the boys, going up to Shirley's, and ladling out the old craperoo about how old Joe Round-heels, who couldn't lick my grandfather and who had just been put away in two over at the Trenton Arena, was primed (I would be starving to death without that word *primed*) to give Jack Contender the fight of his life.

"What are you doing there, Mr. Lewis?" Charles said. "Not writing down something I say."

A good bartender, Charles never pried into his customer's affairs. But he was beginning to break down with me because he liked the idea of getting into my play. I wish Beth had as much faith in me as Charles. "You know what you ought to do, you ought to quit leaning on your elbows and get to work," she was always saying. But Charles was different. He'd tell me something and then he'd say, "You ought to put *that* in your play." We talked about it so long that my work of art came to have a real identity. "If you're going to put me in your show," Charles would say, "please call me Charles. I like to be called Charles. My mother always called me Charles. Charley sounds like—a puppet, or a fat man."

The door swung open and Miniff popped his head in again. "Hey, Charley, still no signa the Mumbler?"

Charles shook his head gravely. "No signa the Mumbler whatsoever, Mr. Miniff." Charles was a snob. It gave him pleasure to exercise his talent for mimicry at the expense of his ungrammatical clientele. Miniff came in and climbed up on the stool next to mine. His small feet didn't reach the footrest at the base of the stool. He pushed his brown felt hat back on his head desperately. He ran his hands over his face and shook his head a few times, his fingers covering his eyes. He was tired. New York is hot when you run around all day.

"Have one with me, Miniff," I said. He waved me off with a small, hairy hand.

"Just the juice of the cow," he said. "Gotta keep my ulcer quiet." From his breast pocket he took a couple of short, stubby cigars, shoved one into his mouth and offered the other one around.

"No, thanks," I said. "If I smoked those six-for-a-quarters I'd have ulcers too. If I'm going to have them, I want expensive ulcers, bottled in bond."

"Listen," Miniff said, "it ain't the hemp. It's the headaches I got. Nervous digestion." He drank his milk carefully, letting it trickle slowly down his throat for maximum therapeutic effect.

"Jeez, I gotta find the Mumbler," he said. The Mumbler was Solly Hyman, the matchmaker for St. Nick's. "I looked everywhere already, Lindy's, both of them, Sam's. Up at Stillman's I hear Furrone can't go Tuesday. Gotta bad toot'. Jeez, I gotta guy to take his place. My bum'll look good in there."

"Who you got, Mr. Miniff?" Charles said, still mimicking.

"Cowboy Coombs."

"Oh, my God," I said.

"He can still go," said Miniff. "I tell ya he c'n stay three-four rounds with the shine, maybe go the limit."

"Cowboy Coombs," I said. "The grandfather of all the bums."

"So he ain't no Tooney," Miniff said.

"Fifteen years ago, he wasn't Tunney," I said.

Miniff pushed his hat back an inch or two on his forehead. His forehead was shiny with perspiration. This Cowboy Coombs thing was no joke. It was a chance to hustle a fast fifty. The way Miniff works he picks up some down-and-outer or some new kid from the amateurs and he angles a spot or two for him, if he can. It's strictly quick turnover. If the bum goes down, Miniff can't do anything more for him anyway. If the kid is good, smarter managers with better "ins" always steal him away. So for Miniff it's mostly a substitution business, running in a bum or a novice at the last minute, so the box office doesn't have to buy the tickets back, or picking up a quiet C by arranging for one of his dive-artists to do an el foldo.

"Listen, Eddie," Miniff said to me, working all the time, "Coombs has got a wife and five kids and they gotta eat. All he's been doin' is spar work the last year or two. The bum needs a break. You could maybe write up something in one of the rags about him. How he got canned for settin' the Champ down in a workout...."

"That's not the way I heard he got canned," I said.

"All right, all right, so it happened a little different, maybe the Champ slipped. I suppose you never write stuff it ain't a hunert percent kosher!"

"Mr. Miniff, you impugn my integrity," I said. The stuff a guy will write to pay his rent and keep himself in whisky! The things a guy will do for 100 bucks a week in America! Eddie Lewis, who spent almost two years at Princeton, got A's in English, had a by-line in the Trib and has twenty-three pages of a play that is being systematically devoured by a little book club of hungry moths who can't tell a piece of literature from a square meal.

"Go on, Eddie, for a pal," Miniff pleaded. "Just one little lineroo about how the Cowboy is back in great shape. You could work it into almost any colyum. They go for your crap."

"Don't give me that Cowboy Coombs," I said. "Coombs was ready for the laughing academy when you had to talk through a little hole in the door to get a drink. The best thing that could happen to Mrs. Coombs and those five kids is for you to climb down off Mr. Coombs' back and let him go to work for a change."

"Aaaah," said Miniff, and the sound was so bitter it could have been his ulcer talking. "Don't sell that Coombs short. He c'n still lick half the heavyweights in the business right now. Whadcha thinka that?"

"I think half the heavyweights in the business should also climb back on their trucks," I said.

"Aaaaaah," Miniff said. He finished the milk, wiped his lips with his sleeve, pulled some of the wet, loose leaves from the end of his cigar-butt, stuck it back between his teeth again, pulled down the brim of his old brown hat, said, "Take it easy, Eddie, see ya, Charley," and got out in a hurry.

I drank slowly, letting the good warm feeling fan out gradually from my belly. The Harry Miniffs of the world! No, that was taking in too much territory. America. Harry Miniff was American. He had an Italian name or an Irish name or a Jewish name or an English name, but you would never find an Italian in Italy, a Jew in Palestine, an Irishman in Ireland or an Englishman in England with the nervous system and social behavior of the American Harry Miniff. You could find Miniffs everywhere, not just the fight game but show business, radio, movies, the rackets, wholesale houses, building trades, blackjack unions, advertising, politics, real estate, insurance—a disease of the American heart—successful Harry Miniffs, pushing their way to the top of steel institutes, oil combines, film studios, fight monopolies; and unsuccessful Harry Miniffs, born with the will but not the knack to catch up with the high dollar that keeps tempting them on like a mechanical rabbit which the whippet can't catch unless the machine breaks down, and can't eat if it does.

"The last one in the bottle, Mr. Lewis," Charles said. "On the house."

"Thanks," I said. "You're an oasis, Charles. An Eighth Avenue oasis."

Someone in a booth had dropped a nickel in the juke slot. It was the only good record in the box, the Bechet version of "Summertime." The haunting tone of Sidney's clarinet took over the place. I looked around to see if it was Shirley. She was always playing it. She was sitting in a booth by herself, listening to the music.

"Hi, Shirley, didn't hear you come in."

"I saw you was talking with Miniff," she said. "Didn't want to interrupt a big important conversation like that."

She had been around for ten or twelve years, but there was still a little Oklahoma left in her speech. She came to town with her husband, Sailor

Beaumont—remember Billy Beaumont?—when he was on the up-
swing, after he had licked everything in the West and was coming to
New York for a shot at the bigtime. He was the boy who crossed the
wise money by going in on the short end of 10–1 to win the welterweight title. He and Shirley rode pretty high for a while. The Sailor was
an unreconstructed reform-school graduate from West Liberty who threw
most of his dough into such routine channels as the fleshpots, the ponies
and the night spots. All the rest went for motorcycles. He had a white
streamlined motorcycle with a sidecar on which, if you were good at
reading print cutting through downtown traffic at sixty miles an hour,
you could make out the words "Sailor Beaumont, the Pride of West
Liberty." That's the kind of a fellow he was. Lots of times, especially in
the beginning when they were still getting along together, I remember
Shirley riding in that sidecar, with her dark red hair flying out behind
her. She was something to look at in those days, before the beers and the
troubles caught up with her. You could still see some of it left, even with
the crow's-feet around the eyes and the telltale washed-out look that
comes from doing too many things too many times. She still had something from the neck down too, even if her pinup days were ten years
behind. She was beginning to spread, just this much, in the rump, the
belly and the bust, but there was something about the way she held
herself—sometimes I thought it was more in her attitude toward men
than anything physical—that made us still turn around.

"Have one with me, Shirley?" I called over.

"Save it, Eddie," she said.

"Not even two fingers, to be sociable?"

"Oh, I don't know, maybe a beer," Shirley said.

I gave Charles the order and went over to the booth. "Waiting for
anyone?"

"For you, darling," she said, sarcastic. She didn't bother to look at
me.

"What's the matter? Hung?"

"Aah, not really, just, oh, the hell with it . . ."

Shirley was in a mood. She got that way every now and then. Most of
the time she was feeling good, a lot of laughs—"What the hell, I'm not
getting any richer and I'm not getting any younger, but I'm having fun."
But once in a while, especially when you caught her alone in the daytime, she was this way. After it got dark and she had had a few, it would
be better. But I've seen her sit there in a booth for hours, having solitary
beers and dropping nickels in the slot, playing "Summertime" or "Melancholy Baby" or another of her favorites, "Embraceable You." I suppose those songs had something to do with the Sailor, though it always
struck me as profane to associate the tender sentiments of those excellent

lyrics with a screwball slugger like Beaumont. He'd lay anything that stood still for thirty seconds. If Shirley even asked for an explanation she got it—on the jaw. He was one of the few professionals I ever knew who indulged in spontaneous extracurricular bouts in various joints, a practice which did not endear him to Jacobs' Beach and brought him frequently and forcibly to the attention of the local gendarmerie. When he finally had a blowout on that hotcha motorcycle of his and left in a bloody mess on the curb at Sixth Avenue near 52nd Street what few brains he had salvaged from ninety-three wide-open fights, the people who took it hard could be counted on one finger of one hand, and that was Shirley.

She reached into her large red-leather purse, took out a little white bag of fine cut tobacco, carefully tapped it out onto a small rectangle of thin brown paper with a practiced hand. She was the only woman I had ever seen roll her own cigarettes. It was one of the habits she brought with her from the hungry years in West Liberty. While she twirled the flat wrapper into an amazingly symmetrical cylinder, she stared absently through the glass that looked out on Eighth Avenue. The street was full of people moving restlessly back and forth in two streams like ants, but with less purpose. "Summertime," she sang under her breath lackadaisically, a snatch here and a snatch there.

The beer seemed to do something for her. "You can draw me another one, Charles," she said, coming up out of her mood a little, "with a rye chaser."

After all these years, that was still one of the pub's favorite jokes. Shirley looked at me and smiled as if she were seeing me for the first time.

"Where you been keeping yourself, Eddie? Over in Bleeck's with my rival again?"

This had been going on for years. It had been going on so long there probably was something in it. Shirley was all right. I liked the way she was about men. She never really let you forget that there were anatomical differences between you, and yet she didn't make a conflict of it. I liked the way she had been about Sailor Beaumont, even if he was a wrongo. There were so many American wives who gave most of their energy to trying to make their husbands vice-presidents or head buyers or something. Twice a week they did him a big favor. That was called being a good wife. Shirley, if she hadn't fallen in love with an irresponsible, physically precocious kid who came in wide-open but had a knockout punch in his right hand, would have made somebody in West Liberty an exceptional wife instead of making Eighth Avenue an exceptional madame.

"Favor us with your presence this week, Eddie," she said. "Come in early and I'll have Lucille fry us some chicken and we'll play a little gin."

"Maybe Friday night, before the Glenn-Lesnevich fight," I said.

"That kid Glenn! A jerk thing Nick did, bringing him along so fast," Shirley said. "Those overgrown boys who get up in the heavy dough because they can sock and can take it—thinking they're King of the May because they got their names in lights outside the Garden, when all they got is a one-way ticket to Queer Street. Glenn draws four good gates to the Garden because the customers know he's going to try, gets himself slapped around by men he's got no business in the same ring with, goes back to LA to be a lousy runner for a bookie or something, and the manager gets himself another boy. That's what he did with Billy. Nick Latka, that crumb!"

"Nick ain't so bad," I said. "Pays me every Friday, doesn't look over my shoulder too much, kind of an interesting feller, too."

"So is a cockroach interesting if it's got Nick's money in the bank," Shirley said. "Nick is marked lousy in my book because he don't look out for his boys. When he has a good one, he's got the dough and the connections to get him to the top, but down under that left breast pocket, he's got nothing there for the boys. Not like George Blake, Pop Foster. Their old boys were always coming back for a touch, a little advice. Nick, when you're winning nothing's too good for you. You're out to that estate over in Jersey every weekend. But when you're out of gas, that's all, brother. You got about as much chance of getting into that office as into a pay toilet without a nickel. I know. I was all through that already, with Billy. And how many has he had since Billy? And now Glenn. And next week maybe some skinny-legged speedball from the Golden Gloves. They're so pretty when they start, Eddie. I hate to see 'em run down."

Now that Billy was gone, I think Shirley was in love with all fighters. She loved them when they were full of bounce and beans, with their hard trim bodies moving gracefully in their first tailor-made full-cut doublebreasteds with peg-top trousers narrowing at the ankles in a modified zoot. And she loved them when the shape of their noses was gone, their ears cauliflowered, scar tissue drawing back their eyes, when they laughed too easily and their speech faltered and they talked about the comeback that Harry Miniff or one of his thousand-and-one cousins was lining up for them. Lots of ladies have loved winning fighters, the Grebs, the Baers, the Golden Boys, but it was the battered ones, the humiliated, the washed-ups, the TKO victims with the stitches in their lips and through their eyelids that Shirley took to her bosom. Maybe it was her way of getting Billy back, the Sailor Beaumont of his last year, when the younger, stronger, faster boys who did their training on Eighth

Avenue instead of on 52nd Street were making him look slow and foolish and sad.

"Well, first one today," Shirley said, and tossed it off, exaggerating
the shudder for a laugh.

She reached into her purse again and took out a very small Brownie
snapshot, slightly overexposed, of a wellset-up kid grinning under a
ten-gallon hat.

"New picture of my kid the folks just sent me."

While I took a dutiful hinge at it she said, "He's the image of Billy.
Isn't he a doll?"

He did look like Beaumont—the same overdevelopment from the
waist up, with the legs tapering down nicely. On his face was a look of
cheerful viciousness.

"He'll be nine next month," Shirley said. "He's with his grandparents
on a ranch near home. He wants to be a veterinary. I don't care what he
does, as long as he stays out of the ring. He can be a card player or a
drummer or a pimp if he wants to. But, by God, if I ever hear that he's
turning out to be a fighter like his old man, I'll go home and kick his
little annyfay for him."

2

When I am in a pub and the phone is for me I am never too happy about
it. It means the natural rhythm of my day is about to be interrupted by
the unexpected. Shirley had gone back to the place, "to make a new girl
feel at home," as she put it, and Beth had dropped in to pick me up. She
was annoyed because I was slightly swizzled when she came in. Beth
wasn't WCTU or anything, but she liked me to do my drinking with her.
She thought I wasted too much time shooting the breeze with Charles
and Shirley and the other characters. If my job didn't take up all my
time, she said, I should plant myself in the room at the hotel and try to
finish that play.

The big mistake I made with Beth was that once when I had her up to
my room—in the days when I still had to impress her—I showed her
that unfinished first act. Beth didn't have too much to say about it,
except for wanting me to get it done. That was the trouble with Beth: she
always wanted me to finish things. I proposed to her once in a drunken
moment and I think secretly she always held it against me for not mentioning the proposal again when I sobered up. I guess she just wanted
me to finish whatever I started.

When I first met her, Beth was fresh out of Smith College, where her
Phi Beta key had been good for a $25-a-week job with *Life,* in their

training squad for researchers. Everything she knew came out of books. Her old man taught economics at Amherst and her old lady was the daughter of a Dartmouth dean. So when I first began to tell her about the boxing business, she thought it was fascinating. That's the word she used for this business—fascinating. This fight talk was a new kind of talk for Beth, and all the time she was professing to despise it, I could tell it was getting to her. Even if only as a novelty, it was getting to her and I was the ideal interpreter of this new world that repelled and attracted her. That's how I got to Beth myself. I was just enough of a citizen of this strange new world to excite her and yet—since Beth could never completely recover from her snobberies, intellectual and otherwise—there was just enough Ivy still clinging to me, just enough Cottage Club, just enough ability to relate the phenomenon of prize fighting to her academic vocabulary to make me acceptable.

I think my talking about trying to write a play on boxing gave her a justification for being interested in me, just as it seemed to justify my staying in the game.

But this is taking us back a year and a half. It's almost another story. In the story I am telling here, Beth is miffed again—her impatience with me had been increasing lately—and somebody wants me on the telephone.

It was Killer Menegheni. Killer was a combined bodyguard, companion, masseur and private secretary to Nick. I don't really think the Killer had ever been responsible for anybody's funeral, but the legend had sprung up that the Killer would have been a featherweight champ if he hadn't killed a man in the ring his third time out. I had looked it up, but no Menegheni, and the *Ring Record Book* almost always gives the boys' right names in parentheses under their professional names. Nat Fleischer, that eminent historian, had never heard of him either. So you could take heavy odds that the Killer's alleged mayhem had no resemblance to any character living or dead, as they always say.

"Hey, Eddie, d' boss wants ya."

"Now, goddamit, Killer," I said. "I'm with a lady. Can't a man settle down to a little companionate drinking without Nick putting his hounds on me?"

"The boss wants ya to get your ass up here," Killer answered. Take away those three- and four-letter essential Anglo-Saxon words and Mr. Menegheni would have to talk with his fingers.

"But this lady and I have plans for the evening," I said. "I don't have to come running every time Nick lifts a finger. Who does he think he is?"

"He thinks he's Nick Latka," said the Killer. "And I never seen d' day he wasn't right."

For the Killer, that was considerable repartee. "Say, you're pretty sharp today," I said.

"Why not?" the Killer said. "I scored with that redhead from the Chez Paris last night. Just seventeen years old. Beauteeful."

The Killer, only five-six in his built-up shoes, was always flashing us the latest news of his daily conquests.

"You would make a good legman for Krafft-Ebing," I said.

"I ain't changing places with nobody. I do all right with Nick."

"Well, I'm glad you're happy," I said. "Pleasant weekend, Killer."

"Hey-hey-hey, wait a minnut," the Killer said quickly. "This deal what the boss wants to see you about. It must be very hot. I'll tellum yer on yer way up."

"Listen," I said, "you can tell him for me"—O Lord, the fear that eats into a man for a hundred bucks a week—"I'll be up in fifteen minutes."

I started back to the booth to break it to Beth. She was always turning down good things to keep Saturday night for me. Saturday nights we'd usually hit our favorite spots together, Bleeck's and Tim's and when we wanted music, Nick's for Spanier and Russell and Brunis, and Downtown Café Society, when Red Allen was there, and J. C. Higginbotham. Sunday morning we'd wake up around ten, send down for coffee and lie around with the papers until it was time to go out for lunch. Beth would kick about the *News,* the *Mirror* and the *Journal* because she was a pretty hot liberal as well as a snob, but some of my best plants were picked up by the tabs and I liked to read the *Journal* for Graham, one of the town's oldest and hardest-working sportswriters.

I don't know if it was love with me or not, but I'll put it this way: I never slept with anybody I was so glad to see in the morning as Beth Reynolds. I've known other girls who were more beautiful, more passionate or more experimental, but who turned out to be a drag in the morning. With Beth, having a drink, seeing a fight, listening to Spanier, going to bed, nursing each other's hangovers, arguing about Wolfe and getting sore at some new stupidity of some old senator's—it was all one, all good, all close, and when you are pushing into your middle thirties and beginning to need a slow count to get up in the morning, that outweighs the dime-a-dozen ecstasies.

Not that Beth wasn't exciting enough, in her own way. She met you with a small, intense passion that seemed surprisingly wanton for a girl with a pretty-plain schoolteacher face, who couldn't see very well without her glasses. I hadn't been her "first man" (Beth's words, naturally, not mine), for that honor had been reserved for an Amherst boy from a distinguished Boston family who had been madly and incompetently in love with her. He had made such a mess of things, apparently, that she had shied away from further intimacies until I came along. I don't quite know yet how I got her to try again. She just decided it for herself one evening. It was the night we had gone back to her apartment after I had taken her to see her first fight. I think she always distrusted me a little for helping make it so successful. That academic, puritanical background didn't stop her from enjoying herself. It just prevented her from respecting herself for what she had allowed herself to do. That's why, when she took off her glasses and the other encumbrances, she was wanton. For only the true Puritan can know that delicious sense of falling from grace that we call wantonness.

More than once, in my cups, I had proposed that we make an honorable girl of Beth. She didn't approve of the way we were living, but she always preferred to wait and see if a similar offer would be forthcoming under the influence of sobriety. But somehow I could never quite muster up enough marital determination to make a legitimate proposal without the nudge of friendly spirits. The closest I could ever come was to say, with what was meant for levity, "Beth, if I ever marry anyone, it's got to be you."

"If you insist on prefacing all your proposals with the conditional conjunctive," she had answered, "you will end up a lecherous old bachelor and I will end up married to Herbert Ageton."

Herbert Ageton was a playwright who had written militant proletarian dramas for the Theater Union back in the early thirties, when he was just out of college and hardly knew how to keep his pipe lit. Much to his horror and indignation, MGM had bought one of his radical plays, and brought him out to adapt it. When he got up to two thousand dollars a week he was analyzed at one hundred dollars an hour by a highly successful female practitioner who made him realize that his proletarian protest against capitalism was only a substitute for his hatred of his father. Somehow the signals got crossed and he came out still hating his father but feeling somewhat more kindly toward capitalism. Since that time he had only been on Broadway twice, with symbolic plays about sex relations which all the critics had panned and all the studios had scrambled for. They turned out to make very good pictures for Lana Turner. Or maybe I was just jealous. Herbert used to call Beth from Hollywood all the time. And every time he came to town he took her to "21" and the Stork and the other meeting places of good-time counter-revolutionists and their opposite numbers.

"Baby," I said, when I got back to the booth, "this is lousy, but I've got to go up and see Nick a minute."

"A minute. Nick and his minutes! You will probably end up out in Jersey at his country place."

That had happened once and Beth would never let me forget it. I had left a message for her at Walker's, but by the time it got through she had taken an angry powder.

"No," I said, "this is strictly business. If I'm not back in one hour..."

"Don't make it too drastic," she said. "If you're back in one hour it will be the first time. You know I could have gone out with Herbert tonight."

"Oh, Jesus, that again."

"How many times have I told you not to say 'Jesus'? It offends people."

"Oh Je—I don't mean Jesus Christ. I just mean Jesus Ageton."

"He's an interesting guy. He wanted me to have dinner at '21' and then come back to his hotel and hear his new play."

"What hotel? Don't tell me. The Waldorf?"

"Hampshire House."

"The poor kid. Have you ever slept with anybody in the Hampshire House?"

"Edwin, when I get you home toinght, I'm going to wash your mouth out with soap."

"Okay, okay, be evasive. Sit tight, honey. I'll go up and see what the Big Brain has on his larcenous mind."

The office of Nick Latka wasn't the tawdry fight manager's office you may have seen on the stage or that can actually be found along 49th Street. It was the office of a highly successful businessman who happened to have an interest in the boxing business, but who might have been identified with show business, shirts, insurance or the F.B.I. The walls of brown cork were covered with pictures of famous fighters, ball players, golfers, jockeys and motion-picture stars inscribed "to my pal Nick," "to a great guy," "to the best pal I had in Miami." On the desk was a box of cigars, Nick's brand, Belindas, and pictures in gold-plated frames of his wife when she was a lovely brunette in a Broadway chorus, and their two children, a handsome, conceited-looking boy of twelve in a military-school uniform, who took after his mother, and a dark-complexioned girl of ten who bore an unfortunate resemblance to her father. Nick would give those kids anything he had. The boy was away at New York Military Academy. The girl went to Miss Brindley's, one of the most expensive schools in the city.

No matter how he talked in the gym, Nick never used a vulgar word in the presence of those kids. Nick had come up from the streets, rising in ordinary succession from the kid gangs to the adolescent gangs that jimmied the gum and candy machines to the real thing. But his kids were being brought up in a nice clean money-insulated world.

"I don't want for Junior to be a mug like me," Nick would say. "I had to quit school in the third grade and go out and hustle papers to help my old man. I want Junior to go to West Point and be an Air Corps officer or maybe Yale and make a connection with high-class people."

Class! That was the highest praise in Nick's vocabulary. In the mouth of a forty-year-old East Side hood, who had been raised in a cold-water flat and wore patched hand-me-downs of his older brother, class became an appraisal of inverted snobbery, indicating a quality of excellence the East Side could neither afford nor understand. A fighter could run up a string of six knockouts and still Nick's judgment might be, "He wins, but he's got no class." A girl we'd see in a restaurant might not be pretty enough to get into the row at the Copacabana, but Nick would nudge me and say, "There's a tomato with class." Nick's suits, tailored by Bernard Weatherill, had class. The office had class. And I remember, of all the Christmas cards I received, picking out one that was light brown with the name tastefully engraved in the lower right-hand corner in conservative ten-point. That was Nick's. I don't know how he happened to choose it or who designed it for him, but it obviously had class.

If Nick thought you had it, he could be a very respectful fellow. I remember once he was chairman of a benefit fight card for the infantile-paralysis fund and had himself photographed turning over the take to Mrs. Roosevelt. This picture, autographed by Eleanor, hung in a position of honor over his head, right next to Count Fleet. The boys used to get a laugh out of that. You can imagine the gags, especially if you are a Republican and/or have a nasty mind. But Nick wouldn't have any of it. Anybody throwing them low and inside at Mrs. R. was sure to get the back of his hand. And it wasn't just because Nick's partner was Honest Jimmy Quinn who had the Tammany connections. Mrs. Roosevelt and Count Fleet belonged up there together, the way Nick saw it, because they both had class.

Nick had made a good living prying open the coin boxes of nickel machines when most of us were home reading the Bobbsey Twins and he had already escaped from the Boys Correction Farm when you and I were still struggling with first-year Latin. By dint of conscientious avoidance of physical work, a nose for easy money, and constant application of the principle Do Unto Others As You Would Not Have Them Do Unto You, he had worked himself up to the top of a syndicate that dealt anonymously but profitably with artichokes, horses, games of chance, women, meat, fighters and hotels, a series of commodities which in our free-for-all enterprise system could be parlayed into tidy fortunes for Nick and Quinn, with large enough chunks for the boys to keep everybody happy. But he was still a sucker for class, whether it was a horse, a human being or a Weatherill sports suit.

The reason he kept me on the payroll, I think, was because he thought I had it too. He had the self-made man's confusion of respect and contempt toward anybody who had read a couple of books and knew when to use *me* and when to say *I*. But whenever he was with me I noticed he cut the profanity down to those words he just didn't have any respectable synonym for. Even Quinn, who had worked himself up through a logical sequence from ward boss to high-level rackets, didn't always get the velvet-glove treatment. And when Nick was dealing with what he considered his inferiors, fighters, other managers, bookies, collectors, trainers, honest but intimidated merchants, the only way to describe his talk would be to compare it with the vicious way Fritzie Zivic used to fight, especially when he was sore, as in the return match with poor Bummy Davis after Bummy had got himself disqualified for conduct even less becoming a gentleman than Zivic's.

Probably the biggest mistake that Nick had ever made in picking class was very close to home. It was his wife Ruby. When Nick was in the liquor business back in Prohibition he had sat in the same seat for George White's *Scandals* twenty-seven times because Ruby was in it. Where Ruby had it over the rest of the line was she was beautiful in an unusually quiet way, like a young matron who would look more at home in a Junior League musical than in a Broadway leg-show. On stage, so the boys tell me, even in the scantiest, she carried herself with an air of aloof respectability which had the actual effect of an intense aphrodisiac. The other girls could dance half naked in front of you and, if you thought about anything, you'd wonder how much it would cost. But seeing Ruby with her black lace stockings forming a sleek and silken path to her crotch was like opening the wrong bedroom door by mistake and catching your best friend's sister.

That's the effect Ruby had on Nick. And the physiological accident that gave Ruby Latka an austere beauty was accompanied by a personality adjustment that developed a quiet, superior manner to go along with the face. The combination drove all other women out of Nick's life. Until then he had been giving the Killer competition, but from the first time he had Ruby he lined up with that small, select group who believe in monogamy and that even more select group who practice it. In fact, the first three years of his marriage Nick had it so bad he hardly ever bothered to look at another woman's legs. Even now, in an environment which, to put it euphemistically, smiled on adultery, Nick never cheated on Ruby unless it was something very special and he was a long way from home. But the ordinary stuff that was always there, the showgirls and the wives who float around the bars when their husbands are out of town, Nick never bothered with. The ones who simply wouldn't have minded never got a play, and the ones who had already made up their minds almost always got the brush. Most of it was the way he felt about Ruby. But what made it easier was the way he worked. He was all the time working, in the clinches, between rounds, always moving in, throwing punches, heeling, butting, elbowing, like Harry Miniff, only it was done on the top floor of a great office building and it wasn't for nickels but for very fancy folding money.

There was a glutton's hunger for money in him. Maybe it was the pinched childhood, the gutter struggle, the fearful itch of insecurity that drove Nick on to his first hundred thousand and his second. And now, without even letting him sit down to catch his breath and enjoy himself a minute, he was pushing toward his third. If it hadn't been for Ruby, Nick would never have had that place in Jersey with the riding horses and the swimming pool and the terraced barbecue pit. Ruby, who had been a working girl all her life, found no trouble at all in double-clutching into a life of leisurely hedonism. Nick would enjoy a swim when Ruby nagged him into it. He liked to get some of the boys out for the weekend and sit up until Sunday morning, playing pinochle. But it's hard to relax when you're possessed by a lean, sharpfaced kid from Henry Street who's always got an eye out to pry the back off another coin machine.

The Killer was on the phone in the outer office when I got there, laying his plans for the evening or vice versa. He had a way of addressing his women in terms of exaggerated endearment that suggested a deeply rooted contempt. "Okay, honey chile . . . Check, sugar . . . You name it, beauteeful . . ." A psychiatrist, observing the Killer's hopped-up promiscuity and his chronic inability to settle down to any female, probably would have described him as a latent homosexual. But the Killer himself wasn't at all reticent about pressing his claim not only to the virility championship of Eighth Avenue, but also to the possession of physiological attributes of heroic proportions. He wore the pants of his snugly fitting suit almost skin tight, so you couldn't help noticing. He had short stocky legs and a four-inch chest expansion which he often showed off, even during normal conversation, by suddenly inhaling deeply and holding his breath. If you have ever seen a bantam rooster penned up with a flock of hens you would have a nice sharp picture of Killer Menegheni.

"Hang on a sec, beauteeful," he said into the phone when he saw me come in. "Cheez, Eddie, hodja come, by way of Flatbush?"

"I always ignore rhetorical questions."

"Cheez, listen to them words," said the Killer.

This had been going on between us ever since we met. The Killer seemed to take my two years in Princeton as a personal affront.

"Better get your ass in there," Killer waved me in. "'D' boss is bitin' his nails."

When I went in, Nick was in his private bathroom, shaving. He had a heavy beard that he always shaved twice a day, leaving a smooth blue patina on his face. He always came to his office in the morning from an hour in George Kochan's barbershop. He was kind of a nut on barbershops. His nails were always trimmed and polished, his black kinky hair was singed and greased and the constant sun-lamp treatments had given his skin a tanned and healthy look. He wasn't a handsome man, but the facials, the oil shampoos and the meticulous grooming gave him a smooth, lacquered appearance.

"Hello, Eddie," he said, with his back toward me, wiping the last of the cream from his face as I came up behind him. "Sorry to louse up your evening this way, but I got no choice." He still pronounced it as *cherce,* but he no longer contracted his *th*'s to hard *d*'s the way the Killer did.

"Oh, that's all right, Nick," I said. "The evening isn't dead yet."

"But it will be," Nick said. "Got a big job for you, kid. Think you're gonna go for it."

He took a handsome leather-encased bottle from the cabinet and turned around to face me as he applied the toilet water to his face and neck. "Great stuff," he said, holding the bottle to my nose. "Smell."

Like most things Nick said, it sounded more like a command than a friendly suggestion. I smelled.

"Hmmmmmmm," I nodded.

"Whatta you use?" Nick said.

"Oh, anything. Mem's, sometimes Knize Ten," I said.

"Hmm," said Nick. He turned back to the medicine cabinet again. "Here," he said. "The best. Old Leather. It's yours."

He handed me a sealed bottle of it. If he liked you, he was always giving away stuff like that. "Aw thanks Nick," I said, "but it's your stuff, you like it. . . ."

"Don't be a sucker," Nick said, and he shoved the bottle into my belly with a gesture so emphatic that it ended the argument. Nick was accustomed to leaning his weight on you, even when he was doing you a kindness. "I've been able to do a couple of little favors for the chairman of the board of the outfit that puts this stuff out—so he sent me a case of it the other day."

Nick was always getting or doing little favors he never elucidated, little favors that meant a quick turnover for some favored party in four, five, maybe six figures. I never knew what they were, and although I had the natural curiosity of anybody working in an atmosphere of big, quick, hushed money, I didn't let myself get too anxious to nose into subterranean affairs of the syndicate. It was a long time ago but I still remembered what happened to Jake Lingle in Chicago. First you get curious, then you try to find out, then you know too much, then you get paid off, then you get knocked off. It happens. So I just assumed that Nick let this toilet-water king in on a horse that was coming in at Bay Meadows, or maybe it was that waltz in the Garden last Friday night when the gamblers cashed in on the short end or maybe it was girl trouble the big shot wanted Nick to get Honest Jimmy to fix up with an assistant district attorney who was a buddy-buddy of his. It could be any one of a dozen things because Nick lived in a mysterious world of secret tips and special favors, a two-way street of silk-monogram intrigue that could lead from the cruddiest gin mill to the smartest house in Sutton Place.

Nick led me back into the office, picked up the dark mahogany box full of slender Belindas, offered me one, snipped the end off his with a silver cigar-cutter, and got down to business.

"I guess you know, Eddie," he said, "I've had the feeling a hell of a long time that your—" he reached for it—"capabilities—hasn't really been extended by our organization. It's like we got a good fast boy—champeenship material—he's fighting four-round curtain raisers all the time. A guy like you, he's got something up here, he can write, he's got whatcha call it, imagination, he needs something he can get your teeth into. Well, Eddie, the dry spell is over. You're out of the desert. I got a little project for you that will really get your gun off."

"What are you handing me, Nick, the Latka Fellowship for Creative Writing or something?"

"Don't worry. Nick never steered you wrong, did he? You're my guy, ain't you? I'm handing you a new deal, Eddie. Forget all about Harry Glenn and Felix Montoya and Willie Faralla and the rest of the bums we got in the stable. Don't even bother with old man Lennert."

That was Gus Lennert, the ex-heavyweight champ who, for want of anything better, was still rated No. 2 in the heavyweight division. Gus wasn't really a fighter any more. He was just a businessman who went to work occasionally in bathrobe and boxing gloves when the price was right. After dropping his crown seven years ago to a rough aggressive boy he could have put away any time he wanted to in his fighting days, Gus had hung up his gloves. He was pretty well fixed with a couple of trust funds and a popular little bar and grill in his home town, Trenton, N.J., called "Gus's Corner." But when we got down to the bottom of the barrel and Mike Jacobs was drawing big gates with heavyweight main events between alleged title contenders who had been spar boys or washed up a year or so before, Gus couldn't resist the temptation to come back for a little of the easy scratch. Under Nick's guidance, Gus had easily outboxed three or four bums who were masquerading as headliners in the Garden. With me beating the drums about how the great Gus Lennert had come back to realize his dream of being the first heavyweight champion to regain his title we were on our way into working poor old Gus into a shot at it.

"Forget Lennert," Nick said. "Get Lennert out of your mind. I got something better. I got Toro Molina."

"I never heard of Toro Molina."

"Nobody ever heard of Toro Molina," Nick said. "That's where you come in. You are going to make everybody hear of Toro Molina. You are going to make Toro Molina the biggest thing to hit the fight racket since Firpo came up from the Argen*tine,* or *teen* or however the hell you say it, and dropped Dempsey into the ringside seats."

"But where'd you get this Molina, who sold him to you?"

"Vince Vanneman."

"Vince Vanneman, for Christ sake!"

As Kid Vincent, Vanneman had been a pretty fair middleweight back in the twenties until he crawled into the wrong bed one night and crawled out again with a full set of *spirochaete pallida,* known to the world as syphilis and to the trade as cupid's measles. The docs didn't know how to clean it up in five and a half seconds, more or less, the way they do today. As a result Vince's case was developing into what the medics called the tertiary stage, when it begins to get to your brain. Pardon me, Vince's brain. But a little thing like a decaying brain cell or two didn't seem to have anything like a deleterious effect on Vince's ability to turn a dishonest dollar. So I was a little surprised that Nick, whose larceny was on such a high level that it approached the respectability of finance capitalism, would get himself involved with a minor-league thief.

"Vince Vanneman," I said again. "A *momser* from way back. You know what the boys call him—The Honest Brakeman. He never stole a boxcar. When Vince Vanneman goes to sleep he only closes one eye so he can watch himself with the other."

When Nick was impatient he had the habit of snapping alternately the thumb and second finger of each hand in nervous staccato rhythm. I've seen him do that when he wanted his man to start carrying the fight to his opponent and the boy couldn't seem to get going. "Listen," he said, "don't tell me about Vanneman. The day I can't handle Vanneman I turn over the business to the Killer. I made a nice deal with Vince. We only give him five G's for Molina and he rides with us for five percent of the profits. The South American jerk, who brought the boy up here, Vince gives him twenty-five hundred and we also cut him in for five percent."

"But if this—what's his name, Molina?—is such a find, what's Vince doing selling out so fast?" I asked. "Vince may be suffering from paresis, but he's not so dumb he doesn't know a meal ticket when he sees one."

Nick looked at me as if I were a high-grade moron, which, in this business, I was. "I had a little talk with Vince," Nick said.

I could picture that little talk—Nick cool, immaculate, quietly implicit; Vince with his tie loosened so he could open his shirt and let his fat neck breathe, the sweat coming out of his fleshy face as he tried to wriggle off Nick's hook—just a talk between two businessmen concerning lump sums, down payments and percentages, just a quiet little talk and yet the atmosphere tense with unheard sounds, the blackjack's thud, the scream torn from the violated groin, the spew of blood and broken teeth.

"Anything I want to do is a hundred percent okay with Vince," Nick said.

"But I don't get it," I said. "Why all this trouble about Molina? Who'd he ever lick? What's so special about Molina?"

"What is so special about Molina is he is the biggest son-of-a-bitch who ever climbed into a ring. Six feet seven and three-quarters inches tall. Two hundred and eighty-five pounds."

"You all right, Nick?" I said. "Not on the stuff or anything?"

"Two hundred and eighty-five pounds," Nick said. "And no belly on him."

"But he could be a bum," I said. "Two hundred and eighty-five pounds of bum."

"Listen for Chri'-sakes," Nick said. "The Statue of Liberty, does she have to do an adagio to draw crowds every day?"

"Come one, come all, see the human skyscraper," I said. "Captured alive in the jungles of Argentina—Gargantua the Great."

"You laugh," Nick said. "Maybe I never went to college, but I sure in hell can add better 'n you. Not two 'n two neither. Two hundred G's and two hundred G's. Tell you what I'm gonna do with you, wise guy. You'll get your straight C every week and on top of that I'll cut you in for five percent of our end. If we do two hundred thousand the first year, you'll make a little money."

"Two hundred thousand!" One hundred thousand was a good year's take for a name who packs the Garden. Anything over that was big-name heavyweights in outdoor shows. "Pass that opium pipe around and let's all take off."

"Listen, Eddie," Nick said, and his voice had the self-satisfied tone it always took on when he took himself seriously, like a self-made Kiwan-

ian explaining his success to his fraternal brothers. "I learned one thing
when I was a kid—to do big you got to think big. When we used to
jimmy those penny machines, for instance, you know, peanuts, chewing
gum, hell, we was always getting caught. Then I got the idea of mug-
ging the collector who went from one machine to another every Friday,
emptying out the coin boxes. It was safer to get him on his way back to
the office at night, and hit the jackpot, than it was to work those machines over in broad daylight and pick up a few pennies. That's what I
mean. If you got to think, think big. What the hell, it don't cost you
nothing to think. So why think fifty grand when you can think a hundred
and fifty grand? Now tomorrow I got this Molina and his spic manager,
Acosta, coming out to the country. You better come too. Bring the broad
along if you want. Take Acosta aside and get the story—you know, how
the big guy was discovered and all that crap. Then we'll sit down together and work out the angles. Wednesday morning I wanna hit the
papers. The suckers open their papers and right away like this" (he
snapped his fingers) "there's a new contender for the championship."

Nick stood up and put his hand on my arm. He was excited. He was
thinking big. "Eddie," he said, "you gotta work like a son-of-a-bitch on
this. You make with the words, I work the angles and if that big Argentine bastard gives us anything at all, we'll all make a pisspot full of
dough."

If I ever got five thousand dollars ahead, I was always thinking, I'd
throw up my job, get a little cabin in the mountains somewhere, take a
year off and write. Sometimes I was going to write a bright, crisp,
wisecracking comedy, the George Abbott type, and make a hatful of
dough. And sometimes I was going to pour out everything I had seen
and learned and felt about myself and America, a great gushing river of
a play that would get me a Pulitzer prize. After the play opened, Beth
and I would take a honeymoon cruise around the world, while I outlined
my next. . . .

"How about a shot?" Nick said. He rose, pressed a button in the wall
near his desk and a panel rolled back, revealing a small, well-fitted bar,
and brought out a bottle of Ballantine's, the twenty-year old.

"To Señor Molina," I said.

"And to us," Nick said.

He filled the two pony glasses again. "That girl you got, she's a writer
too, ain't she?" he said. The only serious reading Nick ever did was the
Morning Telegraph and the *Racing Form* but he always got an earnest,
respectful note in his voice when he spoke about writers. "A smart girl
like that, she must make out pretty good," he said. "What does she make
on *Life*, eighty, ninety a week?"

"You're high," I said. "Took her three years to get up to fifty."

"Fifty," Nick said. "Jesus, a preliminary boy in the Garden gets a hunerd'n fifty."

"Beth figures she'll last longer," I said.

"You oughta marry a dame like that," Nick said. Whenever Nick hit a mellow stretch he liked to concern himself with matrimony and legitimate genesis. "No kidding, you should get yourself hitched. Hell, I was in the saddle with a different tomato every night until I got hitched. You oughta settle down and start having some kids, Eddie. Them kids, that's what makes you want to work like a bastard."

From his inside pocket, Nick drew a handsome leather wallet, initialed in gold, N.L., Jr. "Here's what I'm giving Junior for his graduation—he finishes the lower form up at N.Y.M.A. next week.

I took the wallet and turned it over in my hand. It was from Mark Cross, the best. Inside was a brand-new hundred-dollar bill. "He's a smart kid," Nick said. "Been skipped twice. He's the company commander's orderly or adjutant or whatever the hell it is. Pretty good athlete too. Plays on the tennis team."

You couldn't help liking Nick sometimes, the way he said things. That tennis, for instance. The awe and the wonder of it. Nick, who played punchball on Henry Street against tenement walls decorated in chalk with a childish scrawl of grown-up obscenities, the ball bouncing back into the crowded streets, over pushcarts, under trucks honk-honking drivers' hot disgusted shouting *Git outa there you little sonofabitch;* and Junior white as the saints in his flannels and sportshirt with the school crest over his heart, the warm silence broken only by the sharp crack of racket and ball and the gentlemanly intrusion of the judge on his high cool seat, *Game, to Mr. Latka. He leads, first set, five games to two.* Old Nick and Young Nick, Henry Street and Green Acres, the military school on the Hudson and PS 1 on the corner of Henry and Catherine Streets battleground of Wops and Yids invading Polacks and crusading Micks energetic young Christians brandishing rock-filled stockings crashing down upon the heads of unbaptized children falsely accused of murder committed nineteen hundred years ago. *Your serve. Sorry, take another. Please take two.*

"Killer," Nick called into the outer office, "hang up on that broad and get Ruby on the phone. Tell her to hold that steak for me, I'll be out ina nour."

He tapped me lightly on the side of the jaw with his knuckles. It was one of his favorite signs of affection.

"See ya mañana, Shakespeare."

After Nick left I sat down at his desk to call Beth. There was a small telephone pad near the phone, with Nick's name printed in the upper left-hand corner. There was something in Nick that desired constant re-establishment of his identity. Shirts, cuff links, cigarette lighters, wallets, hat-bands were all smartly initialed. The matchbooks he handed you said "Compliments of Nick Latka."

Nick had been doodling. The top page of the pad was full of large and small ovals representing punching bags: the long sand-filled heavy bags and the smaller, inflated light bags. All the bags were covered with little pencil flecks that looked like miniature s's. I looked at them more carefully and saw that two thin vertical lines ran through them. All the punching bags had broken out in a hive of dollar signs.

As I left, the Killer was just putting on his coat, a formfitting herring-bone with exaggerated shoulders. "Jeez, have I got something lined up for myself tonight," he was saying. "The new cigarette girl at the Horseshoe. Knockers like this. And loves it like a rabbit."

"Killer," I said, "have you ever thought of writing your memoirs?"

Hacking down Eighth Avenue, past the quick lunches, the little tailor shops, the secondhand stores, HONEST PRICES FOR GOLD, past the four-bit barbershops, the two-bit hotels, the Chinese laundries, the ten-cent movies, I thought of Nick, and of Charles and his Jackson-Slavin fight, the magnificent ebony figure of Peter Jackson with his great classical head, his innate dignity, poised and magnanimous in his moment of triumph. Jackson, black athlete from Australia, a pugilist in the great tradition, worthy descendant of the ancient Sumerians, whose boxing contests are depicted in frescoes that have come down to us through six thousand years; and of Theagenes of Thaos, Olympic Champion, who defended his honor and his life in fourteen hundred contests with steel-pronged fists four hundred and fifty years before Christ; of the great British bare-knuckled forefathers who developed the manly art of self-defense; John Broughton, first to give the ring a written code, who, egged on by his impatient backer, the Duke of Cumberland, while being beaten to blindness by a powerful challenger, said, "Tell me where my man is and I will strike him, sir"; Mendoza the Jew, Champion of England, undersized giant-killer who fought the biggest and best his island could boast, bringing a new technique of movement to the slow, savage game; the mighty Cribb and the indomitable champion, Tom Molineaux, the liberated slave who stood up to Cribb for forty bruising rounds and would have won but for a desperate ruse; Englishmen, Negroes, the Irish, Jews, and in our time Americans with Italian names, Canzoneri, La Barba, Genaro; Filipinos, Sarmiento, Garcia; Mexicans, Ortiz, Arizmendi—all sprung from fighting stock, practicing an ancient sport already old in Roman times, a cruel and punishing enterprise rooted deep in the heart of man that began with the first great prehistoric struggles

and has come down through the Iron Age, the Bronze Age, the dawn of
the Christian Era, medieval times, the eighteenth and nineteenth century
renaissance of pugilism, until at last New York, heir to Athens, Rome
and London, has made the game its own, entrusting it to one of its more
successful sons, Uncle Mike Jacobs, unchallenged King of Jacobs'
Beach, perhaps the only unlimited monarch still in business, who, by
crossing the boxing racket with ticket speculation has produced a
hundred-million-dollars-a-year industry that Daniel Mendoza, poor old
Peter Jackson or the blustering John L. would never recognize as their
brave old game of winner take all.

3

Beth drove down with me to Nick's place over near Red Bank, about
forty-five minutes from New York, not very far from Mike Jacobs' own
little Versailles. In fact, if I remember right, he heard of Green Acres
through Mike when he was down there for a weekend five or six years
ago. It had belonged to a millionaire Wall Street broker whose marriage
went on the rocks and who decided to unload it in a hurry. Nick had got
it for around fifty thousand. But there must have been an easy hundred
thousand sunk in it, with the twenty-three-room house, hundred and
twenty acres, swimming pool, tennis court, hothouse, screened-in barbecue, four-car garage and twenty-horse stable.

It was hard to understand what the broker was thinking about when he
built the house. It was neo-Gothic, if you could call it anything, an
architectural Texas-leaguer that fell somewhere between medieval and
modern design, a formal, urban dwelling that looked out of place in the
country and yet would have looked equally incongruous in town. It was
beautifully landscaped, with smartly trimmed hedges bordering the well-
kept lawns dressed up with circular flower beds. We drove around the
house to the garage, where Nick's chauffeur was washing the big black
Cadillac four-door convertible. He was bare from the waist up, and
although there was a bicycle tire of fat around his middle, the chest,
back, shoulders and over-developed biceps were impressive. He looked
up when he saw me and his frank, flattened face opened in a gummy
smile.

"Whaddya say, Mr. Lewis?"

"Hello, Jock. How's everything?"

"Ain't so bad. You know the wife's home with the new kid."

"Yeah? Swell. How many's that make it?"

"Eight. Five boys and three goils."

"Take it easy now, Jock," I said. "You never did know your own strength."

The chauffeur grinned proudly until his eyes, puffy with scar-tissue, pressed together in the grimace of a cheerful gargoyle.

"The boss around?"

"He's out horseback ridin' with Whitey."

Whitey Williams was the little ex-jockey who won a nice chunk of change for Nick at Tropical Park one season when he booted home forty-five winners. Now he took care of Nick's horses for him and taught him how to ride. They were out on the bridle path together almost every Sunday.

"How about the Duchess?"

That was Ruby. Anybody who had been around the place very long knew whom you meant.

"I just took her over to ten-o'clock mass. She'n this big fella from the Argentine."

"Oh, he went, too? What does he look like?"

"Well, if anyone tags him he's got a long way to fall."

"See you later, Jock."

"You bet, Mr. Lewis."

"That's Jock Mahoney," I told Beth as we walked up toward the large lawn that stretched between the main house and the garage, over which Jock, the missus and the seven kids lived in five small rooms. "A good second-rate light-heavyweight in the days when Delaney, Slattery, Berlenbach, Loughran and Greb were first rate. Very tough. Could take a hell of a punch."

"He doesn't talk as if he has a brain full of scrambled eggs," Beth said.

"They don't all come out of it talking to themselves," I said. "Take McLarnin, fought the toughest—Barney Ross, Petrolle, Canzoneri—and his head's as clear as mine."

"This morning probably clearer," Beth said.

I was still thinking about Mahoney. Old fighters will always get me. There is nothing duller than an old ball player or an old tennis star, but an old fighter who's been punched around, spilled his blood freely for the fans' amusement only to wind up broke, battered and forgotten has got the stuff of tragedy for me.

"The only thing soft about Mahoney is the way he laughs," I said. "All you have to do is look at him and he laughs. That's usually a sign you're a little punchy. The time Berlenbach tagged him with the first punch he threw in the third round, Jock was out so completely he went over to Berlenbach's corner and flopped down. But the way he was grinning and laughing, you'd've thought he was home in an easy chair reading the funny papers."

"That's what I don't like about it," Beth said. "The way they laugh."

"When they laugh, Beth, it usually means they're hurt," I said. "They just want to show the other guy that they aren't hurt, that everything's okay."

"I read something about laughter once," Beth said. "The idea was that laughter is just a display of superiority. Laughing when somebody slips on a banana peel, for instance, or gets a face full of pie. Or take the whole line of Scotch-Jewish-darky jokes. The thing about them that makes people laugh is the warm feeling that they aren't as tight as the Scotchman, as beaten down as the Negroes and so on."

"But if we follow that theory," I said, "shouldn't the fellow who does the laughing be the one who throws the punch, not the one who catches it?"

"It's not that simple," Beth insisted. "Maybe the guy who gets hurt laughs to hang on to his superiority—or is that what you said in the first place?"

"That's the trouble with you psychologists," I said. "You can take either side and sound just as scientific."

We had reached the lawn nearest the house, where a row of round metal tables had been set out with brightly colored beach umbrellas rising through the centers. Lying on the grass in the shade of one of these umbrellas was a slight, middle-aged man with gray hair and a sickly white face, eyes closed in the heavy stupefaction of alcoholic sleep. A folded *Racing Form* he had used as an eye-shade had slipped off his forehead. He was snoring strenuously through a badly broken nose, the only punished feature in an otherwise unmarked face.

"There's Danny McKeogh," I said. Around Stillman's they call it "McCuff."

"Is he alive?" Beth asked.

"Slightly," I said.

"He's got a sad face," Beth said.

"He's one of the right guys in this business," I said. "He'd give you his shirt if you needed it, even if he didn't have a shirt and had to go borrow one off somebody else. Which has happened."

"A generous member of this profession? I didn't know there was such an animal."

As we walked along, the volcanic career of Danny McKeogh registered its peaks and valleys in my mind.

He never took a drink until the night he fought Leonard. Danny was a beautiful gymnasium fighter, a real cutie from way back. He never made a wrong move in a gym. He wasn't a cocky kid ordinarily, but he was sure he could take Leonard. Nobody had done it yet, not even Lew Tendler, but Danny felt sure. He studied Leonard in all his fights and even went to see movies of him. Kind of a nut on the subject, like Tunney with Dempsey, only with a different ending. After all the build-up, Leonard knocked him cold in one minute and twenty-three seconds of the first round. Got his nose busted in the bargain. That was curtains for Danny as a fighter. Almost curtains in other ways too. For the next couple of years he gave a convincing imitation of a man who was trying to drink up all the liquor there was in New York.

Then, one day, hanging around the gym with a bad breath and a three-day growth—it was up on 59th Street at the time—he happened to see a skinny litle East Side Jewish boy working out with another kid. Right away Danny decided to get a shave and sober up. It was love at first sight. The boy was Izzy Greenberg, just a punk skinny sixteen-year-old kid then, training for a newsboy tournament. Danny must have seen himself all over again in that kid. Anyway he stayed on the wagon. He worked with Izzy every day for a year or more, boxing with him, showing him, very patient, showing him again—and there's no better teacher in the world than Danny when he's sober. Even drunk he still makes more sense than almost anybody around.

Danny brought Izzy right to the top. He looked like another Leonard, one of those classy Jewish lightweights that keep coming up out of the East Side. Three years of consistent wins and they've got the championship. They travel around the world, picking up easy dough, meeting the Australian champion, the Champion of England, the Champion of Europe, which is not as much trouble for Izzy as slicing Matzoth balls with a hot knife. Then they come back to the big town, and Izzy defends his title in the old Garden against Art Hudson, a slugger from out West. Danny, who always backed his fighters heavily—old-fashioned that way—had his friends cover all the Hudson money they could find. They only found ten thousand dollars. Sixty thousand if Danny lost. But Danny liked the bet, called it easy money.

The first round looked like curtains for Hudson. Izzy left-handed him to death, and that jab of his wasn't just scoring points; it could carve you up like a steak knife. Thirty seconds before the end of the round Hudson went down. Izzy danced back to his corner, winking at Danny, nodding to friends around the ring, waving a glove at the large Jewish following that was letting itself go. He's all ready to go in and get dressed. And Danny's already thinking of how to parlay the ten grand. But somehow or other Hudson was on his feet at nine and rushing across the ring. He was really a throw-back to Ketchell and Papke. All he knew about boxing was to keep getting up and keep banging away. Izzy turned toward him coolly, did a little fancy footwork and snapped out that fast left to keep Hudson away. But Hudson just brushed it aside and banged a wild left to the body and a hard roundhouse right to the jaw.

Izzy was out for twenty minutes. His jaw had been broken in two places. A reporter who was there in the dressing room told me Danny was crying like a baby. He rode with Izzy up to the hospital and then he went out and had a drink. That time he stayed drunk for almost three years.

Then one day at the Main Street gym out in L.A., where Danny looks like any other flea-bitten bum, he spots another little kid, Speedy Sencio. Same thing all over again. On the wagon. Fills the little Filipino full of everything he knows. Cops the bantamweight crown and everything's copasetic until Speedy goes over the hump and starts going downhill. Danny goes back on the flit again.

By this time Danny has made a couple of hundred thousand, gone mostly to the horses. He is also a great little check-grabber and highly vulnerable to the touch, especially when it comes from one of the fighters who used to win for him. Like Izzy Greenberg. Danny put fifteen thousand in a haberdashery business Izzy was starting, and six months later the business went the way of all Greenberg enterprises. He is not nearly the flash in business he was in the ring. But Danny gave him ten thousand more and he went into ladies' wear on Fourteenth Street.

The crash put the finisher on Danny's chips. The only chance he saw of getting it back fast was the horses, and the only way of getting enough for the horses was finding a friend to put it on the cuff. Nick Latka turned out to be the friend, and he seemd to be all cuff where Danny was concerned. Danny didn't know there was a catch to it until he was into Nick for around twenty G's. "Who's worried about it?" Nick had said every time Danny mentioned something about hoping to clean up enough soon to pay some of it back. Then one day Nick sends for Danny and all of a sudden wants his dough. Danny is just back from Belmont, where his tips have been worse than his hunches. So Nick says, "Tell you what I'll do with you, baby. You come to work for me for two fifty a week, building up a stable and handling the boys. You keep a C for yourself and one and a half cuts back to me until we're even. And just to show you how I feel about you, I'll put you down for a bonus of ten percent on everything we make over fifty G's a year."

So that's where Danny's been ever since. Even if he developed another Greenberg or a Sencio it wouldn't be his any more. So the incentive to say no to the bottle is practically nil. Now it's reflex action for him to reach for one in the morning, and he tosses them off in quick nervous motions until somebody puts him to bed. He has never been known to come in loaded on fight night when he is working a corner.

But when he is sober everybody wishes he would take one to relax. He's so sober he gets the shakes. It's really a heroic and terrible effort for Danny to be sober, but he does it, because, for all the disappointments, he's still got his heart in the game. There's nobody hops into a ring at the end of a round faster than Danny and there is something wonderful about the loving way he leans over his fighters, rhythmically rubbing the neck, the small of the back, with his thin, nervous lips close to his boy's ear, keeping up a quiet running patter as he improvises new tactics for the boy's defense and spots holes in the opponent's.

A great manager, Danny McKeogh, in the big tradition of great managers. Johnston, Kearns, Mead. Or at least he was a great manager before Nick Latka brought him into bondage.

As I stood there looking down at him, thinking about him, a fly lit on his nose, was brushed away, only to return to his forehead. Danny shook his head, let a crack of light into his eyes and saw me standing there. He sat up slowly, rubbing his eyes.

"Hello, laddie."

Everybody he liked he called laddie. For people he didn't like, it was mister.

"Hello, Danny. How's the boy?"

Danny shook his head. "Pretty tough," he said, "pretty tough."

"By the way, Miss Reynolds, Mr. McKeogh."

Danny began to tuck one foot under him as if he were going to rise. Beth put her hand out to stop him. "You look much too comfortable," she said. "I'm not used to such gallantry."

That kind of courtesy was part of Danny, drunk or sober. He had that big Irish thing about women, reverent when he mentioned his mother, sore at guys who profaned in the presence of ladies, which was the entire opposite sex in Danny's book, regardless of rep or appearance. But Danny didn't have that other Irish thing, the three-drink belligerence. When he drank himself into a stupor he did so quietly and gradually like the death of Galsworthy's patriarch in *The Indian Summer of a Forsyte*. No fuss and never any fights, even when goaded by a champion like Vince Vanneman. He was one of the few men I've ever known who could pass out and not lose either his cookies or his dignity.

"Seen your new heavyweight yet?" I said.

"No," he said. "I been pounding my ear. You see him?"

I shook my head. "He's gone to mass with the Duchess."

"Well, we'll take a look at him in the gym tomorrow."

"Nick's all excited," I said.

"Yeah," Danny said.

A loud yawn escaped him. "Scuse me, ma'am."

"Who's the biggest guy you ever handled before, Danny?"

Danny thought a moment. "Big Boy Lemson, I guess. Scaled around two-thirty. Looked tough, but he was musclebound, had a glass jaw. I tell ya, Eddie, I don't get excited about these jumbo heavyweights. Hundred 'n eighty, eighty-five, that's all you need to knock out anything, if you know how to punch. Dempsey was only one-ninety at Toledo. Corbett's best weight was around one-eighty."

"Nick sees a sensational draw in this Molina," I said.

"Yeah," Danny said.

That's about the most combative Danny ever got, that "yeah." It would be harder to find two guys further apart in the boxing business than Danny and Nick. Nick was all business. For him the fix was second nature. To Danny it wasn't a sport any more either. It was a trade. He happened to be an honest craftsman. His way was to start from scratch, pitting his brain and his kid's natural talent and ability against all comers. That was too haphazard for Nick. Whether it was horses or fighters, he liked to play sure things.

"You could use a little more shut-eye, Danny," I said. "We'll catch you later."

"Right, laddie," Danny said. There was still the echo of a brogue. He stretched out on the grass again. Beth took my arm and we walked on.

Under the next umbrella sat a couple of gamblers. It sounds like easy generalization to look at a couple of guys you have never seen before and flip your mind down to G like a card-file, right away, "Gamblers." But I would have laid five-to-one that's what they were, if I hadn't learned my lesson a long time ago never to stake my judgment against the professional players'. One of the gamblers had done too well for a long time and it was all in his face and his belly. The other had started out with a very good physique and still kept a little pride in it. Once in a while, when he got into a bathing suit, he probably felt a twinge of self-consciousness about the surplus fat on him and subjected it to the hard mechanical hands of the steam-bath rubber. They were both dressed in easy, comfortable clothes that added up to the kind of country ensemble that looks expensively cheap. The fatter one was wearing a yellow flannel sports shirt that must have cost sixteen bucks at Abercrombie & Fitch. But there was nothing Abercrombie & Fitch about the short hairy arms, the fat neck and the sweat staining the shirt front even in the shade. You would think the Scotch or the British or whoever knitted his socks would have known better than to waste pure wool on such corny patterns.

"Gin," the leaner one said, pushing back an expensive Panama hat from a low forehead tanned from bending over racing programs in the sun near the railing.

The fat man threw his cards down in disgust. "Gin," he said, nodding his head in weary resignation and turning to us as if we had been there all the time, appealing to us as sympathetic onlookers witnessing a catastrophe. "Gin. Every five minutes gin. All the way up from Miami it's all I hear—gin, gin, gin! Three hundred and two dollars he's into me before we hit Balteemore. The cards he gives me, I shoulda got off at Jacksonville."

"You're breaking my heart," the man with the Panama said. "How many you got?"

"Twenty-eight," the fat man complained, and began to turn the cards over sorrowfully.

"Wait a minute, wait a minute, let *me* count," the other man said. His eyes did a quick recap of the fat man's cards. "Twenty-*nine*," he announced triumphantly, "twenty-*nine*, jerk."

"So twenty-nine," the fat man shrugged. "He's cutting my throat by inches and he's worried about a little pinch in the behind."

This fat one, Barney Winch, made gambling his business; but it was also his recreation. His success was due to the fact that he never allowed the business and the recreation to overlap. Strictly speaking, Barney was in the gambling business the way a saloon keeper is in the drinking business, although he never has one himself until the chairs are on the tables and the door is bolted for the night. If Barney were betting on a football game, he would figure out a way to bet on both teams so there was no chance of losing and yet a better-than-even chance of winning on both. That is how he was supposed to have cleaned up on a Southern Cal-Notre Dame game a few years back. First he had laid two and a half to four on the Irish, to win. Then he had turned around and taken Southern Cal and seven points. Notre Dame won by a single point, and Barney collected on both bets. Barney hedged his fight bets the same way, and he never faded in a crap game unless the percentage was with him. If you ever caught Barney betting only one side of a fight or putting a big wad down on the nose of a horse, you would be safe in assuming that these contests had lost their element of chance.

What Barney did for recreation was another story. His hands felt empty when they weren't holding cards. But he wasn't a particularly expert poker player nor invincible at gin. He never cheated at cards because cards was something he did with his friends, and a man like Barney Winch would never give the business to a friend. If *the business* was slang, it was highly literal slang, for it meant to Barney exactly what it had to Webster, that which busies or engages one's time, attention or labor, as a principal serious employment. When something went wrong with Barney's "principal serious employment" there was never so much as a sigh out of him. There was the time Barney had dropped forty thousand because a certain middleweight of Nick's who was supposed to fall down for a price double-crossed his managers and the smart money by staying on his feet and winning the decision. Barney took it philosophically. He shrugged and paid off. The double-cross was one of the risks of the business, like unseasonable rain for the farmer. Only as a little ethical reminder to the disobedient pugilist, a couple of goons were waiting for him outside his Washington Heights apartment when he got home after the fight, anxious to convince him of his mistake. They left him lying unconscious in the hallway with a convincing two-inch blackjack wound in his head.

If it was business, Barney never bellyached. The day he won enough to shoot up into the highest income brackets (if such profits were declared), he could be weeping because he was a sixty-one-dollar loser in a rummy game.

Barney rearranged his new hand, looked it over and shook his head with the clucking sound of self-pity. "Jacksonville," he said, "I shoulda got off at Jacksonville."

Just a hot, quiet Sunday morning at Green Acres, Nick off on the bridle path, Ruby at church and none of the usual Sunday-dinner crowd out of bed this early. We walked out toward the tennis court, where Junior Latka, slender and full of grace and conceit in his white ducks and white jersey with the school crest over the heart, was in the middle of a long and well-played rally with another young man almost his equal. Junior hit a hard deep forehand drive which his opponent had to return as a lob that Junior put away with an overhead smash. The other boy ran back and made a futile pass at it as it bounced high over his head.

Behind the tennis court was a carefully cultivated flower garden where a weather-beaten, runty old man was working quietly on his knees. He looked up when we passed and waited for us to admire his flowers. He had the face of a kid, with big ears and small, grinning eyes.

"The flowers look good this year, Petey," I said.

"T'anks, Mr. Lewis," he said. "I started dem earlier dis year. Dese white bride roses is comin' out better'n I expected."

He went back to his weeding as we walked on. "How old do you think he is?" I said.

"Oh, forty-eight, fifty," Beth guessed.

"He stayed twenty rounds with Terry McGovern before we were born," I said. "He must be crowding seventy. Petey Odell, a great old-time featherweight."

"I suppose he wound up better than most of them," Beth said. "At least he's here in Nick's old fighters' home."

"They come up to Nick's all the time to put the bite on him. I guess it makes Nick feel good to take care of some of them. And of course it pays off. Nick's charities always pay off. They're grateful slobs, these old fighters. Good-hearted, loyal as hell and work like fools. Especially if you show an interest in what they're doing. That Jock Mahoney. I think he loves that Caddy more than he does his wife. All you have to do to make him happy is ask him how he manages to get such a high polish on those fenders. Old Petey's the same way about his garden. If he saw us go by and we didn't say anything about that garden he'd sulk all day. Just a little punchy."

"What a business!" Beth said. The more she saw of it, the less "fascinating" it seemed.

"Mahoney or Hayes, they aren't so bad. They know what day it is. Give them a definite job to do and they'll throw themselves into it. But just the same when you talk to them about anything but the job or maybe their families, you hit something fuzzy, as if they've got a layer of cotton around their brains."

"It's a filthy business," Beth said suddenly. "In your heart you know it's a filthy business."

"Last Friday night you were yelling your head off," I reminded her.

"That's true," she admitted. "I was rooting for the colored boy. He looked so thin and weak compared to the other one. When he started to rally, when he actually had that a big Italian boy groggy, well"—she had to smile—"I guess I got excited."

"It's been exciting people a hell of a long time. Look at Greek mythology—full of boxers. Wasn't it Hercules who fought that very tough boy who grew stronger each time he was knocked down because the earth was his mother? What was his name?"

"Antaeus," Beth said.

"That's why it pays to court a *Life* researcher," I said. "Antaeus. Homer wrote a hell of a piece about that fight. And Virgil covered one of the first great comebacks of a retired champ. Remember how the old champ doesn't want to accept the challenge of the young contender from Troy because he complains he is way out of condition and all washed up, a sort of ancient Greek Tony Galento? But when he's finally goaded into fighting he puts up a hell of a battle, has his man on the verge of a kayo when the King steps between them like Arthur Donovan and gives it to the old champ on a TKO. Of course, Virgil made it sound a little more poetic, but that was the guts of it."

Beth smiled. "You shouldn't be a tub-thumper for a stable of fighters. You should write essays for *The Yale Review*."

"Nick pays me for the tub-thumping," I said. "This kind of talk I have to do for free."

We had almost reached the house. Nick and Whitey Williams were just coming up the driveway, at a slow trot. In contrast to Whitey, who sat his horse as if it were an overstuffed easy chair, and looked as much at home, Nick's seat was very erect, a little ill at ease, and when he posted you felt he was conscious of doing so with perfect form, which always results in something less than perfect in sport technique.

He swung off his horse, a big, deep-chested bay, and handed the reins to Whitey, who led both horses back to the stable. Nick was wearing Irish boots, chamois breeches and a brown polo shirt.

"How long you two been here?" he said pleasantly.

"About half an hour, Nick," I said. "Wonderful day."

"It must be a sweatbox in town," Nick said, gloatingly. "We useta knock the head off the fire plug an' take a shower bath in the street." He gave a little laugh, thinking how far he had come. "Eddie been showing you around the joint?"

"It's perfectly beautiful," Beth said.

"Didja show her the vegetable garden?" Nick said. "We got a thousand tomato plants. Raise all our own stuff. You like corn, miss? I'll betcha never tasted corn like this. Corn like this, you'll never get it in the stores. When you go home take some with you, all you want."

"Thanks very much," Beth said.

"Aah, it's nothing," Nick waved it aside. "This place is lousy with stuff. If you don't take it, my bums will eat me out of it anyway. That Jock Mahoney, he sits down to corn, he doesn't get up till he's finished thirteen-fourteen ears. He'd rather eat 'n . . ." He looked at Beth and stopped. "Even when he was supposed to be trainin', he ate like a pig."

We were back on the terrace. Danny McKeogh was still sleeping, his legs spread apart and his arms outstretched, like a man who had been run over. The gamblers were still hunched over their cards.

"How's it going, Barney?" Nick said.

The fat man's body rose and fell in an exaggerated sigh. "Don't ask. He's murdering me. There oughta be a law against what he's doing to me."

Nick laughed. "No wonder Runyon called him the Town Crier," he said. "Even when he wins, he cries, because it wasn't bigger."

He dropped his hand on my shoulder. "This fella Acosta is inside on the screen porch. This oughta be a good time to talk. Come on in." Then he remembered Beth. "Sorry to grab the boyfriend away," he said with what was for Nick a very courtly gesture. "Ruby oughta be back in a couple of minutes. There's plenty of papers on the terrace if you feel like readin'. And if you wanna drink, just call the butler, the guy with the little black bow tie."

"Who is he, Gene Tunney?" Beth asked.

"Tooney," Nick said, "Tooney gives me a pain in the . . . excuse me, miss, but I'd throw Tooney the hell off the place."

He maneuvered me toward the door. "Just do anything you feel like, take anything you want like it was your own home."

"You boys go ahead," Beth said. "I'll amuse myself."

I watched her for a moment as she started back across the terrace. She was wearing a yellow-brown linen skirt, only a shade darker than her tanned legs and arms. Even in the city, where the only exercise most people get is running for a bus or hailing a cab, she always got down to the courts at Park and Thirty-ninth at least twice a week when the weather was right. She looked very sharp from where we stood, not the dream figure, a little too athletic maybe, a little too thin in the legs and not quite enough in front. But there was something attractively capable about the way she walked. I made a mental note to mention this to her later.

She puzzled me. She was the kind of girl to whom I was always going to say something nice a little later. What kept me back, perhaps, was that she would only half believe what I told her, always holding something in reserve. Maybe it was her upbringing, the kind that demands a strict balance all the time. Maybe it was the old Puritan strain in her. Maybe it was a bad inheritance of fierce convictions. Whatever it was, a nice girl like Beth, good respectable family, good schooling, good brain, was still a question mark to me. Passion and restraint, in equal portions, end up in a no-decision fight.

"She's all right," Nick said. "You got yourself something there. Plenty of class."

4

We walked through the spacious living room, an over-decorated hall of mirrors that looked unlived-in, to the sun-porch. When he saw us, the little Argentinian rose quickly to his feet, stiffly formal, his teeth showing in a rehearsed smile. He was a short dumpy man with a large nose, a swarthy complexion and a half dozen strands of hair angled back from his forehead in a strategic but unsuccessful effort to hide his baldness. He wore spats, a white-checkered vest and the kind of four-button sports suit belted in the back we haven't seen around here in quite a while. On the fourth finger of his short stubby hand was what might have been a ruby.

"Eddie," Nick said, not bothering to introduce me, "this is Acosta. You guys got some work to do, so I'll leave you alone."

Acosta began a little bow and started to say something like "Charmed..." or "Very pleased..." but Nick caught him in the middle of it. The courtesies were all right with Nick, if they didn't get in the way of business. "I dialed out on you," he said to Acosta, "because I don't hafta hear all that crap about the village and the wine barrels. I'm a businessman. I take one hinge at the boy and I see he's got something. I can sell him. But," Nick squeezed my shoulder affectionately, "I want you to give my boy here the full treatment."

"Yes, yes, I understan'," Acosta said, bowing slightly toward Nick again, as if what he had just said had been graciously friendly.

"Don't forget now, the full treatment," Nick said, using the same tone on Acosta he used on the bums around the office. "Including dessert and the finger bowls."

"Meester Latka, he has a very smart head for business," Acosta said to me when Nick left us alone. "Very strong mind, very intelligent. When El Toro and I come to North America I never even have the dream to be the partner of such a big man as Meester Latka."

"Yes," I said.

He reached into his inside pocket and brought forth a silver case from which, with an elaborate gesture, he offered me a cigarette. "Perhaps you do not mind smoking an Argentinian cigarette," he said. "Very mild, very nice smoke. If you will pardon me for saying, I like better than your Chesterfield and Lucky Strike." Again he smiled with his teeth to show that this was not an issue of nationalist rivalry but merely a little joke, and fitted his cigarette nicely into a slender tortoise-shell holder. He spoke better English than the Killer or Vanneman, but with a strong affinity for the present tense and a tendency to louse up his present and past perfects.

"Meester Lewis," Acosta began, "for me to meet you is a very great pleasure. Meester Latka, he has tell me about you the many good things. You are a very great writer, yes? You will make very famous my great discovery, El Toro Molina and his little manager Luis?"

This was said with a little laugh, as if to show we both understood that Luis was not nearly so aggressive and self-seeking as he made himself sound. Luis had shrewd little eyes that appraised you too carefully all the time he was smiling at you. For all the Argentine schmalz, it wasn't too difficult to see him promoting up and down Jacobs' Beach with the best of them, spats and all.

Well, the overture is over and the curtain's going up, I thought.

"Tell you what you do, Mr. Acosta," I said. "Give me the whole thing. From the beginning. Where the guy comes from, how you found him, when he started fighting, the works."

"Please?" Acosta said.

"You know, the whole story, complete in this issue."

"Oh, yes, yes I understan'," Acosta said. "It is very very interesting the story of El Toro and I. Very romantic. Very dramatic. But first if you please I will warn you of something. El Toro Molina, he is a very young boy. He does not have yet twenty-one years. He comes from a very little village in the Andes, above Mendoza. All the people there, they are of very simple minds. Not loco you understan', just of simple minds. All their life they work in the vineyards of the great *estancia* de Santos. Of the world outside, they know nothing, not even of the capital of their state, Mendoza. Buenos Aires, it is not as real as heaven to them, and North America it is as far away as the stars."

Acosta smiled for Toro's innocence.

"So it is of this matter that I will warn you, if you please, Meester Lewis. I cannot make El Toro come to North America without I promise to take care of him with very great *fidelidad*, er . . ."

"Faithfulness," I said.

"Ah, ¿habla usted español?"

"Un poco," I said. *"Muy poco. Seis meses en Méjico."*

"Good, very good," he said warmly. *"Su acento de usted es perfecto."*

"Mi acento es stinko," I said.

"Ah, you have the sense of humor," Acosta said. "In my Argentina we have the saying: A man who cannot laugh is a man who cannot cry."

"On Eighth Avenue life is not so simple," I said.

"Around the Madison Square Garden it is very impressive, yes?" Acosta said. "That is where they make the big business, the ringside ticket for maybe thirty dollars. In my country a hundred pesos. *¡Fantástico!* My ambition it is to see the name of El Toro Molina in the lights of the Garden *marquesina,* this peasant clay that I have carve into work of art. It is my big dream, my big promise to El Toro."

He wasn't kidding. You could see from the intense way his eyes worked that he wasn't kidding. He was a little man, both in stature and achievement and he came from an under-populated, second-rate country. This was his way of dreaming greatness. The way he lived it, Toro Molina was David to his Michelangelo.

"But you must think I am a man of very much wind," Acosta said. "I have talk all this time and I have not tell you this matter of the warning. El Toro, I love him like my son, but he has no head for the business. Only me he trusts to take care of his money. For this he comes with me, to take back the big money to his family in the village. So I cannot tell him of the business of Meester Latka. He will not understan' how I have sell fifty percent to Meester Vanneman and how Meester Vanneman has turn around and sell forty percent to Meester Latka and how Meester

Latka has also buy from me another forty percent. This business El Toro
will not know how to understan'. It will make him very frighten', I
think. So it is better for El Toro if he think the agreement we come to
New York with is not change. It is better if he think Meester Latka is
only my very good friend, a very big North American sportsman. So
when he sees Meester Latka around very many times he has no sospe-
cha, sos . . ."

"Suspicion," I said.

"Exactamente," Acosta said, "suspicion."

"In other words, when I see the boy, you want me to dummy up about
how he is being sliced up like corned beef in a delicatessen," I said.

"Please?" Acosta said.

"Dummy up," I said. "Keep quiet about your little deal with Vanneman and Latka."

"Ah, your slang, they are so colorful," Acosta said. "I would like
before I go back to the Argentine to learn them all."

"Before you go back to the Argentine," I said, "you will learn a great
deal."

"Thank you very much," Acosta said.

"Now let's get back to this work-of-art of yours," I said. "You really
believe you've got a fighter, huh?"

That look came into his eyes again. "Argentina, it is a land of great
fighters," he began. "Luis Angel Firpo would have won the knockout
over Dempsey if the sporting writers had not lift him back into the ring.
Alberto Lovell wins the amateur championship of the world in the
Olympic. But El Toro Molina—he is our greatest, the greatest of all. In
Argentina the mountains are very high, the pampas are very wide, it is a
big country, big cattle, big men, but El Toro—his mother calls him El
Toro because when he is born he weighs twelve pounds ten ounces—he
is *gigantesco,* with the neck and the shoulders of a fighting bull and
muscles in his arms as big as melons and legs as strong as the great
quebracho trees of the Andes."

"Tell me," I said. "Just where did you find this mythological con-
glomerate of fighting bull, mountains, melons and *quebracho* trees?"

"Ah, you mean where have I make my great discovery?"

"Sí, dígame," I said. Nick should dig my *dígame,* I thought. I should
get a couple of extra sawbucks for doing the Spanish version.

"Two years ago I have a little traveling circus in Mendoza," Acosta
began. "There is Miguelito, the clown; there is the bareback riders Señor
and Señora Mendez and their horse; there is Juanito Lopez with his dancing bear; there is Antonio the Magician which is me (one day I will
make a card trick for you); and there is Alfredo el Fuerte, Alfredo the
Strong-one. At the end of his act Alfredo always makes the challenge to

lift up anything that three men in the audience can carry up on the stage together.

"When we come to the little village of Santa Maria in the beautiful wine country of the Andes, we are ask to present our performance in the great patio for the amusement of the de Santos family who have the great *casa de campo* on the highest peak overlooking thousands and thousands of hectares of their beautiful grapes. It is the name day of the head of the de Santos family, and while they watch from the balcony, all the villagers crowd around our little portable stage in the courtyard. Things are passing very excellently. Yes, everything goes very excellently until my last act, Alfredo the Strong-one. Alfredo is a very accomplish strong man, only he has one weakness, which is a very great thirst for champagne brandy. The evening before our performance Alfredo has make a rendezvous with the youngest daughter of the butler of the de Santos *casa*. The next morning when I smell the breath of Alfredo, it is even stronger than he is. I find it out that the little *muchacha* has stolen for him a bottle of champagne brandy from the cellar of the great house with the keys of her father. So when Alfredo makes his challenge to pick up anything three men can carry up on the stage he is already puffing like a big fish in the net. . . ."

"This is all very interesting," I said, "but I'm not doing the life story of your circus. All I need is the stuff on Molina."

"Please," Acosta said, as if I were a heckler climbing up on the stage in the middle of his act, "they are all threads in the same rug, how I have come to make the great discovery of El Toro Molina." He fitted another cigarette into his holder and gave me his cold social smile. "When I see in what weaken condition is Alfredo the Strong-one I am praying to Saint Anthony of my devotion that nothing heavy will come up on the stage. But Saint Anthony does not hear me. Because three of the biggest men I have ever see are carrying up on the stage the biggest barrel of wine I ever see. One of the men is old, of very little more height than I have, but he is almost as wide as he is tall. The other two are young *gigantes* who have over six feet in height and weigh more than Luis Firpo.

" 'Who are those big fellows?' I ask. 'They are the Molinas,' I am told. 'Very famous of this village. The short one is Mario Molina, the barrel-maker, and those are two of his sons, Rafael and Ramon. At all our feast days when it comes to the wrestling, old Mario was always the champion. And now his sons can throw him on his back as easy as you can swallow a grape.' "

"That's good," I said. "That's in the script. I can use that."

"Please," Acosta said. "I will give you what Meester Latka call 'the whole treatment.' Now the big wine barrel is on the stage and if Alfredo

cannot lift it I have promise to pay each of the men who have come up
on the stage one peso. And if, God forbid, anyone in the audience can
come up and equal Alfredo's feat, I have promise to pay five pesos.
Poor Alfredo he puts his arms around the barrel and the sweat is running
down both sides of his nose in two steady streams and I swear on the
faithfulness of my mother to my father I can smell the champagne
brandy. Yes, there is much sweat and much noise but no lifting of the
barrel. All the villagers have begin to shout rude remarks and Alfredo
has much anger in himself and sucks in his breath until the ribs begin to
show through the fat. But still there is no lifting of the barrel. The
villagers are throwing vegetables at Alfredo. Then some one calls out,
'El Toro, we want El Toro' and soon everyone is shouting 'El Toro, El
Toro'!

"Out of the crowd a giant rises up and he seems to get bigger and
bigger as he comes. When he climb up on the stage he move very slow
but very *poderoso*. . . ."

"Powerful," I said.

"Thank you," Acosta said. "Very powerful, like an elephant. He seem
very embarrass. 'I do not wish to come up, señor,' he say to me, 'but it
is the wish of my friends who I cannot insult.' Then, I swear by my
sainted mother, El Toro reach down and lifts the barrel high in the air.
The crowd laughs and shouts *Mucho, mucho, viva* El Toro Molina.
'Who is this fellow?' I ask. 'He is the youngest son of Mario Molina,'
they say to me, 'the strongest man in Argentina.'

"When I pay this young giant the five pesos he has win I say to him,
'Perhaps you will like to come along with me and take the place of my
Strong-one. You will have much money in your pocket and see many
fine cities and everywhere you go beautiful señoritas will marvel at your
strength and be yours for the taking.'

"But El Toro says, 'I wish to stay with my people. I am content here.'

" 'How much are you pay by the *estanciero?*' I say.

" 'Two pesos a day.'

" 'Two pesos! That is but the droppings of the sparrow. From Luis
Acosta you will receive five pesos and when we are performing in Mendoza and the crowds do not keep their hands in their pockets you will
make ten, maybe fifteen, pesos a day. You will come back to Santa
Maria and take the most beautiful girl in the village for your wife.'

" 'You mean Carmelita Perez?' El Toro says.

"At last I have found the soft spot. 'Of course I mean Carmelita,' I
say. 'Who else but Carmelita? You will come back with money enough
to build a house for yourself. For you and Carmelita. And from Mendoza you will bring her a beautiful silk dress as fine as anything worn by
the daughters of de Santos.'

"El Toro looks at me a long time and I can see that my words are working in his head. 'I will ask permission of my father,' he says to me. The father talks it over with Mama Molina who has never travel more than fifty kilometers beyond Santa Maria. She is very much frighten for what will happen to her *infante muy grande,* when he goes down into the great cities. But the brothers Ramon and Rafael they urge the father very much to give El Toro the permission. The brothers have convince Mario to give El Toro the permission. Then there is much embracing and weeping and *Vaya con Dios,* and El Toro lifts his giant body onto my truck and waves good-bye to his family with his enormous hands. I drive down the mountainside with as much speed as I can because I am afraid if El Toro will change his mind."

"Giant son of peasant barrel-maker leaves village in Andes to be strong man in traveling circus," I scribbled. It was one of those stories you could push beyond the sports page. The *Post* or *Collier's* might go for it. There might even be a little extra dough in a piece that gives a name and a personality to the human desire for size and strength. I could start with a mention of the Jews of Palestine and give them Samson. It would sound learned to show how the Greeks worshipped Atlas, Hercules and Titan. How Rabelais dreamed up Gargantua. And now, Toro Molina. For modern times we'd dish up a giant of our own, worthy to stand shoulder to shoulder with great and ancient company. What mighty feats would our giant perform, equaling those of Samson who came down from the hills to champion his subjugated people, Atlas who supported the world on his muscled back, and Hercules who fought his way up onto Mount Olympus! To keep the classical flavor, we could even ring in the *deus ex machina* in the person of Nick Latka, postgraduate hoodlum, soft-shoe racketeer and country gentleman as the means by which a giant peasant from the highest mountains in the New World follows the old pattern from man of the people to hero to demigod and finally joins the deities of contemporary mythology.

"Everywhere I go I have a very big success with El Toro," Acosta was saying while I played with the idea of becoming a god-maker. "The people have never see such bigness, such magnificence of muscles. Because I love El Toro so much I do not give him ten percent of the collection; I let him keep twenty-five percent, for I have promise that when he go back to the village, he will have more money than all the peasants together. But El Toro goes to the great marketplace in Mendoza and like a child he spends every last centavo. For his mama he buys the bandana and for Carmelita a fine black lace gown and for himself a top hat which he brings back wearing on his head. Such a child is El Toro and so little he knows of the world.

"Across the promenade from my circus at the great fair in Mendoza is

my good friend Lupe Morales who is the old sparring partner of Luis
Angel Firpo. Lupe makes the challenge to anyone in the audience to stay
in the ring with him for three minutes. I see the collection of Lupe
Morales and I watch that of El Toro Molina and I am surprise to see that
Lupe who is all wash up in the boxing brings more money than El Toro.
Why am I wasting my time picking up little coins in a side show when I
have in my hands a gold mine?

"So I make a deal with my friend Lupe that he will teach El Toro the
science of the prize fight in return for five percent of all the money El
Toro will make in the ring. When I tell El Toro what I have arrange, he
says he does not like. 'Why should Lupe hit me and I hit Lupe back
when we are not angry with each other?' he says. Poor El Toro, he has a
body like a mountain but a brain like a pea. 'To be angry is not necessary, El Toro,' I say to him. 'The boxing is a business.' But El Toro is
not convince.

"I have much worry because all my life I think, Luis, you are too
clever to die in the province with your little traveling circus. Some day
you will find something equal to your brain and showmanship. And now
it is in my hand. But I am not thinking only of Luis Acosta. I think of El
Toro also, who is become like a son to me. I have see his house in the
village and I know how poor he lives even with their four pairs of arms
of such strength.

"So I say to El Toro, 'I offer you the opportunity to make more money
than you ever dream was in the world. Just to climb into the ring and
box half of one hour you will make five hundred, maybe one thousand,
pesos. Come with me to Buenos Aires and I will make so much money
for you that you will be able to go back to Santa Maria and pay off the
debt on your father's house and hire a maid for Carmelita. You can lie in
bed after the sun is up and cuddle your wife and go to cockfights and sit
at the café and sip your wine. How can you say you are in love if you
are not willing to do this little for the happiness of Carmelita?'

"And so at last I have convince El Toro because in my own language I
am very *elocuente,* although perhaps you cannot tell it from my English
which suffers from a shortness of vocabulary."

"Don't worry about your English," I said. "Compared to the gentlemen who hang around Stillman's, you have the vocabulary of a Tunney.
And he had to sweat for his too."

"You are very kind," Acosta said. "So now I am ready to make my
peasant giant into a champion. Lupe does not know the science of *el box*
like your Tunney or the little heavyweight Loughran who keeps his left
glove in the face of Arturo Godoy in the big fight in Buenos Aires. But
he knows to show El Toro how to put his left foot forward and hold his
left hand out, with the right hand under the chin to protect the great jaw.

He knows to show him how to balance on the balls of the feet, so he is ready to move forward or backward, and he knows to teach him how to lead with his left hand and cross with his right and snap back once more into position. What you call the fundamentals of self-defense, yes? He shows him how to throw the uppercut when he is in close and how to hold his arms in to his body in the clinch, so his opponent cannot hit him in the kidney and the rib. And that is all Lupe can teach, because there is even more to the science than Lupe knows.

"Little by little El Toro learns, for he is always serious in his work and tries to please me very much. In the sparring with Lupe he is very strong because he has the wind of a bull and in the clinch he can toss Lupe around like a feather, and when he has train nearly two months Lupe says now he is ready for the fight in Buenos Aires.

"So at last we are in Buenos Aires, where Lupe Morales has arrange for Luis Angel Firpo himself to box an exhibition with El Toro. When it is finish Firpo tell the newspapers that El Toro is stronger than Dempsey when Dempsey knock him down six times in the first round of their million-dollar fight in the state of New Jersey. So now El Toro Molina already has much fame in Buenos Aires and he is match to fight Kid Salado, the champion of La Pampa. Outside the arena the poster in very large letters has the name El Toro Gigantesco de Mendoza, the Giant Bull of Mendoza. And under this in little letters, 'Under the Exclusive Management of Señor Luis Acosta.' Every time I see this poster, it make me feel very good. How Luis and his giant have come up in the world! We are making everyone sit up and notice. Two days before the fight there are no more tickets to sell. Out of this great piece of peasant clay I find in the mountain I have make the biggest drawing card in South America."

"Okay, okay, but what happened with Salado? This suspense is killing me," I said.

"In the fight with Salado it is ten rounds to a draw, which is all right for El Toro in his first time. You must remember that Salado is a boxer of much experience who knows many tricks and has three times knock out Lupe Morales. For this fight they pay me one thousand pesos, from which I give Toro five hundred, in spite I am taking all the risk by giving up my circus business and putting all my eggs on El Toro Gigantesco. With the five hundred pesos El Toro is very happy, especially when I take him down to the great shopping center on the Roque Saens Pena. I take him to a tailor who makes especially for him a fine brown suit with red and blue stripes which make El Toro laugh with happiness because he has never own a suit of clothes before. 'You see,' I say to him. 'You trust Luis who takes the place of your father, and everything will happen good for you as I have promise.'"

"This is all fine," I cut in, "full of stuff I can use, but we're getting close to chow and we're still down in B.A. Bring me up to date, how you happened to come to town."

"For many many years," Acosta began, "I myself have the dream to come to North America. I cannot bring my little circus. I do not have money enough to go for pleasure. But now that I have El Toro I know it is my opportunity. The people of North America, I have hear, spend much money on the sports. And also they make themselves into big crowds to see something new. My El Toro Gigantesco, I think, if he makes one thousand pesos in one night in Buenos Aires, he can make ten thousand dollars for one fight in North America. The people of North America are—you will excuse me—a little loco when it comes to the number of them who will pay big money to see a heavyweight fight. Lupe remembers from 1923, when he is with Luis Angel Firpo, the night eighty thousand people pay to see our Wild Bull of the Pampas fight Jess Willard when Willard has forty years of age. So I have great confidence that El Toro will make an even bigger success in North America than Firpo who has make in two years here nearly one million dollar.

"When I tell El Toro we will take a boat to North America, he is very frighten. He remembers that the old man of the village says the people of North America do not like the dark skins. The parents of El Toro are of Spanish blood, but there is from the grandfather a little of the *Negro,* perhaps a drop or two. The skin of El Toro is yellow-brown, from standing so many years in the Andean sun. El Toro has heard that in your country they burn the dark ones. He has not the intelligence to understan' that this is not an occurrence of every day.

"So I say to El Toro, 'You know the great house of the de Santos that rises from the highest hilltop overlooking your village and the Rio Rojas. When you come back with me from North America, you will have money enough to build a house of such elegant proportions on the other side of the valley. The people of your village will lift their eyes to the *casa de Molina* and say "Look, it is even greater than the *casa de Santos."* ' To El Toro this sounds like the biggest of all dreams, but he has learn to have faith in his Luis and to follow him like an obedient son. So at last we are here in North America, four thousand miles from the village of Santa Maria. When you put it in the papers, please write how proud is Luis Acosta to introduce to your great country the first authentic giant to climb through the rope and seek the championship of the world."

"Is that all you have to say for publication this morning?" I said.

"One more little thing," Acosta said. "When you spell my first name please be so kind as not to put an *o* in the middle—just the four letters, please: L-u-i-s, pronounce Looeeess."

"I'll remember," I said.

"Thank you very much," Acosta said. He was an intense, self-centered little man who obviously loved to hear himself tell this story over and over again. His personality was compounded of romanticism and materialism, benevolence, acquisitiveness and too many years of unsatisfied vanity, all resolved now in his paternal and profitable creation.

"And now there is just one little personal matter of which I will ask your advice," Acosta said. "It is the matter of the percentage. When I come to New York I have very much difficulty arranging a match for El Toro. To get a good match, you need to have very often your name in the papers. You must have much money for the build-up. And to fight in the Garden, it is necessary to know Mr. Jacobs."

"How long you been around here now, Acosta?" I said.

"We are now in your country nine weeks."

"You're doing all right," I said.

"Twenty-five years in the circus business," Acosta said. "I learn to fool the people and not myself. I see very quick the American boxing business is closed tight for Luis. It is entirely necessary to have partner who has what you call the 'in.' I meet Meester Vanneman in the gymnasium. From the way he talk he is a manager of very big importance. So I sell him fifty percent of El Toro for twenty-five hundred dollars. But a week later I am astonish to hear that Meester Vanneman has sell forty percent of his share to Meester Latka for thirty-five hundred dollar. Then Meester Latka sends for me. Meester Vanneman cannot get El Toro into the Garden, Mr. Latka say to me. He is the only one who has the connection to do that, he say. So he makes me the offer to buy forty percent of my share for thirty-five hundred dollars also. Only, if you will excuse me for saying, it is not exactly an offer. If I do not give him this forty, Meester Latka says to me, I might as well take my El Toro back to Argentina. It seems he has the power to keep me out of the Garden and any other place. So you see, Meester Lewis, for me the position is very difficult. For all my work I am left with only ten percent. And from this I have promise to pay half to Lupe Morales. I did not come for money only, but to me this is a very great disappointment."

I ran through the stockholders in my mind, eighty percent of the manager's end to Latka, which meant 40-40 for him and Quinn, ten for McKeogh, ten for Vanneman, ten for me, five for Acosta, five for Morales, added up to 120 percent. A little complicated. Not as complicated as some of Nick's deals, but well beyond simple arithmetic. Not the kind of equation to figure in your head, unless you had Nick's head, in which case you didn't worry about such mathematical problems as how to cut a pie into five quarters. Either Nick's head or Nick's bookkeeper, Leo Hintz. Leo was a neat, serious, middle-aged man who looked like a small-city bank-teller. In fact that's what he had been, in Schenectady, until his thirty bucks a week made him feel that a change was necessary. Unfortunately for Leo the change he decided to make was a slight alteration in some of his entries, a little matter of a digit here and there that added up to an extra zero on the end of Leo's $1560 a year. Not long afterwards, however, Leo's income was suddenly cut to fifty cents a day, which is what the State of New York pays the inhabitants of Sing Sing prison. Leo was a sort of mathematical genius with a natural talent for quiet larceny, the modern highwayman who has swapped his black mask for a green eyeshade.

"Meester Lewis," Acosta continued, showing his small, white teeth in an anxious, mirthless smile, "since you are so *simpático* I will take the liberty to ask a very big favor. Meester Latka likes you very much, so I am thinking perhaps if you will be so kind to ask him please to make a little bigger my share of the . . ."

"Look, *amigo*," I said. "Don't give me that *simpático* crap. In Mexico every time somebody told me I was *simpático* I got taken. Nick likes me because he needs me. But he doesn't need me that much. You've got your deal. If you want my opinion, you were lucky to come out with ten percent. Maybe that's his idea of the Good Neighbor Policy."

Acosta crossed one short leg over the other, drawing up his pants carefully to protect the creases. He must have been a sharp little business man in Mendoza. Here he was just another peddler. "But ten percent, which I must share with Lupe Morales, is like the droppings of a fly. Especially when it *is* my idea, the big idea of putting boxing gloves on a giant, a conception that will make much money for Meester Latka. He will be grateful, yes?"

"He will be grateful, no," I said. "Now *useful* he understands, but grateful, that's too abstract."

Acosta shook his head in uneasy bewilderment. "You North Americans, you are so direct. You not only say what you mean but you say it immediately. In my country"—he indicated a large circle in the air with his cigarette holder—"we say things like this, instead of"—he bisected his imaginary circle with a sharp downward stroke—"like *that*." He closed his eyes, massaging the right lid with his thumb, the left with his forefinger, as if his head ached. Here he was, four thousand miles from Santa Maria, with only five percent of a dream.

5

When you saw Toro Molina for the first time he was so big you had to focus on him in sections, the way a still camera photographs a skyscraper. The first shot took in no features at all, just an impression of tremendous bulk, like the view a man has of a mountain when he's standing close to its base. Then, as Nick led him into the sun-room, where Acosta and I had been waiting for them, I made an effort to look up at the face which rose a full foot above mine. I felt like a kid in a sideshow peering up at the Tallest Man in the World.

When I stared at Toro that first time the word *giant* that Acosta had been beating me over the head with didn't occur to me at all. It was *monster* that was in my mind. His hands were monstrous, the size of his feet was monstrous and his oversized head instantly became my conception of the Neanderthal Man who roamed this world some forty thousand years ago. To see him move, slowly, with an awkward loping gait, into the sun-room, bending almost double to come through the doorway, was as disconcerting as seeing one of the restored fossils of primitive man in the Museum of Natural History suddenly move toward you and offer a bony hand in greeting. But if anyone were making book on who was the most disconcerted, he would have had to string along with Toro.

Toro acted like a large field animal, a bull or a horse, that has suddenly been lassoed and led into a house. But when he saw Acosta he looked relieved. Acosta said, quickly in Spanish, "El Toro, come over here, I want you to meet a new friend of ours," and Toro came obediently, placing himself a little behind Acosta, as if seeking protection from the pudgy little man who would have to stand on his tip-toes to tap him on the shoulder. That brown suit with the red and blue stripes that Acosta had bought for him in Buenos Aires was pinched in the shoulders; the pants were tight and the sleeves fell short several inches above the wrist. Looking at him more closely as the first shock was wearing off, I remember having the impression of seeing a trained monkey of nightmare proportions dressed up like a man mechanically going through his act under the watchful eye of the organ grinder. Only in this case Luis Acosta didn't need an instrument strapped over his shoulder. He played his own music and wrote his own words and apparently could grind them out tirelessly.

"El Toro," Acosta said (and even the way he snapped the name out and paused a moment reminded me of the way an animal trainer fixes the attention of his beast before giving the command), "shake hands with Meester Lewis."

Toro hesitated a moment, just the way you've seen them do it hundreds of times in the animal act, and then obeyed. I was afraid it was going to be like putting my hand in a meat-grinder, but he didn't grasp it very hard, wasn't sure enough of himself, I guess. Instead it felt like the end of an elephant's trunk pushing into your hand when you're feeding it peanuts, heavy and calloused, unnatural, and with a strange massive gentleness.

"Con mucho gusto," I said, throwing six months of Mexico into the breach.

Toro just nodded perfunctorily. After we shook hands he stepped back behind Acosta again, looking down at him inquisitively, as if waiting for the next command.

"Whadya think of him, Eddie?" Nick said. "Think we oughta start renting him out by floors like the Empire State?"

That was the first of the Toro Molina jokes. This time I laughed, but, oh, how weary I was to become of those jokes about Molina's size!

When Nick made jokes he was feeling good. "Well, did you get everything you want?" he asked me. "Did the little guy talk?"

"To fill a book," I said.

"Hey, that ain't such a bad idea, a book," Nick said. "Maybe one of those comic books. Like this Superman. Know what Superman sells? Eight, ten million copies. At a dime a throw, not bad."

Some day, when they put out a new edition of old Gustavus Meyer's *History of the Great American Fortunes* you may be reading how Nicholas Latka ("illustrious great-great-grandfather of Nicholas Latka III") got his. It may be right in there with the Vanderbilts and the Goulds and the rest of the fancy who knew when to break a law and when to make one.

"Come on out," Nick said. "I wanna show him around to the boys." He nodded toward Toro with a laugh. "Follow me, half-pint."

Acosta leaned over and said under his breath, "Follow him." Toro nodded, in the obedient peasant way he had, carrying out Acosta's imperative literally and walking directly in Nick's footsteps with that slow awkward lope. Suddenly Nick stopped and said, half-kidding, "Tell 'im, for Christ sake, to stop walkin' behind me. Makes me feel like I'm being tracked down by a neliphant."

Acosta translated and Toro must have taken it for censure, for he hurried to catch up with Nick. In his haste, one of his ponderous feet tripped over a lamp wire and he lurched forward, almost losing his balance. He flailed the air clumsily to right himself. He was definitely no Nijinsky. But you couldn't always tell by that. I've seen quite a few flatfooted, awkward fellows look pretty shifty and smart inside the ropes.

"What was that, Eddie," Nick said, "a clean knockdown or just a slip?"

He turned to me with a wink and tapped me playfully on the jaw.

Beth was sitting on the terrace, alone and a little bewildered, for Beth. "Sorry to be so long," I said. "Everything okay?"

"I'm glad I came," she said ambiguously. "But next time I think I'll let you go alone."

Maybe it had been a mistake to throw Beth in with Nick's crowd. She was a girl who had made an easy adjustment from Amherst to New York, but you didn't have to be a clairvoyant to see that this was a world she never knew and didn't want to know. And yet, in spite of herself, she found herself curiously attracted to all this, as to a sideshow of freaks. She telegraphed me a quick smile with a suggestion of panic in it.

"What are the amenities about the hostess in this party?" she asked.

"Oh, Ruby can take her guests or leave them. I kind of like Ruby."

"She makes me nervous. I haven't been able to talk with her. I tried my best, and it wasn't good enough to take her away from the book she was reading."

I took Beth by the arm and led her over to Ruby, who was stretched out on a lawn couch on wheels. When she looked up at us, I said, "What book you reading?"

She held it up for us to see. "It's the Number One Best Seller," Ruby said. It was one of those eight-hundred-page packages with the cover featuring a seventeenth-century Hedy Lamarr bursting her bodice. *The Countess Misbehaved,* this one was called.

Ruby spent most her time in the country reading novels like this Countess business. I know Nick was rather proud of her intellectual pursuits, the way she went through these books week after week. "We've got a hell of a library out there," Nick had told me. "I'll bet Ruby knocks off three books a week. Remembers what she reads too."

So Ruby, who had never exposed her lovely, unlined face to the pressure of literature until she got out in the country and didn't know what to do with herself, had developed an intimate relationship with European history. She could talk with as much authority about the backstair affairs of the hot-blooded ladies-in-waiting at the court of Charles the First as she could about the marital difficulties of Ethel her cook.

When Ruby wasn't consuming her marshmallow history, she was either driving to church in her station wagon or drinking Manhattans. Her life in the country seemed to break up into those three phases. She was sentimental about her religion and retained a schoolgirl's admiration and sense of responsibility to her devotions. The only thing that would get her out of bed before noon was church services, if her hangover wasn't too bad. The nipping usually started around three. I stayed out there through a week once to get some work done, and Ruby would come down for cocktails every evening with a good three-hour start. An outsider might not have been able to tell the difference. She handled it well enough, but her eyes became very set and moist and, depending on what mood she was in when she started drinking, she usually brought the conversation around to religion or sex, working her way up to the latter by way of Metternich's mistress or Napoleon's sister or some other full-bosomed footnote to history. When this happened she had a way of leaning toward you, talking feverishly with her face closer and closer to yours, which made you feel it could happen if you really tried.

This may be an injustice. Nothing ever happened between us and I wouldn't have been too surprised if Ruby had turned out to be as virtuous as she felt on her way home from church on Sunday morning. I wouldn't have been too surprised if she had turned out to be any or all of the things the gossips had her figured for. Her manner was always composed and ladylike, but there was something about her eyes, black and unusually dilated, which left you with the uneasy impression of a deep, controlled instability.

It was this undefined but vivid impression, I think, rather than anything one could be sure of, that started rumors about Ruby. Felix Montoya, the Puerto Rican lightweight, one of Nick's boys, had told me a tall one about something he claimed had happened while he was out training at the place. Nick has his own gym out there with a ring and nice equipment. Felix was there for three weeks when he was getting ready for his title bout with Angott. What Felix told me is that he had Ruby every night except the weekends when Nick came down. What Felix also told me is the part I keep thinking about. Felix paid her the highest compliment he knew when he said that her response compared very favorably with the best Puerto Rico had to offer. But it made him very nervous, he said, when, as they lay in her great double bed, she would reach her arm out to the phone on the bed-table and call Nick in New York. Then, while holding Felix to her with one arm but giving him the sign to be as quiet as possible, she would hold a typical wifely conversation with Nick. "Hello, honey. How's everything in the city? . . . What time will you be out Friday? . . . Anything special you want me to get you for dinner? . . . Sure, I miss you, silly. . . . Be a good boy now. . . . Bye-bye, honey."

Of course that's Felix's story, and Felix sleeps with every woman he meets, if you listen to Felix. If he hadn't left his fighting strength in somebody's bed, I didn't know how else to account for the farce he made with Angott. On the basis of Felix's waltz, I was half inclined to buy his story. But that telephone business was too wild to be credible. Yet, I'd slug toe-to-toe with myself in this one-man debate; it was so bizarre that it didn't seem probable that Felix would have the imagination to dream up such a fantasy.

At any rate, no matter where the needle really pointed, Nick was satisfied. If he were to hear these stories from anyone it would have been the Killer, and Ruby was the only woman in the world about whom the Killer observed strict discretion. So Nick still felt as he had when he married Ruby, that this was the smartest thing he ever did. Those were the words he often used to describe it, as if Ruby were a prize member of Nick's stable. And Ruby was a good wife to Nick, always there when he wanted her, warm and gracious as a hostess, well-spoken, beautifully groomed, with plenty of class in her choice of clothes and her way of wearing them, a good girl who went to church every Sunday and read books.

From where we sat we watched the crowd that had gathered on the terrace and the lawn beyond. Nick's partner, Jimmy Quinn, and his wife and Mrs. Lennert, the wife of the old heavyweight champion, were chatting together. Quinn's face and figure, his baldness, his clothes and the way he had of laughing from his belly, are what we have come to expect from too many Irish politicians. In his youth it must have been a strong, aggressive face, but years of ease and self-indulgence had softened the hard lines with fat and a hearty red complexion, which was really high blood pressure but gave him the cheery, benevolent look of a beardless Santa Claus. He was ostentatiously good-humored and, faithful to the conviction that all Irishmen are great wits, he was addicted to puns and hoary dialect stories. Quinn's concession to country life had been to remove the coat of his single-breasted, three-button suit, and now he was sitting with his collar open, in white suspenders and white arm-garters that hiked up his sleeves, high-laced black shoes and a snap-brim straw hat. Quinn had just said something intended for humor, for he threw his head back and belly-laughed while the women smiled obligingly. When he caught me looking over he waved affably and said, "How ya, young fella?" with his big vote-getting grin. There was nothing mechanical about the cordiality of Honest Jimmy Quinn. He slapped your back, shook your hand and made you chuckle as if he really enjoyed it. He was one sweet guy, Jimmy Quinn, that's what everybody said, one sweet guy. There was nothing in the world Honest Jimmy wouldn't do for you if you asked him, unless you happened to have the misfortune of being a yid, a jigaboo, a Republican or unable to return a favor.

Mrs. Quinn was a formidable, bosomy lady. She always referred to her husband as "the Judge" because he had had the boys put him up for the municipal bench in the early days when he couldn't afford to carry the Party work without being on somebody's payroll.

By contrast, Mrs. Lennert was a plain, quiet woman who looked more like the wife of a truckdriver or a coalminer than of a famous pugilist. She didn't drink. She sat patiently with an attitude of polite boredom, only breaking her silence with an occasional, "Gus, a little quieter," or "Paul, not so much noise," as she kept a motherly eye on her three sons, aged fourteen, twelve and eight, who were out on the lawn throwing a softball around with their old man.

Big Gus was a good all-around athlete who had done a little pitching for Newark before he broke into the fight game. Boxing was just bread-and-butter. His real love was baseball. I don't think the Yanks have played a doubleheader at home for years without Gus and the three kids being up there in their usual seats, behind first base. Gus wasn't the most popular fellow in the sports world because word had gotten around that he would back up from a waiter's check as if it threatened to bite his hand. Gus was a businessman. He knew he had just so many fights left in him, so many purses, and he wanted to make sure he had a little more than enough when he settled down to the restaurant business again.

On the lawn Nick was introducing Acosta and Toro to Danny McKeogh, who appraised them sourly, and to the Killer and the little pekinese-faced hatcheck girl from the Diamond Horseshoe who had just arrived in the Killer's yellow Chrysler roadster. Acosta kissed the doll's hand and bowed easily to the others. Toro stood uncomfortably at his side. The Killer stepped into a fighting pose and feinted with his left as if he were going to lay one on Toro. Everybody laughed except Toro, who just stood there waiting for Acosta to tell him what to do.

When we sat down to lunch in the formal dining room, with its marble statue of Diana with her bow, I took a quick census that totaled twenty-three of us—a typical Latka Sunday dinner. Nick sat at one end of the table, still in riding clothes, Ruby at the other. Next to Nick were the Quinns who flanked a gentleman who maintained a strict anonymity. Then came Vince Vanneman, Barney Winch and his lieutenant. Farther down were the Lennerts, the Killer, the pekinese, Junior and his tennis partner, Danny McKeogh, then Toro and Acosta, with Beth and me on either side of Ruby. The men had not bothered to put on their coats, and Nick tilted back in his chair as he always did in the office, but if the butler, elegant in tuxedo, felt any contempt for this motley assembly, he hid his feelings behind a carefully cultivated deadpan and served each diner, regardless of posture or grammar, with the impersonal solicitude and excessive formality that mark his trade.

The anonymous gentleman had a thick, shrewd face, with dark, heavy jowls set in a permanent expression of inscrutability. Nick did not trouble to introduce him to the company and he sat silently rolling bread-crumbs. When Vanneman spoke to him it was with an awed deference and without any expectation of response. My first guess, later con-firmed, that he was topman in a mob that had muscled in on Nick's racket was based on no more than a hunch. I did learn, subsequently, a little about him. He was wanted for questioning in connection with a murder one of his boys was supposed to have pulled off on the Upper East Side. At one time he had just about cornered the market on first-rate middleweights and he was still a good man to have on your side if you wanted to get the breaks in the Garden. Just what he was to Nick or Nick to him, it would be healthier not to ask.

"Everything you're gonna eat came right off this place," Nick shouted down the table. "It's all our own stuff, even the meat."

"Your own steer, huh?" Quinn said. He turned to Barney and the other gambler, beginning to laugh already. "Hey, fellers, you don't think Nick would give us a bum steer?" He roared with laughter, looking around at everyone to see that they were with him, then repeated himself and was off again. Toro ate his fruit salad hungrily, keeping his head down like a child who has been told not to intrude on adult conversation.

Nick looked down at Toro and nodded. "You're lucky you don't un-derstand English, kid. The rest of us have to laugh at Jimmy's lousy jokes."

The Killer began the laughter like a claque. Everyone looked at Toro, nodding and snickering. Toro stopped and stared around questioningly. From where he sat, it must have seemed as if they were laughing at him. He pressed his thick lips together and his eyes sought Acosta with con-fusion. Acosta said a few hurried words in Spanish and Toro nodded and went on eating. I watched his big face work as he chewed. It wasn't the face of Colossus, noble and magnificent. It was essentially a peasant face with soft brown eyes, heavy-lidded, a bulbous nose, a big, sensu-ous mouth with dark hollows pressing in on either side of it, suggesting some unhealthiness, glandular perhaps, and an elongated jaw. It was a head for El Greco to have painted in his dark, moody yellows, with the model already magnified and distorted by the artist's astigmatism. If he looked up at all, I noticed, he stole quick, furtive glances at Ruby. This was understandable, for Ruby had magnetism in her white diaphanous silk, with back-swept hair and jade earrings swaying as she talked ani-matedly, half Park Avenue, half Tenth.

"Isn't that a swell book?" Ruby was saying. "I can hardly wait to see the movie. Who do you think oughta play Desirée? I read in Danton Walker where it says Olivia de Havilland. Can you see her as Desirée? Paulette Goddard, all the time I was reading I could see Paulette God-dard."

Beth caught my eye for a second but she didn't say anything. I mean she didn't say any of the obvious things you could have said to Ruby. There was something touching about Ruby's discovery of literature, and Nick's pride in this, that made the easy wisecrack catch in your throat. It was like the Dead End Kid who glides up and down in the gutter crying out in wonder *Look at me, I'm dancin'! I'm dancin'!* For Ruby it was *Readin'! I'm readin'!*

"I'm just nuts about history," Ruby said. "It's so much more interesting than what's going on today. I try to get Nick to read sometimes, but he's hopeless."

"Hey, baby," Nick yelled down from the other end of the table, gesticulating with a big cob of yellow corn in his hand. "Everything under control on your end, baby?"

Ruby gave him an indulgent smile and looked at us apologetically. You had a pretty good idea of what there was between them in that smile and that look. Nick was a wonderful husband, a good provider and still nuts about Ruby. She wished he would begin to get over these crudities. All these books, the decorum of social life, the polished manners of the cavaliers had given her a point of view from which to criticize Nick and his loudmouth friends.

"Look at Ruby," Nick laughed. "She thinks I'm making a bum out of myself in front of Albert." Albert was passing the roast beef around again. Not a muscle in his face betrayed his having heard his name brought into this. As he lowered the big silver platter to Nick's place, Nick said, "Just because I eat with my fingers and don't put my coat on, you don't think I'm a bum, do you, Albert?"

"No, sir," Albert said, and moved on to serve Quinn, who took three more pieces of roast beef and two large potatoes.

"There, whaddya think of that, Ruby?" Nick shouted down the table. "The best-dressed guy in the joint and he takes my side."

Nick knew better than this, a little better than this, but he liked to put the mug act on sometimes to show off for his friends and annoy Ruby. It didn't exactly fit with the clothes, the "class" he always wanted or his attitude toward Ruby. I used to wonder at this at first, but I finally decided why Nick seemed to delight in publicly degrading himself sometimes. It provided measurement by which to judge his progress. For he timed these gaucheries to the moment of his most lordly circumstance, such a moment as this when he sat at the head of a twenty-three-piece table, presiding over a lavish feast that would have satisfied the greediest tyrant. "Look," his actions seemed to say, "don't forget that the master of this mansion with the marble statue, the formal butler, his own beef hanging in his own cold-storage plant, is still Nick Latka the hustler from Henry Street."

When we finally managed to get up from the table after an hour of overeating, Nick came over and put his hand on my shoulder. "Want to talk to you," he said. "Let's go out to the sun-house."

The sun-house was just behind the swimming pool, a circular stucco job with no roof. Inside were sun-mats and rubbing tables. Nick took off his clothes and stretched out on his back on one of the mats. He inhaled deeply, seeming to take sun and air in at the same time. His body had a dark even tan and was in wonderful condition for a man in his early forties. It looked lean and energetic everywhere except at the belly, where there was the beginning of a paunch.

"Tell the Killer I want him," Nick said.

I went out and shouted up to the Killer. He came right away. "Wot's on yer mind, boss?" he said.

"That sun oil," Nick said, "that new stuff I got. What's it called?"

"Apple erl," the Killer said.

"Yeah, rub some on me. And bring an extra bottle for Eddie," he called when the Killer had reached the medicine chest.

The Killer handed me a bottle and began to anoint Nick's chest and shoulders. I looked at the label. "Apolloil" it was called. "This not only gives you a tan but it puts vitamins into yer skin," Nick said. "Works right into yer pores. Real high-class stuff. Put out by the same outfit that makes that toilet water I gave yer." He took another deep, healthful breath. "Now lower, Killer. Pour some down there." He looked at me and winked. "It's supposed to be good for that too," he said.

While the Killer rubbed the oil into Nick's thighs, Nick said, "Well, let's get down to business. Acosta give you any ideas?"

"Well, the way he found him is colorful enough," I said.

"I don't want this long-winded crap," Nick said. "You know the fight business as good as I do. It's show business with blood. The boys who fill the house aren't always the best fighters. They're the biggest characters. Of course nothing helps your character like a finishing punch. But the fans like a name they can latch on to. Like Dempsey the Manassa Mauler. Greb the Pittsburgh Windmill. Firpo the Wild Bull of the Pampas. Something to hit the fans over the head with. A gimmick."

"Well," I said, half-kidding, "I suppose we could call Molina the Giant of the Andes."

Nick sat up and looked at me. "Not bad. The Giant of the Andes." He repeated it. "It's got something. We're making money already. Keep thinking."

"You mean this kind of stuff," I said. I ad-libbed: "Up from the Argentine charged the Wild Bull of the Pampas to knock Dempsey through the ropes and come within a single second of bringing the world's championship home with him. Now comes his protégé, the Giant of the

Andes, to avenge Luis Angel Firpo, his boyhood idol."

"Keep talking, baby," Nick said. "Keep talking. You're talking us into a pisspot full of dough."

I thought this would be as good a time as any, so I said, "By the way, Nick, Acosta doesn't seem to happy about the split."

"There's a law says he has to be happy?" Nick said.

"No," I said, "but the little guy did put a hell of a lot into this. He really discovered Molina, gambled on him, and . . ."

"You feel so sorry for him maybe you want to give him your ten percent."

Life was much less complicated when you agreed with Nick.

"No," I said, "but . . ."

"How do you like that little greaseball!" said Nick, a great non-listener when you weren't speaking for his benefit. "He hasn't enough connections to get Molina into a pay toilet in the Garden. Any more crap out of him and we take him down to the boat and kiss him off."

He rolled over and let the Killer massage his back. "Keep your mind on your racket," he said. "I'll take care of mine."

When we came out, everybody had moved down to the pool. The gamblers were at it again, at a table under the awning. Barney Winch, the fatter one, was finally winning. "Only two," he was protesting to the world. "When I gin, he's got only two. What've I done to anybody I deserve such punishment?" Gus Lennert and the three boys were back on the lawn tossing the ball around. "Alla way, Pop," the youngest one was shouting. Quinn was sleeping in a deck chair with his straw hat pulled down over his face. Junior and his guest had apparently gone back to the court. Beth was in the water, swimming a relaxed crawl. The Killer's little pekinese blonde was lying on the edge of the pool working on her tan. She wore black, modern-shaped sunglasses and she had untied the bra of her dainty two-piece bathing suit so as to expose to the sun as much of her provocative little body as possible. Danny McKeogh was talking to Acosta. He looked a little more alive since he had eaten, but from where I stood his watery light-blue irises hardly stood out at all from the white of his eyes, giving his face a deathly quality. He was back on his favorite subject, training. He really knew how to train fighters and liked to work them hard.

"When I was a kid the boys were in much better shape," he was saying. "Imagine any of these punks today going thirty, forty tough rounds like Gans, Wolgast or Nelson? They'd drop dead. They don't like to work as hard as we used to, and they haven't got the legs. Too much riding around, taxis, subways . . ."

Ruby was lying in the hammock reading *The Countess Misbehaved*. Who would play Desirée? On the opposite side of the pool a portable radio was blaring loudly, but nobody seemed to be listening to the comic whose formula jokes were punctuated by the feverish applause of an enthralled studio audience.

I wondered where Toro was. I looked around for him, but I didn't see him right away because he was standing so quietly, staring into the lattice archway of the grape arbor beyond the pool. His enormous head almost reached the top of the arch, and with his back to the sun his extraordinary size cast a mountainous image that overshadowed the entire arbor. I wondered what was in his mind. Did these dark ripe grapes evoke the sight and smell of home, of friendly Santa Maria, of his mother and father, of Carmelita, of the cheers that rose from the throats of fellow villagers when he lifted his wine barrels, of the warmth and security of being born into, working and dying in an isolated, intimate community? Or was Toro's mind computing the conspicuous riches of the Latka estate and dreaming of the day he would return to Santa Maria in triumph to build the castle that would rival the very de Santos villa which the barefooted peasants of his village had always looked up to as the ultimate in luxurious shelter, at least in this life and perhaps in the next?

6

Americans are still an independent and rebellious people—at least in their reaction to signs. Stillman's gym, up the street from the Garden, offers no exception to our national habit of shrugging off small prohibitions. Hung prominently on the gray, nondescript walls facing the two training rings a poster reads: "No rubbish or spitting on the floor, under penalty of the law." If you want to see how the boys handle this one, stick around until everybody has left the joint and see what's left for the janitor to do. The floor is strewn with cigarettes smoked down to their stained ends, cigar butts chewed to soggy pulp, dried spittle, empty match cases, thumbed and trampled copies of the *News, Mirror* and *Journal*, open to the latest crime of passion or the race results, wadded gum, stubs of last night's fight at St. Nick's (managers comps), a torn-off cover of an Eighth Avenue restaurant menu with the name of a new matchmaker in Cleveland scrawled next to a girl's phone number. Here on the dirty gray floor of Stillman's is the telltale debris of a world as sufficient unto itself as a walled city of the Middle Ages.

You enter this walled city by means of a dark, grimy stairway that carries you straight up off Eighth Avenue into a large, stuffy, smoke-filled, hopeful, cynical, glistening-bodied world. The smells of this world are sour and pungent, a stale gamey odor blended of sweat and liniment, worn fight gear, cheap cigars and too many bodies, clothed and unclothed, packed into a room with no noticeable means of ventilation. The sounds of this world are multiple and varied, but the longer you listen, the more definitely they work themselves into a pattern, a rhythm that begins to play in your head like a musical score: The trap-drum beating of the light bag, counterpointing other light bags; the slow thud of punches into heavy bags, the tap-dance tempo of the rope-skippers; the three-minute bell; the footwork of the boys working in the ring, slow, open-gloved, taking it easy; the muffled sound of the flat, high-laced shoes on the canvas as the big name in next week's show at the Garden takes a sign from his manager and goes to work, crowding his sparring partner into a corner and shaking him up with body punches; the hard breathing of the boxers, the rush of air through the fighter's fractured nose, in a staccato timed to his movements; the confidential tones the managers use on the matchmakers from the smaller clubs spotting new talent, *Irving, let me assure you my boy loves to fight. He wants none of them easy ones. Sure he looked lousy Thursday night. It's a question of styles. You know that Ferrara's style was all wrong for him. Put 'em in with a boy who likes to mix it an' see the difference;* the deals, the arguments, the angles, the appraisals, the muted Greek chorus, muttering out of the corner of its mouth with a nervous cigar between its teeth; the noise from the telephones; the booths "For Outgoing Calls Only," *Listen, Joe, I just been talking to Sam and he says okay for two hundred for the semi-final at . . .* the endless ringing of the "Incoming Calls Only"; a guy in dirty slacks and a cheap yellow sports shirt, cupping his hairy hands together and lifting his voice above the incessant sounds of the place: *Whitey Bimstein, call for Whitey Bimstein, anybody seen Whitey . . .";* the garbage-disposal voice of Stillman himself, a big, authoritative, angry-looking man, growling out the names of the next pair of fighters to enter the ring, loudly but always unrecognizably, like a fierce, adult babytalk; then the bell again, the footwork sounds, the thudding of gloves against hard bodies, the routine fury.

The atmosphere of this world is intense, determined, dedicated. The place swarms with athletes, young men with hard, lithe, quick bodies under white, yellow, brown and blackish skins and serious, concentrated faces, for this is serious business, not just for blood, but for money.

I was sitting in the third row of the spectators' seats, waiting for Toro to come out. Danny McKeogh was going to have him work a couple of rounds with George Blount, the old Harlem trial horse. George spent most of his career in the ring as one of those fellows who's good enough to be worth beating, but just not good enough to be up with the contenders. Tough but not too tough, soft but not too soft—that's a trial horse. Old George wasn't a trial horse any more, just a sparring partner, putting his big, shiny-black porpoise body and his battered, good-natured face up there to be battered some more for five dollars a round. There were sparring partners you could get for less, but George was what Danny called an honest workman; he could take a good stiff belt without quitting. To the best of his ringwise but limited ability he obliged the managers with whatever style of fighting they asked for. He went in; he lay back; he boxed from an orthodox stand-up stance, keeping his man at distance with his left; he fought from out of a crouch and shuffled into a clinch, tying his man up with his club-like arms and giving him a busy time with the infighting. Good Old George, with the gold teeth, the easy smile and the old-time politeness, calling everybody mister, black and white alike, humming his slow blues as he climbed through the ropes, letting himself get beaten to his knees, climbing out through the ropes again and picking up the song right where he had left it on the apron of the ring. That was George, a kind of Old Man River of the ring, a John Henry with scar tissue, a human punching bag, who accepted his role with philosophical detachment.

In front of me, sparring in the rings and behind the rings, limbering up, were the fighters, and behind me, the non-belligerent echelons, the managers, trainers, matchmakers, gamblers, minor mobsters, kibitzers, with here and there a sportswriter or a shameless tub-thumper like myself. Some of us fall into the trap of generalizing about races: the Jews are this, the Negroes are that, the Irish something else again. But in this place the only true division seemed to be between the flat-bellied, slender-waisted, lively-muscled young men and the men with the paunches, bad postures, fleshy faces and knavish dispositions who fed on the young men, promoted them, matched them, bought and sold them, used them and discarded them. The boxers were of all races, all nationalities, all faiths, though predominantly Negro, Italian, Jewish, Latin-American, Irish. So were the managers. Only those with a bigot's astigmatism would claim that it was typical for the Irish to fight and Jews to run the business, or vice versa, for each fighting group had its parasitic counterpart. Boxers and managers, those are the two predominant races of Stillman's world.

I have an old-fashioned theory about fighters. I think they should get paid enough to hang up their gloves before they begin talking to themselves. I wouldn't even give the managers the 33⅓ percent allowed by the New York Boxing Commission. A fighter only has about six good years and one career. A manager, in terms of the boys he can handle in a lifetime, has several hundred careers. Very few fighters get the consideration of race horses which are put out to pasture when they haven't got it any more, to grow old in dignity and comfort like Man o' War. Managers, in the words of my favorite sportswriter, "have been known to cheat blinded fighters at cards, robbing them out of the money they lost their eyesight to get."

I still remember what a jolt it was to walk into a foul-smelling men's room in a crummy little late spot back in Los Angeles and slowly recognize the blind attendant who handed me the towel as Speedy Sencio, the little Filipino who fought his way to the top of the bantamweights in the late twenties. Speedy Sencio, with the beautiful footwork who went fifteen rounds without slowing down, an artist who could make a fight look like a ballet, dancing in and out, side to side, weaving, feinting, drawing opponents out of position and shooting short, fast, punches, that never looked hard, but suddenly stretched them on the canvas, surprised and pale and beyond power to rise. Little Speedy in those beautiful double-breasted suits and the cocky, jaunty but dignified way he skipped from one corner to the other to shake hands with the participants in a fight to decide his next victim.

Speedy had Danny McKeogh in his corner in those days. Danny looked after his boys. He knew when Speedy's timing was beginning to falter, when he began running out of gas around the eighth, and when the legs began to go, especially the legs. He was almost thirty, time to go home for a fighting man. One night the best he could get was a draw with a tough young slugger who had no business in the ring with him when Speedy was right. Speedy got back to his corner, just, and oozed down on his stool. Danny had to give him smelling salts to get him out of the ring. Speedy was the only real moneymaker in Danny's stable, but Danny said no to all offers. As far as he was concerned, Speedy had had it. Speedy was on Danny all the time, pressing for a fight. Speedy even promised to give up the white girl he was so proud of if Danny would take him back. With Danny it was strike three, you're out, no arguments. Danny really loved Speedy. As a term of endearment, he called him "that little yellow son-of-a-bitch." Danny had an old fighter's respect for a good boy, and, although it would make him a little nauseous to use a word like dignity, I think that is what he had on his mind when he told Speedy to quit. There are not many things as undignified as seeing an old master chased around the ring, easy to hit, caught flat-footed, old wounds opened, finally belted out. The terrible plunge from dignity is what happened to Speedy Sencio when Danny McKeogh tore up the contract and the jackals and hyenas nosed in to feed on the still-warm corpse.

Strangely enough, it was Vince Vanneman who managed Speedy out of the top ten into the men's can. Vince had him fighting three and four times a month around the small clubs from San Diego to Bangor, any place where "former bantamweight champion" still sold tickets. Vince chased a dollar with implacable single-mindedness. I caught up with him and Speedy one night several years ago in Newark, when Speedy was fighting a fast little southpaw who knew how to use both hands. He had Speedy's left eye by the third round and an egg over his right that opened in the fifth. The southpaw was a sharpshooter and he went for those eyes. He knocked Speedy's mouthpiece out in the seventh and cut the inside of his mouth with a hard right before he could get it back in place. When the bell ended the round Speedy was going down and Vince and a second had to drag him back to his corner. I was sitting near Speedy's corner, and though I knew what to expect from Vince I felt I had to make a pitch in the right direction. So I leaned over and said, "For Christ sake, Vince, what do you want to have, a murder? Throw in the towel and stop the slaughter, for Christ's sweet sake."

Vince looked down from the ring where he was trying to help the trainer close the cuts over the eyes. "Siddown and min' your own friggin' business," he said while working frantically over Speedy to get him ready to answer the bell.

In the next round Speedy couldn't see because of the blood and he caught an overhand right on the temple and went down and rolled over, reaching desperately for the lowest strand of the rope. Slowly he pulled himself up at eight, standing with his feet wide apart and shaking his head to clear the blood out of his eyes and his brain. All the southpaw had to do was measure him and he was down again, flat on his back, but making a convulsive struggle to rise to his feet. That's when Vince cupped his beefy hands to his big mouth and shouted through the ropes, "Get up. Get up, you son-of-a-bitch." And he didn't mean it like Danny McKeogh. For some reason known only to men with hearts like Speedy Sencio's, he did get up. He got up and clinched and held on and drew on every memory of defense and trickery he had learned in more than 300 fights. Somehow, four knockdowns and six interminable minutes later, he was still on his feet at the final bell, making a grotesque effort to smile through his broken mouth as he slumped into the arms of his victorious opponent in the traditional embrace.

Half an hour later I was having a hamburger across the street, when Vince came in and squeezed his broad buttocks into the opposite booth. He ordered a steak sandwich and a bottle of beer. He was with another guy, and they were both feeling all right. From what Vince said I gathered he had put up five hundred to win two-fifty that Speedy would stay the limit.

When I paid my check I turned to Vince's booth because I felt I had to protest against the violation of the dignity of Speedy Sencio. I said, "Vince, in my book you are a chintzy, turd-eating butcher!"

That's a terrible way to talk and I apologize to anybody who might have been in that short-order house and overheard me. The only thing I can say in my defense is that if you are talking to an Eskimo it is no good to speak Arabic. But in what I said I didn't even make Vince lose a beat in the rhythmical chewing of his steak.

"Aaah, don't be an old lady," Vince said. "Speedy's never been kayoed, so why should I spoil his record?"

"Sure," I said, "don't spoil his record. Just spoil his face, spoil his head, spoil his life for good."

"Go away," Vince said, laughing. "You'll break my frigging heart."

The bell brought me back from Newark, from Speedy Sencio with his lousy job in that crapper, and I thought, from Vince Vanneman. Then I saw Vince himself coming in. I realized this must have been one of those times when the mind seems to sense someone before the image strikes the eye so that it appears a coincidence when the very man you're thinking about comes in the door. He was wearing a yellow linen sports shirt, open at the neck, worn outside his pants. He came up behind Solly Prinz, the matchmaker, and gave him the finger. Solly seemed to rise up off the ground and let out an excited, girlish scream. Everybody knew Solly was very goosey. It got a good laugh from the circle Solly was standing with. With the rest of his fingers bent toward his palm, Vince held the assaultive middle finger lewdly. "See that, girls?" he said. "That's what a Chicago fag means when he says he'll put the finger on you." That got a laugh too. Vince was a funny guy, a great guy for laughs, just a big fun-loving kid who never grew up.

Vince came over and ran his hand over my hair.

"Hello, lover," he said.

"Balls," I said.

"Aw, Edsie," Vince pouted, "don't be that way. You've got it for me, baby." He threw his head back in an effeminate gesture, flouncing his fat body with grotesque coyness.

It was another Vanneman routine, always good for laughs. Humor was intended to lie in the margin of contrast between the fag act and Vince's obvious virility. I used to wonder about it.

"Seen him box yet?" Vince said.

"He'll be out in a minute," I said. "Danny's having Doc look him over."

"When you gonna break somethin' in the papers about him?"

"When Nick and I figure it's time," I said.

"Get him, get him!" Vince said. "What are ya, a goddam primmer-donner? Damon Runyon or something? I got a right to ask. I'm a partner, ain't I?"

Edwin Dexter Lewis, I mused, born in Harrisburg, Pa., of respectable churchgoing Episcopalians, nearly two years in the Halls of Nassau with

First Group in English and a flunk in Greek, the occasional companion, intellectual and otherwise, of a Smith graduate and *Life* Magazine researcher, an imminent playwright, clearly a man of breeding and distinction—if not of honor. At what point in what I smilingly refer to as my career was it decided that I was to become a business associate of Vincent Vanneman, two hundred and fifteen pounds of Eighth Avenue flotsam, graduate of Blackwell's Island, egger-onner of beaten fighters, contemporary humorist and practical joker.

"This isn't a partnership," I said. "It's a stock company. Just because we both have a couple of shares of the same stock doesn't make us brothers."

"What'sa matter, Eddie, can't you take a rib any more?" Vince grinned, wanting to be friends. "I just thought maybe when you put something in the paper you c'n drop in a line about me, you know, how it was me discovered the big guy."

"You mean how you muscled in on Acosta?"

"I don't like them words," Vince said.

"Forgive me," I said. "I didn't know you were so sensitive."

"What the hell you got on me?" Vince wanted to know. "Why you always try to give me the business?"

"Take it easy, Vince," I said. "I'll give you a nice big write-up some day. All you've got to do is drop dead."

Vince looked at me, spat on the floor, leaned back on his fat rump and opened his *Mirror* to the double-page spread on the Latin thrush who beat up the bandleader's wife when she surprised them in a West Side hotel.

Behind me a familiar voice was saying, "I wouldn't kid ya, Paul, I've got a bum what'll give yer customers plenty of action. Never made a bad fight in his life."

I looked around to see Harry Miniff talking to Paul Frank, matchmaker for the Coney Island Club. Harry's hat was pushed back on his head as usual and a dead cigar hung between his lips as he talked.

"You don't mean that dog Cowboy Coombs, for Chrisake?" Paul said.

Miniff wiped the perspiration from his lip in a nervous gesture. "Whaddya mean, dog? I'll bet ya fifty right now Coombs c'n lick that Patsy Kline who's supposed to be such a draw out at Coney."

"I need somebody for Kline a week from Monday," Paul admitted. "But Patsy figures to murder an old man like Coombs."

"Whaddya mean, old?" Miniff demanded. "Thirty-two! You call that old! That ain't old. Fer a heavyweight that ain't old."

"For Coombs it's old," Paul said. "When you been punched around fifteen years, it's old."

"I tell ya, Coombs is in shape, Paul," Miniff insisted, but the desperate way he said it made it sound more like a plea than a statement of fact. "And win or lose, he's a crowd-pleaser. Ya know that, Paul. Kline'll know he's been in a fight."

"What about that last one up in Worcester?" Frank said.

"T'row that one out," Miniff dismissed it, reaching quickly into his coat pocket and coming up with a handful of worn newspaper clippings. "Sure, sure, in the record book it's a TKO for La Grange. But read what they said about us in the Worcester papers. Coombs woulda gone for a win if he hadn'a busted his hand on the other bum's head. Here you c'n read about it right here!"

He held the clippings up in front of Paul's face, but the matchmaker waved them away.

"How's the hand now?" Paul said.

"Good's new, good's new," Miniff assured him. "You don't think I'd send one of my boys in with a bum duke, do ya?"

"Yes," Paul said.

Miniff wasn't hurt. There was too much at stake to be hurt: five hundred dollars if he talked Paul Frank into using the Cowboy with Patsy Kline. One sixty-six for Miniff's end. And he could improve that a little if he held out a few bucks on Coombs' share of the purse. Miniff could use that kind of money. The Forrest Hotel, on 49th Street, had put up with Miniff's explanations for six or seven months.

"I'll tell you what I'll do with you, Paul," Miniff said. "If you want to be absolutely sure that your customers get their money's worth before Kline puts the crusher on Coombs..." He paused and looked around with a conspirator's discretion. "Come on out'n the sidewalk," he said, "where we can talk private."

"Awright," Paul agreed, unenthusiastically. "But cut it off short."

Relaxed and poker-faced, Paul moved toward the wide doorway with the undersized, over-anxious director of the destiny of Cowboy Coombs hanging onto his arm and talking up into his face, sweating to make a buck.

Toro had to duck his head to fit through the doorway from the locker room. Usually the boys were so absorbed in their own workouts that they hardly looked up. I've seen the biggest draws in the business working shoulder to shoulder with some fifty-buck preliminary boy and nobody seeming to know the difference. But when Toro came in, everything seemed to stop for a second. He was dressed in black—long black tights and a black gym shirt which would have reached the ankles of the average Stillman boxer. In his clothes, which had been at best haphazardly fit, he had loomed to elephantine proportions. One felt overawed by a shapeless mass. But stripped down to gym clothes, the mass became molded into an immense but well-proportioned form. The shoulders, growing out of the long, muscular neck, were a yard wide but tapered sharply to a lean, firm waist. The legs were massive, with tremendously developed calves, and biceps the size of cantaloupes stood out in his arms. The short-legged Acosta, Danny, and Doc Zigman, the hunchbacked trainer, coming out of the locker room with Toro, looked like stubby toughs escorting a giant steamer. Danny, the tallest of the three, a man of average height, only reached his shoulder.

Toro moved into the big room slowly, shyly, and again I had the impression of a great beast of burden moving along with an obedient eye on its master. Acosta looked up and said something to Toro, and he began to go through warming-up calisthenics. He bent at the waist and touched his toes. He sat on the floor and raised his enormous torso until his head was between his legs. He was limber and, for a man of his size, surprisingly agile, though he didn't perform his exercises with the authority, the zip, of the boxers around him. Again I had the image of an elephant that performs its feats in the circus ring. Slowly, mechanically and with a sullen acquiescence, it executes every command its trainer gives it.

When Danny thought he had warmed up enough, Acosta and Doc prepared him for the ring. They fastened around his neck the heavy leather headgear that protected the fighter's ears and the vulnerable areas of the brain. They fitted over his teeth the hard, red rubberized mouthpiece. With the big sixteen-ounce training gloves on his hands he climbed up to the ring; the bulky headgear and the way the mouthpiece exaggerated the already abnormal size of his mouth gave him the frightening appearance of an ogre from some childhood fairy tale. On the apron, just before climbing through the ropes, he paused a moment and looked over the hundred-odd spectators staring up at him with casual curiosity. He would never face a more critical audience. Some of them were Eighth Avenue *aficionados* who paid four bits to Curley at the door for the privilege of seeing some favorite scrapper knock his sparring partners silly. But most of Toro's audience were professional appraisers who chewed their cigars with cold disdain and sized up the newcomers with shrewd eyes.

"Moliner," Stillman said matter-of-factly, his gravel voice lost in the general hubbub, and Toro climbed into the ring. Toward the ring at a shuffling pace came big, easy-natured George, muttering one of his favorite songs:

> *Give me a big fat woman with the meat shakin' on her*
> *   bones . . .*
> *Give me a big fat woman with the meat shakin' on her*
> *   bones . . .*
> *And every time she shakes it some skinny woman loses her*
> *   home.*

Danny put his hand on George Blount's heavy black forearm to give him last-minute instructions on how he wanted him to fight Toro, the different points of Toro's style he wanted George to test. I saw the Negro nod with his warm, good-humored smile. "You get it like you want it, Mr. McCuff," George said, climbing up into the ring with the business-like air of a laborer punching in for a hard day's work.

The bell rang and George shuffled toward Toro amiably. He was a big man himself, six foot two and around two fifteen, but he fought from a crouch, hunching his head down into his thick shoulders to present a difficult, weaving target. He could be a troublesome fighter, though men who knew what they were doing straightened him up with right-hand uppercuts, reached through his short, club-like arms to score with stiff jabs and stopped him with a hard right-hand over the heart every time he flatfooted in for his roundhouse, haphazard attack. Toro held his long left hand out as Acosta had undoubtedly schooled him and pushed his glove toward George's face in what was supposed to be a jab. But there was no snap to it. George waded in, telegraphing a looping left, and Toro moved as if to avoid it, but his timing was off and he caught it on the ribs. George walked around Toro, giving him openings and feeling him out, and Toro turned with him awkwardly, holding out that left hand, but not knowing what to do with it. George brushed it aside and threw another left hook. It caught Toro in the pit of the stomach, and he grunted as they went into a clinch.

Acosta was leaning against the ropes just below them, tensed as if this was for the championship of the world and not just the warm-up round of a training workout. He shouted something up to Toro in shrill Spanish. Toro charged in, moving his body with awkward desperation, and hit George with a conventional one-two, a left to the jaw and a right to the body. George just shook them off and smiled. Despite the size of the body from which they came, there was no steam to Toro's punches. His fists shot out clumsily without the force of his body behind them. George moved around him again, ducking and weaving in the old-time Langford style, and Toro tried his one-two again, but George easily slipped his head out of reach of the left, caught the slow right on his glove and drew Toro into a clinch again, tying him up with his left hand and his right elbow, but managing to keep his right glove free to work into Toro's stomach.

The bell rang and Toro walked back to his corner, shaking his head. Acosta jumped into the ring, talking and gesticulating excitedly, jabbing, uppercutting, knocking George down in pantomime. Toro looked at him gravely, nodding slowly and occasionally looking around in bewilderment, as if wondering where he was and what was happening.

The second round was no better for Toro than the first. George was moving around him with more confidence now, cuffing him almost at will with open-gloved lefts and rights. Acosta cupped his hands to his mouth and shouted, *"Vente, El Toro, vente!"* Toro lunged forward with all his might, swinging so wildly with his huge right arm that he missed George completely and plunged heavily into the ropes. Some of the spectators laughed. It made them feel better.

Just before the round ended, Danny caught George's eye and nodded. George closed his gloves and crowded Toro into a corner, where he feinted with his left, brought Toro's guard down and cracked a hard right to the point of Toro's jaw. Toro's mouth fell open and his knees sagged. George was going to hit him again when the bell rang. Like a man who drops his hammer at the first sound of the whistle, George automatically lowered his hands, ambled back to his corner, took some water from the bottle, rolled it around in his mouth, spat it out, and, with the same easygoing smile with which he had entered the ring, climbed out again.

Toro leaned back against the ropes and shook his head in a gesture of confusion. For two rounds his giant's body had floundered as if it had lost all connection with the motor impulses in his brain.

Acosta was at Toro's side quickly, wiping the sweat from his large, solemn face while Doc Zigman kneaded the long thick neck with his capable fingers. Then, while Acosta held the ropes apart for him, Toro climbed ponderously out of the ring.

"Didja see that big bastard?" a regular behind me said. "Couldn't lick a postage stamp."

"From one of them chile-bowl countries," said his companion. "El Stinkola, if you understan' Spanish."

I turned to Vince, who was quiet for a change. "You sure know how to pick them," I said.

"Don't jump me," he said. "Nick's the brain and he thinks he can build 'im."

"If we could only get them to decide the championship on form like a beauty contest, Toro would walk away with it. But how can a guy who looks so invincible when he's standing still turn into such a bum when he starts moving?"

"Danny can teach him plenty," Vince said.

"Danny's the best," I agreed. "But if Danny knows how to make a silk purse out of a sow's ear, he's been holding out on us."

"Why don't you try talkin' like everybody else?" Vince said. "All them five-dollar expressions, nobody knows what the futz you're talkin' about."

"In other words, you become nobody by self-appointment," I said.
"You got something there, Vince."

George was leaning against the wall near the ring, waiting to go another round with a new Irish heavyweight from Newark, just up from the
amateurs. I could recognize a couple of lines of the song that seemed to
play continually in his head.

> *Gimme a fat woman for a pillow where I can rest my head . . .*
> *Gimme a fat woman for a pillow where I can rest my head . . .*
> *A fat woman knows how to rock me till my face is cherry red.*

"How do *you* do, Mr. Lewis?" George said when I came up. He
always asked it as if it were really a question.

"How do you feel, George?"

"Ready to go," George said. I had never known him to give any other
answer. The night Gus Lennert banged him out in one round, when Gus
still had something, and George hadn't come to until he was back in his
dressing room, that had still been his answer to "How do you feel?"—
"Ready to go."

"What do you think of Molina, George?"

"Big man," George said.

George never put the knock on anyone. Anger seemed unknown to
him and the common expressions of derision and contempt in which
nearly all of us indulge were never his way. I've often wondered if
George hadn't fought all the meanness and bad temper out of his system,
if it hadn't all been blotted up in the canvas along with his sweat and his
blood.

"Think he'll ever make a fighter, George?"

His black face creased in a wise smile. "Well, I'll tell you, Mr. Lewis.
I'd like to have the job of working out with him all the time. I'd like that
fine."

As I went into the dressing rooms, George was squaring off with the
Irish heavyweight. The big Irish kid fought with a set sneer on his face
and neither knew how to nor wanted to pull his punches. He tore into
George at the bell and whacked him a terrible punch under the right eye.
I saw George smile and work his way into a clinch as the door swung
closed behind me.

Inside, Toro was stretched out on one of the rubbing tables and Sam, a
baldheaded, muscular fat man was working him over. Toro was so oversized for the ordinary rubbing table that his knees reached the end and
his legs dangled down over the side. Danny, Doc, Vince and Acosta
were standing around. Acosta turned to me and began a long-winded,

excitable explanation. "El Toro, today you do not see him on his best. It is perhaps the excitement of his first appearance before such important people. Since the climate is very different from when he fight in Buenos Aires, I think . . ."

"I theenk," said Vince, exaggerating Acosta's accent, "he's a bum. But don't worry, chumo. We've made a dollar with bums before."

"All right. Out of here! I want everybody out of here," Danny said. The only way you could tell he had been at the bottle was that his voice was pitched a little louder than usual. But it wasn't only the bottle talking. It was Vince, to whom he had given the silent treatment ever since that Sencio affair. It was Acosta, who was getting on Danny's edgy nerves. It was Toro, this Gargantuan excuse for a fighter.

Nobody moved. Danny became petulant. "You think I'm talking for my health? I want everybody the hell out of here!"

Acosta drew himself up to his full five-feet-five. "Luis Acosta is not accustom to such insult," he said. "El Toro Molina is my discovery. Wherever El Toro is, I must be also."

"Nick Latka owns the biggest piece of this boy," Danny said flatly. "I work for Nick. A boy can only have one manager telling him what to do. I don't want to hurt no feelings, but I'll see you outside."

Acosta puffed up as if he were going to do something, but he only bowed his head stiffly and went out.

"That's puttin' the little spic in his place," Vince said.

"I said I want everybody out," Danny snapped.

"Listen, I'm one-a the partners, ain't I?" Vince demanded.

Danny never addressed him directly. "I'm responsible to Nick for his fighters' condition. I don't want to have to tell him people are getting in my way."

The word *Nick* dropped on Vince like a sandbag. "Okay, okay, the bum is yours," he said and sauntered out.

"I think I better go take a look at Grazelli's hand," Doc Zigman said. He and Danny were old friends. He knew the order hadn't been for him. "See you later, Danny."

I started to follow him out, but Danny said, "Stick around, laddie. You handle this boy's lingo, don't you?"

I went over to the table and looked down at Toro. *"¿Puede usted entenderme en español?"* I said.

Toro looked up at me. He had large, liquid, dark-brown eyes. *"Sí, señor,"* he said respectfully.

"Good," Danny said. "I've got a few things I want to tell him about that workout before I forget. But we'll wait till Sam gets through. A boy's got to be relaxing completely when he's being rubbed down. That's why I ran those guys out of here."

After Sam finished up, Toro raised himself to a sitting position and looked around. "Where is Luis?" he said in Spanish.

"He is outside," I said. "You will see him soon."

"But why is he not here?" Toro said.

I nodded toward Danny. "He is your manager now," I said. "Danny will take very good care of you."

Toro shook his head and, with wide, thick lips in a child's pout, he said, "I want Luis."

"Luis will continue to stay on with you," I managed to say. "Luis is not going to leave you. But to be a success here you must have an American manager."

Toro shook his head sullenly. "I want Luis," he said. "Luis is my *jefe*."

It's time he heard, I thought. Time for this great hulk of an adopted son to learn the pugilistic facts of life. Better to hear them from me with all the cushion I could give them in my limited Spanish than to pick them up from the gutter talk of Vince and his brothers, as he was sure to do.

"Luis no longer owns you," I said, wishing I had more words with which to make the subtle shadings. "Your contract is divided up among a group of North Americans, of whom Mr. Latka has the largest share. You must do everything he says, just as if he were Luis. He knows much more about boxing than Luis or your Lupe Morales, and can teach you many things."

But Toro just shook his head again. "Luis tells me to fight," he said. "Luis takes me to this country. When we have enough money to build my big house in Santa Maria, Luis will take me home again."

I looked at Danny. "Maybe we better get Acosta back in here to straighten him out," I said.

"Okay," he said. "Call him in. What I got to tell the boy will still be good tomorrow."

I found Luis pacing up and down on the spectators' side of the rings. From the way he looked at me I could see his insides were tied into knots. "Your boy is all mixed up," I said. "He doesn't know what's happening to him. You better go in and get him straightened out."

"You are all jealous of me," Acosta said as we walked back toward the dressing rooms. "You are all jealous because it is Luis who has discover El Toro and so you want to separate us. You do not understand that I am the only one who can make El Toro fight."

"Look, Luis," I said, "you're a nice little guy, but you might as well get straightened out yourself. You can't make Toro fight. There's nobody in the world who can make Toro fight. If anybody comes close, it's

Danny, because there isn't a better teacher in the business than Danny McKeogh."

"But Luis Firpo himself has tol' me how magnificent is my El Toro," Acosta said.

"Luis," I said, "on Sunday I listened to all this crap, because I was trying to be polite. And because I hadn't seen this overgrown peasant of yours yet. But now you might as well have it between the eyes. Even your Luis Firpo was a bum. All he had was a Sunday punch. He didn't know enough boxing to get out of his own way."

Acosta looked at me as if I had insulted his mother. "If you will pardon me," he said, "how do I know that is not just your North American arrogance? Actually Firpo has knock out the great Dempsey that day, but the judges did not want to let the title go to the Argentine."

"If you will pardon me," I said, "that is just pure Argentine horse manure."

Acosta sighed. "For me this is very sad," he said. "Always I have dream of New York. And from the first moment I see El Toro . . ."

"I know, I know," I cut in impatiently. "We've had all that." And then I thought of that epic figure of a man and that big trusting puss being cuffed around by an old pro like George Blount and I was seized by the indignity of it and I said, "Goddamit, Luis, you've pulled him out by his roots. You should've left him there in Santa Maria, where he belongs."

Acosta shrugged. "But it was for his own good that . . ."

"Oh, if you will pardon me," I said, "balls! All your life you were a little frog in a little pond. A little frog with big dreams. And all of a sudden you saw a chance, saddled yourself on Toro's back, to make a big splash in a big pool."

"In my country," Acosta said pompously, "such a remark can lead to a duel."

"Don't take me too seriously, Luis," I said. "In your country I hear you like to shoot off guns. Here we just like to shoot off our mouths."

We had reached the door to the rubbing room. "Now go in there and explain to Toro how Danny is the boss," I said. You could almost hear the air rushing from his deflated ego as he went in. He barely nodded to Danny, who joined me in the hall.

"Luis, ¿qué pasa? What happens? Explain to me. I do not understand," I could hear Toro saying as the door closed.

7

I wanted to walk down to Walker's, which felt like the home team dugout, but Danny couldn't wait five blocks for the first-one-today. So we ducked into the nearest of the gloomy little saloons that tunnel off Eighth Avenue. Danny was one of those fellows who could want a drink so badly that it was an effort for him to make polite conversation until he had the first couple under his belt. When the bartender set it up for him—Jamieson's Irish was his drink—he tossed it off with a quick, nervous motion of his wrist. After the second, he exhaled slowly in a gesture of relaxation. Danny was a thin, taut man who acted as if his nerve ends were on top of his skin. Everything he did, the way he drank, the way he smoked his cigarettes, the tic-like way he had of suddenly brushing his cheek with the back of his hand, the way he talked, had this nervousness in it.

The bartender left the bottle in front of Danny and went on about his business. Every few minutes Danny would pour us another one as we talked.

"Well," Danny said, "don't we have a dilly? Isn't he a beaut?" Danny talked a kind of slang that sounds archaic nowadays. He still said things like "dilly," and he was inclined to refer to beautiful babes as "stunners."

Danny studied the bottle reflectively. "If he just didn't know anything, laddie, that wouldn't be so bad. I've started from scratch before. Bud Traynor was green as grass when I first got hold of him, but at least there was plenty of fight in Bud. Even when he was a dub he was always dangerous. But this ox—" he threw off another one—"he's nothing. Just a big clown. Doesn't even have the moxie for it."

He held up his jigger ceremoniously. Danny liked to drink fast, but with a certain amount of formality. "Happy days," he said.

There was some color in Danny's face now. His eyes were brighter. He wiped his mouth with his hand, and said, "You know, laddie, maybe I caught one too many myself, but I still love this damn game. Even with all the things wrong with it, I love this lousy game. Especially when I have a boxer. Give me a new clever kid and let me bring him along nice and slow like I did Greenberg and Sencio and I'm up in heaven. Happy days," he said.

He seemed to be reading the label on the bottle carefully. "Yes, laddie, maybe I let them reach me once too often, but there's nothing I like better in this world than working a corner when I've got a nice smart boy who can do all the things I ask him. That's the way Izzy Greenberg was, up to the Hudson fight. The Hudson fight took something out of Izzy that's hard to describe, but you're just no good without. I was like that myself after Leonard. You look good as ever in the gym and it's not that you've got any geezer in you when you climb through the ropes. It's just that your confidence is shot. Your chemistry, I guess you'd call it. Your chemistry is changed. That's when I quit. I'd probably be singing nursery rhymes to myself right now if I hadn't called it a day. That's why I never regretted that dough I loaned Izzy to set him up in business. I'd rather lose the spondoolicks than see him get his brains knocked loose. Well, happy days."

From the bar radio we had been ignoring came the call of the starter's signal at the track. Danny brushed his hand against his face in that nervous gesture of his and said, "Wait a minute. I've got something good in the first race."

"In the first at Jamaica," the cold, mechanical voice of the announcer said, "they were off at two-thirty-seven. The winner, Carburetor. Place, Shasta Lad. Show, Labyrinth. The Gob ran fourth. Track, clear and fast. Time one minute, twelve and four-fifths seconds. The winner paid seven-eighty, four-ninety and four-ten."

Danny took a tab out of his pocket and tore it in two.

"Who were you on, Danny?"

"The Gob," he said. "He figured to win that one. Dropping down in class. Only carrying a hundred and fourteen pounds. And the distance was right." He reached for the bottle again. "Well, happy days."

"No, thanks, Danny," I said.

"Go ahead, laddie, keep me company."

"I've got to go up and see Nick after a while."

"Hell with Nick," Danny said. "That's the trouble with this lousy game. Too many Nicks in this lousy game."

"Well, make mine a short one," I said.

"Gotta keep me company," he said. "We're in this together, laddie. Hell with Nick. It's Nick that's driving us to drink, with his lousy freaks he wants us to handle. Happy days."

"It's not just Nick," I said. "I gotta meet my girl later too."

"Now that's a different story, laddie. Never let it be said that Danny McKeogh came between a swain and his ladylove. Here, just let me pour you a drop or two, so I don't have to feel I'm drinking by myself."

He held his jigger up in front of him and stared into it. "It's pitiful," he said, "watching a freak like that. That's what it is, pitiful." He reached for the bottle again. "If there's anything I hate to watch, it's a fighter with no ability. It rubs me the wrong way. If they really want to punish me for my sins, they should find a gym for me in Purgatory and lock me up with nothing but bad fighters." He grinned. He had a nice, boyish grin that made you want to smile with him. He was feeling

better. The liquor was good for him. If only he could quit now, he would
be all right. Nice and easy and relaxed inside, what they mean by that
old definition of happiness: the absence of pain.

Doc Zigman came in and took the empty stool next to Danny.

"Draw a beer for my friend, John," Danny called down to the bartender.

Doc never drank anything stronger than beer. He was dark-complexioned, with a high intellectual forehead and a sharp, sensitive face that
looked damp all the time. Tuberculosis had made his spine rise to a peak
between his shoulders and bent him over as if he were under an unbear-
ably heavy weight. It gave him more the appearance of a scientist or a
scholar than a member of the boxing fraternity. Maybe that was merely
because he was what I always pictured when I thought of Steinmetz. As
a matter of fact, Doc just missed being a legitimate M.D.

The orthopedists tried their best with their rack-like contraptions when
he was a kid, and got nowhere. They only succeeded in keeping him out
of school long enough to smother his dream of becoming a physician.
But what may have hurt more than the "cures" was the progress of his
younger brother, now one of the top surgeons in New York. There are
hints that Doc is not very welcome in his brother's home, and I suppose
it would be easy for a psychoanalyst to trace the feud back to an early
trauma. What's obvious is that it's not very easy to subordinate all your
ambitions to a kid brother, especially if he is favored with a straight
back.

I can't quite remember how he drifted into the boxing racket, but I
think it was through a kid from his block—on the Upper East Side—
who was fighting main events at St. Nick's. Doc worked like a doctor,
more efficiently than a lot of these stuffed-shirts with enough political
pull to get themselves appointed medical examiners for the boxing commissions. I've never seen anybody stop a cut like Doc. In those short
sixty seconds between rounds his long thin fingers worked medical
magic. And it's not only external medicine he knows. He's made a kind
of informal study of punch-drunkenness, with a lot of stuff on concussion and cerebral hemorrhages. The strange thing is that, coming up out
of a tough block and being around mugs so much of the time, he doesn't
sound exactly like Doctor Christian and yet I've heard him talk to doctors about "Parkinsonian syndromes" and "post-traumatic encephalitis,"
and from the way they listened, he must know what he's talking about.

"Well, what do you think of our Superman, Doc?" I said. "How do
you figure him physically?"

"I'll tell you, Eddie, if you want me to level," Doc said. "For one
thing, he's got the wrong kind of muscles. Big square muscles. He's

done a lot of lifting. There's no give, no speed to muscles like that. He's overdeveloped in the biceps. Works like he's a little musclebound. That's sure to slow him up pretty bad."

"Happy days," Danny said.

"How about his size?" I said. "What makes a guy that big? Can that be natural? Or is that something glandular?"

"Well, I wouldn't like to say without knowing more about his history," Doc said, just the way doctors always sound. "But just from looking at him I'd say he's what the Medical Center boys call 'acromegalic.'"

"Is that bad?" I said.

"Oh, it's not serious," Doc said, "but overactivity of the pituitary gland isn't the healthiest condition."

"Well, what are the symptoms?" I said. "Or the syndromes, or whatever you geniuses call it."

"A hyper-pituitary," Doc said, "well, I'll tell you, a hyper-pituitary usually has a misleading appearance. He is abnormally large, and his nervous system sort of hasn't had a chance to keep up with him. So he's apt to act kind of sluggish, kind of dopey, even though his brain may be perfectly okay. It's like the wires between the brain and the body aren't hooked up very good. The chances are he can't take punishment like the shorter, stockier guys. He'll probably go into shock faster. His resistance isn't too good."

"That's great," I said. "That's just great. I can see myself selling that one to the sport desks. 'See Man Mountain Molina, the Hyper-Pituitary, Argentine's gift to medical science.'"

"Happy days," Danny said.

We had struck bottom on that bottle. Danny held the empty up to prove his plight to the bartender. "John," he said.

The bartender turned to bring up another fifth, and set it in front of Danny. Danny reached into his pocket, brought out a wad of bills and handed it over the bar. "Here, John," he said. "When you close take out what I owe you, keep a fin for yourself, stick the rest in my inside pocket and put me in a cab."

"Yes, sir, Mr. McKeogh," John said respectfully. With an air of solid dependability he ripped a strip off a newspaper, scribbled Danny's initials on it, fixed it to the wad with a rubber band and rang up No Sale to deposit it in the cash register.

The starter's call came over the radio again. Danny leaned forward just a little. "The second race at Jamaica. Off at three-ten and one-half. The winner, Judicious. Place, Uncle Roy, Show, Bonnie Boy. El Diablo ran fourth. The time . . ."

While the announcer gave the rest of the details, Danny reached into his breast pocket and tore up another tab.

"Who'd you have that time?" I said.

"Uncle Roy, on the nose," Danny said. He tilted the fresh bottle. "Gentlemen, happy days."

From the other end of the bar a guy in a shabby suit came toward us with the jerky, telltale gait of the punch-drunk. His pug-nose, ageless face bore the marks of his former profession: the eyes drawn back to oriental slits, a puffy ear, the nose spread over his face and a mouth full of store teeth. He threw his arms around Danny's neck and rocked him back and forth with muscular affection. "Hul-la-la-lalo, Danny, old b-b-boy-oh-b-b-boy-oh-boy," he said. As the words came up out of his throat they seemed to stick on the roof of his mouth and he'd twist his head to the side in a spastic motion to dislodge them.

"Hello, Joe," Danny said. "How you feeling, Joe?"

"Oh s-s-s-s-s-swell, Danny, oh-boy-oh-boy-b-boy," Joe said.

When he talked you tried not to watch the muscles in his neck that tightened in the effort of human speech.

"Hey, John," Danny called the bartender, "set up a glass for Joe Jackson."

The way Danny said that name you could tell he still liked the sound of it. He had won plenty of fights with Joe Jackson.

Danny lifted his jigger and tapped it nicely against his old fighter's. "Happy days," he said. "God bless you, Joe."

We had to pretend not to notice how Joe spilled a little off the top as his shaky hand brought the jigger to his lips. He set it down with a laugh. "Boy-oh-boy-oh-boy, that sure h-h-h-h, that sure h-h-h-h-, that sure h-its the spot," he said. He started to laugh again, and then he stopped himself with his mouth suddenly twitching to one side— Doc's "Parkinsonian syndrome"—and he started to say, "Hey, Danny, c-c-c-c-c, c-c-c-c-c—" but this one really stuck to the roof of his mouth, caught up there by some shapeless inhibition that stirred in his punished brain.

"Sure," Danny said. "How's a double saw-buck? You c'n owe it to me."

"I'll p-p-p, I'll p-p-p, I'll let you h-have it back Monday," Joe said.

Joe threw his arms around Danny again. "Thanks a m-million, Danny, oh-boy-oh-boy-oh-boy," he said and he lurched back to his place farther down the bar.

"He's getting worse," Doc said.

"Looks like he's got a one-way ticket to the laughing academy," I said.

"Were you in the house the night he fought Callahan?" Danny said.

"Oh, was he a sweetheart the night he fought Callahan! He was right up there with the gods that night, laddie."

"This must get kind of expensive," I said.

Danny shrugged. "What's the diff? It's only money."

When I got up to Nick's office, his secretary, Mrs. Kane, said would I please sit down and wait, Mr. Latka was in conference at the moment. Mrs. Kane always managed to make Nick's conferences sound at the very least like a meeting with the mayor to decide the city's budget. Her voice always dipped in a respectful little curtsey when she mentioned Nick's name. She was a plump, happy-faced, handsome woman, who, on Nick's insistence, corseted her body into smartly tailored suits. Nick had kept her with him for years, not only for her personal lovalty but because she was Gus Lennert's sister and the wife of Al Kane, who fought as a heavyweight before Nick put him on the payroll as a collector in Prohibition days. Nick figured that with that kind of a family, Emily Kane would have less trouble beating off the wolves. Nick didn't like that kind of stuff around the office. If he overlooked it in the Killer, it was because the Killer, in addition to his numerous other duties, had the leeway of a court jester.

While I was waiting, I wandered down to the little office between the reception room and Nick's sanctum, which said "Executive Secretary" on the door. That's where the Killer hung out. The Executive Secretary was lying on the couch combing back his black shiny hair with a comb he always carried in his breast pocket. The Killer was a vain little man, given to running a comb through his hair so often that it became a kind of nervous habit.

"Hello, Killer," I said, "who's in there with the boss?"

"Copper O'Shea."

"Oh, hell, and she calls that a conference. That isn't even a meeting."

Copper was just one of Nick's legmen. He got that name from the time he put in on the Police Force before one of those seasonal reform shake-ups exposed his connections with the mob. After they took the shield off him, he made it official by going to work for Nick, or rather continuing to work for Nick.

I started into Nick's office, but the Killer waved me back. "Better hold it up. The Boss is pinnin' Copper's ears back. He don't like nobody to go in when he's runnin' off at the mouth like that. I guess he likes everybody to think he's a sweet, lovable character."

"What's the matter with Copper?"

"Aw, the Copper's just dumb," the Killer said. "He don't know howta adjust. That's what the boss says. The Copper's out sellin' the music, see? Well, some of them hash joints, they don't want the music. So

Copper hangs one on the guy. He can't get useta the new way a doin' business, see? This burns the boss. The boss just won't buy the rough stuff no more."

The door opened and Copper O'Shea came out. Like so many of his former buddies on the Force, he was a big man with a hard, beefy face and a belly that hung over his belt. "I gotcha now, boss," he was saying. "I gotcha. I gotcha."

Nick looked mean and aroused. "I only say things once. I don't want you to hit nobody. One more time and you're off my list. You know that, don't you?"

Copper knew it. One thing about Nick, he always kept his word. Whether it was a promise to do you a favor, or to fix your little red wagon, Nick always came through.

Nick just turned away from Copper as if he weren't there any more and put his arm around me. "Come on inside, Eddie," he said with a friendly wink, as he led me into his office. "Sorry to make so much noise about that. Those stupid bastards. All they know about psychology is to pull a guy's coat off his shoulders to tie up his arms and then kick him in the nuts. They'd rather make four bits and crack somebody's skull than make a legitimate buck." He took a Belinda from his silver-edged mahogany humidor, and offered me one. "But I got my lesson learned. Why waste all that time and dough messing around with the cops and the courts, putting in the fix here, paying off a guy there, when I can get richer playing strictly legitimate? Just the juke boxes and the gambling, a couple of concessions and some big money fighters—that's all I need to get along. I don't want to hurt nobody and I don't want to wind up with a nice little room on the third tier. I had that already."

A long time ago Nick had done a ten-month stretch on some kind of technical charge, one of those delicious legal fictions our Justice Department dreams up. Except for the temporary inconvenience, his business had been so well organized that he was able to conduct it smoothly right from his cell by means of visiting-day meetings with his lieutenants.

"Nick," I said, "I've got no ambition to share that tier with you. That's why I'm worried. If you stay with your idea of building this Molina into a big-time heavyweight, I think we've all got a good chance of being held as accessories to a murder."

"You mean Molina's liable to kill somebody?" Nick grinned.

"I mean Molina's liable to catch pneumonia and die from the draft he creates missing all those punches. Seriously, Nick, this guy is a joke. I watched him work this afternoon. He hasn't got a thing. All those big beautiful muscles and he doesn't hit hard enough to break an egg."

"Look, Eddie," Nick said, "I want you to go out and sell Toro Molina. Let me worry about how he lives up to his publicity."

"But you don't seem to understand, Nick. I'm telling you this guy can't lick a lollipop. Why, any professional fighter who knows his trade —even old Gus Lennert—is liable to murder Molina. And I mean the coroner stuff, not the kind you read about in *Variety*."

"Molina will get along all right," Nick said.

"I don't see how you figure that."

"You don't have to see how I figure it." Nick was drawing in the slack of affability now. "Just take my word for it. You go out and plug Molina like you never plugged anything in your life. Man-Mountain Molina. The Giant of the Andes. That crap. And leave the rest to me."

"I can get him space," I said. "I can get him all the space you want, as long as he gives us something. I can alibi a loss here and there, but it's only with consistent wins that we really get snowballing."

"We'll have consistent wins," Nick said. And there was something about the flat, quiet way he said it that made me realize for the first time that Toro Molina, the Giant of the Andes, was going to have consistent wins.

It had been done before. Not every fight, but enough to fatten up the record and put them in the money. Young Stribling had knocked out his chauffeur (known variously as Joe White, Joe King, Joe Sacko, Joe Doktor, Joe Clancy, Joe Etcetera) in practically every town in America.

"But even making them look good is a big order for this barrel-lifter. No kidding, Nick, our god not only has feet of clay, the feet are size sixteens and probably flat at that."

"That gives me an idea," Nick said. "Take him down to Gustav Peterson and get him measured for half a dozen pair of special built shoes. Get 'em made up even a couple of inches longer'n he needs. Get the newspaper cameras down to shoot him trying 'em on. Now that's the side of the street I want you to work. Leave the guy's ring work to Danny. He's a master, even if he hates my guts. Leave the opponent's performances to Vince. You and I both know him for a grifter but that's why he's right for the job. The little guy—" He meant Acosta. "Keep him along for the ride. Someone for the big guy to talk to. But lemme know if he makes any trouble."

"He's all right. He means well."

"The hell with that," Nick said. "That don't sell any tickets. The first time he gets in the way we put him on the boat."

He looked at his watch. "Jesus, I gotta go down and try on a suit." He went to the door and called, "Hey, Killer, tell Jock to pick me up in front of the door right away."

"Okle-dokle," the Killer said. "Where we goin'?"

"Down to Weatherill's. For that fitting you was supposed to remind me of."

"Jeez, boss," the Killer said. "I always remember them things. But I don't know, today I got a lot on my mind."

Nick put on his Chesterfield and winked at me. "Hear what he calls it, Eddie, his mind." He made a fake pass as if to let him have one where he lived.

In the rear seat of the Caddy, Nick leaned back against the seat and blew smoke against the roof. From the fitting he would go to the Luxor for a rub and a steambath and then he was meeting Barney and Jimmy for ribs at Dinty's before going up to see the ball game.

On our way to Walker's, where Nick was dropping me off, he said, "You got the pitch now. Anything else on your mind?"

"We haven't even started," I said. "How do you think I'm going to sell this guy if everybody gets a line on him at Stillman's? All you have to do is take a quick gander and you can see he is from Dixie in B flat with the emphasis on flat."

"Where you want to take him?" Nick asked.

"As far from the wise boys as possible, where the sharpshooters like Parker or Runyon don't knock us off before we get started."

"Ojai," Nick said.

"Where the hell is that?"

"A couple of hours out of L.A. We had Lennert up there for the Ramage fight once. Nice quiet joint. Nobody t' bother you. And now that I think of it, the West Coast is the place to interduce the Man Mountain. They don't get too many good fights out there anyway. They probably won't know the difference. They'll go for stuff like this. They matched Jack Doyle, that Emerald Thrush, and Enzo Fiermonte, one of Madeline Force Astor Dick's husbands. Anybody who paid to see that one will do anything."

"L.A. is all right," I said. "I've always wanted to get a look at L.A."

"I've got a couple addresses I'll give you out there," the Killer said. "Stock girls." He gave the wolf call.

"Leave Eddie alone," Nick said. "He's got to work out there." He put his hands on my leg just above the knee and squeezed the tendons until I jumped. It was a sign of affection. "You've got to really sock it to them out there, kid. Take a nice big cut at the ball. Spend dough. Make them sport editors so goddam sick of your Man Mountain Molina that they'll spread him over a page to get rid of you. Make out like you can't get an opponent for him the first month or so because nobody around there's got the guts to get in the ring with him. You know the routine. Then bring somebody out from the East, a nice soft touch that's never been west of the Rockies before, so nobody knows what a dog he is. Then give him the big build-up about how he's come out to California because he's so tough none of the name fighters in the Garden want to have anything to do with him. Let Vince find you a bum."

I thought of Harry Miniff. This would be a nice way to make a couple of bucks for Harry. "I know a good bum," I said. "Cowboy Coombs."

"Jesus, he still alive?" Nick said.

"Harry was up at the gym trying to sell him this afternoon. He'd be very grateful to make a buck, Harry would."

"How does that Coombs look these days? Will the fans take him serious?"

"The Cowboy has the most menacing scowl of any heavyweight in the business today," I said.

"Okay, I'll tell Vince to get Coombs for us," Nick said. "Come up tomorrow afternoon and pick up the tickets."

"What tickets?" I said.

"The railroad tickets," Nick said. "I'll get you out on the Limited tomorrow night."

"That's kind of on the quick side, isn't it?"

"Why not the quick side?" Nick said. "You tell me the smart boys will begin to catch if we let him hang around here. Then let's make our move fast. I'll have them tickets at four o'clock. So any last-minute business, last-minute humping or anything else you got on your mind, you better get it done tonight."

The shiny black Cadillac dropped me in front of Walker's and cut through law-abiding traffic to shoot out into the clear. Nick carried an honorary badge from the Police Department, so the boys in blue wouldn't give him any trouble.

Things were still pretty quiet along the bar. Just the bums and the strays. The guys who dropped in for the quick ones on their way home from work and the boys who came to spend the evening would be along after a while. Now it was just me and a guy down the bar who looked as if he were studying to be his own worst enemy. The cat that occasionally walked along the bar brushed against him and he patted it absently while staring over the bar with his eyes turned inward in a lonely trance. A couple of ladies of the evening were resting their feet in one of the booths.

Charles set me up with the usual and then slowly wiped the bar in front of me, which was his way of coming around to conversation.

"Well, how are you today, Mr. Lewis?"

"Great, great," I said. "One more and I'll be walking around on my knees."

"I've never seen you take one you don't need," Charles said, which was always the way he put it when a customer anesthetized himself beyond reason.

"Celebrating," I said. "Going to California tomorrow."

"California," Charles said. "I was out there a good many years ago. Worked as helper to a bartender at the old California Athletic Club. That was before you were born."

He drew a couple of beers for two newcomers and came back to his story. "Yes, sir, the California A.C. The greatest heavyweight scrap in the history of the ring was fought at the old CAC. I'll never forget it, sir, if I live to be a hundred. Corbett and Jackson. The greatest white champion and the greatest black champion that even drew on a glove. Fix the picture in your mind, sir. Black Prince Peter and Gentleman Jim. Marvels of science, both of them. As fast as lightweights they were, and for sixty-one three-minute rounds they went at it that night, four hours and three minutes, enough to kill off a dozen ordinary men. When the referee finally stopped it for fear one of the men would drop dead of exhaustion before he'd holler quit, there was hardly a mark on Peter and Jim for ducking, slipping and catching each other's punches. Like pieces of quicksilver they were, and neither one of them slowed down until they had fought thirty of the fastest and most evenly matched rounds anyone will ever see."

Charles wiped the bar shiny where my glass had left its damp imprint. "And all this before five hundred people for a purse of ten thousand dollars, winner take all." He looked at me significantly. "Today the same fight would draw two million dollars into the ball park. But they weren't fighting for money in those days. All the loser got was his carfare home. It was a sport when I was a lad, Mr. Lewis, a rough sport, but a sport nevertheless. None of these ring-around-the-rosie, you-hit-me-and-I'll-hit-you affairs like these heavyweights are often having in the Garden."

"Just a minute, Charles," I said, "I just thought of something. Wasn't that Corbett-Jackson fight a year or so before the Slavin fight you were telling me about?"

Charles looked off vaguely. "I'd better see what that gentleman wants," he said, leaving me to ponder the problem of how Charles could have been in California a year before he left England.

"Charles," I said, when I finally got him to answer my finger, "how can you lie like that? You never saw the Corbett-Jackson fight."

"It's not a lie, sir," Charles insisted.

"Well, what would you call it?"

"A mere stretching of the truth, Mr. Lewis. I did work at the CAC, in Oughty-ought. And some of the old members were still talking about that fight, arguing who'd've won if they had let it go the distance. One day Mr. Corbett stood right up at the bar himself, when he was champion of the world, and gave me his own first-hand description. 'Charles,' Mr. Corbett says to me, and he's standing there just as close to me as you are, 'Jackson had everything. He could beat any heavyweight I ever saw. Try to box him and he'd out-box you. Start slugging and he'd slug you right back. He was the Master, that black wizard, the genuine Nonpareil.'"

"Charles," I said, "you are the truth-stretchingest man I ever met. You stretch it out so far I forget where it started from."

"Dramatic license," Charles shrugged.

I told Charles to put the bottle away because it was beginning to catch up with me and I didn't want to louse up my last night with Beth. I walked back to the Edison thinking about this Molina deal. My mind was already working ahead to the angles. As soon as we hit L.A. I'd get all the sportswriters together and toss a party and fill them full of flit. Deaden their powers of integrity and self-criticism. Then slip them a little something to make their readers feel they were getting their nickel's worth. It didn't have to be true.

8

Beth said she would probably be a little late getting away from the office. So I stretched out on the bed with my copy of *War and Peace*. I have been reading *War and Peace* since I was a high-school senior and have now succeeded in getting almost half way through it. It's not that I haven't found it interesting. But it was written on a large *dacha* in Russia before the age of electricity, motor cars or radios, and sometimes I think I will have to approximate those conditions in order to finish it. I read a couple of chapters and then can't find time to go on. When I'm ready to dip into it again, I have forgotten who Marya Dmitrevna is and have to thumb back two or three hundred pages to pick up the thread. If *War and Peace* has given me trouble, it's nothing I blame on the Count or myself. It's more the fault of the Hotel Edison and my room which overlooks Strand's bar and the horse players who usually assemble on the curb under my window. This is far more conducive to reading *Racing Form* and *Ring Magazine* than Russian literature.

I was lying on my bed with my shoes and socks and shirt off and a glass on the floor where I could reach it when Beth came in.

"Hello, honey," I said.

The sweet name only brought a sour expression to her face. She never liked it.

She looked around for a cigarette and I tossed her one from the bed. She came over and reached down to me to light her cigarette from mine. I put my arm around the back of her legs the way I often did.

I could tell from the way she held herself against my arm that something was wrong. That's the way Beth was. Her passion had its irregular tides. One evening she would come into my arms with a wanton hunger the moment the door was shut and the next evening she had to be as carefully seduced as if it had never happened between us before.

"Darling," I said, "don't be like that. I'm leaving for California to-morrow."

"Oh!" Beth hesitated. "Maybe it's a good idea."

My hand came away from her as if it had a mind of its own. "Well, that's a nice loving send-off."

She sat down on the edge of my bed and deliberately snuffed out her cigarette. Beth could hold a pause longer than was comfortable. I knew I was in for it when she began slowly, "Now, Eddie, don't get sore."

She looked at me seriously and seemed to be debating with herself whether she should say any more. I tried to feint her into a new lead.

"Lots of writers go to California."

"To write?" she asked, and didn't wait for an answer. "Let's get things straight, Eddie. I think it's just about time one of us went out to California."

"You mean for good?"

"I don't know yet. I haven't thought that far. All I know is that we're getting nowhere in New York, because, I guess, you won't let yourself think about where you want to go. The trouble seems to be, I'm the only one who has any idea where you're going. You're always stopping somewhere, to have a drink, to make some soft money, to put off what you ought to do. Just starting, never finishing. This fight business... You know, when you first told me about it, I was fascinated. It seemed to have something, a force, a vitality that's missing in so many other things. But you were in your early thirties then. Now it's the middle thirties, thirty-five, thirty-six, come November. That's a dangerous age, especially in your job, Eddie. A fighter's press agent at thirty-one is kind of an interesting fella. You can see it on book jackets—newsboy, copyboy, reporter, merchant seaman, fighters' press agent, advertising writer. You know how they always sound. But a fighters' press agent at forty, that's a little sad. At fifty, it's very sad. And at sixty you're a bum hanging around those Eighth Avenue saloons boring everybody with the names of great fighters you used to know."

"You've really got my life laid out for me," I said. "Doesn't sound so bad."

"You can't laugh it off, darling. The midtown bars are full of guys like you. They come to town because they have something on the ball. Look at yourself, you've got some talent for writing, but you're too lazy or too frightened or too tied up to develop it."

"Boy," I said, "it's a good thing I'm pulling out of here tomorrow."

"What'll you be doing in California?"

I told her a little about the setup we expected to have on the Coast, about the plans for making Molina, the Giant of the Andes, a household word.

Beth shook her head. "That's exactly what I mean. What kind of a job is that for a guy who . . ."

"Who what? Who doesn't have to go begging for assignments from the slicks? Who doesn't want to hang around the fringe and starve a little? Who wants an easy buck—and lots of them—on the chance of salting away enough to sit down and see what he can write some day?"

"Some day! Some day! Eddie, do you want those two words for your epitaph?"

"Well, what the hell's the difference?" I said. "So I sell Molina. Another guy works for J. Walter Thompson and sells soap. Or he writes perfume ads, telling the girls how this particular poppy juice will make every guy they meet want to lay them. Only he uses ten-dollar words like 'enticing mystery' and 'bewitchment of the night.' He probably went to Princeton too. Or Yale or maybe even Harvard. But if you peek under those beautifully starched white cuffs with the delicate monogram, just above the wrist you will definitely see the shackles. Or take that friend of mine Dave Stempel who published that little book of poems when he was still in school, *The Locomotive Dream*—remember, we read it together?—well, he's out in Hollywood writing stinking Class B melodramas. Where's the difference between that and my job with Nick?"

"But I'm not talking about the ad writer with the starched cuffs. Or Dave Stempel. I'm thinking about you. I mean I guess I'm really thinking about me. I'm a big girl now. I'm twenty-seven. It's time I knew the man I was sleeping with. I never know whether I'm going to bed with one of Nick's boys or someone who can think for himself."

I looked down into the loud and garish night of 46th Street. I could see across the street where old Tommy the bartender was leaning on his elbows talking to Mickey Fabian, a gimpy little gnome who gambled his entire disability pension from World War I every month on his judgment of the relative speed of our four-legged friends. Later on, I'd probably wander over and lift a glass with Mickey and hear how they ran for him at Saratoga. They were my guys. Crumbs, some of them, touch artists and no-goods, but still my guys. Maybe that's what Beth meant. It's part of my racket to sit around the various joints enjoying a friendly powder with the boys. The talk is whether Joltin' Joe has got it any more, and was the Commish justified in tying up both those bums' purses after the waltz last Friday night. A fellow gets to like that kind of life. It's no way to live, but he gets to thinking it is and he can't do without it. I wanted Beth and still I wanted to be free to sit around with the boys, if that's the way I felt. That must have been why I never got around to that proposal unless I had had a few, and after I had them and they worked their quick depressive magic, that was when she knew me better than I knew myself.

"I guess I'm one of Nick's boys," I said. "Oh, sure I like to read a book once in a while and I'm not so dumb I can't see how the profit system takes the manly art out behind the bushes and gives it the business. But I'm strictly a saloon man. Every once in a while I like to pick up the checks all around the table and I like to have enough in my kick to pay my tabs. Nick's dough may look a little soiled but they still exchange it for nice crisp new bills at any window."

"What happens after California?" Beth said.

"Don't know yet. We'll have to see how things break. Probably work our way east knocking over the usual clowns."

"So what you'll really be is a barker for a . . . circus freak."

"For Christ's sakes, what do you want me to do, sell my poems on the corner of Washington Square and starve with the rest of the screwballs? For a hundred a week and a slice of the pie—I bark."

Beth rose from the edge of the bed and said with an air of finality, "Okay, Eddie. But I think you sell yourself awful short. I guess you know what you want. I just wish you wanted a little more."

Then she relaxed into her own self a little and put her arms around me and kissed me quickly. "Take care of yourself."

"You too, kid."

"You're sore," she said. "I hoped you weren't going to be sore."

"I'm not sore," I said. "I'm just . . . ."

"Write me once in a while."

"Sure, we'll keep in touch."

"Hope everything goes the way you want it."

"I'll be okay."

We looked at each other, probably just a second or two, but it seemed longer. There is always that moment when you seem to be able to see in each other's eyes a flash of the things that might have happened if your cards had been a little better or you had played them differently.

"Maybe this breather is just what we needed," I said. "Maybe we can get married when I get back."

"Maybe," Beth said. "Let's see what happens."

"Swell. Be good, coach."

"Good-bye, Eddie."

"See you, Beth."

I stood at the window and watched her go out onto the street. I saw how the boys instinctively turned for a hinge of the gams as she went past. That trim figure of hers never quite looked as if it should belong with her bright and agreeable but untheatrical face. I stayed at the window until her rapid stride was lost in the crosscurrents of human traffic sweeping over the corner.

I bought myself another drink, but it backed up on me. I lay down on the bed again and tried to get back into *War and Peace,* but the scene and the characters had lost contact with me and the words ran into each other meaninglessly. I went over to the dresser and looked at the other books. A Fleischer's *All-Time Ring Record Book,* a two-bit copy of *Pal Joey,* Cain's *Three-in-One,* the *Runyon Omnibus* and an old marked-up edition of *The Great Gatsby.* I picked up the *Gatsby* and turned to one of the passages I had marked. It was that terrible scene where Daisy, Tom and Gatsby finally bring it out into the open. One of the best damn scenes in American fiction, but I couldn't keep my mind on it.

God Almighty, maybe Beth was right. Who was I? Who *had* she been sleeping with? The reader who marked and studied those lines of Fitzgerald? Or the guy who dished out the hyperbolic swill about Joe Roundheels and Man Mountain Molina? What were they to each other, the reader and the raver? Just two fellows who lived under the same skin, strangers sharing a common roof.

I threw the book down impatiently and started dressing for the street. Toro and Acosta were at the Columbia Hotel around the corner. For need of something to do I thought I'd check on whether everything was set with them for the trip tomorrow night.

The Columbia was one of those innumerable hotels in the Times Square area with the same nondescript streetfront, the same lonely people drinking the same cut stuff from the same chromium bars, the same harassed-looking clients, stage actors without parts and managers of derelict prize fighters like Harry Miniff. The lobby of the Columbia seemed to be full of small, shabby groups addressing themselves in sly undertones to the petty conspiracies devoted to the cause of running down a buck without physical effort.

Toro and Acosta had what the Columbia calls a suite, which was a sitting room not much larger than a phone booth leading into a small double bedroom.

"Ah, my dear Mr. Lewis," Acosta said when he came to the door and did his little bow. He looked very dapper in his bow tie and black smoking jacket, with his long-handled cigarette holder and a book under his arm.

"Disturbing you?"

"Please? Oh, no—no, I am just passing the time studying English." He held the grammar out to show me.

"This is one language I'm glad I learned early," I said.

"Yes, the verbs—the verbs are very difficult," Acosta agreed. "But you have a fine language. Not so musical as Spanish perhaps, but very virile, very strong."

"That's us all right," I said.

He led me to the most comfortable chair and bowed me into it with the automatic deference of a headwaiter. "Please," he said. From the bottom drawer of the desk he brought forth a half-empty bottle which he placed on the coffee table with a nice little flourish.

"Please, you will have a little brandy?" he touched the bottle fondly. "I bring this all the way from Mendoza."

"Thanks," I said. "I think I'd better pass. I've been on whisky all day, and this is the only stomach I've got."

Acosta laughed the way men do when they don't understand.

"Well, how do you feel about California?" I said.

"Oh, I am very excite—excited," Acosta said. "All my life I have hear—heard of Los Angeles. Some say it is even more beautiful than our own Mar del Plata. And I think for El Toro it will be very good too. He will have a climate more like he is use to. Here it is so *humedo*. Perhaps that is why he has look so sluggish in the ring."

I had said everything there was to say on the subject of Toro's ability that afternoon, so I didn't grab at this one as it went by.

"Where is Toro, by the way?"

Acosta pointed to the bedroom. "Already in the bed asleep. Poor El Toro. Tonight he feel very bad. He feel he has make this afternoon a very poor showing and he has the wish to go home to Santa Maria. I try to explain to him that now with the interest of Mr. Latka and Mr. McKeogh he will make more money than Luis Firpo. But you know how boys are. Now and then they get the homesickness."

"He doesn't really like to fight? He hasn't really got his heart in it, has he, Luis?"

Acosta had a disarming smile. "The killing instinct, he does not have, perhaps no. But with a man of his strength, when Mr. McKeogh has teach him how to punch . . ."

"Does he get this thing very often, the homesickness?"

"Oh, it is nothing," Acosta assured me. "In the morning after a good sleep he will be hokay. I have the same trouble with him back in Mendoza. When we have first come down the mountain from Santa Maria sometimes he just sits in the truck all day long and I know he has the homesickness very bad. I feel very sorry for him, so one day I go to the daughter of a gypsy fortune teller who has a tent down the way and I say to her, 'In my truck is a young man who is very unhappy. Here is ten pesos for you if you will go into the truck and make him happy.' After that I find the two best ways to keep El Toro from this homesickness is to feed him very much—maybe five times a day—for he can eat like a lion, and to give him the frequent opportunity of girls, for *tiene muchos huevos* and his appetite for the *muchachas* is truly magnificent. It is fortunate for me I find this out, for without the girls I think perhaps it is possible that El Toro goes back to his village and closes the door on his big opportunity."

Acosta's shrewd little eyes glowed with self-importance. Oh, it was not so easy as you think to bring this giant so far up the ladder, they seemed to say. I have had tremendous difficulties to overcome. I have had to use my head.

"Since you have the charge of the public relations," Acosta went on, "there is something I will tell you of El Toro which is of course not for the publications. He comes from such a very little village where the people know nothing of the world. So El Toro in the hands of women of experience is like *arcilla . . .*"

"Clay," I said.

"Thank you. My English has improve a little, yes? To explain how little El Toro knows of the world, one day in Mendoza, when we are still with the circus, Señor Mendez is away having new shoes put upon the feet of the bareback horse. That evening just before the performance El Toro comes to me and says he must see the priest right away, to confess the sin of adultery. In all his life he has never commit the sin of adultery. And now he has very much fear that he will never go to heaven. Like all the people of his village, he believes everything of the Church and would rather go to heaven when he dies than lie down with Carmelita in this present life.

"'With whom do you commit the adultery?' I say to El Toro.

"'With Señora Mendez,' he says.

"'Señora Mendez!' I say. 'But why do you bother with such an old one when the fairgrounds are full of willing *muchachas?*'

"'I did not even want Señora Mendez,' El Toro says to me. 'But she comes into the trunk when I am lying down. She smiles at me and comes over and sits on the edge of my cot. She talks to me and strokes my head and before I realize what has happen, I have commit the adultery.'

"'Do not look so sorry, El Toro,' I say. 'With Señora Mendez you cannot be blame for committing the adultery. Every time Señor Mendez goes into the city for the day, Señora Mendez commits the adultery. Señora Mendez has now almost forty years, and she has been committing the adultery twice a month since she is sixteen. So if it is a sin to be a *contribuidor* to a lady's five hundred and seventy-fifth adultery, it is surely nothing more than the very little tiniest sliver of a sin.'"

"If he pulls anything like that up there," I said, "the public is off him like a shot. We like our heroes to eat wheaties, be good to their mothers and true to their childhood sweethearts."

"You understan'," Acosta said, "I only tell you this now because we are become like one big family."

Just one big unhappy family, I thought.

"I hope I have not make El Toro sound like a bad boy," Acosta continued. "He is only a powerful *joven*—youth with healthy appetites. But I tell you this, since you will have occasion to be with him much in public and perhaps can help to guard him against certain women he will meet who will have interest in him like Señora Mendez."

Siamese twins pulling in opposite directions struggled for possession of my spine. The student of modern American writing, of Fitzgerald and O'Hara, had hired out as male nursemaid to an overgrown adolescent pituitary case who allows himself to be seduced by middle-aged bareback riders.

The heat of the night was heavy in the airless room and the walls were too close to each other. Suddenly I had had enough of Acosta with his ungrammatical long-windedness, his charm, which was largely a matter of teeth, and his protestations of benevolence toward El Toro. If Toro had been the victim of seduction, it was a far more radical seduction than the dallying attention of Señora Mendez.

But maybe this time Toro would make it pay. He had the size. Honest Jimmy had the connections. Nick had the money. I had the tricks. And the American people, God bless them, had the credulity. You couldn't blame them entirely. They were a little punchy too. They had taken an awful pasting from all sides: radio, the press, billboards, throwaways, even airplanes left white streamers in the sky telling them what to buy and what to need. They could really absorb punishment, this nation of radio listeners and shop-happy consumers, this great spectator nation. Only like a game fighter who smiles when he gets hit and keeps boring in for more, they were a little more vulnerable for every encounter. Now perhaps, if the winds are favorable (and if they aren't it may be possible to move wind machines up into the wings), they will be swept on to El Toro Molina, the Giant of the Andes, come down from the mountain heights to challenge the Philistines, like Samson, and avenge a countryman's defeat.

"Well, we'll pick you up tomorrow about an hour before train time," I said.

"Hokey-doke," Acosta said. "We will be very please."

From the bedroom came a loud somnolent groan and the sound of a heavy churning of bedclothes. Acosta went to the bedroom door and looked in. I stood behind him, having a clear view over his shoulder. Toro had kicked off his covers and was lying naked on the bed. The bed was not long enough to accommodate him and a chair had been placed at the end of it to support his feet. This gave an unnatural appearance to the scene. It was as if a tremendous marionette, bigger than life, had been put away between performances. In sleep his face had the set, oversized features of a dummy's head exaggerated for comedic effect.

And I thought, here we are planning his career, patterning his life, taking him to California, matching him with Coombs, surrounding him with managers, trainers, fixers, press agents, and yet he has never been consulted. I could induce the people of America to love him, hate him, respect him, fear him, laugh at him or glorify him, and yet I had never really spoken to him. What were his preferences, his feelings, his ambitions, his most intimate hungers? Who knew? Who cared? As soon ask Charlie McCarthy whether he would object to doing two extra Saturday performances. Toro had been put away for the night. When Jimmy and Nick and Danny and Doc and Vince and I were ready to pull our particular strings in a coordinated effort, the Giant of the Andes would be made to bend his massive torso through the ropes; another tug and his hands would go up in the stance traditional to pugilists for five thousand years; and then he would be guided through the motions calculated to please the cash customers who put their money down to see what is technically supposed to be an exhibition of the manly art of self-defense.

Restlessly Toro rolled over on his side and muttered something in Spanish that sounded like *Sí, sí, Papá, ahora, ahorita*—yes, yes, Father, now, right away. How many thousand miles was Toro from the Columbia Hotel? What little task had his father given him, so trivial and everyday and yet so deeply cut into the section of the brain that never sleeps, that keeps working on like an automatic furnace in a dark, sleep-ridden house?

Perhaps Papa Molina had told Toro to carry the completed barrels out and set them in front of the shop. Toro might have been sitting down to midday *comida* with his brothers and was wolfing his third helping of *pollo con arroz,* while his father, wiping the hot sauce from his mouth with his sleeve and patting his belly indulgently, was saying, "All right, my boys, a good meal for a good day's work. Now back to the shop."

Outside, the street was full of people for whom midnight is noon. Broadway was charged with their insomniac energy. Just as in a protracted visit to a hospital one often begins to feel symptoms of illness, so on Broadway in the early A.M., caught up in the restless overstimulated going-and-coming, you suddenly find your second wind and your eyes snap open in exaggerated wakefulness. So I turned west off Broadway, heading for the row of shabby brownstone houses between Eighth and Ninth Avenues where Shirley's place was.

Shirley lived on the top floor, in one of those flats which turn out to be surprisingly comfortable after you've climbed the dark narrow stairs that look as if they should lead to a tenement. She had the whole floor,

two bedrooms (with coy little boy-and-girl dolls perched at the head of
each bed) a living room, a small barroom and a dinky kitchen. It wasn't
set up as a place where men came to have women. It was really a kind of
informal call house, with the girls going out to work. Only once in a
while, if he were someone Shirley had known a long time, a fellow
could use the extra bedroom. The other part of Shirley's business moved
over the bar that usually kept busy until after the good people had
punched in for their morning work. The shades were always drawn in
that little room and the lighting was so discreetly low that I still remember the oppressive sense of decadence that came over me one morning when I thought I was leaving there around four and came out to face
the blinding, accusing daylight and the sober, righteous inhabitants of an
eight-A.M. workaday world.

I was admitted by Lucille, the dignified colored maid. From the
barroom I could hear Shirley's Capehart, her prize possession, playing
one of her records: Billie Holiday, with Teddy Wilson on piano behind
her, singing, "I Cried For You." It was so dark in the little room that
at first all I could see was the glow of customers' cigarettes and
Shirley behind the bar, with a drink in her hand, smoking one of her
roll-your-owns. She was wearing something long, cut low in front and
zipping all the way up the side that was either an evening gown that
looked like a fancy housecoat or the other way around. She was
singing along with Billie:

> . . . I found two eyes just a little bit bluer,
> I found a heart just a little bit truer.

When she saw me she said "Hello, stranger," and gave me the big
squeeze. She was feeling good tonight.

The record changer had dropped on another Holiday, the slow and
easy "Fine and Mellow," and Billie's voice, lowdown and legato, belonged in the room.

> Love is like a faucet . . .
> It turns on and off . . .
> Love is like a faucet . . .
> It turns off and on . . .

In the loveseat by the window a statuesque blonde with a face that would
have been beautiful if it had been less frozen was trying to fit into the
arms of a runty Broadway comic. Sitting on the floor with his back
against a chair was a big, fine-looking Negro. In the chair, running her
hands through his hair, but not getting much of a play from him, was a

white woman in her late or middle thirties who looked like one of those lushes who come from very good families with plenty of lettuce. As she reached down to embrace the Negro, she brushed her drink off the arm of the chair.

Like any fastidious hostess, Shirley glared. "In about three seconds," she said to me in an undertone the woman should have been able to hear if the flit hadn't stopped up her ears, "I'm going to give that lush the brush."

Leaning over the radio was a slender Latin girl with an unexpectedly beautiful face. "She's my new girl," Shirley said when she saw where I was looking. "Seems like a nice kid."

We had had a talk about Latin girls once and she knew I thought they were the only ones who went into this business without losing their basic love for men or their enthusiasm for the act of love. Anglo-Saxon professionals, as a group, are a sullen, miserable lot who dispatch you with businesslike efficiency or cold-blooded bitterness.

"Come here, Juanita," Shirley said. "I want you to meet an old friend of mine.

"Isn't she something?" she said, as we shook hands. Juanita looked down in embarrassment. She patted the girl's hand fondly. "Have a drink, dear?"

"Coca-cola," the girl said, making it sound Spanish.

While Juanita's eyes were hidden in the glass, Shirley nodded toward her and then raised her eyebrows in a quick questioning gesture. I shook my head. Juanita was obviously an admirable girl, but she wasn't what I had come for.

"How about a little gin? I'm leaving for the Coast tomorrow and I want to try and get even. This is strictly a business call."

"Come into my parlor," Shirley laughed. "You're just in time to pay my bills for the month."

I pulled the oil-cloth off the kitchen table while Shirley got some cold chicken from the icebox.

I dealt. Shirley picked up her cards and said, "Oh, you stinker."

"Sorry dear," I said. "I feel mighty tough tonight."

"Want some beer with the chicken?"

"Mmmm." My mouth was full of chicken. "Damn good chicken."

"I fried it myself. No one else ever gets it crisp enough for me."

Shirley played her hand skillfully and caught me with nine.

We laughed. I was beginning to feel better. I always picked up around Shirley. She generated an atmosphere of health and—yes, security. It was strange after all these years in New York that a gin game in Shirley's kitchen with cold chicken on the table and a beer at my elbow was the closest thing to home I had found in Manhattan.

Half way through the next game, Shirley said quietly, "What gives with you and my rival your last night in town?"

"Oh, hell, I don't know. I'm loused up over there."

"Feel like talking about it?"

Shirley seemed to be paying more attention to her cards than to my troubles, but she always had a knack of listening in a kind of detached, almost disinterested way that made it easier to go into things like these.

"I guess this Molina thing is kind of the payoff," I said. "She wants me to quit the business. Hell, I know it stinks. Just between us, I know Nick's deal doesn't smell like a rose. But at thirty-five you don't start over so easy. I like to see the ready coming in every week."

"How is three?" Shirley said.

"I'm dead," I said. "Twenty-nine. That puts you over, doesn't it?"

"A blitzeroo," Shirley said. "Well, that's the phone bill. Now I have to go after the rent."

I thought she wasn't even listening, but after she made her first discard, she went back to where I had left it, as if there had been no interruption.

"I'll tell you one thing, Eddie, love can't take any kind of a punch at all. If this chick of yours don't like the fight business and you think the business is for you—well, maybe the girl is smart to knock it on the head right there."

"You wouldn't do that," I said.

"Don't be too sure. This fight crowd can lead a lady a hell of a chase. Too much of this sitting around with the boys. The wives and the girl friends don't get much of a shake. I'd never tell nobody else but you, Eddie, but this town damn near loused up Billy and me. If I hadn't been with that sonofabitch—God rest his soul—since I was fifteen I sure in hell would have hit out for Oklahoma."

Like everyone else, I had heard something of the highs and lows in Shirley's relationship with the Sailor, but she had never brought it up before and I had never pressed her. But my leveling on Beth seemed to have loosened something that had been fastened tight inside her.

"You know Billy was a wild kid. He drank a lot before he started boxing serious. I guess we both did back in West Liberty. We were a couple of crazy punks. Every time I read of some kid and his babe robbing some guy who picked 'em up on the road, I think that could've been Billy and me. Billy wanted things awful bad. And I was so stuck on him I would've done anything he said. If he hadn't turned out to be able to get things with his fists, God knows what would have happened to us.

"But one thing I'll say for Billy in those days, he never played around. It wasn't till he hit this town and got to be a name at the Garden and fell in with those creeps who have connections with the clubs. I felt like jumping out the window the first time it happened. It was the night of the Coslow fight that everybody said was going to be such a tough hurdle. Billy won it without even getting his hair mussed. I never went to his fights because I didn't want to see anything happen to him, but I listened on the radio, which was almost as bad. Well, after I hear 'em counting Coslow out I get myself all fixed up because I think maybe Billy wants to celebrate. It turns out he's got his own ideas about celebrating. He doesn't come in till around six in the morning. He stinks of whisky and the smell of another woman is still sticking to him. Next evening when he wakes up it's, Baby forgive me, I'll never do it again. Six weeks later he takes the championship from Thompson in five, and I get the same shoving business all over again. After a while, I got to dreading Billy's winning another fight. Finally he's signed with Hyams and he won't listen to anybody about training—tells Danny McKeogh to duck himself—thinks he can mix fighting with funning around. I guess you remember the Hyams fight. Hyams busted his nose and cut him bad under both eyes. If the referee hadn't stopped it, he probably would've killed Billy. Billy was almost crazy, he had so much guts. Well, that night Billy comes home right after the fight. I keep him in bed for a week and he won't let anybody else come near him but me, not even Danny. And he's just as sweet and loving as a little baby.

"After that I swear to Jesus I used to actually pray that Billy would get licked. Because every time he got licked it was the same thing. He'd come home just as meek as a lamb and I'd have my Billy-baby all to myself again. I'd put cold compresses on his swellings and I'd wash his cuts and read the funnies out loud to him. I know it sounds screwy, but I swear I'd hate to see him get up out of bed."

As she talked, something Willie Faralla told me fell into place. Willie had taken an awful shellacking from Jerry Hyams in the Garden and Willie's state of mind was even worse than the way he looked. So he decided to drop up to Shirley's place and have a little fun. As soon as Shirley saw him with that bad eye and his lip split down the middle, she put him right to bed. She doctored him all evening, and at last, when everybody had gone home, she had climbed into bed with Willie and let him sleep with his head on her breast. Willie stayed there for almost a week, he said. "And the funny part about it was, it was all for free."

Willie was a good-looking kid, and he figured that Shirley just went for him in a big way. Well, a couple of weeks later Maxie Slott gets flattened in a semi at the Garden and he has heard about this Shirley deal from Willie. So he decides to try it. Now Maxie is short and chunky and has a face he could rent out to haunt houses, but Shirley takes him right to her bosom just like Willie, waits on him hand and foot and practically lives in bed with him for a week. And this, to Maxie's amazement, is also for free. After that, any batterred, beat-up pugilist who could even crawl up the three flights checks in at Shirley's. No matter how busy she is, she always has time to bathe an ear or bring down a swollen eye. And though there isn't a day goes by that she doesn't get invited by the best, the only men Shirley ever goes to bed with for love are beaten prize fighters.

Not only for free, as Willie had put it, but really for love, for love of a mean little sonofabitch from West Liberty, Oklahoma, who only belonged to her when he was too bloodied and too ashamed to be seen in public. And Shirley would love him as long as she lived, though sometimes he appeared in the form of the tall, lean Faralla and sometimes in the form of the short, squat Maxie Slott.

"Hey, look at the time," I said. "I've got a big day tomorrow. I mean today."

"You can't take any more, huh?"

"I know when I'm licked, chum. I'm throwing in the towel."

"Okay, take another beer out of the icebox. I'll see what this little visit cost you."

It came to forty-two dollars. "I wish you weren't going to California," Shirley said. "My favorite pigeon."

She walked me to the door. "This Molina you're working with, he's not exactly sensational, is he?"

"How do you know? Someone up from Stillman's tell you?"

"No, nobody told me—not even you. That's what made me wonder. Usually you sell your boys like you thought I was Uncle Mike."

"Well, you've got to promise to keep this under your hat or down your neck or wherever you hide your secrets, but this Molina might give a third-rate lightweight a hell of a battle. But don't say anything. Because I'm going to have him breathing down the champion's neck."

"All I know is what I read in the *Mirror,*" Shirley said.

"Thanks, Shirley, be a good girl."

"Not too good or I'll starve to death." She kissed me on the cheek. "And stay away from those movie stars."

I slapped her fondly. "I'll say one thing for us, we have the sexiest platonic relationship in town."

9

Usually when you get off a train in L.A., you expect that gag about how hard it is raining in sunny California. But this time it was only a light summer drizzle. I would have been glad to get off in a hail storm. Four days and three nights cooped up with this team could seem like a long time. I shared a compartment with Danny; Vince and Doc had another; and Toro and Acosta a third. George Blount, politely Jim Crowed, had an upper out there with the common people. Danny never gave Vince any time at all, and Vince certainly wasn't a fellow I'd pick to be marooned with, either. Luis studied English and told any strangers who would listen long enough about his great discovery of El Toro Molina. Danny and I stayed in our compartment, nipping most of the time, sleeping as late as we could in the morning to shorten the ride. Among the things we settled was who had the best claim to be called the greatest all-time heavyweight, an honor we arrived at by a complicated rating system that included points for hitting power, boxing skill, ability to take punishment, fighting spirit and all-around savvy. That is the kind of thing that begins to happen to you on a train. We came out with Jim Corbett on top and Peter Jackson right behind him. The quietest man in the party was Toro, who sat at the window day after day, looking out at the country phlegmatically, never saying anything. Once, as we roared through the great grazing lands of Kansas, I dropped into the seat beside him and said, "Well, what do you think of it?"

"Big," Toro said. "Like the pampas."

The day before we got in, when the setting sun was coloring the surreal southwestern landscape spectacularly, I noticed Toro sitting with a pad propped up on his knees, with his head bent intently toward something he was drawing. I dropped into the seat beside him to see what he was doing. He didn't even look up. His mind was focused down to the point of his pencil, all the way down to Santa Maria. For the paper was full of rough, half-doodled sketches of village scenes, the bell in the church tower, the uneven row of peasant houses perched on a hillside below a great castle-like mansion that dominated everything below it. And on another hill, on the opposite side of the village, Toro was drawing another great house, even larger. I knew this must be the house Luis had promised him, the dream castle in Santa Maria. The surprising thing about the drawings was that, although they were the most casual kind of pencil sketches, they were not the childish scribbling I would have suspected. They were three-dimensional and revealed a definite sense of form. I watched his heavy-featured face as he added little finishing touches to the sketch. Like everyone else, I had assumed that Toro was just an overgrown, retarded moron. But the drawings made me wonder.

When we pulled into the station I looked around for the cameras, for I had wired ahead to alert the local press on the arrival of the Giant of the Andes. L.A. isn't much of a newspaper town, for all its sprawling size, with only two morning papers, the *Times* and *Examiner*. The *Times'* sports editor was an old elbow-bending partner of mine, Arch Macail, with whom I had covered lots of fights before that non-understanding M.E. caught up with me. So I figured Arch would give us a break. Both papers had their men on the platform all right, but we had a little competition from another athlete, with whom we had to share the spotlight, an All-Midwest high-school quarterback who was coming out to play for Southern Cal, from whom, he had boyishly confided to me on the observation platform one afternoon, he had received the best offer, including a four-year scholarship for his girl.

The photographers got their picture of Toro holding Acosta up on one arm and waving the other hand, with a silly grin on his puss. Then the boys wanted one of Toro carrying Acosta and Danny, but Danny wouldn't play. "Leave me out of this malarkey, laddie," Danny protested. Danny didn't buy this high-pressure stuff.

But Acosta looked into those lenses as if they were the eyes of a long-lost love. It was a big moment for the little Luis, his first public recognition. Vince wasn't exactly camera shy either. He made sure he got his fat face in there, with his arm around Toro's waist, grinning up at him, the first time I had seen him throw the boy a friendly glance. Toro seemed neither pleased nor surprised by the reception. He just played it unself-consciously and deadpan, as if being greeted by newspaper photographers happened every day. You had to like the big guy. A man his size behaving as shyly and reticently as a child in a strange house isn't easy to hate.

"What's the pitch on this big joker?" a young, pudgy-faced reporter asked.

"He just won the South American heavyweight title," I improvised. "He's ready to meet anybody in the world, including the champion."

"Who's he gonna fight here?"

I figured we'd save the Cowboy Coombs announcement and blow that up to another story. So I said, "Anybody the local promoters can get to fight him. We bar nobody."

"What're the immediate plans?"

"To get some of your California sunshine and fresh air. That's the reason we came here, because Doc Zigman, the trainer, says it's the healthiest climate in the world."

That wasn't Eddie Lewis with his lightest touch, but it couldn't do us any harm. L.A. papers always have a little space for visitors loving up their climate.

"Will he be training in town or . . ."

"Ojai," I said. "But we don't want the fans to come up there for a while. We know there must be thousands anxious to see him, but I wish you'd tell them we'll let them know when we're open to the public. Toro's just been through a grueling South American campaign, and, with all this traveling, he needs a good rest."

I figured this would keep the sightseers off our necks till Danny had a chance to smarten him up a little.

"Any chance of Molina's fighting Buddy Stein out here?"

Stein was the best heavyweight developed on the West Coast since Jeffries. The boys who know had told me he had the hardest left hook since Dempsey. Nobody in California had been able to stay with him more than five rounds. If there was a heavyweight alive we didn't want for Toro, it was Buddy Stein.

"We will fight Stein anywhere, any time," I said. "In fact, we're so sure we can take Stein, we'll fight him winner take all."

Stein was pistol-hot, so I thought we might as well cut ourselves in on some of his publicity. It wasn't quite as rash as it sounded because I had it straight from the Garden office that Kewpie Harris, Stein's manager, didn't want any part of any more West Coast fights. Stein was ready for New York, where the money is, and Kewpie wanted either a shot at the championship or an outdoor fight with Lennert and a fat guarantee.

The young reporter scribbled our challenge down on the back of an envelope with a weary, skeptical obedience. Suddenly he turned to Toro.

"You think you can lick Stein?"

"¿Qué?" Toro said.

Acosta talked to him quickly. "The man asks you if you are sure you like California," he said in rapid Spanish.

"Sí, sí, estoy seguro," Toro said.

"Did you get that?" I said. "Yes, yes, I am sure."

Toro was beginning to draw a crowd. "Hey, lookit, there's Superman," a little kid said.

"Let's get out of here," Danny said. "I want to get up to the hotel and take a bath."

"Drop up around six, boys," I told the reporter. "We're having a little tea party."

On our way down the platform we passed the All-Midwest quarterback. "Well, it's a funny thing how I happened to choose Southern Cal," he was telling reporters. "Y'see, I want to be an architect, and one of my coaches—I mean my teachers—told me the best school of architecture in the country is out here at Southern Cal."

When we reached the Biltmore, Vince told George to take the cab
down to the Lincoln, on Central Avenue, in L.A.'s Harlem. I think
George was getting the best of it, at that.

"Sorry we've got to break up this way, George," I said.

"Don't worry about this boy, Mr. Lewis," George said. His eyes
looked as if they were laughing and his whole body shook with a chuckling that came up out of his belly. But I had the uncomfortable feeling
that his laugh was on us.

The cocktail party is America's favorite form of seduction, arranged
by press agents, full of gin and bourbon, paying off in news-space. The
plot is always the same. Come up to my room and have a drink. And
whether the object is physical passion or getting your client's name into
the headlines, the method is standard: to weaken their resistance with
let-me-pour-you-another-one, until they open their arms or their columns
to you in an alcoholic daze. Of course there will always be some ladies,
and members of the working press, who bounce back regularly after
each seduction, holding out their empty glasses, eager to sacrifice themselves again. Often the girls are nice girls and the representatives of the
press are good men who had some talent and some standards once upon
a time.

The little tea party we threw in our suite at the Biltmore to introduce
Toro to the local sports fraternity followed all the rules. Columnists who
arrived as skeptics were ready to take my word for it after an hour of the
amber. There was only one who gave me any trouble, a lank, dyspeptic-
looking fellow from the *News,* the afternoon tabloid, Al Leavitt, who
ran a column called "Leveling with Leavitt." He took his work seriously.
"I'll wait and see this guy before I buy him," he told me. "I've never
seen an oversized heavyweight who could get out of his own way. Back
in the Seventies there was a guy called Freeman, seven feet tall and
three hundred pounds, and he couldn't punch his way out of a paper
bag."

A historian yet! In every town you hit, there's always one jerk like
that, the natural enemy of a press agent, the guy with integrity.

"Write anything you want, Al," I said, pouring him a drink, because
in this business you've got to like everybody. "But remember the farther
out on a limb you get the sillier you'll look when Toro comes through
the way I know he's going to."

Leavitt gave me a slow, knowing smile. But the rest of the boys were
willing to play. I latched Acosta onto Joe O'Sullivan, who ran the *Examiner's* fight column. Luis gave him the full treatment, the whole 7000
miles from Santa Maria to L.A., at three words a mile, and Joe bought it
for a Sunday feature. Charlie King, who ran a little weekly magazine for

the fight fans called *Kayo,* sold at the arenas on fight nights, promised us a front-page picture and a full-column plug. Lavish Lew Miller, who covered fights for the *Times,* passed out, and I had Toro pick him up like a baby and put him to bed. Everything worked out fine. It was a good party. We were off to a good start.

In the morning we hired a car for the drive up to Ojai, all except Vince who was staying in town to work out details of the match with Nate Starr, the matchmaker for the Hollywood Club.

Ojai turned out to be a long valley, full of fruit trees and lots of other kinds of trees I never learned the names of. Mountains rose steeply on both ends of the valley, like the head-and-foot-boards of a giant bed. If you were a country lover, Ojai had it. Its air was the kind you breathe in deeply and hold in your chest, feeling yourself growing healthier every second. We had a couple of cottages at a rich-man's health camp which catered chiefly to business executives who took it into their heads to work a couple of inches off their paunches, and motion-picture directors taking four weeks off to get back into shape to start another picture. The layout was just what we needed: a good gym, an indoor and outdoor ring, a steam bath, good rubbers and plenty of room for road work.

After everybody had unpacked, Danny called the group together on the porch of his cottage and laid down the law. He looked businesslike and athletic in his gray flannel pants, old blue sweater, boxing shoes and baseball cap.

"From here on," he began, "we quit kidding around. I'm in charge as of now. You, Acosta, if there's anything he can't savvy, tell him in your own lingo. Molina, this is your schedule. Up at seven. Roadwork, six or eight miles, alternately running and walking as fast as you can take it without getting exhausted. Then a shower and a brisk rubdown. No monkey business on the road. I'll usually be along with you to show you how I want it. Breakfast at eight sharp, as many eggs as you want, but no pancakes or soft foods. That's out. After breakfast a long rest. You'll walk a mile or so before lunch. After a light lunch, you sleep for an hour and then begin to limber up. Shadowboxing and a couple of rounds of sparring with George comes next. Then a session on the light bag and another on the heavy bag, practicing the punches I'll show you. Then about fifteen minutes of rope-skipping and some calisthenics. Doc'll give you the ones I like best, exercises that'll loosen you up, get you to move around a little faster. No other kind of exercise is worth a damn. Then you'll get on the table for a thorough rubdown. You'll rest from three to five and then take a long walk. Supper will be at six. After supper you can take it easy for a couple of hours. Cards, anything you like. Then a mile walk and lights out at nine-thirty. No liquor. No eating between meals. No women. That's it. Any questions?"

Only Acosta spoke up. "Eight miles a day? I think this is too much for El Toro to run. Since he already is very strong."

"Look, Acosta," Danny cut in, pronouncing his name with an R on the end, "get this in your head once and for all. Strength has nothing whatever to do with it, at least the kind of strength Molina's got. It's speed, headwork, timing, even with the big fellows. Those big, bulging, weight-lifting muscles of his will just get in the way."

Acosta said nothing. The eager, glowing face with which he had first told me his story was glum and disappointed now. Only occasionally, as at the station when the cameras were trained on him, did he show any of his previous animation. The big dream of bringing Toro to America in triumph was rapidly losing its quality of personal achievement for him.

That afternoon they let Toro off easy with a brisk two-mile run. Danny asked me if I wanted to go along, but I told him I wasn't quite ready for suicide yet. Climbing on and off a bar stool was exercise enough for this athlete. Danny always accompanied his fighters on road work. It certainly was one for Ripley. How a guy of his age and his habits could pace a healthy young athlete for six miles was one of the mysteries. Either Danny's guts were made of reinforced steel or an alcoholic diet is not as injurious as its detractors claim it to be. Except for a slight middle-age bulge at the waist, Danny's figure was still lithe and athletic. He ran easily, with a relaxed, springy motion, which was like the movement of a gazelle compared to Toro's heavy lumbering behind him. George followed them, jogging along in a way that made it look as if it were no effort at all.

When they came in, about fifteen minutes later, Danny and George were still running easily, but Toro was all in. He seemed to be favoring his right leg. So Doc put him right on the table and looked him over. "Here it is," he said, fingering Toro's enormous calf. "Just a little Charley. I can rub it out in a few minutes." His long, skillful fingers worked Toro's taut leg muscles. "Better take it easy on running him for a while," Doc said as he worked. "Y'see, these muscles of his are knotty from all that lifting. They go into a Charley easy. They don't slide over each other like you need 'em to in running and boxing."

"What's Nick Latka trying to do to me?" Danny said. "See how much I can take? All that weight and no legs."

"It is perhaps the change of climate," Acosta suggested. "El Toro is not use—"

"Shut up," Danny said.

He hadn't had a drink all day and his face looked drawn. I knew sooner or later Acosta was going to get on his nerves. Danny left Doc to finish rubbing out the charley horse and went back to his cottage to smoke a cigarette. I followed him. He drew on his cigarette a couple of times and crushed it out impatiently. "Son of a sea-cook," he said. "All my life I wanted a good heavyweight, and what do they send me? A big oaf with no legs."

That evening after supper I took a stroll with Toro and Acosta. We walked slowly along the edge of an orange grove. The valley heat still hung in the air. The large, rose-tinted moon was a fifth carbon of the close, hot sun that had beat down on us all day. I walked quietly half a pace to the rear of them, and after a while they began to talk to each other frankly, as if they had forgotten my presence, or perhaps that I could understand. In Spanish, I noticed, Toro wasn't nearly the halting, inarticulate ox he seemed in English. He was able to express himself clearly and with considerable feeling.

"You did not tell me the truth, Luis," Toro said. "You told me I could make much more money and not work so hard as I must in Santa Maria. But to train like this man wants of me is much harder than I have ever worked for my father. And I do not like it as well."

"But the work you do in Santa Maria you must do all your life, until you have perhaps sixty or seventy years," Acosta argued. "Here you must work very hard, it is true. But when you have boxed one or two years you will have enough money to live like a lord in Santa Maria the rest of your life."

"That I could be back in Santa Maria right now," Toro said. "Even without the money."

"You must not talk like that," Acosta scolded. "That is a very bad way to talk. After all I have done for you, to bring you to this country, to put you in the hands of such important managers. How many poor village boys would like to have your opportunity!"

"I would let them have my place, with much pleasure," Toro said.

"But you do not understand," Acosta said, a little impatiently. "None of them have your magnificent physique. This is what you were born for. It is your destiny."

When I got back to the cottage, George was sitting outside on the porch steps by himself, half singing, half mumbling a song that seemed to have no end.

Doc was inside, sitting at a little desk in the front room, his deformed body hunched intently over something he was writing.

"Catching up on your fan mail, Doc?"

Doc turned toward me, slung a thin, angular leg over the arm of his chair, and took a half-smoked cigar from his mouth. "Aw, I'm just making some notes."

"What kind of notes, Doc?"

"Pathological," Doc said, "I guess you call it."

"About punch drunks?" I said.

"That's right. Case histories of punchy fighters. There hasn't been much technical stuff written about it."

"How many really wind up punchy?"

"Well, maybe half the guys who stay in over ten years, but I'd only be guessing," Doc said. "You see, Eddie, the trouble is, nobody's made a scientific survey. Lots of boys are wandering around cutting up paper dolls and there isn't any kind of medical record. Every case I hear about, I write it down in my notebook. Maybe some day I'll do something with it."

"Why not try to put it in an article?" I said. "It'd make a damn interesting piece."

Doc rubbed his damp, high forehead reflectively. "Not without that M.D.," he said. "I know what doctors think of laymen who write books on medicine. If there's anything I don't want to be, it's one of those loud-mouthed quacks with a few fixed ideas. So I'll just stick to my goddam fight racket and let my brother write the books."

He took out a handkerchief, mopped the perspiration that seemed to be constantly on his face and turned back to his notes.

Danny was inside on the bed, studying *Racing Form* with a pencil in his hand and a half-empty bottle of Old Granddad on the table beside him.

"Help yourself, laddie," he said.

"No thanks, Danny," I said. "I'm in the desert for a week. I do this to myself once every year. It's like banging your head against a stone wall. Feels so good when it stops."

Danny reached for the bottle and raised it to his lips. "I was on the wagon when I had Greenberg and Sencio. I stayed on it pretty good when I had Tomkins too, bless his black heart. But I'll be split down the middle if I'll come off the stuff for a big musclebound lummox of a weight-lifter."

He set the bottle down on the edge of the table, so that it threatened to fall at the slightest vibration. Danny absorbed his liquor so well that you had to watch for things like that to realize how far along he was. He returned to the *Form* studiously and encircled one of the names.

"Something good for tomorrow?"

"I'm just checking workouts and speed ratings," Danny said. "Then if they post one of the horses I've spotted, I bet him."

"Your system work?"

"There's only one system that works, laddie. To know who's gonna win."

"What do you play it for, Danny? What's in it for you?"

"Oh, I don't know. Same reason you put salt on your eggs, I guess. Spices things up a little bit." He reached for the bottle again. "A weight-lifter! At my age I get a weight-lifter!" His mouth went to the bottle with desperation.

Danny slept it off in the morning, something he never did when his mind was on his work, but Doc put Toro through his paces. Toro did everything he was told, but there was none of the zip and spring of a man whose body likes to move. His rope skipping was awkward and heavy-footed, with the rope constantly catching on his ungainly feet.

After lunch Danny gave Toro some exercises on the light bag, and then, with the heavy bag for a target, he began to give him pointers on the jab. "I claim a man can't even begin to call himself a professional boxer until he can jab," Danny said. "A good stiff jab throws your opponent off balance. When he's off balance he's a better target for your other punches. The jab isn't just waving your left hand in the other guy's face. You've got to step into your jabs, springing off your right toe and going forward on your left, like a fencing motion or a bayonet thrust. It's all the same idea, straight from the shoulder, with your body behind it always keeping 'em off balance. Like this."

Danny faced the bag, bouncing on the balls of his feet, and even when he wasn't actually moving his body undulated with a weaving, shifty motion, automatically prepared to slip inside a straight right or snap away from a left. His jabs bit sharply into the bag and he recoiled so rapidly into position again that it all became one motion. Then he called George over and demonstrated on him. George allowed the jabs to connect with his face, rolling with them slightly to absorb the shock, but at the same time letting himself be hit hard enough for Toro to be able to see the effect. Then, with George still the target, Danny told Toro to imitate him. Toro lurched forward, drawing his left fist back before pushing it out ineffectually toward George's jaw.

"Never draw back on a punch," Danny said. "That's what you call 'telegraphing.' And you lose part of your force."

Toro tried again. His enormous fist floated slowly into George's face. Danny shook his head dismally and led Toro back to the heavy bag. With his legs spread apart, Danny stood behind the bag, doing his best to transfuse a few drops of his ring wisdom into this dinosaur.

"Mr. Lewis," George said, "you gonna be careful who the big boy fights?"

"Oh, we'll be careful," I said.

"That's good," George said. "He's a pretty nice fella. I wouldn't want to see him get hurt too bad."

"He won't get hurt," I said.

I went over to Danny, who was demonstrating the left jab in shadow-boxing now. "Danny, I'm going into town," I said. "Anything I can do for you?"

Danny wiped his forehead and took a look at Toro. "Wait a minute,"
he said. "I'm going in with you." He called over to Doc, who was sitting
on a bench, reading the papers. "Keep him working on the bag for a
while. George can show him what I mean. Then move him around the
ring for ten-fifteen minutes, no punches, just feeling things out with
George. Then give him some good stiff exercises, as much as he can
stand. Try to keep him up off his heels on the rope-skipping. I'll be back
some time in the morning."

"Okay," Doc said. "Say, Danny, if you see one of them outa town
newsstands, see if you can pick up a New York paper."

"The Giants are still hanging on," Danny said. "What more do you
want to know?"

"A guy likes to keep in touch," Doc said.

"Learn to relax, Doc," I said. "This is a vacation spot. Make like
you're on a vacation."

Doc had a way of smiling that always made me sad.

As we drove out of sight of the camp, Danny said, "Laddie, I just had
to get out of there for a while. There's nothing drives me nuts like trying
to teach a man with no ability. And with that other little guy babbling
Spanish at my elbow all the time, I feel like I'm going off my noodle."

"Think you can get him to go through the motions of looking like a
fighter?"

"Aw, I don't know. I guess I can teach him one or two little things.
But I don't want to think about it till I get back there in the morning."

When we turned off Ventura Boulevard, where the unadorned, rural
gas stations begin to give way to more elaborate lubratoria with an unmistakable Hollywood influence, Danny gave me the address of a
barbershop on Cherokee Avenue.

"But you just had a haircut, Danny."

"This is the address of a fella who will take a bet for me," Danny
said. "I guess I get clipped one way or another, laddie."

After I dropped Danny off, I went up to our rooms at the Biltmore and
got to work. I was making out a list of people I had to call when Vince
came out of the bathroom in his pajamas.

"Hi ya, lover?" he said.

"Hello."

Vince said, "Everything's all right with Starr. We're matched with
Coombs the 26th of next month. That gives you plenty of time to goose
the people, doesn't it, lover?"

"Jesus, six more weeks in this town!"

"What's the matter with this town, honey?" Vince said. "You should
see the poontang down in this cocktail lounge every night. Like shooting
fish in a barrel." He broke wind noisily. "Did you say something, dear?"

He pulled the seat of his pajamas away from his beefy rump and disappeared into the bedroom again.

I settled down to the phone and the business of selling my product. I got Wicherley's Clothes for Men to outfit Toro from head to foot in return for the plugs I promised to give them. I arranged with a furniture store to build an extra-size bed for Toro which I planned to photograph as it was carried through the Biltmore lobby. I sold the Western editor of a national weekly supplement on the idea of a two-page spread, comparing Toro's physical measurements with those of Hercules, Atlas and the giants of antiquity. The angle was to reach out beyond the sports pages, beyond the fight fans to the great public of curiosity seekers. For lunch I took Joe O'Sullivan to Lyman's, where, after the second highball (padded to four on the expense account), I confided the important news that we were considering either Buddy Stein or Cowboy Coombs as the first West Coast opponent for Toro Molina.

Next morning the item headed his column as a scoop. Coombs wasn't as well known to West Coast fans as Stein, O'Sullivan wrote, but he was a strong, experienced heavyweight who had fought the best in the East. This no one could deny. The only detail O'Sullivan had omitted was that he had invariably been on the catching end of all these fights with the best in the East. He had had plenty of experience in the ring. All right, mostly discouraging.

Stein or Coombs, Coombs or Stein. The sports writers kicked that one around for a week or so. When we had pushed this as far as it would go, we got a nice fat two-column for the announcement that Toro Molina, the Giant of the Andes, undefeated champion of South America, would have as his first American opponent none other than Cowboy Coombs, that formidable campaigner who was such a favorite with the fans along the Atlantic Seaboard, a great crowd-pleaser who had been forced to come west because no ranking New York heavyweight would risk his reputation against him.

"Among his many fistic achievements," the article drooled, "Coombs can boast of fighting a draw with the great Gus Lennert." The Lennert fight had been a draw, but it was nine years ago, back in the days when Coombs at least had the vigor of youth, when he had caught Lennert on one of those off nights that every fighter has. But fortunately the people who read the stuff had neither record books nor long memories, and the guys who wrote the stuff liked the color of our Scotch and our chips. All except Al Leavitt, who had a crack in that column of his about how apt Molina's first name was, since it meant bull in English. "It is interesting to note," wrote Leavitt, "that throwing this kind of bull is not the same sport practiced so enthusiastically in Latin countries. Mr. Eddie Lewis, on tour with Bull—sorry, Toro Molina, is a skillful exponent of the

Northern variety." Well, the hell with Leavitt. He was only one voice in
this wilderness. He was the sort of fellow who comes to your cocktail
party, drinks up all your liquor and then goes away and writes as he
pleases. No loyalty. No principles.

I devoted the rest of the day to making the people of California
Molina-conscious. I dusted off some old gags, pinned Toro's name to
them, and phoned them in to some of the boys who had come to our
cocktail party. I picked out the most imposing photograph of Toro to use
on the posters. I had mimeographed sheets made of Toro's life story,
with a tabulation of his physical measurements from the size of his skull
to the circumference of his little toe. I had a girl come in and start a
scrapbook of all the Molina items from the newspapers I had begun
saving the day we hit town. And the funny thing is, as I glanced through
the first few pages of this book, with the big picture of Toro lifting
Acosta off the train, and the Sunday feature on how Luis discovered
Toro lifting barrels in Santa Maria, I had a real sense of achievement.
Whether what I had done was true or not, or whether it would ever do
anybody any good was no longer my concern. Filling up that scrapbook
had become an end in itself, like stamp collecting. That's what made it
so easy to do, what almost sucked me into believing that so good a job
was good in itself.

10

When the sun began to sink down behind the squat, ugly architecture of
downtown Los Angeles, I began to think of some way to spare myself
another social session with Vince. I had sat out the previous evening
with him in the Biltmore cocktail lounge, and though the hunting was as
effortless as he had said, I wasn't ready for indiscriminate mating yet.
Beth's bitter words were still in my head. Damn it, I was making a
living. I wasn't robbing anybody; the lies I told were just ordinary
American business lies like everybody else's lies. They didn't do too
much harm. What did she want of me? What was she being so goddam
righteous about? If there's anything I can't stand, it's a righteous
woman. Of the hundreds and thousands of eligible and relatively willing
females in the city of New York, why did I have to pick on a dame who
wanted to elevate me? Because you wanted to elevate yourself, a small
voice hiding in one of the creases of my mind answered. It wasn't just
her body that made me go for that New England stray. I liked to think so
because it gave me less to worry about. But the first time I talked to her,
I had a hunch that she wanted to elevate me, make me amount to something. It put me on my guard right away. I remember thinking there was
something physically exciting about a girl who could be that pleasant to

look at and still make so much sense. But I wanted her on my terms.

The first time I talked to Beth, all those numbers in the little phone books turned into dogs. They were nice dogs, pretty dogs, from Pomeranians to Russian wolfhounds, but I didn't want them any more. I wanted Beth in a way I had never wanted any woman before. I wanted to enter not only into her body but into her mind, and the satisfaction of one seemed to intensify the satisfaction of the other. Beth gave me a sense of where I was and where I stood in time, and if my job with Nick was like a jail, a comfortable, cushy jail, but still a place of confinement, Beth was my contact with the outside world, who brought some of that world to me each visiting day. It was her world and, out here, it seemed as if it ought to be mine. Beth was my safety valve. And now the valve was shut. I was left to sweat in my own steam.

Vince came out of the bedroom, still in his pajamas. He had slept until one o'clock and then had his breakfast sent up. Now that the match was set, there wasn't much for Vince to do until Miniff arrived and they got together to work out the fight. He had really caught the gravy train this time.

"You know I've been thinking . . ." he said.

"An obvious exaggeration," I said.

"All right, wise guy," he said. "But I didn't get where I am with my beautiful body."

"Where are you?" I said.

"In the Hotel Biltmore," he said. "Room eight-o-one and two. Where the hell are you?"

"In limbo," I said. "The Hotel Limbo. And I don't even know the number of the room."

"You're working too hard," Vince said.

"Well, between us I guess we do a day's work," I said.

"Don't worry about this party." Vince pointed to himself indignantly. "If I don't take care of my end, all them fancy words of yours add up to double-o." He took his pajama top off and bent his soft belly as he tried to touch his toes in a half-hearted gesture of calisthenics. "Jesus," he said, "I'm slipping. Can't even touch my toes any more." He straightened up slowly and put his hands lewdly under his breasts, which were heavy with fat. "Stop staring at me, you naughty boy," he camped in a falsetto and laughed.

"Go get some clothes on, goddam it," I said. "This is an office. Anybody's liable to come in."

"I know what's the matter with you, lover. You wanna keep me all to yourself."

"That's where you're wrong," I said. "I want to keep you all to yourself."

"All to myself," Vince said. "My old man told me never to do that."

"Go get your clothes on," I said.

Vince hesitated and then decided to be friends. For the first time in his life he had a first-class ticket on a fast express and it might pay to get along with the other passengers. "Okay, chummo. I was only kiddin'."

Vince retired to the bathroom. I had to get away from him. I thought of Stempel. I hadn't bothered to get in touch with him yet because I didn't know where he was any more. He had come out for MGM; I remembered that. So I called there and the girl who said *"Metro-Goldwyn-Mayer"* had never heard of him, but she passed me on to the one who said "writers" who told me that Stempel hadn't worked there for several years. Then I thought I remembered having seen his name on a Warners' picture and I called there. Yes, Mr. Stempel had worked there, but not in the last six months. Why didn't I call the Screen Writers' Guild? The Guild secretary had a record of every writer employed in Hollywood. I could reach Stempel at National, she said. National, it didn't seem possible. The author of *The Locomotive Dream,* one of the bright young hopes of my generation, was employed by the studio that specialized in blood-and-thunder Westerns. For me it was almost like discovering that the writing credit on *The Lone Ranger* was Thomas Mann. But anyway I made the call. Yes, Mr. Stempel had been on the lot. "He was checked out this afternoon," I was told. No, the Studio was not allowed to give out any personal numbers.

By this time I had to see Stempel. I had to find out what had happened to Stempel. In desperation I picked up the phone book on the improbable chance that he might be listed. And there it was, easy as falling off the wagon, David H. Stempel, 1439 Stone Canyon Rd. CRestview 6-1101. One minute later I was talking to Stempel himself, his voice sounding exactly as high and boyish and enthusiastic as when I had seen him last.

"For God's sake, Eddie Lewis! From what cloud bank have you descended? Hop in a cab and come on out here."

As I taxied up through the streets of Los Angeles, which resembled small Middle Western cities laid down side by side for miles and miles, I thought of Dave Stempel, David Heming Stempel, and what a demigod he had seemed back in the days when he was first reading his work in progress to us. David Heming Stempel could not have been better cast for a young epic poet if he had been picked out of the actors' directory by an experienced casting director. He was a big man, well over six feet, with that rare combination of size and delicacy. His eyes were light blue, quick to smile and yet intense, and he had a long, slender profile.

After dropping out of school I didn't see Dave again until I ran into him several years later, in Tim's on Third Avenue. He was only a year or two out of college then and *The Locomotive Dream* had made him the most talked-of young poet in America. This had been the first volume of a trilogy he had planned on "Man's inexorable struggle to conquer the Machine," as the dust jacket had put it, and the second volume, *The Seven-Jewel Heart,* had already been announced for "early publication." That night, when I asked him what was new with him, he threw back that magnificent head of his and said, "You know I've always been curious to see what a real mythical kingdom looks like, so I'm going out to Hollywood for a couple of months. See if I can't smuggle out a little of their mythical money. My projects have become an awful strain on those Guggenheims. So I thought it might be an amusing idea to let Metro-Goldwyn-Mayer provide me with a fellowship."

That had been fifteen years ago. For half that time at least, Stempel's publishers had continued to announce the "imminent publication" of *The Seven-Jewel Heart.* I know because I kept watching for it after having practically memorized *The Locomotive Dream.*

My cab turned in at a large medieval-looking stone house. A maid led me through the cold, high-ceilinged living room to a cosy paneled little bar which had nothing to do with the style of the house.

"Eddie Lewis," Stempel said, as if our meeting had a real significance. "My Lord, you've changed, Eddie."

My first impression of Dave was that he hadn't changed at all. The face was still handsomely boyish, the figure tall and slender. The checkered tweed jacket and the polka-dot bow-tie accentuated his youthfulness. It was only when I looked at him more closely, while he shook the cocktails, that I began to see the little alterations time had made. His blond hair was going prematurely gray and thin and something had gone out of his eyes. As a young man he had been full of a bubbling, imaginative gaiety, but it seemed to me as he talked that this had been replaced by a nervous animation. We were reminiscing over the first drink, when Dave's wife entered. I was ready to say hello again, for I had expected the high-strung little mental one with the boyish figure who had published a couple of thin books of verse herself and who had treated Dave with the respectful admiration one only accords to the dead. But this one was a very young woman with bangs, shoulder-length hair, exotic eyebrows, an abundance of Mexican handicraft silver jewelry, fleshy breasts with which she was obviously pleased and a manner that was more like a performance. She could have been a Hollywood stock-girl passing as an intellectual or an intellectual posing as a stock-girl.

"Miki, Eddie's come out here with that giant prize fighter we read about," Dave said.

"I think that's fascinating," Miki said.

"Miki and I go to the fights every Friday night," Dave said. "I love the rhythm of a good fight. I've seen them when they're pure ballet."

"What kind of a character is this giant?" Miki said, stealing a quick, approving glance at herself in the bar mirror as she talked. "It must be madly fascinating to study a person like that."

"Madly," I said.

The man came in, looked at Mrs. Stempel significantly and went out again without a word. "Duck," Mrs. Stempel said, "let's go in to dinner."

Duck and Mrs. Duck sat at either end of a long Spanish Colonial table in the large, formal dining room. After the avocado salad, the maid brought out a bottle of wine wrapped in a napkin and set it down in front of Dave with an air of formality. "Thank God I had the foresight to buy up all the *Graves* I could find," he said as he uncorked the bottle expertly.

He poured a little into a wine glass and asked the maid to bring it down to Mrs. Stempel. He looked down the table at her, waiting for the verdict as she tasted the wine carefully.

"How is it?" he said.

"Not bad," she decided. "Is this the Thirty-three?"

When he said it was, she nodded wisely. "I thought so. The Thirty-three has an extra little..." She paused as if reaching for exactly the right shade of meaning and I wondered if it would be nuance, or even *bonne bouche,* but she ended with "something."

"It's really the funniest thing," Dave said. "I've been studying wines for, well, twenty years and this little minx of mine whose favorite drink when I met her was a lemon coke can tell one wine from another as if she's been at it all her life."

"I've just got a natural taste for it," Miki admitted.

While Dave carved the meat, he said, "Oh, by the way, Miki, I talked to Mel Steiner today."

"Oh," Miki said, and stopped to wait for something that was obviously of great importance. "Well, what did he say?"

Dave turned to me and politely led me into the conversation. "You see, Eddie, there's a little credit dispute on my last picture. A couple of writers who polished my script are trying to ease me out of screen credit. The way we settle these things now is by a Guild Arbitration committee. Steiner's head of the committee."

"Well, what did he say?" Miki pressed him.

"He says the committee hasn't reached a final decision yet. Though it doesn't look like I'm going to get screenplay credit. But I may get an adaptation credit."

"That's simply filthy," Miki said, and then as a lady at a costume ball might do, she let her little pink mask of culture drop for a moment. "I think that stinks," she announced.

"All they did was take my lines and rewrite them," Dave said. "Making sure to take all the rhythm and the poetry out of them."

"Additional dialogue, that's what they should get," Miki said, "additional dialogue."

"You see, Eddie," Dave explained, "to get screenplay credit, you've got to prove that you wrote at least twenty-five percent of the shooting script. So these credit-hounds always try to revise your script at least eighty percent. Writers with the souls of bookkeepers."

The maid filled our glasses again.

"I suppose this is probably all Greek to you," Dave apologized, "but these credits are our bread and butter. I spent nine months at Goldwyn's last year on a script that got shelved, and had to take a salary cut at National. Now if I lose out on this credit, I'm in trouble." A frown creased his high forehead. "Dammit, Miki, how many times do you have to tell that stupid wench not to go to sleep in the kitchen after she's served the main course? You know how I hate to look at dirty dishes."

"I know, duck," Miki said. "She's a Jukes on both sides of her family. But it's so hard to get help to come all the way out here. They're so independent these days."

"What do they think this is, a free country?" I said, laughing to show I was making a joke.

When the maid had removed the coffee cups sullenly and Dave was about to pour our second brandy, Miki said, very charmingly, "If your friend will excuse me, I'll leave you boys alone. You probably have a lot to talk about."

She went over and bit Dave playfully on the ear. "Good night, duck," she said. "Good night, Mr. Lewis. Do come again soon. It's been fascinating."

There was pride in Dave's washed-out blue eyes as her full, confident figure disappeared. "God, she's a great woman," he said. "Don't you think she's a great woman, Eddie?"

"Mm," I said.

"I can't take my eyes off her," he said. "It's been three years and I still can't take my eyes off her. She's given me something, Eddie, something I've been searching for all my life. Without Miki and Irving I would have been a schizo for sure."

"Who is Irving?"

"Irving Seidel, my analyst. He's a great man. He's treated practically everybody I know."

From one of the bookcases that completely covered the walls, Dave pulled out a volume and read a paragraph to me. It was a book by Seidel called, *I Vs. Me*. Dave's library contained practically all the English, Russian and French classics, several shelves on psychoanalysis and most

of the outstanding poetry and fiction of the past twenty years. And
Dave's mind seemed as curious and as hungry for new literary experi-
ences as it had been fifteen years before. He quoted enthusiastically
from a new Yale poet whose work, he said, reminded him "of a Marxist
Gerard Manly Hopkins." He described the subtle relationships in a first
novel by a young Southern girl whose involuted style fascinated him.
And then, pausing to inhale the fumes from his brandy glass, he began
to recite a strange, haunting poem about two robots in a mechanized
utopia who are equipped with human hearts and discover the experience
of love. At first it seemed to lack rhythm and form, and the sound of it
grated on me, but gradually it began to shape itself into a pattern and its
melodies were as unmistakable and provocative as the distorted, disso-
nant themes of Schoenberg.

When Dave paused to refill our brandy glasses, I said, "Never heard
that before. What is it?"

"The prologue to *The Seven-Jewel Heart*," Dave said.

"It's—" I was going to say "fascinating" and then I remembered
Miki. "It's swell," I said. "Have you ever finished it?"

Dave's face was flushed and his eyes went in and out of focus. There
had not been a great deal to drink but suddenly his powers of coordination seemed to switch off. "Almost finished," he mumbled. "Jus' one
more canto. Thasall, jus' one more canto. 'Fi c'd jus' get this town off
my back . . ." He shook his head slowly and began to recite again, un-
intelligibly.

"But why can't you get out?" I said. "What holds you?"

"All I need is jus' one good credit, an' some o' this gold. I need more
gold, Eddie, and then I'll—go to Mexico, six months, maybe a year,
rediscover my soul, Eddie."

"But Dave," I said, "I can't figure it. You've been making big dough
for years. You must have enough to . . ."

"This isn't dough," Dave said. "Dough sticks to your palms. This is a
handful of worms that slip through your fingers. Know what this house
cost me, Eddie? Five hundred dollars a month, six thousand dollars a
year for this unspeakable abortion. And then Louise, a thousand a
month, my fine for committing premeditated matrimony. And then
there's my daughter, Sandy, just starting at Wellesley, a lovely, intelligent girl whose mother refuses to let her contaminate herself by visiting
her disreputable father but somehow brings herself to accept his disreputable lucre, a disreputable five thousand a year. And then there's Wilbur,
who is forty-one years old and who has finally decided what he wants to
be—the brother of a Hollywood writer. One useless brother, three thousand per annum. And don't let me forget my innocent-looking, white-
haired mother-in-law with the cash register ringing in her brain, who

stipulated a yearly retainer of five thousand dollars. These are the weeds, Eddie, that choke the life from the delicate, tender roots of the poetic impulse. The weeds, the weeeeeeeeds . . ." He drew it out into an eerie chant. "That feeds, and feeeeeeeeds . . . upon these poor creative seeds . . ."

I had to go. I had to be away from this. I needed a drink. No, I had a drink. That's what I always thought I needed when I needed something else. I needed air. I needed to get out.

"Dave," I said, "I gotta run. Gotta be up early in the morning. Lot to do."

He begged me to stay, implored me to stay with such repetitious insistence that I felt the great bird had some nightmare fear of being left alone in this little cage. When I kept saying, "Gotta go now, Dave, gotta go," he insisted on going along with me to help me find a cab. He staggered out into the night and walked me down to the boulevard. We waited under a lamppost on the corner, and as a cab pulled into the curb, Dave stood with his legs apart, swinging slowly back and forth, muttering, "Wanna hear my lates', my ver lates' poem, jus' written today, written on National's precious time."

His laugh mounted maniacally. As my cab pulled away, I could see him out of the rear window, lurching out of the glare of the lamplight back into the shadows of darkest Beverly Hills.

"Where ya wanna go?" The heavy, exasperated face of the cab driver turned to me.

"Biltmore," I said.

"Can't make it da Chicago Biltmore?" he said with angry humor.

"What's the matter, you don't like this town?" I said.

"You c'n have this town and seven points. Gimme Chi. Hacking in Chi you c'n make yourself a buck. The customers wantcha to live back in Chi. They leave ya real good tips."

Furiously he shot the cab into high. I was sorry for him. I was sorry for everybody, when you got right down to it. I was sorry for David Heming Stempel. I was sorry for Eddie Lewis. I don't want to be a little sad at forty, and sadder at fifty and a tragic bum at sixty. What was it Beth said: Some day, two words for an epitaph. Who said that? Beth said that. Beth had the courage of her convictions. Why didn't I call Beth? Why didn't I marry Beth? Hello, darling, just wanted to call and let you know I'm getting out of this racket. That's right, not even going back to the training camp. Yeah, I finally did it, made up my mind, rediscovered my poet's soul, no—that's Stempel. Rediscovered something anyway. Coming back on the next train, darling, coming back to you, and by the way, Beth, will you marry me?

I tipped the cab driver from Chi a dollar to brighten his evening and hurried into the lobby to place my call. Person-to-person to Miss Beth Reynolds, R as in righteous, E as in elevate, Y as in yearning. I'm not drunk, my brain rejoiced. I'm not drunk this time. Just a little wine and some brandy, but I'm not doing this because I'm drunk. I'm doing it because I can't stand the failures any more, the fakes, the frauds. I'm doing it because I don't want to be another David Heming Stempel, a poor man's, less-talented David Heming Stempel. I don't want to wander around on my hands and knees searching every corner for my soul as if it were a lost collar button.

"Hello, hello . . . There's no answer?" It was three hours later in New York, which made it two o'clock in the morning there. She had to answer. Where could Beth be at 2 A.M. on a Sunday morning? "All right, then cancel the person-to-person. I'll talk to anybody at the hotel desk. Hello . . . Do you have any idea where I could reach Miss Reynolds? She's away, away for the weekend? . . . Oh . . . well, will you take a message? Just tell her that . . . Oh, never mind, never mind. I'll call again some time."

All the excitement was left behind me in the phone booth. There was a dull, twisting pain in my stomach. I never realized before that jealousy was something you could actually feel in your belly like a green and indigestible apple. Beth was my girl, and now that I wanted and needed her I couldn't even get her on the phone.

I wandered into the cocktail lounge. The Muzak was playing Guy Lombardo. A couple of drunk out-of-town business men who thought they had to be comic as well as spendthrift were pawing a couple of ladies who received their attention with bored, businesslike acceptance. A woman in her thirties was sitting alone at a little table, drinking beer. She looked over in unenthusiastic flirtation as I stood at the entrance. Just another bar, another night, another meaningless woman. I turned and went upstairs.

There were empty whisky and soda bottles on the table in the sitting room, and a stale, sour smell in the air. I looked into the bedroom. All the windows were shut, and the shades were drawn, and it was hot and close in there. Vince's clothes were scattered around the room, his shirt on the bathroom door-knob, his shorts on the floor, while piled rather neatly on one chair were the clothes of a woman. Her silk stockings were folded carefully over the foot of the bed.

Their inconsequential lust had spent itself and they were asleep now, with their heads close together on the pillow. How peaceful they looked together! In the morning they would rise as strangers, with not even a kiss or perhaps a kind word, but tonight they were enfolded together in serene sleep. What misfortune or perversity led this woman to wander so casually into the bed of Vince Vanneman? Vince groaned and rolled over, pulling most of the bedclothes with him. The woman, momentarily uncovered, moved toward him in her sleep, fitting herself against his fat back and rump. It was an instinctive, primeval action, the female seeking warmth and protection from the male, and there was something about its performance in this room under these conditions that bore me down into a bottomless depression.

I couldn't face the morning with this abandoned couple. So I phoned an all-night car-for-hire and drove out of the silent city into the dark, rolling countryside. I drove into Ojai just as dawn was filtering into the valley. Crickets were chirping and the birds were awakening. I tiptoed into the cottage and the room I shared with Doc. Doc was sleeping on his stomach, snoring rhythmically, the covers outlining his deformity. As I slipped into my bed wearily, I remembered it was a good thing I had come out here because I had some photographers due in the morning to cover Toro's training routine. As I sank into sleep, I was thinking of gags and catchy poses I could use for the layout. Just before I went off completely, I remembered somewhere earlier in the evening having told myself I was through with this racket. But it hadn't even entered my mind again as I drove up. Like a well-trained homing pigeon, I had headed straight for my Giant of the Andes. Well, I had made my bed, I guess, and here I was, lying in it.

11

"I got a good idea," the photographer said. "Sit him down on the ground and photograph him with his feet close to the camera, so they'll look a mile high."

We sat him down.

"How about this?" I said. "Stand him up and shoot up at him—the skyscraper angle."

"That's a honey," the photographer said.

We stood him up.

"Now let's get a big close-up, one of those distortion jobs. Shove that big puss right into the lens."

We tilted his head. We posed him with wine barrels, hung him from the branch of a tree like Tarzan. We had him putting away six fried eggs, being massaged by two rubbers at one time. We photographed him with his enormous gloved fist in the foreground, sighting along his forty-inch reach. We caught him "in action" with George, "landing his famous *mazo* punch, which, our caption was going to inform the unsuspecting reader, Toro had developed back in his little Andean winery when he used to drive the bung into the barrel with a single blow of his heavy mallet.

The *mazo* was just a wild roundhouse right swing, which any third-rate professional could parry with his left, and counter with a right that would have caught Toro exposed and off balance. But fortunately for this racket, the fight fan who knows the finer points of the sport is a rare item. Most of them just come for the passive pleasure of seeing one guy beat the hell out of another guy, and if you give them something like a *mazo* punch to chew on, they'll turn cheerfully to their neighbor and say, "Boy, here comes that old *mazo* again."

When we had enough pictures, Danny put Toro through a couple of rounds of shadowboxing. Shadowboxing, working through all the motions of offense and defense, against an imaginary opponent, can be beautiful to watch. With a fast, skillful boy who knows what he's doing, it becomes a kind of modern war dance. The fighter weaves and feints, shoots his punches sharply into the air, pivots and circles. But Toro just plodded dully around the ring, pawing the air.

"Faster, snap it up," Danny snarled.

Toro looked over with the white of his eyes showing in fear. He was afraid of Danny. He knew Danny had no use for him. He made an effort to move faster and sharpen up his punches, but it was just as Danny said: the big knotty muscles were in his way. He breathed hard with the effort of impressing Danny.

"Jesus H. Christ," Danny said.

"But this shadowboxing, it is not natural for him," Acosta hurried to explain. "This does not mean that when he is in the ring with . . ."

"Will you dry up and blow away?" Danny said. Acosta's eager face drew back into a subdued pout. Danny rang the bell impatiently. "All right, George," he called. "Let's get two three-minute rounds." As George shuffled into the ring, Danny said, "Keep him working, keep him busy, don't give him a chance to loaf."

George pushed one glove against the other casually. "You want me to do everything but hit him, that right, chief?"

"Tag him when you see an opening. That'll teach him to cover up. But don't lean on them," Danny said. Then his voice took on the tone of exasperation with which he always addressed Toro now. "Now keep working that left in his face like I told you. And when you see an opening for your right, don't forget to turn your left foot in a little bit and twist your body at the waist. Like this." He demonstrated on Toro. "Now, do you think you can remember that?"

"Okay, I think, yes," Toro said, looking to Acosta for encouragement.

Maybe Danny was too close to see it, but Toro was beginning to bear some resemblance to a fighter. At least he didn't have the stiff, flat-footed stance of an old bare-knuckle bruiser any more. He stepped out on his left foot to jab, still rather mechanically, but you could see he was beginning to get the idea. But the jabs didn't seem to jar George at all, and even when one of Toro's rights connected, George absorbed it effortlessly.

"Arms," Danny emphasized when the round ended, "you're still punching with your arms. How many times do I have to tell you it's body and shoulders and shifting that makes a puncher? Like this." He was a full foot shorter than Toro, but he set his feet, dropped his right shoulder and snapped a straight hard left that landed exactly where Danny meant it to, right under Toro's heart. Toro staggered back, injured and amazed. Knowing Danny, I realized that exasperation and impatience had driven him to throw a much harder punch than he intended.

Toro's large eyes looked hurt. He rubbed the red blotch that was spreading below his heart. "Come on, come on, that didn't hurt you," Danny said. "Now let's see another round. And punch this time."

In the next round Toro threw right hands as hard as he could and George caught some of them just to show Toro how it feels to land solidly, but there still wasn't anything behind them. Toro brought up another of his looping rights and George caught it on his arm, drawing Toro off balance and then moved his left in a straight line toward Toro's chin and Toro staggered back. Danny rang the bell in disgust.

"He can't beat an egg," Danny said.

"I'm worried about that button," Doc said. "That's the damnedest glass jaw I ever saw. Must have his nerves right on the surface there. A lot of these oversized guys have that trouble."

"Pardon me, if I may say one thing, please." Acosta began, "I think perhaps you make the mistake to change Toro's style. This big swing of his which you do not let him do, this is the punch that Lupe Morales . . ."

"Goddam it, you little Argentine windbag," Danny cut in, "if you butt in once more I'm going to bounce you right out on your can. Stop jabbering at me. And for Christ sake stop trying to sell me. You can't change this bum's style any more than you can change the hair-dress on Mike Jacobs' head. You can't change what you haven't got."

"From the first day you are not sympathetic to Toro and me," Acosta said. "You are jealous because all your life you have look for a great heavyweight and it is me, Luis Acosta, who has find him."

"Keep away from me," said Danny, who had a temper but did not like to fight. "Keep away from me. Eddie, get him away from me."

"I have to go into town right away," I said to Acosta. "Miniff and Coombs come in today. Want to ride in with me?"

"Yes, I will come," Acosta said. "I am tired of the insults. I am tired of being push around like a beggar. They do not appreciate me and my El Toro. Maybe they will think different when El Toro has knock out his man Coombs."

Acosta hadn't been told that Coombs was set to make like a swan. The fewer people who know these things, the less loose talk. Toro didn't know either. A fighter usually gives a more convincing performance when he thinks he's on the level.

As we were walking back to the cottage to pick up our things, Toro caught up with us. "Luis, do not leave me here alone," he said in Spanish. "If you leave, I wish to leave too."

"But you cannot leave. You must train for your fight."

"I have trained enough for many fights. I am tired of all this training. When we left Mendoza, did you not promise not to leave me?"

Acosta looked up at him and patted his arm. "Yes, that is what I promised in Mendoza," he said. He smiled sadly. "All right, I will stay."

Toro's big, simple face relaxed into a grateful smile. "And when we have made enough money we will go home together?"

"Yes, we will go home together."

"It is possible that we will go home together this year?"

"Maybe this year, maybe next year."

"Hey, Molina," Doc yelled over, "you know better than to stand around when you're sweating. Hurry up and take a shower. Then get dressed for road work."

As I was getting into the car, Danny leaned his elbow on the window and said, "Expect to be talking to Nick soon?"

"Probably tonight," I said. "I thought I'd call and let him know how things are going."

"I'd lay two to one he knows more about it than you do. He can outfox foxes. But listen, laddie, if you talk to him, tell him I want to lose this Acosta bird. I haven't punched anybody for serious since I quit the ring. If I see a fight coming in a saloon I run a mile. But something tells me if I don't get that little squirt out of here, I'll forget myself."

"But Toro's lost without him, Danny. He needs him for morale."

"If he could only wise up to what a bum he found," Danny said. "It's his walking around with his head in the clouds that drives me nuts. Keeps reminding me what a crook I am."

"You're not a crook," I said. "Whenever you get a free choice, you level. Your real larceny guy is happier when he takes it off the bottom."

"I'll tell you how full of larceny I feel, laddie. This Sunday, I'm going to mass, right along with Molina. First time in over a year. I only go when I do something I don't like."

I didn't go down to the station to meet Harry Miniff and his formidable Eastern heavyweight because sometimes discretion is the better part of public relations. But there was quite a delegation on hand to greet the prominent Broadway sportsman, as Miniff was blithely identified that morning by one of the columnists I had drinking out of my hand. I would like to have seen it, though. Little Miniff, the hungriest of the hungry, as ignored and insulted a man as ever faced daily humiliation on Jacob's Beach, being greeted by Nate Starr, the promoter, and Joe Bishop, the matchmaker, as if he had a stable full of champions; and old Cowboy Coombs, who always looked a little surprised to find himself still on his feet, being treated with the respect usually reserved for more vertical pugilists.

I had given Miniff the pitch by airmail, writing most of his dialogue and warning him urgently not to refer to Coombs as "my bum" in public, as he was inclined to do. "That is all right for those of us who know and love you, but I don't think it will contribute to the success of Toro's debut," I had written. To which Miniff had answered graciously, "Okay, I will give my impersonation of a guy what has all his bills paid and his IOU's called in. And I'll try not call my bum a bum."

According to the evening paper, Miniff had played his part faithfully, if somewhat ungrammatically. There was a picture of Coombs' puffy, flattened face, captioned, "GIANT-KILLER?" and under it a brief interview with Coomb's mentor, in which he said, "This giant don't scare us. We don't fear nobody. We give up a big money match in the Garden to take this fight, that's how confident we are we can walk all over this Man Mountain. The bigger they are the harder they fall."

Late that afternoon Harry came up to the hotel. He had bought a new hat to celebrate his change of fortune, but the way he had already twisted it, with one side up and the other side down, it looked exactly like his old hat. To this day the top of Miniff's head and I are complete strangers. I am sure if you were to look in on Miniff taking a bath you would find him with his hat on. Miniff seemed as determined to go into his grave with his hat on as other adventurers were about their boots.

"Well, how was your trip, Harry?" I said.

"Terrible," Miniff moaned. "Why'd they haveta put this place so far from New York? My ulcers don't like to travel."

"This is the healthiest climate in the world," I said. "This'll make a man of you, Miniff. All this fresh air and sunshine."

"I get dizzy in the sun," Miniff complained.

"Wanna shot?" Vince said, pouring one for himself.

"Whatta you wanna do, kill me?" Miniff demanded. "The milk, I'm strictly on the milk."

"Tell Room Service to send up one Jersey," I told Vince. "We can keep it in the bathroom while Miniff's here. Anything to eat, Harry?"

"Gimme a sturgeon sandwich on rye," Miniff said.

"Sturgeon," I said. "Where the hell do you think you are, Lindy's? This is California."

"Don't they eat in California?" Miniff wanted to know.

"Only nutburgers and cheeseburgers," I said. "How about a nice fruit salad?"

"Fruit gives me hives," Miniff said. From his breast pocket, he took out three short, fat cigars, stuck one in his mouth and passed the others around.

"Ten-cent cigar," I said. "Don't let these write-ups go to your head, Harry."

"I like my old ones better," Miniff said, "but I gotta keep up a front."

"How's Cowboy?" I said. "He understands he's to tell everybody he's betting on himself to knock Toro out? I want to build this up so it sounds like he's fed up with giving a foreigner so much publicity and out to knock his head off."

"But don't get him so steamed up he can't go in two," Vince said. "Got that, I want him to go in two."

"Two!" Miniff said. He pushed his hat back with a quick motion of his hand. "That's too quick. The fans don't like it. They don't get their money's worth. I gotta better idea."

"Shove your ideas," Vince said.

"Gimme a chance," Miniff begged. "Whatsamatter, we ain't got free speech in this country no more?"

"What the hell office you running for you wanna make a speech?" Vince said. "Run as spittoon cleaner and ass wiper and maybe I'll vote for you."

"Aaaaaaaah," said Miniff in rebuttal. It was a gutter sound, a harsh, embittered protest against bigger men with better connections. "I gotta weenie for improving the take and you dial out on me."

"All right, let's have it," Vince said magnanimously. "Ten to one it stinks, but let's have it."

"My bum and your bum," Miniff began, "they fight even . . ."

"Take it away, it stinks," Vince cut in.

"Going into the seventh, eighth, ninth, it's still even," Miniff continued. "Then in the tenth, with thirty seconds t' go, your bum lands and my bum rolls over and plays dead. D'ya buy that?"

"You couldn't give it to me with Seabiscuit for a bonus," Vince said.

"But your bum comes in right under the wire," Miniff's voice rose and accelerated. "It makes more talk. The guy's a hero."

"Just because it's the Hollywood stadium, we don't haveta give 'em a movie," Vince said.

Miniff mopped his forehead with his short fingers in a nervous gesture. "But my way we get a rematch. Eddie writes it up how my bum is convinced he lose on a fluke and wants revenge. Then in the rematch my bum goes in two like you want. What's wrong with that, tell me what's wrong with that?"

"Don't be so shoving hungry," Vince said. "You get seven-fifty for the fight and an extra two-five-o for the act. What more d'ya want?"

"I want it twice," Miniff admitted. "Twice won't do you no harm and we c'n use the difference. We ain't had a fight since Worcester. And the bum has five kids to feed."

"Shove the kids," Vince said. "What does this look like, a relief office? Coombs goes in two. If it lasts too long they'll see what a dog we got. Ten rounds and the ref'll throw 'em out for not trying. Ain't that right, Eddie?"

"I'm afraid it is, Harry," I said. "The longer Toro's in there, the worse he's going to look. And Coombs can't go too many rounds without falling down from force of habit."

"Well, anyway I c'n pay up my back rent," said Miniff philosophically, chewing on his cigar as if it were nourishment.

A week before the fight, the press came up to have a look at our "human skyscraper," as some of the boys were calling him now. The camp was opened to the public too, and there were a couple of hundred sightseers every day, laying down their buck for a hinge at the freak. There were always a good many women in the crowd. There was something about his brute size that seemed to exert a Stone Age influence on the girls. I made a mental note of this for future reference. Atavism, I labeled it.

Everybody seemed impressed as Toro bent and stretched that Brobdingnagian torso. While he was shadowboxing, I went into the dressing room to talk to George, who was lacing up his ring shoes for the last heavy workout he was going to have with Toro before the fight.

"The two-seventeen took my baby away," he was singing under his breath. "The two-nineteen will bring her back some day..."

"George, there's a lot of reporters out there today," I said.

"I understand, Mr. Lewis," he said. And he chuckled again in that way he had of making the whole deal seem ridiculous, profoundly ridiculous, foolish and pointless.

"Toro's supposed to be a hitter," I reminded him.

"Don't worry, Mr. Lewis," George said, "I'll make him look as good as I can." And the low-pitched, good-natured laughter rose from his belly again, untainted by meanness, a warm and compassionate but dis-concerting laugh.

The sparring looked all right. George cuffed him around a little in the first round and tied him up in clinches that Toro was strong enough to break out of. In the next two rounds George mistimed his slips just enough for Toro to catch him with that looping right. George tossed his head, as if to shake off the effect of the punch and fell into a clinch. Just before the final bell, after being short with a right hook, George caught one high on the head and dropped to one knee. It really didn't look too bad. The only funny thing was that when George rose and touched gloves, Toro wanted to make sure George wasn't hurt before continuing.

"What's the hell going on?" Danny said when Toro hesitated.

"He does not have the wish to injure George seriously," Acosta explained.

"Now I've heard everything," Danny said. "Tell him to keep fighting, goddam it, until I hit the bell."

"Is the big joker kidding?" asked the young, jowly reporter who had met us at the train.

"No, he's just afraid of his own power," I ad-libbed. "You see, back in Buenos Aires one of the guys he kayoed spent ten weeks in a hospital and damn near died. Ever since then he's been afraid he might kill somebody." It sounded so good I thought I might as well blow it a little louder. "In fact, it might be a good idea if you sportswriters reminded the referee as a public service that it's his responsibility to the citizens of California to stop his fights before Molina inflicts serious injury. We're out to win as impressively as possible, but we don't want to kill anybody."

"What's the name of this guy he almost killed?" the reporter wanted to know.

I called over to Toro, whose face Doc was wiping with a towel while Acosta was pulling off his gloves. "Toro," I said in Spanish, "what was the name of your first opponent before you came up here?"

"Eduardo Solano," Toro said.

"Got that?" I said, and I spelled it out for the reporter. The next morning he used that for his lead.

Al Leavitt was up there too. "Well, what do you think of him, Al?" I said.

He just shrugged. "I never go by training," he said. "I've seen beautiful gymnasium fighters look like palookas in the ring. And I've seen good fighters who always looked lousy in their workouts."

A wise apple. But he didn't bother me. You always have to figure on one of those. The rest of the press was fine. My book of clippings was getting fatter each edition. The training camp attendance had built nicely. Toro Molina, Inc., was already in the black. And Nate Starr told me the stadium had been sold out for a week. Five-dollar ringsides were being scalped for two and three times their official price. We were ready to move into town.

The first day back in L.A. I took Toro out to MGM for some publicity tie-ups. I had an old buddy out there, Teet Carle, opening doors for me. Toro was wearing the new gabardine Weatherill had cut for him and he looked like a million pesos. He took a child's delight in this sartorial splendor, with his new specially built two-tone shoes and his size 8½ straw hat that would have made Miniff a nice beach umbrella. The pictures we knocked off were right down the old Graflex groove. There must be something about the chemistry of a press agent and a still camera that makes it impossible for them to produce any other kinds of pictures except the ones I set up at Metro—Toro squaring off with Mickey Rooney standing on a box; Toro with a couple of pretty stock-girls in bathing suits feeling his muscles; Toro on the set with Clark Gable and Spencer Tracy showing off the size of his fist. "Two stars see fist that will make Coombs see more stars," I captioned that one.

The Main Street gym, where Toro and Coombs were to put in their final workouts, looks like a shabbier twin of Stillman's in New York. The street is gaudier than Eighth Avenue. It offers cheap burlesque houses and dime movies for adults only, dim and dingy bars with raucous jukeboxes and blousy B-girls, your fortune for a dime, your haircut for a quarter, whisky for fifteen cents, love for a dollar and a five-cent flop.

Outside the entrance to the gym was the usual sidewalk gathering: boxers, managers, old fighters, hangers-on. On the curb a huge, shabbily dressed, fight-scarred Negro swung good-naturedly at a much smaller Negro who had sneaked up to goose him. "Keep away from there, man," the big Negro cried, grinning with a mouthful of gold teeth. It was only then, as he raised his large, punished face, that I saw he was blind.

George went up to him and said, "Whatcha doin', Joe?"

The blind Negro cocked his head. "What you want, man?"

"Punch hands up, brother," George said gaily, "and see if you can still lick Georgie Blount."

"Georgie!" the blind man said. "Where *you* been gate? Gimme some skin, man."

They both laughed as they shook hands. George told him what he was doing out here and then Joe said, cheerfully, "Well, we gave 'em some fights, didn't we, man? We really did it, didn't we, George?"

"You're not kidding," said George. "I still got a dent where you hit me in the ribs."

"Man, oh, man," Joe chuckled. "Them was the days."

George looked at Joe and reached into his pocket. "Here's that saw-buck I owe you, boy. Remember that time in K.C.?"

"K.C.?" Joe said.

"Yeah," George said, and pushed it into his hand.

Joe's grin disappeared into that curiously dead expression of the blind. "Good luck, Georgie," he said. "See you around."

Going up the long, grimy stairway that seems to be the standard approach to every fight gym, George said to me, "That's Joe Wilson, Joe the Iceman, they used to call him. He col'cocked so many of 'em. I fought him four times. He sure could hit you a real good punch. Busted two of my ribs one night out at Vernon."

"How long you been fighting, George?" I asked.

George's eyes narrowed in a private smile. "Tell you the truth, Mr. Lewis, I lost track."

"How old are you, George?"

George shook his head mysteriously. "Man, if I ever told you, they'd take me off the payroll and send me straight to the old folks' home."

Upstairs were the same dirty gray walls, the same lack of ventilation and sanitation and the same milling activity of concentrated young men with narrow waists and glistening skins, bending, stretching, shadow-boxing, sparring, punching the bags or listening earnestly to the instructions of men with fat bellies, boneless noses, dirty sweatshirts, brown hats pushed back on sweaty foreheads, the trainers, the managers, the experts. Only here on Main Street there were even more dark skins, not only black like those that had come to outnumber the whites in Stillman's, but the yellow and brown skins of the Filipinos and Mexicans who poured into the gym from the slums of L.A. For if racing is the sport of kings, boxing is the vocation of the slum dwellers who must fight to exist. When were the sons of Erin monopolizing the titles and the glory: the Ryans, Sullivans, Donovans, Kilbanes and O'Briens? When waves of Irish immigration were breaking over America. Gradually, as the Irish settled down to being politicians, policemen, judges, the Shamrock had to make room for the Star of David, to the Leonards, Tendlers, and Blooms. And then came the Italians: Genaro, LaBarba, Indrissano, Canzoneri. Now the Negroes press forward, hungry for the money, prestige and opportunity denied them at almost every door. In California the Mexicans, fighting their way up out of their brown ghettos, dominate the light divisions: Ortiz, Chavez, Arizmendi and a seemingly endless row of little brown sluggers by the name of Garcia.

In the center ring, throwing punches at the air, ducking and weaving as he crowded an imaginary opponent to the ropes, was Arizmendi himself, who seemed to have inherited not only the strong, stoic face of an ancient Aztec, but the courage and endurance as well.

As Toro climbed through the ropes for a light workout with George, a short, plump, brown-skinned guy in a cheap but spotless white linen suit and white shoes came down to a corner of the ring, raised a megaphone to his lips and began to announce in a Spanish accent, made more inarticulate by too many blows on the head, "Eeen-tro-ducing, ot two hondreed ond seventy-wan pounds, the beegeest heavyweight in the worl'..."

"Who is this clown?" I asked a second who was going to help Doc in the fight Friday night.

"Oh, that's Pancho, one of our characters," the second said. "He's a little punchy. Been around here for years. Thinks he's an announcer. Nobody pays him but he comes in the same time every day just like he had a job. For practice. The guys throw him a quarter once in a while. And the dope spends every nickel he has keeping himself in them white clothes. He once saw an announcer in a white suit and I guess it kind of stuck in his bean."

Coombs climbed into the adjoining ring. He was heavily built and seemed ready to wink at anybody who would smile at him. I watched Pancho raise the megaphone to his lips, throw his head back and close his eyes in ecstasy. "Een-tro-ducing ot two hondred and seex pounds thot great hovyweight from da yeast, Cowboy Coombs."

One of the regulars in the place, an unshaven, baldheaded second with a couple of swab sticks in his mouth, started toward Pancho, and the little Mexican began to back up, half-threatening, "Stay 'way from me, you barstid, stay 'way from me."

"What goes with him?" I asked the second.

"Aw, that's just a running rib," he said. "The fellas know what a nut he is about stayin' so clean. So some of 'em go over and rub their burnt matches down his suit or smudge his white shoes just to hear him holler."

Pancho kept backing and pleading as he worked his way crabwise until he reached the door and darted out. Some of the boys were amused. "Did you see that little greaser run?" Vince laughed.

The next day, the last training session before the fight, we found Pancho at his regular post, busy making those announcements to which no one paid any attention. I just thought Vince was going over to give him a quarter when he started toward him. I didn't realize anything was up until Pancho started backing away frantically just as he did the day before. The whole crowd of us, who had come in together, saw how Pancho retreated until he reached a high stool near the entrance. He drew his feet up, wrapped his arms around himself and pulled his head in like a turtle. "Stay 'way, you stay 'way," he was crying.

"Don't be afraid of me, *muchacha*," Vince laughed, and drew a long streaky line down the arm of Pancho's coat. Pancho stared sorrowfully at the smudge.

Toro was bewildered. "Why did he do that?" he asked in Spanish.

"A joke," I said. *"Un chisto."*

"No entiendo," Toro said. He did not understand. Vince's cruelty was too complex for him. He went over to Pancho, who was still sitting there brooding over the affront.

"Why did he do that to your fine white suit?" Toro said in Spanish.

Pancho answered in the bastardized Spanish of California Mexicans. What he called Vince has no satisfactory equivalent in English profanity.

Toro turned to Acosta and said in Spanish, indicating Vince with his head, "Tell him to give this man ten pesos."

"That is in American money two dollars," Acosta said. "You wish him to have two dollars?"

"I mean ten dollar," Toro corrected himself.

When Acosta relayed this to Vince, Vince kept his hands in his pockets and said, "How does this jerk rate a sawbuck?"

"You give," Toro said.

"Listen to him. Now he's a big shot," Vince said.

"Go on, you cheap skate, give 'im ten bucks," Danny said. It was the first thing he had said to Vince since we hit California.

"Aah, you guys make me sick," Vince said. But he produced.

When Pancho saw his money, he just shook his head. "Go 'way," he said. "You big barstid."

"What's the matter with you, you punchy?" Vince said.

For men in Pancho's condition, that's the chip on the shoulder. "Who ponchy?" he demanded. "I not ponchy. I got job here. I announcer. Maybe you ponchy."

Vince laughed. Toro turned to Acosta again. "Give me ten dollar," he said. He handed the bill to Pancho solemnly. He could not explain what had happened, but some simple peasant intelligence seemed to make him understand that the carefully nourished dignity of Pancho Diaz had been outraged.

While Toro was having his workout I dropped down to Abe Attell's, the dark, narrow saloon and beanery that tunneled under the gym. You could go in there at ten A.M. for a beer and sit around until midnight, watching the old fights on a streaky movie screen. The pictures ran continually, pausing only long enough for one of the bartenders to change reels. A hoarse sound trace of the noises fight fans make when things happen in the ring began to deafen you. Sometimes a young boxer or a sportswriter would sit down to watch a fight, but most of the spectators, who must have seen these same films countless times, were jugheads and shabby ex-fighters just hanging around, waiting for another break, another manager, a chance to pick up beer money sparring with somebody's prospect or working as a second, or waiting to put the bite on an old pal or a newcomer on the way up with money in his pocket.

On the screen, Jack Dempsey, crazy with viciousness, fighting like a man who has tracked down a lifelong enemy, was swarming all over big, slow, flabby Jess Willard, smashing Jess down every time he got up and breaking his ribs, his nose and his heavy jaw. A seedy-looking wino sat down opposite me with his back to the screen and started muttering to himself. When my eyes shifted for a moment from the grainy violence of the screen, he tried to smile, but it was only the unhappy mechanical grimace of a man who is ready to offer a spurious, tentative friendship in return for a fifteen-cent glass of sauterne.

"I seen you somewhere before, ain't I?" he said for openers.

"I've never been out here before," I said.

"Oh, I fought all over, K.C., Louisville, Camden, New Jersey. Young Wolgast." He spoke the name proudly and stopped to watch the effect.

The only Wolgasts in my book were Midget, the flyweight champion, and the great Ad, who knocked out Battling Nelson in forty rounds and finally fought himself into amnesia. But Young Wolgast looked as if he needed a little moral support, and it didn't cost anything to open my mouth and say, "Oh."

"Mushy Callahan," he said. "You know, the great Mushy, I shoulda knocked him out. I had him out on his feet, see, but I didn't know how bad I hurt him and I let him jazz me out of it. I got him laying right on the ropes, all set up for the kayo and I don't go in." The disappointment was still sharp in him, but he couldn't stop himself from pressing down against the point of it with perverse torment. "If I put Mushy away I can write my own ticket. I'm the hottest thing in town, and like a jerk I let him bluff me out of it. I don' know how bad I got him hurt, see . . ."

Mushy Callahan won what they call the junior welterweight championship from Pinky Mitchell back in the middle twenties. So the fight this Wolgast is worrying about must have taken place ten, maybe fifteen years ago. But time is all turned around in Wolgast's head. For two or three seconds in his life he had a glimpse of glory, and down through the shabby years of obscurity, those precious drops of time have grown and grown until they have blotted out the rest of his memory. "I rush him into a corner and clip him with a right uppercut," he was saying, his fist closing in reflex, "and then like a dope I step back, I let him get away, he's out on his feet and I don' even know it."

His head hung down on his chest, heavy with wine and self-disgust. On the screen it was Dempsey and Carpentier now, the first million-dollar gate, curtain raiser on the Golden Age of boxing and gold-plated bunk and ballyhoo. A sharpshooter from Reno moved into New York with the big idea that a fight wasn't just a contest of skill and brawn; it was a dramatic spectacle, and he proceeded to stage it accordingly. So it was Carpentier, the war hero versus Dempsey, the slacker; the fearless French light-heavyweight against the 200-pound bully; the clean-cut, smooth-shaven, gentlemanly veteran, representing patriotism, sports-manship and boxing skill, and the glowering slugger with a three-day's beard who had fought his way up from the hobo jungles. There were the 80,000 high-pressured fans screaming their lungs out for Carpentier because Tex Rickard and his press agents, taking advantage of their simple-minded morality, had been careful to present them a hero to cheer and a villain on whom to vent their volatile anger.

As I got up from my beer, leaving another sauterne for Young Wolgast, the almost-conqueror of Mushy Callahan, the screen had moved on to Philadelphia, with Dempsey and Tunney. Now it was Dempsey, the Horatio Alger boy, a colorful champion who was always in there giving his best, a friendly, quiet-spoken fellow outside the ring, but a furious competitor from bell to bell, facing the aloof, bookish, cautious, undramatic, methodically effective Tunney. That was the Rickard pitch on that one, and the villain of Boyle's Thirty Acres was transformed into the hero of the Philadelphia Sesquicentennial for whom 130,000 people were cheering themselves hoarse, taxing the worn-out sound equipment as I turned my back on this ancient history and came out into the light of the street.

Standing with the sidewalk fraternity outside the entrance to the gym was Harry Miniff. As soon as he saw me come out of Attell's, Miniff ran over and buttonholed me. "Jeez, I gotta see ya about somp'n, Eddie. Walk down the enda the block with me." When he made sure we were far enough away from the others, he began, trotting along to keep up with me and talking up into my face feverishly.

"Eddie," he says, "any time you want I should do something for you, you know me, kid, the shirt off my back."

"Keep your shirt on, Harry," I said. "What do you want?"

"Leave my bum stay in there for a while, maybe seven, eight rounds, how about it, Eddie, for a pal?"

"That's not my department, Harry. You'll have to speak to Mr. Vanneman who does the choreography."

"That Vanneman, if he had a peanut factory he wouldn't gimme the shells," Miniff said.

"Do you realize you are speaking of one of my business associates?" I said.

"Associate," Miniff said. "You call that crumb an associate. Listen, Eddie, for a pal, talk to Vince, get him to leave my bum go six rounds, five, I'll settle for five."

"But what's the difference whether he goes in two or five?" I wanted to know.

"Two, it makes him sound like a washed-up bum," Miniff explained. "Five, that's more of a respectable bum. Five, maybe I can make a few dollars selling the bum to the smaller clubs, Santa Monica, San Berdoo, you know, five, it gives me something to talk about: he was giving the guy a helluva fight for four rounds and the streffis and the strallis, but two . . ." he shook his head despondently, "two don't give me nothin' to work on. Me and my bum'll starve on two."

"Harry," I said, "relax. Leave it alone. Let him go in two. Maybe we'll do business again."

"Hey, I gotta idea," Miniff brightened. "I know a real good bum in Frisco. Tony Colucci. I useta handle him oncet. Great big bastard, almost as big as your bum. You put me on the expense account and I'll hop up there and see if I c'n . . ."

"Quite racing your motor, Miniff," I said. "One bum, I mean one fight at a time. Damn it, now you got me doing it."

Little Harry Miniff, beetle-faced and weevil-legged, was holding on for dear life.

"Okedoke," Miniff said, "but I'm telling you, Eddie, this Colucci'll be sensational. . . ."

12

On the day before the fight I went down to meet Nick, Ruby and the Killer, coming in on the Super Chief. We drove uptown to the Beverly Hills Hotel, where Nick had reserved a bungalow, and had lunch by the pool.

"I've been promising Ruby this trip to California for years, haven't I, baby?" he said. "Nick never failed you yet, did he, baby?"

"No, honey."

She had a new up hairdo, a little fancy for daytime; Ruby was one of those women who belong to the evening and never look quite wholesome by light of day.

"This is really our second honeymoon," Nick said expansively. "I always told you we'd have our second honeymoon in Sunny Cal, didn't I, Ruby?"

"I thought that's what we were doing in Miami last winter," Ruby said.

"Aah, that was nothing," Nick said. "That was just getting in practice for the second honeymoon." He bent over and kissed Ruby, a little roughly. She didn't draw away, but she no longer thought it was ladylike to be kissed in public.

"Killer," Nick said, "go back to the bungalow and get me some cigars."

The Killer, a short, trim figure in his fancy Hawaiian shorts, obeyed.

"You should have brought Toro over for lunch," Ruby said. "How does he look in his new clothes?"

"Haven't you been reading the papers?" I said.

"You've been doing good, Eddie, real good," Nick said. "That Sunday supplement with the full-page picture of Toro opposite that Greek god, that was very okay. I knew what I was talking about, didn't I, kid? That guy is money in the bank."

The Killer was back with the cigars. They came in individual aluminum containers. Nick opened his with tender care. The Killer held the match for him. "New cigar," Nick said. "Made special for me in Havana. Dollar 'n a quarter a piece. Go ahead, Eddie, take all you want."

"Honey, don't you know it's not polite to tell people what everything costs?" Ruby said.

"Listen to her," Nick said, leaning back, crossing his legs and holding that big cigar like a scepter. "Did you ever see a kid from Tenth Avenue get so smart?"

"Nicholas," she said. She put her sunglasses on in a gesture of annoyance and began reading the book she had brought with her. *Three Loves Hath Nancy,* it was called, and from the cover you could see that Nancy was a high-chested, red-headed wench who helped win our country's independence by diverting Cornwallis' attention from one kind of conquest to another.

Three cute-looking girls with slender, tanned young bodies in little dabs of bathing suits walked past us toward the pool and stretched out in the hot sun. "Oh, brother," the Killer observed, "how wudja like to take care of them?"

"How many times I have to tell you, don't talk dirty around Ruby?" Nick said.

"Aw, I'm sorry, Ruby," the Killer said.

"You never did know how to talk in front of a lady," Ruby said pleasantly.

The Killer took it smilingly.

"Nate Starr says he coulda filled the ball park for this fight. Even with Coombs," Nick said. "That shows you what publicity'll do, eh, kid?"

"I wonder what'll happen after they've seen him once," I said.
"They'll come again and like it," Nick promised.
"What if they get wise to us?" I said.
"Then I'll fire you," Nick said cheerfully.

The night of the fight we started off at Chasen's, the place the Hollywood biggies go when they want food, drink or to be seen. There were Nick and Ruby, the Killer and a little stock-girl with a cutie-pie face, the kind that always seems to be in stock. We got down to the stadium in time to see old George box the semifinal. He was fighting a chunky, battle-scarred club fighter, Red Nagle, who came into the ring wearing a faded Golden Glove bathrobe, on the back of which the numerals *1931* could barely be made out. George climbed through the ropes, worked his feet in the rosin and sat down in his corner with a deliberate casualness, an old-timer getting ready to go to work, neither frisky nor afraid.

At the bell the white fighter came out of his corner with a rush that brought a shriek of excitement from the crowd. Red got plenty of work at the club because he scorned any pretense at self-defense and went in swinging. But George calmly side-stepped that first charge and put a sharp left to Red's eye. Red was the kind who takes two to land one, swinging all the time, and George was methodically riding with the punches or slipping inside, countering nicely. But from a distance it must have looked as if Red was murdering George, for the cheers of the gallery gods shook the place with every wild, futile swing. They were pleading with Red to put him out in a hurry.

In the seat next to me sat a broad, beefy-faced fellow with a high-blood-pressure complexion and a big mouth. "Come on, Red, send that boogie back to Central Avenue." He hunched forward in his seat, jerking his shoulders in time with Red's blows. Whenever Red landed, he'd let out an excited, deep-bellied laugh.

George fought in spurts, moving with bored relaxation, pacing himself carefully, never wasting a punch unless he saw an opening and winding up each round with a twenty- or thirty-second flurry to catch the referee's eye. In the fifth round George nailed his man with a right hand as he rushed in, and Red dropped to the canvas with blood dripping from his left eye. But he was up again with a count, brushing the blood away with his glove and rushing George fiercely into the ropes, where he whaled away at him with both hands, not doing much except wearing himself out, for George was catching them on the arms and the shoulders. But the fans loved it. They were on their feet, with their hands megaphoning their violent encouragement, "Attaboy. Get him! Knock him down! Murder that nigger!" A movie comedian's girl in tan make-up, styled sunglasses and a large black straw hat that tormented spectators for three rows behind her lifted her voice to a screech that pierced the general roar, "Kill him! Kill him, Red! Kill him!" And the man next to me added his gravel voice, "In the breadbasket, Red. Those shines don't like it down there."

Working quietly in the clinches, and maneuvering his opponent around so he could look over his shoulder at the big clock that told him how many seconds were left in the round, George was giving that bad eye an unspectacular but thorough going-over. But the white boy kept boring in, forcing the fighting, weak on brains but strong on heart, the kind who have to show how brave they are by jumping up after every knockdown without bothering to take advantage of the count, the kind the fans go crazy about for a while and then don't recognize when they're buying peanuts or papers from them a year or so later outside the stadium.

When the bell ended the last round, Red kept on swinging until the referee grabbed him, but George dropped his hands automatically and shuffled back to his corner to sit down and wait for the decision. George had four of the six rounds on my card, but the referee called it a draw. With his eye a bloody smear, Red threw his arms around George in a broad gesture of sportsmanship and mitted the crowd happily. They gave him a big hand as he left the ring. Most of them thought he had won. There were scattered boos for George as he climbed out through the ropes.

"Nice work, George," I shouted over to him as he passed on his way up the aisle, and he turned for a moment to give me that easy smile. The boos and the cheers, the glory and the name-calling, it was all in a night's work to George. Five minutes from now he'd be in the showers humming one of those songs. An hour from now he'd be down on Central Avenue with his own people, eating fried chicken and chips and laughing softly about the fight, "If that white boy could fight like them people out there thought he could, I wouldn't be sitting here enjoying this bird." Something like that he'd be saying.

The lights were on all over the arena and everybody was standing up, waiting for the main-eventers. The loudmouth next to me pulled the seat of his pants where it had creased into his buttocks and said, "That jigaboo was lucky to get a draw."

Ruby waved across the ring to a platinum-haired star she had known back in the chorus. "Look at Jerry," she said to Nick, "doesn't she look marvelous? I hardly knew her with that new hair."

The air was foul with cigar and cigarette smoke. The ringside crowd were sleek, prosperous actors, directors, movie executives, theatrical agents, songwriters, politicians, insurance men, and their sleek, stylized women and the big-time lawyers who helped to reshuffle them from time to time. I noticed Dave Stempel and Miki, who were sitting near by with a young, tired-eyed heiress and her current Number One boy.

Cowboy Coombs came down the aisle, his broad, scuffed-up puss split with a silly grin of showmanship. Miniff hurried along beside him with a half-smoked cigar clenched in his mouth. The Legion Band, which had been tearing itself apart with a ludicrous version of popular swing that never lost its military influence, stopped for a moment and took off on "The Hall of the Mountain King." That was the cue for Toro to make his entrance. Just one of the little gimmicks I thought up to help the show along. Toro was wearing a white satin bathrobe with an Argentine flag on the shoulder, a symbol of a mountain peak on his back and the gold-lettered words: THE GIANT OF THE ANDES. Danny and Acosta were both wearing white T-shirts with the word MOLINA on their backs. The other two seconds, similarly attired, were both Acosta's size, selected for their diminutiveness to accentuate Toro's height. The staging looked even better than I had hoped. Towering more than a foot-and-a-half over the seconds who flanked him, with the enormous expanse of white satin emphasizing his superhuman size, he moved toward the ring like a strange throwback to the giants of prehistoric time. When he reached the apron of the ring he didn't climb through the ropes in the usual fashion; he stepped over the highest strand. It got the hand I figured on. But Toro forgot to wave, as we had told him to. This was his first appearance before an American crowd—a North American crowd, as he would say—and he looked nervous and bewildered. He knew he hadn't made a good showing with George or satisfied Danny, and he and Acosta had probably swallowed all that big talk we had planted about the formidability of Cowboy Coombs.

They killed the lights, we all bowed our heads and the band gave us The Star-Spangled Banner, with one of those dramatic baritones on the lyrics.

At the bell Coombs tore out of his corner as if he were going to make short work of Toro and fell ferociously into a clinch. They pushed and pulled and pawed their way through the round. All of Coombs' violence was in his face, which he worked pugnaciously, and in the aggressive way he breathed through his busted nose. Toro floundered around, trying an occasional jab and now and then throwing his wild right before his feet were set. The most energy expended in the round came from Acosta, who bent forward as if he were going to jump into the ring himself and kept up a running patter of semi-hysterical instruction, which was far more entertaining than the fight. As the round ended, he leaped into the ring, got in the way of Danny and Doc, put his mouth against Toro's ear and gesticulated excitedly. I could see Danny's face grow taut with irritation.

In the second round they wrestled each other for the first minute, and then Toro pushed his right glove toward Coombs' chest and Miniff's warrior sank slowly to the canvas and stretched out comfortably. At ten he made a half-hearted effort to rise and flopped down again. Toro looked surprised and dragged Coombs back to his corner. That was all in the act too, though Toro didn't know it. I just told him in case he won by a knockout, it was considered good sportsmanship up here to help the man back to his corner yourself.

There were scattered boos from the more observant, but the fans, collectively, seemed to be satisfied that they had seen a quick and decisive knockout. As I pushed my way up the aisle the cash customers were happily expressing their gullibility. "What a build!" "He's got King Kong beat!" "Ya couldn't hurt that guy with a sledge hammer!" "That last one musta hurt!"

But I heard someone behind me say, "How did you call it, Al?" and the answer snapped back, "They ought to give Coombs an Oscar for the Best Supporting Performance of the year."

I looked around and saw it was Al Leavitt, the wise guy from the *News*. I kept going as if I hadn't seen him. Why bother with him? He wasn't even syndicated.

In the corridor, outside the dressing room, a large crowd of hero-worshippers, curiosity-seekers and bandwagon boys were gathering. Inside were the reporters, celebrities and the usual visiting firemen who always manage to find their way to a winner's dressing room after a fight.

As soon as he saw me, Acosta ran over and threw his arms around me. His eyes were wild and he looked as if he were on the stuff, but it was just the over-stimulation of personal triumph. "He win! He win!" he shouted. "My El Toro, is he not everything I say?" Then he ran back and kissed Toro who was lying on the rubbing table. Toro seemed pleased with himself too. "I hit and he go boom," he said several times.

Danny was standing off to one side, eyeing the scene coldly. "Come on, Doc, get him into a shower," he said irritably. "Whatta you want him to do, catch a cold?" His face was very white and his eyes had that washed-out look that always settled in them when he was drinking.

Acosta looked like a busy little tugboat towing a great liner as he led Toro to the showers. "Please, out of the way, out of the way," he shouted importantly, pushing through the dressing-room crowd. At the entrance to the showers, Toro paused and turned to Doc. "This man I knock out, he is not hurt, no? He is okay?"

Doc assured him that Coombs was going to recover. Toro had dropped it in there as if it had been rehearsed. I noticed several of the reporters scribbling it down. "You see, he's scared to death he's going to kill somebody," I explained. "Ever since he almost knocked that guy off back in Argentina."

Al Leavitt was leaning against the door with an unwholesome smile on his face. "As a fighter that Coomb's does a beautiful one-and-a-half gaynor," he said.

"You wouldn't trust your own mother, would you?" I said.

"Not if she was in the fight game," Leavitt said.

"Come on out to Pat Drake's and cool off," I said. "Pat's throwing a little party—just four or five hundred people—up at his joint in Bel Air."

Drake was an ex-chauffeur for Nick back in his boot days who wandered into Hollywood when things got hot in New York, started working extra and went to the top as a rival studio's answer to Bogart.

"Okay, I'll come," Leavitt said, "but I'll still tab it for an El Foldo."

Drake's party was complete with swimming pool, floodlights, buffet, butlers, bartenders, a seven-piece orchestra, celebrities and all the other necessary ingredients of a successful Hollywood party. As usual, Nick had known what he was doing to choose Hollywood for Toro's debut. The Hollywood crowd were sufficiently immersed in sentimentalism, hyperbole and hero-worship to go off the deep end for Toro Molina. Male stars whose faces were altars of a new idolatry crowded around to shake Toro's hand and glamour-coated actresses whose pinups have become a national fetish flocked around like autograph hunters. Dave Stempel rushed up to congratulate me. "Terrific, Eddie, really terrific!" he said. "Like nothing human. Hits like a sledge hammer."

Toro looked astonished and ill-at-ease. A soulful-faced star who was known for her genteel, ladylike roles was smiling up at him over her drink. Ruby came up to me with a cocktail in her hand and said, "I'd better rescue him from that glamour-puss. I hear she's the biggest she-wolf in town. Toro would be just dumb enough to go for her."

A few minutes later Ruby was dancing with him. Nick was inside playing stud with Drake and some other boys. Quite a couple, she and Toro. He was wearing a sharp white Palm Beach, one of those new suits I angled for him. Ruby was wearing a black low-cut, semiformal gown with a large, black onyx cross pointing down the valley between her full breasts. Around her head was a black velvet snood. Her dark eyes were half-closed and her body moved with self-confidence. She was not as symmetrical and fashionably underweight as some of the film stars who had made sex appeal their profession, but there was a mature female luxuriance to Ruby that promised more than the slenderized narrow-waisted figures of the professional body-beautifuls.

I found Danny at the bar, which had been set up under a bright awning near the pool. He was waiting for the bartender to refill his glass. His legs were spread apart to balance himself and he was staring out over the crowd with pale, tired eyes. "Hello, laddie," he said when he recognized me. "You having fun, laddie? I'm getting drunk, laddie. Any objections?"

"How do you think it looked, Danny?"

His face twisted to a bitter smile. "You know what I think, laddie, I think it looked putrid. I think he's the goddamest saddest excuse for a prize fighter I ever saw. I think we're all going to wind up with the Commish taking our goddam licenses away."

"Don't forget Jimmy Quinn and the Commission are like this," I said. "With Jimmy on top. He helps pick 'em."

Danny lifted his drink off the bar. "Happy days, laddie," he said.

Just then Acosta came up to us, ready for more embracing and congratulations. "Is it not true now everything I have say?" He couldn't help laughing as he talked. "El Toro is *magnifico,* no? He give you a big surprise, hey?"

Danny turned away from him without saying anything. Acosta's ebullience was suddenly checked. "I do not understan', please," he protested to me. "Tonight we have the first victory. We celebrate. We are all on the way to a big success. I think perhaps it is time we all are become friends, no?"

Danny turned around and stared at him so long before he said anything that Acosta begin to shift his eyes in embarrassment.

"Go away," Danny said.

Acosta looked frightened, blinked rapidly as if trying not to weep and walked stiffly away.

Danny's rare stands of hostility always left him with a sense of inner discomfort. "I'm sorry," he said, "I'm sorry, laddie, but that little cheerleader is on his way home. He's through tomorrow."

"Nick's going to let him go?"

Danny nodded. "Nick's gonna tell him in the morning. How d'ya say it in spic talk, *adios?* It's *adios* tomorrow for Señor Acosta. *Adios.*"

I watched Acosta puffing up with pride again as he rejoined the party. A famous director and his divorced wife who had starred in his last picture were inviting Acosta to sit down with them. Soon Acosta was doing the talking. The gestures were where I had come in. "And so now my great discovery, El Toro Magnifico, is on his way to the championship of the world," he was undoubtedly saying. He had hitched a ride on a flying carpet and now he was soaring up into the heavens, happily unaware that the carpet was being pulled out from under him.

I wandered over toward the pool. Several couples were in swimming. The Killer was poised on the high-board, showing off his chest development, proud of his muscular little body. Knifing into the water he stayed under a long time. The little mouse who was his for the evening screamed and he broke surface, laughing. She pretended to be insulted but he dove down again and in a moment she was laughing too. In the morning I would hear all about it.

On my way over toward the dancers I passed Toro and Ruby, sitting on a stone bench in the garden. Toro was laughing at something Ruby was saying. It occurred to me that I had never seen him laugh before. "We're having a wonderful time," Ruby said. "I talk to him in English and he answers in Spanish. I've promised to start giving him English lessons."

"She teach me the English," Toro said cheerfully.

"Swell," I said. "Only don't forget Danny's lessons come first."

It was just a very light jab and it didn't seem to hurt her. "He learns very fast," she said. She smiled at him and he became flustered and ran his hand through his hair.

"Hey, Molina, I been looking all over for you," a voice called from across the garden. It was Doc. "I've had a cab standing by for half an hour to take you back to the hotel."

Toro looked at Ruby. "I no tired. I stay."

Doc shook his head. "Know what time it is, after one o'clock. The only fighter I ever saw who could stay up all night and win was Harry Greb. And you ain't Greb."

Toro pushed his big lips out in his child's pout. "But I ask Luis, Luis say I can stay."

"Sorry, brother, Luis has nothing to say about his. I'm the bugler in this outfit and I'm blowing taps."

"I'm leaving in a couple of minutes, Doc," Ruby said. "I'll drop him off if you like."

"It's all the way downtown, Mrs. Latka," Doc said. "I'll take him home with me." He started to pull Toro to his feet. "Let's go, Molina."

I sat on the bench with Ruby as the hunchback led his charge toward the house. She asked for a cigarette and as I leaned toward her to light it for her I was conscious of an evil covetousness in her eyes. And it wasn't for me.

"Nick still in the game?" I said.

"You know Nick. He'll stay there till he comes out a winner if it takes him till tomorrow afternoon."

Nick played everything for blood, a penny-a-point gin game as seriously as no-limit poker.

"I never knew a guy who hates to lose as bad as Nick does," Ruby said. "When a horse he likes runs out or something, for a week or so there's just no living with him."

"I'd hate to be around when he finds he's backed a wrong horse," I said.

13

Next morning, while Toro went to church with Ruby, I took Acosta up to see Nick. With nothing else to write about, the sports pages had given Toro a big play, with one write-up spotting Acosta's running patter of exhortation through the ropes. This public recognition fattened his pride. All the way out to Beverly Hills I had to listen to his vainglorious variations on an already too-familiar theme. "You see, Luis tol' the truth when he say El Toro will make us all very rich and famous," Acosta said as we walked along the row of palm trees to Nick's bungalow.

Nick was having breakfast with the Killer in the patio. He was sitting in his monogrammed bathrobe, smoking a cigar and reading the papers. Acosta gave him his cordial little bow and his most ingratiating smile and began to word one of those flattering greetings when Nick cut him off. Nick always took the quick way.

"Killer, did you find out when that boat leaves for Buenos Air-ees?" he said.

"Thursday midnight from Pedro," Killer said.

"That's the boat you go home on," Nick said.

Acosta looked at him unbelievingly. "Please? I do not understan' . . ."

Nick looked at me. "You wanna tell him in his own language?"

"No, no," Acosta said, desperate-eyed, "I understan' the English. It is just that I do not understan' . . ."

"Well, if you understand English, that's it," Nick said. "Thursday at midnight we put you on the boat."

"No, no, I will not go. You cannot do this. I belong with El Toro. I stay with him!" Acosta cried.

"Shhh," Nick quieted him with his hand. "This is a classy joint. The guy next door is a bigshot. What d'ya want him to think I am, a bum?"

"But El Toro and I, we come together, we stay together, or he goes back with me," Acosta insisted.

"That's not the way it's gonna be," Nick said quietly. "Jimmy Quinn and me, we own Molina. If you want to take your five percent back with you, that's your business. But ninety-five stays here with me."

"But he's mine. He belongs to me. You took him from me. You cannot push me out like this," Acosta screamed.

"We put you on the boat Thursday night," Nick said.

"But why you make me go?" Acosta demanded. "What I do, what I do wrong?"

"You're a pest," Nick said. "You're not satisfied to sit back and take your lousy five percent."

The blood of anger was rising into Acosta's face. "I stay here," he yelled, "I fight. I see a lawyer. I get El Toro back."

Nick calmly poured himself another cup of coffee. "No, you go Thursday. Your visa runs out next week. You can't get an extension on your work visa because we don't need you. My partner's already explained that to a friend of his who's got an in with the State Department. So we only got an extention for Molina. My bookkeeper'll mail you your five percent."

I was sitting off a little to one side, watching the conflict rise to its sorry climax as if it were a play I was seeing from a front-row seat. It would have been nice if my involvement in the action had been cut off cleanly at the fall of the third-act curtain. Nice, but unprofitable. No, I wasn't in the audience, I was on stage, no matter how close to the wings I tired to inch my chair.

"No visa," Acosta said, the fight gone out of him, pursing his small lips as if he were going to cry. "You fix it so I get no visa. You fix it so I must leave El Toro here." The little eyes were moist with frustration now. The jaunty arrogance, the elaborate self-importance had been torn away from him, leaving him as small and scrawny and absurdly pathetic as a defeathered bluejay.

"Now I'll tell you what I'm going to do for you," Nick said. "I'm going to give you a five-thousand-dollar advance against your percentage. You'll get that in cash on the boat Thursday if you tell Toro you want him to stay here with us and that we'll look after him. Have we got a deal?"

Acosta looked at him dully.

"Don't forget, if you don't tell Toro, he stays, and you go just the same," Nick said. "Only without the five G's."

"I understan'," Acosta said.

I couldn't look at his face. Somehow I had the crazy feeling my complicity would increase the more I looked at that face.

"Well, you want that dough?" Nick said. His voice was unemotional, businesslike. "Is it a deal?"

Acosta nodded slowly, almost as if he had become disinterested. "All right, a deal," he said with the boredom of the defeated.

Nick indicated me with his cigar. "Eddie'll sit in with you when you tell Toro," he told Acosta. "Just so I'll know."

Acosta turned around to include me in his distrust of Nick. I could feel myself being dragged from the wings onto the middle of the stage. I looked down at my lap. I wanted to tell him I was sorry, that I wouldn't have done this, that I understood what identifying himself with Toro had meant to him. But what was the percentage? Was there any use dealing myself out of Nick's favor when I couldn't do anything for Acosta anyway?

Some day, if I played my cards right, things would be different. By then, maybe I'd have bought myself enough time off to finish my play. And if it clicked, Beth and I could . . . But meanwhile, here in the hot sun of the patio in Beverly Hills, things were happening the way Nick wanted them to happen and all I could do was vote *Ja*.

The way Acosta continued to sit there after Nick had said everything he had to say reminded me of a badly punished fighter who remains in his corner after the last round is over, waiting for enough strength to rise and climb out of the ring.

"All right," Nick said. "I guess that's it." He beckoned to the Killer. "Take Acosta back to the hotel and stay with him until Eddie comes down."

"But, Meester Latka, this is not right. El Toro . . ."

Nick nodded to the Killer. Menegheni took him by the arm and moved him toward the gate. All the formality was crushed out of Acosta now. There were no good-byes from Nick. The Killer opened the gate with his free arm and pushed Acosta through it.

Nick stretched luxuriously and lit a fresh cigar. He had forgotten all about Acosta. The moist eyes, the crushed look hadn't touched him. He tipped his chair back from the table and opened his robe to let the sun beat down on his chest. "This sun is for me," he said. "Take your clothes off and get comfortable, Eddie. I got some shorts you c'd wear."

"I'm afraid they wouldn't fit me any more," I said.

"I been noticing that," Nick said. "You oughta take care of yourself, kid. There's a swell Finnish bath up on Sunset Boulevard. All the stars take their hangovers there. Sweat all that poison outa your system."

A little while later we were alone together in the steam room, basking in the pleasant enervation of the moist, hot atmosphere. Nick picked up a limp sports section from the level below him and re-read the account of last night's fight. I had done a little business with the guy who had the by-line, and the story read the way we wanted it to read.

"Well, Eddie, we're on our way," Nick said. "The write-ups read good this morning. Real good. Let 'em say Toro's a stinking boxer, call him clumsy if they want to, long as they make the public think he really clouts those guys. That's what they come for, that, and to see some little guy cut him down." He stretched out on his back in an attitude of exaggerated well-being. "This is living, isn't it? California, loafing in the afternoons, money coming in. Latka doesn't throw you any bad ones, does he?"

This was the best job I ever had all right. More money, less to do, and the kick of putting something over. Even Acosta didn't have too much to complain about. Already he had cleared ten thousand, which added up to a lot of pesos for a two-bit circus manager on the village circuit.

"Did I tell you about that kid of mine?" Nick was saying. "He and his partner won the New England scholastic doubles championship. You should see the size-a the cup he got. Must be this big. And it says Nicholas Latka, Junior, right on it." His face softened with an expression of parental pride. "How d'ya like that, Nicholas Latka, Junior, right along with all them high-class handles?"

"Have you picked out a college for him yet, Nick?"

"I'm gonna try to get him into Yale. I've heard a lot about that Yale. It seems to be a real class joint."

The heavy-muscled Swedish masseur opened the door and stuck his head in. "Ready for your massage now, Mr. Latka." I lay there a few minutes longer letting the heat draw the poison through my pores. Later, when I came out into the air after the massage and the cold shower, I felt refreshed. But that feeling only lasted until I got back to the room in the Biltmore that Toro and Acosta shared.

Acosta was sitting at the window looking out. Toro was reading the funny papers, to which he had recently become addicted. The Killer was playing solitaire. He picked up the cards quickly when he saw me come in. "Boy, am I glad to see you! I had a matinee on this afternoon."

He ducked out. Acosta didn't look up from the window.

"Tell him yet?" I said.

He shook his head.

"You better tell him," I said.

He looked at me helplessly. Then he turned to Toro, his face dull with resignation. "El Toro," he said in Spanish, "this Thursday, I must go home."

"But how is that possible? I fight again next week," Toro said.

"You must stay here after I leave," Acosta said.

Toro's comic section slid to the floor. "Luis, what are you saying? Why should I stay without you?"

"Because . . . because it is better that way," Acosta said heavily.

"How—how can it be better?" Toro protested. "You promised we would always stay together. And now you would leave me here with these strangers?"

Acosta rubbed his small hand over his face. "I am sorry I cannot stay with you, Toro."

"You must stay," Toro said. "You must stay or I go too. I will not stay without you, I will not stay."

"El Toro, listen to me," Acosta said, speaking in a flat, measured voice. "You have to stay. It will still be good for you. You will come home as rich as I have always promised. I will come to meet you at the boat."

"Luis, do not leave me, please do not leave me," Toro suddenly begged. "I do not like these people. I am afraid of these people. If you go, I go too."

Acosta looked at me pleadingly. There was nothing left to do but tell him everything, his listless eyes seemed to say.

"El Toro, you cannot go with me. You cannot go because these men own you. They own you now."

Toro's big face studied Acosta, foolish with confusion. "They—own me?"

He had never been aware of the deals and percentage cuts by which Luis had sold part of his contract first to Vince and then to Nick and Quinn. Acosta had thought it would only bewilder him. Now he looked at Toro with the shame of betrayal and did not know what to say.

"How do they own me, Luis?" Toro asked again.

"I sold them your contract, El Toro."

"But why—why did you do that?"

"Because I did not have enough importance to get you up into the big money by myself," Acosta explained. "This way you will fight in the Madison Square Garden—maybe for the championship. This I did for you, El Toro."

Toro's lips puckered. His eyes betrayed a quick, instinctive fear and then narrowed with suspicion. "You sold me, Luis. Then you can buy me back again, please."

"No, that is impossible—impossible," Acosta said, his voice rising irritably. "You must stay here. You must."

Bewildered, Toro shook his massive head. "I thought you my friend, Luis."

"You'll be all right," I interposed. "We'll look after you."

Toro turned to look at me in surprise, as if he had forgotten that I was there. He looked at me for several seconds, without saying anything, until I began to feel embarrassed. He shook his head again, this time with a kind of pity. He said nothing more to either of us. Slowly he went to the window, where he stood, his huge back to us, and looked out at the downtown traffic.

* * *

That Thursday night Vince and Killer came to take Acosta to the ship. Up to the last moment he had been begging me to get Nick to change his mind. He even offered to cut himself down to two and a half percent, if he were allowed to stay. My promises to talk things over with Nick kept him quietly hopeful until the end. What was the use of letting Acosta know there were never any appeals from Nick's decisions? His word was always good, for you or against you.

Neither Vince nor the Killer liked the idea of driving Acosta all the way out to San Pedro, and they treated him more like a man who was being deported for a crime than a man who had been systematically double-crossed. I found myself thinking of a dozen other places I'd rather have been when Acosta said good-bye to Toro. Acosta put his short arms as far around Toro's great waist as they would go.

"Adios, El Toro mio," Luis said almost in a whisper.

Toro just turned away. I stood there trying to think of something to say. He muttered hoarsely, "I thought he was my friend."

"Come on," I said. "I'll take you to a movie."

Toro liked our movies. He was especially fond of music and seemed to enjoy most those big musical extravaganzas with a hundred girls dancing on a hundred pianos in which Hollywood excels.

The newsreel included a feature on Toro himself, training at Ojai, with the inevitable newsreel gags, showing him square off against a flyweight chinning himself on Toro's arm, and ending with his huge face grinning into the camera in a gargoyle full-head close-up. As we left the theatre a group of kids surrounded him and asked for his autograph. But neither the dancing girls nor the little taste of glory seemed to do anything for Toro's state of mind. He withdrew inside himself. On the way back to the hotel, when I tried to break through his silence by saying in Spanish, "Don't worry now. We're all going to be looking out for you," he answered me haltingly in English, as if he refused to share with me the intimacy of his own language. "I wish I go home," he said.

The next day we all took the train down to San Diego for the second fight on Toro's itinerary. Vince had lined up a colored heavyweight by the name of Dynamite Jones, a local pugilist of established mediocrity who had been winning in the border city. In return for five hundred dollars, Jones had agreed to leave in his dressing room what Dynamite he possessed and to accommodate us with a diveroo in the third.

Toro's training in the San Diego gym attracted capacity crowds to every session, even though he looked even more listless than he had at Ojai. Danny was so disgusted he devoted most of his time to the local bars and horse rooms, leaving Doc to continue Toro's education in the manly art. Doc did what he could. He had enough liking for Toro to want to teach him how to take care of himself in case he ever got in

there with someone with the handcuffs off. But Toro lacked either the
primitive drive of a rough-and-tumble killer or the systematized conse-
cration of the athlete. He was lethargic and moody and dreaded the
sweaty monotony of roadwork and the daily grind at the gym. He
obeyed Doc's instructions with reluctant obedience. But except for
learning to hold his left out in the more or less established way, and to
move around with slow, graceless orthodoxy, there wasn't much improvement in his boxing ability. George obligingly permitted himself to
be knocked over occasionally to keep alive the myth of Toro's punching
powers, but our Man Mountain still hadn't learned to hit hard enough to
bother a healthy featherweight.

I had the fight reporter of the only morning paper up to the room a
couple of times and sized him up as a nice guy on the lazy side with
about as much integrity as I had, who would just as soon shove my stuff
in with his name on it as grind it out himself. So I sat up there at the
Hotel Grant, making with the adjectives.

There wasn't a day when I didn't have a qualm or two for what I was
doing. At the same time I had to admit that on the bottom level I was
getting a real kick out of putting this big oaf across as the world's most
dangerous heavyweight. The morning of the fight, for instance, when I
read the copy in the first column of the sports section under Ace
Mercer's by-line, it handed me a laugh, I suppose a laugh of superiority.

> Fresh from his sensational two-round knockout victory over
> highly touted Cowboy Coombs, Man Mountain Molina, the Giant
> of the Andes, 275 pound human pile-driver, faces Dynamite Jones,
> the pride of San Diego, in ten rounds or less at the Waterfront Arena
> tonight.
>
> Although outweighed by eight-five pounds and standing only
> six-feet-one, just a little guy when you're looking down from Mo-
> lina's stratospheric six-foot-seven, Jones and his manager "Whisper-
> ing" Al Mathews have been going up and down cauliflower alley
> grabbing up all the short money they can find. "We ain't afraid of
> nobody," Whispering Al confided courageously to this writer after
> Dynamite's final workout yesterday.
>
> Dynamite is well known to San Diego fans, who have yet to see
> the dusky battler down for the full count. He will be meeting a
> lethal puncher of super-human strength in the Giant of the Andes
> who is already being spoken of as a championship contender...

Jones was a tall, rangy boy with more stuff than I would have expected from a second-rater out there in the sticks. He came out of his
corner as if he really meant to make a fight out of it, with stiff jabs that

made Toro look clumsy and flatfooted. Toro threw a wild right that almost knocked himself down as Jones ducked. The crowd laughed. Ten seconds before the end of the round, Jones feinted to the body, sucking Toro into dropping his hands, and crossed him with a straight right to the jaw. Toro's knees buckled, and if Doc and Danny hadn't jumped through the ropes at the bell, he might have gone down.

The crowd was on its feet, cheering Jones as the colored fighter danced confidently back to his corner. That was part of Toro's appeal of course. They came not only to see the brute flatten his opposition but also with the deeply rooted hope that just once, the little guy, the underdog, the dimly realized symbol of themselves would triumph over the Giant as David the eternal short-ender felled Goliath.

Toro staggered back to his corner in a daze. Doc had to use smelling salts to sharpen his dimming senses.

"What goes with this Jones?" I asked Vince.

"If the jig tries anything," Vince said, "he ends up in the bay."

"Maybe he just wants to make it look good for a round or two and doesn't know how little Toro can take."

"If that jigaboo tries to cross us, we got protection," Vince said. "I got my guy workin' his corner."

That was the first time I realized what a really thorough fellow Vince Vanneman was. It wouldn't win any merit badges for any of us, but if it hadn't been for his foresight things would have turned out even worse than they did.

Jones came out for the second round as if the understanding we thought we had was actually made between two other guys. He wouldn't stand still for Toro to connect with his ponderous rights. As he kept moving around Toro he was scoring with sharp punches that had the crowd on its feet, begging for a knockout, defying the slow-moving giant with bloodthirsty abuse, "Knock the big bum out! Send him back to Argentina! Attaboy, cut him down to your size!"

Fortunately, Jones was a punishing but not a finishing puncher or he would have written an untimely 30 to our whole campaign. But when the second round ended, Toro wandered back to his corner with blood dripping from his mouth and his eyes staring uselessly. Doc worked over him with his educated fingers, massaging the back of his neck, while a handler squeezed a spongeful of cold water over his head, and checked with vaseline the trickle of blood that ran from the corner of his mouth.

"It's the business all right," Vince said.

"Jesus," I said. "This is some tank artist, this Jones."

"My guy's talkin' to him," Vince said. "My guy's a real tough fella. He'll tell that nigger what'll be if he don't splash this round."

The representative of our interests Vince had placed in Jones' corner seemed to be doing plenty of talking. He was leaning through the ropes with his sweaty, larcenous face close to Jones' ear, pouring it to him. But when Jones came out for the third round he was still trying. He knocked Toro off balance with a smart left jab to the mouth and followed up with a straight right that sent Toro stumbling back against the ropes. Any moment I expected to see Toro start caving in, in sections, and my lousy five percent not worth one of Danny's torn-up bookie tabs. It made me realize for the first time how hungry I was for that dough, just as hungry as Nick, or Vince or Acosta out there on the high seas on his way home to the small time. Just like Acosta I found myself up on my feet begging Toro to stay with him.

Jones was getting wild now, with the disobedient urge to knock Toro out. His left hand shot over Toro's shoulder and Toro brought up a looping right from the floor that caught Jones on the chin. It didn't hurt Jones so much as it caught him off balance, and Toro, trying clumsily to follow up his advantage, shoved Jones with both hands, and the colored fighter half-slipped, half-fell to the canvas. As long as he was down the referee (with whom Vince had done a little business) began to count, Jones decided to rest on one knee until the count of six, for he was beginning to be arm-weary from throwing so many punches at his wide-open target.

But when he arose at six, a towel came fluttering up out of his corner. Vince's guy was working overtime to earn his fifty clams. Jones tried to kick the towel out of the ring and go on fighting, but the referee grabbed him and led him back to his corner. Then he came back and raised the hand of our bewildered superman. A terrible roar of protest rose from the crowd. In a second the air was full of flying cushions, programs and bottles. Some of the fans in their wrath started breaking up their seats and hurling the pieces into the ring. With police running interference we hustled Toro back to the dressing room. With a quick fifty to the sergeant, we got away in his police car.

"What happen?" Toro asked me in innocent confusion.

"Don't worry, you won the fight fair," I told him. "It's just that the people aren't satisfied until they see you kill somebody. So they didn't want the fight stopped so soon."

Toro smiled through his bloody lips. "One ponch and he goes boom," he said. "Just like first time."

For once in my life I had no desire to fraternize with reporters. So instead of going back to the hotel or catching a train, we went straight to a garage and hired a car. We drove up the coast until we thought we were safely out of range of the little stink bomb we had exploded and stopped at a small auto-court, or motel, as they like to call them in Cal. The guy Vince had working for us in the other corner was with us too.

His name was Benny. He was one of those ex-lightweights who blow up into heavyweights as soon as they come off the training and get on the beer. As soon as Doc put Toro to bed after a warm bath and light massage, so he'd rest easier, Benny gave us the lowdown on the little comedy (in the Greek sense) that had been going on in his corner. It was a hot night and he was on his third beer when he opened his sweat-stained shirt, revealing a fat, hairy chest on which were tattooed the words, "Pac. Coast lt-wt champ, 1923," and the exaggerated nude figure of a woman called Edna embracing an Adonis-like creature in boxing trunks, boxing gloves and a sailor hat captioned Battling Benny Mannix. The Battler managed to raise the group's morale somewhat by inhaling and exhaling his fatty diaphragm in such a way that the tattooed figures undulated together with impressive realism.

"This jig comes back after the first round cocky as hell, see," Benny began in an injured tone. "'Christ, I didn' know that big fella was such a bum,' he says. 'An' I thought I was layin' down to save myself punishment.'

"'Don't get no fancy ideas,' I tells him, 'or you'll get a helluva lot more punishment 'n you figured on.'

"But when the jig goes out for round two, he's still full of wrong ideas, see? 'This guy's got nothin',' he says, 'I c'n stiffen this guy. The hell with them five C's,' he says to Mathews. 'We c'n make more flattening this joker.'

"Well, I tries to tell him if he keeps up the wise talk he's sucking around for a hole in the head, but the jug don't scare so easy. He's got this giant-killin' on his mind. So when I'm massagin' him I try to squeeze his muscles so they'll go dead on him and when I wipe off his face I accidentally rub some alcohol in his eyes, so when we send him out for Three he's brushing his eyes and he ain't quite the weisenheimer he was when he came in from Two. But even then he's beatin' your guy real bad when he goes down from that slip. So I figures, what the hell, this jig is just wrong enough to get up off the floor and belt the big jerk out. So I sees my chance and throws in the towel."

Danny sucked out the last of a pint bottle of rye. "I don' like it," he said. "Twen'y years in the racket I never have a run-in with the Commish. All that's gotta happen now is I lose my license."

"Aah, shet up your bellyachin'," Vince said. "Always cryin' about your goddam license. Shove the commissions, both of 'em. Leave Jimmy and Nick take care of 'em."

"But damn it, if you're gonna set these fights up, why don't you do it right?" Danny demanded. "The woods are full of bums ready to fall down for a price. But you, the great fixer, gotta pick a guy who likes to win."

"Aah, go shove yourself, spithead," Vince said in rebuttal. "What am I, a mind reader for Chrisake? How the hell should I know what goes on in that dinge's double-crossin' brain?"

"If I lose my license, I'm dead," Danny said. "You, you can always go back to pimping."

"Why you son-of-a-bitch!" Profanity spewed from Vince's fleshy mouth as he lunged heavily toward Danny, starting a wild punch that Danny blocked neatly. Danny made no effort to retaliate as Benny, George, Doc and I grabbed parts of Vince's aroused anatomy and pulled him away.

"Never do that," Danny said quietly, his face strangely white, his thin lips drawn to an angry line.

"Yeah, well, no jerk is gonna call me them names like that," Vince blubbered.

"Whatta you wanna do, wake Molina?" Doc said. "Let the guy sleep. He needs his sleep."

"Aah, shove him too," Vince said. He settled back on the couch with a crumpled copy of *Crime* he had picked up on the train down to San Diego.

I went outside to smoke a cigarette in peace. Across the highway the surf pounded on the beach with relentless monotony. The sky was clear and moonlit. Looking up into it, the tension of the smoke-filled motel room seemed as foolish and far away as an argument you had with your brother when you were eight. In a few minutes George Blount came out and joined me. "Man, oh, man!" he said and chuckled softly.

"One of these days Danny's going to clip him," I said.

"Mister McCuff's like me," George said. "Don' want to fight nobody 'cept for money."

"Why do you think it is, George?" I said. "Why is it most you guys don't go in for these grudge matches?"

"I don' know," George laughed. "Maybe you go roun' punchin' fellows and catchin' punches so long you just get it all outa your system. Maybe every man's got just so many punches in him and when you get rid of 'em all in the ring you just don't want to hit nobody no more."

I walked down the road a quarter of a mile or so with him, not saying much of anything but conscious as always of his deep serenity.

"Boy, we really stank up the joint tonight," I said.

"That fella oughta go home," George said. "That fella oughta go home before something bad happen."

That was easy to say, when all you were getting out of it were three squares and a little pocket money. But Toro Molina had already turned them away in two cities. He was an oil well just beginning to come in and you don't turn off a profitable flow just because your hands are getting a little dirty, not where I come from.

As soon as we read the papers next morning we knew we had troubles. The State Boxing Commission had tied up the purses of both fighters, pending an investigation. The fight we had lined up for Oakland was postponed. Toro couldn't read the papers well enough to learn what had happened, so at least he was happy. Only he wanted to know where the money was that he had earned. Vince slipped him fifty dollars. He had never had a large American bill of his own and he seemed content with it. "Feefty bocks, hokay," he kept saying.

You could have chipped the air up for ice cubes when Nick came in.

"Well, gentlemen," he said, "this is great. This is just great. This is just what we needed, like a hole in the head."

Vince started to blubber and bluster through an explanation, but Nick's hard, sharp voice knifed through his defense.

"I'm not interested," he said. "When I was a kid I learned one thing and I learned it good. Never do nothing halfass. Whatever it is, if you're gonna do it, do it. The kid who stole an apple off the pushcart and ran away, he's the dope the cop always caught. The guy who followed the old man home, bopped him in the hallway and took his whole goddam pushcart, he's the one who got away. That's been a principle with me ever since. Like this build-up we're giving Molina. You say you slipped the nigger two-fifty to lay down. (It had been five hundred when I heard it, but maybe Vince held out the other half.) Hell, make it worth his while. It's worth it to us. Don't be a piker. Think big. Give 'em a grand. Only give it to 'em after the fight. No dive, no dough. You got that? Now this time I let it go. Maybe this sun is making me soft in the head, but I let it go. Next time you fumble you're out on your ass."

"Yeah, but we gotta contract," Vince pouted.

"Sure we gotta contract," Nick agreed. "But give me trouble and see how quick I tear up the contract. I got Max Stauffer," he said, mentioning the Darrow of corruption. "You louse me up and right away Max has ten reasons why the contract's no good that'll stand up in court." He opened his chest drawer and paused discriminatingly over his impressive collection of handpainted ties. "Now screw, both of you," he said. "Pat Drake is bringing a couple of big men over from the studio, and you guys don't look dressed good enough."

The investigation dragged on for a couple of weeks and I had a job on my hands trying to make it look as good as possible in the papers. One of the things working for us was the convincing way Toro reacted to the charges. "Me no fight feex," he insisted. "I no crook. I try hard."

Vince also expressed indignation that his professional integrity should be impugned. The whole thing wound up with the Commission exonerating Toro and his managers completely, but finding Benny Mannix guilty and suspending his license to second fighters in the State of California for twelve months. Benny had admitted throwing in the towel because he had placed a large bet on Toro, which he was afraid he might lose. This handful of verbal sand in the eyes of the Commission hiked our overhead up five hundred bucks, which was Benny's price for taking the rap. The Commission ruling was only binding so far as California was concerned, so Vince sent Benny on to Las Vegas, where we had a date with a full-blooded Indian Miniff had dug up for us by the name of Chief Thunderbird. Chief Thunderbird, Miniff was insisting with characteristic whimsicality, was the heavyweight champion of New Mexico.

Now that the Commission loosened the strings on the San Diego purse, Toro wanted his money. He wanted to send a chunk home to the family in Santa Maria. He wanted them to realize down there what a rich man he was becoming in North America. But Vince explained to him that there couldn't be any payoff until Nick's bookkeeper Leo figured out Toro's net take after overhead and managerial cuts had been deducted. "Meanwhile here's another fifty," Vince said. "Any time you need money, just ask me."

Toro was very pleased. He had all the money he wanted. All he had to do was ask Vince. And as soon as his percentage was figured out, he would send enough to his father to begin building that home that was going to put the de Santos mansion to shame. Perhaps he would even go back for a vacation—I held out the hope that this was possible when he was well-enough established—and sanctify his relationship with the lovely Carmelita.

While we were waiting for the Commission to make up their minds about that San Diego business, I was walking down Spring Street with Toro one afternoon. Toro could never go by a music store without stopping to press his nose against the window and gaze wonderingly at the radios, phonographs and musical instruments. This time he said, "I come back pronto," and darted into a music store. In a few minutes he returned with a portable radio in his hand, loudly broadcasting a swing band. "Feefty dollar. I buy," Toro said happily. People kept turning around to stare at us, not only for Toro's size but for the volume of the unexpected music.

"Toro, turn that thing off," I said. "Nobody plays a radio in the street."

"I like carry music," Toro said.

Beth should see me now, I thought, playing nursemaid to an elephantine idiot. Everywhere we went, Toro carried that silly radio around, always turned on with the volume up. When we went to a restaurant he placed it tenderly on an empty chair and smiled at it lovingly as he ate while it filled the room with the nasal music of cowboy songs. "In Santa Maria no music in box," he said. "I bring back many to my village for give away."

I don't think Toro knew there was any way of changing those bills. You either had to buy something for fifty dollars, it seemed to him, or you might as well throw it away. He blew the second fifty all at once in the arcade of the hotel and hurried to show me his latest acquisition. It was a tiny gold key in a miniature heart-shaped gold lock.

"Who's this for?" I said.

"For Señora Latka," he said.

I looked at it more closely. On the back of the lock was engraved in small letters, "The key to my heart."

"You can't give her this," I said.

"Why not?" Toro wanted to know. "She nice lady. I like very much."

"Her husband likes her very much too," I said.

"I like her too," Toro protested. "She nice to me. Good lady. Go to church every Sunday."

Well, finally there was nothing to do about it but take him up to Beverly Hills, so he could present his little trinket to Ruby. Nick was out playing golf with Pat Drake, as it happened, and she was home alone. Although the sun was shining, we found her inside drinking her way through a batch of sidecars. "Why, Toro, that's sweet of you, that's awfully sweet of you," she said, and she pinned the locket over her heart in a provocative gesture.

While I drank along with her for a little while, Toro just sat there silently staring at her in simple-minded shamelessness. She was a stunning woman, with the agelessness of the full-blown voluptuary. Though her behavior was above reproach and almost studiously ladylike, I wondered if it was the influence of the sidecars which made me sense that Toro's presence was stimulating her to a more animated charade than usual.

Just as we were leaving, Nick came in with Pat Drake and he seemed pleased to be able to show off his giant protégé to the film star. If he were at all disturbed by Toro's present to Ruby there was no hint of it in his reaction. "The guy shows pretty classy taste," he said good-naturedly, looking at the locket. He poked Toro playfully in the ribs. "All set for that guy in Oakland, Man Mountain?"

"I ponch. He go boom," Toro said.

14

In Oakland we polished off in four a character called Oscar DeKalb and in Reno an alleged heavyweight by the name of Tuffy Parrish collapsed from a vicious slap on the chest, which added another five thousand to the take of the corporation. By the time we came into Las Vegas, "with the new scourge of the heavyweights, the Giant of the Andes, seeking his fifth straight knockout victory," the East was beginning to rise to the bait and AP wanted fifty words on the outcome of the Chief Thunderbird fight.

"Turn that goddam radio off," Danny said on our way up to the hotel. The more success we had the more irritable Danny seemed to be getting. Larceny just didn't come naturally to him the way it did to Vince. He fought it all the time.

Toro was still hanging on to his radio. Jazz, cowboy music, spirituals, Latin songs—he didn't seem to care what it was as long as it was something that came out of a box he could carry around.

As soon as we were settled, Doc and George took Toro out to stretch his legs. Danny ducked out to find a place to bet a couple of good things he thought he had at Belmont. Vince was on the phone trying to get hold of a broad he used to know in Las Vegas and I was in the bathtub reading the *New Yorker* when Miniff popped in.

By the time I finished the story and came out with a towel around my middle, they were already in an argument.

"But this Mex is no second-rate bum," Miniff was insisting. "He's a first-rate bum. Why, he coulda been a contender if he was managed right."

"You mean back in the days of Corbett?" I said.

Miniff's ferret eyes turned on me reproachfully. "Aahh," he said in rebuttal. "He's oney twenty-eight year old. Whaddya thinka that?"

"I think in that case he must have fought his first professional fight when he was six," I said. "I looked him up in the record book."

"He's a real tough bum," Miniff said. "Six-four, weighs two-twenny-five. He's a man-mountain hisself. He'll look real good in there with your guy. Lettum go for seven, huh boys?"

"One round, pal, one round," Vince said.

"One round!" Miniff wailed. "Nail me to the cross, go ahead crucify me, one round! Seven rounds, it looks like your bum is knocking over real opposition. One round, it's a farce. That's what it is, a lousy farce."

"Keep your voice down," I said. "Do you want the whole town to know what round we got it greased for?"

"Seven rounds, I could maybe make myself some money with this Indian," Miniff whimpered. "Whatsamatter with you guys, you never wanna let me make no money?"

"For Chrisake you're gettin' a thousand from the club and another five from us for the act," Vince said. "Three months ago your ass was hanging out. What more d'ya want?"

"For goin' so quick I wanna grand," Miniff said. "One grand for the hoomiliation."

"Listen to him, he wants," Vince said to me with righteous derision. "A punched-up greaseball he picks up in a poolroom and alluva sudden he wants!" His mouth opened in a mocking laugh.

Miniff did want. He wanted desperately. He never seemed to be able to get out of the petty-cash department.

"I'll tell you what I'll do with you," Vince turned to Miniff in sudden imitation of Nick. "I'll give you an extra two-fifty you c'n keep for yourself. Your bum don't have to know anything about it. That way you come out the same as when you split an extra five down the middle."

And that's the way they settled that, with Vince saving us two bits (which he probably pocketed) by convincing Miniff to hold out on his fighter. The next afternoon I was in our room sipping a rye highball and bending over a hot typewriter whipping up some porridge about this fight's being for the Latin Heavyweight Championship of the World when Miniff came in crying the blues louder than ever. It was a hot fall day, but he still kept his hat on and the heat of the sun plus his own internal fires brought the shine of perspiration to his small, unhealthy face. All the way through the bedroom Miniff kept up his miserable soliloquy. "No wonder I got the bite in the belly. It's these bums, these stinking bums. Oh, Jesus, I wish I had as much money as I can't stand them bums."

"What's the matter, Harry?" I said. "Relax." I pointed to the bottle. "Help yourself."

"The amber?" He recoiled in horror. "I haven't got enough troubles! Why, my ulcer is havin' ulcers! You wanna know why, you take this bum of mine, this Chief Thunderbird he calls hisself."

Vince was still lying in bed, in his underwear, sleeping off a big night. He rolled over irritably. "Whatsmatter? Whatsmatter?" he said.

"My bum, he's off his nut," Miniff said. "He says he don' wanna quit to your bum. Alla sudden he talks like he ain't already been belted out thirty-eight times already."

"What's the matter, doesn't he think he's getting enough dough?" I said.

"It ain't the dough," Miniff said, and then he hesitated as if he were ashamed to say it. "He says it's his pride."

Vince sat up in bed, scratched his hairy chest and reached for a cigar. "Pride, for Christ sake! Whaddya mean, pride?"

"That's what he says, pride," Miniff shrugged. "He hasn't got to eat, he has to have pride yet. The whole trouble starts when he sees this Molina work out in the gym yesterday. 'Why, he's a bum like me,' he says right away. And then, you know these punchy guys, he begins to get sore about it. He's almost as big as your guy, so he gets to thinking how different things'd been if his managers had greased things for him the way you's doing with Molina. Gets to feelin' real sorry for hisself, see? An' on toppa that, some a his relatives off the reservation is comin' in to see the fight. He says he's ashamed for 'em to see a dog like Molina belt him out in one. He says for dough he don' want it, he says. He says he's still got his pride."

"Shove his pride," Vince said. "You think he's the only tanker in Las Vegas?"

"But the fight's the night after tomorrow," I said. "We got all this publicity working for us. There's seventy-five hundred already in the house. We're out of pocket if this sensitive fellow doesn't keep his word like a gentleman."

Miniff wiped his forehead nervously. "The aggravations I gotta put up with from these stumblebums."

"Maybe you could slip the guy a mickey," Vince suggested.

"Whatta you think I am, a crook?" Miniff demanded. "Eighteen years in the business, I never got mixed up in no rough stuff. No mickeys and no beatin' up guys. I got principles."

"You're breakin' my heart," Vince said. "You're breakin' my heart. Oney I'm gonna break your little neck if this creep-a yours gives us any trouble."

Miniff's hairy little hand shoved his hat back farther on his head and wiped his face in a convulsive gesture.

"I tell ya the guy won't budge." He turned to me as the more reasonable listener. "I'm talkin' to a wall. His brain is jammed like somebody dropped a rock in the machinery."

"Tell you what you do," I said. "Bring the fellow here after his workout this afternoon. Maybe we can get somewhere with him."

In a couple of hours Miniff was back with his problem child. He looked like a full-blooded Indian, all right, a tall, powerfully built man, with the long, impressive head of a Navajo warrior. In another time, you couldn't help thinking, he might have been a great tribal chieftain, but now he was just another scuffed-up pug, the nobility of his face hammered into a caricature of the eternal palooka, the high-bridged, Roman schnoz pushed into his face, ears on him that would look like cauliflowers even to a cauliflower and sunken eyes overhung with scar tissue.

Only he had a way of fixing you with those eyes, sort of proud-like and melancholy that made you want to look away.

"What seems to be the matter, Chief?" I said.

"Molina don't knock me out," he said.

"Why, you good-for-nothing bum," Vince said. "What record are you protecting, for Christ's sweet sake? I suppose you never took a dive before. Why, you been in the tank so long you're starting to grow fins."

The Indian seemed numb to abuse. He didn't say anything.

"It's just business," I said. "There's no disgrace to it, Chief."

The Indian just sat there looking out at us from the depth of his battered dignity. Miniff screamed, Vince threatened and I reasoned, but he just shook his head. Miniff was right, it was just as if a rock had fallen into the mental machinery and the brain had jammed. He sat there immune to abuse, bribery and the danger of physical violence. Maybe it was only a dim protest against a life of profitless punishment that made him slam his mind against us and refuse to submit to further humiliation at the hands of these white-faced jackals riding high on the towering shoulders of an oversized, overrated bum.

The morning of the fight the Indian was still holding out and all of us were jittery—all, that is, except Toro, who was really beginning to think that boxing came as naturally to him as Luis Acosta had once told him it did. I ponch and he go boom—that's the way it seemed to Toro as one opponent after another flopped down beneath his ludicrous onslaught.

As soon as Nick got in, we ran over to his suite to dump our troubles in his lap. The manicurist was just putting the finishing touches on his nails as we entered. Ruby met us at the door on her way downstairs to the beauty parlor, although she looked more as if she had just stepped out of one. The Killer was on the phone making a date for Nick with Joe Gideon, who ran the casino downstairs. Apparently the syndicate had an interest in the joint.

"So you two geniuses can't handle one dopey fighter," Nick said. "What would you do if I wasn't around? You know, that's why eventually we have to have all the money." He looked at his trim, polished fingernails. "Tell Miniff to send his boy to me."

We went over to the arena, where Toro and the Chief were weighing in. Vince whispered the word to Miniff, who passed it on to the Indian under his hand. At first, Miniff told us, Thunderbird didn't want any part of it. But Miniff impressed him with what a big man this Latka was and hinted that he might be interested in buying Thunderbird's contract and taking him East to fight in the Garden. Hope is the blind mother of stupidity, and the big jerk went for it.

I went back to the dressing room and sat with Toro while he put his clothes on after the weigh-in. He had hit the scales at 279, four pounds more than the last fight. Toro was putting on the gray, double-breasted plaid I had picked out for him in L.A. He looked at himself in the mirror and smiled at the well-groomed, well-tailored figure he presented.

"You look mighty sharp there, boy," I said.

"You take picture?" Toro said. "I send picture to Mama and Papa to show them I am dress up like a de Santos."

"Sure, we'll send all you want," I said.

"Señora Latka, she is also here?" Toro asked me as we left the dressing room.

"Yes, she's here with Nick," I said.

"I go see her now," Toro said.

"Take it easy. You'll see her when you see Nick."

"We go for walk. We talk."

"I noticed that," I said. "I suppose Nick's noticed it too. What do you find to talk about?"

"We talk . . . nice," Toro said.

"In Spanish," I said. "Tell me in Spanish."

"The Señora is very kind and sympathetic," Toro explained. "She is more like the ladies of Argentina. I like to go to church with her. And after church I tell her something about the life of my village. About my family. About the *Dia del Vino,* the first full moon of the harvest time, when the fountain in the village runs wine for all to drink and even the village beggars stagger like lords."

Maybe that was all it was, I thought. Ruby, in her instinctual way of reaching out to men, was more like the women of Toro's village. Perhaps Ruby was only supplying the personal touch which the rest of us were too lazy, too selfish or too busy to supply. But the fear—completely unjustified by anything I had seen and lurking only in the evil back-alleys of my mind—that her touch might become too personal prompted me to say, "Go a little slow with her, Toro. I've seen Nick when he's mad. I wouldn't want him mad at me."

"But there is nothing wrong in what we do," Toro said in Spanish. "She is a good woman. She goes to church. We do no one any harm."

We walked back to the hotel together. "This man I fight tonight—big fellow?" he said.

"Yes, he's big," I said, "but you ought to beat him, all right. Just keep throwing punches."

I wondered how Nick was making out with that Indian. The Indian wasn't much, easy to hit and as musclebound as Toro, but he was more of a fighting man, with better coordination, and I hated to think what he might do to Toro if he held out on his refusal to go in under wraps.

Ruby was still down in the beauty parlor, so Toro went up to his room to put away those three chops that would have to sustain him until fight time. I thought it would be interesting to see how Nick was jockeying the Indian, but when I put my head in the door Nick told me this was strictly between him and the boy and to go take a powder for myself. At the bar I met Miniff, who hadn't been allowed in either. "Jeez, I'm worried," he said with a sigh of venality. "You gotta admit it, my bums has always been reliable. When I say they go, that's when they go. If this jerk crosses me, it's terrible for my reppatation."

About half an hour later, the Indian came down. Miniff beckoned him to the privacy of the men's room off the bar.

"Well, what happened? Give," Miniff begged.

"He told me I shouldn't say nothing to nobody," the Indian said.

"But you're not gonna ootz us out of that extra dough? You and Nick got together?"

"He's a pretty smart fella," was all the Indian would say.

Half an hour from fight time I was still as much in the dark as the cash customers. When Benny Mannix came in from the Indian's dressing room to go through the motions of watching Doc bandage Toro's hands, I asked him if he knew what was going on.

Benny shook his head with irritable bewilderment. "It beats the hell outa me. Know what the guy does? He takes me aside 'n tells me to go out 'n get him a little piece a chicken wire. Chicken wire, the guy wants! So a couple minutes later when I run down the wire, he says, 'That's good. Now go get a pair of pliers and meet me in the can.' I think the guy's crossing over to the silly side a the street, so I try to con him out of it. 'Okay,' he says, 'okay, after the fight I'll just tell Nick you din wanna cooperate.' 'You mean this is Nick's idea?' I says. 'Who else aroun' here has any ideas?' this Thunderbird comes right back. So I shut my mouth before I catch any more flies and I meet him in the can with the pliers like he asks."

"Wait a minute, Benny," I said. "Let me smell your breath."

"I should drop dead this second if it ain't like I'm telling you," Benny says, offended that I should doubt his veracity. "So when we get into the crapper together he says, 'Now cut off a little piece.'

" 'How small?' I says.

" 'Small enough to fit 'n my mouth,' he says.

" 'What the hell?' I says.

" 'Now have you got a rubber on you?' he says.

" 'A rubber?' I says. 'Sure, but . . .'

" 'Okay, now slip the wire into the rubber,' he says. 'There, that's it. Now keep it in yer pocket, an' when you put the mouthpiece in my mouth make sure you got this underneath it so it'll lie flat against my gums.' "

"Holy Jesus," I said.

"I seen 'em do a lot-a tricks but this is a new one on me," Benny said.

So that's the way it was when the fight began. The first time Toro held his left in the Indian's face, the chicken wire did its work and the blood began to trickle out of one corner of his mouth. But it wasn't bothering him yet. He fought back. He could punch a little with his left hand and he let it go a couple of times, forcing Toro back. The customers stood up and yelled. It looked as if the Indian could take him. Again you could feel the mass frenzy to see the giant punished and humiliated. Men who were good to their mothers and loved their children shouted encouragement for the Indian with passionate hatred for the hulking, inept figure who retreated before him. But every time Toro pushed his left glove into the Indian's face, blood came forth to meet it. By the end of the round he looked as if he had stopped an oncoming truck with his face.

Miniff and Benny did what they could for the cuts between rounds. The Indian came out of his corner with a looping right hand that made Toro grunt, but in the clinch that followed, Toro pawed at his opponent's face and the Indian's mouth became a bloody mess. Toro's gloves were sticky with it too and each time he brushed the Indian's face they left an ugly red blot. The Indian kept boring in, but the blood pouring out of his mouth was beginning to bother him. Before the round was half over his mouth and Toro's gloves were so soggy they made a sickeningly squashy sound when they came together.

"Stop the fight, stop the fight," some of the ringsiders were beginning to yell. Women hid their faces behind their programs. The Indian sprang out of his corner with show-off courage, but his face was a bloody mask. He missed a wild swing which sprayed the white shirt of the referee and some of the ringsiders beneath him. Toro backed away and turned to the referee with a question in his eyes. He had no stomach for this. The more tenderhearted among the fans, and those who had wagered on an early knockout were on their feet now, chanting "Stop it, stop it!" The Indian, seeing the referee move toward him, shook his head and charged in recklessly. But the referee caught his arm and led him, apparently under protest, back to his corner. It was all over. The Giant of the Andes had scored his sixth consecutive victory by a TKO.

Toro crossed himself as he did before and after every fight. Then he went across the ring to see if the Indian was all right. The Indian, his mouth still bleeding profusely, rose to embrace Toro. The crowd loved it, all their blood-thirst suddenly run to sentimentality. Toro got a fair hand when he left the ring. But everybody stood up and cheered or applauded the Indian as he climbed down through the ropes with his mouth wadded with blood-soaked cotton. The Indian smiled through his pain and mitted the crowd happily. The boys from the reservation, up in the bleachers, screamed his name exultantly and he responded with a wave that was full of pride.

Nick looked over at me and winked. "Good fight," he said. It had looked convincing, all right. I wondered what touch of sadism in Nick made him dream up a gimmick like that. Maybe it was just a hard, sound business idea. There was no blood-lust in Nick, just money-lust.

"That was too bloody," Ruby said. "I hate to see a fight like that."

"Aah, that was nothing," Nick said, pleased with Ruby's reaction. "Ruby misses all the knockouts," he said. "She's always hiding her eyes under her hand."

"I hate to see those boys get hurt," she said. "At least I'm glad it wasn't Toro."

I walked back to our dressing room. Toro was lying on the table getting a rubdown. Danny was slumped in a chair, staring at the floor. He had been drunk ever since we got to Las Vegas.

Vince fell into a burlesque pantomime of Danny's condition. In this act of condescension, performed for my benefit, there was more than a hint of comradeship between us. You and I are the guys who keep this show going, the grimace seemed to say. And I suddenly realized with a sickening shock that my old hostility to Vince, boldly unconcealed on the train going west, had been pushed further back in my mind and discreetly suspended as our common interest in the success of our venture inevitably drew us closer together.

"What you doing tonight, son?" Vince said. "How about me 'n you going out and getting into trouble?"

I was Vince's friend. It was a terrible thought. All my insults had bounced off him harmlessly. Their pointed vulgarity had only succeeded in making our relationship more intimate than it would have been if I had merely ignored him. Vince, suffering the unbearable loneliness of the gregarious heel, had taken me for a friend.

"Tell me where you're going to be so I'll be sure not to go there," I said.

"Catch me at the Krazy Kat around twelve," Vince said, just as if I had begged to accompany him. "That's where these divorce dames hang out. Let's have ourselves a little poon hunt."

That's the way nearly everyone talked along the streets I worked. That's the way I was beginning to sound myself. But somehow I heard Vince's words one by one in all their forlorn and godforsaken vulgarity, coming out of that fat white neck rising over the open yellow sports shirt. They were not familiarly meaningless phrases, but separate counts indicting me for my degradation. Instead of meeting the charge head-on, I sidestepped and walked over to the rubbing table and looked down at

Toro. Doc was massaging a red splotch along his ribs where the Indian had let those right hands go.

"Nice fight, Toro," I said.

"Too much blood," Toro said. "No like bleed heem too much."

"He's worried about the other guy," Doc said. His damp, homely face creased into a cheerless smile.

"How about the Indian?" I asked Doc. "Think he's okay?"

"I guess he'll live," Doc said. "But I'll bet he'll be eating his dinner through a straw for the next couple of days. Those blood vessels in his gums are probably cut all to hell."

I went across the hall to have a look for myself. If the club doctor was going to send him to the hospital I ought to know it. The headlines even popped into my mind—a box on the sports page—MOLINA TKO VICTIM RUSHED TO HOSPITAL. For a second I was horrified to realize this was a daydream, or rather a night dream of vicious wishfulness.

Over in the other dressing room, the house doc was still working over the Indian. A small crowd of handlers and well-wishers were grouped around the table, their tense, silent faces turned toward the Indian's terrible mouth.

Miniff was standing at the sink, with his shirt off, washing off his hands and face. For once he was without his hat and his small bald head looked naked and pathetic with nervous blue veins trellising across it. He was so short that he had to stand on tiptoes to look into the mirror.

"How's your boy?" I said.

"He ain't mine no more," Miniff said. "Soon as I pick up my check and pay him off, I kiss him off for good. I want no part of him."

"This is the first time I ever saw you throw away a dollar," I said.

Miniff picked up the short, straggle-ended cigar butt he had placed carefully on the edge of the sink, and shook his head. "I never want to go through nothing like this again. That bum like to drove me crazy. I don' want no part of him. That screwball almost gets me in wrong with a big man like Latka and then he lets 'em chop his puss up like a hamburger when he coulda stretched out on the canvas in round one, nice and comfortable, like he was home in bed. I'll never figure that one."

"He had to save his pride," I said.

"Pride!" Miniff seemed to chew the word and spit it out again. "Would you let your mouth get cut to ribbons when allatime you could let yerself down easy without even scraping an elbow?"

"I don't know," I said. "Maybe I wouldn't know."

"Pride, nuts," Miniff said.

The doc had decided to send the Indian to the hospital for a couple of days. Nothing serious, just superficial hemorrhages, but he didn't want to take any chances.

I rushed out to make sure there were a couple of photographers on hand to catch the Indian being loaded into the ambulance. That was the kind of publicity that falls into your lap. You can't buy it and you can't dream it up. A small crowd of busybodies pressed around him. A couple called out, "Attaboy, Chief!" The Indian waved feebly. He must have been pretty sick from swallowing all that blood. In his own stupid, and unnecessarily brutal, martyrdom, he had won his victory. To us it had been just another little skirmish in the long campaign, but the Indian had given his blood in a cause neither Nick nor Miniff nor Vince could ever understand.

15

I didn't bother to go back to the dressing room. Danny had already drunk himself beyond companionship, and the realization that I had drifted into Vince's zone of intimacy had me back on my heels. I left the arena and started on a lonely prowl for a quiet place to buy myself a drink. But the first bar was too much of a crum-joint, the next too crowded, the third too desolate, and so it went until I found myself at the end of the short street that led right into the desert.

It was a mild night with millions of stars in the sky. The quiet took me away from the meaningless noise of many months, away from the bars and the jukes. I had to think. It was a long time since I had tried to think. In the fight game, I didn't think; I merely got bright ideas, hot flashes, used them, kept the wires burning. When I was a kid I used to raise turtles. I'd pick one out of its bowl and instantly it would draw in its head and feet and become a cold, dead lump. A moment before it had been a live, scurrying thing. I'd drop it down into another bowl and its head would pop out; its feet would shoot forth and it would be scrambling around again. It had no idea where the hell it was going, but moved with frantic, aimless haste, exactly as I had been dropped down and had kept going in the fight game. For some reason I couldn't understand, and only at odd, out-of-the-way moments protested against, automatically my brain would begin to spark, my legs would start working, and I'd be off on my feverish, pointless journey around and around my little bowl.

I put my hand to my mouth. I didn't know why for a moment, and then I remembered Chief Thunderbird. I had no chicken wire pressed up against my gums, but I was flicking myself with steel-tipped self-reproach in a last-minute effort to hang on to what was left of my pride. The events of the evening passed before me in all their tawdry melodrama. Nick, Vince, Danny, Doc, and Toro, that monstrous figure I had helped create. I had to get away from all of them; I had to rack up on this rat race before the trap was sprung. How had Beth described my job? Interesting at thirty, a blind alley at forty, a last refuge for a bum at fifty.

Beth's words. Beth and her damned New England conscience following me all the way out here into the desert. How much had I ever wanted Beth? Were we ever "meant for each other," like lovers on the screen? Had I ever wanted to marry Beth? Were my occasional marital tendencies merely the automatic reflection of Beth's need for permanence? The tentative, the casual relationship was all against her upbringing. Back of all her dissatisfaction with me was her dread of uncertainty, aimlessness and impermanence. Far away from her in a world she could never make herself know, I was rootless and rotting.

I wanted to hear Beth's voice again. I think I even missed the brisk impatience with which she liked to dismiss me. I walked back along the neon-glowing street until I came to a little saloon called Jerry's Joynt. I kept on walking past the bar to the phone booth in the rear. I gave the operator Beth's number. The circuits were busy; it would be a few minutes, she said. I went back to the bar to wait. All the customers seemed either silently morose or garrulously unhappy.

A fellow in cowboy boots down the bar was telling the bartender about our fight. "Best goddam fight I ever saw," he was saying. "The goddam bloodiest fight I ever saw. Boy, you shoulda seen it, Mike."

Next to me a seedy little drunk was confiding his domestic troubles to a half-listening truck driver with a union button on his cap.

I turned the volume way down on everybody and tried to listen to my own thoughts. What a setting for a play a place like this would make! Gorky's *Lower Depths* with an all-Las Vegas cast. Beth would approve of my thinking in terms of a play instead of a fight fix.

The phone was ringing. I rushed to answer it.

"Hello. On your call to New York City. The circuits are still busy. Do you wish me to call you again in twenty minutes?"

Another twenty minutes, another drink, another hard-luck story from the guy who didn't want to go home to his wife. I don't know why I drank. Drink makes some men talk honestly and well; it urges other to foolish lies. Drink slows my rhythm, depresses my nerves, releases fears that crawl inside me. I thought with envy of Toro sleeping up there at the hotel in serene ignorance, Man Mountain Molina, the Hyper-Pituitary of the Andes, who would remain asleep when he woke in the morning. As I thought of Toro I recalled, with that trick compartmentalization of the free-associating mind, a reading assignment in freshman English: John Milton's *Samson Agonistes,* the great giant in the hands of his enemies who had put out his eyes and exhibited him in chains for the amusement of the Philistine crowds.

But how could Samson's plight be compared to Toro's, with all those stumblebums flopping on their flattened faces for him? What danger was he in? Danger? A red light flashed in my mind. I was seized by an inescapable foreboding, and yet, for the life of me, I could not imagine what could possibly happen to him. Was that red light really in my mind or was it just the flashing red tubing outside the window spelling out the words "Jerry's Joynt"?

The bell in the booth was ringing insistently. I lurched toward it and finally had the receiver off the hook. Yes, yes, this was Mr. Lewis. Could I have my party now?

With the door closed I could hardly breathe in the booth. The closeness made me dizzy, made the walls float around me, around and around in my head.

"Hello, *hello,* darling."

"Hello, Eddie. What's been happening to you?"

"I know, I know. I've been meaning to write you . . . But this has been such a rat race . . . I started a long letter to you in L.A. . . . ."

I didn't need television to see Beth shaking her head on the other end of the phone, half amused, half resigned.

"Eddie, sometimes I think you just want to be a character."

"How's everything been, Beth? You could have written me too, you know."

"Things have been awfully calm, Eddie. Nothing much has been happening. I've just been working and coming home early. Doing a lot of reading."

"You weren't home reading the Saturday I called you up at 2 A.M."

"Oh, I was probably away for the weekend. I've been going out to Martha's a lot."

Martha was a roommate of Beth's at Smith who had made quite a splash as a fashion designer. Martha had never been very subtle about what she thought of me. I knew it wasn't going to help my cause any to have Beth out at Martha's.

"Martha's finally decided to give up her job and get married. An awfully nice boy from Brookline. You wouldn't know him. She actually wants to settle down and raise a family."

"What the hell are we talking about Martha for? How about us, baby? All this time away from each other and we haven't even started talking about you and me."

"Is there anything new to say about us, Eddie?"

"Well, I've missed you like all hell. But you're right, I guess that isn't very new."

"I've missed you too, Eddie. I really have. I wish I didn't, though. I feel it's kind of a weakness of mine . . . to want you any more."

"Now listen, Beth. Why make a problem out of it? We're in each other's hair for good. Why don't you relax and admit it?"

"You sound awfully sober. Are you sober tonight, Eddie?"

"More than sober, baby. I've been thinking. This fight we had tonight just about gave me a bellyful. I'm just about ready to tell Nick to find himself another boy."

"Just about ready, Eddie? Eddie, aren't you ever going to *be* ready?"

"Sure, sure. I'm ready, but you know how Nick is. You just don't go up to him and quit. You've got to ease yourself out."

"But you've been easing yourself out ever since I've known you."

"Just wait, Beth. I'll prove it to you. I ought to be back in a few months. Wait for me, Beth."

"Wait for Nick, you mean. Oh, Eddie, walk out on him. Please. It's easy, believe me."

"I will. I'm going to. But I've got to feel my way. You don't understand. I'll need every nickel I can get out of it. Then . . ."

"All right, Eddie. Get all the nickels you can. Keep on kidding yourself."

"For Christ's sake, Beth, what else can I do? Just wait and you'll see."

"I don't know what else you can do. I honestly don't. Let me know when you've had enough. Good-bye, Eddie."

She hung up while I was saying "Good-bye." I pulled the folding door of the booth open and stepped back into the hubbub of Jerry's Joynt. I moved over to the bar to have another drink. Maybe I shouldn't have called Beth. Maybe I should have gone straight to Nick to turn in my uniform, climb down off the gravy train and head east. Maybe I should have talked only to myself and made up my mind, once for all, to do what I had to do. Well, after all, there were a few things still to be said to Nick, and this was the time to get them off my chest before making my getaway.

The party at Nick's suite looked like a Cecil DeMille production of how modern robber barons entertain themselves. Coming in cold out of the loneliness of my one-man jag I had an impression of big, prosperous thickskinned mammals of the masculine variety laughing loudly from expansive bellies, of women who were Aphrodites of the make-up box, all eyebrow pencil, eyeshadow, lipstick, hair-dos and perfume that incited you to conventional passions. Floating toward me, cool and ladylike, was Ruby, wearing a black tulle evening gown and a Spanish comb in her hair, sensual in a removed and stately way. Ruby's eyes had a strange luster and she walked with a telltale but successful effort at steadiness.

"Well, it's about time you showed up, Eddie," she said, and she kissed me affectionately on the cheek. "Come on over and I'll pour you a drink."

Looking at Ruby and then hearing her talk never failed to surprise me. She was like a common show girl who walks on stage into a high-born, glamorous part, but for whom the dramatist has neglected to write any lines.

"We were all hoping you'd bring Toro," Ruby said.

"Toro's a country boy," I said. "He needs his rest. This stuff won't do him any good, Ruby. He's confused enough as it is."

She looked up at me, but I wasn't sure whether she got it. That was another thing about Ruby. She could look at you steadily with those enlarged dark pupils in what would appear to be a reaction of profound intelligence, but it was only an elaborately convincing charade of intelligence.

"He's such a sweet boy," she said. "Takes his religion so seriously. I just love to go with him Sundays. Honestly we can all learn a lot from people with simple faith like that."

"Yeah," I said, reaching for my drink, "I guess we can. Where's Nick, Ruby? I've got something to tell him."

"Over there," she indicated with her head. "With that fat fella in the corner."

Nick had a glass in his hand too, but he must have been nursing it all evening. Nick was too smart and too organized; his pattern was woven too tightly for promiscuous drinking. Nick drank when he needed a drink to put someone at ease. Now in the small, sloppy, unraveling hours of the morning he managed to remain remarkably dapper, sober and wide-awake. His tailor-made, sharkskin suit fitted him almost too perfectly, and his lean, closely shaven dark face seemed even sharper than ever in contrast to the bleary, sagging countenances of his guests.

"Hello, Shakespeare," he said, glad to see me.

"Nick," I said, "I want to talk to you."

"So do I, kid," he said. "Let's go out on the balcony for a couple of minutes."

He stood on the balcony with his legs apart, blowing smoke into the night.

"I wish these jerks would start clearing out of here," he said.

He offered me a cigar, but I refused it. I had been smoking Nick's cigars for years and blowing smoke rings to spell Nick Latka or Toro Molina or whatever he had on his mind.

"Nick, I . . ." I tried to begin.

"I know what you're going to say," Nick interrupted. "And I'm ahead of you. You think you ought to have a raise. Well, you're not going to get a fight out of me. You've done a hell of a job, Eddie. You actually have the public believing this bum's a great fighter. I'm a bullish sort of a guy, but I didn't think the fans would buy him so fast. You been away from the East, so you don't know what's been happening. We're ready to get out of this chicken-feed circuit. Charley Spitz in Cleveland says he's got five thousand on the line for Toro to fight anybody—Joe Floppola. The customers just want to see him. In Chi, we can get a fifteen-thousand guarantee against forty percent of the gross for him to go with Red Donovan. Red's manager, Frank Conti, owes me a favor. Then with a win over Donovan, who's beaten some pretty fair boys, Uncle Mike will be ready to bring us into the Garden. Quinn was out to see Mike already and they talk about putting Toro in with Lennert two months after the Lennert-Stein fight Thursday night."

"But you own 'em both," I said. "Isn't it bad business to let one eliminate the other, when . . ."

"I'm still ahead of you," Nick said. "Don't forget I haven't got nothing to do with Toro yet, officially. I've still got Vince and Danny fronting for me. So after Toro gets a win over Lennert, Gus retires—which he wants to do anyway—and you announce that Quinn and me have bought up Toro's contract from Vince and Danny. Could anything be simpler?"

"But Gus has always been on the level," I said. "Gus never went into the bag for anybody in his life. What makes you think you could get Gus to . . ."

"I already been through all that with Gus just before I came out," Nick said. "Gus is thirty-three next month. He's been in the ring fifteen years. He's not thinking of his career any more. What he wants is a couple of real money fights, enough for him to take things easy the rest of his life, good investments, a couple of good annuities, so his kids will be all right. We got his financial setup all figured out to his satisfaction and Mrs. Lennert's. You know, she's always been a little sore at me for talking him into coming back. She wanted to keep him in that hamburger stand of his, even if he was making peanuts. Well, we showed her how in two fights Gus can make himself around a hundred thousand dollars. With Stein in the ball park, Uncle Mike figures to gross around four hundred G's, with Gus getting twenty-five percent. That's a hundred divided between us and Jimmy. I decided on account of it's Gus, and he's racking up we'll leave him take two-thirds without deductions. That's around sixty-five thousand for openers. Then with Toro in the Garden we ought to do a hundred 'n fifty G's easy. On account of

Toro's getting such a build-up from knocking over Lennert, I figure he ought to be satisfied with ten percent, which puts Lennert's cut at fifty-five thousand, leaving Gus around thirty-six G's."

A couple of times I tried to break in on this overwhelming flow of grosses and percentages with the beautiful speech I had worked out on my way over to Nick's after my talk with Beth. But this was like trying to fight an Armstrong—leaning on you, crowding you, never giving you a chance. It was no use. Nick's adding-maching mind kept right on computing each fight in dollars and cents.

"So sixty-five and thirty-six, Gus has got his hundred thousand fish. The win over Gus makes Toro a logical opponent for Buddy Stein and then we're really in the tall grass, with a million-dollar gate, if we play it smart. So, Eddie, I want you to know I realize what you mean to this deal. Of course, five percent of Toro's slice of a million bucks—if we make it—that isn't Chiclets. But meanwhile I'm putting you down for one-five-o per week, and we'll push it to two hundred right after the Lennert fight."

Six hundred a month, that was a respectable improvement over my old job on the *Trib,* and with Lennert and Stein coming up after Cleveland and Chicago, Toro could stand to gross around $250,000 for the year, which would mean a nice little $12,500 on top of my regular $7,500. $20,000! How many guys in America would throw up a job that averaged them four hundred bucks a week just because the job pinched their souls a little bit? Hell, even Beth could see the wisdom of that. And it wasn't as if I were mortgaging myself to Nick for life. Why, another couple of years of this, with maybe a hike to $25,000 the second year, and I'd have enough of those little green coupons to take things easy, get that play out and wrap it up, if I feel like it. And meanwhile, think of all the valuable material I was getting. Why, my plans weren't changed, my integrity was still intact, I was just racking up gradually instead of all at once, like Gus Lennert, who figured to take an awful beating from Stein for his sixty-five thousand, coast through the Toro fix for an easy thirty-six and then live out his days on a farm like a country squire. I was just thinking like a moon-struck freshman when I was out there on the edge of town deciding to blow Nick off.

This wasn't selling out. This was just playing it smart.

16

With Dynamite Jones and Chief Thunderbird finally salted away in the record books as early knockout victims of Toro Molina, we thought we needed an easy one. So for Denver Toro's opponent was a "Negro protégé of Sam Langford's who has faced the best in his division." Of course, he turned out to be our own Georgie Blount.

But I had to start earning my dough again when a local reporter—another Al Leavitt—came up with the discovery of George's identity. That is what makes a press agent's ride so nerve-racking. Just when you think you're freewheeling down a four-lane highway, some jerk tosses a handful of tacky truths in your path.

But a smart guy takes trouble in stride and puts it to work for him. So right away I gave out a story, capitalizing on the fact that George had been a sparring partner who had had a row with Toro when he claimed that Toro had knocked him out when they were only supposed to be having a light workout.

> No ordinary spar-boy (I worked my plant into the leading Denver sports column), Blount has stood up to some of the outstanding heavyweights in the country, including Gus Lennert, who won a close, split decision over the Harlem Panther. So in an unprecedented act of insubordination for a sparring partner, George challenged the Giant of the Andes to go into a room with him, lock the doors and have at it in a regular old-fashioned knock-down dragout. The Molina board of strategy frowned on this impromptu (and unprofitable) rivalry, however, and so tomorrow night Denver fight fans will be treated to the privilege of sitting in on the first grudge match in the Argentine Behemoth's spectacular American career of seven straight knockouts over such formidable opposition as Cowboy Coombs, Dynamite Jones and Chief Thunderbird, undisputed champion of the Southwest until the Man Mountain stopped him in Las Vegas recently in three torrid rounds.

At the weigh-in, the day of the fight, George, doing his best to play his little part for the Latka Repertory Theatre, wouldn't shake hands with Toro.

We had told Toro that George had quit his job with us because he really thought he could beat him, but even so Toro could not comprehend George's discourtesy. "Why he no shake hands?" he asked. "George my friend, no?"

It takes real talent to lose as convincingly as George did that night. Nobody Toro had fought had shown him off to such good advantage. From the way Toro moved his shoulders and set his feet, George could tell just when Toro's punches were going to start. All he had to do was move in toward the blows instead of going away from them, as he would have ordinarily. The force of his body smashing against Toro's fist made a sound that could be heard all over the arena. Nobody hearing that impact could doubt Toro's prowess as a puncher. And when George fought back, he was careful to avoid that big glass jaw that was such an open and tempting target.

In the fourth round George exposed his belly to a particularly resounding wallop from Toro and permitted himself to be counted out. Magnanimously forgiving in victory, Toro insisted on helping George back to his corner, where, in a gesture right down the fans' cornball alley, he offered him his hand. There was something almost mystical about Toro's ability to perform just the right gesture without realizing how well it fitted into our act. It was an old plot, but the fans, going for the grudge match with their mass talent for self-hypnosis, bought the happy ending just as if it were Saturday night at the Double Feature.

Relieved to see that George had recovered so quickly, Toro waved to the cheering crowd and jumped down from the ring. George followed him, moving with his familiar, deliberate ease, an ambiguous smile on his massive face.

When we pulled out of Denver, George was left behind to make it look kosher. A couple of days later he caught up with us in K.C., where we were getting ready to knock off another tanker.

"George, how did Toro feel to you in that fight?" I asked.

George smiled with his mouth, but his eyes kept their seriousness. "He just can't bang," he said. "And when a heavyweight can be reached and he can't bang . . ." George shook his head. "You better watch the big fella, Eddie. Watch him close, man, before something real bad happens."

But the only thing that happened in K.C., in Cleveland where we filled the Municipal Stadium, and in Chicago where we did close to $80,000 with Red Donovan, was to add three more to our string of knockouts and sign the papers for the big fight with Lennert in the Garden.

Toro's cut for the eighteen minutes of alleged fighting must have been around $20,000. But all he had been seeing of it were the 50's and C-notes that Vince came up with whenever Toro put the zing on him. After the Chicago fight, though, Toro smelled money. "You give now, I send my papa for build big house," he told Vince. Vince reached into his pocket, pulled out a wad and peeled off five hundred-dollar bills.

"Any time you need dough, just ask me," he said with unusual affability.

Next morning when Toro and I were walking down Michigan Boulevard, we passed the Lake Shore National Bank.

"*El banco grande!*" Toro said.

"One of the biggest," I said.

"I go in," Toro said.

"What are you going to do, put your five in the bank?"

"I come back pronto," Toro answered.

When he came out he had a fistful of Argentine bills. Over two thousand pesos. "Look how much money," he held it up to me happily: "This feel like real money."

The day we got to New York, Toro achieved immortality—at least for one week. He made the cover of *Life*. And if this wasn't honor enough, he was urged to come up on the floor and take a bow when Joe E. Lewis spotted him at a ringside table at the Copa with Vince and me. My job was a breeze now. I didn't have to scrounge any more. Reporters came looking for us. Even when Runyon devoted a full column to ridiculing the whole Man-Mountain build-up, ending by describing Toro as the Ghastly Gawk of the Andes, the undisputed Side-Show Champion of America, it didn't really put the whammy on us. In America a knock is just a plug that lets itself in the back door. Nick had guessed right, as usual. Toro's freakish size, plus the knockout record we were compiling for him, was tapping the public's incredible credulity.

Just before he was ready to leave for Pompton Lakes with Vince, Danny, Doc and George to start training for the Lennert fight, a white, special-body Lincoln phaeton appeared at the hotel entrance. The afternoon before, when he was supposed to be resting, Toro had sneaked off and ordered this little number at a mere five G's. Apparently he wasn't such a meatball that he couldn't find a way to get around Vince's reluctance to declare a dividend. It wasn't in his nature to learn how to throw a left hook without telegraphing it, but it hadn't taken him long to find out how to join the great American fraternity whose password is "charge it."

When he heard what the grunt for this white job was, Vince wanted to send it right back to the floor. Toro pouted and protested, "My car, my car, I buy!"

"Let him have have it," I told Vince. "Why get the guy sore over a lousy five thousand bucks when the real dough's starting to roll in? Leo can take it off the income tax, for transportation. And meanwhile a white Lincoln is publicity."

So Toro drove off to Pompton Lakes with his portable radio, his entourage, and Benny Mannix at the wheel of the Lincoln phaeton. As I stood on the curb in front of our hotel watching them lose themselves in the morning traffic, a phrase popped into my head, the last line of that Wolcott Gibbs' profile on Luce in Timestyle, "Where it will end, knows God!"

I had been back in town two days already without seeing Beth. Her excuses seemed to be on the level, and yet they were the sort she would have found some way to finesse in the days when we were clicking together.

With all that time behind us, I hadn't thought I could slip back so quickly into the old role of hopeful suitor. I even found myself sending her flowers all over again.

On the morning of the third day I called Beth and said, "Look, I'm going nuts. When am I going to see you?"

Something in my voice must have reached her, for she said, almost too calmly to please me, "How about right now? Come on over and have breakfast, if you like."

On my way over I picked up a box of candy. It was a silly thing to do. What seemed more sensible was to stop at a bar on Sixth Avenue for a courage-cup.

Beth opened the door and said, "Hi, Eddie," in her direct and friendly way. Her attitude seemed crisp rather than cool. But she had never been demonstrative until the moment of demonstration itself. Like most women, she had a way of setting her own emotional climate.

"Make yourself comfortable, Eddie. I've got to rush back and save my toast. I still burn it!"

She was wearing smartly tailored beige lounging pajamas that made her figure look stylishly, rather than merely, thin. I followed her through the book-lined room with the familiar modern furniture, past the combination radio-phonograph whose illuminated dial had been the only glow of light in the darkness of our first night. Alone with Beth again after all those uncertain months, I could feel growing in me the desire to break down her reserve, to force her back to the spontaneous response I had drawn from her before. But even surrounded by these erotic landmarks, the radio, the studio couch, the thick yellow rug, I had the strange sensation that I was feeling all this for the first time. I felt the same excitement, the same longing, the same curiosity about her as in the beginning.

She served breakfast on a little table by the window in the kitchenette, with eggs boiled just three minutes the way she knew I liked them, crisp bacon and the buttered toast that she always had to scrape. As we sat there together I wished more than ever before that this could be every day. Something—I still couldn't give it a name—had blocked my setting this up on a permanent basis when it was still in my hands. What had stopped me? At this moment marrying Beth seemed like the most natural thing in the world. I am going to count slowly up to ten and then I'm going to make the first sober proposal of my life, I thought.

"Well, how was your trip, Eddie? Was it fun, was it interesting?"

You mind-reading, subject-changing vixen, I thought, jabbing me off balance just when I'm getting set to throw my best Sunday punch.

"Oh, you know," I said. "Same old squirrel cage."

"But you love it," she said. "Why don't you admit it instead of acting as if you were too good for it, as if you were just slumming?"

"For Christ sake, Beth, let's not start that again."

"Okay, I'm just getting awfully tired of all these people knocking what they're doing but keeping right at it year after year."

"This is a goddam serious way to begin a day."

"Don't you remember?" she said, smiling to take the curse off it, "I'm always more serious before I've had my first cup of coffee."

"I remember," I said.

She looked at me sympathetically. She had never looked at me that way before and I resented it. What if I just got up and grabbed her the way I used to do? Some atavistic conviction that male force could prevail where everything else had failed must have driven me on.

"Eddie, what are you doing?"

Almost from the moment it began, it ceased to be instinctive. It had already become a self-conscious effort, but somehow it couldn't be stopped. It seemed as if I had to bull it through, even though I already felt the terrible futility of this approach.

"Eddie! For God's sake!"

"Beth—darling—please . . ."

"Stop it, Eddie! Stop!"

She was pushing me away. The strength in her mind and in her body was holding me off. My own body felt heavy and slothful in defeat. I felt limp and spent, the body hunger gone as completely as if it had been appeased instead of rudely frustrated.

"The coffee," Beth said. "The coffee's boiling over."

She brought two cups back to the table. I felt her accidentally brushing against my shoulder as she set mine down and I edged away.

"This is the moment I hate," Beth said as she sat down. "The messy time."

I didn't say anything. I felt terribly angry with her. And yet I was conscious of being unreasonable. After all, she wasn't one of Shirley's girls.

It was typical of Beth to pitch the conversation to its true level, to say exactly what she meant about exactly what had happened.

"Eddie, I've had plenty of time to think it over. Nights when I missed you—I'm terribly used to you, in lots of ways—almost afraid to start over again with somebody else—and yet there were days when—I might as well tell you this, I've been straight with you on everything else—days when it was a relief to have you out of my life—It wasn't getting anywhere."

"When I called you from Las Vegas," I said, "I wanted to marry you. I've always wanted to marry you, Beth."

"Yes, I think you have, Eddie. But not ever enough to do it. I always had the feeling if it were going to happen I'd have to sit down, pick the day and make you go down for the license. Marriage is an old-fashioned thing, Eddie. I guess even a gal like me, who's been on her own for years, wants someone to come along and just carry her off."

The coffee had a sour taste. I always used to kid Beth about her coffee. "So this is the . . . blow-off?"

"Eddie, you know I—hate those words. Not the words themselves, but what they stand for. Why are you afraid of being soft—ashamed to show what you really feel for people—afraid to try anything better than you're doing—for fear you'll be a flop? The play, for instance . . ."

"I've been thinking about that play. I've got some of the scenes worked out in my head, I . . ."

"Eddie, I hate to say this—it probably sounds so smug—but you're never going to do that play. You've been telling me scenes from that play from the first night we met. You've been talking it right out of existence. You won't finish that play any more than you'll quit the fight business. You just haven't the courage to do it."

"Thanks," I said. "What is this, tell-off day?"

"I guess it did come out a lot clearer than I expected," Beth said, apologetically. "I've been mulling it over so long. But I wish we could have worked it out, Eddie. I wish we could have. You know that, don't you?"

"Sure," I said. "This is how the story ends, can't we be friends. It's been set to music."

I wanted to call the wisecrack back, wanted to show her I was bigger than that, wished I could think of something to say that would send me out of there a generous, understanding citizen. But I didn't seem to have it in me. I went out with the smallest, meanest, foul ball of a parting shot I could think of. "Well, I suppose Herbert Ageton is a better bet at that. After all, he's had a hit on Broadway."

"Oh, damn you, Eddie, damn you!" Beth cried out, and her eyes were suddenly full of angry tears. "You're such a heel! What makes you such a heel? Eddie, you of all people! You make me so God-damn mad sometimes."

I felt exhausted, I felt exhausted with the effort of having all these years tried to keep my marriage to Beth in suspension. I never wanted to let go of it and I never wanted to face the consequences of holding on. But finally, now, when I was forced to let go, where did that leave me? Maybe I was lucky to be rid of her, always harping at me, trying to reform me, make me quit the fight game. I wanted to get out of town. I didn't want to stay in the same town with her, even a real big town like N.Y. Real big. I knew better than to say "real big." I knew better than a lot of things. But it was easier. Danny and Vince and Doc and George, they said "real big." Why should I be any different, why should I be any better, what was so special about me that I should look down on those guys? But I did look down on them, and why shouldn't I? I knew more, I understood more, I felt more. Who else in this crowd of bums, lushes and grifters worried about Toro, wondered what he was feeling, saw him in any real perspective? Who noticed when he was lonely, bothered to walk around town with him, tried to give him some guidance? And yet Beth called me a heel! She had the nerve to call me a heel!

I took a train out to the camp. I felt better as soon as I got off. I was back in my own world, or at least in a world I felt equal to.

Benny Mannix met me at the station. His venal, unattractive puss made me feel at home. "How's everything going, Benny?"

"T'ings ain't so bad, kid. We got a nice setup here."

"How's Danny behaving himself?"

"Danny, he's kinda tapering off. Oney had a pint so far today."

"Sounds like he's almost on the wagon. And how's my boy getting along? Toro."

Benny shrugged. "Da bum tries, you gotta give 'im dat. He didn't look too bad wit' Chuck Gussman dis afternoon. That's this new light-heavy we got in from Detroit who fights kinda on the style of Lennert."

It was just after dinner when I got there, and Danny was sitting out on the porch with Doc and some of the other sparring partners. Danny was reading the *Morning Telegraph*. He looked almost sober.

"Still trying to beat 'em, Danny?"

Danny grinned. "I gave that up a long time ago, laddie. I'm just along for the ride. But this Shasta Rose"—he tapped the racing form—"if she don't run away with the Maryland at Laurel tomorrow I'm gonna . . ."

"Turn in your chips and quit," I interrupted.

Danny shook his head and smiled. ". . . throw these lousy form sheets away and play my own hunches."

"He couldn't do any worse if he picked 'em blindfold," Doc said. "He's the bookie's friend, Danny is."

Everybody laughed at Danny. At a training camp it seems as if everybody is waiting to laugh at everybody else. There was a dice game starting in the parlor and Doc, Gussman and the other boys on the porch joined it.

"That Gussman, he knows how to handle himself for a kid," Danny said as the new light-heavy went in. "Kinda reminds me of Jimmy Slattery, when he was gettin' started, a regular Fancy Dan, not quite as fast as Jimmy maybe, but he's got natural ring sense. If I could take him in hand 'n teach him to sharpen up his punching a little . . ."

Danny sighed and looked off into the gathering dusk. "Boy, to come into New York with a real fighter again, to walk down 49th Street and have all the guys come up and say, 'Saw your boy take that guy last night, Danny. You really got yourself something there . . .'"

"Why don't you sign this Gussman?" I said. "Why don't you bring him along?"

"What's the percentage, laddie?" Danny said, dead-voiced again. "If the guy's too brittle and he don't work out, I've wasted a lot of time. And if he looks good, Nick moves in and takes over, and pretty soon the kid has to throw one or he wins one he don't deserve. The hell with that. Nick's got me by the short hairs, laddie. Sure it's my own fault, but when did that ever make a guy like it any better?"

"Anyway," I said, "I'm glad to see you looking so sharp."

"Yeah," he said, "I'd like to win this one. I'd really like to beat that Lennert."

This had been Nick's idea, to bring Danny back to his job by not letting him know the Lennert thing was in the bag. Danny knew Lennert hadn't done any business before, so it wasn't too difficult to convince him. And since he had never learned as much about the fight business as he had about fighters, he bought the line that Nick didn't care who won this time because he owned them both. Danny was a sucker for most of the fighters he had handled, but Lennert was the exception. Lennert was a businessman, not a miser exactly, just careful about his money. If some old pug came along whom Lennert had licked and put the arm on him for a sawbuck or two, Lennert had been known to stall on the ground that the guy was a boozer who would just drink the dough away. But Danny didn't care what the guy did with the dough, figuring it was only money and that was none of his business. That was the difference between them. When Lennert made his comeback, he figured he knew as much about conditioning and strategy as Danny and insisted on being his own boss. Pretty pigheaded, Lennert was. When he came back he made no bones about being in it purely for the high dollar and not to take any unnecessary chances. Once in a while, for instance, Danny would want Gus to go in and carry the fight to an opponent whom Gus would be content to stay away from and counterpunch, winning an easy decision on points without extending himself when he might have been able to do something more spectacular. That wasn't honest prize fighting, in Danny's book, but then, even though one would never know it from some of the things he had had to do, Danny had a sense of purity, of real nobility about the game that an ordinary pro like Lennert wouldn't understand. Lennert went in for boxing the way he ran his diner in Trenton, not robbing anybody, just cutting them as close as he could without stepping over the line.

"You don't really think Toro could take Lennert if they're both sent in to win?" I said.

"Don't be too sure, laddie," Danny said. "Let's not kid ourselves, Gus hasn't got much any more. That beating he took from Stein didn't do him any good."

"I never thought he could take that much any more," I said.

Lennert had looked like his old self against Stein until he began to run out of gas. From the seventh on, Stein had had him down in every round, but couldn't keep him there. The referee was just about ready to stop it when the fight ended. Lennert was still on his feet, but no longer able to defend himself. He had collapsed on his way to his dressing room.

"He showed a hell of a lot more guts than I thought he had," I said.

"That was business," Danny said. "He was figuring how much bigger the Molina fight would draw if Stein didn't knock him out. So he let Stein beat his brains in, to make an extra ten or fifteen G's. That's Gus. I know him. He don't care about being a hero. All he's worried about is how much dough he can lay aside to retire on."

"You think Stein really slowed him up?"

"I saw him the next day, when he came up to the office to pick up his money," Danny said. "I thought he was acting kind of funny, sort of slow-like, like something was hurting him in his head or something."

"I heard Stein hit him so hard Gus cracked his head on the floor," I said. "Gus is a pretty old man to take those pot-shots in the head the way Stein throws them."

"He's lucky Toro can't hit," Danny said. "I guess that's why he picked him for the bow-out. He figures Molina can't do any more 'n lean on him once in a while or maybe stamp on his toes with those size fifteens. But believe it or not, laddie, I think I got Toro working a little better. I been spending a lot of time with him this week. I got him throwing a pretty fair right uppercut, and he's getting so he don't just wave that left hand like it was a flag."

"Danny, you could teach a wooden Indian to box."

"Well, at least a wooden Indian wouldn't buckle every time you tap him on the jaw." Danny laughed. "I think I got a pretty good defense worked out for Toro's jaw this time. Only if he wants to look any good in there, he's gotta pay a little more attention to his training." Danny rubbed the back of his hand across his cheek nervously. "That's why I'm glad you came down, laddie."

"I'm just the word man," I said. "What have I got to do with it?"

"You can talk to him. Maybe in his own language he'll listen better."

"Sure I'll talk to him. What do you want me to talk to him about?"

"About Ruby. You better talk to him about Ruby."

"Ruby? What goes with Ruby?"

"I don't know," Danny said, "but I got ideas."

"You mean Ruby and Toro? No, Danny, I can't buy that. Why, Toro doesn't know enough . . ."

"How much do you have to know, laddie?"

"Jesus, are you sure, Danny? Toro is no intellectual giant, but I didn't think he'd be dumb enough to fool around with what belongs to Nick."

"Well, all I know is he's been driving over there in that goddam Lincoln of his every chance he gets. I been letting Benny take him out for rides. You know he's worse than a kid with a new toy with that thing. Well, Benny told me the big sap's been slipping him dough to drive over to Green Acres. And Toro goes inside and doesn't come out for an hour. Well, I don't know, maybe I got a dirty mind, but if Toro isn't getting in, Ruby's not the girl I've heard she is."

"Jesus!" I said. "I hope you're wrong. I'd hate to think what'd happen to Toro if Nick ever catches onto that one."

"It's a funny thing," Danny said. "You'd think a guy as smart as Nick would keep a little closer check on a broad like that."

"They all got their weak spots, the smartest of 'em," I said. "And, for Nick, I guess it's believing Ruby's a real high-class dame."

"Well, you better talk to him," Danny said. "Even if Nick doesn't catch, that kind of business won't do him any good in there with Lennert. And I want to beat Lennert. I just want to see if I can do it with this lunk."

Doc came out on the porch. When he smiled he did not stop looking sad, but merely superimposed the smile over the permanently tragic lines of his face. "How about a little two-handed pinochle, Danny?" he said. "You might as well lose it to me as to the books."

"Don't gimme that," Danny said. "I'm the champion pinochle player of Pompton Lakes."

"Since when could a Mick ever beat a Jew-boy at pinochle?" Doc said, and winked at me.

I sat on the porch alone for a while, half listening to the guys inside talking to their dice. I thought of Toro and George walking out there on the back road and wondered what they found to say to each other, Toro with his pidgin English and his child's mind and George making his own music deep in his throat. "There it is, boys, the hard way!" someone called out, with the gloating laughter of the triumphant. I was tempted to go in and fade that guy. He sounded like the kind of fellow who took so much pleasure in winning that he pressed himself too far.

But I supposed I should wait and talk to Toro. Goddamit, since when was I Toro's keeper? What business was it of mine whether he hung the old horns on Nick? That's just it; it was my business. It wasn't my inclination; it wasn't my personal interest; it was simply my job, my five percent interest to see that Toro stayed away from trouble.

"*¿Qué tal, qué tal, amigo? ¡Buenas noches!*"

Toro had loomed up on me, his gums showing in a clownish smile. I hadn't realized how glad he would be to see me. He seemed actually relieved to have me back. I hadn't thought anything about it, but this had been the first time we had been separated since Acosta left. Toro didn't speak enough English to have a real conversation with the others, and anyway those who bothered with him at all treated him with the belittling kindness one might bestow on a trained dog. We talked for a while about the little things, the quality of the food at the camp, the peace of the countryside after our hectic tour, how hard Danny and Doc were working him, the album of pictures of him in fighting poses I had promised to prepare for his family. In a little while Benny came out with the message, "Doc says it's time fuh yuh tuh hit da sack."

"I'll go up and sit with you while you're getting ready for bed," I said.

It was a large, sparsely furnished room with a comfortable-looking old-fashioned wrought-iron double bed. As soon as he came in Toro turned his radio on with the volume up. An elocutionist for the NAM was talking about the unique opportunities for self-made men who believed in the American Way. But Toro didn't seem to care what it was, as long as it was loud. I wandered over to his bureau. There was a pile of papers under his comb and brush. I picked them up and looked at them. They were quick pencil sketches that Toro had drawn, primitive in perspective but with surprising force and humor. The first was obviously Vince, all neck and fat in the face with little eyes and a large cruel mouth. The next one was Danny, with an exaggerated flattened nose and with X's for eyes. He was bent over a bar. The next was Nick, looking considerably more hard-boiled and sinister than I had thought him. It made me realize for the first time what Toro must have thought of him. Toro had always seemed perfectly docile in his presence, as if he had no feelings in the matter. But the sketches seemed to bespeak a resentment, even a kind of understanding of these men that Toro either had hidden or was unable to express. No matter how crude these sketches were, they showed a certain limited talent that no one would have expected from this lumbering giant. But the artistic quality of the next picture was considerably lower. It was a schoolboy's amateurish and sentimental attempt to draw a beautiful woman. The woman was obviously meant to be Ruby, though a younger, more slender, more ethereal and completely romanticized version of Ruby. The snood she wore around her head, instead of creating an effect of the exotic as Ruby actually intended it, gave her in Toro's picture a spiritual, almost Madonna quality. It was clearly a work of love, marred by the mawkishness that such works often have.

When Toro caught me looking at it, I thought he was going to be angry, but he was only embarrassed. There seemed to be no anger in Toro. All the violence in his nature had shot out into big bones, into girth and heft.

"You draw very nicely, Toro."

Toro shrugged.

"Where did you learn to draw so well?"

"In my school when I am a little boy. My teacher show me."

I held up the sketch of Vince. "This one very good," I said, finding myself mimicking Toro's basic English. Then I looked at the one that was supposed to be Ruby. "This not so good."

"So beautiful as the Señora I cannot make," Toro said.

"And if you know what's good for you, you won't try to make the Señora either," I said.

"No me comprende," Toro said.

He wasn't just an overgrown lummox now; he was all the natives I had ever known who retreated into the convenient dodge of not understanding the language. "No me comprende," they say, and they look at you with what is clearly designed to be their most stupid expression, though their eyes betray them with a faintly mocking defiance.

"You'll comprende all right if Nick catches you fooling around with his wife," I said.

A deep hurt came into Toro's eyes. "No fool around. The Señora my friend. She treat me very nice. She like talk with me. She no laugh at the bad English. With the Señora I am not, not . . . solitario."

"Lonely," I said. "Why should you be? Who the hell is lonely when they're with the Señora?"

Toro's large, passive eyes brightened with resentment. "No es verdad, no es verdad," he broke into Spanish. "No one else is with the Señora. The Señora herself has told that to me."

"Listen, you stupid bastard," I said, "I'm trying to help you, the way Luis would have tried to help you. Help you, help you! Understand?"

Toro's face became sullen and unfriendly. "Luis no help. Luis no friend. Luis leave me here alone. He sell me like a novillo to the butcher. Only the Señora, she treat me like a man." Only he used the word *hombre,* which has a special ring of pride in it.

"That's what I'm afraid of," I said. "That she'll treat you like too much of a man."

"The Señora my friend," Toro insisted. "The Señora and you and George my only friend."

And none of them can do you any good, I thought. Your only friend is the man who puts you back in the wine-barrel business in Santa Maria before it's too late.

17

The next afternoon, while Toro was pawing his way through his workouts with George, Gussman and a couple of other obliging carcasses, I decided to run over to Green Acres and take a personal reading on Ruby. Driving up the long, winding approach to the house I passed the chauffeur, Jock Mahoney, in an old turtleneck sweater and cap, looking as if he had just run right off a page of Frederick Lewis Allen's *Only Yesterday.* Jogging at his side was a tall young fellow in gym pants and a dirty sweat shirt.

"What you doing, Jock, getting in shape for Delaney?"

Mahoney grinned good-naturedly. "Delaney wouldn't be so tough now. But, Jesus, fifteen years ago . . ." He shook his head and smiled at his memory of a bad thirty minutes. "I thought I was back in my old man's saloon, fighting three-four guys at once."

The young man doing roadwork with Jock had a fresh, neatly chiseled face that would have been handsome enough for Hollywood. But its symmetry was marred by an expression of disdainful self-confidence. "Eddie Lewis—meet the kid nephew, Jackie Ryan," Jock said.

"Come on, Jock, for Chris'sake, ya want me to catch cold?" Ryan demanded.

"Okay, okay. You jog on, I'll catch up to yuh," Jock said affably. He looked after him proudly. "He's gonna be the best fighter we ever had in the family. You shoulda seen him win the Golden Glove welterweight champeenship of Joisey. Nick's got him on the payroll. Just wants him tuh fill out 'n develop for a year. He's a comer, Mr. Lewis. But, Jesus, he's a hotheaded young sonofabitch. Thinks he knows all the answers awready. He ain't a bad kid when you get to know him, a course. And a comin' champ if I ever seen one. If I c'n just keep him away from the broads. You know how them kids are when they're seventeen—too big for their britches."

I started to inch the car forward. "Well, take care, Jock. The kids okay?"

"They'll be beatin' up their old man any day," he called after me happily as I drove off. Ryan didn't acknowledge my wave as I passed.

I found Ruby out on the chaise longue on the sunporch, reading a book. She was wearing ornate lounging pajamas, and even though this was just a weekday in the country, her glossy black hair was elaborately dressed. A half-filled box of dates was on the nearby table.

"Hello, Eddie," she said. "Long time no see."

I looked around for a chair. She made room for me beside her.

"Good book, Ruby?"

She held it up. The title was *Maid-in-Waiting;* its wrapper displayed a dashing-looking fellow in a beplumed hat looking roguishly over the shoulder of a young lady with impudent breasts. "I liked last month's selection better," Ruby said. "But it's in my favorite century. I'd've just loved to live in the seventeenth century. All those off-the-shoulder gowns. The women were so much more—distingay. I think the men were a lot more attractive too."

I wondered what Ruby would have been doing in the seventeenth century. Probably pretty much what she was doing now, only maybe as a mistress of a big madeira king or a power in the spice racket in the Indies. But actually, Ruby's was a seventeenth-century marriage. Or even a fourteenth. Boccaccio had followed her into more than one boudoir.

"Nick coming out tonight?"

"You know Nick. He usually calls half an hour before he's coming and expects me to have a big roast-beef dinner waiting for him."

"I guess Nick's a pretty demanding fella."

"Oh, Nick's okay. I haven't got any kick against Nick. I never have to *ask* him for things, like some of the girls I know. Nick's sweet in a lot of ways. But . . . ."

"But?"

"What do I tell you all this for? You'll probably just repeat it to Nick."

"Now wait a minute, Ruby, I . . ."

"I don't know why you should be any different. Everybody else does. That little louse Killer, I'm afraid to open my mouth when he's around."

"You're not comparing me with the Killer, for Christ sake?"

"No, you're a gentleman, Eddie. At least if you have an affair, you don't go around telling everybody about it, play by play. That's what I like about this seventeenth century. Everybody had just as good a time, but they had some manners about it."

There was something about the way her full, red lips moved that was for adults only. Somehow, everything Ruby did became a sensual act. She looked at me with her enlarged pupils, possibly just a physical affliction, some sort of astigmatism commonly mistaken for passion. Again I had the feeling—just a vibration as they say in the mental-telepathy racket—that it could be managed. That it was there if I wanted it.

"You know, you stimulate me," she said. "Nick brings home nothing but ignoramuses. Me, I'm different. I like people I can learn something from."

"Just what do you figure you can learn from Toro, Ruby?"

The look in Ruby's eyes hardened. "Just what do you mean by a crack like that?"

I shrugged. "I don't know. If the shoe fits, I guess . . ."

"And I considered you a gentleman," she said. "I thought you were different. But he's got you stooling for him just like the rest of his mob."

"Now listen, Ruby, this is strictly between us. Nick doesn't even know I'm here."

"Not much! And I thought we were just having a nice little talk about books and stuff. And all the time you're just snooping around like a private dick."

"Nick will never know I was here," I insisted. "I just wanted to remind you, Ruby, Toro is just a big, awkward goof. I hate to see him stumble into something he can't handle."

"Maybe Nick won't know you're here," Ruby said. "But just the same you're doing Nick's work. You're seeing that nothing happens to Nick's property. Just like all the rest of his mob. Well, goddam all of you. That goes for Nick too. Leaves me out here all week, with no one to talk to but a punch-drunk chauffeur and a fairy butler."

"Ruby, I don't care what you do. That's your pleasure. I'm just trying to look after Toro."

"You can keep Toro," Ruby said. "Tell you the truth, I'm sick of Toro. I'll admit I was a little curious about him at first, but you have nothing to worry about any more. If you came here to tell me not to lead your little boy astray, you can go back to your office and grind sausage about how your great Man Mountain is going to wipe the floor with poor old Gus Lennert."

"When're you going to leave our fighters alone?"

"You will please get out of this house at once," Ruby said with imitation hauteur, and then something gave way in her mind and she began to scream, "Get out of here, you cheap louse, you cheap, little louse! Get out of here, you bastard!"

Ruby's shrill profanity followed me through the house as I hurried to the marble hallway. But the butler opened the door for me and bowed me out with a wise smile.

When I saw Nick a couple of days later in New York having lunch at Dinty Moore's with Jimmy Quinn and the Killer, he was in high spirits. Off the advance sale it looked as if we were going to get our $150,000 house, just as he had figured. Even the Garden fans who suspected Toro's record was padded with tankers were curious to see how he'd shape up against a first-rater like Lennert.

As part of the build-up, I brought an ex-champ down to the camp to be photographed looking Toro over. Afterwards I'd write up a little statement we'd plant in the papers about how he had visited both camps and picked Toro to win by a knockout because of his superior punching power and the streffis and the strallis and the voraspan.

The joker on our junket was Kenny Waters, ex-heavyweight champion, but definitely a third-road-company champ, a clown who would have been back digging ditches if he hadn't come along just at the time when the line on the heavyweight chart had flattened out. The title had been awarded to him while reclining flat on his back, crying foul. A year later he had lost his crown to Lennert, on a night when Gus still retained some of the vigor of youth. This defeat, ignominious as it had been at the time, still entitled him to speak with authority—no matter how counterfeit—about any contest in which his conqueror was involved. For this ex-champion it was a chance to bask for one more precious moment in the warm sun of publicity. To see his name in print just once more with his four-star civilian rank *former-champion-of-the-world,* I'm sure he would have been glad to pay *us* for his services.

I was up in my room writing Kenny Waters' eyewitness comparison of Toro and Lennert when Benny came in to tell me that some gee from Argentina was here to see me.

"Damn it, I'm busy," I said. "I promised the *Journal* I'd have this crap in by four o'clock."

"Well, dis guy's a big dealer," Benny said. "He's got a car, it looks like they put wheels on a speedboat. He drove it alla way up from Argentina."

"Tell me I'll be there in a minute. Keep him happy till I come down."

I finished up Waters' piece in a hurry. This is great, I thought, a ghost writer for a ghost, a stooge for a stooge. While I laughed at this idea, a thousand little gnats of conscience whined in my head.

Waiting for me in the sitting room was a tall, swarthy, smoothly groomed fellow with two neat little mousetails of a moustache, in his early thirties, and a squat, dark-complexioned, stolid-faced, middle-aged companion in a baggy brown suit.

"Allow me to introduce myself, Carlos de Santos," the younger man said, rising gracefully and speaking English with barely a trace of Spanish intonation.

"This is Fernando Jensen," de Santos said. "He is the sports editor of our famous newspaper, *El Pantero*. We have come to root for our countryman in the big fight."

"In our country, there is very great interest in this fight," Jensen began ponderously, drawing from his pocket a folded and finger-worn clipping from *El Pantero* to show me his feature article on Toro's career. "El Toro Brings New Glory to Argentina," it was headed. "I wish to send back a daily report on El Toro's condition and activities," he continued. "You see, our country is a very proud country. We have a Strength-and-Health program to build up the bodies of our young men. Before I left I have written an editorial in which I consider El Toro Molina as the symbol of Young Argentina."

"Fernando here is a very serious fellow," de Santos added jokingly. "You shouldn't pay too much attention to everything he says." His brown eyes seemed to be laughing. "Can we see El Toro now? I have a gold watch I want to present to him in behalf of his fellow Santa Marianos."

Toro was just drawing on his running togs when we came in. He looked surprised when de Santos embraced him so warmly. Even though the young *estanciero* was obviously accepting Toro as an equal now, Toro still treated him with the shy deference of an obedient *paisano*. While de Santos gave Toro the latest home town news, with a breeziness that did not succeed in overcoming Toro's obvious unpreparedness at this sudden familiarity, I went out to round up the reporters and photographers. News had been pretty slow around the camp and this was just what we needed to cover up the general sluggishness of Toro's workout.

We even got the newsreels out that afternoon for de Santos' presentation of the gold watch. The fantastic strength of the Molina barrelmakers had long been a legend in Santa Maria, de Santos said, and now the entire village was praying and burning candles for El Toro to bring back the championship of the world. If El Toro defeated Lennert, the de Santoses were going to fill the village fountain with wine and declare a two-day holiday.

That had everything. It couldn't have had more schmalz if I had dreamed it up myself. And I noticed that young de Santos, for all his playboy chatter, had managed to work in his commercial for de Santos wines, which were just beginning to hit the North American market.

While the newsreel men wrapped up their cameras, and de Santos and Jensen were telling the reporters they had also brought with them fifty thousand dollars raised by a group of de Santos' wealthy friends to bet on Toro, Toro just stood there in a daze.

"Well, this must be a pleasant surprise," I said to Toro. "Now you'll have someone to talk to."

"He wishes me to call him by his nickname, 'Pepe'," Toro said unbelievingly. "Imagine me, an *aldeano*, addressing a *de Santos* as Pepe!"

He showed me the gold watch with its sentimentality engraved on the back. "To El Toro with pride and affection from the House of de Santos."

"And he asks me to call him Pepe," Toro repeated. "In his whole life my father has spoken to Carlos de Santos only once. But you have heard his son with your own ears asking me to call him Pepe." It was more than he could comprehend. "I have much luck, Eddie. Just like Luis promise. I have everything I want—money, honor, people like me, and young Carlos de Santos asks me to call him Pepe." He pressed his lips together in a simple gesture of determination. "I must beat this Lennert. I must show my countrymen they have not come all this way for nothing."

"You'll beat Lennert," I said. "You're a cinch to beat Lennert."

"One ponch, I hope he go boom," he said.

The camp was too quiet for Pepe that evening. There was nothing doing but the regular nightly crap game. So he suggested that I take him and Fernando into town and show them the sights. The three of us squeezed into the Mercedes-Benz he had brought up from B.A. Pepe, it developed, was a dirt-racing driver as well as a polo player and pilot, and the way he pushed that M-B into the city seemed to combine all those accomplishments. It was not without a certain fear that I realized I was in the hands of a playboy. A playboy in my book is not the carefree, luxury-loving character that word usually calls to mind. It is someone trying to escape from the neurotic riptide of an overabundance of money and an insufficiency of responsibility.

First we had to go up to the suite they were keeping in the Waldorf Towers so Pepe could change into more suitable clothes. He indicated an impressive display of bottles on the table. "I'll be out in a jiffy, old fellow. Help yourself." The Scotch was Cutty Sark. There was also some champagne brandy, some Holland gin and a couple of bottles of Noilly-Prat.

Fernando was ready in a couple of minutes, but Pepe must have been in there at least half an hour. When he finally appeared, he looked like one of those ads the tailors alway show you when you are selecting a style that never comes out looking on you as it did in the picture.

"Now where shall we go, boys?" Pepe said, with an empty, festive smile.

"Depends what you're looking for," I said. "Music, celebrities, girls?"

"Who's interested in music and celebrities, eh, Fernando?" Fernando smiled heavily. Pepe produced a gold cigarette case, filled with *Players,* and selected one gracefully. "Don't worry, my friend," he said to Fernando, winking at me happily, "I will swear to your wife you spent every night at the training camp."

Pepe tipped his way to ringside tables, ordered the waiters to keep the wine flowing and fell verbosely in love with each successive blonde who came on to dance, sing, or smile across her cigarette tray. It was apparent that he was to have a happy and costly Broadway debut. Early in the morning at the Copa, he was saying, "The one second from this end—who looks like a little golden kitten—do you suppose she would like to come up to the apartment for a nightcap?"

"Look, Pepe," I said—he had already offered me a large guest house all by myself whenever I came down to Santa Maria—"that little tramp takes a hinge at your layout in the Towers, and you're in trouble."

"But she is so beautiful. For her I would not mind a little trouble . . ."

When the party broke up, the garbage collectors who herald the dawn in New York were banging and scraping the cans on the sidewalk as if in protest against the more fortunate citizenry with cleaner jobs at more convenient hours. On the corner of Eighth Avenue I bought the morning papers from an old woman with a shawl around her head. Automatically, I turned to the sports sections as I walked back to the hotel.

The *News* had given the de Santos story a nice play. "Argentine Scion Arrives to Cheer Former Employee, Toro Molina. Brings $50,000 to wager on Ex-Barrel-Maker of Famous De Santos Vineyard."

And further down, I read, "Toro Molina faces the acid test of his spectacular career this Friday night when the undefeated giant gets a chance to try his celebrated *mazo* punch on the formidable ex-champion, Gus Lennert."

I recognized my own words, words I had written so many times they began to assume the weight of truth. On the bottom of the same page was a large cigarette ad in which a recently crowned middleweight champion was advising his fans to smoke a well-known brand because it was the only cigarette that didn't affect his endurance. I thought of all the people involved in this pious lie: the fighter, the copywriter, the advertising and cigarette executives, the newspaper publishers and finally the great mass of readers themselves who acquiesce and make a lie, for all practical purposes, as easy to live by as truth.

How could I be blamed for pushing my product, the Giant of the Andes: Who was I to crusade for integrity? I was just trying to live in the world with a minimum amount of friction and pain. If this town was so stupidly credulous as to fill the Garden to see a harmless oaf maul a burned-out ex-champion, who was I to turn them away at the door?

What if I did know better? What if I even saw the fight game for what it was, a genuinely manly art, dragged down through the sewers of human greed? What could I do about it?

But whom was I arguing with? Who said I had to do anything about it? I was looking up toward the sixth floor of Beth's apartment hotel. What was I doing a dozen blocks away from my own joint off Times Square? Her light was on. At five o'clock in the morning, her light was on. Now I realized why my mind wasn't letting me rest. This wasn't a Hamlet soliloquy; it was my running argument with Beth. I peered through the locked glass doors into the hallway. The dreary shapeless figure of a middle-aged woman was scrubbing the floor. I had seen her there for years on my way to and from Beth's apartment.

I kept looking in at the scrubwoman while trying to make up my mind. How would Beth receive me? Would she see this as an act of determination daring enough to sweep away her resistance? Or would it seem to be just another alcoholic performance by a restless drunk who wandered through the gray canyons of the city's dawn in pursuit of a will o' the wisp—his decency?

Her window was a small rectangle casting its yellow shaft into the drab morning. There shines my conscience, I thought, one small compartment in this great edifice of darkness. And as I watched it, in a kind of hateful reverence, it suddenly went out. Down the empty street came a bony milk-horse calop-calopping wearily on the echoing pavement. His day had begun again. Back in harness with his blinders on. In that instant I remembered that I had to be out at the camp by nine o'clock to meet some out-of-town sportswriters who were coming in to interview Toro.

18

I shaved, showered, tossed a couple of coffees down and called the Waldorf to see if the Argentine delegation was going out with me. Fernando answered the phone. Pepe had just gone to bed. He had left a call for four that afternoon. But Fernando wanted to go with me. He thought it would be a good idea if Toro, in his interview, said something about the growing importance of the national sports movement in Argentina. So for one hour on that bumpy local, with an off-key version of the Anvil Chorus pounding in my head, I had to hear about the growing enthusiasm for *Argentinidad*. Our Giant of the Andes was only supposed to be a national hero. But this self-appointed ambassador from south of the Amazon seemed determined to make him a hero of nationalism as well.

Toro was sitting on the porch listening to his radio and idly drawing faces in the margin of a newspaper. Training was over except for some light exercises in the afternoon and there wasn't much for him to do.

"Why you leave last night?" he said. "Lots of people come and ask questions. I do not know what to say."

I had never seen him in such a mood. The strain was beginning to tell. This was the first fight for which Danny and Doc had really put the pressure on, and the daily grind building up to the nervous tension of the tapering-off period had twisted even Toro's stolid intestines into the usual pre-fight knot.

Even with the reporters, to whom he usually showed a peasant amiability, he was irritable and uncommunicative.

"It's a good sign," Doc observed. "He's in the best shape he's been so far. Down to two-sixty-eight. It's the first time he's had an edge. Danny has really been working the hell out of him. Trained him like he would for an old-time fight. Had him chopping wood, climbing trees and hopping fences besides his regular work."

"I'd like to see the big bum make a good showing," I said. "Those boys in the press row who can't be had will really be gunning for him."

"If you ask me, Danny's done miracles with him," Doc said. "At least this time he oughta look like a pro. He's finally got him punching a little bit and he's moving around a little better, getting off his heels."

After lunch Toro was supposed to lie down, but he told Doc he couldn't sleep. He was too nervous about the fight. He said he wanted to take a drive in his car. Danny, edgy with the terrible effort at sobriety he always made when he was taking his work seriously, jumped Toro irritably.

"Don't try to kid your Uncle Danny. I haven't let you out in three weeks, so now you want to run over and get Ruby to take care of you."

Toro's face tightened with anger. "You say that, I keel you, you son-of-beetch..."

"Tell you what I'll do," I stepped in. "Maybe the ride'll do Toro good. So I'll go along with him. Okay?"

They both agreed. Fernando was ready to come along, but for some reason Toro didn't want him. Even in Spanish he could never find the words to express his suspicion of his aggressively patriotic countryman. For Toro, phrases like "the power and glory of Argentina" had no meaning, no matter how many flowery adjectives were used to establish him as a symbol of *Argentinidad*. To him Argentina was the village of Santa Maria.

"Please," Toro said, when we were on the open road, "I go to see the Señora."

"Toro, I am your friend. What goes with you and the Señora?"

"I want to see her," Toro pouted. "I see her today."

"Maybe I can help you. But you've got to tell me more about it. I'll guard your secret like a confession. I promise."

"I have already confess to the sin of *adulterio*," Toro said. "But I cannot stop. I am in love with the Señora. I want the Señora for my wife. I want to bring her home to Santa Maria to live with me in the big house I build on the hill."

"But, Toro, *estás loco*," I said. *"Completamente loco*. Don't you realize she's married? Have you forgotten Nick, of all people?"

"It is not real marriage," Toro insisted. "She has tell me whole business. It is not real marriage before the Church. It is only civil marriage."

"But what makes you think the Señora wants to go with you? Has she told you? Has she promised you?"

"She says only maybe, it is possible," he admitted. "But she says she is in love with me, only with me. I will take her back to Santa Maria. And Mama will teach her how to cook the dishes I like. And we will be very rich with the money I make in the ring."

"That's great," I said. "That's the end of the movie, all right. Only you left out one little detail. Nick. What are you going to do about Nick?"

"The Señora is very intelligent. The Señora will find a way to tell him what has happen."

What could you do with a dope like that except clam up and enjoy the scenery?

Toro told Benny to drive to Green Acres. "Dat okay?" Benny asked me. Maybe it was just nasty curiosity on my part, masquerading as high purpose, but I let him go.

When no one answered the front door, we went around to the back and let ourselves in through the screen porch. There was no one in sight, so I followed Toro up the stairs. He seemed to know where he was going. At the end of the second-floor hall was Ruby's suite—she and Nick had separate apartments—an upstairs sitting room decorated completely in white. At the far end of the room, facing us, was a white piano. A man was sitting on the bench at the piano, but he wasn't playing. He had his back turned to it and his head was thrown back as if he were a mute going through the emotions of singing grand opera. We didn't see Ruby at all until we were half way into the room. From where we stood, her head had been hidden by the top of the piano.

When he noticed us, the man jumped up and I saw it was Jackie Ryan, Jock Mahoney's kid nephew. "Get outa here! Get the hell outa here," he was yelling. Ruby's voice, shriller than I had ever heard it, screamed. Even quicker than I could, Toro seemed to grasp what had been going on.

"¡Puta!" he shouted. "¡Estás una puta, una puta!"

He made a frenzied, awkward lunge for her, but Ryan who barely came to his shoulder, rushed forward and drove his fist into Toro's stomach. The punch caught Toro by surprise and sent him reeling backward. Then he lowered his head, amazingly like a fighting bull, and started to charge.

"Get out, get out," I ordered Ryan.

"Yes, for God's sake, all of you," Ruby screeched. "You too, Jackie."

"Okay, okay, I'm going," Ryan said and swaggered out with an air of casualness.

"Come on, Toro. We better go, too," I said. But he didn't hear me.

The first wave of Toro's fury was spent now. He turned to Ruby unbelievingly. "Puta," he said. "Why you do this? Why you do this bad thing? And all the time you tell me Toro is the only one . . ."

"You lummox," Ruby shouted. "You filthy, sneaking lummox."

Her lips were unusually red in her pale, frightened face. But as she stood there in her silk lounging pajamas, her superb, unimaginative self-control began flowing back into her.

"Why you do this bad thing to Toro?" he persisted. "Why? ¿Por qué?"

"None of your business," Ruby said. "None of your goddam business. Just because I let you come up here a few times, you think you own me. All you men try to own me."

"But all the time we talk about Santa Maria. Maybe you go with me, you say."

Ruby looked at him without pity. "I had to tell you something, you baboon. Do you think I'd leave all this for a lousy little hole in Argentina? Spend my life with a dopey tenth-rate bum!"

Toro stared in bewilderment. "Toro no bum. Toro fighter. All the time win. Best fighter Nick has in whole life."

Ruby laughed. She had to get back at him. After what had happened she had to do something to put him in his place.

"Listen, you slob," she said slowly. "You couldn't beat Eddie here if it wasn't fixed. Every fight you had in this country was fixed. All those bums you're so proud of beating, they were paid to take a dive, every one of them."

"Dive?" Toro said, frowning. "I not understand. Explain me what you mean, dive?"

"You poor sap," Ruby said. "Those guys you beat were letting you win—didn't you know that?—letting you win."

Toro's large eyes half closed in pain. "No!" he roared. "No! No! I no believe. I no believe."

"Ask Eddie," Ruby said. "He ought to know."

Toro turned to me desperately. *"Dígame,* Eddie," he begged. *"La verdad. Solamente la verdad. Dígame."*

Having to stand there and swing that body blow to his simple pride suddenly seemed to compound my crime. But there was no room to weasel out. "It's true," I said. "Your fights were fixed. They were all fixed, Toro."

Toro ran his hand slowly over his face as if his head held a terrible aching. Looking at him, you had the crazy impression that the whole front of his face had been beaten in.

He turned and rushed out. Downstairs, he charged out through the screen door, ran around the house and started wildly down the street. I jumped into the car and told Benny to follow him. We let him go for almost four blocks. He was beginning to run out of gas. He lacked the athlete's coordination to run easily on his toes. Gradually he slowed down to an awkward workhorse trot. We parked the car about fifty yards ahead of him, and as he came abreast we tried to herd him into the back seat.

"Go 'way, go 'way, you make me look like fool," he shouted.

"G'wan, get in dere," Benny said. He pushed Toro toward the car. He had nothing but contempt for him. The exertion had sapped Toro's power to resist. Wearily he submitted and climbed into the back seat.

All the way out to the camp, Toro sat huddled in the corner, staring down at his massive hands.

"Listen, for Christ sake," I said. "We were only trying to help you. Trying to get you that dough you wanted."

There was no response from Toro, no indication that he had heard me.

This wasn't in the script. Toro wasn't supposed to have any sensibilities, any capacity for humiliation, for pride, or indignation. He was merely the product: the soap, the coffee, the cigarette.

"Honest, Toro, we weren't trying to make a fool out of you. We just wanted to make sure you got the right start. It happens all the time."

But Toro wouldn't hear me. He just sat sullenly in the corner, his eyes turned inward in shame.

When we reached the camp, Danny and Doc were sitting out on the steps with George and some of the boys.

"Hello, big fella," George said. "Have a nice ride?"

Toro stood on the landing, dwarfing all of us. Looking up at this inept and angry giant, his inarticulate wrath was terrible to see.

"You think you make joke of Toro, huh?" he accused us all. "You make big fool of Toro?" He went on into the house.

"What's eating him?" Danny wanted to know.

"Ruby just gave it to him straight about how he beat all those fellas," I said.

"Serves him right for nosing around the Duchess," Doc said. "It serves him right."

"Maybe we shoulda told him," Danny reflected. "It stinks bad enough without smelling it up with more lies."

"Aah, you guys sound like a lot of old women," Vince said. "He'll be all right. I'll go in and slip him another five hundred. That's the best kind of medicine."

But a few minutes later, when Vince returned, his fat neck was reddened with anger. "He says he don't want the dough. The jerk. And six months ago his ass was hangin' out. How d'ya figure a slob like that?"

When it was time for supper Benny went up to call Toro, but he wouldn't come down. Then George took a crack at it because he was closer to Toro than the others, but he came back alone too. So I went up to see what I could do. Toro was standing in front of his window, staring out into the gathering darkness.

"Toro, you better eat something," I said.

"I stay here," Toro said.

"Come on, snap out of it. We've got a beautiful steak waiting. Just the way you like it."

Toro shook his head. "I no eat with you. You make joke of Toro."

Then he turned around and confronted me. "This fight with Lennert? This fix too?"

"No," I lied. "This one is on the level. So if you beat Lennert, you have nothing to be ashamed of."

I was sorry to have to keep on with it, but I was in so deep there was no way out of this circle of lies. We were in a tight spot. The mood he was in now, he was liable to do anything in that Lennert fight. If he thought the fight was in the bag, he might even spill it to the Commission and that would be the end of the Lennert and Stein gravy. We could even wind up before a Grand Jury. I wish I could have had a choice, but there I was. I had to make him believe this fight was on the level.

Toro drove his enormous right fist into the open palm of his other hand. "I win this fight," he threatened. "I show you Toro no joke. You no have to fix for Toro. This time you no laugh behind me."

"Okay, okay," I said. "Now come on down and get yourself some steak."

19

HEAVYWEIGHT RIVALS IN CRUCIAL BATTLE TONIGHT—MAKE FIGHT PREDICTIONS

"Toro to Get Boxing Lesson and First Licking," says Ex-Champ

by
GUS LENNERT

I feel confident I will snap the Man Mountain's winning streak tonight. Although I have plenty of respect for his strength and punching ability, I expect to out-box and out-general him in our 15-round bout in the Garden. Giving away 75 pounds doesn't frighten me. He may be a giant, but giants have been licked before. Don't forget Goliath. The bigger they are, the harder they fall. I have never been in better shape and am betting on myself to dispose of this Argentine invader and go on to become the first ex-champion to regain his crown.

"I Will Knock Him Out in Five Rounds," says Argentine Giant

by
TORO MOLINA

When I was in Argentina I have heard already of Gus Lennert. He was Champion-of-the-World then. Even though he no longer holds the title, I realize he is still a great fighter and the most dangerous opponent I have faced. But I will be surprised if he is still there for the sixth round. My advantage in weight, age and strength should wear him down in the early rounds. After that I am counting on my *mazo* punch to put him away. I predict that this fight will be one more step up the ladder toward my goal of achieving what my idol, Luis Angel Firpo, came so close to doing—bringing the championship to Argentina.

I read back over these brilliant pieces of creative writing I had just knocked out. Not bad, I thought. As convincing as this stuff ever is. Toro's essay was a rewrite of one I had written a year earlier for a French middleweight, but who'd know the difference? Certainly not the suckers who read the stuff. The other one sounded more like Lennert than Lennert himself. Next thing I know he'll begin to think he's Tunney and want me to write his speeches on Shakespeare to give the boys at Harvard.

Next, I dreamt up a follow-up piece for Gus on "How I Got Licked," for the morning after the fight. Usually I had to knock out those first-person post-mortems in that high-tension interval between the end of the fight and the *Journal's* deadline. But this time I figured I might as well clean up all the literary labors at once. So I batted out something that began, "In my thirteen years in the ring, I have stayed with the best of them. So I can honestly say this Argentine Giant is the most powerful puncher I ever faced. I look for him to take the mighty Buddy Stein and go on to the championship."

Most of the time you just threw this stuff together, slapped the guy's name on it and shoved it in. But Gus was exasperatingly particular about the way his name was used. Wise to all the angles on how to gather unto himself that extra buck, Gus saw a profitable sideline for himself as a spot commentator on the big fights. He had even suggested that I might be able to work up a daily column for him. On the chance that there might be something in it for me, I had promised to take these by-line pieces out to him to check them over before I sent them through.

Gus lived in a modest white frame house in a middle-class section of West Trenton. His wife met me at the door in an apron. She was just getting the boys' lunch ready, she said. With the purse from the Stein fight and his savings, Gus must have had at least a hundred G's in cash and securities, but I don't think they had ever had a cook. Gus liked to make you think it was because he was so fond of the missus' cooking. But what he was really fond of was that lettuce in the cooler.

Gus was sitting in the breakfast nook in a worn, red bathrobe, an old pair of pants and bedroom slippers, with a lot of papers spread out in front of him. His hair, sharply receding from his forehead and showing signs of gray at the temples, was unkempt, as if he had just gotten out of bed. He hadn't bothered to shave, in the old fighters' tradition that the extra days' growth was an additional protection to his face. He looked much older than when I had last seen him at Green Acres. You would have put him down for closer to forty than thirty. The Stein beating seemed to have taken something out of him. I could count where the six stitches had been taken after Stein had split his right eye in the fourteenth round.

When I came in he frowned at me as if his head was hurting.

"Goddamit, you sure take your own sweet time getting out here," he greeted me.

"Sorry, Gus," I said. "I missed the ten-o'clock train. Hope it didn't inconvenience you."

"Well, we still got telephone service," he said. "Thank God I can still pay my phone bills. You could of called Emily. I got up at nine-thirty especially to be ready for you. What's a matter, too much celebrating last night?"

"Hell, no, I was in the sack before midnight. I wanted to be sure and be in shape for the fight tomorrow night."

I thought that might get a rise out of him, but he didn't even smile.

"I had a lousy night," he said. "Must a been three o'clock before I could get to sleep. Finished two whole murder mysteries. That's why I coulda used the extra hour this morning."

"I'm sorry," I apologized again. "I guess I should have called you, Gus."

"Well, that's the way it is," Gus said in a voice surly with self-pity. "When you're on top the phone never stops ringing. But when you're on your way out, nobody gives a damn."

From the kitchen came a loud, boyish screech, and then a general hubbub. Gus jumped up, opened the door and shouted in, "For God's sake, Emily, how many times do I have to ask you to keep them quiet? I knew I shoulda gone to the hotel last night. Now are you gonna make 'em shut up or do I have to come in there and knock their heads together?"

He came back to the table, closed his eyes and pressed his fingers against the right side of his forehead.

"Feeling okay, Gus?"

"Just a lousy headache," he said. "Hell, no wonder, the racket those kids make around here."

He squeezed his eyes together and massaged the triangle between his eyebrows.

"Jesus, it looks like I have to do everything." He picked up some of the pages in front of him, on which there were long rows of figures. "I pay a business manager two hundred bucks a month to handle my investments and he can't even add right." He tapped the papers irritably. "Found two mistakes already. And these fifty G's I make tonight, he's trying to sell me on the idea of putting it in annuities. Annuities is a lot of bunk. I been figuring it up and it don't pay. I carry a hundred thousand straight insurance. That's the only kind to have. If I got fifty thousand to invest, I'd rather put it in something like Treasury Bonds."

He was starting to figure out how 2.9 percent of fifty thousand compared with setting up a trust fund. You could see he loved to write those big figures down and multiply them.

"Look, Gus," I said. "I've got a lot to do yet today. Want to take a gander at this stuff?"

He read it over as if he were Hemingway guarding his literary reputation, with his pencil poised critically over each word, occasionally shaking his head and rereading a sentence. "This line here," he quibbled, "'Don't forget Goliath.' That don't sound good. Maybe some people don't even know who Goliath is."

"Anybody who reads the *Journal* and doesn't know who Goliath is," I said, "deserves to read the *Journal*."

"If you wanna succeed in this writing business," Gus insisted, "you gotta write so everybody can understand you."

"But since you're comparing Goliath to Toro, it'll remind everybody who he is."

"Goddamit, why does everything have to be an argument," Gus said, his voice rising. "My name's going on this, so I guess I can have it the way I want it."

He took my copy and began correcting it, erasing several times. "There," he said, "that's a little more like it."

I looked at it and said nothing. What he had written was, "Don't forget how David overcame Goliath." He went through the rest of the copy, making his petty and niggling changes and handed it back without looking at me.

"There," he said. "Every goddam thing I've got to do myself."

I kept quiet. But I couldn't figure why he was under so much pressure for a fight he was going to throw.

He stood up, rubbed his head again, and walked me to the door. "How does the house look?"

"Even Jacobs can't kick. Nothing but some three-thirties left and they'll be gone by fight time. It's a hundred and fifty easy."

"If it wasn't for those goddam taxes I'd make myself some money," Gus said.

"I wish I were paying those taxes," I said. "Well, see you, Gus. Take it easy."

"I just hope it looks all right," Gus said. "That big clown better fight enough to make it look good. All I need now is for the Commish to smell a rat and tie up our purses."

"Stop worrying," I said. "It'll be all right. It's money in the bank. You haven't got a thing to worry about."

As the front door closed behind me, I could hear the Lennert kids cutting up in the kitchen again. "For God's sake, will you keep those damn kids quiet?" Gus shouted. "How many times do I have to tell ya? I got a headache!"

*   *   *

Toro had driven into town with Pepe and Fernando. He wanted no part of us. Fernando, moving in, took him up to the suite at the Waldorf. We didn't see him until the weigh-in at noon.

"Howya feeling?" I said.

Toro looked away. He wasn't talking to any of us.

"Don't forget now, a good lunch around three o'clock," Doc said. "But remember, no fats, no gravies and no lemon-meringue pie."

But Toro wouldn't acknowledge Doc either. Fernando rubbed Toro's back possessively as he stepped off the scales in his shorts. "We will take care of him," Fernando assured us.

Gus got on the scales wearing an old towel that had printed on it in faded letters, *Hotel Manx*.

"Well, anyway, Gus, after this fight you oughta be able to go out and buy yourself a towel of your own," Vince said as Gus stepped down.

Most of the boys laughed. But Gus was a humorless man at best and this afternoon he was not at his best.

"At least I don't do nothing worse than swipe hotel towels," he said. It was not so much what he said as the irritable way he said it that infected the atmosphere.

Toro was waiting to step onto the scales as Gus stepped off. This is a moment of importance in the drama of any fight. The reporters watch the faces of the principals to see if the underdog betrays any fear of the favorite, or for those displays of bravado that may be part of a preconceived plan of psychological warfare, or for a sign of some highly publicized hostility, or for that exchange of smiles and good wishes that never fails to delight the sentimentalists.

But between Toro and Gus nothing happened at all. Gus just stepped on and stepped off with the indifference of a man punching in for work in the morning. Not to greet Toro wasn't snubbing him any more than the man punching in shows any discourtesy by ignoring the fellow behind him. But as Gus walked away, Toro watched him from the scales. Reporters who had no way of knowing what had happened to Toro in the last forty-eight hours may have described his eyes as being full of hate. But Gus had no special significance for Toro as an individual. He had simply become the most immediate target for Toro's exploding resentment against a world which had tricked and belittled him.

An hour before the fight you could feel the tension growing in the Garden lobby: the late ticket seekers, the sharp-eyed scalpers, the busy little guys making last-minute book, eight-to-five on Toro, five-to-nine on Lennert, playing the percentages.

Around nine, Toro came down from the Waldorf with Pepe and Fernando. Danny wanted to throw them out. Strangers in a dressing room always made him even more nervous. But Toro was stubborn. "They are my friends," he insisted. "If they go, I go too."

Danny had never paid much attention to what Toro said before, but this time Danny sensed something in Toro that was not to be denied, something wild inside him that wanted violence.

Usually Toro had waited to go down to the ring with the patient amiability of a prize Guernsey standing by to make its appearance at the county fair. But this time he asked how much longer it would be every few minutes. And finally when Doc told him to start warming up with a little shadowboxing, Toro lashed out at his imaginary opponent with a fury none of us had ever seen in him before.

Lennert was first to enter the ring. As he worked his feet slowly in the rosin box, he responded to the cheers of his supporters with a tight, cheerless smile. His face was ghastly white in the glare of the ring lights.

Toro's white satin bathrobe with the blue trim and the Argentine flag on back got a tremendous hand as he climbed through the ropes. He didn't jackknife over the top rung as I had had him do for the previous fights. Something about that omission vaguely worried me. It was a trivial but significant protest against the kind of circus presentation we had set up for him. I didn't know what could happen, but I had the same sense of apprehension a playwright would feel if one of his actors began the play by speaking unfamiliar lines that were not in the script.

I kept my eyes on Toro while the announcer introduced the usual celebrities, followed by some future attractions—the "highly regarded lightweight from Greenwich Village who has emerged victorious in seventeen consecutive contests," the Bronx middleweight "who has recently established himself as a fistic sensation and who never fails to make a spectacular showing," and several other boys whom Harry Balough managed to describe with artless and incongruous pomposity. Toro sat on the edge of his stool, anxious to begin. Even when a great cheer went up from the crowd and Buddy Stein swung through the ropes and mitted the crowd in a broad, ham gesture, Toro paid no attention. Stein was dressed sharply in a loud checked sports suit that set off his wide shoulders and his trim waist. The body that tired sportswriters were always comparing to Adonis' moved with jaunty arrogance. He trotted over to Lennert's corner and, instead of the conventional and perfunctory handshake, kissed him on the forehead. The crowd laughed and Stein laughed back. They loved each other. Then he skipped across the ring to shake hands with Toro. Toro just let him lift his glove. He still didn't seem to see him. He didn't see anybody but Lennert.

The ring was cleared now. The referee brought the fighters together for final instructions. Gus stood quietly with a towel draped over his head, looking bored as he listened to the routine warnings about foul punching and breaking clean he had heard hundreds of times before. Toro fixed his eyes on his opponent's feet, nodding sullenly as the referee went through his spiel.

Then they were back in their corners, with their bathrobes off, alone and stripped for action. Toro turned to his corner, in a gesture of genuflection and crossed himself solemnly. Lennert winked at a friend in the working press. The crowd was hushed with nervous excitement. The house lights went down and the white ring was sharply outlined in the darkness.

At the bell, Gus put out his gloves to touch Toro's in the meaningless gesture of sportsmanship, but Toro brushed him aside and drove him into the ropes. This aroused the fans' erratic sense of fair play and they booed. Gus looked surprised. Toro was leaning on Gus, flailing his arms with ineffectual fury. When the referee separated them, Gus danced up and down, flicking his left into Toro's face and preparing to counter with the clever defensive timing that everyone expected of him. But Toro rushed him into the ropes again, not hitting him cleanly, but roughing him up, punishing him with his great weight, clutching him with one arm and clubbing him about the head with the other.

That was the pattern of the first round. Lennert wasn't able to make Toro fight his fight. His movements were listless. He lacked the strength to stand off Toro's wild rushes.

Toro looked even more aggressive as he came out for the second round. Up from the floor he lifted a roundhouse uppercut, the kind Gus had easily blocked and countered a thousand times. But this time he seemed to make no effort to avoid it and it caught him on the side of the head.

He shouldn't let Toro hit him that easily, I thought. Nobody is going to believe that. But I had to admit Gus put on a very good show. He actually seemed hurt by the blow. At least he fell into a clinch as if to avoid further punishment. Toro kept on trying to hammer at him even in the clinch. He wasn't what we'd call an infighter, but he had enough strength to pull one of his arms free and club away at Gus' back and kidneys. Gus was talking to him in the clinches, mumbling something into his ear. I wondered what he could be saying. Perhaps, "Take it easy, boy. What you so steamed up about? You're gonna win." Whatever it was, Toro wasn't listening. In his clumsy, mauling way, he was taking the play away from Gus. As we had figured the fight, Gus would outbox Toro for the first two or three rounds and then ease himself out around the sixth, whenever he caught one that would look good enough for the K.O.

But Toro wasn't giving him a chance to show anything. He was fighting him as if possessed, as if he had to destroy Gus Lennert. Just before the round ended, Toro rushed Gus again, clubbing the smaller man viciously, and his gloved fist came down heavily on top of the ex-champion's head. It wasn't a punch known to boxing science, just the familiar downward clubbing motion that cops like to use. Gus sagged. Toro clubbed him fiercely again and Gus sank to his knees. The bell sounded. Gus didn't look badly hurt, but he didn't get up. He remained on one knee, frowning and staring thoughtfully at the canvas. His seconds had to half-carry, half-drag him back to his corner.

"He's a bum, he wants ta quit," someone yelled in back of me.

Smelling salts, massage at the back of the neck and a cold wet sponge squeezed over his head brought Gus around by the time the warning buzzer sounded for round three. He opened his eyes and then closed them again and shook his head slowly as if trying to clear it.

"He's faking," the guy said behind me. "Look at him, he wants ta quit."

Several other skeptics took up the cry.

At the bell, Toro ran across the ring. Gus tried to hold him off with a feeble jab, but Toro just pushed it aside and brought his fist down on Lennert's head again. Gus dropped his hands and turned to the referee. He was muttering something. Whatever it was, the referee didn't understand and motioned him to fight on. Toro clubbed him again. Gus stumbled back against the ropes and sat down on the middle strand with his head buried in his arms. There was a wild look in Toro's eyes. He was going to hit Gus again, but the referee slid between them. Gus continued to sit on the ropes, cowering behind his gloves. The way it looked to the fans, he hadn't really been badly hurt. It looked as if that guy behind me was right. It looked as if he were doing an el foldo, all right. I couldn't figure it. Gus had more sense than to quit without going down. Even if he wanted to go home early, he had enough ring savvy to give the crowd the kind of kayo they paid to see. But he just kept sitting there on the rope, with his head bowed in his arms as if he were praying. The referee looked at Gus curiously. Then he raised Toro's hand and waved him back to his corner. The crowd didn't like it. The guy behind me was yelling, "Fake!" The cry began to spread. Apparently just enough had leaked out about Toro's record to make some of the cash customers hypercritical. Lennert's handlers jumped into the ring and led Gus back to his corner. He slumped down on his stool and his head fell forward on his chest. Part of the crowd had begun to file out, muttering their disappointment to each other. But thousands were still standing around, booing and crying, "Fake!"

"This act oughta bring vaudeville back," the comic behind me shouted. People around him were still laughing when Gus suddenly pitched forward and slid off his stool. His head hit the canvas heavily and he lay still.

The powerful lights beating down on Gus' inert, expressionless face gave it a ghostly hue. A couple of news cameramen shoved their cameras at him through the ropes and flashed their pictures. The crowd wasn't booing any more. Around the ring curiosity seekers were pressing forward for a closer look.

The house doctor, portly, genial, inefficient Dr. Grandini, bustled into the ring. The handlers grouped themselves anxiously around the doc. This sort of thing didn't happen very often and they were frightened.

The guy behind me who first started yelling "Fake!" was pushing past me to get a better view of Gus. "He's hurt bad," he was telling a companion. "I knew there was something funny the way he sat down on those ropes."

"He just can't take it any more," his companion declared.

"I seen him put up some great battles here in the Garden," someone said.

"Well, he sure stunk up the joint tonight," said a gambler who had bet Lennert to stay the limit.

Barney Winch, and one of his lieutenants, Frankie Fante, came along.

"Hi, there, Eddie," Barney grinned behind his fat cigar. "How's my boy?"

"Looks like something's wrong with Gus," I said.

"Come on, Barney," Fante said. "We c'n see it at the Trans-Lux. We gotta meet those fellas outside."

"Have a big night?" I asked Barney.

"Not bad," Barney said.

Not bad, for Barney, meant twelve, fifteen thousand, maybe twenty.

They were carrying Gus out now. They carried him up the long aisle to the dressing rooms, with his white face staring sightlessly at the fans who had been abusing him with their cynical catcalls a few minutes before.

In our dressing room, Pepe was inviting everybody to be his guest at El Morocco. Vince had managed to place the fifty grand for him and Pepe wanted us all to help him start spending it. But Toro was more excited than anybody else. He grabbed me when I came in and shouted, "Toro no joke. Toro real fighter. You see tonight, huh?"

"Everyone in Argentina will be talking about you tonight," Fernando said, coming in from somewhere. "This is a great victory for *Argentinidad,* for the pride of Argentina."

For the pride of Toro Molina, I thought. That's all that was at stake, and that's enough.

Doc came in from the hall. Nobody had missed him in the excitement.

His hunchback and his damp, pale face framed in the doorway, he looked like a herald of doom. His nasal voice knifed through the celebration din.

"Gus is still out," he said. "He's going to the hospital."

20

We all drove over to St. Clare's Hospital in Pepe's car. I wished it had been just a cab, for somehow it seemed profane to use a jazzed-up Mercedes-Benz when you were going over to visit a guy in critical condition. Nobody said anything. Even Pepe knew enough to be quiet.

In the waiting room Doc talked to one of the nurses. The patient was still in a coma, she said. Lennert's doctor had called in a brain specialist. It was a hemorrhage of the brain; that's all she could tell him.

Doc came back and gave us the news. "Is that . . . ? Is that . . . ?" everybody wanted to know. Doc didn't know either. "I heard of cases recovering," he said. "Like when a scab forms on the brain. The patient lives, only he's got paralysis agitans; what we mean when we call a guy punchy."

Some people feel better when they keep talking. That's the way Doc was. Danny just sat in a corner biting his lip and fingering his hat. Toro held his crucifix in his hands. His eyes were half-closed and his face was a mask. His lips moved slowly. He was saying his beads.

"I didn't think Toro could hit him hard enough for this," I said to Doc.

"Chances are, Toro had nothing to do with it," Doc answered. "Gus probably came out of the Stein fight with those hemorrhages, see. Multiple hemorrhages. They can be awful small, no bigger than a pinpoint. But it just takes a little tap to start them. Or even getting a little too excited would be enough to do it."

"Gus was talking about a headache when I saw him the other day," I said.

"That sounds like it," Doc said. "That could be it."

"Jesus," I said.

"I heard of guys recovering," Doc said.

A little while later Mrs. Lennert and her two eldest sons came out of the elevator. They went right by us, down the corridor to Lennert's room. Toro looked up as they passed and then hung his head again. With his grave bent head, his sad brown eyes and the beads clutched desperately in his enormous hand, he looked like a battered monolith.

About two o'clock in the morning they wheeled Gus down the hall to the elevator. Mrs. Lennert was crying. Doc went over and asked one of the interns what the score was. He came back worried. "They're going to try to relieve the pressure," he said.

"What do you mean, try?" I said.

"Well, these brain things are tricky," he said. "You see, they've got to try to drain off the excess cerebrospinal fluid . . ."

"Goddam it, quit trying to show off your medical knowledge and tell me so I can understand," I said.

"Okay, okay," Doc said, "I thought you wanted me to tell you."

He was always sensitive on this point, but I couldn't help it. Danny came over and said, "What're the odds on this thing upstairs, Doc?"

"I wouldn't want to say," Doc told him.

Danny went back to his corner, sat down and started leafing through a *National Geographic* he didn't seem to be looking at.

At three o'clock Pepe and Fernando got tired and decided to go back to the Waldorf. They wanted to take Toro with them, but he just shook his head and bent over his beads. A little later Nick and the Killer came in. Nick was wearing a double-breasted blue pin-stripe and a somber tie. He must have dressed for the occasion. He looked very serious and yet I had the feeling his attitude was as carefully put on as his clothes. The expression on the Killer's face was a carbon of Nick's, only not quite as convincing. Nick walked over to the window where I was looking out over the monotonous rooftops.

"Do the best you can with the stories in the morning papers," he said.

"Jesus," I said, "how can you worry about the angles with Gus up there with a tube in his head?"

"I feel bad too," Nick said. "But someone's gotta keep his head. This could look very lousy for us. If the papers play up the angle that Gus was all through after the Stein fight . . . You know what I mean."

"Sure I know what you mean. Try to make 'em think Gus was a suitable opponent and not a beat-up old man with his brains full of blood."

"Take it easy," Nick said.

I could feel the pressure lifting when I blew off at Nick. After all, if anything happened, that's where the blame lay. It was Nick's baby. All I did was make the public buy it. If it hadn't been Eddie Lewis, Nick could have had ten other guys.

The hours ticked by. Nick paced restlessly, the Killer moving with him, slightly behind him, like a well-trained dog. A reporter from the *News* came up. Nick gave him what he wanted. "Gus has got off the floor plenty of times before," I heard him say. "But I'll be in his corner right to the end."

He didn't say anything about being in Toro's corner too. That wasn't public knowledge yet. I was all set to break the news of Nick's purchase of Toro's contract after Gus announced his retirement. If Gus kicked off, I found myself thinking, we'd better hold up the contract story until people began to forget a little bit.

Jesus, Gus was still on the table with the surgeons trying to get his brains back together, and here I was, burying the guy. Not only burying him, but beginning to work out a way to cover Nick. What do you call that, reflex action, psychological conditioning, or just plain depravity? Writing Gus off and realizing I was already working out the best way to sell his death to the public, it didn't come as quite so much of a shock when Doc came in and told us.

"I've lost not only one of the best fighters I ever had but one of the best friends I ever had," Nick was telling the reporters. "As Lennert's manager, I want to say that I don't blame Molina. He fought clean. It was just one of those things."

He isn't mourning, he's working, I thought. He isn't saying farewell to Gus. He's too busy protecting himself in the clinches. The credo of Henry Street, the *Weltanschauung* of the guys on the corner.

But why wasn't I speaking up to tell them this wasn't one of those things, that this was murder, that Gus Lennert had been sacrificed to human greed, his own included? No, I kept my mouth shut. Protecting myself in the clinches, too. An accessory before the fact. As the reporters turned from him, Nick looked over at me in what was almost a wink, a conspiratorial sign. After all, we were both in the same stable.

A photographer from the *Mirror* moved in and flashed a picture of Toro. Simultaneously it flashed in my mind that the picture wouldn't do us any harm; it caught Toro in an effective pose of repentance, saying his beads.

I had to lead Toro out. He was in a trance. Lennert's death wasn't filtered for him, as it was for us, through protective screens of sophistication and rationalization. Toro took it head on. He had killed a man. He wandered in fear and shock as the victim of an auto accident sleepwalks away from the wreck.

Mrs. Lennert came out while we waited on the curb for a cab. Nick was sending her home in his car. Toro went over to her. "I sad. All my life, sad. All the money I make tonight I give you. Every cent I give. I no want the money."

"Get away from me, you murderer, you," Mrs. Lennert said. She wasn't crying. "The fight was fixed and you still had to kill him. You had to show everybody how tough you are. The fight was fixed so poor Gus could get home early because he was sick, and you, you couldn't even wait. You had to kill him. You filthy, dirty murderer."

Then she began to cry. It was an ugly, retching cry, because there was still so much anger in it. Her sons helped her into Nick's car. As they drove off, Toro stood there, staring after them with his mouth hanging loose. He bowed his head and began to mutter, "Jesus Christo . . . Jesus Christo . . . Jesus Christo . . ." We had to push him into the cab.

No one said anything for several blocks. Finally Danny broke the silence with something unexpected. "You know, when a guy goes, you feel like you owe it to him to say something real nice. But Gus, Gus was never much of a fella in my book. Only now I kinda wish he was. Because in a way, you don't feel quite as bad about losing a pal as losing a guy you never got around to liking."

"I liked Gus, *olav hasholem*," Doc said. "He sure was one hundred percent with his wife and kids."

"You and that Jew-heart of yours," Danny said. "You like everybody."

We pulled up in front of St. Malachy's, the little church that's squeezed in among the bars and cheap hotels of Forty-ninth Street. The garbage men were dragging the big cans along the pavement to their big churning truck. A drunk still living in the night before staggered past and wandered off toward wherever he was going. A hooker whose face wasn't meant to be seen in the daylight passed us slowly on the way home to catch up on her sleep.

I have never been much for churches, but I felt easier when we got the sexton to let us inside. The quiet and the candlelight created a better atmosphere for thoughts about the dead. Toro and Danny lit candles to the Virgin Mother. Then Toro went into the sacristy to find the priest.

"I oughta confess too," Danny said to me. "If I hadn't had a grudge against the guy, I never would have whipped Toro into the shape he was in. I came up to the fight with hate in my heart, laddie. Maybe that's what did it, God help me!"

But Danny didn't confess, unless you would call me his confessor. He went over to another altar, stuffed a pocketful of bills into the offering box, and knelt in prayer.

Doc was sitting in one of the rear pews with his head bent. I went over and sat next to him while we waited for Toro to finish. "I had a strong hunch Gus had the canaries in his head after Stein," Doc said. "I knew something was wrong with him. I coulda said."

Sure you coulda said, I thought. Danny coulda said. I coulda said. Poor old Gus, counting his annuities, coulda said. We were all as guilty as Cain. All but Toro, in there in his spiritual sweatbox, carrying our burden. Yes, if the Father were really hep, Toro would be learning that he was just an innocent bystander, just the boy who happened to be around when the mob decided to cash in on a rundown ex-champion whose name still retained some of its marquee magic.

Toro returned from the confession booth, lit another candle to the

Virgin Mary and dropped on his knees in front of the shrine. He stayed that way for several minutes. When we came out onto the street again, a cold gray light was settling over the city. A few early risers were going to work with sleep-heavy but freshly shaved faces.

"I'm going home and crack my best bottle of Irish," Danny said. Home was a room-and-bath he kept in a shabby hotel off Broadway.

"I better call my mother," Doc said. "She worries about me."

When we dropped Danny off, we bought the morning papers from a listless middle-aged newsboy. Gus and Toro had the headlines. On the front of the *News* were big pictures of Gus lying on the canvas, Gus on a stretcher being carried to the ambulance, and Toro with his head bent, saying his beads. I turned to the story on Page Three. The Boxing Commission would investigate the death, but as far as the Chairman could see, "It seems to be a tragic accident for which nobody is to blame."

Well, maybe so. And maybe Jimmy Quinn had gotten to the good Commissioner. Maybe the Commissioner didn't actually have his hand out. Maybe he just wasn't very bright.

The story went on to say that Toro would be arraigned on the usual manslaughter charge. I hustled Toro down to the headquarters of our city's finest. Toro was frightened when they brought him before the police judge. He didn't understand what I meant when I told him all this was mere technicality.

The bail was nominal, just a G to save the face of the Department with those taxpayers who think prize fighting is organized mayhem and should be run out of bounds. But Toro had the peasant's fear of official-dom. If it were necessary to pay out all this money, he reasoned, the government must consider him a criminal.

I took him up to the suite in the Waldorf Towers, thinking Pepe and Fernando might be able to cheer him up, but he just sat there in a daze. Pepe talked about Santa Maria and the great three-day celebration they would have when Toro made his triumphant return.

"But I kill a man," Toro said, "I kill him."

"My friend," Fernando said smoothly, "there are some things worse than death. There is weakness and cowardice. That this poor fellow should die is most unfortunate, of course. But think what you are doing for our country! Every youth from Jujuy to Tierra del Fuego will want to be big and strong and victorious like the great El Toro Molina."

Toro's enormous, vulnerable chin lay on his chest. "But I kill this man. I do not even talk with him before, and I kill him."

"Maybe you should come back to Santa Maria before you fight again," Pepe suggested. "You can be my house guest."

"But I kill this man," Toro said. "For no reason, I kill him."

"Pepe is right," Fernando said. "After a few months' rest, you can have a tune-up fight in Buenos Aires. Perhaps we can bring down a Yankee, some second-rater..."

It made him smile to think of this public demonstration of Argentine supremacy. But Toro wasn't with him. Toro shook his head slowly. "I go home now. I fight no more. That I do not injure any other man."

Personally, I think I would have given up my cut in the Stein fight to see him go home. But Nick had him signed for the Stein fight in the ball park. And Nick was a stickler for contracts, when they worked his way.

The next day we all attended the funeral over in Trenton. Nick took care of all the expenses, and he really did it right. Everybody agreed that, as funerals go, it was just about tops. Nick was one of the pall-bearers, along with five ex-champions. Nick's floral wreath was in the form of a huge squared ring of white carnations with red carnations spelling out the words, "God Bless You, Gus." At the grave, the minister told us what a great man Gus had been, a man who never abused his strength, a home-loving, God-fearing, clean-living champion whose life should be a model to young America. After Gus was laid to rest, everybody stood around telling one another what a great guy he had been. Even people who had been up and down Jacobs' Beach for years, putting the knock on him, were slobbering about what a pal they had lost.

As I came out of the cemetery with Toro, I saw Nick helping Ruby into their limousine. He was wearing a black homburg and looked distinguished, if you didn't see him too close. She was very attractive in black with a black chiffon snood. If she noticed Toro, she gave no indication. The Killer drew a fur car robe over them. I looked in at her as the car drove away. Her face was somber, to befit the occasion.

Pepe and Fernando took Toro back to the hotel with them. He didn't seem to be coming out of it. I went down the street to a beer joint I had made a mental note of as we approached the cemetery. Some of the trade from the funeral had had the same idea. Danny was in the corner with a very full load. He hadn't changed his clothes since we dropped him off at the hotel the morning before, and the front of his suit was spotted because his hand had not been steady enough. His face looked bloodless; the light blue irises of his eyes were so washed out that they blended into the whites. The Irish gift for parlaying a deep sense of guilt into a marathon drunk had possession of Danny. "Never liked the bastard," he was saying to whoever would listen. "Never liked the bastard. So what? Drink to 'im anyway. Whatsamatter, anything wrong with that? Maybe you think I got no right to drink to 'im, huh, Mister? Well, le's drink to 'im anyway, even if he was a selfish, tightwad bastard."

An Irishman at a funeral who can't love the guy they're burying is in a terrible way. Especially when he figures he's been credited with an assist in putting the deceased where he is.

I didn't want to go from bar to bar with Danny and maybe run into fight reporters who would be trying to pump me on the Lennert business. So I went back to my room. I tried *War and Peace,* but I had forgotten who Marya Dmitrevna was again, and I didn't have enough patience to go back and find out. I tossed that aside and started reading "The Rich Boy" by Fitzgerald, but it was too probing for the way I felt. I wondered what Beth was doing. I could imagine what she thought now that this had happened. But dammit, people are getting themselves killed all the time.

What was I thinking? I was just tired from the strain of the last few days. I closed the door to the bathroom. I raised the shades to let more light into the room. I wished I could call Beth. I didn't have Beth to call any more. I should have married Beth. I shouldn't have kept this lousy job so long. I should have written my play. Well, maybe it still wasn't too late.

I didn't want to stay in my room alone any longer. I walked over to Fifty-second Street, where the music was hard and loud and restless to the breaking point, a musical score to accompany the doubts and frustrations and villainies of Eddie Lewis, I thought.

Next morning I went up to the office to pick up my weekly retainer. Nick was talking to Kewpie Harris, who had Buddy Stein. Nick was wearing a soft-brown English tweed with a black armband. After Kewpie left, Nick went to his mirror and inspected himself carefully. Then he turned to me.

"Do you see a blackhead here?" He pointed to a spot near his mouth. It was there all right, but what did he think I should do, squeeze it out for him? He must have thought so, for he said, "Don't bother with it, Eddie. Oscar down in the barber shop has a way of taking 'em out without leaving a mark." He went back to his desk and swung his feet onto it.

"I just been trying to talk Kewpie into cutting it thirty-thirty when we go against Stein," Nick said. "He wants it thirty-three and a half—twenty-six and a half. He says Stein's beaten better fellas. I have to give him that, but not even Stein and the champ 'd draw like Stein and Molina. I figure with any kind of breaks we ought to do a million four, maybe a million six if we get really lucky. That means a nice half a million for us to kick around."

"In other words about three hundred thousand for Toro himself," I said.

"Or in other words at least twenty-five thousand for you personally," Nick answered.

"There's a slight hitch," I said. "Toro wants out. He told me he doesn't want to fight any more. He wants to go home."

"Who cares what Toro wants? He's got a contract with me. And I've got a contract with Mike and Kewpie for the ball park June nineteenth. Toro's gonna be there if we have to carry him into the ring."

"Maybe you better talk to him," I said.

"I got more important things to do," Nick said. "Ruby and I are going to Palm Beach for six weeks. I haven't been spending enough time with her lately. A wife like I got, you just can't treat her like any dumb broad. She says we gotta have companionship." He looked proudly at the picture on his desk, a photograph taken many years earlier. "Jesus, it used to be all a wife needed to keep her happy was a new fur coat every year and a rub-of-the-brush once in a while. Now she's gotta have companionship." He tried to pass it off as a joke, but his respect for Ruby was too deep. "She even wants me to read her goddam books."

He went to the door and called out, "Hey, Killer, tell Oscar I'll be down in ten minutes." He went to the humidor and gave me one of his cigars. I tore the band off it and was going to throw it away when he said, "Read it, read it." It said, "Made exclusively for Nick Latka by Rodriguez, Havana."

He took his double-breasted herringbone overcoat off a hangar and gave it to me to hold for him. "Oh, by the way," he said as he slipped his arms through, "break the news of my buying the Molina contract from Vanneman a couple of weeks after I'm gone. I don't have to tell you how to handle it. You know. Everything in good taste. Class, Eddie."

He put his hand on my arm confidentially. "You know, Eddie, it may sound cokey, but we could go as high as two million with this fight. God knows I never wished Gus any hard luck, but . . . well, this thing that happened isn't doing us any harm. Some of these columnist boyscouts who've been wondering out loud about Toro's opposition. Well, you can't make it look any squarer than killing a guy, can you?"

"No, that should quiet any suspicions," I said.

"Nobody would ever believe a guy checked out while trying to take a dive," Nick said. "So we'll have that going for us."

"Yes, that's a break," I said.

"And it makes your job a helluva lot easier, selling that *mazo* punch. You know how the public is, they'll all be there to see if maybe he can kill another guy."

"Yes, it's great," I said. "Lennert sure did us a favor. We had no more use for him anyway. He might as well be pushing up daisies."

But Nick wouldn't even permit me the luxury of anger. "I know how you feel, kid," he said. "I guess you think I'm doing handsprings because Gus went out when it could do us the most good. Hell, I always took care of Gus. I threw him everything I could. But I figure, when a thing happens, it happens. We still gotta live. That's my psychology."

21

Next morning we broke the story of the Stein-Molina fight. It broke big all right. Nick hadn't overestimated the value of the Lennert tragedy. Every heavyweight fight is a simulated death-struggle. Those fans who rise up in primeval blood-lust and beg their favorite to "Killim! Killim!" may be more in earnest than they know. Death in the ring is not an everyday occurrence, not every month or even every year. But it always adds a titillating sense of danger and drama to all the matches that follow. For the sadism and cruelty of the Roman circus audience still peers out through eyes of the modern fight crowd. There is not only the conscious wish to see one man smash another into insensibility, but the subconscious, retrogressive urge to witness violent tragedy, even while the rational mind of the spectator turns away from excessive brutality.

These psychological factors, combined with Stein's authentic viciousness and Toro's bogus savagery, made their coming bout another Battle of the Century. Even the sportswriters, who were calling Toro the "Man Monstrous" and "El Ponderoso," had to admit that the Stein fight would be worth seeing as Toro's first real test. And the hacks, who are always along for the ride, were pulling out all the stops, conjuring up the Dempsey-Firpo thriller and passing on to their readers our pitch about Toro's ambition to avenge the defeat of the Wild Bull of the Pampas.

When the phone rang, I was lying in bed, wondering how Nick figured to do business with Kewpie Harris and Stein. It was Fernando. I must come right over. Toro had just seen the papers. He was very angry. He said he was not going to fight Stein. He was not going to fight anybody. He was going home.

I threw my clothes on, grabbed a cab and hurried over to see Toro. I wasn't as convincing as I should have been because I didn't entirely blame him. But I tried to show him how there was no way out of the Stein fight. Nick and the Garden had his name on the dotted. The Stein clause had been written into the Lennert contract. If he took a run-out powder now, Toro would end up in the river, wrong side up. And since he had come this far, it didn't seem sensible to pass up the six-figure dough finally coming his way.

But all Toro said when I wound up my oratory was, "No. I go home."

Pepe and Fernando tried to reason with him too, but he just sat there, shaking his huge, solemn head, saying over and over again with maddeningly childish monotony, "No. I go home."

I told Pepe to take him out to a midnight movie, or a call house or whatever else he could think of—anything to get Toro out of himself. But there seemed to be no temptations left for Toro any more. All he wanted was to be away from us, to be home and at peace again. If it had been up to me, I think I would have let him go. But I knew, for his own good, he had to stay. He didn't know Nick and the boys as well as I did, friendly fellas until you crossed them.

Toro, unconvinced, finally went to bed and I returned to the hotel. It was a little before three when Fernando called me again. Toro had disappeared. He must have sneaked out into the corridor while they thought he was sleeping. He had left with a suitcase and his portable radio, which would seem as if he was leaving for good.

I tracked Nick down at the Bolero, an East Side night club the syndicate owned. He was surprisingly calm. I had forgotten that essentially he was a man of action. He rose to occasions like this. "No, don't call the police," he said, answering my question. "It would look too lousy. Might hurt the gate. We'll find him ourselves. I'll send some of the boys out. He's too well known to get very far."

Nick's boys checked all the outlets of the city, the stations, airports and bus terminals, to see if Toro had bought a ticket. Fernando remembered that Toro had made some kind of a threat to go back to Argentina alone if he had to. So Benny, Jock Mahoney, Vince, the Killer and I drove to the waterfront in the white Lincoln. We cruised past the docks of all the lines that had ships going to South America. We asked the watchmen if they had seen him. One of them told us that the American Fruit Company had a freighter leaving in the morning for Buenos Aires —at Pier Six. We rushed down. We stopped at the entrance to the pier, and all of us got out and looked around. There was only a quarter moon and the waterfront was draped in a gray-black fog. The lights on the freighter looked yellow and blurred.

Suddenly Benny called out, "Hey, I think I see the bastard." He sprinted toward the huge sliding door that blocked the entrance to the pier. We followed him. It was Toro, all right. He must have been waiting for the gate to open in the early morning. He started running when he saw us. I joined the chase with the others. I was part of the pack running the quarry down. Toro's movements were as ponderous outside the ring as in. Jock and the Killer caught up with him quickly, grabbed at him and slowed him down. Benny, Vince and I ran up and surrounded him. Toro tried to break out of the circle, but Benny held him from behind, and Jock and Vince closed in from the sides. Toro shook them off, and for a moment he was free, but he had only taken a few steps when they were on him again. He cursed us in Spanish and kept shouting, *"Ya me voy. Ya me voy,"* I'm going. The Killer reached up and drove his small fist into Toro's face. Toro roared and wrenched his shoulders back and forth to break our grips but we held on and began to drag him toward the car. He struggled furiously against being pushed back into his Lincoln. In the darkness our milling figures, above which he towered, must have looked like ancient hunters grappling with some prehistoric beast. Suddenly the great beast went limp, and we half-pushed, half-lifted him into the car. Benny slipped his blackjack back into his pocket. "The son-of-a-bitch won't lam no more tuh-night," he said.

Next morning I talked things over with Nick. He was leaving for Florida that afternoon. "Tell you what you do," he said. "Take the big dope and the two greaseballs and go out and have some fun. The Killer will get you all the gash you want. Do anything as long as you don't let that big bum knock up a high-school girl or get himself a dose. When he's had his fun, take him out to the country and start training. Maybe that's what he needs to get over this Lennert business." He gave me a thick roll of bills. "That oughta cover it. Entertainment. I'll get Leo to take it off the income tax."

Pepe liked the idea and there was nothing Fernando wouldn't do for his country. So we started that afternoon. Pepe broke out a case of champagne and the Killer sent up six girls, including a couple of spares, in case some of them went flat, he said. What we started that afternoon may have lasted a week or maybe it went for three, I never knew for sure. I think I remember Pepe betting Toro a hundred dollars he couldn't drink a bottle of champagne without stopping and Toro falling asleep on the floor and Pepe having one of the girls wake him up in a way that made us laugh. I think I remember all of us breaking in on Fernando and catching him in his BVD's, the old-fashioned kind, shoes, socks and garters, looking like the straight man in a pornographic movie. It seems to me there was a showgirl of Amazonian proportions sent up expressly for Toro, and I think we all watched and cheered them on. There was a night in Philadelphia, or maybe it was Boston, for I guess we were moving around, when we all seemed to be in a large bed together. I think it must have been in a house because I vaguely remember a mirror on the ceiling. There was a girl named Mercedes who came from Juarez and claimed to be one of Pancho Villa's numerous daughters, who taught us, among other things, the Mexican anthem, and there seemed to be an endless switching of partners and good-natured comparing of notes. There were girls who were spiritlessly accommodating and there were girls who were impersonally tempestuous. There were girls who would submit to the most extreme indignities but would not allow their ears to be assaulted with profanity. There were girls who did not hesitate to assume conventional postures but primly drew the line at variations. And there were girls who indulged in entertainments that are not to be described. For some reason I remember a girl named Olive who talked a lot about her little son, Oliver, and who, at the moment when it could be least appreciated, suddenly burst into tears. I remember a pretty little Irish girl who wouldn't go into the bedroom with Toro because he frightened her. And there was a prematurely gray woman of obvious breeding whom we picked up in the hotel lounge falling down drunk and who confided to me that she had had a secret yen for Toro from the first time she read about him. There was the morning I came downstairs for breakfast and found it was dark outside and already time for cocktails. I went back to our rooms and there was Toro, nude, asleep on a bed. Fernando was snoring in the other bed. He looked very ugly with his bloated face and his squat, hairy body in his underwear. But Toro, even in that disheveled hotel room, among the stale glasses and the mashed cigarette butts, didn't belong in the backwash of a debauch. He was too big for the room, too big for the bed, stretched prone like a tremendously larger-than-life statue that had somehow come loose from its base and toppled over. I wondered if I should wake Toro, so he could eat something. Fernando could lie there until he rotted, for all I cared. I wondered where Pepe was. I was pretty wide awake for so early in the morning. Or was it evening? Awake. A wake. A wake for Gus Lennert. We are really having us a wake, Gus. I'm awake, a wake, a wake for Gus Lennert. The Mexican Indians bury their dead and get drunk in the cemetery and sing songs and tell bawdy stories and have themselves a time. And who is to say there's a better way? But that is a pure wake, like the drunken wake of the Irish, and this is a lewd wake, a wake for the depraved and degraded, a wake to call forth devils and summon witches, a stewed crude nude lewd debauch of a wake, to copulate ourselves into such deadening stupor that we no longer see the self-accusing fingers of guilt pointing at our eyes.

Toro was lying on the bed in his immense nakedness. It was evening instead of morning and I was wondering if I should rouse him. He was sleeping heavily. As I watched, he rolled over on his side. *"Ya me voy, Papá. Ya me voy,"* he was muttering. Let him sleep, I thought, let him sleep, let him think he's home.

When I came out of it, I didn't know where I was. The inside of my mouth felt like lumpy cotton and a maddening tom-tom was beating in my head. "Take this," Doc said. "It'll settle your stomach." It wasn't my stomach coming up; it was remorse. I could feel it heaving up from my belly, that terrible, dragging, end-it-all sense of remorse. The restless succession of women, no more remembered than chain-smoked cigarettes, Fernando with his garters, the daily seduction of Toro Molina, the whole empty, frenetic saturnalia closed in and threatened to crush me.

A picture on the bureau came slowly into focus. It was staring at me, a nice, cool face, staring at me. My picture of Beth. I was in my own room. "Where is everybody?" I said.

"You saw Pepe off at the boat last night," Doc said. "He's coming back with a crowd in time for the Stein fight. Fernando has gone out to Pompton Lakes with Molina. We'll just sweat him out the next couple of weeks."

"How about Danny?"

"Danny's down there too. But I don't think we better count on Danny too much. Danny's been on the flit so long he's sweating alcohol."

Doc put his hand on my forehead and then he felt my pulse. His hands were amazingly alive, damp and nervous, and yet strangely reassuring.

"Thanks, Doc."

But I guess I didn't have to thank him. Doc liked to play doctor.

I didn't bother going out to the camp very often. Nothing much was happening there. When you visit a camp you can tell right away what the morale is, whether the place is taut and businesslike, or loused up with lushes and gamblers, whether it's dully methodical, slothful and lackadaisical or keyed-up and confident. The atmosphere around Toro was listless. Usually it's either the purpose of the manager or the energy of the fighter that sparks a camp. But this time Danny was squandering his time and his money in the grog shops and the horse rooms, and Toro walked through his workouts like a somnambulist.

When he talked about Toro, George shook his bronze-molded head. "I'm worried about him," he told me. "He fights like a zombie. He just ain't there at all. That's no way to get ready for Stein. The big fella's gotta be *up* to stay in there with Stein."

I went out again for the last workout before they came into town and I could see why George was worried. This kid, Gussman, giving away around eighty pounds, had to pull up so he wouldn't knock Toro's head off right in front of the reporters. Toro was hog-fat in the belly because Fernando had more or less taken over the camp by default, and let the big slob put away too much fattening food.

The day before the fight there wasn't a hotel room to be had in New York. Fans had driven in from all over the country. A delegation from Stein's home town came in on a special train, with everybody from the Mayor to the favorite madam, and took over a midtown hotel. *Variety's* list of "In's" was almost twice as long as on an ordinary Wednesday. Pepe and his Argentine delegation of assorted millionaires, politicos and playboys staged a big luncheon at the Ritz. The Argentine Consul General welcomed his countrymen, and Fernando spoke for the Argentine

Athletic Association. The Giant of the Andes was rising in the fistic firmament, he said, just as Argentina herself, the land of giants, was rising in the Pan-American firmament. They must have applauded that one for two full minutes. Throughout all the speeches, Toro's name was waved like a flag, the blue-and-white of our contentious neighbor to the south. Then Toro was called on to say a few words. His face was stolid. There was no belligerence in him, nationalistic or otherwise. "I do my best," he said. "Then I go home."

All the Broadway restaurants were full of guys talking fight, laying or taking the nine to five on Stein. There must have been an easy million ready to change hands by six o'clock.

By seven there was already a tremendous crowd milling around the ball park. There was the last-minute scramble for tickets, the scalping, the squatters' rush for the unreserved section, the gamblers working the suckers right up to the opening gong. Walking up and down in front of one of the entrances was a blind man with a tin cup and a sandwich sign over his shoulders. "Kid Fargo," it said, "Former Heavyweight Contender. Used to Spar with Jack Dempsey."

The smart money was going on Stein because it had to ride with him until he was licked. There hadn't been a puncher like him since Dempsey. But there was plenty of Molina money, from people impressed by mere size, ballyhoo and the manslaughter of Gus Lennert.

Lumbering into the ring were the first of the brace of muscular mediocrities Uncle Mike always foisted on his public when he knew the main attraction was so good he didn't have to bolster it with expensive preliminaries. The Stadium was a sellout, all the way up to the gallery gods on the top tier who paid five dollars for the privilege of being able to say that they had attended a ring classic. And even above them were the thousands of curious bargain hunters who paid top-story dwellers a dollar to watch the spectacle from the windows or rooftops. And beyond them were the millions of radio listeners in swank metropolitan apartments, lower middle-class homes, slums, small-town houses and farms from coast to coast.

The ringside—or what Uncle Mike cagily called ringside—fanned out for three hundred rows, a true cross-section of the prosperous, including the Governor, the Mayor, the chief of Police, Broadway headliners, Hollywood stars, and all the representatives of the best legal and illegal rackets, the Wall Street boys, industrial tycoons, the socialites, insurance men, advertising executives, judges, prominent lawyers, bigtime gamblers and the top mobsters who never get their name in the papers. Nobody who was anybody was missing a chance to be seen at ringside.

The crowd was laughing at the antics of two barrel-chested incompetents who were waltzing through the curtain-raiser. "Turn out the lights, they wanna be alone," a big voice bellowed from the mezzanine. It still got laughs. Someone ought to write new material for the fight fans. The same old saws to express the old derision, the displeasure with blood-less, painless, actionless battle. "Can I have the next dance?" . . . "What we got, da Ballet Russe?" . . . "Are you bums brother-in-laws?" . . . "Careful, you goils might hoit each other!" But the protests were still relaxed and good-natured. The crowd was working up to its excitement slowly. The catcalls were still without real contempt. The most high-tensioned of all American sports crowds hadn't roused itself yet. It was still behaving as if this were merely a sport.

I went back to the dressing room to see Toro. Fernando and George were helping him get ready. Danny was there too. He was mumbling. He was trying to tell Toro something. But Fernando pushed him away. Toro removed his clothes slowly, as if reluctant to change into a fighter again. He didn't say anything to me when I came in. He wasn't saying anything to anybody.

"I think he's full of geezer tonight," Doc whispered to me. "He's had the trots all day."

"Maybe he's just scared this'll be another Lennert," I said.

"I just hope it isn't the other way," Doc said.

Pepe came in with some of his Argentine pals. They all made a fuss over Toro, gave him the big embrace, told him how much money they had going on him and went out to enjoy the semifinal. They were full of ready laughter and carefree rooting-section enthusiasm. Toro didn't say anything to them. It was just as George said: he wasn't really there at all.

Nick came in with the Killer and Barney Winch. All three were wear-ing tailored camelhair topcoats. Toro was sitting on the table in his bathrobe. Doc was rubbing his back.

Nick set himself in front of Toro. "Listen, you bum," he said in a hard, quiet voice. "I just wanted to let you know something. My wife's told me all about you."

Toro looked up slowly, waiting for the blow like a slaughterhouse steer.

"She told me you came over to the house one day and tried to get fresh with her. I ought to kick your head in, you double-crossing crud, you. But I don't have to take the trouble. This fight tonight is the first one you ever fought for me on the dead square. So I don't have to mess up my manicure on you. I can just sit out there in the front row and have the pleasure of seeing Stein beat your goddam brains out. I hope he kills you."

He slapped Toro once sharply across the face. Toro just stared at him.

For several minutes after they went out, Toro continued to stare stupidly into space. Chick Gussman, who was fighting the six-round special, came in after a win by TKO in three, exhilarated by his showing. He tapped Toro playfully and said, "Looks like a big night for the Latka stable, kid." But Toro didn't even see him. The semifinal was over in a hurry, and it was Toro's turn to go down. For the first time since I could remember Danny wasn't in shape to work the corner, so Vince took over with Doc and George, who was holding the bottles.

"Well, good luck, Toro." I tried to put something into it, but my voice sounded flat and hollow. My hand was extended and Toro took it in a soft handshake. That was when I noticed he was trembling.

Buddy Stein entered the ring first. The crowd roared and screamed its approval as he danced around in a blue silk bathrobe with a white bath towel draped over his head. He reached down over the ropes with his taped hands and shook hands with lots of people, Jack Dempsey, Bing Crosby, Sherman Billingsley... A beautiful blonde in the third row pursed her lips as if she were kissing him, and he winked. There were more women than usual tonight. Both fighters were good draws with women. Stein was dark, curly-haired, unusually handsome for a fighter. He had one of those broad-shouldered, narrow-hipped builds, tapering down to surprisingly graceful legs. He was a vain bully boy with the personality of a show-off and the stage presence of the matinee idol accustomed to adoration. He had often been complimented on his smile —the Stein grin, it was called sometimes—though actually it was the nasty smile of a man who had found a way of channeling his natural cruelty into a profitable career.

In spite of the hamming and clowning with the crowd, Stein was a serious practitioner of assault and battery, trained to a sharp fighting edge. He pranced around the ring with an ominous, pent-up vigor, warming up with short, shadowboxing hooks that shot viciously into the air.

The reception for Toro was friendly but reserved, and there were a few scattered boos from skeptics and from old Lennert fans who clung to the primitive notion that the ex-champion's death was in some way due to an excess of brutality on Toro's part. Actually, as Doc and George pulled off his flashy bathrobe, I was reminded once more of the enormity of the joke nature had played on this giant. His colossal shoulders, bulging muscles and record chest expansion would seem too great an advantage against even the most formidable opponent, and yet his menacing physique contained a gentle, placid disposition with less fighting instinct than the average ten-year-old boy, and considerably less aptitude.

The huge floodlight system over the stadium dimmed out and the ring became an intense white square cameoed in the vast darkness. The announcer requested one minute of silence for "Old Gus, a real champion who went down fighting, with the Great Referee counting over him the Fatal Ten."

The stadium went black as the impatient fans stood up in a touching demonstration of bogus bereavement, while the bell tolled ten with sound-effect impressiveness.

As the lights over the ring came on again, and the announcer had finally introduced all the famous fighters and identified the contestants with needlessly elaborate formality, the mass tension surged, and a barbaric roar rose from 80,000 throats. The referee gave them final instructions and sent them back to their corners to await the opening bell. As their handlers drew their robes from their shoulders at last, the contrast in their sizes brought an excited gasp from the crowd. Toro, almost six feet eight, weighing nearly two hundred and eighty pounds, looking a little fleshy around the waist, crossed himself and waited for the bell in a kind of docile bewilderment. Stein, an even six feet, with a hard, lithe, rippling body, weighing one-ninety-six, shuffled his feet back and forth with restless impatience and worked his shoulders from side to side as if he were already in there flailing away at his mammoth adversary.

"Kill 'im, Buddy," the blonde in the third row begged in a shrill, unpleasant voice.

The bell brought Stein streaking across the ring to face Toro moving slowly out of his corner. Toro held his left out in the mechanical defense Danny had taught him. Stein felt him out carefully, showing considerable respect for Toro's advantages in weight and reach. He flicked stinging jabs into Toro's face, feinted with his right and held his famous left as if he were going to let it go, but he wasn't taking any chances yet. Toro was boxing rigidly, pushing his long left toward Stein's head and keeping the smaller man at a distance. Toro had finally learned the rudiments of boxing, but his execution was clumsy and had no zing. His footwork was slow but correct, and once he followed up a left jab with a right cross that managed to reach Stein's ribs. Stein smiled and snapped Toro's head back with a sharp jab. Stein's jab looked harder than Toro's best punches. Buddy pressed his lips together and a sneer came over his face as he shot another jab in. The pain aroused Toro slightly and he tried a one-two with elementary timing. The left reached Stein's face, but the right, the *two*, lobbed harmlessly into the air as Stein slipped it neatly and drew Toro into a clinch. Nothing much seemed to be happening in the clinch, but when the referee came between them Toro's eye was reddened and blinking. It looked like a thumb job. Stein had been around; he was very cute. As they separated, Stein held out his gloves in a broad gesture of sportsmanship. Toro, momentarily blinded, failed to reciprocate and touch gloves. The crowd booed his ungentlemanly conduct. In tonight's drama they had cast him for the villain.

Some of the bleacherites began to clap their hands rhythmically to show their impatience. "Quite stalling," they yelled. Stein, with the sensitivity of the vain, moved in to satisfy them. He started a right to Toro's body, and when he saw the big arms go down, he suddenly pivoted and let the left hand go for the first time. It caught Toro hard on the side of the jaw. Toro sagged. I was sitting close enough to see how his eyes turned in. Stein danced back to his corner at the bell, hamming it up a little with his chest out. Toro walked back to his stool slowly and sat down like a man with a bellyful of beer.

Stein was waiting for him as soon as he got up again. He was speeding up his tempo now. Toro tried to box him again, but Stein feinted, exactly as he had done before, sucked Toro out of position and crashed his left into Toro's reddened eye. A lump was swelling over it with abnormal rapidity. At that moment I wanted to be away from this, away from what could only be the relentless tormenting of a helpless freak. But something gripped me with terrible fascination, just as did all 80,000 of us, waiting in a kind of deathwatch for what already seemed inevitable.

It had ceased to be a contest; it was a bullfight, a thrilling demonstration of man's superiority over the beast, the giant, the great shapeless fear. The voices of the onlookers were growing tight with excitement. "Work on that eye!" "Close that right eye for him!"

Stein obliged. Measuring Toro coolly, he smashed the swollen eye. Toro's heavy lips parted in pain, revealing the ugly orange mouthpiece. Staring balefully at his attacker with his one good eye he had suddenly become a grotesque and incredible throwback to Cyclops. Stein was working him over with methodical viciousness now. The short, savage blows pounded Toro with sickening monotony. When the bell ended his punishment for sixty seconds, Toro hesitated foolishly for a moment, trying to decide in which direction his corner lay. The referee guided him back to his stool.

Doc's fingers digging into Toro's limp neck, the water George poured over Toro's head and the smelling salts Vince held to his nose gave the giant a semblance of recuperation with which to face the next round. But Stein was stabbing him with animal fury now. His lips were drawn tight over his mouthpiece and his eyes had a homicidal intensity. You could almost feel the pressure of the accumulating cruelty of the crowd closing in on the ring. "Get him! Get him!" "Knock him out!" "Kill 'im!" the cries mounted in hysteria. The lump over Toro's right eye had risen to the size of an egg. Stein drove Toro back with another straight left that was beginning to split Toro's mouth. Then, with all his might, he jabbed at the lump, smashing it as if it really were an egg, but an egg full of blood. Instantly the right side of Toro's face was a crimson splotch.

"That's the way, Buddy. Kill 'im!" the blonde in the third row screamed.

I looked over at Nick, who was sitting with Ruby in the front row, directly across the ring from me. He was just sitting there, pulling clamly on a long cigar and watching the proceedings with a kind of bored attentiveness I had seen on his face hundreds of times at the training camps. Ruby was wearing a spectacular black felt hat with a band of spangles around the crown, framing a powder-white face with fierce dark eyes and a deep red mouth. From where I sat, she seemed to be enjoying herself.

Another savage shriek was torn from the throat of the crowd and people all around me jumped up to see Stein catch Toro in a corner, where he rained rights and lefts at his head until Toro began sliding down the ringpost to squat ludicrously on the floor. Some people laughed. The referee pointed Stein to a neutral corner, where he bounced crazily, waiting to get at Toro again. "Stay down, Toro, stay down," I shouted. But for some inexplicable reason of that dogged, semi-conscious brain, Toro pulled himself up and tottered heavily toward Stein. The bell postponed the slaughter for another minute.

In his corner, Toro lay back against the ropes drooling blood from his torn mouth and gasping for breath, exhausted from the terrible punishment he was absorbing. His one half-open eye closed in an agony of weariness. Doc's fingers did their best. With all their strength they pressed together the lips of the cut over the right eye to try to stem the bleeding. Then Doc patted collodion over the wound and it seemed momentarily to congeal. Meanwhile George tried to rub some life into the huge, muscle-bound, all-but-useless legs, and Vince shouted profane instructions into his swollen ears.

After all this preparation, Stein tore across the ring at the bell and knocked Toro down again with the first punch. All of Doc's work had come undone and the cut above the eye dripped blood into the dirty canvas. There was no point, no honor in continuing this demonstration of a big man's hopeless inability to compete in coordinated viciousness with a smaller man of proved superiority. When Toro got up again I don't think he even intended to try. His face was a gory mess and he stumbled forward to receive more blows, a broken and battered hull of a man foundering on a sea of pain, relentlessly buffeted by the angry waves of blows, and borne up only by some unknown fund of pointless endurance.

The crowd was screaming for a knockout now, begging for it, pleading for it, a wild-eyed cheering section of bettors who were riding on a

Stein knockout, of fans inspired with an angry sense of misplaced justice who resented Toro for his fraud-fattened record and mistook this beating for the revenge of integrity, and finally the vast audience of the frustrated and the browbeaten who could not help taking a deep vicarious pleasure in being in on the final transformation of an overpowering giant into a pitiful wreck of human flesh.

Somehow Toro weathered that round, dragged himself back for first aid and staggered out glassy-eyed to offer himself up to Stein once more. Why didn't they stop it? Why didn't Doc stop it? Doc must have been under orders from Nick to let it run. What about the referee? Well, for one thing they don't like to stop a heavyweight fight too soon because the big boys are supposed to be able to take it. And then I remembered another thing. Vince had said something about laying eight G's to five that Toro would still be there for the eighth. Vince and the referee, Marty Small, had done business before. Marty didn't have to do anything crooked, just let Toro keep going as long as he could. Vince would take care of the rest.

For three more minutes, with the roar of the crowd pitched to a manic fury, Stein cut the crippled giant down. Toro tumbled over and writhed to a kneeling position and when he rose with his knees shaking, Stein knocked him down again. He rolled over onto his knees with his battered head pressed against the canvas. Then with a perverse and useless courage, he struggled to his feet again. With one hand on the ropes, he kept himself from falling. His other arm hung limply at his side. Blood poured from both eyes, and a new stream of blood gushed from his mouth. Swaying back and forth, in blind and helpless bewilderment, he waited for the little man to attack him again. Stein leaped in with a powerful right to the body that made Toro bend over. Then he straightened him up with a paralyzing left to the jaw. Toro toppled over. He fell so awkwardly that his ankle twisted under him. With horrible concentration, he lifted himself to his knees. He crawled forward on his knees, slipping in his own blood, like a dying beast. His mouth was open and the lower part of his jaw hung hideously loose. "Jaw's busted," I heard someone say. The big orange mouthpiece flopped out of his mouth and rolled a few feet ahead of him. For some reason he did not understand, he crawled painfully toward it and tried to stuff it back into his mouth in a slow-motion gesture of futility. He was still fumbling with his mouthpiece when the referee finished his count and raised Stein's hand. Buddy danced around happily, mitting his gloves over his head to acknowledge the ovation of the crowd. Toro was still trying to stuff the mouthpiece back into his mouth when Vince, Doc and George dragged him back to his corner.

22

Satisfied and quiet now, the crowd was filtering slowly toward the exits. Going up the aisle I met Nick and Ruby, the Killer with one of his girls, Mr. and Mrs. Quinn and Barney Winch.

"Did you ever see a worse bum?" Nick said.

"We should swap him to Harry Miniff for an old jock strap," Quinn laughed.

"Nice talk in front of the girls," Nick said, taking Ruby's arm.

"But there goes your meal ticket," I said.

Nick drew me closer. "Don't worry, kid. I made a deal with Kewpie Harris. We've got a piece of Stein."

"Come on over to the Bolero, Eddie boy," Quinn said. "Just ask for my table."

"I don't feel like it tonight," I said.

"I can get you fixed up with something nice in the show," the Killer said.

"I'm not in the mood tonight," I said.

I went back to the dressing room. Toro was sitting on the rubbing table with a bloody towel over his head. Doc was still trying to check the flow of blood from his nose and mouth. Toro's smashed and swollen face hung limply on his chest. He was trembling. The reporters pressed around him, oblivious of his condition in their eagerness to round out their stories.

"When was the first time he hurt you, Toro?"

Toro muttered through his torn mouth. "Jesus Christo . . ."

"What punch was it that gave you the most trouble?"

"Jesus Christo . . ." Toro said.

"Like to have a return match?"

"Jesus Christo . . ."

"Where the hell is Grandini?" Doc said. "George, go down the hall and see if you can find Dr. Grandini. He better have a look at this jaw."

Toro's head shook slightly from side to side like a man with palsy. The lumpy, sliced flesh over his eyes was turning purple and the broken jaw hung open.

"Lie down," Doc said. "Better lie down."

Toro just sat there in blind agony, shaking his head slowly. "Jesus Christo . . ." he whispered.

They took him up to Roosevelt Hospital, and set his jaw for him. I went over to see him in the morning. His upper and lower jaws had been wired together; his cuts had been stitched; he was taking liquids through a glass straw. The lumpy discolored bruises on his face made him look more like a huge gargoyle than ever.

There was something he was trying to say to me. He tried to mutter through his wired teeth and his swollen, lacerated lips, but no sound came. Finally I caught some of the words forced from his throat. "I go home now. My money . . . money . . ."

"I'll get it for you," I said.

On the way out I passed Vince in the hall.

"Well, this is the last place I ever expected to see you," I told him.

"Aah, what's-a-matter with you, you think you're the only white man in the outfit? You think you got an exclusive on seeing the guy?"

"What's your angle, Vince? Don't tell me you're just coming in to cheer him up. That's not my Vince."

"I just thought maybe I could help the guy," Vince said.

"I didn't know you knew that word," I said.

"There's a lotta things you don't know, chum," Vince said and went in.

Well, it was a funny racket, I thought. I've seen boys beat each other so that neither would ever be as good again and then throw their arms around each other in an embrace of genuine affection. I've seen a father sit tight-lipped in a corner and let his son bleed like a pig for ten rounds and then, when it was all over, take his boy's disfigured face in his hands and burst out crying. They were unpredictable, the toughest of them, whimsically and inconsistently tender. Maybe that was Vince. Maybe somewhere in that fat, coarse face, in that fat, lewd brain, was a hidden core of humanity I had missed, or that had never been tapped before.

I went up to the office to see about the money for Toro. Nick was home sleeping off a late night, the Killer said. "That's where I shoulda stayed," he complained. "Christ what a night! Didja ever have a Chinese arobatic dancer, Eddie? I thought I seen everything, but . . ."

"Killer," I said, "how can I get Toro's dough for him?"

The Killer looked disappointed. "Talk to Leo," he said. "He's in this morning."

I went down the hall to see Nick's bookkeeper. He was working over a ledger. He looked small, pale and devoted, the way bookkeepers are supposed to look, except for his eyes, which were put there to warn you.

"Busy, Leo?"

"Well, I'm breaking down the take on the fight," he said.

"What was the exact gross?"

"One million, three hundred and fifty-six thousand, eight hundred ninety-three and fifty cents."

"I promised Toro I'd pick up his money for him," I said.

"I'll have to look it up in the file," Leo said.

He thumbed through his file professionally, LATKA, LEWIS, MANN, MOLINA . . . "Here it is." He licked his forefinger and removed several sheets from the file. He studied them carefully.

"There's a small balance," he said.

"A small balance? Are you kidding?"

"It's all down here in black and white," Leo said.

I reached for the sheets and stared at the rows of figures, all neatly typed and itemized. My eye ran down a column of astronomical figures. There was $10,450 for training expenses, $14,075 for living expenses and $17,225 for publicity and entertainment. There were items, all beautifully padded, for equipment, sparring partners, transportation, personal amusement, phone calls, telegrams and good old miscellaneous. There was a little matter of $63,500 in cash, alleged to have been advanced to Toro by Vanneman. And, finally, there were the managerial commissions, the Federal and State taxes and "personal gratuities for favors rendered." By the time all this had been duly subtracted from purses which totaled almost a million dollars, there was a small balance, all right. Exactly forty-nine dollars and seven cents.

"Wait a minute," I said. "This is highway robbery. Vince never advanced Toro any sixty-three thousand. You must mean six thousand."

"That's the way I got it from Vince," Leo said. "He gave me all the tabs."

"So Toro winds up with forty-nine dollars and seven cents," I said. "What are you guys so generous for? What do you leave him the five sawbucks for?"

"You can add it up yourself if you want to," Leo said.

"I know you can add, Leo. I've seen you add for Nick before. I've seen you subtract too."

"Everything is in order," Leo said. "I can show these books to anybody."

"Sure," I said. "You've got those numbers trained, Leo. You got those numbers jumping through hoops for you."

"If you have any beefs, talk to the boss," Leo said. "But you can't find no bugs in my books. I'll show my books to anybody, any time."

I jumped into a cab and hurried over to Nick's apartment on East Fifty-third. It was around noon. Nick was having his breakfast, alone in the dining room in a silk midnight-blue bathrobe with a large N.L. embroidered over the breast pocket in Spencerian script.

"Nick," I began, "I've just been talking to Leo."

"Yeah?" He was crumbling his toast carefully into his soft-boiled eggs. "Did you get yours all right, kid? You should be in for around seventeen G's."

"But, Nick. What about Toro? All Toro's got is forty-nine bucks. A broken jaw and forty-nine lousy bucks."

"What's it got to do with you, Eddie?"

"What's it got to do with me, I..." What *did* it have to do with me? Where were the words to bridge the unbridgeable? To reconcile the unreconcilable?

"You just can't do that to a guy, Nick. You just can't let him get beat to death and then leave him with a hole in his pocket."

"Listen, Eddie, the slob got paid off. You can see it on the books."

"I know," I said. "I just saw the books. I know Leo and his books."

"Then it's just tough titty, isn't it?" Nick said.

"Jesus, Nick, after all, the poor son-of-a-bitch is human. He's..."

"It's just tough," Nick said.

"For Christ's sake, Nick. For the sake of Jesus Christ, you can't do this."

"Go back to bed, Eddie," Nick said, reaching calmly for his coffee. And the terrible thing about it was the way he said it. I knew he still liked me. I knew, God forgive me, he thought I had class. He was always going to count me in. "Go back to bed and sleep it off. You're spoiling my breakfast."

I went back to the hospital to see Toro. "You mustn't stay very long," the nurse said, outside his room.

"How is he getting along?"

"He's under sedation. Still suffering from shock. His left side is partially paralyzed, but the doctor is confident it's only temporary."

Toro was lying on his back, staring up at the ceiling. His face was a mass of blue and purple blotches. He turned his head slowly when he heard me enter.

"*¿Mi dinero?* My money...my money?"

I shook my head. I didn't know what to say.

His eyes searched me frantically. "*¿Mi dinero...dinero?*"

I don't know why I should have been the one to tell him. But I figured I was the only one who would take the trouble to break it to him easy.

"Toro, I...I don't know how to tell you this, but...it's gone. Toro, it's all gone. *Se fue.*"

"*¿Se fué?*" Toro muttered through his wired teeth. "No. *No es posible. ¿Se fué?*"

"*Lo siento,*" I said. "Toro, *lo siento.*" That's what the Spanish say for "I'm sorry," but it means literally, "I feel it," and that was the way I meant it.

A wrenching groan came up out of Toro's throat. He stared at me unbelievingly for what seemed at least a full minute. Then he turned slowly away from me and stared into the wall. Suddenly his great shoulders began to heave and he was shaken by dry, guttural sobs. It was a terrible thing to see a man of such size crying so desperately.

Finally I said, "Toro, I'm terribly sorry. I wish there was something I could do." Then I thought of my own seventeen thousand. "Say, I've got an idea! I can let you have five thousand dollars." I was going to say "ten," but some little bookkeeper in my brain cut it in half for me. "At least that would get you home."

"But it . . . is all my money . . . all . . . all . . . I make it all . . ."

"Sure, sure," I agreed, "but what can you do? They've got you coming and going. Be smart and take the five, Toro."

He turned from the wall and glared at me.

"Vaya," Toro whispered hoarsely. "Go. All of you . . . Go away from me."

All of you. What did Toro mean, *all of you?* He must have me mixed up with the others. I was Toro's friend, the only one who cared, the only one who sympathized. And yet, he had said *all.* He had said *all of you.*

"But, Toro, I'm your friend, I want to help you, I . . ."

"Go," Toro whispered. "Go . . . go . . . go . . ."

As I walked slowly down the corridor, Vince appeared. He was wearing a big wrap-around camel's hair overcoat.

"Hello, lover," he said.

"Vince," I said. "I can't believe it. Don't tell me you're coming to look in on Toro again."

"Sure," he said. "He's my boy now. I gotta see how quick I can spring him. We got big plans together."

"You mean, you and Toro?"

"Yeah. I just bought his contract back from Nick this morning. Just because he loused himself up in town doesn't mean there isn't plenty of scratch to be picked up in the sticks."

"But he's through, Vince. He's all washed up."

"For the Garden, sure. But I figure we can still pick up a nice piece of change going back over the same territory, in reverse. This time the hometown fans'll put their bucks down to see the local boy beat hell outa the giant. We got a name that's still a draw and we don't even have to bother to rig anything. I already got him booked with Dynamite Jones for the Bull Ring at Tijuana. We'll let the people guess maybe last time it was a tankeroo and this time Jones is going in without the handcuffs. I bet we do twenty thousand."

"Vince, you're crazy! What makes you think Toro wants to go on fighting, after last night?"

"You're not thinking so good today, lover. He's got to fight. He's broke."

I thought of Speedy Sencio. I thought of all the broken and burned-out fighters the Vince Vannemans of the world were forever patching up and shoving back into the ring. But I was too disgusted to think of anything to say.

"You know, I'd like to cut you in, kid," Vince was saying. "After all, me and you're good pals. But, well, to level with you, Eddie, you been on the flit too much this last trip. I haven't got the dough to throw around like Nick. I just don't think you're worth it any more. But if I change my mind, I'll let you know." He reached out and pinched my cheek. "No hard feelings, though, huh, lover?"

He sauntered down the hall toward Toro's room. I stood there helplessly. I wasn't good enough for Vince.

There was only one more little thing I could do for Toro, I thought. Pepe and Fernando could take him home with them. Pepe would provide for him. I ducked into a phone booth in the hospital drug store and called the Waldorf Towers. The hotel operator transferred me to Information. The De Santos party checked out at noon, I was told. Their forwarding address was the Hotel Nacional in Havana.

I wandered back to my room. Something led me to the closet. I opened my trunk. The bottom drawer was full of old stuff, articles, press clippings, letters—I couldn't even remember why I had kept them—and down in the middle of all this mess, there it was, *And Still Champion* by Edwin Dexter Lewis, three names, to give it class.

The pages were yellowing. But that didn't matter. I could get them retyped. As I looked at the title page I had a dream's-eye view of the Theatre Guild poster in front of the theatre. I started to read the first act. I tried to make myself believe in it. But what was the use? How long could I go on kidding myself? The dialogue was forced. The characters were props. The bones of the plot stuck out all over. And this was the blank check to fame I had been holding out for myself all these years. The Pulitzer Prize number! All I had written was the first act of a bad play. Just twenty-three pages of a play that was going back into the bottom drawer of my trunk, where it belonged.

I pushed the trunk back into the closet again. It felt frighteningly insecure to be without my play. What was I now? Just what Beth said I was, just another guy working for Nick.

It was early in the morning when I found my way to Shirley's. Lucille was cleaning the bar room and Shirley was playing solitaire.

"Eddie," she said. "You look like hell. You look like the kid's last fight. What in God's name is the matter with you?"

"The worst of them all," I said. "The biggest heel of them all. The only one who knew right from wrong and kept his goddam mouth shut. The only one who knew the score, knew what was going on and still kept his hands in his pocket. The worst, the worst, Shirley, the worst of all."

Shirley came over and looked up into my face.

"Come on," she said. "Forget it. It's time for bed."

When I awakened, the room was dark, the shades were drawn and I didn't know whether it was day or night. All I knew was that there was a woman in bed with me, and for a moment I thought it was Beth. I fumbled for a match to light a cigarette, and when I lit it I realized with a shock that I was in the room into which Sailor Beaumont and other beaten fighters had crawled in search of solace and relief from pain.

Shirley? What was I doing with Shirley? Shirley never went to bed with me. Shirley only took to bed her badly beaten fighters. Just a succession of substitutes for the Sailor. Everybody knew that.

I know the goddam trouble with me, I thought. Enough brains to see it and not enough guts to stand up to it. Thousands of us, millions of us, corrupted, rootless, career-ridden, good hearts and yellow bellies, living out our lives for the easy buck, the soft berth, indulging ourselves in the illusion that we can deal in filth without becoming the thing we touch. No wonder Beth wouldn't have me. A heel, she called me, a heel, the biggest heel of all.

"I know the goddam trouble with me," I suddenly said aloud.

"Eddie, honey, what's the matter with you? Stop fighting yourself. Whatever it is, don't worry about it," Shirley said quietly.

Her bare arm went around my neck and her generous breasts pressed against me soothingly.

"Go to sleep now. You'll feel better when you get up."

But even as I floated off into warm, cowardly sleep, I realized why it was that she had taken me into her bed at last.